ISLANDICA

A SERIES RELATING TO ICELAND AND THE

FISKE ICELANDIC COLLECTION

CORNELL UNIVERSITY LIBRARIES

Edited by Kristín Bragadóttir

VOLUME LI

Morkinskinna: The Earliest Icelandic Chronicle
of the Norwegian Kings (1030–1157)

Translated with Introduction and Notes by
Theodore M. Andersson and Kari Ellen Gade

Morkinskinna

The Earliest Icelandic Chronicle
of the Norwegian Kings
(1030–1157)

Translated with Introduction and Notes by

THEODORE M. ANDERSSON

and KARI ELLEN GADE

ISLANDICA LI

Cornell University Press

Ithaca and London

First published 2000 by Cornell University Press
Cornell Paperbacks edition, 2012
Printed in the United States of America

Morkinskinna. English.
Morkinskinna : the earliest Icelandic chronicle of the Norwegian kings (1030–1157) / translated with introduction and notes by Theodore M. Andersson and Kari Ellen Gade.
p.   cm. — (Icelandica ; 51)
Includes bibliographical references and index.
ISBN: 978-0-8014-7783-6
I. Andersson, Theodore Murdock, 1934–   .   II. Gade, Kari Ellen.   III. Title.   IV. Series.
PT7279.M4E5   2000
839′.68—dc21   99-43299

Cornell University Press strives to use environmentally responsible suppliers and materials to the fullest extent possible in the publishing of its books. Such materials include vegetable-based, low-VOC inks and acid-free papers that are recycled, totally chlorine-free, or partly composed of nonwood fibers. Books that bear the logo of the FSC (Forest Stewardship Council) use paper taken from forests that have been inspected and certified as meeting the highest standards for environmental and social responsibility. For further information, visit our website at www.cornellpress.cornell.edu.

Contents

Foreword

With this volume of *Islandica,* we note with sadness the death of P. M. Mitchell on 27 March 1999. Mitchell's tenure as series editor of *Islandica* stands among the many enduring contributions that he made to Old Norse and Icelandic studies.

After having served as professor of German and Scandinavian literatures at the University of Illinois, Urbana-Champaign, Mitchell was appointed curator of the Fiske Icelandic Collection, Cornell University Library, in 1986, relinquishing that position in 1993.

Bridal-Quest Romance in Medieval Iceland, by Marianne E. Kalinke, which appeared in 1990, was the first *Islandica* volume to have been published under Mitchell's editorship. Mitchell had earlier written *Halldór Hermannsson* (1978) and co-compiled with Kenneth H. Ober *Bibliography of Modern Icelandic Literature in Translation, Including Works Written by Icelanders in Other Languages* (1975) and, with Marianne E. Kalinke, *Bibliography of Old Norse-Icelandic Romances* (1985).

Kristín Bragadóttir, head of the National Section of the National and University Library of Iceland, became series editor for *Islandica* on 1 January 1998. Kristín Bragadóttir has collaborated closely with colleagues at Cornell University Library, principally during the *SagaNet* project for the creation of an Icelandic National Digital Library of saga manuscript images. She is active in the fields of Old Norse and Icelandic literatures.

Patrick J. Stevens
Curator, Fiske Icelandic Collection
and Managing Editor, *Islandica*

Preface

Morkinskinna marks the birth of a full-scale royal chronicle in a Scandinavian vernacular. But despite its key position in Norse-Icelandic letters it has suffered surprising neglect over more than a century of intense research in the field of Icelandic literature generally and the kings' sagas in particular. There is no normalized edition or annotated edition, nor is there a translation into any language. We have sought to remedy this deficiency by making the text available in English and providing some initial orientation on the source problems and the literary context of *Morkinskinna*. We hope that this first step may hasten the appearance of a standard edition in Icelandic with the necessary aids.

Our text is eclectic, drawing on alternative manuscripts where the main manuscript defaults, in the interest of producing a complete narrative. At the same time, we have attempted to make clear what precisely is in the main manuscript and where we have supplemented it from cognate redactions. Passages enclosed by asterisks denote illegible passages in the main manuscript, and the reader should consult the "Textual Notes" for details. Our aim has been to serve both the reader who wants a full account of the period covered by the text and the student who needs a discrimination of sources. We have tried as well to provide the necessary background in notes and appendices. Many of the problems are difficult to resolve, and we have not as a rule reached new or rigorous conclusions. We have tried rather to lay out the questions for future scholars. Most particularly we are aware of the preliminary nature of the "Explanatory Notes," which supply a bare minimum of information. In another five or ten years we could probably have worked out a proper commentary, but for the moment we are more interested in promoting some familiarity with the text before another century passes.

The prose in *Morkinskinna* is closely connected with the poetry and in many cases derives directly from the stanzas. The available editions of the verse generally rely on other manuscripts, such as those of *Heimskringla* and *Fagrskinna*, and therefore do not always reveal the basis of the narrative in *Morkinskinna*. To compensate for the missing critical edition we have elected to include the Norse originals of the stanzas in our prose translation. The Old Norse versions of the stanzas are accompanied by Old Norse prose paraphrases and English translations. The edition of the verse is based on the main manuscript, supplemented by other manuscripts to be discussed below. With respect to the Old Norse texts, our edition reflects the language at the stage when the poetry was composed (ca. 1035–1150) rather than the language of the thirteenth-century manuscript. Thus "er" is rendered "es," later lengthened forms (e.g., "Úlfr," "sjálfr") are given in their earlier nonlengthened versions, and so forth. Stanzas marked with asterisks indicate stanzas that occurred in defective sections of the *Morkinskinna* manuscript and have been added from *Flateyjarbók*. Information about emendations, variant readings, and earlier critical and diplomatic editions is detailed in the section "Notes on Stanzas."

The project was initiated by Andersson under the generous and convivial auspices of the Stanford Humanities Center in 1992–93. He gratefully acknowledges the leisure provided by this grant and the genial atmosphere created by the director, Wanda Corn, and the associate director, Charlie Junkerman, as well as a number of colleagues, most immediately his partners in *otium*, Michael Fellman and Marleen Rozemond. During that year he finished the translation of the prose text, but despite the ideal working conditions, completion of the project was nowhere in sight. Gade then assumed the responsibility for the verse and provided both the translations and a new edition based on the texts in the *Morkinskinna* manuscript. The remaining work on introduction, notes, and appendixes was carried out collaboratively from the fall of 1994 to the fall of 1996. During this rather extended period we have of course become fond of our text and hope that in its present form it may gain the wider circulation that it surely deserves.

T. M. A.
K. E. G.

Bloomington, Indiana

Abbreviations

ÅNOH	*Aarbøger for nordisk oldkyndighed og historie*
Ágrip	See *ÍF* 29.
ANF	*Arkiv för nordisk filologi*
APS	*Acta Philologica Scandinavica*
ASC	The Anglo-Saxon Chronicle: *Two of the Saxon Chronicles Parallel with Supplementary Extracts from the Others.* Ed. Charles Plummer. 2 vols. Vol. I: *Text, Appendices and Glossary.* 1892. Rpt. Oxford: Oxford University Press, 1952.
Bisk	*Biskupa søgur.* 2 vols. Copenhagen: S. L. Möller, 1858–78.
Blöndal	Sigfús Blöndal. *The Varangians of Byzantium.* Trans. and rev. Benedikt A. Benedikz. Cambridge: Cambridge University Press, 1978.
Cleasby/Vigfusson	Richard Cleasby and Gudbrand Vigfusson. *An Icelandic-English Dictionary.* London: Oxford University Press, 1874; rpt. 1957.
DMA	*The Dictionary of the Middle Ages.* Ed. Joseph R. Strayer. 13 vols. New York: Charles Scribner's Sons, 1982–89.
EAK	Ernst Albin Kock, ed. *Den norsk-isländska skaldediktningen.* 2 vols. Vol. I. Lund: Gleerup, 1946.
EHD	*English Historical Documents.* Vol. II: *1042–1189.* Ed. David C. Douglas and George W. Greenaway. London: Eyre & Spottiswoode, 1953.
F	*Fríssbók: Codex Frisianus. En Samling af norske konge-sagaer.* Ed. C. R. Unger. Christiania [Oslo]: P. T. Mallings forlagsboghandel, 1871.
Falk *Kleiderkunde*	Hjalmar Falk. *Altnordische Kleiderkunde, mit besonderer Berücksichtigung der Terminologie.* NVAOS. No. 3. Kristiania [Oslo]: Jacob Dybwad, 1918.
Falk "Seewesen"	Hjalmar Falk. "Altnordisches Seewesen." *Wörter und Sachen,* 4 (1912): 1–122.
Falk *Waffenkunde*	Hjalmar Falk, *Altnordische Waffenkunde.* NVAOS. No. 6. Kristiania [Oslo]: Jacob Dybwad, 1914.
FJ	Finnur Jónsson, ed. *Morkinskinna.* SUGNL 53. Copenhagen: J. Jørgensen & Co., 1932.
Flat	*Flateyjarbók: En samling af norske konge-sagaer med indskudte mindre fortællinger om begivenheder i og udenfor Norge samt annaler.* Ed.

	Guðbrandur Vigfússon and C. R. Unger. 3 vols. Oslo: Malling, 1860–68.
FmS	*Fornmanna sögur eptir gömlum handritum útgefnar að tilhlutun hins norræna fornfræða félags.* 12 vols. Copenhagen: Popp, 1825–37.
Fritzner	Johan Fritzner. *Ordbog over det gamle norske sprog.* 3 vols. Kristiania [Oslo]: Den norske forlagsforening, 1886–96.
Fsk	*Fagrskinna.* See *ÍF* 29.
Heimskringla (1991)	*Heimskringla,* ed. Bergljót S. Kristjánsdóttir, Bragi Halldórsson, Jón Torfason, Örnólfur Thorsson. 3 vols. Reykjavík: Mál og menning, 1991.
HH	Henry of Huntingdon: *Henrici Archidiaconi Huntendunensis Historia Anglorum.* Ed. Thomas Arnold. Chronicles and Memorials of Great Britain and Ireland during the Middle Ages, published by the authority of Her Majesty's Treasury, under the direction of the Master of the Rolls. 1879. Rpt. Wiesbaden: Kraus, 1965.
Hkr	*Heimskringla:* See *ÍF* 26–28.
HT(N)	*(Norsk) Historisk tidsskrift*
ÍF	*Íslenzk fornrit.* Reykjavik: Hið íslenzka fornritafélag.
	Vol. 1 (pts. 1 and 2): *Íslendingabók; Landnámabók.* Ed. Jakob Benediktsson. 1968.
	Vol. 2: *Egils saga Skalla-Grímssonar.* Ed. Sigurður Nordal. 1933.
	Vol. 3: *Borgfirðinga sǫgur.* Ed. Sigurður Nordal and Guðni Jónsson. 1938.
	Vol. 4: *Eyrbyggja saga.* Ed. Einar Ól. Sveinsson and Matthías Þórðarson. 1935.
	Vol. 5: *Laxdæla saga.* Ed. Einar Ól. Sveinsson. 1934.
	Vol. 6: *Vestfirðinga sǫgur.* Ed. Björn K. Þórólfsson and Guðni Jónsson. 1943.
	Vol. 7: *Grettis saga Ásmundarsonar.* Ed. Guðni Jónsson. 1936.
	Vol. 8: *Vatnsdæla saga.* Ed. Einar Ól. Sveinsson. 1939.
	Vol. 9: *Eyfirðinga sǫgur.* Ed. Jónas Kristjánsson. 1956.
	Vol. 10: *Ljósvetninga saga.* Ed. Björn Sigfússon. 1940.
	Vol. 11: *Austfirðinga sǫgur.* Ed. Jón Jóhannesson. 1950.
	Vol. 12: *Brennu-Njáls saga.* Ed. Einar Ól. Sveinsson. 1954.
	Vol. 13: *Harðar saga.* Ed. Þórhallur Vilmundarson and T. Bjarni Vilhjálmsson. 1991.
	Vol. 14: *Kjalnesinga saga.* Ed. Jóhannes Halldórsson. 1959.
	Vols. 26–28: *Heimskringla.* Ed. Bjarni Aðalbjarnarson. 1941–51.
	Vol. 29: *Fagrskinna-Nóregs konunga tal.* Ed. Bjarni Einarsson. 1984.
	Vol. 34: *Orkneyinga saga.* Ed. Finnbogi Guðmundsson. 1965.
	Vol. 35: *Danakonunga sǫgur.* Ed. Bjarni Guðnason. 1982.
Islandske Annaler	Gustav Storm, ed. *Islandske annaler indtil 1578.* Christiania [Oslo]: Grøndahl & søns bogtrykkeri, 1888.
KLNM	*Kulturhistorisk leksikon for nordisk middelalder.* Ed. Lis Jacobsen et al. 22 vols. Copenhagen: Rosenkilde & Bagger, 1956–78.
Litteraturhistorie	Finnur Jónsson. *Den oldnorske og oldislandske litteraturs historie.* 2 vols. Copenhagen: Gad, 1894–1901.

LM	*Lexikon des Mittelalters.* Ed. Robert Auty et al. Munich: Artemis-Verlag, 1980——.
MHN	*Monumenta Historica Norvegiae: Latinske kildeskrifter til Norges historie i middelalderen.* Ed. Gustav Storm. 1880. Rpt. Oslo: Aas & Wahl boktrykkeri A.s., 1973.
MLR	*Modern Language Review*
MM	*Maal og minne*
MSE	*Medieval Scandinavia: An Encyclopedia.* Ed. Phillip Pulsiano. New York: Garland, 1993.
Neckel/Kuhn	*Edda: Die Lieder des Codex Regius nebst verwandten Denkmälern.* Vol. I. Ed. Gustav Neckel. 4th rev. ed. by Hans Kuhn. Heidelberg: Carl Winter Universitätsverlag, 1962.
NGL	*Norges gamle love indtil 1387.* 5 vols. Vol. I: *Norges love ældre end Kong Magnus Haakonssøns regjerings-tiltrædelse i 1263.* Vol. II: *Lovgivningen under Kong Magnus Haakonssøns regjeringstid fra 1263 til 1280, tilligemed et supplement til første bind.* Ed. R. Keyser and P. A. Munch. Christiania [Oslo]: Chr. Gröndahl, 1846–48.
NN	Ernst Albin Kock. *Notationes Norroenae: Anteckningar till Edda och skaldediktning.* Lunds universitets årsskrift. N.s., sec. 1. Vols. 19–39. Lund: Gleerup, 1923–44.
NVAOS	Skrifter utgitt av Det Norske Videnskaps-Akademi i Oslo
Orðtakasafn	Halldór Halldórsson. *Íslenzkt orðtakasafn.* 2 vols. Reykjavík: Almenna bókafélagið, 1968–69.
OV	Ordericus Vitalis. *The Ecclesiastical History of Orderic Vitalis.* Ed. and trans. Marjorie Chibnall. 6 vols. Oxford Medieval Texts. Oxford: Clarendon Press, 1969–80.
RH	Roger de Hoveden. *Chronica Magistri Rogeri de Houedene.* Ed. William Stubbs. 4 vols. Chronicles and Memorials of Great Britain and Ireland during the Middle Ages, published by the Authority of Her Majesty's Treasury, under the direction of the Master of the Rolls. 1868. Rpt. Wiesbaden: Kraus Reprint Ltd., 1964. Vols. I–II.
Riant	Paul Riant. *Expéditions et pèlerinages des scandinaves en Terre Sainte au temps des croisades.* Paris: Imprimerie de Ad. Lainé et J. Havard, 1865.
Skj I-IIA, I-IIB	Finnur Jónsson, ed. *Den norsk-islandske skjaldedigtning.* Vols. IA-IIA: *Tekst efter håndskrifterne.* Vols. IB-IIB: *Rettet tekst.* 1908–15. Rpt. Copenhagen: Rosenkilde & Bagger, 1967–73.
SI	*Scripta Islandica*
SnE	*Edda Snorra Sturlusonar: Edda Snorronis Sturlæi.* Ed. Jón Sigurðsson et al. 3 vols. 1848. Rpt. Osnabrück: Zeller, 1966.
SS	*Scandinavian Studies*
Sturlunga saga (1988)	*Sturlunga saga,* ed. Örnólfur Thorsson et al. Reykjavík: Svart á hvítu, 1988.
SUGNL	Samfund til udgivelse af gammel nordisk litteratur
U	C. R. Unger, ed. *Morkinskinna: Pergamentsbog fra første halvdel af det trettende aarhundrede. Indeholdende en af de ældste optegnelser af norske kongesagaer.* Oslo: Bentzen, 1867.

UHV   *Untersuchungen zu Handel und Verkehr der vor- und früh-
               geschichtlichen Zeit in Mittel- und Nordeuropa. Teil I: Methodische
               Grundlagen und Darstellungen zum Handel in vorgeschichtlicher Zeit
               und in der Antike: Berichte über die Kolloquien der Kommission für die
               Altertumskunde Mittel- und Nordeuropas in den Jahren 1980 bis 1983.*
               Ed. Klaus Düwel, Herbert Jankuhn, Harald Siems, and Dieter
               Timpe. (= Abhandlungen der Akad. der Wiss. in Göttingen.
               Philol.-hist. Kl., Ser. 3, No. 143). Göttingen: Vandenhoeck &
               Ruprecht, 1987.

VGT   Ingvald Reichborn-Kjennerud. *Vår gamle trolldomsmedisin.*
               NVAOS in five parts: (1) 1927, no. 6:1–284; (2) 1933, no. 2:
               1–212; (3) 1940, no. 1:5–221; (4) 1944, no. 2:3–263; (5) 1947,
               no. 1:3–253.

WJ   William of Jumièges: *The Gesta Normannorum ducum of William of
               Jumièges, Orderic Vitalis, and Robert of Torigni.* Ed. and trans. Elisa-
               beth M. C. Van Houts. 2 vols. Oxford Medieval Texts. Oxford:
               Clarendon, 1992–95.

WM I–II   William of Malmesbury: *Willelmi Malmesbiriensis monachi de ges-
               tis regum Anglorum.* Ed. William Stubbs. 2 vols. Chronicles and
               Memorials of Great Britain and Ireland during the Middle Ages,
               published by the authority of Her Majesty's Treasury, under the
               direction of the Master of the Rolls. London, 1887.

Morkinskinna

Introduction

The Narrative

Morkinskinna is the first compendious collection of Norse kings' sagas, covering the period 1030–1157 (originally 1177). Earlier kings' sagas were either in the form of brief epitomes or individual biographies. The epitomes go back about a hundred years to the time of the first Icelandic historians at the beginning of the twelfth century, Ari Þorgilsson and Sæmundr Sigfússon. Ari writes a mysterious passage in his extant *Íslendingabók* (*ÍF* 1, 3) indicating that this book is a revision of an earlier version "minus the genealogies and kings' lives." The debate on what exactly may have been included in these kings' lives is inconclusive, but they must have been the point of departure for the later tradition of royal biography. At about the same time, Ari's contemporary Sæmundr Sigfússon (1056–1133) must have written a similar epitome, perhaps in Latin. A poem from ca. 1190 ("Nóregs konungatal"; *Skj* IA, 579–89) reviews ten kings from Haraldr hárfagri on "as Sæmundr inn fróði [the Wise] told." That seems to indicate that Sæmundr gave some account of the Norwegian kings from Haraldr down to Magnús góði (858–1047). The dimensions of this account are no clearer than in Ari's case.

At the end of the century, this Icelandic initiative was supplemented with three short histories written in Norway, two in Latin and one in Norwegian: the *Historia de Antiquitate Regum Norwagiensium* by Theodoricus monachus (ca. 1180), the *Historia Norwegiae* (of uncertain date), and *Ágrip af Nóregs konunga sǫgum* (ca. 1190). Theodoricus covered the period from Haraldr hárfagri to Haraldr gilli. The *Historia Norwegiae* contains geographical and legendary matters as well as a brief overview of historical kings down to Óláfr Haraldsson († 1030). *Ágrip* tells the story of the kings from the time of Haraldr hárfagri down to the point at which *Morkinskinna* ends (1157), but like *Morkinskinna*, it is defective at the end and may originally have continued down to 1177. In the standard editions, Theodoricus numbers 65 pages and *Ágrip* 50 pages. Exactly how these Norwegian works were connected with the Icelandic tradition is uncertain, but they may well derive in the final analysis from Ari and Sæmundr.

1

Royal biographies on a larger scale began later. The first, Eiríkr Oddsson's *Hryggjarstykki, was written in Iceland sometime in the middle of the twelfth century. The most recent investigation, by Bjarni Guðnason (1978), argues that it focused exclusively on Sigurðr slembir († 1139) and cannot therefore have been extensive. It was some time before Eiríkr's model caught on, and it was not until the 1190s that book-length biographies were composed. They singled out the conversion kings Óláfr Tryggvason (995–1000) and Óláfr Haraldsson (1015–1030). Two monks at the monastery of Þingeyrar, Oddr Snorrason and Gunnlaugr Leifsson, composed biographies of Óláfr Tryggvason, and about the same time there was a biography of Óláfr Haraldsson ("The Oldest Saga of St. Óláfr"), of which only six fragments are extant. In the late 1180s and probably again in the first decade of the thirteenth century, the Abbot of Þingeyrar, Karl Jónsson, began—and either he or someone else completed—a biography of King Sverrir Sigurðarson (1177–1202). By 1210 or so, there were thus substantial kings' sagas for the periods 995–1030 and again for 1177–1202. It seems likely that the author of *Morkinskinna* knew these works and that part of his project was to fill in the blank period between 1030 and 1177.

Unlike the earlier epitomes, and unlike Snorri's *Heimskringla* from a decade or so later (ca. 1230), *Morkinskinna* is not a surveyable series of royal biographies, each with a discrete focus on a single monarch. In the first place, very close to 60 percent of the text (through Ch. 52) is devoted to the lives of King Magnús Óláfsson and King Haraldr Sigurðarson; in addition, these lives are intertwined. We are told first of Magnús's succession to the throne and early reign (Chs. 1–8), then of King Haraldr's Mediterranean adventures (Chs. 9–13), then of the shared reign of Magnús and Haraldr down to the time of Magnús's death (Chs. 14–26). Only at this point does the text turn exclusively to Haraldr, relating his Danish and Swedish campaigns and ultimately his illfated attempt on England.

But most of the material in these chapters is episodic in nature, often narrating encounters with individual Icelanders (Chs. 30, 34, 36, 38, 40, 41, 43, 46, 47). The proportions are also skewed by the disproportionately long tale of Haraldr's dealings with Hákon Ívarsson (Ch. 42). Roughly 70 percent of the narrative in this section is given over to the *þættir* (episodic stories) of Icelanders and the story of Hákon Ívarsson. What tradition had to tell about Haraldr, aside from these anecdotal digressions, bore on his early adventures, his sometimes tense dealings with his nephew Magnús, his campaigns against King Sveinn Úlfsson of Denmark, and his invasion of England. The nodes of tradition on Magnús were his succession, his military campaigns in Denmark, and his sturdy diplomacy in contending with his aggressive uncle Haraldr.

The author clearly sees these careers not so much in terms of political history as in terms of character study. Haraldr's confrontations with Gyrgir, Magnús, Hákon Ívarsson, Einarr þambarskelfir, a succession of Icelanders (notably

Halldórr Snorrason), and Jarl Tostig profile a particular personality. The same is true of Magnús, though in much less detail and with a contrastive emphasis on the religious auspices of his father, St. Óláfr, Magnús's steady reliability, and his devotion to peace. Despite the paucity of moral commentary, it seems clear that the underlying theme is moral in nature.

In contrast to the abundance of tradition on Haraldr stands a corresponding dearth of information on his son Óláfr kyrri, who is the beneficiary of only two mid-sized chapters despite a reign of twenty-seven years. The second of these two chapters recounts a *þáttr*-like incident that seems so uncharacteristic of the sanguine and tranquil Óláfr that the reader may seriously question whether it was originally associated with him or his father. Very little that was deemed "saga-worthy" seems to have been transmitted about Óláfr, certainly nothing that was harmful to his reputation. Adventures, military campaigns, and dynastic struggles, which made up the bulk of the tradition about Magnús and Haraldr, were apparently considered to have been gratifyingly absent from Óláfr's reign. In other literary traditions, such an agreeable respite might have given rise to the biography of a great statesman, but there is very little hint of such a portrait in *Morkinskinna* or in any other source on Óláfr kyrri. This missed opportunity says much about the action-dependence of saga narrative and the limitations of that literary form.

With the advent of Óláfr's son Magnús berfœttr (Chs. 55–59), we return to the man of action and the military and expeditionary narrative that was characteristic of Haraldr Sigurðarson. The stock of motifs is also similar, beginning with Magnús's dynastic contentions, moving to his campaigns in the British Isles and in Gautland, and concluding with his fatal venture in Ireland. The dynastic section relates his uneasy truce with his cousin Hákon, who was accepted by the Þrœndir as their king. The situation is reminiscent of the division of the realm between Haraldr and Magnús. On Hákon's death, the realm might be expected to reunite, but the Þrœndir persist in their drive for independence by taking a certain Sveinn, son of Haraldr flettir, as their king. Magnús now concedes no claim of kinship or kingship to Sveinn and moves forcefully against the Þrœndir by routing their troops and hanging their leaders Steigar-Þórir and Egill of Forland. That part of the narrative is reminiscent of Haraldr harðráði's contention with Einarr þambarskelfir over the fealty of the Þrœndir, ending as it does with the murder of Einarr.

The similarities in outline between "Haralds saga" and "Magnúss saga" are obscured because the latter is only 15 percent the length of the former and because the multiple *þættir* in "Haralds saga" tend to obscure the plotline in that story. The only portion of "Magnúss saga" that might be termed a *þáttr* is the story of Sveinki Steinarsson, which is told with such verve and wit that it seems to have independent status. Sveinki is the original foster father of Magnús's rival pretender Hákon. He therefore belongs in the context of the dynastic struggles and represents the last impediment to Magnús's sole rule over

Norway. Finally, Magnús's rule concludes on the same note as Haraldr harðráði's—death while on a foreign adventure in the west. Snorri Sturluson recognized the kinship and summed up Magnús in the following words (ÍF 28,
218): "He was a bold, warlike, and enterprising man, in every respect more
similar in temper to his grandfather Haraldr than to his father."

The succeeding section of some twenty chapters (60–81) again describes a
divided rule shared by Magnús berfœttr's two sons Sigurðr and Eysteinn (after
the early death of their younger brother Óláfr). Again, the focus is on contrastive characters, illustrated by Snorri's remark on Magnús's heritage. Sigurðr adheres to the tradition of his great-grandfather Haraldr harðráði, while
Eysteinn takes after his grandfather Óláfr. Just as Haraldr received a disproportionate share of the narrative compared to his more peaceable nephew
Magnús, so Sigurðr emerges in the spotlight at the expense of his stay-at-home
brother Eysteinn. Only four chapters (64, 65, 68, 73) are centrally concerned
with Eysteinn, and two others (70–71) are evenly divided between Sigurðr and
Eysteinn. Sigurðr has the double advantage of undertaking a great Mediterranean crusade adventure at the beginning of his life and of outliving Eysteinn
at the end.

The adventure pattern duplicates the brilliant youth of Haraldr harðráði,
and the shared rule duplicates Haraldr's uneasy relationship with Magnús.
The uneasiness is summarized in two dramatic narratives at the very center of
this section, occupying a bit more than 25 percent of "Magnússona saga." The
first, "Þinga saga" (Ch. 70), relates an extended legal battle between the brothers, and the second (Ch. 71), a "flyting," or verbal joust, in which they compare
their achievements. The concluding section after Eysteinn's death is anecdotal
but contains none of the þættir of Icelanders that characterized Haraldr harðráði's career. Most of the incidents are very brief and serve to illustrate the
lapses of mental stability that plagued Sigurðr's mature years.

Sigurðr is succeeded only very briefly by a half-brother of somewhat doubtful lineage, Haraldr gilli, but Haraldr succumbs quickly to a pretender of
equally doubtful parentage, Sigurðr slembir. The following narrative on Sigurðr (Chs. 84–93) is not original with the author of Morkinskinna. All or large
parts of it were narrated in the lost book by Eiríkr Oddsson titled *Hryggjarstykki. Whether for this reason or because the events were recent enough to
be in more proximate memory, this part of the narrative does not subscribe to
the patterns of adventure and dynastic tension that dominated earlier sections
of the story. Sigurðr's challenge to the infant sons of Haraldr gilli takes the
form of raids and killings among their supporters.

When the contending forces finally meet in the Battle of Hólmr inn grái
(Holmengrå), Sigurðr makes a distinguished stand but does not fall in battle
like Haraldr harðráði or Magnús berfœttr. Instead, he is captured and dies a
martyr's death by torture. The remainder of the story returns to the theme of
dynastic conflicts and accounts for the death of two of Haraldr gilli's sons,
Eysteinn and Sigurðr. The narrative is clearly aimed at the emergence of Ingi

Haraldsson as sole ruler, but the manuscript breaks off before the succession is stabilized.

The Manuscripts

Morkinskinna Manuscript (MskMS)

MskMS is kept in Det kongelige bibliotek in Copenhagen under the signature Gamle kongelige samling 1009 fol. Very little is known about the prehistory of the MS. In 1662 it was sent from Iceland to King Frederick III of Denmark by Bishop Brynjólfur Sveinsson. The name "Morkinskinna" ("rotten parchment") was given to it by Þormóður Torfason (Torfæus) who borrowed the MS in 1682 and used it as one of the sources for his *Historia Rerum Norvegicarum* (see FJ iii–iv; Louis-Jensen 1977:62–63).

In its present form, the MS consists of thirty-seven leaves. It originally contained seven quires: four eight-leaf quires, one nine-leaf quire, and two six-leaf quires (FJ iv–v). The entire seventh quire is missing, and the MS ends abruptly in the middle of Chapter 100 of the "Saga of Ingi and his Brothers." In addition to the missing seventh quire, MskMS contains the following lacunae:

1. Six leaves: "The Saga of Haraldr and Magnús" (Chs. 1–12; FJ 14.3–70.24; U 7.21);
2. One leaf: "The Saga of Haraldr and Magnús" (Chs. 26–30; FJ 141.16–148.36; U 46.32);
3. One leaf: "The Saga of Haraldr and Magnús" (Chs. 31–35; FJ 169.22–177.39; U 59.21);
4. One leaf: "The Saga of Sigurðr jórsalafari" (Ch. 61; FJ 348.17–19; U 163.12);
5. One leaf: "The Saga of Haraldr gilli and Magnús blindi" (Ch. 82; FJ 400.26–27; U 198.32).

MskMS has been dated to the end of the thirteenth century or a little earlier, and it was copied by two professional scribes who appear to have worked on the MS simultaneously. It has not been established where in Iceland it was written (Louis-Jensen 1977:63–64). The two hands are distributed as follows in the extant portions of MskMS:

Hand I: leaves 1–9 (FJ 1–169.27; U 1–59.21);
Hand II: leaves 10–17 (FJ 178.1–258.13; U 59.22–108.4);
Hand I: leaves 18–25^r, l. 11 (FJ 259.1–338.22; U 108.4–157.8);
Hand II: leaf 25^r, ll. 11–48 (FJ 338.22–342.2; U 157.8–159.14);
Hand I: leaf 25^r, l. 48–leaf 37 (FJ 342.3–462; U 159.14–237).

The sections written by the second hand contain several marginal additions and textual corrections by the first scribe. Hand I is more archaic than hand II, but the second scribe consistently preserves certain archaic spellings not found in the parts copied by the first hand (for example, the spelling "of" instead of "um"). On the whole, the orthography in MskMS is characterized by archaic features, which has led some scholars to believe that it reflected the conventions of an old archetype dating back to the first third of the thirteenth century (FJ v; but see Louis-Jensen 1977:64). The archaic forms appear to be distributed fairly evenly throughout the MS, and they occur in the *þættir* as well as in the main corpus of the text, although some *þættir* seem to be characterized by a greater number of such forms than others (e.g., "Hreiðars þáttr heimska"; see Jón Helgason 1934:14). We have also observed the tendency that the orthography in the poetry, as well as in direct speeches, is more archaic than the orthography in the main corpus of the text. As of yet, there is no comprehensive study of the orthography in MskMS, but Finnur Jónsson gives a summary and discussion in the introduction to his diplomatic edition (FJ v–viii; see also Foote 1955:67, 71–75).

The Later Flateyjarbók (Flat)

During the last half of the fifteenth century, three quires containing the "Saga of Haraldr and Magnús" were added to the Flateyjarbók compilation (Gamle kongelige samling 1005 fol. from around 1387; for a more detailed discussion, see Louis-Jensen 1969, 1977:65–66). The new addition was apparently commissioned by the then owner of the Flateyjarbók compilation, Þorleifur Björnsson of Reykhólar in northern Iceland. The text of that addition corresponds very closely to that of MskMS, and a comparison between the two shows that most changes in Flat consist of slight expansions of the text, the insertion of alliterating formulas, changes from indirect to direct speech, the replacement of archaic words and phrases, and a simplification and modernization of the syntax. In addition, some of the stanzas contained in MskMS have been left out in Flat.

As Jonna Louis-Jensen has shown (1969; 1977:66), the addition to Flateyjarbók appears to go back to an older MS from the second half of the fourteenth century, of which two fragments have been preserved (AM 325 IV ß and AM 325 XI, 3 4^(to)). It is unlikely that this MS comprised all the sagas of the Morkinskinna compilation; rather, it seems to have contained the "Saga of Haraldr and Magnús" only (ibid.). In the present work, the text of Flat has been used to fill in the first three lacunae in MskMS (*MskMS).

Hulda (AM 66)

The MS known as "Hulda" ("the hidden MS") or by its signature, AM 66, contains the sagas of the Norwegian kings from Magnús góði to Magnús Erlingsson (1035–1177). The MS consists of 142 leaves, and the first quire (six leaves) is lost. AM 66 was written by one hand and has been dated to the last part of the fourteenth century. (For a more comprehensive discussion, see Louis-Jensen 1977:7–10.) According to Louis-Jensen (1977:7), that hand is the same as (or at least is closely related to) a hand found in two diplomas (AM Fasc. III, 5, and III, 6) issued in 1375 at the monastery Munkaþverá in Eyjafjörður in northern Iceland.

Hrokkinskinna (Hr)

"Hrokkinskinna" ("wrinkled parchment"; Gamle kongelige samling 1010 fol.) consists of ninety-five leaves. The first ninety-one leaves contain the sagas of the Norwegian kings from 1035–1177 and were written at the beginning of the fifteenth century. (For a comprehensive discussion, see Louis-Jensen 1977:10–13.) In the sixteenth century a four-leaf quire was added to the MS that contained an incomplete version of "Hemings þáttr Áslákssonar" (ibid., 10). The main part of the codex appears to have been written by one hand, also found in a diploma issued in 1423 at Lögmannshlíð in Eyjafjörður in northern Iceland. That diploma is a receipt from Ingibjörg Loptsdóttir to Magnús Jónsson, the owner of the farm Grund in Eyjafjörður. Marginal notes in the MS suggest that Hr at one point belonged to Ingunn Arnardóttir († after 1427), the wife of Magnús Jónsson of Grund (ibid., 11–12). Because the scribe of Hr apparently was in the employ of Magnús Jónsson, his wife could have been the first owner of the MS (ibid., 12).

Earlier MSS and the Relations between MskMS, Flat, AM 66, and Hr

*H

Hr is not a copy of AM 66, but the two MSS go back to a lost exemplar, *H (see Louis-Jensen 1977:13–15). It is impossible to determine whether *H was an original or a copy of an earlier MS. The date of AM 66 (the third quarter of the fourteenth century) provides a *terminus ante quem* for *H, and comments in the texts of Hr and AM 66 suggest that the exemplar must have been compiled after 1268, most likely after 1280 (ibid., 13). The text of the kings' sagas in *H (as evidenced by the texts of Hr and AM 66) was ultimately based on Snorri's *Heimskringla* (see the detailed discussion by Louis-Jensen 1977: 16–61), supplemented by prose and poetry from a version of *Morkinskinna* (ibid., 62–94; see below).

m and Msk2

As stated above, the text of the "Saga of Haraldr and Magnús" in the later part of Flat follows that of MskMS fairly closely. But because Flat in places has readings in common with *H that differ from those of MskMS (see Louis-Jensen 1977:70–72), neither *H nor Flat can be copies of that MS; rather, both versions must go back to a common exemplar, m, that again derives from an older MS (Msk2), which also was the exemplar of MskMS. Louis-Jensen (1977:72) envisions those relations as follows:

<pre>
                            *Msk2
       ───
       MskMS   ────────────────────────
                                    m
                         *H   325-Flat
</pre>

The MSS of *Heimskringla*

A comprehensive discussion of the MSS of Snorri's *Heimskringla* and their relations falls outside of the scope of this work (for a more detailed discussion, see Louis-Jensen 1977:16–43). But because the oldest version of *Morkinskinna* (ÆMsk) served as a source for that work, and because later MSS of *Heimskringla* were interpolated from a later version of *Morkinskinna* and have been used to supplement the text of MskMS in the present work (notably *Fríssbók*), the overview below has been added to clarify the relations between the most important MSS of *Heimskringla* as well as the connections between MskMS and the later MSS of *Heimskringla* (see "The Relations between Msk2 and the *Morkinskinna* Text in Hkr x-y," below).

Kringla (K)

K was destroyed in the fire in The University Library in Copenhagen in 1728. Except for one leaf (Perg. fol. nr. 9, I), preserved in Kungliga biblioteket in Stockholm, Sweden, the MS survives in copies only. The remaining leaf allows for a dating of K to 1260–1280, and the MS was written in Iceland (*ÍF* 28, lxxxiii–lxxxvi; Louis-Jensen 1977:16–17).

AM 39 fol. (39)

This MS consists of forty-three leaves written by one hand. It has been dated to around 1300 and was written in Iceland (*ÍF* 28, lxxxvi–lxxxvii; Louis-Jensen 1977:18–19).

Codex Frisianus or Fríssbók (F): AM 45 fol.

This MS contains the sagas in *Hkr* I (*ÍF* 26) and III (*ÍF* 28) plus "Hákonar saga Hákonarsonar" (see *ÍF* 28, lxxxvii–lxxxviii; Louis-Jensen 1977:19–21). It has been dated to the beginning of the fourteenth century and seems to have originated in a scriptorium in southern Iceland (possibly the same scriptorium that produced 39). It was apparently brought to Norway at an early date. F contains sections from a version of *Morkinskinna* (after the "Saga of Haraldr and Magnús") and incorporates stanzas, as well as *þættir* and smaller anecdotes, not found in K and 39. For an overview of the material included in F from *Morkinskinna*, see Louis-Jensen 1977:87–88.

Eirspennill (47): AM 47 fol.

In AM 47 are contained the last chapters of "Óláfs saga helga," the sagas in *Hkr* III (*ÍF* 28), as well as "Sverris saga," "Bǫglungasǫgur," and "Hákonar saga Hákonarsonar" (see *Eirspennill* v–xxiv). It has been dated to the beginning of the fourteenth century (see *ÍF* 28, xc; Louis-Jensen 1977:21–24). Like F, AM 47 contains substantial material from a version of *Morkinskinna* (see the overview in Louis-Jensen 1977:37, 39) and the MS was probably also sent to Norway from Iceland shortly after it was written.

Jöfraskinna (J)

Except for four leaves (Perg. fol. nr. 9, II) and fragments (AM 325 VIII 3d 4to; NRA 55A), this MS was lost in the fire of 1728. It was of Icelandic provenance and has been dated to around 1325. Jöfraskinna survives in a copy (J2) from the end of the seventeenth century made by Ásgeir Jónsson (see *ÍF* 28, lxxxviii–lxxxix; Louis-Jensen 1977:24–28). Interpolations from *Morkinskinna* are also found in J (see Louis-Jensen 1977:38).

Gullinskinna (42): AM fol. 42

The entire MS burned in the fire of 1728 and survives in a seventeenth-century copy, also by Ásgeir Jónsson (see *ÍF* 28, xc–xci; Louis-Jensen 1977: 28–31). Material from *Morkinskinna* is contained in AM 42.

The relations between the MSS of *Heimskringla* discussed above can be schematized as shown (see *ÍF* 28, xciv; Louis-Jensen 1977:35):

original (?)

x					y
K	x^1		47	J2	42
39	F				

The Relations between Msk2 and the *Morkinskinna* Text in Hkr x-y

Both branches of the *Heimskringla* MSS have been interpolated from a version of *Morkinskinna*. The Hkr x branch (F) contains the same series of interpolations from *Morkinskinna* as the y branch (42, 47, J2), but in addition, F (Hkr x) incorporates text from *Morkinskinna* that, in some cases, replaces the text of *Heimskringla* (Louis-Jensen 1977:83). A comparison between the relevant sections of MskMS and F shows that the two manuscripts ultimately must be derived from the same exemplar (Msk2), but because the *Morkinskinna* text of F, as well as that of Hkr y, relies on a shorter version than that of MskMS, the *Morkinskinna* exemplar of Hkr x and y appears to have been an abbreviated

version of Msk2 (ibid., 90). According to Louis-Jensen (1977:93), the relations
between the different versions can be schematized as follows:

Msk2

MskY   MskX

y   F   MskMS   m

y¹   y²   *H   Flat

42, 47, J2

Fagrskinna (Fsk)

Fagrskinna has been preserved in two versions, Fsk A and B. Both exemplars
burned in the fire of 1728, but they have survived in copies from the latter part
of the seventeenth century. Whereas the first MS (Fsk A) was completely destroyed, one leaf of the latter (Fsk B), which was removed from the compendium before it was sent to Copenhagen, has been preserved in Riksarkivet,
in Oslo, Norway (NRA 51; for a more extensive discussion, see *ÍF* 29, lxi–lxv).
Fsk B has been dated to around 1250, and it must have been older than the extant MS of *Morkinskinna* (MskMS). The palaeographic evidence suggests that
Fsk B was written in Trondheim, Norway. The copies of Fsk A indicate that the
lost exemplar was written during the first half of the fourteenth century in
southeastern Norway.

Fsk A and B survive in the following MSS:

A: AM 52 fol.; AM 301 4ᵗᵒ; AM 303 ⁴ᵗᵒ (all copied by Ásgeir Jónsson).
B: NRA 51; UB 371 fol. (copied by Ásgeir Jónsson between 1657 and 1707); AM 51
fol.; AM 302 4ᵗᵒ (copied by Eyjólfur Björnsson [1666–1746]).

A comparison between the texts of Fsk A and B shows that A contained a fuller
text and more skaldic stanzas than B. Furthermore, B has lacunae and the MS
apparently ended with our Chapter 87 (*ÍF* 29, 330).

The Oldest Morkinskinna (ÆMsk)

Scholars now agree that both *Fagrskinna* and *Heimskringla* drew on an older, no
longer extant version of *Morkinskinna* (ÆMsk) for the sagas of those Norwegian kings whose lives span the years 1035–1177 (see "The Narrative," above,
and Louis-Jensen 1977: 66–70). The relations between ÆMsk, *Fagrskinna,*
Heimskringla, and MskMS can be schematized as follows:

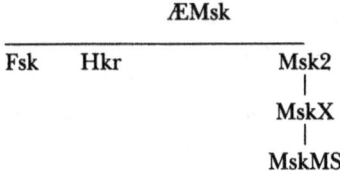

Although a comparison between the texts of *Heimskringla, Fagrskinna,* and MskMS shows that the three versions in places correspond almost verbatim, both *Fagrskinna* and *Heimskringla* fail to record the many *þættir* and smaller anecdotes that characterize the narrative of MskMS. That is also true of a number of skaldic stanzas (see "The Oral Sources," below). Because most of these episodes (as well as the stanzas) occur in Hr, AM 66, in those portions of F that follow Msk X, as well as in the "Saga of Haraldr and Magnús" in Flat, it has been suggested that the text of *Morkinskinna* was heavily interpolated at the stage of Msk2 (see the discussion in Louis-Jensen 1977:69–70 and the introduction to Finnur Jónsson's diplomatic edition). According to that opinion, then, the extant version of *Morkinskinna* (MskMS) would bear scant semblance to ÆMsk, which would seem to be better represented by the versions of *Fagrskinna* and *Heimskringla.* In the present work, the issue of interpolation is addressed in "The Narrative," "The Poetic Corpus of ÆMsk and the Question of Interpolation," and "The Oral Sources."

The Native Sources

Morkinskinna ("rotten parchment"—so named by Torfæus and now used both as a name for the manuscript and as a title of the book) is the least well publicized of the early Icelandic sagas, despite its compendious dimensions. It has been published in two scholarly editions that reproduce the orthography of the manuscript: a nineteenth-century edition by C. R. Unger (1867), and an early twentieth-century edition by Finnur Jónsson (1928–1932). In addition, there is a phototypical edition of the main manuscript (GKS [Den gamle kongelige samling] 1009 fol.) by Jón Helgason (1934), but there is no reader's edition. *Morkinskinna* has not appeared either in the standard Íslenzk fornrit series or in the popular Íslendingasagnaútgáfur. It was not included among the works translated in the German Thule series, and it has not been translated into a modern Scandinavian language. Under these circumstances, we surmise that the book is not much read except by scholars.

But even scholars have been chary in their attentions to this text. C. R. Unger's introduction was very brief, while Finnur Jónsson and Jón Helgason confined themselves to about twenty pages on the main points. Only one scholar, Eivind Kválen, developed a central interest in *Morkinskinna,* but his

views gained little favor and are almost never referred to in the current literature. The best work has been done obliquely in books devoted primarily to
other texts, for example, in Gustav Indrebø's study of *Fagrskinna* (1917) or
Bjarni Aðalbjarnarson's study of a variety of kings' saga problems (1937). The
most important recent contribution may be found in Jonna Louis-Jensen's
study of two related kings' saga redactions, *Hulda* and *Hrokkinskinna* (1977).
We will begin here with a summary of Bjarni Aðalbjarnarson's forty-page review of the main problems.

His point of departure was an analysis of the connection between *Morkin-*
skinna and *Ágrip af Nóregs konunga sǫgum*, a brief history of the Norwegian kings
from Haraldr hárfagri to Ingi Haraldsson (†1161) or, perhaps, to the accession
of King Sverrir (1177); we cannot be certain because the concluding chapters
are missing from the only manuscript. The probable date of composition is
around 1190. There are numerous verbatim correspondences between *Ágrip*
and *Morkinskinna*. Bjarni Aðalbjarnarson noted forty-three significant correspondences, but the count will vary somewhat depending on the counter.

A number of explanations have been offered, among them that the author
of *Morkinskinna* drew on *Ágrip*, or that both authors used parallel sources, or
that *Morkinskinna* was later interpolated from *Ágrip*. The likelihood of common sources seems questionable because the two works date from the dawn of
Norse history writing, and it is uncertain what the lost common sources may
have been at such an early date. Interpolation from a very brief work like *Ágrip*
also seems inherently unlikely because *Morkinskinna*, which provides a fuller
history, hardly stands to gain from incorporating passages from the much
more cursory *Ágrip*. And yet Bjarni Aðalbjarnarson made a good case for believing that interpolation is the right answer. His analysis shows that the interpolations often produced an awkward text in *Morkinskinna*. One symptomatic
instance may suffice to illustrate the case.

Ágrip (Ch. 38) tells us that when King Haraldr Sigurðarson returned from
his Mediterranean adventures, he approached King Magnús's adviser Úlfr
stallari disguised as a messenger. The episode reappears in *Morkinskinna*
(Ch. 8) out of context, because it is related before the tale of Haraldr's adventures in the south. The interpolator is obliged to locate the episode at this
juncture rather than after Haraldr's return because Úlfr stallari accompanied
Haraldr on his campaigns and could not have been attached to the service of
King Magnús during that time. The most palpable contradiction in the *Morkin-*
skinna version occurs when Úlfr addresses King Magnús in the following terms,
even before he has engaged in his foreign adventures: "He also said that Haraldr was a wise man with a great following, and that he had accomplished many
great deeds abroad, which would be long remembered." That sentence appears to be lifted directly from *Ágrip* because it is foreign to the context in
Morkinskinna, in which the "great deeds abroad" have not yet been related.

Bjarni Aðalbjarnarson was able to adduce a number of similarly telling examples. In addition, he pointed out (1937:145–46) that *Morkinskinna* some-times echoes passages from one of the sources of *Ágrip*—the *Historia de Anti-quitate Regum Norwagiensium* of Theodoricus monachus. Since there is no pat-tern of direct borrowing from Theodoricus, these echoes are best explained as the result of incorporations from *Ágrip*. A further indication of interpolation had already been observed by Gustav Indrebø (1917:22–30). He noted that the author of *Fagrskinna*, who relied heavily on *Morkinskinna*, consistently omits the passages that seem to be derived from *Ágrip* from his account. Indrebø concluded that the author of *Fagrskinna* must have used an uninterpolated redaction of *Morkinskinnna*.

Bjarni Aðalbjarnarson also weighed the possibility of lesser interpolations from *Knýtlinga saga* and *Orkneyinga saga*, but despite an extensive narrative parallelism, he did not believe that *Morkinskinna* made direct use of the sepa-rate *Hákonar saga Ívarssonar (see below). In the case of a close correspon-dence with *Ljósvetninga saga*, he judged (in contrast to Jón Helgason 1934:14–15) that *Morkinskinna* was primary. These matters will presently be considered in some detail.

One of the most salient features of *Morkinskinna* is that it includes a large number of semi-independent tales (*þættir*) not found in the related texts of *Fagrskinna* and *Heimskringla*. Bjarni Aðalbjarnarson lists sixteen such *þættir*, which, based on their loose connection with the royal biographies and some tautologous wording, may have existed in separate redactions prior to the composition of *Morkinskinna*. It has generally been assumed that some or many of these *þættir* were interpolated during the period between the original redaction of *Morkinskinna* (ca. 1220) and the extant MS (ca. 1275). But the *þættir* and incidental episodes are so numerous that it seems unlikely that they are supervenient as a rule. We would have to believe that for some reason, in-terpolation became epidemic in *Morkinskinna* manuscripts but that this epi-demic spared the manuscript traditions of *Fagrskinna* and *Heimskringla* dur-ing the same period. It seems more likely that *Morkinskinna* was characterized by anecdotal digressions from the outset, although this proclivity may have opened the door to further insertions at a later date.

Bjarni Aðalbjarnarson was cautious in assuming an extensive interpolation of *þættir*, but he did point out (1937:158) that the story of the Norman knight Giffarðr (Ch. 58) is built around an interpolation from *Ágrip* (Ch. 48) and may therefore have been added at the time of the interpolation. He was also open to the idea that six *þættir* not found in *Flateyjarbók* ("Auðunar þáttr," "Sneglu-Halla þáttr," "Halldórs þáttr Snorrasonar," "Hreiðars þáttr," "Brands þáttr ǫrva," and "Íslendings þáttr sǫgufróða") were later interpolations in *Morkin-skinna*, but Louis-Jensen (1977:77–78) argued that three of them are identi-cally placed in the transmission branches represented by *Morkinskinna* and *Hulda-Hrokkinskinna*. Since it is unlikely that two interpolators would hit on the same order, the placement may go back to the original *Morkinskinna* redaction, and the *þættir* may have been omitted in *Flateyjarbók*. This observation substantially alters the likelihood of wholesale interpolations in *Morkinskinna* and places the onus of proof on those who hold to the idea of interpolation.

Bjarni Aðalbjarnarson's concluding discussion is devoted to the more substantial sources of *Morkinskinna*, notably Eiríkr Oddsson's **Hryggjarstykki*. Since **Hryggjarstykki* is not extant in its original form but only in extracts found in *Morkinskinna, Fagrskinna,* and *Heimskringla,* most of the analysis has been devoted to determining the extent of the lost book. Bjarni Aðalbjarnarson reviews the arguments for the period 1130–1139 (the death of Magnús blindi and Sigurðr slembir), 1130–1161 (the death of Ingi Haraldsson), or 1130–1177 (a possibility maintained by Eivind Kválen). He finds plausible reasons in support of the first two alternatives but very little to recommend Kválen's extension of the book down to 1177. He also reviews the evidence, argued chiefly by Finnur Jónsson, for prior biographies of individual kings. He concedes the possibility of such lost sagas but considers them to be quite hypothetical.

The reconstruction of **Hryggjarstykki* is a particularly difficult problem, but it is of some moment because this text appears to be the earliest Icelandic "saga" and is one of only three books referred to in *Morkinskinna*. The others are a version of *Knýtlinga saga* (Ch. 53 at note 11) and a work called "jarla sǫgur" (Ch. 4 at note 1), corresponding to what we now know as *Orkneyinga saga*. Bjarni Aðalbjarnarson found the problem sufficiently vexed that he returned to it in the third volume of his *Heimskringla* edition (*ÍF* 28, lxiv–lxvii). Here he reviews both the indications that **Hryggjarstykki* ended with the death of Magnús blindi and Sigurðr slembir and the indications that Eiríkr Oddsson may have carried the story down to the death of Ingi Haraldsson (1161). He tries to harmonize the conflicting evidence by suggesting that the first redaction of **Hryggjarstykki* extended only to the death of Sigurðr slembir but that Eiríkr later composed a continuation to the year 1161. There were thus two redactions in circulation.

Given the problematic nature of the question, we are fortunate to have a particularly thorough and well-balanced reassessment by Bjarni Guðnason (1978), who arrived at rather different conclusions. He argued that **Hryggjarstykki* covered a very short period indeed (1136–1139). There is then a gap in the story until 1142. For the period 1142–1177, Bjarni proposes the interesting hypothesis that there may have been a written narrative in which Abbot Karl Jónsson of Þingeyrar had a hand (1978:26–28). We may of course ask why the author of *Morkinskinna*, who was so careful to identify Eiríkr Oddsson's **Hryggjarstykki*, would have failed to identify a book by such a prominent writer as Karl Jónsson, but he may well have had other written sources that he failed to identify. The question then is why the author would have singled out Eiríkr Oddsson, among all his sources, for special mention. Perhaps he referred to Eiríkr as the most ancient of his sources, just as Snorri Sturluson singled out Ari Þorgilsson but failed to mention the authors of *Morkinskinna* and *Fagrskinna,* on which he was substantially more dependent. This surmise is particularly attractive if Bjarni Guðnason (1978:144) is correct in placing the composition of *Hryggjarstykki as early as 1146–1155.

In any event, Bjarni makes a strong case for believing that the book was exclusively focused on Sigurðr slembir and derived a hagiographic emphasis from its focus on the martyr's death suffered by Sigurðr. This focus is well supported by a closely parallel narrative of Sigurðr's final battle and death in Saxo Grammaticus's *Gesta Danorum* (Bjarni Guðnason 1978:65–66). The account is so close that although it has often been assumed to be only an oral variant, Bjarni Guðnason is able to argue persuasively that Saxo had a copy of *Hryggjarstykki in front of him as he worked. Since Saxo concentrates on the finale of Sigurðr's martyrdom in 1139, that may well have the high point and conclusion of Eiríkr's little book.

The apparent focus on Sigurðr slembir raises the interesting question of the political orientation in *Morkinskinna.* There is evidence, to be reviewed below, that the author was particularly sympathetic toward King Ingi Haraldsson and that this part of the story may have been brought to Iceland by King Ingi's Icelandic followers. Yet Sigurðr slembir, who was intent on dethroning Ingi and his brothers, is given heroic coverage in the text. It seems likely that *Morkinskinna* is not to be regarded as pro-Ingi or as pro-Sigurðr. Both men had their partisans in Iceland, and it is not unusual for Icelandic sagas to give two antagonists their due in equal portions. Sigurðr spent a winter with Þorgils Oddason in Saurbœr and had close Icelandic connections (Bjarni Guðnason 1978: 119–31), but that would not have diminished Ingi's reputation in Iceland. One of Ingi's special partisans, Þorvarðr Þorgeirsson, in fact married his daughter to Sigurðr slembir's grandson (Bjarni Guðnason 1978:93).

More politically telling are Sigurðr's Danish connections, which seem to have been communicated to Eiríkr Oddsson by a certain Ketill prófastr, for whom we have a Latin life, the *Vita Ketilli.* Bjarni Guðnason speculated that Eiríkr Oddsson could have encountered Ketill while the latter was provost at St. Mary's in Ålborg in 1147–1148 (1978:139). Sigurðr slembir seems to have recruited the Danish kings Erik Emune (1134–1137) and Erik Lam (1137–1146) in his attempts to win Norway—or perhaps the recruitment was reversed. In any case, since Sigurðr made common cause with the Danes, Bjarni Guðnason (1978:137) believes that they would have had good reason to promote his reputation to the point of saintliness. The ultimate inspiration for a hagiographic account of Sigurðr's life could therefore well have been Danish. The author of *Morkinskinna* saw no reason to abandon this seventy-year-old account because it did not square with the pro-Ingi sympathies in his own circle.

Although *Morkinskinna* refers directly only to three texts, there are unresolved connections with several others. Most prominent among these is a *Hákonar saga Ívarssonar, which survives only in fragments. These fragments have many points in common with a chapter in *Morkinskinna* titled "Concerning King Haraldr and Hákon" (Ch. 42). The similarities begin, in fact, somewhat earlier (Ch. 35), with the description of the death at King Haraldr's hands of Einarr þambarskelfir and his son Eindriði. Here there are some verbatim correspondences, which, however, are not such as to convince previous critics of a textual link. After the death of Einarr and Eindriði, the author of *Morkinskinna* tells us that Finnr Árnason went to Denmark and took service with King Sveinn. At this point he inserts a series of *þættir* or *þáttr*-like episodes:

1. "Auðunar þáttr"
2. the story of King Haraldr and Úlfr auðgi
3. "Brands þáttr ǫrva"
4. the story of King Haraldr and Ingibjǫrg Halldórsdóttir
5. the story of the Icelander who narrated King Haraldr's adventures
6. "Þorvarðs þáttr krákunefs"

Here the story of King Haraldr and Hákon Ívarsson begins. It might be broken down into the following episodes:

1. King Haraldr's fleet is trapped in Lófufjǫrðr (Halland) with an inadequate supply of water, but Haraldr uses a snake to locate a source of water on an island.
2. Hákon's father, Ívarr hvíti, gives the skald Sigvatr a rather reluctant hearing.
3. Ívarr's son Hákon is introduced.
4. Hákon goes on harrying expeditions with Finnr Árnason.
5. Hákon joins forces with King Haraldr at the Battle of Niz (1062).
6. Haraldr captures Finnr Árnason and provokes him into a memorable exchange of words.
7. King Sveinn, having been defeated in the battle, takes refuge with a poor couple.
8. King Haraldr's Icelandic follower Þórólfr mostrarskegg tries to cap the victory with a private exploit and suffers a humiliating defeat.
9. King Haraldr offers Hákon marriage to King Magnús's daughter Ragnhildr and a jarldom.
10. When it becomes clear that Haraldr will not keep his pledge of the jarldom, Hákon departs in anger and kills one of the king's stewards.
11. In the service of the Danish king, Sveinn Úlfsson Hákon kills the obstreperous Ásmundr Bjarnarson.
12. Hákon receives a jarldom in Halland, is defeated by King Haraldr, but is able to recapture his banner and take some measure of revenge.

A number of these narrative elements (1, 4–5, 7, 9–11) recur in the fragments of *Hákonar saga* (lettered A–D below), but in a different order and with differing details. There are several breaks in the narrative, but it proceeds as follows:

A. Hákon Ívarsson is described as a brilliant youth comparable only to Einarr þambarskelfir's son Eindriði. He goes on harrying expeditions, on one occasion with Finnr Árnason (as in *Morkinskinna*, episode 4). King Haraldr becomes tyrannical, but Einarr employs his considerable power in defense of the Þrœndir. One day Haraldr recites a threatening stanza as he observes Einarr amidst his retinue (echoed in Ch. 33 of *Morkinskinna*).

B. The details are unclear, but the Þrœndir seem to have arranged for a meeting between Hákon and King Haraldr, perhaps as part of a peace-making effort. In any event, Finnr Árnason is instrumental in establishing peaceful relations between King Haraldr and Þrœndalǫg. Haraldr urges Ragnhildr to attend him at court. She perceives that there is strong pressure and accedes. Hákon comes to Haraldr's Christmas celebration, as had apparently been planned, and he and Ragnhildr seem a natural match. It is clear that this was the plan, but when Finnr Árnason presses the king, he is evasive (cf. 9–10 above). Haraldr defers to Ragnhildr, and Hákon addresses her in person. In response, she speaks at length about her lineage and the impossibility of marrying beneath her station (Ch. 42 near note 18). Hákon asks Haraldr for the title of jarl but is refused. He goes to Denmark and is welcomed by King Sveinn (cf. 11 above), who is having difficulty with his nephew Ásmundr. The fragment breaks off here, but the story is clearly moving toward the intervention of Hákon against Ásmundr as it is told in *Morkinskinna*.

C. King Haraldr levies troops and summons Hákon for a campaign against the Danes. Since Hákon is referred to in this passage as Haraldr's *mágr* (in-law) and a jarl, it is clear that Haraldr eventually agreed to the marriage with Ragnhildr and to the conferral of a title. Perhaps in this version Hákon angered King Sveinn by killing Ásmundr Bjarnarson and then returned to Norway, where his friends in Þrœndalǫg finally prevailed on King Haraldr to grant the title of jarl, or perhaps Ormr Eilífsson had died, thus making the title available. The preparations for the campaign are described with special attention to the vessels and several stanzas by Þjóðólfr. Haraldr sails his ships into Lófufjǫrðr and harries. The Battle of Niz appears to begin immediately thereafter, and the author draws on stanzas by Steinn Herdísarson and Þjóðólfr. Hákon is conspicuous in the battle.

D. After the battle the king thanks his troops, in particular Hákon, though many suspect that he is not pleased with the universal praise heaped on Hákon. King Sveinn rewards the poor farmer who gave him shelter after the battle, but punishes the farmer's wife for her hard words. During the following winter the men at Haraldr's court continue to praise Hákon, with the result that the king takes a dislike to him. Hákon returns home well rewarded but has an inkling of the king's envy. After his departure the discussion of his preeminence begins once again. During the course of these discussions it emerges that Hákon saved King Sveinn in the

Battle of Niz. King Haraldr gets wind of this rumor and gathers an expedition against Hákon.

Clearly, the same story is being told in both versions, but with considerable discrepancies. *Morkinskinna* has nothing to say about the diplomatic maneuvers between King Haraldr and the Þrœndir, in which the story of Hákon is embedded in the saga version. It begins instead with Hákon's youth and the campaign leading up to the Battle of Niz, picking up the betrothal story only after the battle has been fought. Furthermore, in *Morkinskinna* the episode in Lófufjǫrðr appears to be separated from the Battle of Niz, to which it is immediately prefatory in the fragments. Whether *Hákonar saga included the exchange of words between King Haraldr and Finnr Árnason is uncertain. Both texts told of King Sveinn's refuge with a poor couple, but *Morkinskinna* does not make it clear that Hákon was instrumental in Sveinn's escape from the battle. Again, it is not clear whether *Hákonar saga included Þórólfr mostrarskegg's ill-fated exploit.

Other parts of the story are also less than congruent. In *Hákonar saga, Hákon's quarrel with King Haraldr over the betrothal to Ragnhildr and his departure for Denmark precede the Battle of Niz. In *Morkinskinna*, Haraldr offers the betrothal and a jarldom as a reward for Hákon's service at the Battle of Niz. That perhaps clarifies why the motif of Hákon's secret complicity in Sveinn's escape from the battle has no place in *Morkinskinna:* there is as yet no link between Sveinn and Hákon and no reason for Hákon to have divided loyalties.

The story of Ásmundr Bjarnarson may have been similar in the two accounts, but there is no suggestion of the campaign in Gautland in *Hákonar saga. According to *Morkinskinna,* this campaign is part and parcel of the hostilities between King Haraldr and the Gautar, but *Hákonar saga makes it appear that King Haraldr launched an attack against Hákon in eastern Norway and that the Gautish campaign may have been a result of Hákon's falling back across the border into Gautland.

Until recently, there has been a degree of unanimity to the effect that there is no textual connection between *Hákonar saga and *Morkinskinna* and that the resemblances are oral in nature. Bjarne Fidjestøl (1982:16–17; also Poole 1991:67–68) questioned this consensus and found it unlikely that two texts in such proximity to each other should be entirely independent. The hypothesis of independence also fails to explain the verbatim correspondences in the opening scenes focused on Einarr þambarskelfir, tenuous though these may be. Fidjestøl thought it more likely that the author of *Hákonar saga knew *Morkinskinna* but did not make extensive use of it because he was engaged in the writing of a fuller saga. If this view is correct, *Morkinskinna* is entirely dependent on oral transmissions.

Fidjestøl's hypothesis makes good sense. It is hard to imagine that the author of *Morkinskinna* could have referred to *Hákonar saga and so jumbled the narrative, while leaving few echoes of the text before him. It is more comprehensible that the author of *Hákonar saga recast the story completely on the basis of a more thorough inquiry into the relevant traditions and a deeper reflection on the logic of the story. He perhaps shaped it as a continuation of *Hlaðajarla saga (a lost account of the earls of Lade in Þrœndalǫg), connected the incident in Lófufjǫrðr with the Battle of Niz, and psychologized at length about envy and good faith in the relationship between Haraldr and Hákon. The differences between his version and what we find in *Morkinskinna*, having to do more with narrative sequence and emphasis than with the substance of the story, are typical of what are often referred to as "oral variants" (cf. Gísli Sigurðsson 1994:30–41).

The term is somewhat misleading because it is clear that the stories were not finally formed in tradition and that the variation has as much or more to do with authorial intervention as with the vagaries of transmission. The author of *Hákonar saga saw the potential for a heroic biography, but the author of *Morkinskinna*, whose genius is perhaps more episodic than epic, saw the potential for a digression on personalities and values. He seems to have been less interested in the political conflict between King Haraldr and Hákon and more interested in the domestic drama played out between Hákon and Ragnhildr, the conflict between love and status. This interlude is extraordinary because domestic analysis is so rare in saga literature and unparalleled elsewhere in *Morkinskinna*.

The conclusion of Hákon's story appears in *Ljósvetninga saga* (*ÍF* 10, 103) as well. We must therefore also consider how this passage relates to *Morkinskinna*. Björn Sigfússon once suggested (*ÍF* 10, xxxvii) that both texts borrowed the episode from a lost section of *Hákonar saga, but if the case made for believing that *Hákonar saga postdates *Morkinskinna* is sufficient, *Morkinskinna* must have the original text and *Ljósvetninga saga* may well be the borrower. The parallelism runs as follows:

Morkinskinna	*Ljósvetninga saga*
It was rumored that King Steinkell would also block the river mouth with a naval blockade. King Haraldr believed these rumors and began to hack away the ice around his ships. As they were at this work, somebody said: "No one does his job like Koðrán's killer." He was referring to Hallr Ótryggsson, who had killed Koðrán Guðmundarson, and Hallr was there in King	After that Brandr traveled to the court of King Haraldr Sigurðarson and stayed with him, as did Hallr Ótryggsson. He was in his army east in Gautland when King Haraldr fought Jarl Hákon Ívarsson. When King Haraldr was ready to leave, his ship got frozen in the ice between the ships. King Haraldr said: "Nobody wields a stronger ax than Hallr, Koðrán's killer." There was

Haraldr's army. Þormóðr Eindriða-son jumped up and delivered Hallr's death blow because he could not stand to hear the praise of Koðrán's killing. Þormóðr was distantly related and the nephew of Guðmundr Eyjólfsson, Koðrán's father. When the men crowded about and wanted to kill Þormóðr, the ice broke under them and there was a great tumult because many men were on the point of drowning. King Haraldr's son Magnús came to Þormóðr's aid and asked that he be spared. He offered a settlement because Þormóðr was in his crew, and a reconciliation was reached. Subsequently Þormóðr went south to Denmark and from there to Greece and wanted to take imperial service . . . .

a man named Þormóðr, the son of Ásgeirr and a kinsman of the Mǫðrvellingar. He was on the ship of Magnús, the king's son, and had recently arrived from Iceland. He was plotting against Hallr's life. And when the king said "Koðrán's killer," Þormóðr rushed at Hallr and delivered his death blow, and then leapt onto Magnús's ship. King Haraldr was furious and ordered an attack on them. But as they crowded in on Þormóðr, the ice broke beneath them, and many drowned. Magnús got away and had Þormóðr ferried abroad. He didn't interrupt his journey until he got to Constantinople, where he took service. The king and his son were later reconciled.

Both the wording and the close correspondence in narrative sequence suggest that there is a direct textual connection. The author of *Ljósvetninga saga* omits certain retrospective details that are clear from his previous narrative, but otherwise follows *Morkinskinna* closely. It is, of course, possible that the direction of the borrowing is the reverse and that *Ljósvetninga saga* has the original text, but the episode forms a natural conclusion to the tale of Hákon in *Morkinskinna* and is in line with the source indications elsewhere in the text. Þormóðr Eindriðason appears as Þormóðr Ásgeirsson in *Ljósvetninga saga*, but Snorri (*ÍF* 28, 165) confirms the patronymic Eindriðason and makes him the grandson of Guðmundr ríki's sister. The information therefore looks as though it originates in Guðmundr's region of Eyjafjǫrðr, where, as we shall see, the author of *Morkinskinna* is likely to have worked. It is puzzling how the author of *Ljósvetninga saga* arrived at the differing patronymic Ásgeirsson, since that saga too is almost certainly rooted in Eyjafjǫrðr. In any case, Þormóðr appears to figure in the texts as the ultimate source of the story. The story looks integral in *Morkinskinna* and a little like an afterthought in *Ljósvetninga saga*, where it stands in the close vicinity of another probable literary borrowing from *Þorgils saga ok Hafliða*. In all probability, then, the text in *Morkinskinna* is primary and not a literary loan. The total literary debts incurred by the author of *Morkin-*

skinna may therefore amount to no more than *Hryggjarstykki, very incidentally a version of *Knýtlinga saga,* perhaps *Orkneyinga saga,* and one further text to be discussed below.

The relationship of *Morkinskinna* to *Orkneyinga saga* has not been clearly worked out and may well defy any solution. The reference in *Morkinskinna* is as follows (Ch. 4 at note 1): "King Magnús put Rǫgnvaldr Brúsason in authority to the west in Orkney and gave him the title of jarl. During Magnús's reign great strife broke out between Rǫgnvaldr jarl and Þorfinnr jarl, his uncle, and there were many history-making events, as is told in the 'Sagas of the Jarls.'" *Orkneyinga saga, Morkinskinna,* and *Heimskringla* show a number of shared phrasings. Bjarni Aðalbjarnarson (1937:151) pointed out that in most cases, *Heimskringla* probably borrowed from *Morkinskinna* and *Orkneyinga saga* from *Heimskringla.* Where *Morkinskinna* has a separate correspondence with *Orkneyinga saga* not found in *Heimskringla,* it would seem likely that *Morkinskinna* is borrowing from *Orkneyinga saga,* but the situation is complicated by the fact that *Orkneyinga saga* (*ÍF* 34, 55) mentions a *Magnúss saga góða. That may be no more than a reference to the section on Magnús in *Heimskringla,* but it may also be a reference to a lost separate *Magnúss saga góða. In the latter case, the correspondences in *Orkneyinga saga* and *Morkinskinna* may reflect drafts on a common source.

There is the distinct possibility of one further written source used but not identified by the author of *Morkinskinna.* The bitter legal dispute between King Sigurðr jórsalafari and King Eysteinn is told at some length (Ch. 70). It is referred to in our text as "Þinga saga," the heading used in MskMS. It has separate status because it is transmitted in this manuscript, as well as in *Hulda* and *Hrokkinskinna,* and in a shorter version ("Þinga þáttr") in four other manuscripts (*Eirspennill, Jöfraskinna, Gullinskinna,* and *Flateyjarbók*). The relationship of these texts was analyzed by Gustav Storm in 1877 and again by Jonna Louis-Jensen in 1977:94–108. Storm printed the differing versions in adjacent columns so that the differences are easily surveyable in his edition. He believed that "Þinga saga," as it appears in MskMS and *Hulda-Hrokkinskinna,* was primary, but Louis-Jensen (1977:99–105) argued that this version derives from an older version of "Þinga þáttr."

Both agree that the original version was a separate text composed as early as 1200 and worked into *Morkinskinna.* Storm believed that the original version was Icelandic because of misunderstandings of Norwegian law. Louis-Jensen, however, could find no reason why such a specialized text on Norwegian law should be written in Iceland and therefore located it in Norway. She cautiously suggested (1977:108) a certain Bjarni Marðarson († after 1223) as the possible author. That "Þinga saga" was originally a separate composition is suggested by the redundant introduction at the beginning of Chapter 70, which provides information that has already been given in Chapter 60: "When Jerusalem-

Sigurðr returned to Norway, the three brothers ruled and divided the land among themselves."

"Þinga saga" does not quite exhaust the list of putative literary sources for *Morkinskinna*. There remains the question of the semi-independent *þættir* that appear in the text. Given that these tales are not always obviously germane to the main narrative, that some seem stylistically or otherwise independent, and that some are missing in cognate redactions, scholars have long suspected that they were not all to be found in the original *Morkinskinna* and may have been interpolated at various stages between 1220 and the date of MskMS. If this is true, the interpolated *þættir*, like *Ágrip*, may be regarded in some sense as literary sources. Bjarni Aðalbjarnarson (1937:154–55) tabulated sixteen such *þættir*, and Heinrich Gimmler (1976:63–65) added a list of twenty-eight shorter pieces. For the sake of inclusiveness, we may begin with this latter list:

1. "Karls þáttr vesæla" (Ch. 1)
2. Haraldr heals a woman in Constantinople (Ch. 9)
3. "Þorkels þáttr dyrðils" (Ch. 15)
4. King Magnús receives three rings from a man who counseled him at the Battle of Hlýrskógsheiðr (Ch. 16)
5. King Magnús bestows a jarldom on Ormr Skoptason (Ch. 17)
6. "Þrándar þáttr upplendings" (Ch. 18)
7. King Haraldr mocks King Magnús's brother Þórir (Ch. 19)
8. "Arnórs þáttr jarlaskalds" (Ch. 21)
9. King Haraldr heals a boy's memory (Ch. 22)
10. King Magnús and Margrét (Ch. 23)
11. An Icelander shares in the discovery of Hákon jarl's treasure (Ch. 34)
12. King Haraldr tests the loyalty of his district chieftains (Ch. 35)
13. "Úlfs þáttr auðga" (Ch. 37)
14. King Haraldr heals Ingibjǫrg Halldórsdóttir (Ch. 39)
15. King Haraldr meets a fisherman (Ch. 44)
16. King Haraldr hangs the murderer of King Tryggvi Óláfsson (Ch. 45)
17. King Óláfr kyrri and the crow fellow (Ch. 54)
18. Magnús berfœttr and Sveinki Steinarsson (Ch. 56)
19. "Þinga saga" (Ch. 70)
20. "Þórarins þáttr stuttfeldar" (Ch. 72)
21. King Sigurðr jórsalafari and Óttarr birtingr (Ch. 74)
22. King Sigurðr and Erlendr gapamunnr (Ch. 75)
23. King Sigurðr and Áslákr hani (Ch. 77)
24. King Sigurðr and the whore (Ch. 78)
25. King Sigurðr and Bishop Magni (Ch. 80)
26. Sigurðr slembir's stay with Þorgils Oddason in Saurbœr (Ch. 85)

27. Einarr Skúlason displays his poetic skills (Ch. 97)
28. The slaying of Geirsteinn (Ch. 98)

Bjarni Aðalbjarnarson considered most of these episodes to be too slight to have had a separate written existence (1937:158). Most of them focus primarily on the kings whose lives are being told, and with the exception of 11 and 20 ("Þórarins þáttr stuttfeldar"), they lack the defining feature of the *þáttr*— an Icelandic protagonist. Heinrich Gimmler (1976:65–66) disagreed and thought it quite possible that these "borderline cases" already existed in written form when the author of *Morkinskinna* went to work.

Bjarni Aðalbjarnarson (1937:154–55) had identified sixteen *þættir* that might have existed as independent entities. Four of them can be found on Gimmler's list: "Sveinka þáttr Steinarsonar" (Gimmler 18), "Þinga saga" (Gimmler 19), "Þórarins þáttr stuttfeldar" (Gimmler 20), and "Einars þáttr Skúlasonar" (Gimmler 27). If the remaining twelve on Bjarni Aðalbjarnarson's list are added to Gimmler's twenty-eight, the grand total is a startlingly high forty episodes. If we are prepared to believe that the author had forty ready-made episodes on file, we may wonder to what extent he was obliged to inquire into living tradition at all. He might appear rather in the light of a compiler of written anecdotes.

If, on the other hand, we believe that some of his material must necessarily come from tradition—the same tradition that must underlie any written versions he had—then it becomes questionable why we should assume that the *þáttr* transcriptions were made by someone other than the author himself. Although we can never be certain whether an episode is first- or second-hand, it seems more straightforward to credit the author unless there are strong indications to the contrary. What Gimmler's supplementary list illustrates most clearly is that the author was given to an episodic mode of composition. That is quite in line with recent thinking on how the family sagas came into existence. They, too, it is surmised, resulted from a concatenation of episodes drawn from tradition (Clover 1986).

The borderline cases singled out by Gimmler are not, however, the focus of the discussion on prior written *þættir*. The crucial cases are the ones listed by Bjarni Aðalbjarnarson:

1. "Þorsteins þáttr Hallssonar" (Ch. 20)
2. "Hreiðars þáttr heimska" (Ch. 24)
3. "Halldórs þáttr Snorrasonar" (Ch. 30)
4. "Auðunar þáttr vestfirzka" (Ch. 36)
5. "Brands þáttr ǫrva" (Ch. 38)
6. "Íslendings þáttr sǫgufróða" (Ch. 40)
7. "Þorvarðs þáttr krákunefs" (Ch. 41)

8. "Sneglu-Halla þáttr" (Ch. 43)
9. "Stúfs þáttr blinda" (Ch. 47)
10. "Odds þáttr Ófeigssonar" (Ch. 48)
11. "Ívars þáttr Ingimundarsonar" (Ch. 65)
12. Ásu-Þórðar þáttr" (Ch. 68)

Bjarni Aðalbjarnarson distinguished carefully between the problem of whether these are independent stories initially set down without reference to *Morkinskinna* and the problem of whether they are later interpolations. "Auðunar þáttr" and "Sneglu-Halla þáttr" exist in separate redactions in *Flateyjarbók*. A separate version of "Stúfs þáttr" appeared in *Árbók Háskóla Íslands* (1912), and a separate version of "Ásu-Þórðar þáttr" appeared in *Sex sögupættir* (Reykjavik, 1855). Without going into detail, Bjarni Aðalbjarnarson remarks that the versions in *Morkinskinna* are generally abbreviated in relation to the other redactions. This was the conclusion reached by Björn M. Ólsen in his edition of "Stúfs þáttr." In other words, these *pættir* seem to have been edited for inclusion in *Morkinskinna*. Bjarni notes (1937:156) that judging from certain manuscript catalogues, other variant versions beyond these four may exist as well but that they have not been published.

We observed above that six of these *pættir* ("Hreiðars þáttr," "Halldórs þáttr Snorrasonar," "Auðunar þáttr," "Brands þáttr ǫrva," "Íslendings þáttr sǫgufróða," and "Sneglu-Halla þáttr") are missing in *Flateyjarbók*. That led Bjarni Aðalbjarnarson (and others) to question whether they were in the original redaction of *Morkinskinna*. Louis-Jensen (1977:77–78) later argued that they were just as likely to have been omitted in the *Flateyjarbók* redaction. With respect to the other six *pættir*, Bjarni Aðalbjarnarson (1937:157) was completely agnostic on the question of whether they originated with the first redaction or were added later.

Heinrich Gimmler was much less cautious and assumed without much discussion that all twelve *pættir* were likely to be independent compositions and interpolations as well (1976:61): "Their authors, along with the interpolators who inserted them in *Morkinskinna*, are unknown." That phrasing seems to suggest that all the *pættir* were later interpolations, but Louis-Jensen's argument seems to shift the burden of proof to those who believe in wholesale interpolation. The original author clearly cultivated an episodic style, and strong reasons are needed to demonstrate that any particular episode is not part of his conception. That does not, of course, preclude the possibility that a number of the *pættir* were composed separately by other writers, but there seems no strong reason for believing that they were not included in *Morkinskinna* from the outset. Real evidence has been adduced only in the case of the little story about the knight Giffarðr (in Ch. 58) and "Karls þáttr vesæla," which Louis-Jensen (1977:80–81) regards as an interpolation. But even these cases may be subject to doubt (on the Giffarðr episode see Gade [forthcoming]).

The Poetic Corpus of ÆMsk and the Question of Interpolation

This section addresses the issue of interpolation and gives an estimate of the extent of the poetic inclusions in ÆMsk. The discussion will, we hope, shed some light on the issue of interpolation (prose and poetry) at the various stages of the *Msk* transmission and also on the function of poetry in the prose narrative of the earliest version of *Msk*.

The safest criterion for determining whether a stanza was part of ÆMsk is the incorporation of that stanza in approximately the same narrative environment in *Hkr* and *Fsk*. But because both Snorri and the author of *Fsk* demonstrably subscribed to individual editorial policies involving a critical sifting of the poetic corpus of their exemplar, such an approach is certainly not foolproof. Snorri, for example, frequently replaced stanzas from ÆMsk that he must have considered unspecific with other and more pertinent stanzas, and sometimes stanzas with "unspecific" content were excluded altogether. Furthermore, both Snorri and the author of *Fsk* almost consistently excluded stanzas in *fornyrðislag* for historical verification, although the prose of *Hkr* shows that some of those stanzas must have been part of Snorri's exemplar. The problem of establishing the poetic corpus of ÆMsk based on the stanzas included in *Hkr* and *Fsk* is further compounded by the fact that after the beginning of "Magnúss saga berfœtts," *Fsk*, with a few exceptions, ceases to incorporate stanzas into the prose narrative, and the presence of such stanzas in the *Fsk* exemplar can only be established by information incorporated into the prose. The stanzas that occur in the *þættir* and smaller anecdotes as intrinsic parts of the narrative are consistently omitted in the main MSS of *Hkr* and in *Fsk*. The following discussion therefore focuses on those sections of MskMS that are common to all three versions.

The Saga of Haraldr and Magnús (Chs. 1–52)

If we include the stanzas from *Flat* that occur in the lacuna of MskMS (*sts. 1–52, 80–82, 98–99), the "Saga of Haraldr and Magnús" contains 156 stanzas, twenty-two of which are found in *þættir* and smaller anecdotes (sts. 73–79, 104–5, 119–31). Of the remaining 134 stanzas, ninety (67 percent) have been incorporated in *Hkr* (eighty stanzas; 60 percent) and/or *Fsk* (seventy-four stanzas; 55 percent). *Hkr* cites sixteen stanzas that are not included in *Fsk*, and conversely, *Fsk* gives ten stanzas that were rejected by Snorri. According to that count, MskMS contains forty-four stanzas that are not included in the two later compilations. All of those stanzas occur in either Flat, Hr, or 66 and must have been part of Msk2.

The stanzas incorporated into *Fsk* and *Hkr* from ÆMsk have one thing in common: they all contain specific information (personal names, place names, numerical or chronological information, "pregnant remarks," etc.) that serve to verify similar information in the prose text. Conversely, the stanzas in MskMS that are not included in *Hkr* or *Fsk* are frequently conspicuous for their lack of specific information (sts. 21, 33–34, 40, 51, 53, 138, 155). In four instances, Snorri retains the prose environment but replaces the stanza in question with a stanza that he clearly felt better suited the prose environment (sts. 4, 27, 37, 137), and three times *Hkr* and *Fsk* fail to quote a stanza but incorporate information from the stanza into the prose.

In the episode that details the funeral voyage of Magnús góði from Denmark to Norway, for example, st. 80 describes the Norwegians traveling north with the corpse of Magnús. That stanza is left out in both *Fsk* and *Hkr*, but *Fsk* changes the prose to include the following sentence, derived from st. 80 (*ÍF* 29, 249): "Einarr þambarskelfir með Þrœndaher fór *með líki Magnúss konungs norðr* til Níðaróss [emphasis added]" (Einarr þambarskelfir and the army from Trøndelag traveled *north* to Nidaros *with the corpse of King Magnús*). In the description of the aftermath of the Battle of the River Ouse, MskMS adds a stanza (st. 141) to document that the English earls fled to the stronghold York ("dunðu jarlar undan . . . *til borgar*" [emphasis added]). That information is not included in the prose of MskMS (or *Fsk*), but Snorri adds the following sentence derived from the stanza (*ÍF* 28, 181): "Valþjófr jarl ok þat lið, er undan komsk, flýði upp *til borgarinnar* Jork" (emphasis added) (Jarl Waltheof and those men who were able to escape, fled *to the stronghold* York). Similarly, the place name "Hrafnseyrr" (Ravenseer) in st. 154, which describes the point of departure of the Norwegians from England after the Battle of Stamford Bridge, is absent from the prose of MskMS and *Fsk* but was incorporated into the prose of *Hkr* (*ÍF* 28, 197), undoubtedly from st. 154, which consequently must have been part of ÆMsk.

A brief look at the stanzas that must have been contained in ÆMsk but are omitted or replaced by the author of *Fsk* and Snorri shows that many share features that must reflect the tastes of one specific individual, namely, a delight in battle descriptions involving beasts of battle feasting on corpses. Consider the following examples:

St. 27 (replaced by Snorri):
Later the king launched a weapon storm [battle] that the Wends will remember; the lord scorched rust-red corpses of pirates at Wollin. The bloody wolf pulled the fast-fried body from the fires; the greedy slayer of the hall [fire] flickered on heathen foreheads.

St. 32 (not in *Fsk* or *Hkr*):
King, you caused the Wends distress by the clear Skotborgará [Kongeå]; lord, the fortune you achieved with half the troops was famed. Relative of the stout king, famous among men, there lay a corpse heap higher than the far-traveled family of wolves could climb; you were victorious.

St. 33 (as above):

The courageous king stacked a corpse pile from wolves' food so high—I praise the life of that brave lord of the people—that the steed of the wife of Yggr [Óðinn] of the river bone ["Óðinn of the river bone (stone)" = giant; "wife of the giant" = giantess; "steed of the giantess" = wolf], wandering all night, could not climb over it, even if it wanted; fallen men were spread far and wide.

St. 40 (as above):

The sandy bodies of Sveinn's men drift from the south to the shores; people see where corpses float far and wide off Jótland's [Jylland, Jutland] coast. The wolf drags the corpse pile from the water and tears bodies in the bays; Óláfr's son put an end to the eagles' fast.

St. 87 (as above):

The king gave the brood of eagles Danish blood, Huginn's [raven] banquet [blood], to drink; I heard the lord waged war by Þjólarnes. Far and wide the eagle's kin stalked over the corpses of the fallen; the wolf ate the flesh of the Jótar [people of Jylland, Jutland] as he pleased, may he enjoy that.

St. 138 (as above):

The rain of wounds [blood] fell far and wide on the fields and the vikings waded in warriors' blood; there the wolf got its fill.

Another common characteristic of the stanzas in MskMS not found in *Hkr* and *Fsk* is that these stanzas often belong to a sequence of two or more stanzas used to punctuate or to recapitulate a major battle. Such is the case with sts. 32–33 (the Battle of Lyrskovshede); 113–14 (the Battle of the River Niz); 139–40 (the Battle of the River Ouse); 151–53 (the Battle of Stamford Bridge). In all these instances, the course of the battle has already been described in prose and documented in poetry (usually similarly in the three versions). The stanzas provide poetic retrospective views on the previous events and do not add new or specific information. Such stanzas are omitted in *Fsk* as well as in *Hkr*.

Sometimes MskMS contains stanzas that would appear to be at odds with the prose environment or are positioned awkwardly in the narrative. Such is the case in the following instances:

St. 24: The prose has just established that Magnús became joint ruler of Norway and Denmark and proceeded to stay the winter in Denmark: the stanza states that Magnús "later" came to rule all Norway and Denmark.

St. 142: The prose describes Haraldr marshaling his army after encountering the English at Stamford Bridge; the poetry belatedly notes that he ordered his men to disembark (at the River Ouse) and that a great army marched against him from the south.

St. 143: On that same occasion, prior to the battle, the stanza prematurely announces the death of Haraldr.

The stanzas discussed so far fall into one or more of the six following categories: (1) "stanzas replaced in *Hkr*" (sts. 4, 27, 37, 137); (2) "stanzas of unspecific content" (sts. 21, 33–34, 40, 51, 53, 138, 155); (3) "stanzas that do not fit the prose environment" (sts. 24, 142–43); (4) "sequences of stanzas punctuating battle" (sts. 32–33, 113–114, 139–40, 151–53); (5) "stanzas with beast of battle imagery" (sts. 27, 32–33, 40, 87, 138); and (6) "stanzas paraphrased in the prose of *Hkr* and *Fsk*" (sts. 80, 141, 154). Whereas the presence of the latter three stanzas, as well as of sts. 4, 27, 37, 137 (replaced by Snorri) in ÆMsk, seems to be secure, we can only speculate as to the inclusion in that MS of the remaining stanzas discussed so far. It would appear, however, that stanzas subsumed under categories 2, 3, and 4 above would have been prime candidates for omission by compilers whose focus was on factual information and a tight narrative.

As already mentioned, the author of *Fsk* and Snorri fail to include the *þættir* and smaller anecdotes that characterize the narrative of MskMS. Furthermore, *lausavísur* and personal asides are included in their compilations only when the stanzas occur as integral parts of the main narrative (for example, sts. 45, 83, 91, 98–99, 132–35, 144–46). Such editorial policies could explain the failure to include st. 82, which details the personal grief of Oddr kikinaskald after the death of Magnús góði, and the same tendency may serve to explain the selection of the stanzas in the two compilations from one of the longer sequences of stanzas in ÆMsk, namely, from Sigvatr's "Bersǫglisvísur" ("The Unvarnished Verses"; our sts. 5–20).

Whereas *MskMS (according to *Flat*) gives sixteen stanzas from that poem, *Hkr* lists nine (the first of which is not in *MskMS), and *Fsk* has five. The selections made by the author of *Fsk* and by Snorri show that the two compilers focused on the issue at hand, namely, on Magnús's vengeful behavior and on Sigvatr's warnings about the possible dire consequences of his hard-handed policies against the farmers of Trøndelag. The stanzas from "Bersǫglisvísur" in *MskMS not found in the *Hkr-Fsk* versions all have in common that they are personalized statements by Sigvatr—concerning, in most cases, the prehistory of Sigvatr's relationship to Óláfr Haraldsson, Magnús's father (sts. 5–7, 11), and to Magnús himself (st. 10). The poem must have undergone critical editing in both *Fsk* and in *Hkr*, and as the table below shows, the two authors differed in their opinions on which stanzas to include:

St	8	9	12	13	14	15	16	17
Fsk			x	x	x	x	x	
Hsk	x	x	x	x	x	x	x	x

The last two stanzas (sts. 19–20) that allegedly belonged to Sigvatr's "Bersǫg-lisvísur" are recorded in *Flat* only. St. 18 is quoted in *F* (which includes only this stanza), where it is stated that "Sigvatr then composed that *flokkr* which is called 'Bersǫglisvísur,' as it is told in 'Óláfs saga [helga].' This is the last [stanza]" (*F* 177). According to Louis-Jensen (1977:84), that stanza was inter-polated into *F* from MskY, and because the prose in *F* states that this is the last stanza of the poem, she suggests that the two last stanzas (our sts. 19–20) were interpolated into *Msk* at a later point. She finds that possibility supported by the content of the two stanzas, which, in her opinion, have a different focus from the other stanzas in the "Bersǫglisvísur" because they express Sigvatr's hope of personal gain.

If we look at sts. 19–20 in the context of the rest of the poem, however, and in particular in the context of the personalized stanzas that were left out in *Fsk* and *Hkr*, they form a natural conclusion to Sigvatr's plea:

St. 5a: Throughout his lifetime, I stayed with the lord who gave his faithful liege-men gold and the ravens slaughter; he became famous.

St. 6: I followed your father faithfully, that generous king, who wanted my service; now people rejoice in the peace. There was no gap in the ranks where I stood proudly in the midst of his men with the sword; one should make the forest denser with brush.

St. 7: Magnús, with great courage your father forced his way with his company through the throng where men fought. Fiercely he defended the inheritance of kings, and keen hearts quivered at that; thus Óláfr advanced.

St. 10: Young lord, I was with you that autumn when you came from the east; king, you alone can secure the whole country; that will be heard. The country-men thought they had caught the bright heavens with their hands when you claimed the lands, prince, and were alive.

St. 11: I let Magnús's father hear the hidden words of the king's enemies that my ears heard; how they plotted deceit. I carried each message with a candid heart, because I did not betray my liege lord; I knew then there was danger.

St. 18: I thus hope matters will take a good turn for Óláfr's son; they say that the cautious man's business must wait until late in the evening; between us two all is well. Magnús, I am well disposed; I wish to live and die with you, generous one; you protect Haraldr's hawk isle [Norway] with the sword.

St. 19: Óláfr, not lacking in lordly splendor, graced me with rings; the dealings of the stout king were bountiful. Throughout his lifetime, I always bore the gold of the mover of sea-warriors [war king] on both arms, and I was seldom afraid.

St. 20: Sigvatr's soul will be yonder in Hǫrðaknútr's hall unless generous King Magnús welcomes the skald with great warmth. I followed the fathers of both; I was still totally beardless then: my tongue brought me gold as a youth.

In sts. 5–7 and 10–11 Sigvatr establishes his credentials, as it were, by reca-pitulating his service to Magnús's father (sts. 5–7) and to Magnús himself (st. 11), and he emphasizes his role as adviser to Óláfr (st. 10). In st. 18 he ex-presses the hope that his mission will be received well by Magnús. Sts. 19–20 contain a veiled threat: Óláfr rewarded him lavishly for his role as royal coun-sellor (st. 11), and Sigvatr was not forced to divide his loyalties between Óláfr and Knútr (to bear arms), but he will not hesitate to do so and to throw in his lot with Knútr's son, Hǫrðaknútr, unless Magnús reacts favorably to his plea (st. 20). There is no reason to assume, then, that sts. 19–20 were not part of the "Bersǫglisvísur." The fact that the stanzas may not have been part of the *F*-exemplar (MskY), which, as Louis-Jensen points out (1977:91), has been ab-breviated, does not mean that they were not part of Msk2. Furthermore, be-cause these stanzas, as well as sts. 5–7, 10–11, and 18, concern themselves with the personal rather than with the factual aspects of Sigvatr's plea, they could have been at cross purposes with the editorial policies of Snorri and the author of *Fsk*. Hence, we cannot exclude the possibility that all of the sixteen stanzas cited in *MskMS belonged to Sigvatr's "Bersǫglisvísur" and that they were part of ÆMsk.

The second sequence of stanzas in MskMS that are not recorded in *Fsk* and *Hkr* are the "Gamanvísur" ("Jesting Verses"; sts. 58–63), which Haraldr Sigurðarson allegedly recited on his way back to Russia from Greece. All of those stanzas (including st. 58) were omitted in *Flat*, but sts. 59–63 are given in Hr and AM 66, ensuring their presence in Msk2. *Fsk* and *Hkr* cite the first stanza of these verses (st. 59) with the following comment (*ÍF* 29, 237; *ÍF* 28, 89): "Í þessum ferðum orti Haraldr gamanvísur ok eru [*Hkr*: saman] sextán ok eitt niðrlag at ǫllum. Þessi er ein" (During this journey Haraldr composed his jesting verses, sixteen stanzas [in all], with the same ending. Here is one of them). MskMS lists five stanzas, with a slight change in the introductory prose (FJ 85, U 14): "Ok í þessum ferðum orti Haraldr gamanvísur ok eru sextán ok eitt niðrlag *at flestum, þó eru hér fár ritnar*. Þessi er ein" (emphasis added) (Dur-ing this journey Haraldr composed his jesting verses, sixteen stanzas in all, with the same ending *in most, though only a few are recorded here*. Here is one). The statement in MskMS that most of the "Gamanvísur" had the same ending (not all, as in *Fsk* and *Hkr*) must have been occasioned by the fact that st. 61, which enumerates Haraldr's accomplishments, does not contain the refrain of the other stanzas. The compiler of *H, faced with the conflicting information of Msk2 and *Hkr*, retained the *Hkr* prose and replaced ll. 7–8 in st. 61 with the re-frain, with the result that this stanza, which claimed to list eight of Haraldr's accomplishments (and did so in the MskMS version), only enumerated six in the *H version. The question is, then, whether MskMS accurately reflects the ÆMsk version, which was then abbreviated and slightly changed in *Fsk* and subsequently adopted by Snorri, or whether sts. 59–63 were added in Msk2 by an interpolator who changed the ÆMsk prose to accommodate the content of st. 61.

A look at the stanzas themselves and their prose environment indicates that the latter must have been the case. First, it is doubtful whether all the stanzas belonged to Haraldr's poem: some of them (or parts of them) are given elsewhere and attributed to other poets (see "Notes to Stanzas"). It appears that whoever added the stanzas was at pains to include as many as possible and drew heavily on oral tradition (not necessarily connected with Haraldr) to do so. Second, the sequence of the stanzas is mixed up: st. 59, which describes Haraldr leaving the scene of battle at Stiklastaðir in 1030, certainly belongs before st. 58, which describes his exploits in Sicily. It is not clear why the author of ÆMsk, if he knew st. 59, would have chosen st. 58 as an example of the "Gamanvísur" rather than st. 59 or, for that matter, st. 62, which addresses the exact moment of composition ("I was born where the Upplendingar [people of Opplandene] bent the bows; now I let my fleet, loathed by farmers, float among the skerries"). Third, in all the versions, including MskMS, st. 58 is accompanied by the prose comment that the poem was dedicated to Elisabeth of Russia (*ÍF* 29, 237–38, *ÍF* 28, 89; FJ 85, U 14). Thus, that statement must have been part of ÆMsk, and it is not clear why, if all the stanzas were included in ÆMsk, this prose insertion followed st. 58 rather than st. 63. Finally, the statement in MskMS to the effect that "only a few are recorded here" ("eru hér fár ritnar") is suspect in itself. The verb "ríta" (to write, record) is otherwise used only three times in MskMS, twice to describe Eiríkr Oddsson's composition of *Hrygg (FJ 419; U 210) and once in connection with a section that appears to have been interpolated from *Ágrip* (FJ 17: "sem fyrr var ritat" "as was previously mentioned" [written]). We must conclude, then, that sts. 59–63 could have been added in Msk2 by an interpolator who wanted to augment the *Msk* text with as many stanzas of the "Gamanvísur" as possible.

A further instance of possible interpolation into Msk2 is st. 156. That stanza, which is the last stanza in "Haralds saga," is inserted to document that Óláfr kyrri became sole ruler of Norway upon the death of his brother Magnús. It is not recorded in *Hkr* or *Fsk*, but the second half-stanza (st. 158) occurs later in a sequence of stanzas (sts. 158–60) in MskMS as well as in *Fsk* to illustrate that Óláfr defended Norway against Sveinn of Denmark. Curiously enough, a later scribe must have noted the doubling of the stanzas, and in a clumsy attempt to cover up, he changed the first line of st. 158, as well as the prose, by replacing the verb "verr" (defends) with "ferr" (travels). Because *Fsk*, Hr, and AM 66 (which give both stanzas) retain the correct wording of st. 158 ("mætr hilmir verr malmi"), that change must have been made at a stage between Msk2 and MskMS (MskX?). Thus it seems that st. 158 was part of ÆMsk and was copied in the same environment into *Fsk;* that st. 156 was added in Msk2 by an interpolator and that both sts. 156 and 158 were copied into *H; that a later scribe, who noticed that the second half-stanza had been quoted twice, changed the first line of st. 158, as well as the wording of the accompanying prose, to create the impression that we are dealing with two different stanzas.

The remaining two stanzas in MskMS (sts. 29, 49) not recorded in *Hkr* or *Fsk* contain factual information, and there is no apparent reason why they should have been omitted in these two compilations. St. 29 verifies that the Battle of Lyrskovshede occurred south of the Skotborgará (Kongeå), near Hedeby. That information is incorporated verbatim into the *MskMS prose prior to the Ótta episode and is derived directly from the stanza (FJ 38: "fyrir sunnan Skotborgará"; st. 29: "fyr sunnan Skotborgará"). *Fsk* leaves out the place name, but Snorri (*ÍF* 28, 41) retains it and changes the wording to correspond with that of *Ágrip* (*ÍF* 29, 35), which also includes the place name: "við Skotborgará á Hlýrskógsheiði" (by the Kongeå at Lyrskovshede); cf. *Ágrip* "á heiði þeiri, er Hlýrskógsheiðr heitir, er liggr við Skotborgará" (at that heath called Lyrskovshede, which is adjacent to the Kongeå). Neither *Hkr* nor *MskMS incorporates the stanza at this point, and the reason for that is clear: in addition to the information about the Kongeå, the stanza also states prematurely that Magnús won the battle ("My valiant friend of warriors [king] was victorious south of the Skotborgará [Kongeå]"). It could well be that Snorri, then, having documented the place of battle through *Ágrip*, felt it unnecessary to include the stanza at a later point to verify the same information.

St. 49 occurs in a prose section that details Haraldr's itinerary from Russia to Greece. According to the prose, he went from Russia to Wendland, Saxony, France (the latter documented in st. 49), and from France to Lombardy (documented in the stanza in note 9.7), Rome, and Apulia, where he embarked on the voyage to Greece (st. 50). *Fsk* and *Hkr* omit the detailed itinerary and only mention Haraldr's departure from Russia and his arrival in Constantinople, which is documented by st. 50 in *Hkr* (that stanza is missing in *Fsk*). The author of *Fsk* must have thought it unnecessary to include stanzas to verify Haraldr's route to Greece. It could be that Snorri, having no further information about Haraldr's alleged campaigns in France and Lombardy, decided to exclude these stanzas, as well as the accompanying prose, from his narrative. It is also possible, however, that this section was added in Msk2 by an interpolator.

To sum up: The sections that the MskMS version of the "Saga of Haraldr and Magnús" have in common with *Fsk* and *Hkr* contain 134 stanzas. Ninety of those stanzas are included in one or both of the latter compilations and must have been part of ÆMsk. There is direct evidence that an additional seven stanzas in MskMS belonged to ÆMsk; thus 72 percent of the stanzas (minus those that occur in *þættir* and smaller anecdotes) in the extant *Msk* version of the "Saga of Haraldr and Magnús" must have been present in the oldest version. Common to all the stanzas from ÆMsk that were copied into *Fsk* and *Hkr* is that they provide concrete information that support the prose narrative. Thus, none of the stanzas in MskMS with unspecific content is found in those two compilations. Furthermore, both the author of *Fsk* and Snorri inserted stanzas directly into the narrative to achieve a point-by-point documentation of events, whereas in MskMS, sequences of two or more stanzas tend to be added to the narrative at the conclusion of a battle, giving a poetic and general recapitulation of the events. No such stanzas were incorporated into *Fsk* or *Hkr*. That is also the case with stanzas that provide an insight into the sentiments and opinions of persons extraneous to the main narrative. It is, of course, possible to argue that such stanzas were not part of ÆMsk; rather, they were interpolated into Msk2 by a person with an interest in personal asides (cf. the many *þættir* and anecdotes), who liked to conclude the high points of narrative with a poetic epilogue, and who, as it would appear, was fascinated by the the imagery of wolves and eagles feasting on enemy corpses. The fact remains, however, that there is scant evidence to suggest that the *Msk* version of the "Saga of Haraldr and Magnús" was subject to a large-scale interpolation of stanzas at the stage of Msk2.

The Saga of Óláfr kyrri (Chs. 53–54)

The "Saga of Óláfr kyrri" is one of the shortest of the kings' sagas, and the information about Óláfr must have been scant. Snorri was forced to augment his narrative with interpolations from *Ágrip*, and Msk2 was also interpolated from that compilation. One of the main poetic sources of information about Óláfr was Steinn Herdísarson's "Óláfsdrápa," and that poem was apparently well known to the author of ÆMsk (see p. 266) as well as to the later interpolator.

The "Saga of Óláfr kyrri" in MskMS contains fourteen stanzas. One of those stanzas (st. 166) is recorded in the episode about Óláfr and the crow man (Ch. 54) and is included in MskMS, Hr, AM 66, and F. Of the remaining thirteen stanzas (eleven of which come from Steinn's panegyric), five (38 percent) are recorded in *Hkr* or *Fsk* and must have been copied from ÆMsk (sts. 157–59, 163–64); seven are given in Hr, AM 66 (or F) and must have been part of Msk2 (sts. 161–62, 165–70); and one stanza (st. 160) is given in MskMS only.

One anonymous stanza (st. 165) is recorded in both MskMS and in *Hkr* but in different contexts. Snorri uses the stanza to document that Óláfr mobilized Norwegian troops against Sveinn of Denmark, and he incorporates it prior to our st. 157 (*ÍF* 28, 202). St. 165 is also found in *Ágrip* (*ÍF* 29, 41), and the prose of MskMS shows that this entire section, including the stanza, was lifted from that work. Hr and AM 66 follow *Hkr* at this point, but F cites the stanza twice, once according to *Hkr* (*F* 254) and once in the same prose environment (from *Ágrip*) as in MskMS (*F* 259). Thus, we must be dealing with two independent interpolations from *Ágrip* in *Hkr* and *Msk*, and furthermore, the interpolation in the latter must have taken place at the stage of Msk2.

Sts. 160–62 in MskMS are appended to a sequence of stanzas (sts. 157–59;

also in *Fsk*) from Steinn's "Óláfsdrápa" pertaining to the tension between Norway and Denmark after the death of Haraldr Sigurðarson. Whereas sts. 157–59 simply confirm that Óláfr prepared to defend Norway against Sveinn (all three versions concur), sts. 160–62 document actual hostile encounters between the two forces. No battles between the Danes and the Norwegians are mentioned in other sources, but there is evidence that Snorri must have been familiar with the content of these stanzas. St. 162 states that both Óláfr and his brother, Magnús, took part in the mobilization of the Norwegian forces and the subsequent meeting with Sveinn. However, both MskMS and *Fsk* place the unrest after the death of Magnús (see Ch. 51; *ÍF* 29, 290, 297). Snorri, on the other hand, rearranges the narrative, has Magnús participate in the negotiations with Sveinn (*ÍF* 28, 201), and places his death after the peace agreement between Norway and Denmark (*ÍF* 28, 202). Snorri could have made that change independently based on his knowledge of Steinn's poem, but it could also be that one or more of these stanzas were part of his exemplar, and that Snorri, who had no further information about the alleged skirmishes between the Norwegians and the Danes than the sparse details offered by the poetry, decided to omit the stanzas from his narrative (see the comment on st. 49, above).

The remaining stanzas (sts. 167–70) are recorded in Hr, AM 66 (all stanzas), and F (sts. 167–69) and must have been part of Msk2. They are variations on the same theme, namely, Óláfr's generosity, and they form a natural sequence to the preceding episode about Óláfr and the crow man (p. 284): "He gave him good gifts and forgave the land taxes for the land he lived on. . . . There are many examples reported on how generous King Óláfr was in his gifts of money. He also bestowed all sorts of treasures, as the skald Steinn mentions." Thus it could well be that the *þáttr* about the crow man and the stanzas were inserted into *Msk* at the same time. Whether that took place in ÆMsk or in Msk2 is impossible to ascertain, but because neither *Fsk* nor *Hkr* makes any reference to Óláfr's generosity, the whole section, including the *þáttr*, could also have been the work of a later interpolator.

We may conclude, then, that there is clear evidence to the effect that "Óláfs saga" in *Msk* was augmented by a later interpolator and, furthermore, that the interpolations took place in Msk2. The interpolations consisted of sections of prose and poetry from *Ágrip*, and it is possible that additional stanzas from Steinn Herdísarson's "Óláfsdrápa," as well as the episode about Óláfr and the crow man, were interpolated at that time. Because Snorri apparently rearranged the narrative of *Hkr* to account for the information given in st. 162, however, sts. 160–62 could have been included in ÆMsk.

The Saga of Magnús berfœttr (Chs. 55–59)

This section of MskMS contains fifty stanzas. Four of those stanzas (sts. 202–5) occur in the *þáttr* about the Norman knight Giffarðr and do not concern us here. Of the remaining forty-six stanzas, fourteen (30 percent) are given in

Hkr (twelve) or *Fsk* (eight) and must have been part of ÆMsk; the other thirty-two stanzas are all given in Hr, AM 66, or F (= Msk2). Twenty of the thirty-two stanzas are composed in the meter *fornyrðislag* and belong to Gísl Illugason's commemorative eulogy to Magnús berfœttr. None of these stanzas is cited in *Hkr* or *Fsk*. (Gísl's panegyric is discussed separately below.)

Chapter 57 of MskMS cites two half-stanzas (sts. 185–86) that are used to corroborate the statement in the prose that Magnús rid Norway of pirates and outlaws. Those stanzas are introduced as follows in MskMS (p. 297; FJ 315; U 142): "Þess getr hann [Bjǫrn krepphendi] ok, at Magnús konungr ruddi land sitt víkingum ok illþýðisliði" (He [Bjǫrn krepphendi] also mentions that King Magnús rid the land of pirates and rabble). The first half-stanza is misplaced and belongs to a stanza describing the hanging of Steigar-Þórir, which Snorri introduces at its correct place (the whole stanza; *ÍF* 28, 217). As far as Magnús's punitive activities are concerned, the other versions read as follows: "Hann gørðisk maðr ríkr ok refsingasamr, hvárttveggja innan lands, ok þó mest útan lands" (*Fsk, ÍF* 29, 306: "He became an imperious man and quick to punish disobedience at home, but more so abroad"); "Hann friðaði vel fyrir landi sínu ok eyddi ǫllum víkingum ok útilegumǫnnum" (*Hkr, ÍF* 28, 218: "He maintained peace in the land and suppressed all vikings and outlaws"). A closer look at the text of *Hkr*, however, reveals that this particular passage is taken from *Ágrip* (*ÍF* 29, 45): "ok friðaði vel fyr landi sínu ok eyddi ǫllum víkingum ok útilegumǫnnum" (and maintained peace in the land and suppressed all vikings and outlaws). Thus *Hkr* copies *Ágrip* verbatim, and the half-stanzas in MskMS (sts. 185–86) are not part of the *Hkr* narrative. St. 185 occurs elsewhere, however, in its correct context. The sentence in *Fsk* is taken directly from ÆMsk (*ÍF* 29, 306; FJ 315; U 142): "ríklundaðr maðr ok refsingasamr bæði innanlands ok útanlands" (an imperious man and quick to punish disobedience at home and abroad). The question is whether the section that contains sts. 185–86 in MskMS originally belonged to ÆMsk, too, or whether it was interpolated into Msk2.

The wording of *Hkr* and *Ágrip* on the one hand, and that of MskMS on the other, would seem to suggest a common source. That circumstance leaves us with two possibilities: we must assume either that both Snorri and the interpolator of Msk2 independently decided to copy *Ágrip* at this point, or that the passages in ÆMsk and *Ágrip* go back to a common source, namely, a written account about Magnús (*Magnúss saga). If the first were the case, it is not clear why the interpolator would incorporate the phrase "ruddi land sitt víkingum ok illþýðisliði" ("rid the land of pirates and rabble"; cf. *Ágrip, Hkr* "eyddi ǫllum víkingum ok útilegumǫnnum" "suppressed vikings and outlaws") and leave out the rest of the sentence (*Ágrip, ÍF* 29, 45): "ok var maðr herskár ok rǫskr ok starfsamr ok líkari í ǫllu Haraldi fǫðurfeðr sínum í skaplyndi heldr en fǫður sínum" (and he was a warlike man, brave and active and in all respects he was more like his grandfather, Haraldr, in disposition than his father). That information was copied verbatim into *Hkr* (*ÍF* 28, 218), and we would expect that the interpolator, too, would have included the comparison between Magnús and Haraldr if it were part of his exemplar.

If, however, the comment about Magnús's punitive actions as well as the stanzas were part of ÆMsk, it is easy to see why Snorri, who clearly knew Bjǫrn's "Magnússdrápa" much better than the author of ÆMsk (see below), would have changed the narrative. Once he realized that the stanza was both misquoted and misplaced in his exemplar (see "Notes to Stanzas"), he replaced that section with a corresponding section from Ágrip. The author of Fsk, who at this point abbreviated the text and almost entirely ceased to incorporate stanzas in support of the narrative, retained the comprehensive sentence from ÆMsk about Magnús's activities at home and abroad but omitted further elaboration on those issues.

As it emerged from the discussion above, st. 185 from Bjǫrn's "Magnússdrápa" was not only misplaced but was also misquoted, most likely in ÆMsk. Further stanzas from that poem are used to document the sequence of Magnús's harrying in the islands on his first expedition to the west (sts. 188–90). Snorri also documents Magnús's devastations with the relevant stanzas from Bjǫrn's poem, but a comparison of Hkr and MskMS again shows that although the author of ÆMsk certainly knew Bjǫrn's poem, his recall of the sequences of stanzas, half-stanzas, and lines was imperfect. Thus Magnús's itinerary in MskMS and Fsk (= ÆMsk) differs slightly from that of Hkr. F follows MskMS rather than Hkr at this point. In one instance in MskMS, we can detect the "corrective" hand of a later scribe, possibly the same person who changed the first line of st. 158 in the "Saga of Óláfr kyrri." St. 190 describes Magnús harrying in the Mull of Kintyre ("þioð raN mvlsc til møþi" "the men of Mull fled exhausted"). That information is incorporated into the prose (FJ 317; U 143): "Þa lagþiz M[agnús] konvngr meþ heriN vt a Mvlsc" (Then King Magnús took his army out to "Mulsk"). The corrupt form "mvlsc" was copied into the prose from the poetry, and because F retains the correct reading in both cases ("mylsk" and "vt at Myl"; F 270), that "correction" must have taken place either in MskX or in MskMS itself. Thus, textual changes must have been made at two different stages in the Msk transmission: once in Msk2, where the text was augmented with interpolations from Ágrip and with some additional stanzas, and once at a later stage and by an incompetent scribe who must have been particularly concerned with the relations between prose and poetry.

The next stanza in MskMS that is not found in Hkr (Fsk has no stanzas at this point) is st. 187. The content of the stanza is negligible ("The proud-minded feeder of wolves [warrior] embarked on a swift journey to the west; the king disbarred the peace; the stiff prows sliced the wave"). It does not corroborate the information in the preceding prose, namely, that Magnús and Erlingr of Orkney accompanied Magnús on the journey west. The prose of Fsk follows MskMS (ÍF 29, 307 = ÆMsk), but Snorri changes the narrative and includes a section on the jarls Páll and Erlendr. There is no evidence that the stanza is a later interpolation.

The last two *dróttkvætt* stanzas that are incorporated into MskMS as historical verification are sts. 206 (about the Gautish campaign) and 220 (about the Battle of Ulster). None of these stanzas presents specific information. St. 206 documents that Magnús fought in Gautland and is the first in a sequence of stanzas (sts. 207–10) inserted after the Giffarðr episode to conclude the narrative about the Battle of Fuxerna. It contains the usual imagery of beasts of battle ("the Gautish torso lay beneath the yellow claw of the old eagle"). St. 220 merely states that Magnús ordered his troops to disembark and that he fought a battle; no details about the place of battle or the identity of the enemy are given. Although we cannot ascertain whether the stanzas were part of ÆMsk, they have all the characteristics of stanzas that were at cross purposes with Snorri's editorial policy.

Six stanzas are given as *lausavísur* and are attributed to anonymous Norwegians (sts. 178, 217) or to Magnús berfœttr himself (sts. 212–14, 218). St. 178 recapitulates the conversation between Steigar-Þórir and Sigurðr ullstrengr and is paraphrased in the prose of *Hkr* (*ÍF* 28, 216) and *Fsk* (*ÍF* 29, 304). The execution of Steigar-Þórir and Egill is documented in detail in prose and poetry in all three versions, and because both Snorri and the author of *Fsk* were fond of recording pregnant remarks in poetry (see sts. 23, 106, 108, 149, 181), there is no reason why this stanza should not have been incorporated into their narratives if it were part of their exemplar. The prose is derived verbatim, however, from the poetry (= ÆMsk), and it is strange that the author of ÆMsk did not record the stanza if he knew it. We are faced with the following two possibilities: (1) the author of ÆMsk did not know the stanza, followed a prose narrative that recorded the verbal exchange between Sigurðr and Þórir, and the stanza was added by the interpolator of Msk2; (2) the stanza was part of ÆMsk but was omitted in *Hkr* and *Fsk*.

Sts. 212–14 come from a love poem allegedly composed by Magnús berfœttr. In MskMS, the stanzas follow the section about the peace treaty between Norway and Sweden and the marriage of Magnús to Margréta of Sweden. Thus, the stanzas form a natural appendix to that episode: the information about Magnús's marriage to the Swedish king's daughter is followed by a poetic recapitulation of his earlier attachment to the "emperor's" daughter. If Russell Poole (1985:116–18) is right, st. 219, which is quoted in *Fsk*, also belonged to that poem, and if that were the case, sts. 212–14, too, could have been part of ÆMsk. Poole further argues that st. 79, which in MskMS is attributed to Magnús góði, actually belonged to Magnús berfœttr's poem. It is curious that that stanza, which deals with Magnús's love for the sister of an unknown king (Edgar of Scotland?) is used to introduce the erotic *þáttr* about Magnús [góði] and Margrét, whereas sts. 212–14 occur as an appendix to the marriage of Magnús [berfœttr] and Margréta. It could well be that the poetic insertions (and, consequently, also the *þáttr* about Magnús and Margrét in Ch. 23), were the work of one person, who took a lively interest in the amorous affairs of kings and their retainers (cf. the triangle Haraldr harðráði–Maria–

Zoë [Chs. 12–13]; Magnús and Margrét [Ch. 23]; Haraldr and Ingibjǫrg [Ch. 39]; Ívarr Ingimundarson and Oddný [Ch. 65]; Sigurðr jórsalafari and Sigríðr [Ch. 70]; Sigurðr and Cecilia [Chs. 80–81]).

Magnús's love stanza in MskMS is followed by two stanzas (sts. 215–16) whose presence is entirely unmotivated. They describe a sea voyage and are prefaced by the following statement: "The skald recited the following about King Magnús at sea." The only reason for the inclusion of the stanzas must be an interest in nautical imagery. A similar two-stanza insertion occurs in the "Saga of Haraldr and Magnús" (sts. 21–22): "Next we are told that at one time King Magnús was sailing along the coast. . . . Here there is some reference to his campaigns." Neither *Fsk* nor *Hkr* incorporates the stanzas at this point, but because Snorri uses st. 22 in a similar context in the next chapter (*ÍF* 28, 34), at least that stanza must have been part of ÆMsk.

We may conclude, then, that there is no direct evidence to suggest that any stanzas in *dróttkvætt* meter in "Magnúss saga berfœtts" were interpolated into Msk2, although the absence of st. 178 from the narratives of *Hkr* and *Fsk* is rather conspicuous. The content of sts. 186–87, 206, and 220 is unspecific, and although no evidence can be adduced as to their presence in ÆMsk, it could well be that Snorri found them unsuitable as historical verification. That is also the case with sts. 215–16, which have no historical value at all and must have been added for purely personal reasons (reflecting the author's predilection for nautical scenery). As far as sts. 212–14 are concerned, they form an integral part of the *Msk* narrative, and because st. 219 (which most likely belonged to the same poem) demonstrably did belong to ÆMsk, it is likely that sts. 212–14 (as well as st. 79?) were added by the same author.

None of the twenty stanzas from Gísl Illugason's "Erfikvæði Magnúss berfœtts" is given in *Hkr* or *Fsk,* and most scholars believe that they are later interpolations. In MskMS (and in Hr, AM 66, and F) these *fornyrðislag* stanzas are distributed as follows:

Sts. 172–77: Steigar-Þórir's rebellion and Magnús's intial response to that unrest
Sts. 182–83: Magnús's reconciliation with the people who had supported Þórir
St. 191: The capture of Lǫgmaðr on Skye
Sts. 195–98: Recapitulation of the Battle of Menai Strait
Sts. 199–201: Description of Magnús's return to Norway ("sailing")
Sts. 207–10: Recapitulation of the Battle of Fuxerna

Sts. 172–74 refer to Magnús's actions upon hearing about the uprising of Þórir: "When King Magnús learned of this, he gathered troops and ships. Then he traveled north against Þórir and his followers with a great host. Gísl Illugason, who was then with the king, spoke as follows." *Fsk* appears to follow *Ágrip* or a similar source and records only that Magnús encountered Þórir and his men in Trondheimsfjorden (*ÍF* 29, 304): "then Magnús sailed into the fjord."

Hkr follows the *Msk* text but omits the stanzas (*ÍF* 28, 215): "King Magnús learned of these happenings and at once gathered troops and proceeded north to Trondheim." The only indication that Snorri knew the stanzas is the comment that Magnús went "north to Trondheim" (st. 173 gives Oslo as Magnús's point of departure).

According to MskMS, Magnús convened an assembly after arriving in Trondheim, proceeded to waste the surrounding countryside by fire, and Egill and his men fled north (sts. 175–77). Snorri here reverts to the narrative of *Fsk* (*Ágrip*) but incorporates the Bjarkøy incident (*ÍF* 28, 215), which in MskMS and *Fsk* (*ÍF* 29, 305) follows the capture of Þórir and Egill. After st. 177, MskMS also picks up the *Fsk* (*Ágrip*) text and doubles back to incorporate the events as told in the other versions. Thus it is impossible to know whether or not sts. 175–77 (and the prose, which is clearly derived from the poetry) were part of ÆMsk, or whether ÆMsk read like *Hkr*. (*Fsk* apparently did not follow *Msk* at this point.)

According to MskMS, Magnús became reconciled with his enemies after the execution of Þórir and Egill, and sts. 182–83 are cited as evidence (p. 291; FJ 305; U 136): "Ok eptir þessi verk fór Magnús konungr aptr *inn í Þrándheim* ok *refsaði* þar mǫrgum *mǫnnum*, en þeir víkusk til hans miskunnar. *Svá segir Gísl*" (emphasis added) (After these events King Magnús went back *to Trondheim* and *inflicted penalties on* many *men*, but they threw themselves on his mercy *as Gísl says*). *Fsk* makes no mention of further actions by Magnús, but *Hkr* includes the following section (*ÍF* 28, 218): "Magnús konungr helt síðan suðr til Þrándheims ok lagði *inn í Þrándheim*, veitti þar stórar *refsingar* þeim *mǫnnum*, er sannir váru at landráðum við hann. Drap hann suma, en brenndi fyrir sumum. *Svá segir* Bjǫrn enn krepphendi" (emphasis added) (King Magnús then proceeded south to the Trondheim district and *to Trondheim* and *inflicted* heavy *penalties on* those *men* who had been found guilty of treason against him. He killed some and burned the houses of others. *This is reported* by Bjǫrn enn krepphendi). There can be no doubt that Snorri at this point adopts the *Msk* prose, but he replaces Gísl's *fornyrðislag* stanzas with a *dróttkvætt* stanza from Bjǫrn krepphendi's "Magnússdrápa" that provides additional information about killing and burning in Snorri's version of the event. Thus sts. 182–83 must have been part of ÆMsk.

Both *Hkr* and MskMS contain a *dróttkvætt* stanza by Bjǫrn to document that Magnús captured Lǫgmaðr during his first expedition to the west (st. 190; *ÍF* 28, 221–22). However, MskMS appends yet another stanza from Gísl's poem (st. 191a–b), which states that Magnús kept Lǫgmaðr in his company. That information is repeated in the prose (FJ 318; U 144): "Ok áðr létti, tók Magnús konungr hann hǫndum við skipasǫgn sína, ok gaf honum grið, ok var hann með konungi nǫkkura hríð" (Before the matter was concluded, King Magnús captured him with his crew, but he spared him and kept him in his company for some time). The prose of *Fsk* repeats the first part of the sentence in

MskMS, but the information from the stanza is omitted (*ÍF* 29, 307): "ok áðr en hann létti [*sic*] tók Magnús konungr hann með skipasókn sína" (and before he [Lǫgmaðr] concluded his journey [*sic*] King Magnús captured him with his crew). *Hkr,* however, reads as follows (*ÍF* 28, 221): "En at lykðum tóku menn Magnúss konungs hann með skipasǫgn sína, þá er hann vildi flýja til Írlands. Lét konungr hann í járn setja ok hafa á gæzlu" (But in the end King Magnús's men captured him with his crew when he prepared to flee to Ireland. The king had him put in irons and kept him under guard). Again, it seems that the information in *Hkr* was derived from Gísl's stanza, which then must have been part of ÆMsk. The prose in *Fsk,* however, indicates that *Fsk* does not follow ÆMsk but a common exemplar.

The slaying of Hugh of Shrewsbury (Hugi enn prúði) in Menai Strait is commemorated by *dróttkvætt* stanzas (193–94) in both MskMS and *Hkr.* Snorri reverses the order of the two stanzas. MskMS then adds four stanzas from Gísl's poem (sts. 195–98) to recapitulate the battle and Hugh's death. The stanzas fall into the category "stanzas that punctuate a battle," and they contain no information that is reflected in the prose of *Hkr.*

After the campaign Magnús spent the winter in the Hebrides and, according to MskMS, returned to Norway the next summer: "The next summer he sailed north to his realm in Norway, as Gísl reports." Then follow three stanzas (sts. 199–201) describing Magnús's sea voyage. *Fsk* (*ÍF* 29, 309) and *Hkr* (*ÍF* 28, 225) correspond fairly closely to MskMS as far as the prose is concerned, but none of these versions includes the sequence of stanzas in MskMS. It is impossible to ascertain whether the stanzas were part of ÆMsk.

In MskMS, the Battle of Fuxerna and the first leg of the Gautish campaign are concluded by a sequence of stanzas, the first of which is in *dróttkvætt* meter (st. 206; see above), whereas the remaining four stanzas belong to Gísl's "Erfikvæði" (sts. 207–10). Again, there are no indications in the prose of *Fsk* and *Hkr* that the stanzas belonged to ÆMsk.

As the discussion above has shown, it is difficult to say when the stanzas from Gísl's poem were incorporated into the *Msk* narrative. Because the prose of *Hkr* occasionally betrays knowledge of the content of these stanzas, it appears that some of them must have been part of ÆMsk. It is equally clear, however, that Snorri did not consider stanzas composed in *fornyrðislag* suitable for the purposes of historical verification, and at one point he retains the prose of ÆMsk but replaces the pertinent stanzas with another stanza in *dróttkvætt* meter.

Whereas the "Saga of Haraldr and Magnús" in *Fsk* incorporated 55 percent of the stanzas found in MskMS and *Hkr* retained 60 percent, the percentages in the "Saga of Magnús berfœttr" are much lower (15 percent and 26 percent, respectively). Even if we omit the twenty stanzas from Gísl's poem from this count, the percentages in this saga are still considerably below those in the "Saga of Haraldr and Magnús" (*Fsk* 27 percent, *Hkr* 40 percent). We suggested above that one of the reasons for this low count could have been that many of the stanzas in MskMS that could have been part of ÆMsk are unspecific and do not contain information that could be used to verify the content of the narrative. A look at the "Saga of Haraldr and Magnús" and the "Saga of Magnús berfœttr" certainly confirms that the narrative of the former relied much more heavily on information from poetry than that of the latter. In *Hkr*, for example, the stanzas in the "Saga of Magnús berfœttr" are used to document Magnús's harrying in Halland (= ÆMsk), the names of the participants in the uprising against Magnús (= ÆMsk), Magnús's reconciliation with his enemies (substitution of stanzas from ÆMsk), Magnús's harrying in the isles (= ÆMsk), and the Battle of Menai Strait (= ÆMsk). *Fsk* is even more parsimonious. After an initial cluster of stanzas in the episode about Steigar-Þórir's uprising and death (our sts. 171, 179, 180–81), the remainder of the saga contains only three stanzas.

Even stanzas that must have been part of ÆMsk and are included as historical verification in *Hkr* were omitted in *Fsk*, which either leaves out the episodes altogether or summarizes the content in brief prose passages. It is interesting that *Fsk* at this point chooses to incorporate stanzas that are integral parts of the narrative, among them two anonymous stanzas and three *lausavísur*, rather than stanzas that are cited for historical verification. It could well be that the author had access to a written saga about Magnús berfœttr that contained most of the stanzas given in *Fsk* and, furthermore, that that saga also underlay the narratives of *Ágrip* and ÆMsk. That would account for the similarities in the wording of the three versions and also explain why *Fsk* suddenly ceases to incorporate stanzas into the prose (assuming that *Magnúss saga contained few stanzas).

Such a supposition is further strengthened by the fact that the one stanza quoted in all the compilations, namely, Steigar-Þórir's *lausavísa* (st. 179), contains the same mistake in *Ágrip*, *Fsk*, and MskMS (and in Hr, AM 66, and F, securing the same reading for Msk2). In all versions, line 2 reads as follows: "fœrðum einn við stýri" ("færðum": F, 47, 66; "fœrðum": MskMS, Fsk B; see *Skj* IA, 434). Only *Hkr* has the correct reading "forðum," probably owing to Snorri's familiarity with skaldic poetry. Even if we assume that the reading of ÆMsk ("fœrðum") was copied into *Fsk* and Msk2, we would be hard put to explain the reading of *Ágrip*. Because *Ágrip* could not have copied ÆMsk, and ÆMsk did not copy *Ágrip*, the only possible explanation must be that the erroneous wording in the two versions goes back to a common exemplar.

The stanzas in MskMS (Msk2) fulfilled clearly defined functions. Moreover, unlike the stanzas in the "Saga of Haraldr and Magnús," their function is more literary and structural than historical. If possible, stanzas are used to introduce and to conclude important campaigns and battles (the campaign against Steigar-Þórir: sts. 172, 182–83; the first expedition to the west: sts. 187, 199–201; the Battle of Menai Strait [conclusion only]: sts. 195–98; the Gautish campaign: sts. 206–10; the second expedition to the west [beginning only]:

sts. 217–18). None of these stanzas contains much factual information about the campaigns themselves, and none of them is found in *Hkr*. Their function and content correspond to that of "stanzas punctuating battles" in the "Saga of Haraldr and Magnús." Magnús's love stanzas (which appear to have been part of ÆMsk) and the stanzas about Magnús's sailing (sts. 215–16) provide asides that must reflect the personal taste of the author. If the author of ÆMsk had access to a written narrative about Magnús berfœttr and inserted skaldic stanzas into that narrative to augment and support the story-line, that is, if the choice of stanzas were dictated by the information in an encoded text rather than the text being derived from information culled from the stanzas (as in the "Saga of Haraldr and Magnús"), we would expect to find both an awkward fit between prose and poetry and a certain redundancy (a detailed prose account documented by stanzas of a fairly general content). Indeed, the relationship between prose and poetry in this part of MskMS is often both redundant and awkward.

The Saga of Sigurðr jórsalafari (Chs. 60–81)

Twenty-two stanzas are incorporated into the extant portions of the "Saga of Sigurðr jórsalafari" in MskMS. Eight of those stanzas (sts. 235–42; also recorded in Hr and AM 66) are found in *þættir* or smaller anecdotes ("Ásu-Þórðr," Ch. 68; "Þingasaga," Ch. 70; "Þórarinn stuttfeldr," Ch. 72; "Sigurðr and Ingibjǫrg," Ch. 73; "Erlendr gapamunnr," Ch. 75). *Hkr* cites ten of the remaining fourteen stanzas (71 percent), and *Fsk* one only (our st. 231). The stanzas given in *Hkr* (= ÆMsk) all verify the itinerary of Sigurðr's crusade and contain either place names or factual information.

In addition to the ten stanzas recorded in *Hkr* (sts. 222, 224–29, 231–33), the extant portions of MskMS document Sigurðr's journey with another four stanzas (sts. 221, 223, 230, 234), three of which belong to Þórarinn's "Stuttfeld-ardrápa." St. 221 initiates the expedition and describes how people flocked to Sigurðr to join him in his venture, but the stanza is out of place. The prose reads as follows (p. 313): "and when the men were prepared, he had a total of sixty ships, as Þórarinn stuttfeldr says." The stanza that verifies the number of ships (st. 222, from the same poem) is inserted later in the narrative, after Sigurðr's departure from Norway.

Snorri smoothes out the discrepancy by omitting st. 221 and inserting the information about the sixty ships prior to st. 222 (ÍF 28, 239). *Fsk* abbreviates the prose in *Msk* and omits both stanzas (ÍF 29, 315). It would appear that the information in the prose must have been derived from st. 222, and because that stanza must have been part of ÆMsk, there is no apparent reason why the prose statement about the sixty ships should not have been followed by the stanza from which that information was taken. However, the information about the sixty ships is also in *Ágrip* (*ÍF* 29, 47) without the corroborating stanza, and it could have been taken over from a written exemplar.

According to the prose, st. 222 should have been given in place of st. 221, and st. 221 should have been inserted prior to the sentence about the sixty ships (p. 313): "Many district chieftains and other powerful men readied themselves for this expedition with King Sigurðr." That is the sequence in Hr and AM 66 (*H), but because *H at this point combines the narratives of *Hkr* and *Msk*, it is impossible to say whether the *H text reflects Msk2 (< ÆMsk) or a later revision of Msk2 (F follows *Hkr*). The fact that sts. 222–23 in MskMS are introduced by the name of the wrong poet (Þorvaldr blǫnduskald rather than Þórarinn stuttfeldr; thus *H and *Hkr*) suggests that this section of MskMS has been subject to revision. Furthermore, the prose of MskMS shows clear indications of having been interpolated from *Ágrip*. Compare the following sentences (not in *Fsk* or *Hkr*): "ok hafði með sér fjǫlmennt ok góðmennt ok þó þá eina, er fara vildu" (*ÍF* 29, 47: "He took with him a select and numerous company, but only men who were themselves intent on making the voyage"); "Hann hafði með sér fjǫlmennt ok gott mannval, ok þó þá eina er sjálfr vildu fara ok veita honum fylgð ok fǫruneyti" (FJ 338; U 156: "He took with him a select and numerous company, but only men who were themselves intent on making the voyage and giving him support and companionship"). Thus it could be that st. 221 was added when the text was interpolated from *Ágrip*, or that sts. 221–22 were misplaced during the revision.

St. 223, which also belongs to "Stuttfeldardrápa," follows immediately upon st. 222 and verifies that Sigurðr went from Norway to England on the first leg of his journey. Snorri retains the prose but replaces the *tøglag* stanza with a stanza in *dróttkvætt* (*ÍF* 28, 240) that contains more specific information (Sigurðr stayed the winter in England). It is likely that st. 223 was part of ÆMsk.

St. 230, a *dróttkvætt* stanza from Halldórr skvaldri's "Útfarardrápa," is the first stanza in a sequence of three (sts. 230–32) describing Sigurðr's ruse to capture the cave in Formentera. Sts. 231–32 are also given in *Hkr*, but Snorri replaces st. 230, which provides little factual information, with a stanza from Halldórr's "Útfararkviða" that contains the place name "Forminterra" (*ÍF* 28, 245). That place name also occurs in the prose of MskMS but without the accompanying stanza. *Fsk* retains the prose of *Msk*, albeit in abbreviated form, but gives no stanzas in support of the information given in the prose (except our st. 231; *ÍF* 29, 316–17). But whereas *Hkr* follows the itinerary and sequence of events given in MskMS (= ÆMsk), *Fsk* deviates from the other narratives by omitting the name Sintra, by placing the capture of the galleys after the capture of Lisbon (and the unnamed Sintra), and by omitting the capture of Ibiza, which is documented in prose and poetry in the other two versions (see *ÍF* 29, 316–17; *ÍF* 28, 241–47). Again, it is possible that *Fsk*, as well as ÆMsk, ultimately derived their narratives from a shorter, written version of Sigurðr's pilgrimage, which in ÆMsk was augmented by stanzas from Halldórr's and Þórarinn's poems. The text of *Ágrip* is very abbreviated at this point, and apart from the interpolation from *Ágrip* noted above, there are no similarities between the prose of *Ágrip* and the other versions, apart from the information about the sixty ships in the introductory section to the saga.

St. 234 is incorporated into MskMS to document Sigurðr's return to Norway and the Norwegians' joyful reception of him. There are only two lines left of the stanza, and their meaning is hard to discern. The same two lines are copied into Hr and AM 66, and they must have been part of Msk2. If the couplet had been added in Msk2, one would at least expect it to make sense, and the fact that it does not suggests that the lines were copied in this abbreviated form from an earlier version (ÆMsk?). The function of the couplet in the narrative is to form the conclusion of Sigurðr's voyage.

To sum up: *Hkr* includes a high percentage of the stanzas found in the extant portions of the "Saga of Sigurðr jórsalafari" in MskMS. All the stanzas contain concrete information about Sigurðr's expedition to Palestine, and they must have been part of ÆMsk. In two instances, Snorri apparently rejected stanzas from ÆMsk and replaced them with stanzas he must have felt were more pertinent. The initial section of the "Saga of Sigurðr jórsalafari" in MskMS was interpolated from *Ágrip,* but the extent of that interpolation is limited to part of one sentence. It is possible that the stanzas in that section were misplaced during the revision and that the wrong name of the poet was added by mistake. The prose of MskMS, as well that of *Fsk,* contains factual information that is not corroborated by poetry, and the narrative of *Fsk* indicates that the author could have drawn on a version of the "Saga of Sigurðr jórsalafari" that differed slightly from the source of *Hkr* and MskMS.

The Saga of Haraldr gilli and Magnús blindi (Chs. 82–83)

In MskMS, the extant portion of this saga is very short, and the texts of *Hkr, F,* and *Fornmannasǫgur* show that the saga must have contained more stanzas than the seven stanzas presently preserved in the MS (see Ch. 82a; *Ágrip* has a lacuna here). *Fsk* and *Hkr* incorporate three of these stanzas (43 percent), and the remaining four are found only in MskMS (Hr, AM 66, and F follow *Hkr*). The three stanzas common to all versions (sts. 243, 246–47) contain factual information and place names (the siege of Bergen, Haraldr's campaigns on Hven and Læsø), and must have been part of ÆMsk.

The other four stanzas in MskMS are found in the same section of the saga (sts. 244–45, 248–49). The first two stanzas verify the prose statement that Haraldr gilli became sole ruler of Norway after the maiming of Magnús Sigurðarson, and the second pair is appended to sts. 246–47 and recapitulates the sacking of Hven and Læsø described in those stanzas. The relevant passage in MskMS reads as follows (FJ 402; U 199): "En Haraldr konungr var þá einvaldi alls Norégs um vetrinn, ok gaf ǫllum sættir, er hafa vildu, ok tók marga þá til hirðvistar, er verit hǫfðu með Magnúsi konungi. Svá segir H. [+ sts. 244–45]. Nú er Haraldr einn konungr í Nóregi" (King Haraldr was sole king of all Norway that winter. He granted terms to all those who wished to have them and took many into his retinue who had served with King Magnús. In the words of H. [+ sts. 244–45]. Haraldr was now sole monarch in Norway).

The corresponding information in *Fsk* (*F* 29, 326) is brief and limited to one sentence ("and Haraldr then subjugated the entire country") followed by the section with genealogical information that occurs after st. 249 in MskMS. *Hkr* gives the same prose statements as MskMS, however, although in reverse order and with a long section on the sacking of Konungahella by the Wends (Chs. 9–11) in place of sts. 244–45 (*ÍF* 28, 288, 296): "Síðan var Haraldr einn konungr yfir Nóregi, meðan hann lifði. [+ chs. 9–11]. En Haraldr réð þá einn landi eptir um vetrinn ok gaf ǫllum mǫnnum sættir, er hafa vildu, tók þá marga menn til hirðvistar, er með Magnúsi hǫfðu verit" (Thereafter Haraldr was sole monarch in Norway while he lived [+ chs. 9–11]. But Haraldr ruled the country alone that winter and granted terms to all those who wished to have them. He took many into his retinue who had served with Magnús). Hence, both MskMS and *Hkr* contain a doubling of the statement that Haraldr became sole ruler of Norway, and the wording of the two versions is sufficiently similar to posit a common source (ÆMsk). Because ÆMsk did not include the chapters on the Wends in Konungahella (Snorri must have gotten that information from Jón Loptsson), there is no reason why that MS should have contained two statements about Haraldr's becoming sole ruler of Norway unless both or one of the stanzas were inserted in between, and the presence of sts. 244–45 (or at least one of those stanzas) is thus secured for the oldest version of *Msk*. Snorri replaced the stanzas with the section about the Wends and retained the two statements from ÆMsk (but in reverse order). *Fsk* merely states that Haraldr subjugated the country, omits the stanza(s), as well as the information about Magnús's earlier retainers, and proceeds directly to the section containing genealogical information, placing sts. 246–47 and the surrounding prose after the death of Haraldr gilli (*ÍF* 29, 329).

Haraldr's campaign in Denmark is documented in all three versions by two *dróttkvætt* stanzas from Einarr Skúlason's "Haraldsdrápa I" (sts. 246–47), but MskMS adds two stanzas in *tøglag* from Einarr's "Haraldsdrápa II." All four stanzas contain the relevant place names ("Hveðn," sts. 246, 248; "Hlésey," sts. 247, 249). Sts. 248–49, then, are completely redundant because the prose has already been confirmed by sts. 246–47. Thus the stanzas could have been omitted by Snorri and the author of *Fsk*, but it is equally possible that they were interpolated into *Msk* at a later point, especially because, in MskMS, they are mistakenly attributed to Halldórr skvaldri. It is difficult to imagine that the author of ÆMsk, who apparently knew Einarr's "Haraldsdrápa II" and correctly assigns st. 243 to that poem, would have made such a mistake (unless st. 243

was part of a written exemplar). Because Hr, AM 66, and F follow *Hkr*, we cannot know whether these stanzas were part of Msk2.

We may conclude, then, that at least four (57 percent) or perhaps five (71 percent) of the stanzas included in the extant portions of the "Saga of Haraldr gilli and Magnús blindi" in MskMS were copied from ÆMsk. Furthermore, it is clear that both Snorri and the author of *Fsk* continue to adhere to the policy of including only *dróttkvætt* stanzas with factual information (here: place names), and that the latter, as was the case in the "Saga of Magnús berfœttr" and the "Saga of Sigurðr jórsalafari," abbreviates the narrative and leaves out stanzas. Whether *Fsk* at this point followed an abbreviated version of Eiríkr Oddsson's *Hryggjarstykki is impossible to ascertain (see "The Native Sources" above).

The Saga of Sigurðr slembidjákn (Chs. 84–93)

In this part of the narrative, all three compilations (*Fsk, ÆMsk,* and *Hkr*) are based on different versions of the same written work, namely, Eiríkr Oddsson's *Hryggjarstykki (Bjarni Guðnason 1978:54–55; see also "The Native Sources"). It is doubtful whether that work contained skaldic stanzas, but the texts show that Eiríkr must have based part of his narrative on information gleaned from Ívarr Ingimundarson's "Sigurðarbǫlkr" (ibid., 47, 89). MskMS incorporates forty-five stanzas of that poem (excluding st. 280), of which two (sts. 259, 262) are found in *Fsk* and *Hkr* and must have been part of ÆMsk. An additional seven stanzas from the same poem are included in *F* (sts. 266–67, 269–70, 274, 277–78) and are consequently secured for Msk2. The remaining thirty-six stanzas of "Sigurðarbǫlkr" are transmitted in MskMS only. (Ívarr Ingimundarson's poem is discussed separately below.)

Aside from the stanzas from "Sigurðarbǫlkr," the "Saga of Sigurðr slembidjákn" in MskMS contains eleven stanzas, none of which is recorded in *Fsk*. Snorri, however, gives six of those stanzas (sts. 263–65, 276, 279–80; 55 percent; = ÆMsk). Four of them contain factual information about the battles at Minne and Sörbygden and the skirmish at Portør and are used to corroborate the prose (sts. 253–55, 276). The remaining two stanzas are *lausavísur* (attributed to Sigurðr himself: st. 279; anonymous: st. 280). It could well be that one or both of those stanzas were part of *Hrygg.

MskMS also cites two *dróttkvætt* stanzas (sts. 296–97) to document the Battle of Holmengrå, as well as a sequence of three *dróttkvætt* stanzas to conclude that battle (sts. 303–5). None of those stanzas is included in *Hkr* or in Hr, AM 66, or F, which follow Snorri's narrative verbatim. Because Eiríkr Oddsson's description of Sigurðr's and Magnús's last stand in Hvaler is based on eyewitness accounts, and the prose exemplar of ÆMsk (*Hrygg) clearly contained no stanzas, we may ask at what point in the *Msk* transmission sts. 296–97 and 303–5 were incorporated.

There is an extremely awkward fit between the prose narrative and the content of the first two stanzas. They are incorporated into a section that describes the fall of Magnús blindi and the heroic stance of his followers. The stanzas that belong to Kolli's praise poem to King Ingi admittedly do mention that Magnús fell ("The red snowflakes of the roar of steel [battle, blood] drifted before war-eager Magnús fell," st. 296). In addition, however, they prematurely announce the death of Sigurðr (st. 296) and praise Ingi and his legitimate claim to the Norwegian throne (sts. 296–97). Those statements accord badly with the preceding prose from *Hrygg (p. 384): "Hreiðarr fell backward onto the deck with Magnús on top of him. Everyone agreed that he had followed his lord well and valiantly, and any man who earns such a reputation should be praised. Loðinn of Línustaðir fell there, along with Sigurðr's front-rank warrior Brúsi Þormóðsson, as well as Ívarr Kolbeinsson and Hávarðr fægir. This is told in King Ingi's praise poem." As the content of sts. 296–97 shows, these events are *not* told in Ingi's praise poem, and the stanzas must have been added by someone who felt that a battle ought to be documented by skaldic evidence, but was unable to come up with stanzas that would fit Eiríkr's prose. It is not strange, then, that the stanzas, if they were part of ÆMsk, would have been omitted by Snorri (he did include sts. 263–65 from the same poem), but the stanzas could also have been incorporated into *Msk* at a later point in the transmission.

Sts. 303–5, from Bǫðvarr balti's "Sigurðardrápa," form the conclusion of the Battle of Holmengrå in MskMS and the end of the "Saga of Sigurðr slembidjákn." Again, there is an awkward fit between the content of the stanzas and the narrative they supposedly illustrate. Bǫðvarr's poem is a eulogy to Sigurðr munnr; apart from the stanzas mentioning the deaths of Sigurðr and Magnús (which *Hrygg had already discussed in detail in an eyewitness report), they contain no information pertaining to the events that took place during the battle itself or its aftermath. The stanzas fall into the category "stanzas that conclude a battle," but they are hardly a fitting epitaph for the king whose last stand they allegedly commemorate: "you had Sigurðr slain . . . the oppressor of princes died" (st. 303). As was the case with sts. 296–97, these stanzas, too, must have been added to a preexisting written narrative as a literary and structural device by someone who adhered to specific narrative norms, and it is not unlikely that some of the stanzas were remembered and included because of their imagery: "The very corpse heap floated ashore and you, brave king, concluded the fast of Muninn [raven, hunger]. . . . The brood of the wolf thoroughly enjoyed the encounter with the eagles in wide Langeyjarsund [Langösund]" (st. 297); "you have satiated many a horse of the sorceress [wolf]" (st. 304); "the wolf reddened its teeth on the dead troops" (st. 305).

The incorporation of the stanzas from Ívarr Ingimundarson's "Sigurðarbǫlkr" presents a special problem in the *Msk* transmission. If we proceed by the evidence of the MSS alone, it would appear that two stanzas of that poem (sts. 259, 262) were part of ÆMsk; seven (sts. 266–67, 269–70, 274, 277–78) were interpolated in Msk2; and the remaining thirty-six were incorporated at a later stage (MskMS?). However, because both Snorri and the author of *Fsk* avoid citing stanzas in *fornyrðislag* as historical verification, the texts of these works cannot be used as a yardstick to determine the extent of poetic interpolation in ÆMsk (*Hrygg). Furthermore, the stanzas incorporated in F may not reflect the actual number of stanzas in Msk2: not only did the compiler in places follow *Hkr*, but the version of *Msk* represented by the exemplar of F (MskY) appears to have been an abbreviated version of Msk2 (Louis-Jensen 1977:89–93). The problem of determining the corpus of stanzas in ÆMsk is compounded further because, as the texts of *Hkr* and *Fsk* show, Eiríkr Oddsson drew on information from "Sigurðarbǫlkr." Hence, verbal correspondences between the stanzas and the prose in *Hkr* and *Fsk* may go back to *Hrygg and not to an interpolated ÆMsk.

The first stanza from "Sigurðarbǫlkr" in MskMS (st. 250) confirms the prose statement that Sigurðr was raised by a priest called Aðalbrikt (the form "Albrict" in the prose appears to be a later scribal corruption), but the stanza does not corroborate what it is supposed to, namely that "[i]t appeared to some people that he was the priest's son, as Ívarr Ingimundarson said in the poem that he composed about Sigurðr." The same prose is found in *Hkr* but not in *Fsk*, and Snorri could have taken his information from the stanza. However, because of the lack of correspondence between prose and poetry, it appears that the stanza was interpolated into the *Hrygg prose, but it is impossible to determine at what stage in the transmission that interpolation occurred.

Sts. 251–56 document Sigurðr's participation in the slaying of Þorkell fóstri in Orkney; his banishment to Scotland and his stay with King David (sts. 252–53); and his participation in four battles (sts. 254–56). It is strange that the MskMS prose fails to include the following information from the stanzas: the name of the Scottish king ("David," mentioned in st. 252; "Dáfinnr," st. 253); the years of his stay ("five years," st. 252; the prose has "some time"); and the number of battles ("four," st. 256; prose: "several battles"). *Fsk* omits any reference to Sigurðr's early years, but Snorri retains most of the prose while omitting the information about the battles (*ÍF* 28, 298). If the factual information about Sigurðr's adventures in the west had been part of Snorri's exemplar (ÆMsk), there would no reason for him to omit it from his prose. He does, however, include the information about Þorkell fóstri (st. 251 and *Hrygg?) and Sigurðr's reception at the Scottish court ("he was much esteemed"; so also MskMS: "in great honor," and st. 253). He also provides one piece of information that is not contained in the MskMS prose, namely, the name of the Scottish king (sts. 252–53). That name does not appear to have been part of *Hrygg (cf. *ÍF* 34, 117), and it could well be that Snorri got the name from either st. 252 or st. 253. If st. 252 had provided the information, however, we would also have expected him to include the "five years." That he did not, sug-

gests that st. 253 could have been his source. That stanza also documents Sigurðr's high standing at the Scottish court, which, as we have seen, is mentioned
in the prose of *Hkr* as well as in MskMS. It is tempting to suggest, then, that
sts. 251 and 253 were part of ÆMsk, and that sts. 252 and 254–56 were added
by a later interpolator. Such a reconstruction is supported by the fact that
whereas the latter stanzas are introduced by the formula "svá segir Ívarr" (according to Ívarr), st. 251 is prefaced by "þat er sagt" (it is told), and st. 253 is
introduced by the archaic formula "sem skaldit sagði" (as the skald said),
which seems fairly conspicuous squeezed in between two stanzas introduced by
"according to Ívarr." The reason the name of the Scottish king was not included in the prose of ÆMsk (if st. 253 was part of that MS) could be that the
author failed to draw the connection between the "Dáfinnr" of the stanza and
the name "Davíð."

Sts. 257–61 describe Sigurðr's journey to Rome (st. 257) and Jerusalem
(st. 258), the oath concerning his paternity (st. 259), and his return via Greece,
France, and Saxony (st. 260) to Orkney (st. 261). *Hkr* leaves out this detailed
itinerary and only mentions that Sigurðr went to Palestine and to Jordan,
where he "visited the holy shrines, as is customary for pilgrims" (*ÍF* 28, 297).
That particular sentence is common to *Hkr* and MskMS and must have been
part of ÆMsk/*Hrygg. It also echoes the wording of sts. 257–58, but it is unclear whether that wording derives from *Hrygg or from the presence of the
stanzas in ÆMsk. What is clear, however, is that some (if not all) of the stanzas
in this section of MskMS are later interpolations. St. 259 states that five bishops partook in the oath concerning Sigurðr's paternity, and the prose places
that event in Palestine. However, the same stanza is recorded in both *Fsk* and
Hkr at a later point in the narrative to document that five bishops swore to
Sigurðr's paternity in Denmark (= ÆMsk, *Hrygg). MskMS, too, retains that
episode, with the result that the oath is given twice in that MS—once in Palestine (supported by st. 259), and once in Denmark, in accordance with the
other versions (minus the stanza).

Furthermore, there is a discrepancy between the sequence of events presented in MskMS and in *Hkr*. According to the latter, Sigurðr left Norway, went
on his pilgrimage, traveled for a while as a merchant, returned to Orkney
where he participated in the killing of Þorkell, was exiled to Scotland, and
went from Scotland to Denmark (*ÍF* 28, 297–98). Although we cannot exclude
the possibility that ÆMsk and *Hkr* at this point followed divergent versions of
*Hrygg, it is fairly clear that the version in MskMS has been reworked by some-
one who not only interpolated stanzas from "Sigurðarbǫlkr" but also changed
the sequence of the narrative to conform to the sequence of stanzas in that
poem. It is highly unlikely that anyone who quoted stanzas from memory
would impose the sequence of stanzas on a written narrative; rather, we should
expect that the sequence of events in the written narrative would evoke the
content of the individual stanzas. It seems reasonable to assume, therefore,

that the person who interpolated the stanzas into the *Msk* text was working from a written copy of "Sigurðarbǫlkr," and that the sequence of stanzas in that written version caused him to change the order of events in the prose to conform to that of the poetry. That interpolator was certainly not familiar with the content of his exemplar, because he failed to realize that st. 259 actually occurred later in the narrative, and it is difficult to reconcile such blatant incompetence with the skillful narrator who composed ÆMsk.

St. 262 is recorded in both *Fsk* and *Hkr* (ÆMsk) and is used to corroborate Sigurðr's election as king by the people of Sogn and Hordaland (*ÍF* 29, 330; *ÍF* 28, 298). A comparison of the three texts shows that the stanza is slightly misplaced in the MskMS narrative, and that the wording of the first two lines has been changed. Instead of occurring right after the event it is supposed to verify ("He headed north for Hordaland and convened a thingmeeting of the farmers. They submitted to him and gave him the title of king. Then he went inland to Sogn and over the mountains to Fjordane. Most people responded favorably"), the stanza is found after the coronation of Haraldr gilli's sons. To remedy that slip-up, the interpolator was forced to add the following sentence after the stanza (FJ 414; U 207: "Hér víkr hann [Ívarr] svá til at því sem fyrr var sagt, at þeir *tóku við* Sigurð slembi at konungi" (emphasis added) (literally translated as: "Here he [Ívarr] makes reference in such a way to that which was mentioned earlier, that they *accepted* Sigurðr slembir as king"). Not only is the sentence ungrammatical, but it echoes the wording of the first two lines of our st. 262 in *Hkr* and *Fsk* (*ÍF* 29, 330; *ÍF* 28, 302): "*tóku við* mildum ‖ Magnúss syni" (emphasis added) ([they] *accepted* the generous son of Magnús), which in MskMS is rendered as "tóku síðan ‖ Sigurð til landa" ([they] elected Sigurðr to rule the lands). There can be no doubt that ÆMsk must have read as follows: "Tóku við mildum ‖ Magnúss syni . . . . Hér víkr hann til, at þeir tóku við Sigurð slembi" ([they] accepted the generous son of Magnús . . . . Here he makes reference to the fact that they accepted Sigurðr slembir). The change in the wording of the stanza must have been occasioned by the wording of the first two lines in the interpolator's exemplar. That he was unable to recast the statement accompanying the stanza in ÆMsk as a grammatical sentence suggests that we are dealing with a scribe who was used to copying a written text but was unfamiliar with the actual process of written composition.

Sts. 266–69 occur at the beginning of Chapter 89 and describe Sigurðr's return to Norway in the summer of 1138. Sts. 266–67 and 269 are also recorded in *F.* A comparison with *Hkr* and *Fsk* shows that the prose introducing that chapter is derived from *Hrygg* but that the stanzas and their surrounding prose are independent additions. The text of *Hkr*, however, suggests that Snorri must have been familiar with the content of the stanzas, as well as with a prose text similar to that of MskMS. The initial prose of *Fsk* and MskMS (=*Hrygg) states that Sigurðr went from Orkney to Denmark, but st. 266 mentions that the people of Trøndelag and Møre revolted against Sigurðr.

MskMS accordingly incorporates that information into the prose (the MskMS allusion to Sigurðr's stay in "Suðrlondum" [the lands in the south] is obscure and could be a corruption of "Suðrlandi" ["Sutherland"; cf. *ÍF* 34, 115]) and maintains that Sigurðr stayed away "since he knew there was no support in Norway." Sts. 267–68 describe Sigurðr's sailing to Sweden, and they are introduced by the following statement "He [Ívarr] told of the time Sigurðr left Norway and went to Sweden in the following stanzas. . . . Then he came to the realm of the King of the Danes." That information is not incorporated into *Fsk*, which at this point follows a version of *Hrygg, but Snorri takes account of both prose and poetry (*ÍF* 28, 309: "That summer Sigurðr slembidjákn came east across the sea to Norway. But when he heard of the mishaps of his kinsman Magnús, he seemed to know that he would have little support in Norway. He therefore sailed the outer course south along the coast and arrived in Denmark." It would appear, then, that this information was part of Snorri's exemplar (*Fagskinna* indicates that it did not come from *Hrygg), and that st. 266 and at least some of sts. 267–69 must have been part of ÆMsk. Sts. 267–69 are characterized by nautical imagery that recalls the similar sequence of stanzas (sts. 199–201) in the "Saga of Magnús berfœttr."

St. 270 (also in F) mentions Sigurðr's alliance with the Danes. The stanza must have been part of Msk2, but there is no indication in the *Hkr* prose that it was cited in Snorri's exemplar. That is not the case in sts. 271–72 (MskMS only), whose content is paraphrased in the prose of all three versions. The prose must have come from *Hrygg, however, and in MskMS the stanzas are introduced de facto with the following comment "Ívarr makes mention of the battle waged at Ærø, already noted." Thus, the person who incorporated the stanzas into the prose had difficulties placing them in their correct environment, probably because the prose of *Hrygg had Sigurðr proceed directly from Orkney to the Danish campaign, as recorded at the beginning of Chapter 89.

Although it is impossible to ascertain at what point sts. 271–72 were interpolated into *Msk*, there are clear indications that Snorri must have known st. 273. According to that stanza (and the accompanying prose), Sigurðr held a second battle east by "Mœri," against the Wends. Snorri, who must have failed to recognize the obscure place name, replaces it with Mǫn (Møen) and states that "he [Sigurðr] also held a battle by Møen against the Wends and was victorious" (*ÍF* 28, 309). That battle is not mentioned in *Fsk* and would appear not to have been mentioned in *Hrygg. Thus, the prose of *Hkr* betrays knowledge of the content of sts. 266–69 and 273.

Sigurðr's subsequent activities in Halland are documented in sts. 274–75, the first of which is given in F (= Msk2). The prose of *Hkr* and *Fsk* shows that the stanzas must have been paraphrased in the text of *Hrygg as well, and we cannot know whether they were part of ÆMsk. That is also the case with sts. 277–78 (also in F), which describe Sigurðr and Magnús's slaying of Benteinn Kolbeinsson at Lista in Norway.

The remaining stanzas of "Sigurðarbǫlkr" are recorded in MskMS only. They can be divided into the following three groups: (1) stanzas that document the killing spree of Sigurðr and Magnús along the Norwegian coast in the spring of 1139 (sts. 281–88); (2) stanzas that describe the return of Sigurðr and Magnús to Norway in the late autumn of the same year (sts. 289–91); (3) stanzas that pertain directly to the battle by Holmengrå and the deaths of Sigurðr and Magnús (sts. 292–95 and 298–302).

As far as the first group is concerned, *Hkr* and *Fsk* show that these stanzas also served as a source for Eiríkr Oddsson's version of the events. It is difficult to say anything about their possible presence in ÆMsk, or in Msk2, for that matter, but there are clear indications that both prose and poetry were subject to the editorial activities of the interpolator who was at work in Chapter 84.

St. 281b verifies that Sigurðr killed a father and two sons in Vågan. That information is also related in the prose: "He emerged at Vågan, where he seized the priest Sveinn and his two sons and had them all killed. Ívarr recounts this" (p. 379). According to the prose wording, we would have expected the stanza to follow immediately after the reference to Ívarr, but instead we find the following ungrammatical sentence (FJ 425; U 214): "En næsta vetr eptir er Benteinn var drepinn, at Sigurðr var á valdi Háleyja" (*sic*) (literally translated as "The next year after Benteinn was killed, that Sigurðr was at the mercy of the 'Háleyjar'"). That elliptical statement was meant to reflect the information in st. 281a, according to which Sigurðr stayed among the "Háleyjar" (miscopied in the stanza) "the next winter." Furthermore, the first line in that stanza has been changed, obviously by someone who failed to understand the *kenning* for "winter" (see the note on st. 281). It would appear, then, that we are dealing with a two-layered interpolation into the *Hrygg text: first st. 281b was added to document the slaying of the priest and his two sons "as Ívarr recounts," then the second interpolator, who had access to the whole stanza, added the (ungrammatical) information about Sigurðr's stay in Hålogaland and diligently copied the wrong form of the ethnic name ("Háleyja" for "Háleygja") into the prose text.

Sigurðr's next attack took place in Vik on the northwestern coast of Norway (according to all versions), but the scribe who added the stanza in support of the prose failed to notice that the stanza (st. 282) contained the wrong place name ("Vågan"). A similar discrepancy can be detected in the next stanza, where the prose reads "Hvalsnes" (so also *F* 331, but corrected in the MS), while the stanza correctly has "Valsnes." The prose introducing the next two stanzas (sts. 285–86) reads as follows (FJ 427; U 215): "Þá fór hann suðr á Mœri fyr útan Þrándheimsmynni, ok tók þar Heðin harðmaga ok Kálf klingruauga ok lét Heðin undan ganga, en drap Kálf. Þat segir Ívarr, at hann tœki Finn hǫndum" (Then he went south to Møre past the mouth of Trondheimsfjorden and seized Heðinn harðmagi and Kálfr klingruauga. He let Heðinn off but killed Kálfr. Ívarr recounts that he captured Finnr). St. 285 indeed recounts that Sigurðr captured Finnr, but it also states in no uncertain terms that he killed him, and that his death took place east at Kville by Oslofjorden: "The valiant war leader met ambitious Finnr east at Kvildir [Kville]; they caused the crafty offerer of the spear storm [battle, warrior], Ulfr's heir, to lose his life." The slaying is related later in all three versions, and the wording makes it clear that the information in the prose was derived from st. 285 (*ÍF* 29, 333; *ÍF* 28, 313): "Sigurðr and his men went east to Viken and captured Finnr [*Fsk, Hkr:* "east at Kville"], the son of Sauða-Úlfr, as he was collecting land dues. They hanged him, then sailed south to Denmark."

There can be no doubt that just as st. 259 was misplaced in the text (resulting in a repetition of the oath vouching for Sigurðr's paternity), st. 285 was inserted into the prose as part of the sequence of stanzas available to an interpolator who was unaware that his prose exemplar recorded Finnr's death at a later point in the narrative. Furthermore, the new prose environment created by him shows that he was unable to incorporate the information from the poetry into the prose: the sentence "[þ]at segir Ívarr, at hann *tœki* Finn *hǫndum*" (emphasis added) (Ívarr recounts that he captured Finnr) is clearly taken from st. 286 ("Vann fyr Mœri ‖ mildingr *tekinn* ‖ Heðin með *hǫndum*" (emphasis added); "The king captured Heðinn by Møre") and pertains to Heðinn, not to Finnr. Hence, the stanza about Heðinn, as well as the corresponding prose, must have been part of his exemplar, and he retained that prose, replacing the name Heðinn with Finnr, and inserted st. 285 before st. 286. Whether st. 285 occurred later in the text in conjunction with the hanging of Finnr is impossible to say, but the fact that the prose of both *Fsk* and *Hkr* retains the wording of the stanza, and that the phrase "east at Kville" occurs later in the text of MskMS ("You taught me that when you killed my brother Finnr east at Kville"), suggests that the place name could have been willfully deleted by the reviser, who wished to cover up his mistake and make it appear as if the text were dealing with a different Finnr. Thus, it seems that some of the stanzas detailing Sigurðr's rampage along the coast of Norway were part of an earlier version of *Msk* (ÆMsk? Msk2?), and that they were reworked by a later scribe who had access to a written version of "Sigurðarbǫlkr." As to sts. 287–88, which conclude Sigurðr's expedition and describe the battle at sea, it is impossible to say when they were inserted into *Msk*.

The stanzas in the second group (sts. 289–91) describe the return of Sigurðr and Magnús from Denmark to Norway in the autumn of 1139, and they contain factual information incorporated into the prose: Sigurðr and Magnús return from the south (st. 289); they have thirty ships (st. 290); Sigurðr munnr and Ingi set out to meet them (st. 291). The prose in *Hrygg must have been derived from the poetry, but it contains additional information not recorded in the stanzas (e.g., Ingi had twenty large ships). Otherwise, there is no awkward fit between prose and poetry, and we cannot exclude the possibility that these stanzas were part of ÆMsk. The only trace of the later reviser is found in the prose text, where the phrase "en hon var laugardaginn áðr" ("and it [Saint Martin's Day] fell on the Saturday before") clearly represents an attempt to rationalize "í Hvǫlum við Hólm inn grá" ("in Hvaler by Holmengrå"; thus *ÍF* 29, 334; *ÍF* 28, 316) in the other versions.

St. 292 introduces a sequence of battle stanzas (sts. 292–94) describing the onset of the battle by Holmengrå and containing vivid imagery with little factual information. As such, the stanzas constitute a separate poetic narrative, adding color to the matter-of-fact prose statement to the effect that "they fought a battle, as is told here." St. 295 provides the additional information that the people of Jutland, who had accompanied Sigurðr and Magnús to Norway, fled the scene of battle with eighteen ships. That information is also given in the prose of all three versions (*ÍF* 29, 334; *ÍF* 28, 316) and was apparently part of *Hrygg.

Sts. 298–302 address the conclusion of the battle and the subsequent capture, torture, and execution of Sigurðr slembir: after Sigurðr's ship was cleared, he jumped overboard (st. 298); he was captured in the water (st. 299); he sang the psalter and prayed for his enemies while being tortured (st. 301); he died without having been shriven after he finished singing the psalter (st. 302). Most of this information must have been part of the eyewitness reports available to Eiríkr Oddsson, and both Snorri and MskMS follow *Hrygg at this point. (*Fsk*, for some reason, omits this part of the narrative.)

Whoever incorporated these stanzas into the *Msk* narrative was at great pains to achieve a correspondence between prose and poetry, but he was not always successful in that respect. St. 298, for example, states that Sigurðr jumped overboard after his ship had been cleared, but that information is given in the next section of the prose, which seems to follow that of *Hrygg fairly closely. It is evident, however, that Snorri must have had a text similiar to that of MskMS before him, because he rearranges the prose, adding the information from st. 298 where that stanza occurs in MskMS, and omitting it from the subsequent narrative. A look at the text of *Hkr* also shows that Snorri incorporated the wording of st. 298 into his prose and changed that of *Hrygg (*ÍF* 28, 317): "Sigurðr slembidjákn hljóp *á kaf af skipi sínu*, þá er hroðit var" (emphasis added) (Sigurðr slembidjákn jumped into the sea from his ship when it had been cleared); cf. "Hrauzk und jǫfri . . . snekkja með stǫfnum || þás skjǫldungs sonr || *af skipi sínu* || sóknfœrr *á sjá* || sunds kostaði" (emphasis added) (The warship was cleared from stem to stern beneath the king . . . when the battle-crafty king's son, leaping from his ship, tried swimming in the sea). It also seems that the wording of st. 299 could have influenced that of *Hkr*: (cf. "varð tekinn," "was captured," st. 299; "var tekinn," *ÍF* 28, 318; "var handtekinn"; FJ 436; U 220). It is very likely, then, that these stanzas indeed were part of one of Snorri's exemplars (ÆMsk).

As the discussion above has shown, it is almost impossible to ascertain which stanzas of "Sigurðarbǫlkr" were part of ÆMsk and which were later interpolations. Both Snorri and the author of *Fsk* chose to include sts. 259 and 262, and their reasons for doing so are clear: st. 259 verifies that Sigurðr believed he had a legitimate claim to the Norwegian crown, and st. 262 documents that the people of Sogn and Hordaland acknowledged that claim by electing him king. Because the prose of *Hkr* occasionally betrays that Snorri must have had access to a version of the "Saga of Sigurðr slembidjákn" that contained at least some of the stanzas included in MskMS, it seems safe to assume that Æsk must have included more stanzas of "Sigurðarbǫlkr" than are accounted for in *Fsk* and *Hkr*. The stanzas in question documented Sigurðr's stay with the Scottish king, his return to Scandinavia and subsequent campaigns in Denmark in the summer of 1138, and the Battle of Holmengrå in December of 1139.

Our investigation also shows that stanzas from "Sigurðarbǫlkr" must have been incorporated into the *Msk* text at various stages of the transmission. Whether we are dealing with a three-tiered (Æsk, Msk2, MskMS) or a two-tiered interpolation (Æsk, MskX, MskMS) is impossible to say. It is clear, however, that the first interpolator (or first two interpolators) was well versed in skaldic art and tried to harmonize the incorporation of the stanzas with the information provided by the written text (*Hrygg). Because he obviously was unwilling to change that narrative, inclusion of the poetic text in places proved problematic. Sometimes the prose contained more information than the stanzas, and the stanzas, although they certainly were pertinent to the situation described in the prose, failed to document what they were supposed to verify. At other times, the prose of *Hrygg condensed the content of several stanzas into one brief statement, and it was difficult to position the stanzas in the narrative without having to resort to recapitulation ("as was noted earlier"). Because Eiríkr Oddsson's narrative also drew on information from "Sigurðarbǫlkr," there is less tension between the prose of *Hrygg and the stanzas from "Sigurðarbǫlkr" than between *Hrygg and the unrelated stanzas from Kolli's and Bǫðvarr's poems. In the latter case, the stanzas were unsuitable as historical verification simply because they had not been the source of the prose text (*Hrygg) in the first place. The tension between prose and poetry in this part of MskMS clearly demonstrates the difficulties facing an interpolator who attempted to augment a written narrative with skaldic stanzas.

The *Msk* version of the "Saga of Sigurðr slembidjákn" was last reworked by a scribe who seems to have had access to a written copy of "Sigurðarbǫlkr." During that revision, the written (?) copy of the poetry took precedence over the prose and poetry of the exemplar. Not only was the sequence of events changed in accordance with the sequence of stanzas in the poem, resulting in a doubling of episodes (the oath, the slaying of Finnr Sauða-Úlfsson), but the text of the stanzas was tampered with; the scribe's attempt to accommodate new poetic insertions with accompanying prose resulted in awkward and sometimes downright ungrammatical sentences. We cannot determine at what exact point in the *Msk* transmission this last revision took place, but the changes are so incompetent that it is unlikely that they were made by the interpolator of Msk2. Rather, it would appear that they occurred in MskMS itself.

The Saga of Ingi and His Brothers (Chs. 94–100)

This last (and incomplete) saga in MskMS contains fifteen stanzas, three of which are found in smaller anecdotes involving the skald Einarr Skúlason (sts. 315–17; Ch. 97). *Hkr* incorporates eight of the remaining twelve stanzas (sts. 307–14; 67 percent), all of which provide concrete information about Eysteinn Haraldsson's dealings with the Norwegian farmers (sts. 307–8) and his subsequent raids in Orkney and England (sts. 309–14). *Fsk* omits the sections on Eysteinn but records the last three stanzas (sts. 318–20; 25 percent), showing that 92 percent of the stanzas in MskMS must have been part of ÆMsk.

The only stanza in this portion of MskMS that is not recorded in *Hkr* and *Fsk* is st. 306, which consists of two lines documenting Eysteinn's return to Norway: "The lord, liberal and bold, was eager to journey east." Those lines come from Einarr Skúlason's "Runhenda," a poem composed in honor of Eysteinn. The author of ÆMsk was certainly familiar with that poem (sts. 307–8, 310–14 also belong to "Runhenda"), and there is no reason to believe that the couplet was a later interpolation. Thus, it would appear that all the stanzas in this part of MskMS must come from the earliest version.

Concluding Remarks

The main results of our investigations of the textual transmission of *Morkinskinna* and the question of interpolation of stanzas can be summarized as follows:

1. *Hkr* and *Fsk* on the average incorporate between 51 percent (excluding stanzas in *fornyrðislag*) and 61 percent (including stanzas in *fornyrðislag*) of the stanzas in the extant version of *Msk* (MskMS), but ÆMsk must have contained an even higher percentage of stanzas than this comparison allows for.

2. Although it is clear that some stanzas must have been added in Msk2, there is no evidence that *Msk* at any point in its transmission was subject to a large-scale interpolation of skaldic stanzas.

3. *Msk* must have been interpolated twice: once in Msk2, as evidenced by stanzas common to MskY (F) and MskX (MskMS, *H, Flat), and once at a later stage. It is possible that the latest interpolation, which mainly entailed the addition of stanzas from Ívarr Ingimundarson's "Sigurðarbǫlkr" and corresponding "adjustments" of the prose narrative, took place in MskMS itself (scribe 1?).

The comparison of the use of poetry in MskMs, *Heimskringla,* and *Fagrskinna* has revealed that the compilers of the latter two compendia were consciously selective in their use of the poetic corpus of ÆMsk, and that they included only stanzas that provided concrete information with a direct bearing on the events narrated in the prose. In both compilations, then, skaldic stanzas were used as historical verification. ÆMsk, however, is a completely different matter. The author certainly drew on skaldic stanzas for historical information, especially in the "Saga of Haraldr and Magnús," and it is obvious that skaldic poetry was an art with which he was thoroughly familiar. Not only was he able to cite a great number of stanzas from memory, but he understood the stanzas and their complex diction (a rare accomplishment in the thirteenth century) and took great pleasure in their imagery and in the stories they told. That circumstance serves to explain the seemingly superfluous stanzas describing ferocious beasts of battle and ships struggling on the wind-swept sea, and also the fact that he went to great pains to incorporate new stanzas into a codified written narrative (*Hrygg). It is more than likely that the many þættir and smaller anecdotes about skalds and the composition of skaldic poetry in Morkinskinna reflect the interests and knowledge of the same author, namely, the author of ÆMsk.

This person, then, was more of a storyteller than a critical historian like Snorri and the author of Fagrskinna. He was at home in the traditions of prose and of poetry, but his interest seems to lie in the stories and the stanzas themselves rather than in their historical value. That circumstance could account for the relatively low esteem in which the Morkinskinna compilation appears to have been held by later historians. The skaldic stanzas in some cases allowed the author to construct a narrative; in other cases, they stood alone and constituted an independent poetic narrative or provided a personal aside. At the same time, it is clear that he used the stanzas for specific structural purposes: narrative high points were prefaced by skaldic stanzas; the sequence of events in those episodes was documented by skaldic stanzas; and sequences of stanzas were used as conclusion and recapitulation. When faced with a written account such as *Hryggjarstykki, he continued to adhere to his principles of composition. He was not recording history but telling a story in which skaldic stanzas were supposed to be an integral part.

The Oral Sources

Finnur Jónsson (1928:esp. xxxviii) took the view that most of Morkinskinna is based on a series of lost royal biographies. We have also seen that the þættir, to a greater or lesser extent, are commonly believed to be taken over from prior written versions. In this way it is possible to defer the question of oral sources and roll them back to a stage sufficiently anterior to Morkinskinna that they appear to become marginally relevant. Bjarni Aðalbjarnarson (1937:169–73), however, while not rejecting the possibility of lost kings' biographies, did not find much evidence to support the hypothesis. Gustav Indrebø (1939:72–76) was even more doubtful and was inclined to use the working hypothesis that *Morkinskinna* is the original work of a single author. It may well be that *Morkinskinna* rests chiefly on oral sources, and yet that alternative has not been explored, partly because the references to such traditions are so sparse. A number of them cluster about the story of Sigurðr slembir toward the end of *Morkinskinna*. They are presumably taken over from references in *Hryggjarstykki and do not shed direct light on the method of composition in *Morkinskinna* proper. They will therefore be discussed separately.

We may begin with the references to six identified source men. The earliest is a certain Oddr Gellisson (Ch. 5 at note 8), who is credited as a source of information on the Battle of Hlýrskógsheiðr (1043): "There was a man named Oddr Gellisson with the king. He told some parts of these events." This attribution is inserted just after the preparations for the battle and the battle itself. The whole narrative is somewhat extravagant, involving, as it does, the miraculous intervention of St. Óláfr, improbable odds, and superhuman feats on Magnús's part. And yet the mention of Oddr Gellisson is dropped in such a casual and uncalculated way that it does not have the look of a protestation. The reference to Oddr does not survive in either *Fagrskinna* or *Heimskringla*, but there seems to be no reason to doubt that such a man existed, was present at the battle, and mediated information about it. Since most of the source men mentioned in *Morkinskinna* are Icelanders, it seems likely that Oddr was also an Icelander, but he cannot be traced. Since 175 years elapsed between the battle and the composition of *Morkinskinna*, it is perhaps not surprising that Oddr's account eventually took on such legendary overtones.

The next reference to oral sources features no less an authority than Haraldr Sigurðarson. The author tells of Haraldr's escape after the Battle of Stiklastaðir (1030) and adds (Ch. 9 at note 4): "King Magnús and others in Norway knew of this story. But from now on the story of Haraldr's travels is what Haraldr himself, and the men who accompanied him, told." That Haraldr was a deeply interested custodian of his own tale is illustrated by "Íslendings þáttr sǫgufróða," in which Haraldr monitors the accuracy of an Icelander's retelling. This retelling has been exploited by scholars (Ch. 40, note 1) to argue that such tales could take on the dimensions of extensive and integrated sagas. The Icelander concludes by explaining that he learned the story from Halldórr Snorrason, piece by piece, at a series of assembly meetings. When the reference at hand tells us that the story of Haraldr's travels was transmitted by Haraldr himself "and the men who accompanied him," those men would have included Halldórr Snorrason most prominently of all.

The story of Haraldr's adventures is certainly no less fanciful than the story of Magnús's victory at Hlýrskógsheiðr, despite Haraldr's critical vetting of the Icelander's version. But again, the legendary dimensions may be explained by the lapse of 140 years between the onset of Haraldr's tale and the writing of *Morkinskinna*. What is most noteworthy about the reference, taken in conjunction with

"Íslendings þáttr sǫgufróða," is the documenting of something approaching a total biography. The traditions about Haraldr seem to have flowed more abundantly than other royal traditions, and we may suspect that Haraldr had a hand in this. He may have been the chief patron of his own legend and have nurtured a total narrative. It seems clear that he also had special relations with Icelanders, who were in a position to maintain the narrative. Exactly how Haraldr's literary project originated is hard to know, but he evidently equated fame with story and probably determined the nature of royal narrative for succeeding generations. His questing in foreign lands, for example, seems to have become both a royal imperative for Sigurðr jórsalafari and Magnús berfœttr and a negative model for Óláfr kyrri and Eysteinn Magnússon. Similarly, Haraldr's sense of literature may have had a formative influence on how the kings' saga as a genre ultimately evolved. It is interesting to note that much as Haraldr owed his literary life to Icelanders, the sort of adventure tale formed in his image had very little influence on the sober native traditions that must have been evolving simultaneously in Iceland and eventually produced the very different family sagas.

That the traditions about Haraldr Sigurðarson were not entirely centralized is illustrated by a reference further along (Ch. 9 at note 11): "A great multitude of Norsemen were already there [scil. in Constantinople] and were called Væringjar. There was an Icelander named Már, who was the son of Húnrøðr and the father of Hafliði Másson. He was a distinguished chieftain. He was very suspicious about whether everything these foreigners [scil. the Væringjar] said was true. He made it a point to speak with Halldórr Snorrason, who was in the company of the Haraldr who called himself Norðbrikt. Már wanted to speak with Haraldr, but Haraldr wanted nothing to do with him. Már got nowhere with him. Then he left Constantinople, thinking it was not unlikely that major events were in the offing."

This passage is interesting because it is so trivial in comparison to the panoramic view of Haraldr's adventures implied in the previous reference. We are told, in effect, that Már wanted to participate in the action in which Halldórr Snorrason was involved, but was excluded. It is understandable that word might be passed down the generations about how some particular information was acquired but odd that we should be told how information was withheld. Már Húnrøðarson and Halldórr Snorrason were from great families in neighboring districts. One senses some literary jealousy. The gist of the incident is that one family was privy to the great story of Haraldr Sigurðarson, while a neighboring family had lost an opportunity to participate in these great events. Then as now, literature was a proprietary matter, and Már's family would not forget that it had come within an eyelash of sharing a great literary moment.

The next reference pertains to events of 1046, when King Magnús bestowed half his realm on his uncle Haraldr Sigurðarson. The passage is as follows (Ch. 14 at note 11): "They both stayed in Norway, each with his own retinue. This is the way it was told by Þorgils, a prudent man, and he said that he had

been told the story by Guðríðr, the daughter of Guthormr, the son of Steigar-
Þórir. He said that he had seen the maple bowl and the cloak that King Haraldr had given Þórir. The latter had by then been cut into an altar cloth. The
skald Bǫlverkr confirms this matter." (Bǫlverkr's relevant stanza is cited here.)

Þorgils is not as mysterious as he appears. In both *Fagrskinna* (*ÍF* 29, 245) and
Heimskringla (*ÍF* 28, 101), he is identified as Þorgils Snorrason, who died in
1201. The passage accounts for an important historical event and how it was
transmitted from 1046 down to the time of *Morkinskinna*. Steigar-Þórir became
an old man and ended on Magnús berfœttr's gallows in 1094. He was the first
to accept Haraldr's claim to the Norwegian throne and would have been an
eyewitness to the division of the realm. His son Guthormr was King Eysteinn
Magnússon's father-in-law (*ÍF* 28, 256) and could have outlived Eysteinn, who
died in 1122. His daughter Guðríðr could have lived into the second half of
the twelfth century and could have told Þorgils Snorrason (and many others)
of events going back to the reign of Haraldr Sigurðarson.

We know nothing further of Þorgils Snorrason and Guðríðr Guthormsdóttir, how they knew each other, or why they dealt in old traditions, but they
may exemplify for us how Norwegian royal traditions crossed to Iceland and
how historically minded people could have maintained a narrative continuity.
Steigar-Þórir was at the center of the political stage for fifty years, and his family could have known the events of these years in great detail. There are no references in *Morkinskinna* to sources about Magnús berfœttr, but the enmity
between Magnús and Steigar-Þórir would surely have kept traditions about
Magnús alive among Steigar-Þórir's descendants.

Although there are no references to traditions about Magnús berfœttr, his
saga does include reference to an incident involving Magnús's follower Giffarðr and an Icelander named Eldjárn (Ch. 58 at note 6): "There is a little tale
to tell of him [*scil.* Giffarðr]. They had stormy weather in the North Sea, and
Giffarðr was little help. He was always leaning over the gunwale while the
others bailed. There was an Icelander on board from Húsavík. His name was
Eldjárn, and he had come back from Constantinople. Once as Eldjárn went to
bail and saw Giffarðr sprawled there, he recited a stanza." (The stanza follows.)
Giffarðr takes offense at this stanza and summons Eldjárn before an English
borough-reeve when they reach shore. At the hearing, Eldjárn recasts the
stanza and thwarts the charge against him. This incident would have taken
place around the year 1100.

As has already been indicated, Bjarni Aðalbjarnarson (1937:158) suggested
that the story of Giffarðr was intertwined with the account of Magnús's campaign in Gautland, which is interpolated from *Ágrip*. The Giffarðr incidents
are therefore unlikely to have been incorporated prior to the interpolation
from *Ágrip*. There is no space to probe this proposal in detail, but it does not
seem altogether compelling. It seems perfectly possible that the account of the
Gautland campaign and the story of Giffarðr were present in the original
Morkinskinna and were merely rephrased according to *Ágrip* (see "The Native

Sources," above). If so, Eldjárn, like Már, was part of the tangle of tradition-bearers ultimately available to the author of *Morkinskinna*. Though invoked only in connection with Giffarðr's seasickness, Eldjárn may have been well informed about other events around 1100 and may have disseminated other historical lore when he returned to Iceland.

The last named informant peculiar to *Morkinskinna* is a certain priest named Sigurðr, who, we are told, later became a bishop in Bergen (Ch. 80 at note 1). Sigurðr was a witness to the reprimand lodged by Bishop Magni against King Sigurðr jórsalafari when he divorced his queen late in life, about 1130. Bishop Magni addresses the king as follows (ibid.): "'Why have you decided to do this in our bishopric, sire, and thus disgrace God's law and Holy Church and our bishopric? Now I shall do what I am obligated to do and forbid you to commit this sin, in the name of God, St. Peter the Apostle, and all the saints.' While he said these words he stood straight with his neck extended as if he were prepared for the king to strike him with his sword. Sigurðr, who later became bishop, related that he seemed to see no more of the heavens than a piece of parchment because the king was so monstrous in his rage."

Unlike Már and Eldjárn, Sigurðr was a Norwegian informant. Again, we do not know how his observation of King Sigurðr's wrath survived the decades down to 1220 before appearing in *Morkinskinna*, but it is not impossible that he related his experience to Guthormr Þórisson or Guðríðr Guthormsdóttir, who could then have relayed it to Þorgils Snorrason or any one of a number of Icelandic informants.

These source references span the century from Haraldr harðráði himself after 1030 and Oddr Gellisson in 1046 to Sigurðr in 1130, but the reports of informants seem to cluster particularly around Sigurðr slembir († 1139). In the short space from Chapter 88 to Chapter 93, *Morkinskinna* reports no fewer than four individuals who were presumably named as sources in Eiríkr Oddsson's *Hryggjarstykki: a certain Hákon magi, who is registered as the chief source (Ch. 88); Guðrún, the granddaughter of Ari at Reykjanes, who helped Sigurðr through a winter in northern Norway (Ch. 90 at note 4); Gyríðr Birgisdóttir, sister to Archbishop Jón Birgisson, who had information on Sigurðr's final battle from Bishop Ívarr Kálfsson (Ch. 92 at note 5); and a certain Hallr Þorgeirsson, who witnessed Sigurðr's martyrdom (Ch. 93 at note 2). The density of references in this late part of the text might seem to suggest that sources were more abundant for more recent periods of history, but it may only mean that Eiríkr Oddsson was assiduous in registering his informants, perhaps on the model of Ari Þorgilsson. In *Morkinskinna* proper, the source references are evenly distributed throughout the text and do not suggest an increase or decrease in the availability of source material.

So far, we have noted only the named sources, but there are other, more general references that illuminate the nature of the oral transmissions. Haraldr Sigurðarson may in some sense be the author of his own saga in prose, but he was also the focus of a rich poetic tradition, and we are told (Ch. 13 at note 9) that there were "many" *drápur* about him. That may be something of an exaggeration, but there is no doubt that Haraldr was much celebrated in verse. The extent to which this verse had a separate and self-contained existence apart from prose traditions and to what extent the verse interlocked with prose (*Begleitprosa*) has been the subject of scholarly debate. That they may well have interlocked is suggested by the use of Þorgils Snorrason's prose testimony alongside Bǫlverkr's verse testimony on the matter of how Magnús and Haraldr divided the realm (Ch. 14 at note 12). Such a specific tradition on this matter tends to make references to more general traditions plausible. Thus, there is little reason to doubt the reference to stories about Haraldr and Magnús a few pages later (Ch. 18 at note 6): "Both kings remained in Norway and had not a few differences, as is often heard when stories are told about them."

In a few instances, traditions seem to adhere to particular objects, as in the report that Þorgils Snorrason (Ch. 14 at note 12) "had seen the maple bowl and the cloak that King Haraldr had given Þórir." *Morkinskinna* later reports (Ch. 26 at note 10): "We are told that she [King Magnús's mother] gave King Sveinn a precious plate worked in gold." By analogy, we may suppose that "we are told" is no empty phrase and implies that the ultimate source of the information is someone who actually saw the precious plate. Such objects could even end up in Iceland. When Bishop Magnús Einarsson visits King Haraldr gilli (Ch. 83), he is presented with a drinking horn and two royal cushions. On his return to Iceland, Bishop Magnús houses these valuables in the church at Skálaholt, where presumably they are viewed by a great number of Icelanders, who are also told the story of how they got there.

In some episodes, no source is identified but is nonetheless implied. When, for example, we are told that Sigurðr slembir spent a winter at Saurbœr (Ch. 85 at note 1), there is no reference to the individual who reported on that winter, but we can be quite certain that the tradition was handed down in the household of Sigurðr's host Þorgils Oddason. Or when Þorsteinn Hallsson requests permission of King Magnús to name a son after him (Ch. 26 at note 3), we can be certain that both the name and the story were handed down in Þorsteinn's family. Þorsteinn was, in fact, the great-grandfather of the Bishop Magnús Einarsson, who was so richly honored by Haraldr gilli. The tale of Hákon Ívarsson (Ch. 42) concludes with another Icelandic episode: the killing of Hallr Ótryggsson by Þormóðr Eindriðason in revenge for the killing of Koðrán Guðmundarson. Just how well this tradition was maintained in Iceland is documented by *Ljósvetninga saga*, which tells the whole feud leading up to the killings of Koðrán and Ótryggr.

Although such traditions were abundant and presumably commanded great interest, we know disappointingly little about how they were told and how they were received. Tales and anecdotes must have been in constant circulation and under constant discussion, and we would happily give several middling sagas in exchange for the minutes of such a discussion. But even in this dark area,

Morkinskinna sheds a few thin shafts of light. After the story of how King Haraldr discovers water for his troops while trapped in Lófufjǫrðr, the author comments (Ch. 42 at note 3): "The device was preserved in memory because it seemed wise and ingenious." That comment begins to address the question of why some traditions were preserved while others were not. They had a better chance of surviving if they could engage the listener's sense of "wisdom and ingenuity." There was something like an intellectual test, and one question put to a tradition was whether it said something interesting about human intelligence. That is perhaps the central interest in the traditions handed down about Haraldr Sigurðarson.

But there could presumably be a moral as well as an intellectual weighing of traditions. After the author has told of King Haraldr's capture of Finnr Árnason and King Sveinn's escape from the Battle of Niz and recounted the hospitality (as well as the scorn) accorded him by a poor couple, he concludes by assessing the "meaning" of these stories in surprising detail (Ch. 42 at note 14):

> This tale [King Sveinn's escape] is only for the fun of it and worth telling only because it illustrates wisdom and witlessness. On the other hand, when the exchange of words between King Haraldr and Finnr jarl was told, the man who had the power showed mercy, and there was honor in that action and no lack of authority. But the jarl showed how fearless he was. He was unable to do otherwise than to speak what was on his mind, and in that he demonstrated loyalty. He spoke only well of King Sveinn since he had been in his service, but he spoke angrily to King Haraldr, whom he had opposed. But King Haraldr treated what he had to say like so many childish words, and that has been the view of everyone ever after.

This may be as close to literary criticism as Norse saga literature gets. It provides the foundation for a discussion of values—mercy, honor, authority, fearlessness, candor, loyalty, and moderation. Here we are concerned not only with the evidence that traditions were told and transmitted but that they also became the subject for reflection.

What, then, was the oral basis for *Morkinskinna?* Although the references are very limited in number, they suggest several conclusions. There were, apparently, oral sources for the whole extent of *Morkinskinna,* from the early adventures of Haraldr Sigurðarson after 1030 down to the events of the mid-twelfth century (and presumably beyond). These sources could range from snapshots of random moments, such as Már's attempt to penetrate Haraldr's mystification in Constantinople or Sigurðr's observation of King Sigurðr jórsalafari's wrath when confronted by the demands of the Church, to full-scale narratives, such as the Icelander's account of King Haraldr's adventures over a series of evenings. Neither pattern seems to exclude the other. Although the saga of Haraldr Sigurðarson seems both full and well articulated in its various biographical phases, very little was transmitted from the rather longer reign of Óláfr kyrri, aside from some character traits. And yet even from Óláfr's time, there is a curiously out-of-the-way *þáttr* about the king and the crow fellow (if this is correctly associated with Óláfr). Why some kings received so much fuller attention than others is unclear. We have suggested that Haraldr may have had a special interest in fostering his own legend. Perhaps Óláfr had no such interest. Or perhaps a king's literary fate depended on the chance presence of literarily or historically interested persons in his own circle.

In the study of the family sagas, which provide a more abundant narrative material, there has been some discussion of whether the oral prototypes were fully articulated stories or loose anecdotes that could be understood to belong to an "immanent whole" (Clover 1986) but were never presented as a whole until they reached the written stage. The composition of *Morkinskinna* seems to lend support to the notion of an oral tradition comprising disconnected episodes, which were not necessarily joined in a prior tradition. The author seems to have "collected" oral materials from a variety of sources and set them down in a somewhat arbitrary way not dictated by a preexisting biographical structure but guided only by a rough chronology. The biographical structure that eventually emerged was more the work of *Fagrskinna*'s author and of Snorri, who tried to simplify the episodic disorganization of *Morkinskinna* by stripping the *þættir* away, clarifying the political issues, and emphasizing the underlying biographical features.

By contrast *Morkinskinna* seems unstructured, and we may ask whether, in fact, the composition is unified from beginning to end by any particular concept. Yet the little passage of "literary criticism" cited above suggests strongly not only that the transmitters of oral lore applied critical concepts but that the saga writer was given to such assessments. Since we do not have full sources against which to measure the author's concerns, we must in some sense work backward and judge the author's stance by comparing it to the political-biographical outlook in *Fagrskinna* and *Heimskringla*.

In the first place, the term "kings' saga" seems less appropriate to *Morkinskinna* than to any other example of that genre that went before or after. There is some reason to believe that the author knew some version of *Óláfs saga helga* and *Sverris saga*, because he seems to have designed his work to bridge the chronological gap between them. He may also have known the versions of *Óláfs saga Tryggvasonar* by Oddr Snorrason and Gunnlaugr Leifsson (see notes 1.7 and 9.5). All of these kings' sagas were constructed biographically, and three of them were at least mildly hagiographical. That was also the model afforded by *Hryggjarstykki. And yet the author of *Morkinskinna* departed radically from the available model. He tends to jumble the portraits so that they do not emerge as sharply defined biographical sketches. The lines are blurred most conspicuously by the insertion of forty *þættir* or *þáttr*-like digressions. The best and longest of these are as much about Icelanders as they are about Norwegian kings, so that even the national focus of *Morkinskinna* wavers. Is the book about Norwegian kings, or is it about the Icelandic experience of Norwegian kings?

Morkinskinna is the first Icelandic historical work that resolutely brings the Icelanders into play, both as participants in the larger events of European history and as the poets who recorded significant moments in that history and thus facilitated the work of later historians. There is an Icelandic assertiveness about *Morkinskinna* that sets it apart from all other kings' sagas.

We may therefore ask whether the events described are seen through an Icelandic interpretive lens or even whether *Morkinskinna* betrays a general interpretive posture. Down to the year 1130, there seems to be an overall organizational principle. The six kings in this period (Haraldr Sigurðarson harðráði, Magnús Óláfsson góði, Óláfr Haraldsson kyrri, Magnús Óláfsson berfœttr, Sigurðr Magnússon jórsalafari, and Eysteinn Magnússon) seem to be categorized under two types: adventurer kings who earn fame and fortune abroad (Haraldr harðráði, Magnús berfœttr, and Sigurðr jórsalafari), and peaceable kings who devote themselves to domestic projects (Magnús góði, Óláfr kyrri, and Eysteinn Magnússon). Although the author devotes considerably less space to the latter group, whose tranquility was not the stuff of adventure tales, he seems to have a preference for them. Magnús góði is explicitly and implicitly compared to Haraldr harðráði and has much the better of it. Haraldr emerges as autocratic and deceitful despite his legendary accomplishments. The uneventfulness of Óláfr kyrri's career is by no means held against him, while Magnús berfœttr seems choleric and rash and beyond the control of his advisers, who judge any given situation better than he does. Sigurðr jórsalafari's spectacular adventures are counterbalanced by his later episodes of madness, and the author makes his preference for his peace-loving brother Eysteinn quite distinct in the famous flyting that he stages between the two brothers.

That an Icelandic writer should arrive at this categorization seems understandable given the historical situation just prior to the writing of *Morkinskinna*. The period 1215–1220 was characterized by considerable tension between Iceland and Norway because of commercial disputes (Andersson 1994). The tension culminated in a plan by Skúli jarl to mount a naval expedition against Iceland. The plan did not materialize, but feelings ran high. We can readily imagine that Icelanders around 1220 would have taken a negative view of Norwegian monarchs who engaged in military adventures abroad. It hardly seems unlikely that an Icelandic author chronicling Norway at this time might have written into his text a condemnation of adventurism and a strong commendation of a peaceful domestic policy.

After the death of Sigurðr jórsalafari in 1130, this polarity of temperaments collapses. Sigurðr slembir could certainly be recruited for the adventurer model, but he seems to have inherited the reputation of a martyr from *Hryggjarstykki and had strong ties to Iceland. Haraldr gilli might have qualified as a peaceful stay-at-home but seems to have been wanting in wisdom and public service, compared to some of his predecessors. In contrast, King Ingi Haraldsson seems truly to have engaged the author's sympathies, and we will explore the reasons below.

Time and Place of Composition

It is generally agreed that *Heimskringla* was written in the years 1225–1235. There is also agreement that Snorri made use of both *Morkinskinna* and *Fagrskinna* in writing his history. *Fagrskinna* is therefore dated somewhat earlier and *Morkinskinna* earlier still. But there are some indications that *Morkinskinna* cannot have been written much earlier than about 1220.

At the end of the story of Haraldr Sigurðarson, the author describes how his son Óláfr kyrri rewards Skúli, the son of Haraldr's ally Tostig, with properties near Konungahella and Niðaróss. To this information is appended the following genealogy (end of Ch. 51):

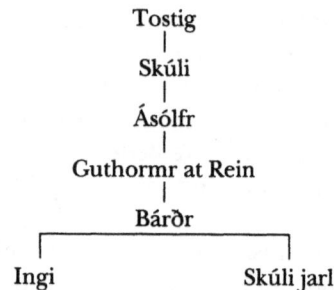

Tostig
|
Skúli
|
Ásólfr
|
Guthormr at Rein
|
Bárðr
┌──────────┴──────────┐
Ingi   Skúli jarl

The genealogy is thus brought down to the time of *Morkinskinna*'s composition. That Skúli is referred to as "Skúli jarl" shows that the passage must have been written sometime after 1217, when Skúli received the title of jarl. This may serve as a *terminus post quem* for the writing of *Morkinskinna*.

A further indication is provided by the genealogy of King Sigurðr jórsalafari's queen, Málmfríðr (Ch. 66):

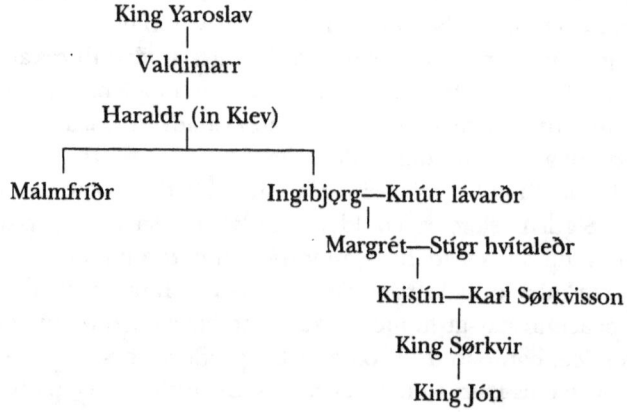

King Yaroslav
|
Valdimarr
|
Haraldr (in Kiev)
┌──────────┴──────────┐
Málmfríðr   Ingibjǫrg—Knútr lávarðr
|
Margrét—Stígr hvítaleðr
|
Kristín—Karl Sørkvisson
|
King Sørkvir
|
King Jón

The author writes: "Margrét was married to Stígr hvítaleðr, and their daughter was Kristín, who was married to Karl Sørkvisson, King of the Swedes. Their son was King Sørkvir, the father of King Jón." King Jón reigned from 1216 to 1222 and was succeeded by King Erik Eriksson (1222–1229). Since the author mentions Jón but not his successor, it is most reasonable to assume that he was writing before 1222.

Bjarni Aðalbjarnarson (1937:136) notes one other passage that may shed light on the date. After the death of King Óláfr Magnússon, the author includes the following genealogical information (Ch. 69): "King Óláfr's mother Sigríðr was the daughter of Saxi from Vík. Sigríðr was the sister of Kári from Austrátt, who was called Kári King's Brother. He was a powerful and popular man. Saxi in Vík had another daughter named Þóra. She bore a son who was named Sigurðr and was later alleged to be Magnús's son and was called Sigurðr slembidjákn. Kári King's Brother was married to Borghildr, the daughter of Dagr Eilífsson. Their son was Sigurðr Austrátt, a district chieftain and the father of Jón, who was married to Sigríðr, the sister of King Ingi Bárðarson." The genealogy may be outlined thus:

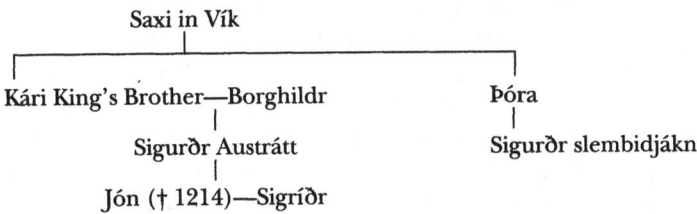

Bjarni Aðalbjarnarson speculated that the author stopped with Jón because he was not yet apprised of the marriage of Jón's daughter Baugeið to Ásólfr jarlsfrændi at Austrátt in 1221 or 1222. These various dating indices place the composition between 1217 and 1222.

More difficult is the question of location. No one doubts that *Morkinskinna* is Icelandic, but the exact location in Iceland is uncertain. Most of the internal evidence points to northern or northwestern Iceland. Eivind Kválen (1925a: 46–53) favored a location at the monastery of Munkaþverá in Eyjafjǫrðr, but Sigurður Nordal (*ÍF* 2, lxviii) assigned it to Borgarfjǫrðr without detailing the evidence. This evidence accrues from references to individuals in a particular region. Thus, the reference to Már Húnrøðarson (in Húnavatnsþing), or to Þorgils Snorrason (at Skarð in Dalir), or to Þorsteinn Gyðuson at the end of "Auðunar þáttr" (on Flatey in Breiðafjǫrðr) might point to the northwest. But a number of other references tend to circumscribe Eyjafjǫrðr. The protagonist of "Hreiðars þáttr" is at home in Svarfaðardalr northwest of Eyjafjǫrðr. Þjóðólfr Arnórsson, whose family lore looms large and who may also be the source of "Brands þáttr ǫrva," belongs in Eyjafjǫrðr proper. The story of the feud that led to the killing of Koðrán Guðmundarson and his avenging by Þormóðr Eindriðason also belongs in Eyjafjǫrðr. "Odds þáttr Ófeigssonar" is located in Reykjadalr, northeast of Eyjafjǫrðr. Eldjárn from Húsavík may be from the same region.

The interweaving of sources from northwestern and northern Iceland is readily comprehensible because the leading families of these districts inter-married and interacted from the 1150s on. Hvamm-Sturla, the patriarch of the Sturlung clan, Ari at Reykjahólar, Þorgils Oddason at Saurbœr, and Þorgeirr Hallason in Eyjafjǫrðr were particularly prominent in this network. The liter-ary activity in the west is usually given precedence, but the monastery at Munkaþverá in Eyjafjǫrðr was engaged in literary work as early as the 1150s (Abbot Nikulás Bergsson's *Leiðarvísir*).

An incident that is often taken to illustrate the literary dominance of the west is a visit that Sturla Sighvatsson paid to his uncle Snorri Sturluson in Reykjaholt in the summer of 1230 (*Íslendinga saga* I, 329). We are told that he was much preoccupied with having the "saga books" compiled by Snorri copied down. The passage is usually understood in the context of Snorri's work on *Heimskringla*, while Sturla's interest is considered incidental or even in-dicative of the radiation of saga writing from the western center of Reykjaholt to other parts of the country (Sigurður Nordal 1953:245).

Sturla Sighvatsson's family had moved to Grund in Eyjafjǫrðr in 1215 when Sturla was sixteen years old. If *Morkinskinna* was composed at Munkaþverá in the period 1217–1222, just a few miles from Grund, Sturla would have been coming of age at just that time. Apparently, he developed literary interests, and it could have been under the influence of *Morkinskinna* that these interests blossomed. It was also under the influence of *Morkinskinna* that Snorri Sturl-uson's interest in the post-Olavian Norwegian kings blossomed. He had a copy of *Morkinskinna* from which to work, though we do not know how he came into possession of it.

The indications on the location of *Morkinskinna* are sparse and not adequate to anchor the book in any particular region. Sigurður Nordal thought, for lack of any obvious alternative, that it could have been written in Borgarfjǫrðr, but we know of no literary activity there prior to Snorri's work. It could also have emanated from the monastery at Þingeyrar in the northwest, where, in the previous generation, Oddr Snorrason, Gunnlaugr Leifsson, and Karl Jónsson had written important sagas, but there is nothing in *Morkinskinna* to suggest a connection with Þingeyrar.

The weakest aspect of the argument for Munkaþverá is that it is not as con-spicuous a literary center as was Þingeyrar in the early thirteenth century. Only *Víga-Glúms saga* is routinely assigned to Munkaþverá in the decade 1220–1230, but Dietrich Hofmann (1972) made a strong case for dating *Reykdœla saga* in the period 1207–1222. It relates events to the northeast of Eyjafjǫrðr and could be assigned with some plausibility to Munkaþverá, the nearest monastery to

Reykjadalr. More recently, Ólafur Halldórsson (1987:ccxxxix) suggested quite tentatively that the author of *Færeyinga saga* may have been from Eyjafjǫrðr and worked in the years 1210–1215. A fourth saga, *Ljósvetninga saga,* is centrally concerned with events in Eyjafjǫrðr and almost certainly originated in the monastery at Munkaþverá, but it is customarily dated in the middle of the thirteenth century. There is, however, no evidence that forbids an earlier date, and *Ljósvetninga saga* makes reference to the same chieftain in Eyjafjǫrðr also mentioned in *Reykdœla saga* (Þorvarðr Þorgeirsson †1207). There is no reason why both sagas should not be assigned to Munkaþverá around 1220. We have seen above that *Ljósvetninga saga,* in all probability, copied a passage out of *Morkinskinna.* Given the way that passage is positioned in *Ljósvetninga saga,* it could be an interpolation. If it is original, it might suggest that the two texts are closely linked and may have been set down at the same time and in the same circles. If these three family sagas (*Víga-Glúms saga, Reykdœla saga,* and *Ljósvetninga saga*) can be connected with Munkaþverá around 1220, there is every reason to believe that Munkaþverá was an active literary center at this time and could have produced a work such as *Morkinskinna.*

There is also some evidence that *Morkinskinna* shows a political bias that is in line with the views of the leading chieftain in Eyjafjǫrðr, the same Þorvarðr Þorgeirsson who is mentioned in *Ljósvetninga saga* and *Reykdœla saga.* It is apparent that the author of *Morkinskinna* favors King Ingi over his brothers Sigurðr and Eysteinn. The comparison is explicit at one point (Ch. 97 at note 6): "King Sigurðr was altogether a very overbearing and contentious man in his youth, and his brother King Eysteinn was not very different except that he was also a very covetous man. King Ingi was in poor health. His back was crooked and one foot was withered so that he was very lame, but still he was very popular with the people." This direct comparison must, however, be omitted from the argument because it appears to be an interpolation from either *Ágrip* (Ch. 59) or the source of *Ágrip.*

Setting this passage aside, there are other indications of a pro-Ingi bias. The author places his own positive estimate of Ingi in the mouth of the papal legate Cardinal Nicholas (Ch. 99): "During the reign of the brothers Cardinal Nicholas came north from Rome to Norway on the orders of the pope. The cardinal visited his wrath on King Sigurðr and King Eysteinn, and they were obliged to make their peace with him. But he was always on good terms with King Ingi." When Nicholas returns to Rome, becomes Pope Adrian IV (1154–1159), and shows special favor to Norwegian visitors, we are to understand that this represents a diplomatic triumph for King Ingi. We cannot, however, be certain that this comment was not taken over from *Ágrip,* which is defective here.

The killing of King Sigurðr is justified on the grounds of provocation and is charged largely to the account of Grégóríús Dagsson. The killing of King Eysteinn is told only in *Fagrskinna* (*ÍF* 29, 340–41) and *Heimskringla* (*ÍF* 28,

345–46), but the texts are very similar and may well reflect the wording of *Morkinskinna*. Here, too, no blood stains the hands of King Ingi. His retainer Símon skálpr tracks Eysteinn down in the woods and kills him there. For this deed, he earns only infamy. *Fagrskinna* (*ÍF* 29, 340) states tersely that he "earned ill repute because of this matter." *Heimskringla* (*ÍF* 28, 345) says that Símon skálpr was greatly despised for this deed, but then adds an interesting additional note: "Some say that when King Eysteinn was captured, Símon sent a messenger to King Ingi, and the king bade Eysteinn stay out of his sight. This is the way King Sverrir had it written down, but Einarr Skúlason composed the following." (A half-stanza follows.) *Fagrskinna* has the half stanza but not the note on King Sverrir.

We know nothing about a composition in which King Sverrir would have recorded an alternate version (see Bjarni Aðalbjarnarson in *ÍF* 28, lxiii–lxiv). Nor do we know whether the comment originates with *Morkinskinna* or represents an addition by Snorri. If the remark derives from *Morkinskinna*, it shows that the author opted for the version that is most favorable to King Ingi, even though it stood in opposition to an official version established by King Sverrir. If the remark was added by Snorri, we may still conclude that a version authorized by King Sverrir was in circulation but was rejected by the author of *Morkinskinna* in favor of a version that leaves King Ingi completely unblemished. Can we also surmise an underlying opposition to Sverrir?

Another indirect indication of a special preference for King Ingi can be found in the introduction of Erlingr skakki (Ch. 95 at note 3). Erlingr is clearly presented as the man of the future, and his loyalties are in no doubt: "Erlingr was a wise man and a great friend of King Ingi. With the king's sponsorship he was married to Kristín, the daughter of King Sigurðr jórsalafari." He gains fame by duplicating King Sigurðr's voyage through the Mediterranean to Constantinople and the Holy Land (end of Ch. 95): "Their luck held all the way to Norway, and their journey was much praised. Erlingr skakki was deemed to be a much more important man than before, both because of his expedition and his marriage. He was a man of great wisdom, and his friendship inclined most to King Ingi."

We may ask now where King Ingi's special partisans were located in Iceland. The most conspicuous of these partisans was none other than Þorvarðr Þorgeirsson. In *Prestssaga Guðmundar Arasonar* (I, 101–2) we learn that he went to Norway at the age of eighteen, in 1158, and killed one of King Ingi's retainers. The matter was patched up, however, and Þorvarðr in turn became King Ingi's retainer, thus developing a close relationship with him. It was so close that when Þorvarðr returned to Iceland after Ingi's death in 1161, he vowed never to serve another king.

At the same time, he urged his brother Ari not to join Ingi's enemies. Ari Þorgeirsson was attentive to his brother's wishes and took service with Erlingr skakki in 1165. He proved to be no less faithful an adherent to his lord than

Þorvarðr, to the point that he sacrificed his life in Erlingr's service. The jarl acknowledged his sacrifice in the following words (I, 105): "It is certain that he
was the man who served me best, and I am left with none who has the same
courage. Of all of you he was the only one to give his life voluntarily to save
mine. I will never be able to repay his kinsmen for the injury they have suffered
on my account." When Þorvarðr learned of Ari's death, he composed a commemorative poem, "thinking that was the best way to be consoled for Ari's
death and record his courage in poems that were widely circulated." In addition, we learn from *Sturlu saga* (I, 75) that Þorvarðr's nephew Einarr Helgason
died in the service of Magnús Erlingsson at the Battle of Íluvellir in 1180. The
family therefore had a remarkable tradition of service to King Ingi, Erlingr
skakki, and Magnús Erlingsson, the three figures who seem to emerge with
special luster at the end of *Morkinskinna*. There is no family more likely to have
sponsored a laudatory chronicle of their deeds in Iceland.

The family lived in Eyjafjǫrðr and had a long-standing affiliation with the
monastery at Munkaþverá. Þorvarðr's father, Þorgeirr Hallason, retired and
died there in 1171 (I, 107–8). Þorvarðr himself is referred to as "munkr" in
two sources (Gustav Storm, *Islandske annaler*, pp. 123, 182) and may also have
withdrawn to Munkaþverá. (He died in 1207.) One of his brothers, Ingimundr, was famous for his love of books (I, 112). We have seen that Þorvarðr
composed a poem in memory of his brother Ari, and he is mentioned in two
sagas that may plausibly be attached to Munkaþverá—*Ljósvetninga saga* and
Reykdœla saga. There may, therefore, very well have been a literary streak in the
family and the possibility of literary sponsorship. The attachment of the family to the monastery at Munkaþverá might even help to explain the mixture of
secular and devout tonalities in *Morkinskinna* (Meissner 1902:48 and Kválen
1925a:51–53). It can only be speculation, but given Þorvarðr's devotion to
Ingi and the pro-Ingi slant at the end of *Morkinskinna*, it seems reasonable to
look for the ultimate inspiration of the book in Þorvarðr's family. The accu-
mulation of *þættir* would also accord well with the tradition of taking service in
the Norwegian retinue exemplified by Þorvarðr, Ari Þorgeirsson, and Einarr
Helgason. That brings us no closer to the exact identity of the author, but it
does suggest something about the environment in which the author worked.

Finally, we might raise the question of political inspiration. We have seen
that the earlier sections of *Morkinskinna* may be interpreted as promoting a
sound domestic policy against a tradition of foreign adventurism. We have
seen, too, that Norwegian interference in Icelandic affairs was likely to have
been a lively issue in the period 1215–1220. Political intimations would, therefore, not be unexpected in *Morkinskinna*. The favor lavished on Ingi and, at
least preliminarily, on Erlingr skakki may reflect not only a personal loyalty
on the part of the author but also a political viewpoint. There is reason to believe that the author knew *Sverris saga*, which celebrated Sverrir's victory over
Magnús Erlingsson in 1177 and the rise of a new dynasty, embodied in Hákon

Hákonarson at the time *Morkinskinna* was composed. It is possible that *Morkin-skinna* is in part a counterpoise to the rise of King Sverrir. It reverts fondly to the earlier period of King Ingi, an era of cordial relations between the Icelanders and the Norwegian king, and an era in which there was no threat of Norwegian intervention. In short, *Morkinskinna* may be designed not only to fill the gap between *Óláfs saga helga* and *Sverris saga* but also to counteract a new danger posed by Sverrir's dynasty.

Toward a Profile of the Author

It is dangerous to speak of a single author in the case of a work that has, more often than not, been regarded as a composite. The most extreme "analyst" position was taken by Finnur Jónsson in the introduction to his edition (1928–1932), and the most consistent single-author argument was made by Gustav Indrebø (1939:72–76), but even Indrebø was quite guarded in his conclusions. It is clear that *Hryggjarstykki was incorporated into *Morkinskinna,* whatever the exact dimensions of that text may have been. Although no one is likely to assume a whole series of anterior kings' sagas, as Finnur Jónsson did, the possibility remains that one or more such sagas were available to our author, for example, a *Magnúss saga berfœtts. Particularly tenacious has been the belief that many of the *þættir* are independent compositions that were incorporated either by the author himself or by later copyists. The problem of interpolated stanzas is dealt with in "The Poetic Corpus of ÆMsk and the Question of Interpolation," but we are concerned here with the author in his prose incarnation. For that reason, we may also set aside the interpolations from *Ágrip* because they are not substantial enough to alter the authorial signature of the work as a whole. Despite these uncertainties about what belongs to the original author and what is either borrowed or supervenient, we will proceed hypothetically (and only hypothetically) on the assumption that the original *Morkinskinna* was largely the work of one individual and that there are, as a consequence, individual peculiarities in the text.

The traditional approach to textual uniformity is linguistic, an attempt to establish whether style, syntax, vocabulary, and idiom are consistent throughout. This is, however, a specialized study on which no beginning has been made and which we cannot undertake here. Every so often, the text does seem to echo itself, suggesting that the author has particular habits of phrasing that are apt to recur. This is, of course, not the only explanation for repetitions; it is possible that the author took over a bit of phrasing, for example, in a ready-made *þáttr,* then duplicated it elsewhere. Nonetheless, the easiest explanation may be that the author had his own mode of expression and was inclined to revert to it.

We may compare, for example, a passage in Chapter 1 (at note 10) with a much later passage in Chapter 36 (at U 62). The first reads: "The king replied: 'Why did you make so bold as to come here? Do you think you are luckier than other men? Do you think you will be able to display your goods when others can't even save their lives?'" The latter passage from "Auðunar þáttr" reads: "King Haraldr asked: 'Are you such a foolish man that you have not heard of the war being waged between these two countries? Or do you think that your good fortune is such that you can travel freely with treasures where others can hardly get off unscathed though it is a matter of life and death?'" It may be that the phrasing in Chapter 1 is taken over from "Auðunar þáttr," but it seems more likely that this is simply the way a particular author chose to stereotype a particular situation.

Later, in Chapter 1 (at note 16), Karl vesæli captures a boat by pitching the occupant overboard: "Karl grabbed him by the shoulders and pitched him overboard, then rowed off in the boat." That phrasing echoes Sigurðr slembir's handling of two captors in Chapter 86: "He gripped them both by the shoulders and plunged them overboard, taking them down with him." In this case, the latter incident was almost surely taken from *Hryggjarstykki, whence it was also adopted in *Fagrskinna* (ÍF 29, 327) and *Heimskringla* (ÍF 28, 299). *Fagrskinna* and *Heimskringla* agree almost exactly in their wording and must reflect the wording in *Hryggjarstykki, but the phrasing in *Morkinskinna* is slightly different and closer to what we find in Chapter 1. This was apparently the way our author preferred to articulate the situation.

In a third example, the author seems to have a predilection for the image of ice in describing an advancing army. In Chapter 50, we read: "They waited accordingly, and as the army drew nearer and they saw more clearly, everything looked like gleaming ice" (FJ 272.10–11: "ok allt var á at sjá sem ísmǫl væri"). That passage occurs in the context of Haraldr harðráði's last campaign in England, but it recurs in Magnús berfœttr's confrontation with Sveinki Steinarsson in Chapter 56 (at note 1): "Then a company of men was sighted, and it looked like gleaming ice because they were so well equipped with weapons and chainmail" (FJ 307.27: "ok var sem á ísmǫl væri at sjá"). Not much can be deduced from such stray echoes, but perhaps a thorough study of language patterns might reveal something about the author's idiosyncracies.

On rare occasions, the author does emerge in the first person: Chs. 24 (U 42.27; FJ 134.21), 32 ([from *Flat*]: FJ 170.10), 50 (U 118.3; FJ 276.16), 59 *bis* (U 153.32; FJ 333.15; U 156.4; FJ 337.1), 65 (U 167.6; FJ 354.6), 93 (U 221.24; FJ 437.28 [fairly clearly from *Hryggjarstykki]), 98 (U 232.2; FJ 453.27), and 100 (U 234.34; FJ 457.32). These lapses into the first person are not specifically characteristic of *Morkinskinna*. There are a couple of instances in *Fagrskinna* (ÍF 29, 261, 364) and a dozen in *Heimskringla* (ÍF 26, 3, 328 *bis*, 332, 346; ÍF 27, 157, 241; ÍF 28, 137, 188–89, 332, 341, 366). What is interesting about the occurrences in *Morkinskinna* is that they are so evenly distributed over the biographies of Haraldr harðráði (Chs. 32, 50), Magnús berfœttr

(Ch. 59), Sigurðr slembir (Ch. 93 [from *Hryggjarstykki]), Eysteinn Haralds-son (Ch. 98), and Sigurðr Haraldsson (Ch. 100). They occur also in the quasi-independent *þættir* attached to Haraldr harðráði ("Hreiðars þáttr") and Eysteinn Magnússon ("Ívars þáttr"). They do not, therefore, have the appear-ance of being residues from separate sources, despite the instance from *Hryggjarstykki. Again, not much can be made of such scattered evidence, but as far as it goes, it does not suggest heterogeneous authorship.

If we therefore follow Indrebø and hypothesize a single author, it becomes incumbent on us to piece together an authorial personality. This is a long-term task to which we can contribute only a few preliminary suggestions. Perhaps the most palpable authorial characteristic is a consistent lack of interest in chronology throughout the book. No year is ever specified, and there are few references to relative chronology, the age of an individual, or particular days in the church calendar. Some such references clearly come from skaldic stan-zas and others look to be inserted from *Ágrip* or annalistic sources. In all, there are no more than a score of such indications.

Toward the end of Chapter 2 (at note 5), which describes Sveinn Álfífuson's attempt to reconquer Norway, we learn that "the next winter King Sveinn . . . died south in Denmark," but "the next winter" stands in no relation to any pre-vious chronological guidepost. The same paragraph reports the death of King Knútr (the Great): "That same summer he died west in England." We know from English sources that Knútr died on November 13, 1035, but there is no way to divine that date from *Morkinskinna*. The chronology may in fact be in-terpolated from *Ágrip* (*ÍF* 29, 34), which reads: "At that time Sveinn had died in Denmark, and likewise his father Knútr in England."

Chapter 4 (at note 6) relates the attempt by Queen Álfífa to poison King Magnús Óláfsson, with the mistaken result that King Hǫrðaknútr (miscopied as "Hákon") is poisoned instead. At this point, *Morkinskinna* provides a whole paragraph of chronology, saying that the event took place in the sixth year of King Magnús's reign, that King Haraldr (Harefoot) had died in England two years earlier, that King Knútr died "the same spring," and that King Edward (the Confessor) was then anointed on the first day of Easter. All of this is so un-characteristic that it looks like an interpolation from an English source related to the *Anglo-Saxon Chronicle*, which tells us that Hǫrðaknútr died in a paroxysm while at drink in 1042, that Haraldr Harefoot died in Oxford in 1040, and that King Edward was anointed in Winchester on the first day of Easter in 1043.

In Chapter 5 (at note 13), the text pinpoints the Battle of Hlýrskógsheiðr on the afternoon of Michaelmas (September 29), but that information is merely lifted from st. 39. Similarly, in Chapter 37 (at note 3) the author remarks on Magnús's twentieth birthday, but in so doing he merely paraphrases st. 44 (see note 7.3). In Chapter 14 (at note 4), we learn that Steigar-Þórir agrees to give Haraldr harðráði the royal title at the age of fifteen. We have noted that there was abundant oral tradition about Þórir, and this specific mention of age could well have been transmitted in a stanza marking Haraldr's accession.

Chapter 26 (at note 6) is devoted to the death of King Magnús, which is fixed three nights before the feast of Simon and Jude (October 28). That looks more like an annalistic entry than a skaldic reference. There is no further mention of chronology until Chapter 42 (at note 10), at which point the author dates the Battle of the River Niz in the evening of St. Lawrence's Day (August 10). Since the battle was a momentous one, duly noted in the Icelandic annals (1062), and since "Laurentius" might be a hard fit in a skaldic stanza (though "Lafranz" might do), an annalistic source again seems most likely.

At the beginning of Chapter 49, there is again a full paragraph on the chronology of the royal succession in England in 1066. We are told that the events occurred in the twentieth year of King Haraldr's rule, an item of information that could have been inserted from *Ágrip* (*ÍF* 29, 39). There follows a precisely dated order of events: King Edward dies on the fifth day of Christmas; on the seventh day, the English acclaim Harold; on the eighth day, Harold is anointed (ending the line of "Æthelstan the Good"). That looks too precise to be explicable by anything but a written English source, although William of Malmesbury (I, 280) gives different dates. He records that Harold was crowned in London on Christmas Day, with an immediate contradiction to the effect that Harold "seized the crown" on January 6. Snorri (*ÍF* 28, 171) also specifies January 6. There was clearly some confusion about these dates, but the author of *Morkinskinna* (or an interpolator) must have had access to English information at first or second hand.

Further along in the same chapter (at note 9), Haraldr harðráði invades England and fights a preliminary battle against the jarls Morkere and Waltheof. The battle is assigned to the day before St. Matthew's Day (September 21), specified as a Wednesday. That is to say, the battle fell on Wednesday, September 20. At the beginning of Chapter 50, Haraldr marches his army against York, and the day is given as Sunday. The information in these latter two instances may well come from the same source as the information on Harold's succession.

There are two chronological references in the saga of Magnús berfœttr (Ch. 59). The first tells us that Magnús had ruled nine years when he set out on his fatal expedition to Ireland, a figure that may well come from *Ágrip* (*ÍF* 29, 47), which informs us that Magnús reigned for a sum total of ten years. A couple of pages later, the battle is set on the day before the feast of St. Bartholomew (August 23). It is interesting that the designations of particular days seem to cluster on the British Isles, perhaps suggesting once more an English source. But Magnús berfœttr's death just before St. Bartholomew's Day is registered in the same style as Magnús góði's death before the feast of Simon and Jude and may come from the same Norse source.

The next chronological indications pertain to Magnús berfœttr's sons Sigurðr, Eysteinn, and Óláfr. We are told at the beginning of Chapter 60 that Óláfr was only three years old at the time of the succession and, immediately thereafter, that he lived only twelve years after the succession. The wording of this paragraph is clearly taken over from Chapter 51 of *Ágrip* (*ÍF* 29, 47), which also tells us that Óláfr survived his father by only twelve years. There is an interesting discrepancy in Óláfr's age at the time of his death. *Ágrip* gives his age as seventeen, but by *Morkinskinna's* reckoning he would have been fifteen (3 + 12). Since *Morkinskinna* so clearly echoes *Ágrip* at this point, it is perhaps easier to assume a calculation error than a second source.

Ágrip also appears to underlie the chronological reference at the end of Chapter 63, indicating that Sigurðr jórsalafari was twenty when he returned from his Mediterranean voyage and that his brother Eysteinn was a year younger. The categories of information match *Ágrip* (*ÍF* 29, 49), which states: "En heim í Nóreg sœkir hann um Ungeraland ok Saxland, of Danmǫrk eptir þrjá vetr, er hann fór ór landi, ok fagnaði allr lýðr kvámu hans. Þá var hann tvítøgr, er hann kom aptr í land ór þessi ferð, ok var orðinn enn tíðasti. Vetri var Eysteinn ellri þeira brœðra, en Óláfr þá tólf vetra gamall" (He took the route home to Norway through Hungary, Saxony, and Denmark three years after his departure, and all the people welcomed his arrival. At the time when he returned from this journey he was twenty and had become very famous. Eysteinn was the older of the two brothers by a year, and Óláfr was then twelve years old). *Morkinskinna* (FJ 352.9–14) states: "Ok nú eptir .iii. vetr frá því er Sigurðr konungr fór ór landi átti allr lýðr honum at fagna í Nóregi. Hann var þá tvítøgr at aldri ok var orðinn inn frægsti af ferðum sínum ok stórlyndi. Vetri yngri var Eysteinn konungr, bróðir hans" (And now three years after King Sigurðr departed, all the people could welcome him back to Norway. He was then twenty years of age and had gained great fame because of his voyages and his magnificence. His brother King Eysteinn was a year younger).

Again, the verbal similarity between the two passages is unmistakable and cannot be coincidental, but there is another discrepancy in information. *Ágrip* makes Eysteinn a year older, *Morkinskinna* a year younger than Sigurðr. This latter is likely to be a simple error. But if the author of *Morkinskinna* knew *Ágrip* and knew therefore that Óláfr died at the age of seventeen, why did he (at the beginning of Ch. 60) give Óláfr only fifteen years of life? The author of *Ágrip* apparently thought that Óláfr was aged five at the time of the succession and then lived another twelve years. The author (or interpolator) of *Morkinskinna* lost two years somewhere in the calculation. That blunder seems more likely to be the work of a superficially involved interpolator than the author. If so, perhaps the interpolator realized that there was a problem and omitted the mention of Óláfr's age at the time of his death in order to make the problem less obvious. Whatever the case, there is a clear lack of chronological precision in *Morkinskinna*. In *Heimskringla*, Snorri corrects the record almost pedantically (*ÍF* 28, 257).

The next king to receive chronological attention is Haraldr gilli, who (in Ch. 86) is reported to have been slain the night after the feast of St. Lucy (December 13). The last sentence of the chapter supplements this information with the note that Haraldr reigned for sixteen years after the Battle of Fyrileif. *Ágrip* has a lacuna at this point, but the final note on Haraldr's reign may well have come from that source, especially because it seems out of context in *Morkinskinna*. The style of reporting Haraldr's death day is, however, reminiscent of the reports on the death of Magnús góði (three nights before the feast of Simon and Jude) and Magnús berfœttr (the day before the feast of St. Bartholomew) and may come from the same annalistic source.

A signpost near the beginning of Chapter 92 dates the Battle of Hólmr inn grái (Holmengrå) and, hence, also the death of Sigurðr slembir, the day after St. Martin's Day. The source for that information is almost certainly *Hryggjarstykki, because the phrasing in *Fagrskinna* (*ÍF* 29, 334) and *Heimskringla* (*ÍF* 28, 316) matches closely.

At the beginning of Chapter 100, we are told of a meeting between King Sigurðr and King Eysteinn designed to force King Ingi into retirement. The text notes: "At that time Ingi and Sigurðr had ruled Norway for nineteen years." There is a lacuna in *Ágrip* at this point, but we have seen that previous mentions of regnal duration in the case of Haraldr harðráði and Magnús berfœttr may have come from *Ágrip* (*ÍF* 29, 39, 47). This may also be true of Haraldr gilli's sixteen-year reign, although the corresponding passage in *Ágrip* is lost. *Morkinskinna* goes on to relate that the conspiracy of Sigurðr and Eysteinn resulted in a battle in Bergen in which Sigurðr was killed: "The battle was fought two weeks before the feast of St. John the Baptist [June 24] and that was a Friday." Once more, the style is akin to the reports on the death of Magnús góði, Magnús berfœttr, and Haraldr gilli, and the source may well be the same.

The upshot of this surprisingly brief chronological survey is that the indications in *Morkinskinna* are most likely to derive from skaldic verse, from some English or Norman record, from annalistic sources that noted the death days of Norwegian kings and the dates of important battles, from *Ágrip*, and in one case at least, from *Hryggjarstykki. In the case of *Ágrip* in particular the chronological notes are likely to be be interpolations, and this could also be true of the special English dates. If the inserts from skaldic verse, English sources, *Ágrip*, and *Hryggjarstykki are subtracted, the original author of *Morkinskinna* is left with no more than the death days of four kings (Magnús góði, Magnús berfœttr, Haraldr gilli, and Sigurðr Haraldsson) and the days on which a few battles were fought: the Battle of Hlýrskógsheiðr, the Battle of the River Niz, perhaps the Battle of the River Ouse, Magnús berfœttr's last battle, the Battle of Holmengrå, and Sigurðr Haraldsson's last battle. An author's interest in chronology could hardly be more exiguous or less methodical.

There has never been any doubt about the author's Icelandic identity. Eivind Kválen (1925a) argued the point on the basis of the author's knowledge of Iceland and relative unfamiliarity with parts of Norway, but a more obvious line of argument might proceed from the preponderance of *Íslendinga þættir* in the book. These *þættir*, if they are substantially the work or the inclusions of the original author, are the clearest windows on his Icelandic perspectives and sympathies. No other book about the Norwegian kings gives such attention to the Icelandic presence in Norwegian history.

Above and beyond a disproportionate presence, we may suspect that there is sometimes a particular Icelandic slant on Norwegian history. There are, for example, occasional, and perhaps surprising, overtones of something that resembles Norwegian patriotism. Thus in Chapter 2 (at note 4), we find a Norwegian stand against Danish tyranny (a posture that recurs throughout the story of hostilities between Norway and Denmark): "They [*scil.* the Norwegians] all desired rather to be free under King Magnús than to suffer the tyranny of the Danes any longer." Perhaps an Icelandic writer is genuinely aligning himself with Norwegian interests, but given the tensions that characterized relations between Norway and Iceland in the period just before the composition of *Morkinskinna,* it is tempting to imagine that an oblique defense of Icelandic independence also inspires these words. Possibly the emphasis on regional liberties in relation to the central monarchy, for example, the strains between Magnús góði and the Þrœndir, between Haraldr harðráði and Einarr þambarskelfir, and between Magnús berfœttr and Steigar-Þórir or Sveinki Steinarsson could be construed in the same way. It is, in any case, remarkable how the authorial sympathies seem to gravitate toward Einarr, Þórir, and Sveinki in their contests with royal power. But even the unblemished Magnús góði must listen to some harsh oratory (Ch. 3 at note 4) and learn to accommodate the self-perceived rights of the Þrœndir.

In the *Íslendinga þættir,* the discourse on political independence can be more direct. In "Hreiðars þáttr," the Icelandic protagonist is rewarded with an island off Norway and immediately proclaims himself as diplomat and peacemaker (Ch. 24 at note 21): "With that I will link Norway and Iceland." Linking implies fundamental separateness. Furthermore, King Magnús promptly buys the island back from Hreiðarr in order to avoid any friction between Hreiðarr and the Norwegians, thus implying that it is best to maintain the separateness. The respect for national autonomy is also dramatized in the contrast between Haraldr harðráði's grasping designs on Denmark and England and King Magnús's deliberate renunciation of Norwegian claims on those countries. If there is an underlying foreign policy statement in the book, it is that nationalisms and regionalisms are to be respected. Foremost in the author's mind was presumably his own nationalism.

The author is thus by implication an Icelander, but an interesting subtheme makes him more explicitly so. Insistently in the first two chapters, and recurring in the later chapters, is a concern with how the "people" relate to the Norwegian crown. The word for "people" in these contexts is *þegnar* (thanes), suggesting a legal or contractual bond between the king as lord and his sworn adherents. In the opening chapters the theme is struck four times (notes 1.11, 1.20, 1.25, 2.3) in connection with the loyalty of the Norwegian people toward the absent king Magnús. It is sounded again in Chapter 19 (at note 2), in which

Haraldr lays claim to the throne only to be told at a popular assembly that King Magnús already has the allegiance of his "þegnar."

These passages apply overtly to internal Norwegian affairs, but like the echoes of Norwegian patriotism above, they may also reverberate with a special Icelandic consciousness. That the Icelanders could consider themselves the *þegnar* of the Norwegian king is suggested by a passage in "Gísls þáttr Illugasonar," which seems to have originated at the beginning of the thirteenth century. Here Jón Qgmundarson addresses the king with the words (*ÍF* 3, 337): "We are just as much your thanes (*þegnar*), lord, as those who live in this country." The same sentiment is echoed in *Ljósvetninga saga* (*ÍF* 10, 97) from the same period as *Morkinskinna*. Here the Norwegian king (Haraldr harðráði) is asked for leave to kill some offending Icelanders, but he responds: "I am not here to kill my people (*þegnar*), and if someone undertakes to do so, it will be paid back." When the Icelanders spoke of the relationship between king and thanes, they may very well have reflected on their own status as well as that of the Norwegians.

This drift is nicely illustrated in Chapter 30 ("Halldórs þáttr Snorrasonar"), which centers on the troubled relationship between Haraldr harðráði and his Icelandic thane Halldórr. Haraldr obliges him to swallow a penalty drink, which Halldórr does with an ill grace and the sharp comment (at note 6): "It may be, sire, . . . that you can get me to drink, but I can tell you that Sigurðr sýr [Haraldr's father] could not have forced Snorri goði [Halldórr's father]." Haraldr is greatly angered by this slur on his status and genealogy, which so aggressively argues Icelandic equality, but the author of *Morkinskinna* maliciously allows him to confirm the point a few pages later. Here King Haraldr deprives one of his Norwegian district chieftains of a captaincy in order to turn the ship over to Halldórr. The Norwegian protests, but Haraldr replies (at note 8): "His ancestry in Iceland is no worse than yours is in Norway, and not much time has elapsed since those who now live in Iceland were Norwegians themselves."

The author gives voice here to conflicting feelings about the standing of the Icelanders. On the one hand, he seems to be insistent on a sort of dual citizenship for the Icelanders in the interests of achieving equality. On the other hand, he takes a fierce view of Icelandic independence and relishes a series of humiliations heaped on King Haraldr by Halldórr Snorrason. Halldórr is at once an outstanding warrior, with an unequaled record of valor, and at the same time Haraldr's most rebellious thane.

Both fidelity and contentiousness seem to be important in the author's system of values. Fidelity is embodied in another Icelander, Úlfr stallari, who apparently renders perfect service with none of Halldórr's bristling defiance and, as a result, is rewarded with a handsome royal eulogy over his grave (FJ 265.27–28): "Here lies a man most loyal and devoted to his lord." The little chapter "A Dear Friend of Tryggvi Óláfsson" (Ch. 45) seems to be inserted for the sole purpose of celebrating a nameless man who can never recover from the grief over the loss of his king. Magnús blindi is given perhaps the least flattering

portrait of any king in the book, but his death becomes the occasion for celebrating the loyalty of a certain Hreiðarr Grjótgarðsson (Ch. 92 at note 2):
"Hreiðarr fell backward onto the deck with Magnús on top of him. Everyone
agreed that he had followed his lord well and valiantly, and any man who earns
such a reputation should be praised." This comment may well be taken over
from *Hryggjarstykki and is also found in *Heimskringla* (ÍF 28, 316), but it ac-
cords well with the thematic sentiment in *Morkinskinna*. The series of retainer
anecdotes attached to Sigurðr jórsalafari in his years of declining sanity
(Chs. 74, 75, 77) illustrate how devotion to a monarch's welfare overcomes
fear. A final parable of exemplary service is the unfinished story of Grégóríús
Dagsson at the end of the book.

In contrast to these idealizations of loyal service, the author included a series of *þættir* that function as a sort of opposition literature. "Halldórs þáttr" is
the most obvious case, but there are others that suggest a programmatic resistance to King Haraldr (notably "Odds þáttr Ófeigssonar" [Ch. 48] or "Sneglu-
Halla þáttr" [Ch. 43]) or exemplify a moral or intellectual superiority on the
side of the Icelanders (for example, "Auðunar þáttr" [Ch. 36] or "Brands þáttr
ǫrva" [Ch. 38]). The author is thus animated by conflicting ideals of service
and national and personal autonomy. If it were permissible to translate these
ideals into some speculation on the author's identity, we might guess that he
was an Icelander with a powerful sense of his own national and individual heritage who spent time in royal service, absorbed the appropriate ethic, but at
the same time experienced the strain between self and service that inheres in
such a position.

A career in armed service would certainly accord well with the author's manifest interest in military matters. The interest emerges in the disproportionate
attention to military tactics and descriptions exemplified by the Battle of
Hlýrskógsheiðr, Haraldr harðráði's Mediterranean campaigns and artifices,
the warfare between Denmark and Norway, Hákon Ívarsson's campaign in
Gautland, Haraldr's campaign in England, Magnús berfœttr's last battle in Ireland, and Sigurðr jórsalafari's itemized Crusade voyage. This predilection is re-
inforced by the observation that when there is no warfare to relate, the author
is apt to fall silent, as in the reign of Óláfr kyrri.

The author's interests are, however, not exclusively military or feudal. He
has a clear side-interest in commercial and financial matters. Several of the
þættir are, in effect, about how Icelanders make their fortune ("Hreiðars þáttr,"
"Auðunar þáttr," "Þorvarðs þáttr krákunefs," or "Stúfs þáttr blinda"). "Karls
þáttr vesæla" at the very outset of the book is not generally included in the *þáttr*
gallery, but it is very much in the same style. It tells the story of how Karl rises
from a salt burner to a wealthy merchant, together with his brother Bjǫrn
(Ch. 1 at note 9): "They were brothers without much family background, but
still ambitious to get ahead." Ultimately, Karl becomes a major player in international diplomacy. The rise from poverty to prominence on the international
scene is recapitulated in "Auðunar þáttr." A more modest example of this

theme is found in Chapter 34, in which an unnamed northern Icelander observes the unearthing of a buried treasure and talks himself into a share. The discoverer becomes wealthy with trade investments, but he ultimately becomes too conspicuous, is found out by the king, and has his money confiscated. The Icelander, however, makes himself useful to Einarr þambarskelfir and is able to get himself off to Iceland.

The fullest tale of commercial triumph is "Ásu-Þórðar þáttr" (Ch. 68). It is the pecuniary equivalent of the commonplace of the romantic Icelander who goes abroad and charms the queen. Here the Icelander falls in with an older wealthy widow, is both romantic and practical, makes his fortune, and achieves a visible presence in the highest circles. This rise is tricky and fraught with danger; the possibility of failure is illustrated by the story of Úlfr auðgi (Ch. 37), whose wealth originated with an ancestor, Álmsteinn, who was a slave but understood the art of investment and became wealthy. But wealth does not eradicate ancestry, and King Haraldr deprives Úlfr of all but one of his farms. It appears that although a Norwegian rising above his rank may fail in the delicate financial game, the author is inclined to argue that an Icelander is more apt to succeed.

The author's values are by no means wholly mercenary. In one area he seems to have a particularly strong moral commitment, the area of incest. It is the central issue in three separate episodes. In Chapter 23, the comely Margrét at Stokkar is threatened by the unwanted attentions of King Magnús, but on the supernatural advice of St. Óláfr, she eludes the king by feigning a liaison with a relative of his. Because of the incestuous implication, Magnús, who was previously immovable, desists immediately.

In Chapter 65, the story of how King Eysteinn cures Ívarr Ingimundarson's lovesickness, incest bars any access to the woman Ívarr loves because she is married to his brother. King Eysteinn has no scruples about facilitating a divorce (contrary to church doctrine in the early thirteenth century), but he unhesitatingly abandons any thought of intervention as soon as he learns that Ívarr would be in the position of marrying a sister-in-law. Finally, in Chapter 70 ("Þinga saga"), King Sigurðr Magnússon trumps up a mission for Ívarr of Fljóðar so as to clear the way for sleeping with his wife Sigríðr, who is technically his aunt by marriage. As a consequence, Sigríðr's brother, Sigurðr Hranason, provokes a heated confrontation with the king, which leads to a protracted and highly charged quarrel, ultimately between King Sigurðr and his brother King Eysteinn. Sigurðr Hranason's challenge to the king may have much to do with family honor, but the vehemence may in part be linked to the problem of incest, which appears to be a particularly sensitive issue in this text. Those who reject incest (King Magnús, Ívarr Ingimundarson, Sigurðr Hranason) occupy a clear moral high ground.

Most interesting of all, for our purposes, is the author's obvious preoccupation with literary matters. Not only is he skilled in skaldic verse and the first large-scale collector of verses (see "The Poetic Corpus of Æsk and the

Question of Interpolation"), but he has a rare narrative verve. He is eager to tell stories, and though his work has not been much appreciated, it is both lively and dramatic, with a masterful handling of dialogue in more than a few passages. He is a narrator by preference, with very little interest in what we might call scientific history. But beyond his narrative art and his poetic expertise, he shows a curiosity about literary transmissions that appears nowhere else in Icelandic literature. A typical instance occurs in Chapter 17, in which King Magnús appoints Ormr (Skoptason) to a jarldom, although Ormr once spared the life of his enemy King Sveinn. The author does not bother to provide the name of Ormr's father (as *Fagrskinna* does), but he is eager to explain the moral of the story (FJ 103.2–3): "This is told to show how unlike other men the king was in making such a fine demonstration and judging that the quality of the man was more important than the enmity that separated them."

In Chapter 42 the author tells the story of how King Haraldr, lacking water for his troops, induces maximum thirst in a snake, then ties a thread to its tail so that it can lead the men to water. At this point, the author steps back and ponders how such an incident could have been remembered (FJ 205.8–9): "The device was preserved in memory because it seemed wise and ingenious." Further along in the chapter, Haraldr captures Finnr Árnason, who treats him to a memorable tongue-lashing. Just before the final repartee, the author once more ruminates about the survival of the anecdote (FJ 214.1–3): "Then Finnr made a vicious comment that was later remembered because it indicates that he was so angry that he could not control his words." A third time in the same chapter, when a poor woman berates her king without knowing that the king himself is standing before her, the author cannot restrain himself from commenting on her words (FJ 214.23): "At that point the woman spoke a very foolish word: 'Woe to us—we are miserably provided for since our king is both halt and cowardly.'"

In an incident in Chapter 68, rather similar to the one involving Finnr Árnason, the chieftain Ingimarr takes leave of King Eysteinn with a biting insult, but Eysteinn does not react (FJ 364.18–22): "King Eysteinn did nothing to impede his journey and took no notice of his foolish words. He let his goodness and intelligence prevail as was always the case." Of all the saga authors, this one seems most clearly to be reflecting on his own narrative matter and the words he is setting down. In doing so, he betrays a new ruminative consciousness about the act of writing. It is perhaps not surprising that he includes the little account of how an Icelander told the story of Haraldr harðráði's foreign adventures (Ch. 40), that account which has always been prized as the chief source of our information about the practice of Icelandic oral narrative.

How, then, should we imagine our author? He was an Icelander, most probably a northern Icelander. His idea of literature was story and anecdote. He was not primarily a historian but a teller of tales, and the tales delighted him. He had access to a few books, primarily *Hryggjarstykki, but for the most part he relied on a large variety of oral sources communicated to him by Icelanders and presumably Norwegians as well. A century after Ari, he was no longer much preoccupied with the accuracy of these sources, but he did reflect on how and why they were transmitted. He was not academically analytical but was transported by the imagined scenes of past events. If Snorri was the Thucydides of Norse history, our *Morkinskinna* author was the Herodotus.

He was also Herodotean in his cosmopolitanism. His imagination swept not only Norway, Denmark, southern Sweden, and the eastern and western shores of England and Scotland, along with Ireland, but also recreated court and campaign life in Constantinople, Russia, and the periphery of the Iberian Peninsula. He was sufficiently absorbed by the conduct of warfare and the protocol of relations between liege and lord that we may ask ourselves whether he was not himself in foreign military service. He seems also to have been a practical man, who combined a sense of adventure with an interest in trade, commerce, and investment success, as had been the custom of ambitious Scandinavians ever since the Viking Age.

But wherever his foreign military and commercial activities may have taken him, he remained a passionate Icelander, who liked to chronicle the success of his countrymen at foreign courts. He did not confine himself to accounts of individual daring and parables of superior character. He seems also to have had a larger perspective on foreign relations, the sanctity of agreements, and the importance of moderating royal ambition. In particular, he seems to have been concerned with the relationship of the Icelanders to the Norwegian crown, which is the gist of many *þættir*. But perhaps his most signal contribution to the history of saga writing was to broaden the narrative repertory and widen the horizons of saga art. Whatever came before *Morkinskinna* looks parochial by comparison, and whatever came afterward was obliged to take the wider parameters into account. The first reaction (in *Fagrskinna* and *Heimskringla*) was to shrink back from such universal dimensions, but the author of *Morkinskinna* eventually had his way. His book may perhaps be regarded as the ultimate model for the great compilations of a later era, *Sturlunga saga, Óláfs saga Tryggvasonar in mesta, Hauksbók,* and even *Flateyjarbók.* With *Morkinskinna* the individual biography and the ideal of defensible history gave way to the ideal of comprehensive and panoramic narrative.

Contents of *Morkinskinna*

Morkinskinna

1. *Here Begins the Saga of King Magnús and King Haraldr*

(FJ 1; U 1) We begin the story at the time when King Yaroslav ruled Russia together with Queen Ingigerðr, the daughter of King Óláfr the Swede.[1] She was a very wise woman, and fair to look at. It is told that King Yaroslav had a splendid hall constructed in magnificent style, ornamented with gold and precious stones. He manned it with excellent fellows, tried and true to a high degree. He adorned their equipment and war gear in accordance with their standing so that everyone found that the outfitting and arrangement of the hall matched the hall itself. It was hung with precious fabrics and costly tapestries.[2] The king himself was in noble raiment and sat on his throne.

He invited many of his distinguished friends and arranged a splendid feast. Then the queen entered the hall with a fair retinue of ladies. The king rose to meet her and greeted her warmly, saying: "Where have you seen such a splendid hall, so fittingly adorned by a following of men such as are assembled here, and, in addition, decorations of such opulence?"

The queen replied: (FJ 2) "Lord, this hall is well appointed, and it must be almost unexampled that such splendor and expense should conspire in a single residence, along with such a number of excellent chieftains and valiant men. Nonetheless, the hall in which King Óláfr Haraldsson sits is superior, even though it only stands on posts."[3]

The king responded angrily to her: "Such words are insulting, and once again you are yielding to your love for King Óláfr." And he struck her in the face. She said: "The difference between the two of you is much greater than I can properly express in words."

She departed in anger and told her friends that she wanted to take leave of his kingdom and not be subject to such shame any longer.[4] Her friends intervened and asked her to be calm and to relent. In reply she said that the king should first compensate her. The king was now informed that she wished to depart, and his friends asked him to smooth things over. (U 2) He acquiesced and asked for a reconciliation, saying that he would grant her whatever she wished. In reply she said that she would accept these terms. (FJ 3) She stipulated as follows: "You shall send a ship to King Óláfr in Norway, for I have learned that he has a young son out of wedlock. Invite the boy here and provide for his upbringing and fostering, because it is confirmed in the case of you two that it is the less distinguished man who fosters the other's child."[5]

"You shall have what you ask for," he said, "and I will rest content that King Óláfr is the greater man. Nor do I consider it a dishonor to foster his child."

The king sent a ship to Norway, and the men who were dispatched met with King Óláfr and delivered the message from their king and queen. He replied: "I will gladly accept the offer. I think that my son could be in no better hands than those of King Yaroslav and his queen, whom I know to be a most excellent woman and well disposed toward me." After that he sent his son Magnús east with them, where he was honorably received by king and queen and was raised there in the retinue with no less love and affection than their own sons. Some people rejected him and thought it was inappropriate to raise a foreign prince there. (FJ 4) They represented that to the king, but to no effect because the king took no account of such things.

He often participated in the amusements of the king's hall and soon came to be skilled in many games and accomplishments. He walked along the tables on his hands with much agility, thus demonstrating great physical prowess.[6] The people who liked his being so precocious were in the majority, but one retainer, who was somewhat up in years, took a dislike to him. One day as he was passing along the tables and came by this courtier, he gave him a shove and *toppled the boy from* the table, saying that he wanted none of his nuisance. People expressed different views; some sided with the boy, others with the courtier.

On the same evening, when the king had gone to bed, the boy stayed behind in the hall. As the retai*ners sat there* and drank, Magnús went up to the courtier in question. He held a little ax in his hand and struck the courtier his death blow.[7] *Some of his tablemates wanted to seize the boy immediately and kill him* and thus avenge the courtier. But others were opposed and wanted to test how much *the king loved him. Then a man took the boy in his arms and ran with him* to the building in which the king was sleeping. He tossed him into the king's bed and said: "Take better care of your little fool *another time.

The king replied: "You often speak to his discredit, but what has he done to deserve it?* (FJ 5) The retainer answered: "He has given ample cause and has killed your retainer." *The king asked how that had come about*, and he told him.

Then the king said: "A royal deed, foster son," (U 3) and he burst out laughing. "I will settle the compensation for you." *Then the king arranged the payment with the heirs* and paid over the fines immediately. Magnús remained in residence with the king's retinue and was brought up with great affection.

He was *more and more to everyone's liking the more his age and intelligence advanced.*

*At this time there was hostility between Sveinn Álfífuson and King Yaroslav because King Yaroslav correctly judged that the Norwegians had betrayed Saint Óláfr. For a time there was no trade between them.[8] There was a man named Karl, and another named Bjǫrn.[9] They were brothers without much family background, but still ambitious to get ahead. They had been salt burners in their early years and had made money from that occupation. Now it had turned out that they were wealthy merchants, popular and confident men, though Karl was the leader in all their dealings.

In their line of business they had a large trading vessel. One summer they sailed it south to Saxony. Then they went to Denmark and intended to sail from there to England. (FJ 6) Then Karl spoke up and addressed his shipmates: "I want to inform you of my intention, because the voyage is taking a different turn from the one you expect. I intend to make a trading voyage into the Baltic, but because of the declarations of King Sveinn and King Yaroslav and the hostility between them, the voyage is hardly without risk. I want to tell you that I am determined to make the voyage, but I will give you the option of choosing a different course, and you are free to leave my ship. Let the Danes, Germans, and Englishmen here hire onto other ships and go wherever they prefer."

A Norwegian replied: "This takes us very much by surprise. We would not have signed on with you in the first place if there had been talk of this. But because you are successful men and we have a liking for you yourself, and it is not unlikely that you live under a lucky star, we feel that we have an obligation to follow your lead." That was the course they chose. They sailed with him to the Baltic and anchored at a big market center with the intention of purchasing what they needed. But as soon as the natives realized that they were Norwegians, they refused to trade with them. It was shaping up for a battle, and the natives were ready to attack.

When Karl saw that things were turning bad, he addressed the natives: "It will be judged bold and rather reckless if you, in the king's name, injure or rob foreigners who come with articles for trade and do nothing to disturb your peace. You have no way of knowing whether the king will thank you for it or not, and it would be wiser for you to await the king's decision in this matter." That pacified the natives, and no attack was made on the Norwegians. (U 4) But Karl could see that this would not be the end of it, and he made his way to see the king. (FJ 7)

There is no information on his trip until he came before King Yaroslav and greeted him. The king asked who he was. "I am a Norwegian of no great account," he said, "and I and my companions have come here well supplied."

The king replied: "Why did you make so bold as to come here? Do you think that you are luckier than other men?[10] Do you think you will be able to display your goods when others can't even save their lives? What Norwegians suffer at my hands is never so bad that they don't deserve worse."

*[Karl said: "Lord, not everyone should be cut over the same comb. I am an insignificant salt burner even though I have made some money at it. I have always known where my advantage lay, but I was never against King Óláfr in my heart."

"I rather expect," said the king, "that you will turn out like all the other Norwegians."

The king ordered that he be taken and put in irons, and this was done. Then the king told his foster son Magnús about it and asked how the two of them should deal with the Norwegians. Magnús replied: "You have not taken counsel with me much before now, foster father, but I think that Norway will find its way into my possession rather slowly if you go about killing everyone who comes from there. You are no doubt well-intentioned, foster father, because the Norwegians may all rightfully be called my thanes,]*[11] but I think there might well be more promising ways to proceed than to antagonize everyone who comes from there." The king said that was well spoken and that he would abide by his advice.

In the morning the king called Karl before him and spoke to him as follows: "You look to me to be favored by fortune, and Prince Magnús wants you to be granted a truce. You now have two options available, either to go to your ship, for which I will provide wine and victuals, and conduct your trade as you wish, (FJ 8) or spend the winter with me. But you should know for a certainty that when spring comes, some difficulty will be in store for you."

Karl said: "I am not well equipped to deal with that, but I am not inclined to turn down an honorable invitation and I will take a chance on your good fortune. It may still turn out well even though some difficulty is involved."

He now took his place in the retinue. The king often conversed with him and found him to be an intelligent man. As spring drew near, it happened one day that the king and Karl were in conversation. The king said to him: "Here is a sum of money for you to take over and, together with it, a difficult mission. With this money you will suborn the district chieftains in Norway and all such men as are of any importance and wish to be the friends of Magnús the son of Óláfr.[12] You are a prudent man even though your family background does not amount to much."

Karl said: "This is not a job for me. The man who carries out such missions and must deal with such superior forces and execute such grand designs should be of great distinction and have profound wisdom."

(U 5) The king said: "My experience tells me that you are the right man, but I judge it likely that you will be put to a considerable test. It is unclear whether you will make it through safely or not. But even if you refuse, it may be that you will not have to wait long before you run into trouble."

"I'll risk it," said Karl, (FJ 9) "considering your luck and counsel."

Karl set sail westward with his crew, and they arrived in Denmark. Then Karl addressed his shipmates: "It occurs to me that we had no permission for this voyage to the Baltic, and there is every reason to think that the king will have a case against us. It is my advice that we part company here and that everyone should go his own way. You should travel to England or other trade centers, and each one should find his own way to Norway. In that manner our voyage will be less obvious, but otherwise there will be some risk both to our property and lives. But I will proceed inland to visit a wealthy friend of mine who lives here, and I leave my property in your keeping."

His brother Bjǫrn leaned toward him and spoke softly: "I never knew you had a friend here, and I suspect there is some deception involved. Tell me what it is because I am suspicious."

Karl told him the whole story and asked him to attend to their property, but Bjǫrn said that he did not want to take leave of him in such a difficult situation. "It seems to me more advisable," said Karl, "that I should take sole possession of the king's money, though I expect that things might turn out well if we both have the courage for the task."

It was decided that both should go, and they arrived in Vík. They set about studying the men in order to judge which ones were King Sveinn's friends and which ones were less well disposed toward him. It was hard to distinguish, but they felt they could make out to some extent what people thought. Then they went to see Einarr þambarskelfir and took up the matter with him. They showed him the money and gave a clear account of Prince Magnús's message. Einarr replied: (FJ 10) "I have always disliked the bribery of the magnates in this realm since Knútr (Cnut the Great) did it, but on the other hand I am very interested in Prince Magnús's case, and for that reason I will certainly commit myself to travel east before Whitsun."

They departed and came to town[13] before Palm Sunday. There they took lodging with a certain Grímr enn grái (the Gray). Word of their travels had gotten around to some of the more important men. Grímr fell into conversation with them and asked: "Do you not know of those men who have been traveling around the land in secret offering money to the chieftains? You seem to be about their size." They said they knew nothing about them.

The next day a meeting was convened, and (U 6) King Sveinn's steward spoke to the effect that he had gotten some information concerning men who wanted to deprive the king of his land by treachery. They were alleged to have come to the town and taken lodging with Grímr enn grái. He said that anyone who hid them would forfeit his life. The men returned home and told Grímr what had been said.

"If there is any truth in the idea that you are these men, I have always been devoted to King Óláfr and wish to serve his son Magnús as well. For that reason it is advisable for you to tell me the truth."

Then Karl said, "You have guessed correctly—we are the men."

"Then be off (FJ 11) as quickly as you can," said Grímr, "and I will stay behind in the snare."

"On no account," said Karl, "one of us will stay behind with you. It matters little whether we return as long as Prince Magnús knows what the situation is and who his friends are in this country."

Bjǫrn said: "Whether you want to leave or stay, I will not separate from you."

"It cannot be," said Karl. "One of us must go to tell Prince Magnús because he needs to know. You are free to stay behind if you wish."

Bjǫrn said: "I am less well suited, for you are in every way superior." Karl did not object to staying behind, though neither choice seemed attractive.

Bjǫrn now traveled east in secret, favored by the luck of King Óláfr and Magnús, and brought the journey to a successful conclusion. Then he told King Yaroslav and Magnús what had been achieved in Norway, who had accepted the money in a spirit of friendship, and on whom Prince Magnús could depend. King Yaroslav said that a great deal had been accomplished, though much was left unfinished.

Back in the town a meeting was summoned, and it was announced that King Sveinn had come to town and that the Eyrarþing was convened,[14] to which all the propertied men were bidden. The king stood up at the thingmeeting and spoke: "What previously gladdened our hearts may now seem not to amount to so much. I have learned that men (FJ 12) have come to this country and are traveling about with money to suborn the chieftains and magnates with the intention of making the land defect from us. I have also learned that these men have come to this very town and are housed with Grímr enn grái. It is now advisable to surrender the men. Whoever received them will have done so in ignorance."

Grímr made answer to the king and stated that the men were not in his house. The king said: "Grímr, your case is worse than we thought since you are intent on hiding the men, for they are surely there. Your choices are now going to be more restricted than they might have been otherwise."

"That is in your hands, sire," he said, "but I will say only what I wish to say."

The king threatened to torture Grímr for a confession, and when Karl saw that this would be carried out, he stood up and spoke: "Sire, I am the man (U 7) your words refer to, but there is less in this matter than meets the eye. Such things are often *exaggerated. Grímr is ignorant and guiltless with respect to this affair*."

The king said: "I know precisely who you are, a very successful man in many ways. And if you will tell me (FJ 13) who accepted money, *I will pardon you*."

Karl said: "If insignificant men have accepted money, it makes no difference, but if important men have done so and I identify them, that will lead to great tension and bloodshed in the country. I don't want to be responsible for the death of so many men, and for that reason I will say nothing."

The king said: "You will be obliged to speak whether you wish to or not, if not voluntarily, then under severe torture." He had him put in irons and set four men to guard him in a house.

The meeting broke up, and the king paid no attention to Grímr enn grái. Karl sat in his irons with his guards by him. He spoke up: "It must be said that your lot is a hard and unenviable one since you must guard me with nothing to amuse you and nothing to drink. Is the king so stingy with you *that you can get no pocket money to buy a drink?"

They replied: "We don't want to criticize him, but we think there are more liberal men than King Sveinn*, even though he cannot be expected to give everybody money." "Look here," said Karl, "I can't take it with me and I can't see any better use for the money than to make the people with me a bit less miserable. I don't blame you for guarding me since you are obliged to do what the king commands."

Then he gave them some money and told them to buy some beer. They were eager to do as he said (FJ 14) and sat down to drink. *After a bit Karl tasted the drink with them* and said: "That's poor stuff, you should rather go and buy some mead." They do *[so and sit down to drink.

After a while Karl spoke up again: "Go and buy some wine, boys, that's the best drink. Let's enjoy life while we can. I'll give you whatever money you need." They said they hadn't seen many people face death that way.

"Everybody's got to die sooner or later," said Karl. "That's something everyone has to contend with." Then the wine came. They drank deeply, and nobody held back. Eventually everyone dropped off to sleep.[15]

After that Karl made his way out, but his hands were tied behind his back and his feet were fettered. He worked his way over to where the ax of one of the guards lay, turned on his back, and rubbed his hands against the blade until he severed the cords. Then his hands were free, but his feet were fettered. Still, the irons were loose, and he got out and down to the docks and to a privy under which the tide flowed. There he got the irons off one foot, though at the cost of hacking away the heelbone. He bound the fetter to the other foot. Then he took a board up from the floor and dove into the sea.

At this point a guard woke up and ran out. He thought he saw a glimpse of Karl down on the docks. He also saw that a board was disturbed in the privy and thought that it had been moved recently. He told the men that their captive was gone. The next thing that happened was that the alarm was sounded all over town. People ran in all directions through the town and the ships in search of him, but he could not be found. The king put a price on his head and condemned anyone who helped him to the loss of property and life. He also set a watch everywhere to make sure that Karl was caught.

When most of the tumult had died down in the town and morning had come, Karl saw a man in a boat on the river. He swam away from the ships in that direction, and before the man realized it (FJ 15), Karl jumped into the boat next to him. Karl grabbed him by the shoulders and pitched him overboard, then rowed off in the boat. He was an accomplished athlete.[16] Nothing more was learned of Karl, and they gave him a nickname and called him Karl vesæli (Luckless).

King Sveinn called a meeting in the town and gave an account of the difficulties that were besetting the country. Then he announced his departure south to Denmark to meet with King Knútr. Kálfr Árnason was to accompany him. He had been promised a jarldom by King Knútr if he would topple King Óláfr, and his credit was so great that he was privileged to moor his ship next to the king's ship whenever or wherever they went into port. The next day King Sveinn set sail with his district chieftains, but Kálfr left a little later because his preparations were delayed. The king's ship got out ahead, and Kálfr's men started rowing when the breeze died down.

They caught sight of a boat rowing ahead of them, and there was a cloak visible in the boat. They headed for it, and as they drew near, a man jumped up from under the cloak, dove overboard, and made for land. That was Karl vesæli. He wound up on land, with the cloak left behind in the boat. Kálfr got into the boat and made for shore while the longship sailed on ahead. Kálfr set out after Karl so that they could both see each other. Kálfr called to him to wait. Karl replied that he had no intention of waiting—"You betrayed a king to whom you were much more obligated than you are to me."

"I will not betray you," said Kálfr. "That I swear by God and Saint Óláfr."

"You will lose more than I will," said Karl "if you kill me in spite of this oath, so I will risk it."

He did so, and Kálfr now took him into his custody and said that he would protect him: "But I don't trust all of my men to conceal you if we anchor next to the king. We will therefore anchor at some distance from him." As soon as Kálfr and his men caught up, the king sent messengers to him and asked him to come as quickly as he could, for Kálfr had put in at a considerable distance from the king's ship. They then made their way to the king's ship. (FJ 16)

The king said: "Welcome, Kálfr. Anchor next to us. The others will make room for you in the mooring."

Kálfr said: "Lord, you grant me too much honor when you ask distinguished men to leave the mooring for us, but if I moor first, then there can be no objection."

The king said: "Did you find Karl vesæli today? That's the sort of good fortune that is apt to come your way." Kálfr said that he had not found him.

"All the same," said the king, "take care not to deceive us now."

"I will not deceive you," said Kálfr.

Then the king said: "Do you see the ax inlaid with gold out by the gunwale? Get me such an ax from England."

Kálfr burst out in anger: "That is a perilous mission, and it seems to me that for the moment you have no lack of axes, wherever they come from, even if they are not all inlaid with gold."[17] Then Kálfr jumped into his boat and rowed to his ship. He told his men to head out—"We have been in bad company too long already, serving this king and getting little in return compared to what King Knútr promised us. Now, Karl, we will be mindful of your appeal on behalf of Magnús Óláfsson and make amends in any way we can for what has been done."

They sailed east to Russia to meet with Magnús. He and King Yaroslav were overjoyed to see Karl. He told them all about his travels, then placed Kálfr's case before Magnús and explained how Kálfr had helped him. Magnús said: "The matter you raise is of far too great importance to be quickly decided, and it is somewhat beyond your scope because Kálfr is charged with having borne weapons against King Óláfr, my father. Since we are expecting Einarr þambarskelfir and other friends to arrive shortly from Norway, I will seek counsel from them with respect to Kálfr. If fortune grants it, we will come to power with their aid. I know of no man in Þrœndalǫg who is much wiser than Kálfr, and it will not be easy to guard against his guile."

Karl said: "Kálfr will now swear to you that he did not strike your father King Óláfr. If you should assume power in Norway, I expect that you will have great forces at your command, and if you believe that my journey to Norway advanced your cause, then I imagine that (FJ 17) in your bounty you might do something for my sake. In my view I owe Kálfr my life."

"Your conduct is laudable," said Magnús.

Then the king and Magnús took up the matter between them. And because they thought they owed Karl some reward for his journey and the perils he had suffered, they felt obliged to do something for his sake. They sent for Kálfr, for whom Karl had already secured a truce. Kálfr then swore an oath that he had not struck a blow at King Óláfr, and he committed himself to support Magnús faithfully and to perform all the tasks that Magnús assigned him.

Now we pick up the story at the point where King Sveinn was headed south along the coast, as was previously mentioned.[18] But the Þrœndir gathered in council and decided to choose all the best men in the country and send them east to Russia. Einarr þambarskelfir and Sveinn bryggjufótr were in command, and with them the best men of Þrœndalǫg.[19] At that time God gave ample proof of King Óláfr's sainthood, and many saw the truth of his status and realized their error and the wickedness they had committed. They thought the best way to make amends for what they had done was to compensate his son. They journeyed east to the court of King Yaroslav.

Kálfr Árnason and Karl had left the East. Before leaving, Karl had received many excellent gifts from King Yaroslav and Magnús, and many other tokens of their esteem. Kálfr had also promised to meet Magnús as soon as he learned of his whereabouts after leaving the East. Einarr þambarskelfir and his men now arrived at the court of King Yaroslav and Queen Ingigerðr. They presented their business and the message with which they were charged from the best men in Norway, to wit, their entreaty that Magnús should go to Norway and assume control over his land and people.[20] The king was receptive and said there was no man in Norway whom he trusted as much as Einarr: "But we are nonetheless apprehensive about how faithful the Norwegians are to Magnús, given the evidence in the case of his father."[21]

At that time Rǫgnvaldr Brúsason was with King Yaroslav and was in charge of the Russian defense forces. He was a very valiant and popular man, (FJ 18) and was much honored by the king. King Yaroslav raised the matter with the queen, telling her that the most distinguished men of Norway had arrived and wished to confer the Norwegian royal title on Magnús and support his claim to power. She responded: "I do not begrudge Magnús the royal title in Norway and the attendant honors, but his father received such ferocious treatment that I am very suspicious about the Norwegians' willingness to grant him authority, what with the opposition of King Knútr's family and Álfífa, who is the worst of them all and has the fiercest disposition. We should discuss this more fully before Magnús sets out and have firmer commitments if this plan is to go forward."

Einarr and his men asked the king a second time to represent their view to the queen so that they might take Magnús along with them, as indeed the king himself had advised in the first place and as they had agreed in accordance with his proposal. Einarr said it would not be kingly to change his mind so quickly without cause. Rǫgnvaldr Brúsason also supported Einarr and his men in this matter. We are told that for a long time their entreaty was not granted.

Then the king said: "That is indeed the nature of my message to you, and I am most eager that my foster son Magnús should receive the honor due him, but I am apprehensive about Álfífa's malice, Knútr's power, and the treachery of his countrymen. Even though you are well-intentioned, as I am sure you are, it can still happen that the Þrœndir will betray him as they did his father."

Einarr replied: "It is understandable, sire, that you should be apprehensive about our plan, but it is crucial that the boy should get his inheritance and that his honor should be as great as possible. It is also the desire of everyone in Norway to rid themselves of the evil rule and oppression that now prevails."

The queen said: "We will not stand in the way of Magnús's honor and prevent him from getting his inheritance, but you, Einarr, will understand our fear that the Þrœndir may become as arrogant as before. Because of my love for Magnús, I would never part with him if there were less at stake, but you, Einarr, are a famous man and stand in high repute. You were not in Norway when King Óláfr fell. You also command powerful forces and are yourself chief among the magnates in Norway. (FJ 19) If you will agree to be Magnús's regent and foster father, we will risk it, but with the stipulation that you and twelve others of our choosing will swear oaths of loyalty to him."

Einarr answered: "Although it might seem to some that it is undue pressure to demand oaths from us in a foreign land, I think the country will be ruled better if we accept your condition. It is certain that many will find it ridiculous that we have journeyed all the way from Norway to swear an oath of twelve,[22] but we are nonetheless willing to make this concession and promise him our full support."

Then twelve most distinguished men swore oaths that they would back Magnús as king in Norway and support him with complete devotion and bolster his rule in every way. They remained in the East during the summer engaged in these negotiations, then left Russia taking Prince Magnús with them. Rǫgnvaldr Brúsason went with them. They went westward in the frost of winter to the open water, then manned their ships and crossed the sea to Sweden and sailed up the coast to Sigtúnir (Sigtuna), where they landed and took the land route to Helsingjaland (Hälsingland). In the words of Arnórr:

*1. Nú hykk rjóðanda reiðu   vasat ellifu allra
     rógǫrs (þvít veit gǫrva)   ormsetrs hati vetra
     (þegi seimstafir) segja   hraustr þás herskip glæsti
     seggjum hneitis eggja: Hǫrða vinr ór Gǫrðum.

"Nú hykk segja seggjum reiðu rógǫrs rjóðanda hneitis eggja, þvít veit gǫrva; þegi seimstafir. Ormsetrs hati vasat allra ellifu vetra, þás hraustr Hǫrða vinr glæsti herskip ór Gǫrðum."

Now I shall tell men of the preparations of the battle-brave colorer of the sword's edges [warrior], because I am well informed; let the gold staves [men] be silent. The enemy of the snake lair [gold, generous king] was not quite eleven years of age when the audacious friend of the Hǫrðar [people of Hordaland] handsomely outfitted his warships from Russia.

Here the indication is, as one can hear, that Magnús Óláfsson was eleven when he came to Norway, and that was in the beginning of winter.[23] Again:

*2. Þing bauð út enn ungi   salt skar húfi héltum
     eggrjóðandi þjóðum   hraustr þjóðkonungr austan
     fim bar hirð í hǫmlur   báru brimlogs rýri
     hervæðr ara brǽðis: (FJ 20)   brún veðr at Sigtúnum.

"Enn ungi eggrjóðandi bauð þjóðum út þing; fim hirð ara brǽðis bar hervæðr í hǫmlur. Hraustr þjóðkonungr skar austan salt héltum húfi; brún veðr báru brimlogs rýri at Sigtúnum."

The young edge colorer [warrior] commanded the troops to gather for the expedition; the able retinue of the eagle's sustainer [warrior] bore their arms to the rowing stations. The audacious, mighty king cut the ocean from the east with the frost-covered keel; stiff winds carried the mover of the wave flame [gold, generous king] toward Sigtúnir [Sigtuna].

Now news of Magnús's journey westward came to Norway, and a great body of men came out to meet him. Kálfr Árnason was their leader, but many others who had been opposed to King Óláfr followed his lead. Kálfr and Einarr became Magnús's counselors and foster fathers. They were the most powerful men in all of Þrœndalǫg. Einarr was a great warrior and a preeminent man. Kálfr was wise in counsel. They now traveled west across the border mountains and came down into Þrándheimr.[24] Right away there was a mustering of forces from all the districts, and the closer a man was to Magnús, the better he felt. Magnús and his followers now went out to the coast to the town of Niðaróss. The Eyrarþing was convened without delay and was attended in great numbers. Men came from all the districts of þrœndalǫg, and the title of king was conferred on Magnús Óláfsson, and the land and people were committed to his care.[25] He appointed his retinue and established himself in Niðaróss with a great multitude of followers and great joy and festiveness.

2. Concerning Sveinn

Having learned of these events, King Sveinn came west to Vík together with his mother Álfífa. They immediately sent out the levy arrows and convened a thingmeeting.[1] King Sveinn mobilized troops and appointed the ship crews, telling the men that the Þrœndir had set up a king in opposition to him and that he was obliged to defend his country. He concluded his speech by asking approval of his request by the popular assembly, but the reaction to his speech was very uneven. Some said that they did not want to bear arms against King Magnús Óláfsson, and some said that they wanted to fulfill their naval obligations, as they were obliged, but did not want to go themselves because they claimed that they did not owe such service.[2] The masses were silent, but they were of a mind with the people who spoke up and were no better disposed. King Sveinn said: "The company gathered here cannot be counted on to do battle. (FJ 21) And for my part I can say that I will not fight against King Magnús if I do not have a more reliable army than this one."

Then the Danish chieftains who were with him made long speeches, all to the same effect, namely that they reproached the Norwegians for having betrayed King Sveinn and contriving to make the country defect from him. They said he had no choice but to sail south back to Denmark to gather forces with the aid of Hǫrðaknútr, his brother, and the elder Knútr, his father. He could then bring that army to Norway and burn and waste far and wide. In that way he could pay the Norwegians back for their treachery. That plan was adopted, and King Sveinn sailed away south to Denmark with no further ado, accompanied by his mother Álfífa and all the Danes who had been with him in Norway.

Back in Norway King Magnús established his rule as far as his father's power had extended, and he subdued the land without a battle and with the consent and agreement of all the people, rich and poor.[3] They all desired rather to be free under King Magnús than to suffer the tyranny of the Danes any longer.[4] In the words of Skúli:

*3.   Flýði fylkir reiði   létat Nóregs njóta
       framr þjóðkonungs ramma   nýtr þengill gram lengi
       stǫkk fyr auðvin okkrum   hann rak Svein af sínum
       armsvells hata gellir: sókndjarfr fǫðurarfi.

"Framr fylkir flýði ramma reiði þjóðkonungs; armsvells hata gellir støkk fyr auðvin okkrum. Nýtr þengill létat gram njóta Nóregs lengi; sókndjarfr rak hann Svein af sínum foðurarfi."

The prominent ruler ran before the powerful wrath of the mighty king; the contender of the enemy of the arm expander [ring, generous king] fled from our generous friend. The capable king did not let the nobleman enjoy Norway for long; battle-brave, he expelled Sveinn from his patrimony.

And again:

*4.   Eignask namt þú óðal þegna
allan Nóreg gotna spjalli
mangi ryðr þér mildingr annarr
Mœra gramr til landa œri.

"Gotna spjalli, þú namt eignask allan Nóreg, óðal þegna; Mœra gramr, mangi annarr mildingr ryðr til landa œri þér."

Companion of warriors, you conquered all Norway, the inheritance of free men; lord of the Mœrir [people of Møre], no other generous king as young as you acquires lands.

The next winter King Sveinn, the son of Álfífa, died south in Denmark. It is told that when King Knútr the Great learned of King Magnús's arrival (FJ 22) in Norway, he said: "It may be that we won't have a peaceful summer at home if the family of old 'Stout Legs' has returned to the country." That same summer he died west in England.[5]

After him his son Haraldr was king of England. In Denmark his other son, Hǫrðaknútr, was proclaimed king a second time. For a while Hǫrðaknútr and King Magnús Óláfsson were involved in a great deal of strife and warfare. Knútr considered that Magnús had taken over his hereditary lands, which his father Knútr had possessed after the fall of King Óláfr. But King Magnús said that he was entitled to vengeance against the Danes for the original treachery of Knútr's family against his father and their seizure of lands when Óláfr had left the country to escape Knútr's onslaught, only to succumb to his treachery later on. He said that he would avenge these actions if he could, with the luck of his father, Saint Óláfr, and the support of his countrymen.

When the warfare between the kings had gone on for a time, each succeeded in wreaking much damage on the other. This was a burden on the farmers, and they were eager to improve relations between the kings. The farmers from both realms assembled and consulted wisely and propitiously on behalf of the kings, who were both young men, amenable and willing to be guided by their followers. They arranged a meeting at the River Elfr (Götaälv). The kings arrived there at the agreed time and made peace between themselves and their countrymen. That peace was to be maintained as long as they both lived, and both kings swore oaths to that effect. Each promised to be a brother to the other in all their dealings. The peace and treaty were formulated in the oath to the effect that if Magnús died without progeny and Hǫrðaknútr lived longer, he was to have possession of all Norway with peace and good will. The same was stipulated if King Knútr died childless and King Magnús lived longer. In that case King Magnús was to possess all of Russia[6] and be the lawful heir of Knútr as if they had been equal brothers.

Oaths were sworn by twelve of Magnús's foremost men and by another twelve of Knútr's men. It was stipulated that all the chieftains who swore oaths (FJ 23) should observe this agreement as long as any of them was alive. They were to support and maintain the power of the one who lived longer, and until that time they were to support both of them. That agreement was modeled on the one that Knútr the Great and Edmund made in England, to the effect that the one who lived longer would have the land. Then the kings parted with the greatest cordiality.[7]

Now we turn to a feast held to the east in Vík, where both Kálfr Árnason and Einarr þambarskelfir were present with King Magnús. Einarr arranged the seating of the guests, while Kálfr took Einarr's seat and turned his attention to the king. For it was Einarr's habit always to sit beside the king. When Einarr saw that, he went to his customary seat and stood at Kálfr's shoulder, since he failed to move, and said, "The old ox should be put in his stall before the calf"—then he slid down between them. Nothing more was said.

One time when they were sailing along the coast, they went from the ships onto the land with a small band. They saw another small group approaching them and had no idea who they were, whether friend or foe. They told the band to stay together until they knew whether they needed any help, and they discussed what to do. Then Einarr þambarskelfir said: "I think it is a good idea to form up and be prepared for whatever happens." The king put Einarr in charge, and the formation was drawn up. Then Einarr glanced around and could not see Kálfr Árnason anywhere in the band. He searched for him and found him in the underbrush. He had drawn his sword and was tying it to his hand as tightly as he could with bast. Einarr asked, "Why are you doing that, Kálfr?"

"The local people will have no chance to mock me for running from my weapons, and I will stake my life on it."

"It's much more likely that you lack neither valor nor boldness," said Einarr, "and nobody questions your courage." It turned out that the approaching group was peaceable.[8] (FJ 24)

3. Concerning King Magnús's Round of Feasts

King Magnús now made his way around the country, was entertained, and got acquainted with the people.[1] He soon became powerful and popular, and was more mature in strength and wisdom and authority and every form of manliness than his years would indicate. He was a very handsome man, very amenable to his friends when he got positive advice. But with respect to slander and deception he was deaf and could clearly see and understand what was said to him.[2] But there was much talk of the men who had supported his father King Óláfr against the Þrœndir and of the others who had induced the land to defect from him. Many distinguished men in Þrœndalǫg were alleged to have been against King Óláfr, and King Magnús was judged to be without spirit because he always had these men at his table, and some of them even in private consultations, such as Kálfr Árnason.

The king took some notice of such talk and took a harsher view of the Þrœndir because of these representations. One time when Magnús was at a feast in Þrándheimr and his foster father Einarr and Kálfr Árnason were with him, the king said to Einarr: "Let us go in to Stiklastaðir (Stiklestad) today so that you can tell me exactly about the events that took place there—where the king fell and where the foremost men stood. Tell me where everything happened."

Einarr said: "Sire, ask Kálfr to do this—he is likely to know. He was closer to these events and will be much more familiar with them. He will be able to describe where the important events occurred."

Then the king said to Kálfr: "Come with me in to Stiklastaðir and tell me in detail about these events."

Kálfr said: "It is up to you, sire, but I cannot see that it serves any purpose. You are surely very mindful of what happened there even if the account is not repeated. It is better, sire, to maintain the trust of one's friends, who are completely devoted, as they should be, to your service. It doesn't seem to me that this state of affairs stands to be improved."

The king said, "We will make the trip."

When Kálfr saw that the trip was resolved, he said (FJ 25) softly to his page: "Go out to Egg (Egge) as fast as you can and tell my men to make my longship ready with men and arms right away. Every necessity and all my valuables should be on board by nightfall."

Now King Magnús and his followers rode to Stiklastaðir, and many other people as well. And when they arrived, the king asked in detail about the events and what had happened at each spot. Kálfr told the king what he asked, but not a word more. It seemed to people that his knowledge was precise.

They covered the field where the battle had taken place extensively.

Then King Magnús said: "Where did my father King Óláfr fall?"

"Here," said Kálfr. And he thrust his ax shaft toward the spot.

The king said: "Where were you at that point?"

"No further than where we are standing now, sire," said Kálfr.

The king said: "Your ax might have reached my father then." The king turned away, and his face went red as blood. Kálfr mounted his horse, and he and the king parted company.

Kálfr then rode to his residence in Egg and boarded his longship. He headed immediately out of Þrándheimr and west across the sea to Orkney.[3]

Þorfinnr jarl ruled Orkney at the time and was married to Kálfr's sister Ingibjǫrg Árnadóttir. Kálfr left the country in the way that has now been described because of the king's wrath. Thereafter the king became much harsher toward the Þrœndir so that some lost all their property, others left the country, as Kálfr did, and some paid fines.

The farmers did not suffer that gladly and assembled in Þrándheimr to discuss the matter among themselves, wondering whether the king would show them no moderation. They said that they had mounted resistance on lesser matters: "It is a great shame if the Þrœndir should have less benefit of the law than other Norwegians. Our kinsmen and ancestors are most certainly a thing of the past—those who did not relinquish their prerogatives beyond what the law prescribed. The Þrœndir have long been known as the heart of Norway, and now a decline has set in that causes their land to be overrun by arms. The Þrœndir used to be powerful men, but now they are to be the slaves of the king's steward here in Norway."[4]

Some of King Magnús's friends were standing by and discussed the matter among themselves, consulting on what course of action to take. They agreed (FJ 26) that it was unclear how much the farmers would tolerate if the situation continued unchanged. It seemed needful to his friends that someone tell the king the upshot of their conversation, and everybody urged someone else to tell the king what he himself did not want to say. They finally solved the problem by putting markers in a cloth and drawing lots to determine who should speak. It was the lot of Sigvatr the skald that came up.[5] Sigvatr had been with King Óláfr for a long time, and now he was in King Magnús's retinue. He composed the poem [*flokkr*] that is called "Bersǫglisvísur" (Unvarnished Verses), and here are some of the stanzas:

*5.   Vask með gram (þeims gumnum   fullkerska sák falla
      goll bauð dróttinhollum)   (fráneggjum sonr gránum
      (nafn fekk hann) (en hrǫfnum   gaf margan val vargi)
      hræ) þess konungs ævi: verðung (konungs sverðum).

"Vask með gram, þeims bauð dróttinhollum gumnum goll en hrǫfnum hræ, ævi þess konungs; hann fekk nafn. Sák fullkerska verðung falla; sonr konungs gaf gránum vargi margan val fráneggjum sverðum."

Throughout his lifetime, I stayed with the lord who gave his faithful liegemen gold and the ravens slaughter; he became famous. I saw the vigorous company fall; with keen-edged swords, the king's son gave the gray wolf the choice of the fallen.

This concerned King Óláfr and told what was known of his great deeds. Then he considered in his verse what he had to say and what course of action he proposed:

*6.   Fylgðak þeim (es fylgju)   vasat á her (með hjǫrvi)
      fémildum gram (vildi)   hlið (þars stóðk í miðjum
      (nú eru þegnar frið fegnir)   hrœsinn) (skal með hrísi)
      feðr þínum vel (mína):   (hans flokki) (við þjokkva).

"Fylgðak þeim fémildum gram, feðr þínum, vel, es vildi fylgju mína; nú eru þegnar fegnir frið. Vasat hlið á her, þars stóðk hrœsinn í miðjum flokki hans með hjǫrvi; við skal þjokkva með hrísi."

I followed your father faithfully, that generous king, who wanted my service; now people rejoice in the peace. There was no gap in the ranks where I stood proudly in the midst of his men with the sword; one should make the forest denser with brush.

*7. Gekk við móð enn mikla   varði hart (en hjǫrtu
     Magnús allt í gǫgnum   hugfull við þat skullu)
     ferð (þars flotnar bǫrðusk)   (Óláfr réð svá) jǫfra
     faðir þinn liði sínu: (FJ 27)   erfðir (framm at hverfa).

"Magnús, faðir þinn gekk við móð enn mikla liði sínu allt í gǫgnum ferð, þars flotnar bǫrðusk. Varði hart jǫfra erfðir, en hugfull hjǫrtu skullu við þat; Óláfr réð svá at hverfa framm."

Magnús, with great courage your father forced his way with his company through the throng where men fought. Fiercely he defended the inheritance of kings, and keen hearts quivered at that; thus Óláfr advanced.

From this point he turned his attention to the most distinguished chieftains in Norway, noting that they held to the laws in dealing with the farmers.

*8. Hét (sás fell á Fitjum)   þjóð helt fast á fóstra
     fjǫlgegn (ok réð hegna   fjǫlblíðs lǫgum síðan
     heiptar rán) (en hánum)   (enn eru af þvís minnir)
     Hákun (firar unnu):   Aðalsteins (búendr seinir).

"Hákun, sás fell á Fitjum, hét fjǫlgegn ok réð hegna heiptar rán, en firar unnu hánum. Síðan helt þjóð fast á lǫgum fjǫlblíðs fóstra Aðalsteins, enn eru búendr seinir af, þvís minnir."

Hákon, who fell at Fitjar, was called the good: he punished hostile looting and people loved him. Later men have maintained the laws of Æthelstan's friendly foster son; the farmers are slow to relinquish what they still remember.

*9. Rétt hykk kjósa knáttu   Haralds arfi lét haldask
     karlfolk ok svá jarla   hvardyggr ok sonr Tryggva
     af þvít eignum lofða   lǫg (þaus lýðir þágu)
     Óláfar frið gáfu: laukjǫfn (at þeim nǫfnum).

"Hykk karlfolk ok svá jarla knáttu kjósa rétt, af þvít Óláfar gáfu frið eignum lofða. Hvardyggr Haralds arfi ok sonr Tryggva lét haldask laukjǫfn lǫg, þaus lýðir þágu at þeim nǫfnum."

I feel that both farmers and jarls chose rightly, because the two Óláfrs brought peace to people's properties. Haraldr's audacious heir and Tryggvi's son upheld the just laws that men received from the two namesakes.

Then it was pointed out that when King Magnús came to Norway, he proceeded peacefully and prudently in all matters, so that people welcomed him with open arms.

*10. Ungr vask með þér þengill   himin þóttusk þá heiðan
      þat haust (es komt austan)   hafa (es landa krafðir
      einn stillir mátt alla   lofðungs burr) (ok lifðir)
      jǫrð hegna (svá fregnisk):   landfolk tekit hǫndum.

"Ungr þengill, vask með þér þat haust, es komt austan; stillir, mátt einn hegna alla jǫrð, svá fregnisk. Landfolk þóttusk þá hafa tekit hǫndum heiðan himin, es krafðir landa, lofðungs burr, ok lifðir."

Young lord, I was with you that autumn when you came from the east; king, you alone can secure the whole country; that will be heard. The countrymen thought they had caught the bright heavens with their hands when you claimed the lands, prince, and were alive.

When Sigvatr had indicated, as is stated here, how much joy the people felt at first when Magnús (FJ 28) came to Norway and what love the people showed for him, and how they had made him responsible for telling the king what had been said and what was important for him to know concerning the treachery of the farmers against the king, saying that he had done the same for his father King Óláfr, he composed the following:

*11. Fǫður Magnúss létk fregna   mál bark hvert af heilum
      folgin jǫfurs dolga   hug (þvít eigi brugðumk)
      orð (þaus eyru heyrðu   (ek vissa þá) (ossum)
      ór) á svik hvé fóru: (ótta) (lánardróttni).

"Létk fǫður Magnúss fregna folgin orð jǫfurs dolga, þaus eyru heyrðu ór; hvé fóru á svik. Bark hvert mál af heilum hug, þvít eigi brugðumk ossum lánardróttni; ek vissa þá ótta."

I let Magnús's father hear the hidden words of the king's enemies that my ears heard; how they plotted deceit. I carried each message with a candid heart, because I did not betray my liege lord; I knew then there was danger.

*12. Skulut ráðgjafar reiðask   hafa kveðask lǫg (nema ljúgi
      (ryðr þat konungr) yðrir   landherr) búendr verri
      (dróttins orð til dýrðar)   endr í Ulfasundum
      dǫglingr við bersǫgli: ǫnnur an þú hézt mǫnnum.

"Dǫglingr, ráðgjafar yðrir skulut reiðask við bersǫgli: þat dróttins orð ryðr til dýrðar, konungr. Búendr kveðask hafa ǫnnur verri lǫg, nema landherr ljúgi, an þú hézt mǫnnum endr í Ulfasundum."

Lord, your counselors must not get enraged at the unvarnished words: that royal command will pave the way for glory, king. The farmers claim they have another and less good law, unless the liegemen lie, than you promised people earlier in Ulfasund [Ulvesund].

Then he asked the king to remember what he promised the people when he first came to Norway. He related the views of the people according to their words, indicating that he was not judged to have kept his word in every respect. He said that his friends were fearful about what would happen and how long the country would be secure if things continued in the same vein.

*13. Gjalt varhuga veltir
    viðr (þeims nú ferr hiðra)
    þjófs (skal hǫnd í hófi)
    hǫlða kytt (of stytta):

vinr emk (varmra benja
vǫrnuð býðk) en hlýðið
(tármútaris teiti)
til hvat búmenn vilja. (FJ 29)

"Veltir þjófs, gjalt varhuga viðr hǫlða kytt, þeims nú ferr hiðra; hǫnd skal of stytta í hófi. Vinr emk: býðk vǫrnuð varmra benja tármútaris teiti, en hlýðið til, hvat búmenn vilja."

Toppler of the thief, beware men's talk that now comes hither; the hand must be measured by moderation. I am a friend: I warn the appeaser of the hawk of the tear of warm wounds [tear of warm wounds = blood; hawk of blood = raven; appeaser of the raven = warrior], but you must heed what the farmers want.

*14. Hverr eggjar þik hǫggva
    hjaldrgegna bú þegna
    ofrausn es þat jǫfri
    innanlands at vinna:

engr hafði svá ungum
áðr bragningi ráðit
rán hykk rekkum þínum
(reiðrs herr konungr) leiðask.

"Hverr eggjar þik hǫggva bú hjaldrgegna þegna? Ofrausn es þat jǫfri at vinna innanlands. Engr hafði áðr ráðit ungum bragningi svá; hykk rekkum þínum leiðask rán; reiðrs herr, konungr."

Who urges you to slay the stock of battle-brave men? It is insolent of a king to harry in his own country. No one had earlier given a young ruler such advice; I think your troops are tired of plunder; people are angry, king.

*15. Hætts (þats allir ætla)
    (áðr skal við því ráða)
    (hárir menn) (es heyrik)
    hót (skjǫldungi at móti):

greypts (þats hǫfðum hneppta)
heldr (ok niðr í feldi)
(slegit hefr þǫgn á þegna)
(þingmenn nǫsum stinga).

"Hætts hót, es heyrik, þats allir hárir menn ætla at móti skjǫldungi, áðr skal ráða við því. Heldr greypts, þats þingmenn hneppta hǫfðum ok stinga nǫsum niðr í feldi; þǫgn hefr slegit á þegna."

It's an impending danger when all mature men, as I hear, intend to rise against the king; we must prevent that. It's rather grim when lawmen hang their heads and cover their noses with their cloak; men are dumbstruck.

*16. Hverr eggjar þik harri
    heiptar strangr at ganga
    (opt rýðr þegnum þýðum
    þunn stál) á bak málum:

fastorðr skyli fyrða
fengsæll vesa þengill
hœfir heit at rjúfa
hjaldrmǫgnuðr þér aldri.

"Hverr eggjar þik, heiptar strangr harri, at ganga á bak málum? Opt rýðr þunn stál þýðum þegnum. Fengsæll fyrða þengill skyli vesa fastorðr; aldri hœfir þér at rjúfa heit, hjaldrmǫgnuðr."

Who urges you, pugnacious lord, to go back on your promises? You frequently redden slender steel for gratified warriors. A prosperous king of the people must be true to his word; it never befits you to break your pledges, battle increaser [warrior].

*17.   Eitt es mál þats mæla   Rán mun seggr (ef sína
       minn dróttinn lét sína   selr út) í því telja
       eign á óðal þegna   (flaums at fellidómi
       ofgask búendr gofgir: foðurleifð konungs greifum).

"Eitt es mál, þats mæla: 'minn dróttinn lét eign sína á óðal þegna.' Gofgir búendr
ofgask. Seggr mun telja rán í því, ef selr út sína foðurleifð konungs greifum at
flaums fellidómi."

Everybody agrees: "my lord appropriated men's ancestral properties." Proud farmers revolt. A man will call it plunder if he parcels out his patrimony to the king's
counts according to precipitate rulings.

"I fear that if it continues in the same way, Magnús will lose the land to the
chieftains." And he recited another stanza:

*18.   Syni Óláfs biðk snúðar   erum Magnús vér vægnir
       (síð kveða aptans bíða   vildak með þér mildum
       óframs sok) (meðal okkar   (Haralds varðar þú hjorvi
       allts háligt) svá mála: haukey) lifa ok deyja.

"Biðk syni Óláfs svá snúðar mála; kveða óframs sok bíða síð aptans; allts háligt
meðal okkar. Magnús, vér erum vægnir; vildak með mildum þér lifa ok deyja; þú
varðar Haralds haukey hjorvi."

I thus hope matters will take a good turn for Óláfr's son; they say that the cautious man's business must wait until late in the evening; between us two all is well.
Magnús, I am well disposed; I wish to live and die with you, generous one; you protect Haraldr's hawk isle [Norway] with the sword.

(FJ 30) Then he noted how much honor King Óláfr had done him when he
was in his retinue:

*19.   Óláfr lét mik jofra   goll bark jafnt of allan
       órýrr framask dýrða   aldr hans (ok vask sjaldan
       (urðu drjúg ens digra   hryggr) á hvárritveggja
       dróttins þing) með hringum: hendi flotna sendis.

"Óláfr, órýrr jofra dýrða, lét mik framask með hringum; ens digra dróttins þing
urðu drjúg. Of allan aldr hans bark jafnt goll flotn sendis á hvárritveggja hendi, ok
vask sjaldan hryggr."

Óláfr, not lacking in lordly splendor, graced me with rings; the dealings of the
stout king were bountiful. Throughout his lifetime, I always bore the gold of the
mover of sea-warriors [war king] on both arms, and I was seldom sad.

And again:

*20.   Sigvats es hugr hizig   fórk með feðrum þeira
       Horðaknúts í garði   (fekk mér ungum tunga
       mildr nema mjok vel skaldi   golls) (vask enn með ollu
       Magnús konungr fagni: óskeggjaðr þá) beggja.

"Sigvats hugr es hizig í garði Horðaknúts, nema mildr Magnús konungr fagni
skaldi mjok vel. Fórk með feðrum þeira beggja; þá vask enn með ollu óskeggjaðr:
tunga fekk mér ungum golls."

Sigvatr's soul will be yonder in Hǫrðaknútr's hall unless generous King Magnús welcomes the skald with great warmth. I followed the fathers of both; I was still totally beardless then: my tongue brought me gold as a youth.

The words of admonition directed to the king in the poem were to the effect that he should observe the laws that his father had established and that he had guaranteed to the people when he came to Norway. He reminded him that he had promised a truce to everyone when he received the royal title, even if they had previously been opposed to his father King Óláfr.

Now the king considered the counsels and admonitions that the skald Sigvatr had couched in the poem. There were also many distinguished men of good will who supported this excellent advice with strong arguments. And because the king was both wise and amenable,[6] he controlled himself despite his strong feelings. (FJ 31) Then a thingmeeting was convened and was attended by many people. At first a rather large number of burdens were imposed on the farmers. Then a man named Atli stood up and said only the following words: "My shoes pinch me so that I can't move from the spot."[7] The king's friends considered these words and what they might mean. Thus the thingmeeting adjourned for that day, and the king asked them all to reconvene the next morning. People seemed to detect in the king's words that God had softened his temper and that harshness had turned to mercy.

The next day people were surprised that the king was so mild and that he addressed his countrymen so gently, the Þrœndir as well as the others. The king promised everyone peace and good will, and he fulfilled the promise better and better as time went on. For that reason he acquired great fame and popularity, and for the second time he reconciled himself with the farmers and forswore the great wrath that he harbored against all of them because they had broken the peace and gone to war against the sainted King Óláfr, his father. From then on King Magnús was so dear to the Norwegians that the people loved him with all their hearts, and he was called Magnús the Good.

4. Concerning King Magnús

King Magnús put Rǫgnvaldr Brúsason in authority to the west in Orkney and gave him the title of jarl. During Magnús's reign great strife broke out between Rǫgnvaldr jarl and Þorfinnr jarl, his uncle, and there were many history-making events, as is told in "The Sagas of the Jarls."[1] With the aid of King Magnús he voyaged westward and had a great and fair following from King Magnús's retinue. He brought the king's letters and seals to Kálfr Árnason to let him know that Kálfr would be welcome in Norway and would regain all his property if he would support Rǫgnvaldr jarl. Kálfr answered that he found it risky to rely on King Magnús's steadfastness. He said that he had made trial of it once before when he had befriended Magnús to the best of his ability but had been slandered so that he could no longer maintain himself. Rǫgnvaldr jarl said: (FJ 32) "You may have heard that the king has once again set aside his case against all the men who combined to dethrone his father, and I can truly state that you will enjoy great honor with the king if you choose to return." Kálfr pretended not to hear what Rǫgnvaldr jarl was saying and drew away from the jarl's ships into a concealed cove not far from the jarl's fleet.

Then Rǫgnvaldr and Þorfinnr joined battle and attacked each other fiercely. Kálfr had a clear view and saw them clash. The engagement was to Rǫgnvaldr jarl's advantage, and many of Þorfinnr's men were killed, while he himself was driven to shore. He saw where Kálfr was concealed and said: "What now, Kálfr, do you value the king's letters more than your kinship with me? Show your courage and join in to support us."

Kálfr said: "It will be as you ask, but I wanted to establish how important it was to you which side I chose."

Kálfr now entered the battle with Þorfinnr, and there were great losses on both sides. In that engagement Rǫgnvaldr attacked so vigorously that his ship ran up onto Þorfinnr's ships, so that Rǫgnvaldr found himself firmly stuck. Þorfinnr and his men attacked him, but Rǫgnvaldr jarl made his escape onto another ship and fled. Then the fleets separated. The battle was fought at Rauðabjǫrg.[2] We can report that after the battle, Kálfr harried widely and became a great viking.

Next we are told that at one time King Magnús was sailing along the coast. According to Arnórr jarlaskald:

*21. Síðan vas þats suðr með láði   samnask bað til hverrar hǫmlu
      siklingr ýtti flota miklum   (hræðask menn við ættarklæði
      skíði vas þá skriðar of auðit   Gjúka) (þótti gǫfugt eiki
      skorðu (renndi Visundr norðan):   gerzkum malmi) Peitu hjalma.

"Síðan vas, þats siklingr ýtti miklum flota suðr með láði; skíði skorðu vas þá of auðit skriðar; Visundr renndi norðan. Bað Peitu hjalma samnask til hverrar hǫmlu; menn hræðask við ættarklæði Gjúka; eiki þótti gǫfugt gerzkum malmi."

Later the king set out south along the coast with a large fleet; then the ski of the ship prop [ship] was granted speed; Visundr [bison] swept southward. He commanded the helmets from Poitou [warriors] to man every rowing station; men were alarmed by the ancestral garments of Gjúki [legendary king, armor]; the ship was splendidly adorned with Russian steel.

*22. Ljótu varp á lypting útan   stirðum helt fyr Stafangr norðan
      lauðri (bifðisk goll et rauða) (FJ 33) stálum (bifðusk fýris álar)
      fastligr hneigði furu geystri   uppi glóðu élmars typpi
      fýris angr ok skeiðar stýri: eldi glík í Danaveldi.

"Ljótu lauðri varp á lypting útan; goll et rauða bifðisk; fastligr fýris angr hneigði geystri furu ok skeiðar stýri. Helt stirðum stálum norðan fyr Stafangr; fýris álar bifðusk; élmars typpi glóðu uppi, eldi glík, í Danaveldi."

The horrible sea spray splashed onto the deck; the red gold trembled; the relentless grief of pine wood [wind] submerged the swift-moving ship and the ship's rudder. You steered the stiff prows south past Stafangr [Stavanger], the eels of pine [ships] trembled; the mast tops of the storm steed [ship] glowed like fire in the realm of the Danes. ·

Here there is some reference to his campaigns. The king arrived in the Limafjǫrðr (Limfjord) with his troops, and when Hǫrðaknútr learned of that, he immediately came out to meet him with a great company, with music, elegance, and pomp. He invited King Magnús to his court, and Magnús accepted. Everyone joined together to make the journey to King Hǫrðaknútr's court. When they came to the hall, King Knútr said to King Magnús: "You should enter before me, sir, and have precedence in all honor and service."[3]

King Magnús said: "I see exactly where this is headed. When I am in Norway and you come to visit me, I will enter first and take precedence in all honor and service, but now that I have come here, it is up to you to go first, sit first, drink first, and have precedence in all matters pertaining to honor and service. For it seems most likely to me that both peoples will be most attached to their own king, and it will cause no envy on either side if it is done in this way." Hákon [*sic;* F: Knútr][4] said that it was up to him, then went in and sat on the high seat with King Magnús next to him.

Then Álfífa entered the hall and welcomed King Magnús warmly, saying that she wished to honor him in every way. She poured for him and asked him to drink. King Magnús said: "Hákon [Knútr] should drink first and have precedence in every form of service." Then she gave the horn to Hákon [Knútr], and he drank it off, exclaiming, as he cast the horn aside, "shouldn't have," but he got no further and gave his death groan.[5] This demonstrated Álfífa's treachery toward King Magnús because she intended the fatal drink for him. But she (FJ 34) vanished instantly so that she could not be punished.

· This event took place in the sixth year of King Magnús's reign. It was the death of Hákon [Knútr], who had become king of both Denmark and England.[6] Two years earlier his brother King Haraldr had died west in England. He was the son of King Knútr the Great, and at that time the brothers had succeeded to the throne after their father. After Haraldr's death, Hákon [Knútr] became heir to England and ruled both countries for two years. But the same spring that Hákon [Knútr] died Edward the Good (Confessor) became king. He was the son of Ethelred by the same mother. Their mother was Emma, the daughter of Richard, Duke of Rouen, and the sister of Robert Longspear, the father of Duke William the Bastard. Edward was anointed king the first day of Easter.

King Magnús sailed home to Norway from the feast that had been planned in this way. One day as he sat in his hall and people were talking about recent events, the tables were removed and the king stood up to speak: "As God and Saint Óláfr are my witnesses, I shall now assume power in Denmark according to the agreement with King Hákon [Knútr], or die in the attempt." In the words of Arnórr:

*23. Afkárlig varð árla   at framm í gný grimmum
      orðgnótt (sús hlaut dróttinn)   grafnings und kló hrafni
      fylgði efnð þvís ylgjar   fúss lézk falla ræsir
      angrtælir réð mæla: feigr eða Danmǫrk eiga.

"Orðgnótt, sús dróttinn hlaut, varð árla afkárlig; efnð fylgði, þvís ylgjar angrtælir réð mæla: at ræsir lézk fúss falla framm feigr und kló hrafni í grimmum grafnings gný eða eiga Danmǫrk."

The eloquence allotted to the king soon became sincere; the oath that the destroyer of the she-wolf's grief [hunger, warrior] swore was fulfilled when the king declared himself ready to fall, doomed, beneath the raven's claw in the raging din of the shield [battle], or else conquer Denmark.

That summer King Magnús went south to Denmark with a great company and traveled throughout the country. He cultivated the people and made his dispositions with due regard for law and decency. Then he sailed to Vébjǫrg and convened a thingmeeting. At that meeting he was accepted as king of all Denmark, and no one spoke against him. He then proceeded through the realm and appointed chieftains to share his rule, and he stayed in Denmark through the winter. As Arnórr said: (FJ 35)

*24. Náði siklingr síðan   engr hefr annarr þengill
      snjallr ok Danmǫrk allri   áðr svá gnógu láði
      (máttr óx drengja dróttins   (bráskat bragnings þroski)
      dýrr) Nóregi at stýra: barnungr und sik þrungit.

"Snjallr siklingr náði síðan at stýra Nóregi ok allri Danmǫrk; dýrr máttr drengja dróttins óx. Engr annarr þengill hefr áðr þrungit und sik svá gnógu láði barnungr; bráskat bragnings þroski."

The daring king later came to rule Norway and all of Denmark; the precious power of the lord of men increased. No other king previously forced so much land under his yoke at an early age; the ruler's fitness did not fail.

Mention is made of King Magnús's voyage from Norway to Jutland when he [Arnórr] recited this stanza:

*25. Segja munk hvé Sygna   setti blíðr at breiðu
      snarfengjan bar þengil   (brynþings meginhringa
      (hallr vas hrími sollinn   fús tók ǫld við œsi)
      hléborðs) Visundr norðan: Jótlandi gramr branda.

"Munk segja, hvé Visundr bar snarfengjan Sygna þengil norðan; hallr hléborðs vas hrími sollinn. Blíðr gramr setti branda at breiðu Jótlandi; ǫld tók fús við œsi brynþings meginhringa."

I shall recount how Visundr [bison] carried the resourceful king of the Sygnir [people of Sogn] to the south; the slope of the sea board [ship side] was bulging with frost. The benevolent king set the prows toward broad Jótland [Jylland, Jutland]; eagerly the people received the wielder of the mighty swords of the byrnie assembly [battle, battle sword, warrior].

The third summer he returned to Norway. As he lay anchored in the Elfr (Götaälv) by Konungahella, a young gentleman from Gautland came to him. The man's name was Sveinn, and he was the son of Jarl Úlfr sprakaleggr and the lady Ástríðr, who was the sister of two kings, Knútr the Great and Óláfr the Swede.[7] Her father was King Sveinn Forkbeard and her mother was Sigríðr en stórráða (the Imperious), who had previously been married to King Eiríkr enn sigrsæli (the Victorious).

Sveinn had been in Sweden for some time with his kinsman King Ǫnundr Óláfsson. Sveinn made diplomatic overtures and gained the friendship of King Magnús. He sought some form of honorable appointment, for example, that Magnús might give him the sort of fief to which his birth entitled him, because his father Úlfr had been a jarl in Denmark, but Sveinn had received no compensation from King Knútr for the killing of his father. He now promised King Magnús to be wholly devoted to him if he would honor him with some fief to administer, though he did not press the point aggressively. King Magnús heeded Sveinn's words and judged that he was a wise man and worthy in appearance. (FJ 36) He thought that his loyalty and friendship would be in line with his appearance. King Magnús therefore took him into his following, and he stayed with the king for some time.

One day when they were drinking together, the king gave him his cloak, which was cut from the most precious material, and along with it a bowl of mead, with which he asked him to drink a toast. "And herewith," said the king, "I will give you the title of 'jarl' and that part of Denmark that I desire to delegate when I come there." Sveinn took the cloak but did not put it on. He gave it immediately to one of his men and turned bright crimson. But he himself put on an Icelandic fur cloak. When Einarr þambarskelfir saw that, he said, "Too great a jarl, too great a jarl, foster son."[8]

The king replied angrily: "You think I have precious little judgment and no knowledge of men since you think some are too great to be jarls and some not enough to be men." Einarr let the matter go and said no more.

But the next day before mass was sung, the king took a reliquary with the holy relics in it and bade Jarl Sveinn step up and swear an oath of fidelity to him. He did as the king requested. When the jarl laid his hands on the reliquary, King Magnús formulated the oath to the effect that he should be faithful to the king, increase his authority in every way and diminish it in none, and that he should be faithful and subject to him in all things as long as they both lived. Hence the skald's stanza:

*26. Sjalfr vas austr í Elfi   réð Óláfs sonr eiðum
     Ulfs mǫgr ok hét fǫgru   (átt hafa þeira sáttir
     þar réð Sveinn at sverja   skemmra aldr an skyldi)
     sínar hendr at skríni: Skánunga gramr hánum.

"Ulfs mǫgr vas sjalfr austr í Elfi ok hét fǫgru; þar réð Sveinn at sverja sínar hendr at skríni. Óláfs sonr, Skánunga gramr, réð hánum eiðum; þeira sáttir hafa átt skemmra aldr an skyldi."

Ulfr's son was east in Elfr [Götaälv] in person and made fair pledges; there Sveinn swore his fidelity on the reliquary. Óláfr's son, the king of the Skánungar [people of Skåne, Scania], formulated his oaths; their settlement had a shorter life than it should have.

After that Jarl Sveinn stayed with King Magnús. When the summer was coming to an end, they traveled south to Denmark, and King Magnús transferred power and authority to the jarl (FJ 37) in Jutland, where the power of all Denmark is centered. It is farthest from the Norwegian realm and closest to the Wends and Saxons, who have always waged war on the Danes. Then King Magnús returned to Norway and stayed in Niðaróss during the winter. He celebrated Christmas there. King Magnús possessed a ship that his father had owned and commanded, and which was called Visundr (Bison).[9] It was a ship that King Óláfr was accustomed to sail everywhere if he did not travel by land.

Concerning Jarl Sveinn it can now be related that after Christmas in Vébjǫrg he convened a thingmeeting. He made a speech in which he said that it would not be unfitting for the Danes to serve him rather than the king of the Norwegians, "for my origins and family are here, as you know, and my nature and temper are familiar to everyone. It is difficult to serve under a Norwegian king, even though it may be, as everyone knows, that he is a good king. I therefore wish to ask for my ancestral name and be king in Denmark. In return I will promise you my support and, in addition, gifts and my full affection." At that thingmeeting the Danes gave him the title of king, and Sveinn took possession of the visitation rights and tax collections over most of Denmark.

King Magnús learned of the news at the beginning of spring. During the summer he summoned half the levy in Norway with arms and provisions and sailed south to Denmark at the beginning of summer. When King Sveinn learned that, he had no confidence in his forces and left the country. He went into Sweden to meet his kinsman King Ǫnundr and raised troops during the summer. When King Magnús arrived in Denmark, he punished the Danes for having taken another king, and he fined many. Some fled their property and left the country. Some he had killed. Then he sailed across to Wendland and arrived with his army at Jóm (Wollin). There they landed, harrying and burning both settlements and people. They wreaked great destruction and accomplished great deeds.[10] As Arnórr says:

*27.   Vann (þás Vinðr of minnir)   búk dró bráðla steiktan
       vápnhríð konungr síðan (FJ 38)   blóðugr vargr af glóðum
       sveið of ám at Jómi   rann á óskírð enni
       illvirkja hræ stillir: allfrekr bani hallar.

"Konungr vann síðan vápnhríð, þás Vinðr of minnir; stillir sveið of ám illvirkja hræ at Jómi. Blóðugr vargr dró bráðla steiktan búk af glóðum; allfrekr bani hallar rann á óskírð enni."

Later the king launched a weapon storm [battle] that the Wends will remember; the lord scorched rust-red corpses of pirates at Wollin. The bloody wolf pulled the

fast-fried body from the fires; the greedy slayer of the hall [fire] flickered on heathen foreheads.

Then King Magnús led his army back to Denmark. When they arrived at Ré
(Rügen) in Vestland, they encountered a great number of large viking ships,
and they joined battle immediately.[11] The victory went to King Magnús. According to the skald's stanza:

> *28. Fúss lét á Ré ræsir
> rammþing háit Glamma
> virðum rauð fyr víðu
> Vinðlandi gramr branda.

"Fúss ræsir lét háit Glamma rammþing á Ré; gramr rauð branda virðum fyr víðu
Vinðlandi."

The ready ruler held a powerful assembly of Glammi [sea king, battle] in Rügen;
the lord reddened swords on warriors off wide Wendland.

When King Magnús came to Smálǫnd (the Danish Islands), he sent the Norwegians home, but he himself stayed behind.

5. Concerning the Declaration of War against King Magnús and Concerning the Duke

That same autumn, when King Magnús was in Jutland, he received word that
a Wendish army was marching against him with the justification of taking revenge. Without delay King Magnús levied troops throughout Denmark and
marched against the Wends night and day at top speed. He did so because he
was told that the Wendish army was proceeding without restraint, burning and
wasting as soon as it entered King Magnús's realm.

King Magnús met them south of Skotborg River (Kongeå), and here the
story must be suspended because not everything can be told at once.[1] King
Magnús was troubled because the discrepancy in numbers was great. Indeed,
it is said that the advantage was no less than sixty to one, but the king refused
to retreat on any account. There was nonetheless a very apprehensive feeling
among the Danes, and they thought they were headed for a fall.

At another point the story relates that there was a powerful duke named Otto
south in Saxony, a man of enormous wealth. He was a kinsman of the emperor's, as well as being his foster son and long-standing friend.[2] He was a
valiant man (FJ 39) and a great warrior, so that his match could scarcely be
found. King Magnús had a sister in Norway whose name was Úlfhildr. She was
the daughter of King Óláfr, a fair woman in appearance and highly intelligent.
Once when Duke Otto and the emperor, his kinsman, were in conversation, the
emperor spoke as follows: "I intend to send you north to Norway to meet with
her brother King Magnús and ask them for her hand in marriage, provided that
the woman seems to you to live up to her reputation and the marriage seems

to be an honorable one for me." The duke said that he would undertake any trip the emperor proposed.

After that he sailed to Norway and arrived in Vík. King Magnús was not in residence, but Álfífa was there in Vík and prepared a banquet for the duke because he was a very wise and distinguished man. One day as they were drinking, the duke asked Álfífa whether King Magnús's sister was there in her house. Álfífa said that she most certainly was. The duke said that he would like to see her, and Álfífa made no objection. One day at table Álfífa had her daughter decked out with great splendor. She was not King Sveinn's sister by the same father. When the duke went to table, this girl sat next to him, with no lack of gold and precious ornaments, not unlike a god set out on an altar.[3] The duke looked at her for a time and conversed with her, judging that neither her speech nor her intelligence was outstanding, and that she was not so fair as he had thought or had been told. He therefore made no mention of his mission and did not think that this marriage was fitting for the king. But Álfífa presented her as King Magnús's sister.

The duke returned home unimpressed by the woman. And when he met with the emperor, he told him about his mission and said that the woman amounted to much less than they thought. The emperor said: "In gratitude for your good will and for the sake of our friendship and kinship I wish to send you again to ask for her hand, this time for yourself on the strength of my request. It may be that the king will grant (FJ 40) you this marriage if I ask him. Even if you did not find the woman to be what you expected or what we had been led to believe, still it seems to me that most people would judge it to be an honorable marriage because it confers kinship first of all with Saint Óláfr and secondly with her brother King Magnús."

The duke set out on a second trip. When he arrived in Norway, King Magnús was there. They met and the king welcomed him warmly because he had heard many good things that redounded to his credit. When the duke and king conversed over drink, the duke asked if the king had any sisters by the same father.

"Indeed," said the king, "I have a sister named Ragnhildr, the daughter of King Óláfr."[4]

The duke said: "I would like you to permit me to see and speak with her."

"I will certainly permit that," said the king.

The next day King Magnús and Duke Otto went to the place where she sat at drink. She stood up to greet her brother and the duke. The duke sat by her, and as they conversed, he quickly realized that this woman was far superior to the previous one, who was also presented as King Magnús's sister, both in intelligence and beauty. When he had talked to her for the length of time that suited him, he and the king took their leave. The duke realized that he had been tricked and that Álfífa had intended to deceive him with respect to the marriage if he had not been on his guard. He took counsel with himself about whether he should woo her for himself or the emperor. He could see that the emperor would find the woman suitable for himself in every way, but still he chose to woo her on his own behalf on the emperor's authority.

King Magnús responded by saying that an equal match for her would be long in coming and that it was uncertain whether her marriage could wait that long. "But if the court and my mother agree, the proposal is worth considering, for we have heard many excellent and noteworthy things about you."

The duke now sought out the princess (FJ 41) and the king assiduously, and many great chieftains supported him. He recommended himself with gifts and demonstrations of friendship for the people. Eventually the king acceded, and Úlfhildr was married to him with great pomp. Then they went south to Saxony to the fortified towns that he controlled. He was an exceedingly wealthy man, both very generous and very courageous.

The duke did not go to meet with his kinsman the emperor or pay visits to him or his men, but kept to himself at home. The emperor sent messengers to Duke Otto and issued a friendly invitation, saying that he wished to meet with him. But the duke said that he was much preoccupied and could not make the trip just then because of the difficulties in which his people found themselves. He said that great hostilities had broken out in his realm. The messengers who had been sent out now returned and told the king what the situation was.[5]

We are told that one evening the duke was sitting with his friends in the hall, and Úlfhildr was sitting beside him in the high seat. They thought they saw a man entering the hall door with a Danish hat on. He went forward to the high seat, then back out without saying a word.

The duke addressed the duchess: "Did you recognize that man, princess?"

She replied: "Shall I tell your grace what I think?"

"You should do so with my permission," he said.

She replied: "It looked like my father's beard where the shadow from the hat ended on the lower face, and it may be that my brother Magnús is in need of your assistance."

Duke Otto had just recently left the battlefield and was severely wounded, with the wounds not yet healed, but he said right away: "We must give King Magnús such assistance as we have available or can muster."

The princess said: "You are not in a very sound state just now, lord, unless my father Saint Óláfr should heal you more quickly than seems likely."

"That should be no impediment," he said, "and I have every confidence that I will suffer no harm if what you say is true and Saint Óláfr himself was here." He jumped up from his seat and bade the knights (FJ 42) arm themselves as quickly as possible. Then the princess took a belt that had belonged to King Óláfr and placed it on the duke's wounds. It immediately healed all the injuries, and he never again experienced pain from these wounds.

Duke Otto then proceeded with his forces until he reached King Magnús on Hlýrskógsheiðr (Lyrskovshede). The king received his brother-in-law with every attention and was overjoyed that he had come. The pagans, as already indicated, had a huge army, so that there was a great discrepancy in numbers and great unrest among the Danes, who said that their king was heading them for disaster. For this reason the king was grieved and pitied the dismay that he observed in his men. But he said that he would never retreat as long as there was anyone to follow him and support his view. He thought the prospects were better now that Duke Otto had come to lend assistance.

King Magnús was accompanied by Einarr þambarskelfir, his foster father. He spoke to the king and advised him to pay close attention to what the Danes were thinking, "because you are very dependent on the help they give you."

One evening the king and Einarr adopted the device of circulating secretly among the soldiers in disguise.[6] The soldiers did not recognize them in their changed appearance. They heard one of the Danes saying the following words: "Where do they intend to fight?"

Another said: "I know exactly—here by the river."

Then the first one said: "I would like to be close to the woods. Then those who want to fight can fight, and those who are afraid can hide."

Then Einarr said to the king: "There you can hear, lord, that this Dane speaks for many others. It would be my advice to draw up the army in such a way that they cannot reach the woods as quickly as they would like." The king said that it would be done accordingly.

At a short distance from that place there was a little farm. Einarr suggested to the king that they go there and arrange that the farmer suffer no injury because he was a poor man. They did so. The farmer gave them a warm welcome and served good wine. After that the king lay down and quickly fell asleep. He immediately experienced a dream or some similar revelation. He thought he saw his father on a white horse, and he thought that his father addressed him: "Get up quickly and marshal your army. It is sufficient to do battle (FJ 43) against the pagans because I will fight on your side. When you hear Glǫð ring north in Þrándheimr, you need wait no longer, for that will be my signal trumpet today."[7] After that the king awoke and told his foster father Einarr that they had been promised victory, and he said that their path to the farmer's house had been a propitious one. Then they returned to the army and saw that the men lay covered by their shields. The king bade them arise.

There was a man named Oddr Gellisson with the king.[8] He told some parts of these events. The duke urged the king to fight and said that he had a good feeling that they would be victorious. The army spent the night in arms on Hlýrskógsheiðr because the army of the Wends could be expected from any direction. King Magnús now called aloud and ordered the men to get up: "We will win the victory because Saint Óláfr will go into battle with us." At that moment they all heard the sound of bells in the heavens above them, and Magnús, together with all the Norwegians, recognized that the sound was like the one in Glǫð north in Þrándheimr. With that the army shed any sign of fear and everyone reflected on these miracles. None feared for his life no matter how many pagans there were.

King Magnús stripped off his chainmail and wore nothing but a silken shirt. He had an ax in his hand, which his father had owned and which was called Hel.[9] In the midst of this tumult a farmer came forward among the men and said that he had business with the king. Some of the men jostled him, and others pushed him toward the king and cleared the way for him. Einarr recognized the man and gave him leave to proceed.

When the farmer came before the king, the king said, "What is your wish, farmer?"

He said: "I wish to tell you my dream. I thought I saw King Óláfr riding on a white horse in his full royal robes. He said he would lend you assistance and instructed you to draw up a long battle line with the deepest ranks in the center. He said that you should station yourself there and that you should let your wings encircle the Wendish formation so that they (FJ 44) will be unable to escape. He said he would show his banner before the army, and lest you have any doubt about my report, I have true tokens to confirm it." With that he showed the king tokens that he could not fail to recognize. The king was greatly cheered and gave the farmer a large reward.

King Magnús assigned his brother-in-law Otto together with his troops to one wing, but he himself remained in the center as his father had instructed. There was a man in the Wendish army who wanted to join battle in the evening, and he opened the engagement. He is described as very big and strong, with magical powers that made him invulnerable to steel.[10] He advanced so fiercely against King Magnús's battle formation that it could not withstand him. He hewed to the left and right and gave many men a quick death. He laid low whatever he encountered and demanded to know where the king of the Norwegians was.

Then a certain man addressed the king. He was tall in stature, handsome, and somewhat up in years. "Why do you let this foe slaughter your men like cattle?"

"Is there somebody who can put a stop to it?" asked the king.

Then the elderly man replied: "You left home at the head of a great army before you could foresee everything that lay in store for you."

The king said: "It may be as you say, but I will take any good advice you have to give me."

The man said: "Aim your ax Hel at him with my help."

The man then placed himself before the king and struck a great blow on the champion's helmet so that he toppled before him. He wore a short mailcoat, which now slipped off him. Beneath it the king delivered a blow with the ax Hel, and it almost cut the man in half.

The pagans who had previously been most forward now sought to pull back, but the king did not wait for the banners, and a great slaughter ensued. The Wends were chased down to the river, and King Magnús pursued them with his troops so that the Wends fell like underbrush being cleared. King Magnús hewed with both hands gripping his ax Hel. He wore neither helmet nor chain mail nor any protective arms. When the Wends came to the river, they put up some resistance and fought for a while. Then King Magnús enveloped them with the wings of his army, and it ended (FJ 45) with their being driven into the river so that their formation was broken by slaughter. The king pursued with his troops, and the slaughter was so great that the report will seem hard to credit when it is told that the heaps of slain in the river were so high and dense that it was possible to step from corpse to corpse and thus cross the river.[11]

The king and Duke Otto thus pressed the rout. It is told that the device on which the Wends had counted turned to their greatest disadvantage. They had placed many oxen in the forward ranks with spears tied on their back and blinders before their eyes, but the cattle advanced a little, then turned back on their own men so that they were trapped beneath the herd of oxen and in the very midst of King Magnús's army.[12] Thus they suffered huge loss of life. The ones who did not lose their lives escaped by flight.

King Magnús now pressed his pursuit of the Wends, not waiting for the standards, and he hewed left and right, slaughtering men like cattle, but the army lagged behind. He pressed ahead so hard by himself that no one could keep pace with him, though some people recount that he had twelve companions and failed to notice that he had distanced himself so far from the army. When he had proceeded thus for a while, he realized how incautious it was. He returned to his army, and everyone was overjoyed to see him, since they had feared his fall greatly. King Magnús thanked his brother-in-law warmly for his support, and all his men as well. It was the consensus of the Wends who escaped that if everyone had fought like the handsome man in the silken shirt, not a man would have escaped. There is the following stanza about the battle:

*29.   Minn vá sigr fyr sunnan   unði ótal Vinða
       snjallr (Heiðabý) spjalli   Ellu konr at fella
       (nær frák skarpa skœru)   hvar hafi gumnar gǫrva
       Skotborgará gotna: geirhríð fregit meiri. (FJ 46)

"Minn snjallr spjalli gotna vá sigr fyr sunnan Skotborgará; frák skarpa skœru nær Heiðabý. Ellu konr unði at fella ótal Vinða; hvar hafi gumnar fregit gǫrva meiri geirhríð?"

My valiant friend of warriors [king] was victorious south of the Skotborgará [Kongeå]; I heard of a hard skirmish near Heiðabýr [Hedeby]. Ella's kinsman [Magnús] took pleasure in killing countless Wends; where have men heard of a greater spear storm [battle]?

Then they shared out the spoils of battle, and from the great treasure the king took several rings. That was the only time his desire for wealth was evident, but he also distributed great wealth to many others. He asked those men who had given him good counsel to visit him, saying that he would reward them when he returned to Norway. They fought this battle on the eve of Michaelmas, and they had not fought long when the enemy ranks broke.[13] King Magnús's troops were so widely dispersed in the pursuit that for several miles the slaughter was so thick that every brook and stream was blocked up and diverted from its course. No one knew how many heathens fell. According to Sigvatr:

*30. Hykk í hundraðsflokki   vítt lá Vinða flótti
       Haralds bróðurson stóðu   varð (þars Magnús barðisk)
       (hrafn vissi sér hvassast   hǫggvinn valr at hylia
       hungrbann) framast manna: heiði rastar breiða.

"Hykk Haralds bróðurson stóðu framast manna í hundraðsflokki; hrafn vissi sér hvassast hungrbann. Vinða flótti lá vítt; hǫggvinn valr varð at hylja heiði rastar breiða, þars Magnús barðisk."

I believe Haraldr's nephew stood foremost of all men in the mighty army; the raven knew its hunger would be sated most rapidly. The Wends who had fled lay scattered far and wide; the sundered corpses of the fallen covered the heath for miles where Magnús fought.

This was the greatest battle in the North, both with respect to casualties and especially in light of the great miracles performed by Saint Óláfr, enabling such a small force to overcome such a great army with the loss of only a few men who could not be healed. The king himself exposed himself to the weapons of the pagans without armor, and no one dared to attack him, protected as he was by God's mercy and his father's intercession. In Arnórr's words:

*31. Óð með øxi breiða   þás of skapt (en skipti
       ódæsinn framm ræsir   skapvǫrðr himins jǫrðu) (FJ 47)
       (varð of hilmi Hǫrða   (Hel klauf hausa fǫlva)
       hjǫrdynr) ok varp brynju: hendr tvær jǫfurr spenndi.

"Ódæsinn ræsir óð framm með breiða øxi ok varp brynju; hjǫrdynr varð of hilmi Hǫrða, þás jǫfurr spenndi hendr tvær of skapt, en skapvǫrðr himins skipti jǫrðu; Hel klauf fǫlva hausa."

The indefatigable king pressed on with the broad ax and shed his byrnie; sword din [battle] erupted around the lord of the Hǫrðar [people of Hordaland] when the king tightened both hands around the ax haft and the native ruler of heaven allotted land; Hel split pale skulls.

He goes on to say:

*32. Skjǫldungr lézt við skíra valdit   vári lá þar valkǫstr hæri
       Skotborgará Vinða sorgum   (vas þér sigr skapaðr) grams ens digra
       yngvi vas sá frægr es fenguð   virðum kunnr an víða runnin
       fǫrnuðr þinn við helming minna: varga ætt of klífa mætti.

"Skjǫldungr, lézt valdit Vinða sorgum við skíra Skotborgará; yngvi, sá fǫrnuðr þinn,

es fenguð við helming minna, vas frægr. Vári grams ens digra, virðum kunnr, þar
lá valkǫstr hæri an víða runnin varga ætt mætti of klífa; sigr vas þér skapaðr."
King, you caused the Wends distress by the clear Skotborgará [Kongeå]; lord, the
fortune you achieved with half the troops was famed. Relative of the stout king,
famous among men, there lay a corpse heap higher than the far-traveled family of
wolves could climb; you were victorious.

And again:

*33.   Svá hlóð siklingr hávan   at áleggjar Yggjar
        snarr af ulfa barri   allnáttfǫrull máttit
        (hrósak hugfulls vísa)   (ǫld lá vítt) (þótt vildi)
        hrækǫst (fira ævi):   vífs marr yfir klífa.

"Snarr siklingr hlóð svá hávan hrækǫst af ulfa barri—hrósak ævi hugfulls vísa
fira—at allnáttfǫrull marr áleggjar Yggjar vífs máttit klífa yfir, þótt vildi; ǫld lá vítt."
The courageous king stacked a corpse pile from wolves' food so high—I praise the
life of that brave lord of the people—that the steed of the wife of Yggr [Óðinn] of
the river bone ["Óðinn of the river bone [stone]" = giant; "wife of the giant" =
giantess; "steed of the giantess" = wolf], wandering all night, could not climb over
it, even if it wanted; fallen men were spread far and wide.

The brothers-in-law now parted. Duke Otto went home to Saxony and remained in his realm. When the emperor realized that the duke did not intend
to visit him, he sent men to him a second time with the message that he would
visit him on his rounds and that Otto should prepare to receive him. When the
messengers delivered this communication, it was easy to see that it did not
please the duke greatly. He was not keen on the prospect but prepared the reception all the same. The emperor came at the appointed time. When he saw
the princess, he was deeply impressed by her beauty and courtliness, and it
seemed to him that the duke had given a wrong account of her. The emperor
became rather dejected, and that was quickly apparent to the duke because he
served at table. The rest of the people followed their leader's example and also
became downcast.

In the evening when the duke and the princess (FJ 48) went to bed, she
asked him what the emperor's dejection could mean: "I thought it would be a
friendly gathering when you and your kinsman met, because you told me that
the two of you were very affectionate and that there was no one to whom you
attached greater importance than the emperor. Now tell me if it is true, as I
suspect, that I am somehow involved and that you have not conducted matters
in a way altogether pleasing to him. I may not have been so fortunate as to get
the marriage originally intended, and that may be in part your doing. Even if
this is the case, I advise you to approach him tomorrow and ask why he is so
unhappy. Though the emperor may respond to your words harshly, you should
nevertheless be gentle and kind to him and place the whole matter, both as it
pertains to you and to me, in his hands. If he is well disposed, as I surmise, you
will benefit from it, because I believe him to be a distinguished man. If he does

otherwise, it is still up to him, and he is likely to have his way in any event. My approach will therefore serve you best."

He said that he had done as she supposed—"and in all likelihood it is best to follow the advice you offer."

In the morning he broached the topic with the emperor and said: "Why are you so taciturn, lord? We wanted to arrange this reception for you with the greatest friendship and affection, as our duty dictates."

The emperor replied: "It is strange indeed that you have become so arrogant that you should ask about this when you have betrayed me."

The duke answered: "This is a sorry state of affairs. You sent me to King Magnús in Norway to ask for the hand of his sister on your behalf. But at that time I did not meet with King Magnús because he was abroad. I was shown a girl and was told that it was his sister, but she did not seem to me worthy of your rank, either in intelligence or appearance. With that I returned and told you exactly how things stood. Then you sent me a second time to woo her for myself. When I came to Norway this time (FJ 49), I met with King Magnús and saw this woman. At the time, lord, it struck me that it would be grievous to forgo this marriage, all the more so because you had granted your permission. Now I beseech your mercy and God's because it came about in this way. I place both my affairs and those of the princess in your hands."

After a while the emperor said: "I have the feeling that it happened in this way because God is content that you should enjoy this treasure. I also suspect that I have exercised my rule as long as the joy of it lasted. Given your situation, I wish to confer the whole realm and the imperial title and all the attendant honors on you. I will join those who abandon the life of this world and accept what God's mercy allots to them." We are told that Otto now became emperor in Saxony.[14] He and the princess had a son named Magnús, who was a most handsome man. The man who had been emperor did exactly as he had promised, and that is the end of the story.

6. King Magnús in Jutland

King Magnús Óláfsson spent the winter in Jutland. The following summer Jarl Sveinn came to Denmark with a fleet, and King Magnús went out to meet him. They met at Helganes (Helgenæs) and immediately joined battle.[1] The battle lasted the whole night and ended with Sveinn's rout. He got away onto the land with all those who escaped with their lives, but all the ships were lost and the greater part of the army was killed. In Arnórr's words:

*34. Dǫrr lét drengja harri   létat hilmir hneiti
      drjúgspakr af þrek fljúga   Hǫgna veðr í gǫgnum
      (glœddi eldr af oddum)   (jǫrn flugu þykkt sem þyrnir)
      almi skept á hjalma: þél harðara sparðan. (FJ 50)

"Drjúgspakr drengja harri lét fljúga dǫrr, almi skept, á hjalma af þrek; eldr glœddi
af oddum. Hilmir létat sparðan hneiti, þél harðara, í gǫgnum Hǫgna veðr; jǫrn
flugu þykkt sem þyrnir."

The shrewd lord of the people vigorously loosed elm-shafted spears against the
helmets; fire sparked from the spear points. The king did not spare the sword,
harder than a file, throughout Hǫgni's [legendary king] storm [battle]; steel flew
as thickly as thorns.

*35.   Hizig laut (es heitir   mætr helt mǫrgu spjóti
       Helganes) fyr kesjum   Mœra gramr í snœri
       (sukku sárir rekkar)   odd rauð aski studdan
       Sveins ferð (bana verðir):   ǫrr landreki dǫrrum.

"Sveins ferð laut fyr kesjum hizig, es heitir Helganes; bana verðir rekkar sukku
sárir. Mætr Mœra gramr helt mǫrgu spjóti í snœri; ǫrr landreki rauð aski studdan
odd dǫrrum."

Sveinn's troops fell before the spears yonder at the place called Helganes [Hel-
genæs]; doomed warriors sank down wounded. The glorious king of the Mœrir
[people of Møre] held the strap of many a spear; the brave ruler reddened the ash-
shafted spear point.

*36.   Uppgǫngu vann yngvi
       ítrlógandi gnóga
       (gerði hilmir Hǫrða
       hjǫrþey) á Skáneyju.

"Ítrlógandi yngvi vann gnóga uppgǫngu á Skáneyju; hilmir Hǫrða gerði hjǫrþey."
The king, the famous spender, pushed far into Skáney [Skåne, Scania]; the lord of
the Hǫrðar [people of Hordaland] raised a sword breeze [battle].

This battle was also mentioned by the skald who stated:

*37.   Keppinn vannt (þats æ mun uppi)   yngvi fekktu ǫll með hringum
       Yggjar veðr (meðan heimrinn byggvisk)   (jarl vissi sik foldar missa)
       (valgammr skók í vápna rimmu)   þjóðum kunnr (en þú tókt síðan)
       viðr Helganes (blóðugt fiðri):   þeira flaust (við sigri meira).

"Keppinn vannt Yggjar veðr viðr Helganes, þats æ mun uppi meðan heimrinn
byggvisk; valgammr skók blóðugt fiðri í vápna rimmu. Yngvi, þjóðum kunnr, fekktu
ǫll flaust þeira með hringum, en þú tókt síðan við sigri meira; jarl vissi sik missa
foldar."

Fiercely you fought a storm of Yggr [Óðinn, battle] near Helganes [Helgenæs]
that will always be remembered while the world is populated; the corpse buzzard
[bird of prey] shook bloody wings in the strife of weapons [battle]. King, famous
among people, you captured all their ships from stem to stern, and then you won
an even greater victory; the jarl knew he had lost his land.

Here it is stated that King Magnús seized all their ships and that Jarl Sveinn
fled to Gautland and from there to Sweden to join his kinsman, the king of the
Swedes.

7. King Magnús's Stay in Jutland

King Magnús stayed in Jutland for another winter. That winter, a little before
Christmas, Jarl Sveinn Úlfsson came down from Sweden to Denmark with his
army and sailed directly to Jutland to meet King Magnús. He intended to do
battle for the realm again if it were not surrendered to him without a struggle.
This time they met south of Áróss (Århus) in Jutland and joined battle.[1] It was
of short duration because Jarl Sveinn had a smaller army, and King Magnús
was vouchsafed victory, now as always. There Sveinn lost his whole army and
all his ships, and he escaped onto land with only a few men. In the words of
Þjóðólfr: (FJ 51)

*38. Flýði jarl af auðu   réð herkonungr hrjóða
      ótvínn skipi sínu   hneitis egg í sveita
      morð þars Magnús gerði   sprændi blóð á brýndan
      meinfœrt þaðan Sveini: brand (vá gramr til landa).

"Ótvínn jarl flýði morð af auðu skipi sínu, þars Magnús gerði Sveini meinfœrt
þaðan. Herkonungr réð hrjóða hneitis egg í sveita; blóð sprændi á brýndan brand;
vá gramr til landa."

The fearless jarl fled from the slaughter off his empty ship, where Magnús barred
Sveinn's escape. The war king reddened the sword's edge in gore; blood splattered
on the whetted weapon; the lord strove for lands.

*39. Vas fyr Mikjálsmessu   en fyr jól varð ǫnnur
      marggrimm háið rimma   óhlítulig lítlu
      fellu Vinðr en vǫnðusk   (upp hófsk grimm með gumnum
      valtafni þar hrafnar: gunnr) fyr Árós sunnan.

"Marggrimm rimma vas háið fyr Mikjálsmessu; Vinðr fellu, en hrafnar vǫnðusk þar
valtafni. En fyr jól varð ǫnnur, lítlu óhlítulig, fyr sunnan Árós; grimm gunnr hófsk
upp með gumnum."

A terrible battle was fought before Michaelmas; Wends fell, and the ravens grew accustomed to corpse food. Yet, before Christmas, another [battle] ensued, by no
means undecided, south of Áróss [Århus]; grim fighting erupted among men.

It is evident in this verse that King Magnús and all his men called Sveinn
a "jarl," although he himself and his friends called him "king."[2] Arnórr jarlaskald composed the following about the battle:

*40. Sveins manna rekr sunnan   vitnir dregr ór vatni
      sǫndug lík at strǫndum   (vann Óláfs sonr bannat)
      vítt sér ǫld fyr útan   (búk slítr vargr í víkum)
      Jótland hvar hræ fljóta: valkǫst (ara fǫstu).

"Sǫndug lík Sveins manna rekr sunnan at strǫndum; ǫld sér, hvar hræ fljóta vítt fyr
útan Jótland. Vitnir dregr valkǫst ór vatni; vargr slítr búk í víkum; Óláfs sonr vann
bannat ara fǫstu."

The sandy bodies of Sveinn's men drift from the south to the shores; people see
where corpses float far and wide off Jótland's [Jylland, Jutland] coast. The wolf

drags the corpse pile from the water and tears bodies in the bays; Óláfr's son put an end to the eagles' fast.

> *41. Skeiðr tók Bjarnar bróður
>   ballr Skánungum allar
>   (þjóð reri þeirar tíðar
>   þingat) gramr með hringum.

"Gramr, ballr Skánungum, tók allar skeiðr Bjarnar bróður með hringum; þjóð reri þeirar tíðar þingat."

The king, grim toward the people of Skáney [Skåne, Scania], captured all the ships of Bjǫrn's brother [Sveinn] from stem to stern; men rowed thither at the right time.

Jarl Sveinn escaped onto the land and saved himself, while King Magnús seized all the ships and the treasure. Jarl Sveinn went from his landing place all the way to Sweden and stayed there during the winter. King Magnús now landed in Skáney and did battle with the farmers, killing many of his enemies. In the words of Arnórr (FJ 52):

> *42. Vítt hefk heyrt at héti
>   Helganes þars elgi
>   vágs enn víða frægi
>   vargteitir hrauð marga.

"Hefk heyrt, at héti vítt Helganes, þars enn víða frægi vargteitir hrauð marga vágs elgi."

I have heard it was called wide Helganes [Helgenæs] where the wide-famed wolf pleaser [warrior] cleared many moose of the sea [ships].

After that King Magnús went south, as is stated here:

> *43. Svik réð eigi eklu
>   allvalldr Dǫnum gjalda
>   lét fullhugaðr falla
>   Falstrbyggva lið tyggi.

"Allvaldr réð eigi gjalda Dǫnum svik eklu; fullhugaðr tyggi lét Falstrbyggva lið falla."

The ruler did not repay the Danes scantily for their treason; the daring king caused the host of Falstermen [men of Falster] to fall.

From there he returned and made a landing on Fjón (Fyn), where he harried and killed a number of people because of their treachery, for he was intent on discouraging the treachery of the Danes. Arnórr the skald makes mention of this attack:

> *44. Næst rauð frán á Fjóni   minnisk ǫld hverr annan
>   (fold sótti gramr dróttar)   jafnþarfr bláum hrafni
>   (ráns galt herr frá hánum)   (ǫrt gat hilmir hjarta)
>   hringserks lituðr merki: herskyldir tøg fylldi.

"Næst rauð hringserks lituðr frán merki á Fjóni; gramr dróttar sótti fold; herr galt
ráns frá hánum. Minnisk ǫld, hverr herskyldir, jafnþarfr bláum hrafni, fylldi annan
tøg? Hilmir gat ǫrt hjarta."

Next, the colorer of the ring shirt [byrnie, warrior] reddened the shining standards in Fjón [Fyn]; the lord of the retinue made a landing; people were repaid
for their robbery of him. Can men recall, which war king, of equal benefit to the
black raven, was barely twenty years of age? The king got a stout heart.

Here there is a reference to King Magnús's completing his twentieth year, and
he turned twenty the following spring.[3] His fame now spread widely through
the lands because of his power and good fortune in battle, and because of the
great gifts he dispensed. It could well be said that everyone loved him dearly
except his enemies.

Now that King Magnús had taken possession of all Denmark according to
the aforementioned agreement he had made with Hǫrðaknútr, and now that
he was more or less free of hostilities, he sent his messengers with letters west
to England to meet with Edward the Good (Confessor), who had ascended the
throne of England after his brother King Hákon [*sic; F:* Hǫrðaknútr]. (FJ 53)
These letters contained the message that King Magnús and Hǫrðaknútr had
sworn oaths that each would inherit the other. And now it had come about, as
everyone knew, that Knútr had died first and that King Magnús was his rightful heir. King Magnús said that he now wanted to inquire of King Edward
whether he would have to go to war over England or whether Edward wished
to do as the Danes had done and observe the rightful treaty between them. In
that case King Magnús would have equal possession of England and Denmark
with Edward's consent after the death of Hǫrðaknútr [MS "Hordakara"], inasmuch as these lands came into his possession after the death of his brother
Haraldr, who had been king of both countries before he died.

When King Magnús's men came to England and entered the presence of
King Edward, they communicated his message and delivered his letters.[4] Having read through King Magnús's letters, King Edward prepared letters in response to the effect that he and his kinsmen had lost his father King Ethelred
when he was a child,

and because of my youth my brother Edmund succeeded to the throne before me
according to the law of our land. And after that, the prior King Knútr arrived in
the country and levied battle with a Danish army in an attempt to win England, our
patrimony, and thus it happened that he became king of England with my brother
Edmund. But not much time passed before King Edmund died, and some said that
it was the work of Knútr the Old. At that time King Knútr took possession of the
whole realm, not so much because it was rightfully his as because he was covetous
and aggressive.

And even though I was the son of King Ethelred and Queen Emma and the
rightful heir to England, still I was deprived of my land. My stepfather Knútr then

offered to support me in conquering the land, but I preferred to have faith in God's mercy and to believe that he would have given me the throne if I were deserving of it. (FJ 54) But I did not wish to bloody Christian hands and bodies for this cause.

A few more moments of King Knútr's authority in this life passed before he died. Then his sons were elected, first Haraldr. I was again dispossessed and deprived of all my ancestral honor, but I was content as long as God desired that this man should be in power. It was not long before King Haraldr died and the other son of Knútr the Great, Hǫrðaknútr, succeeded to the throne. He was my brother by the same mother and became king of both Denmark and England. Thus for the fourth time a king was chosen to rule the land while I had no status. I remained like the son of a nobleman who has no expectation of inheritance, but no one can claim that I rendered less good service or behaved more proudly toward my brother Hákon [*recte* Hǫrðaknútr] than those knights who were without noble birth on either side.

Then my brother Hǫrðaknútr died, and it was the wish and decision of all the men of the land to elect me king. That was the desire of the chieftains in the first instance, and of all the people as well. It was deemed that I had lived without my patrimony or the honor due me for some time. I was then anointed with the royal chrism and enthroned. I swore the oath during my anointment that as long as God in heaven allowed me to remain king, I would maintain God's law and the law of the land in all things and rather die in the defense of law and justice than endure the aggression of evil men. I therefore rule this land in God's name and according to the law of the land, to render justice to all and suppress violence.

And now, King Magnús, you wish to deprive me of this land, which is my rightful inheritance, only because you think your lands are not sufficiently far-flung, although you rule your patrimony in Norway and have also acquired Denmark, but you now covet my realm and propose to attack me in England as well. Nonetheless, the likelihood is that I will not gather forces against you. But you will not be called king of England before you have severed my head, and no service will be rendered to you in this land before that is done.

The men who had been sent by King Magnús now returned and showed him King Edward's letters. When King Magnús had heard and read (FJ 55) King Edward's words and understood how long he had suffered such grief before succeeding to the throne, because of the power and aggressiveness of others, he grasped how devoted he was to God and refrained from an undertaking designed to inflict war on him. He said that in truth his realm was sufficiently large provided that God would allow him to rule it. He said further that the only thing he would increase by killing such a chieftain and godly man as King Edward was his chance of losing what was worth a great deal more, to wit, his hope and trust in almighty God. Now each of them governed his realm in honor and triumph.

8. How King Haraldr Set Sail When He Came to Skáney

In the autumn when King Magnús was in Skáney with his ships, they observed one day how a ship sailed from the east along the coast. It was all ornamented in gold above the water line and carried splendid dragon's heads fore and aft. The sail was of fine fabric sewn double and of the costliest manufacture.[1] When this sighting was made, people thought it was remarkable news. As for the cargo, the ship was loaded with ruddy gold, and all the weathervanes glistened like gold, as did the dragon profiles.[2] On board there were stout men clad in precious materials.

King Magnús immediately weighed anchor and went out to meet them in order to learn of their journey. When the messengers met up with them, these men turned toward land and furled their sail. They rowed to the king's fleet and laid to with their splendid vessel near the king's ship. The captain addressed King Magnús's counselor Úlfr stallari but concealed his name.[3] He spoke on behalf of Haraldr Sigurðarson as if he were his messenger. He inquired how King Magnús would receive his uncle if he should come to visit him. He said that there was reason enough to receive him well, in the first place because of their kinship and his loyalty to his father King Ólafr. He asked (FJ 56) the counselor to present this to King Magnús. He also said that Haraldr was a wise man with a great following, and that he had accomplished many great deeds abroad, which would be long remembered. He said that he was wealthy and possessed of great treasures.[4] The one who claimed to have been sent by Haraldr said: "He can be of great assistance to his kinsman, but it could turn out to be dangerous and difficult if he is not received with honor and esteem." The counselor was receptive to the man's words and thought the message was well presented. The man was tall and of noble appearance as far as he could tell, but his view was always partly obscured.

The counselor retraced his steps to the king, who responded well and gladly to the news. "I expect much good from all my friends and followers," said the king, "but most of all from my uncle, both with respect to advice and other forms of support, and I would be very glad if he came to me." After the king had responded in this way, the counselor returned to the ship and gave the captain his answer. Then Haraldr went on shore together with him to meet King Magnús, and this time he did not conceal his identity. At that moment the counselor recognized the tall and stately man with whom he had spoken—it was Haraldr Sigurðarson, who was now recognized by several others as well. King Magnús himself went forward to meet him, together with his whole company, and gave him a very warm welcome. Many people were very eager to know about him and to hear the tales he could tell, and King Magnús afforded him a most cordial reception.

9. Concerning Haraldr's Travels

We will now turn from the story of King Magnús and tell of Haraldr's travels, first of all what happened to him after the fall of King Óláfr. Haraldr's genealogy is said to have been the following. Haraldr hárfagri (Fairhair) had a son who was named Sigurðr hrísi (the Illegitimate). He was the father of Hálfdan, the father of Sigurðr sýr (Sow), the father of Haraldr. These ancestors were all kings of (FJ 57) Hringaríki in Norway. Sigurðr sýr was married to Ásta, the daughter of Guðbrandr. She had previously been married to Haraldr grenski. They had five or more children. Guðrøðr was the oldest, then Hálfdan, then Ingibjǫrg, then Gunnhildr. Haraldr was the youngest. This Haraldr was the captain of the aforementioned ship and had recently come from the East.[1]

As has already been told, Haraldr Sigurðarson was at Stiklastaðir with King Óláfr and earned high repute. He was seriously wounded in the battle, and Rǫgnvaldr Brúsason removed him from the battlefield and placed him with a farmer to be healed. That farmer had a grown son, who gave an account of what he knew after the Battle of Stiklastaðir, namely that twelve men "came to my father," he said, "and carried a wounded man into his house. The one who spoke for them was very handsome and had light-colored hair. Then they departed, and a little later my father sent for me and asked for my horse. I did as he said, and my father came to me leading a tall man in a red cloak. I had the impression that he was young. He had covered his head with a hood, and for that reason I could not see his face.[2] My father told me to accompany him until he told me to turn back. We went on for some time. Then he turned to me and recited the following and laughed":

> *45. Nú lætk skóg af skógi
>   skreiðask lítils heiðar
>   hverr veit nema verðak
>   víða frægr of síðir.

"Nú lætk skreiðask skóg af skógi lítils heiðar: hverr veit, nema verðak víða frægr of síðir?"

Now I'm slinking from wood to wood with little honor: who knows if I won't become famous far and wide in the end?

The farmer's son told still more of their travels. "We rode ahead mostly northward as far as I could tell. Then we met up with the same men who had come to my father's house. They greeted the man in the red cape with the name of Haraldr. Then," the boy said, "I saw his face clearly. He was a fit man, pale, impressive, with heavy eyebrows, and with a rather fierce expression. He gave me a knife and belt on parting, and I returned to my father's house."[3] (FJ 58)

King Magnús and others in Norway knew of this story. But from now on, the story of Haraldr's travels is what Haraldr himself, and the men who accompanied him, told. Then Haraldr went east to Sweden and from there to Russia, as Bǫlverkr said[4]:

*46. Mildingr straukt of mækis   en gramr né frák fremra
      munn es lézt af gunni   friðskerði þér verða
      (holds vannt hrafn of fylldan   austr vast ár in næstu
      hrás) (þaut vargr í ási):   ǫrðiglyndr í Gǫrðum.

"Mildingr, straukt of mækis munn, es lézt af gunni; vannt of fylldan hrafn hrás holds; þaut vargr í ási. En, ǫrðiglyndr gramr, vast ár in næstu austr í Gǫrðum; né frák friðskerði verða fremra þér."

Generous king, you wiped the sword's mouth [sword edge] when you had finished the fight; you filled the raven with raw meat; the wolf howled in the hill. And, pugnacious king, the following years you spent east in Russia: I never heard of a peace diminisher [warrior] more distinguished than you.

This is what Þjóðólfr said:

*47. Austrvinðum ók
      í ǫngvan krók
      vasat Læsum léttr
      liðsmanna réttr.

The East Wends were forced into a tight corner: the terms of the army were not easy on the Polish people.

Haraldr soon became the commander of King Yaroslav's defense forces and received great honor and respect, to a large extent for the sake of his brother King Óláfr, but also for his own sake.[5] He won great glory in the service of the king against a foreign army that attacked the realm. They both campaigned for a time with Jarl Eilífr, as Þjóðólfr says:

*48. Eitt hǫfðusk at
      Eilífr þars sat
      hǫfðingjar tveir
      hamalt fylkðu þeir.

The two chieftains acted in accord where Eilífr ruled: they marshaled their troops in a wedge-shaped formation.

The longer he spent in the East, the greater was the fame that he achieved. King Yaroslav and Queen Ingigerðr had a daughter named Elisabeth. The Norsemen call her Ellisif. Haraldr bespoke her hand in marriage and said that they were familiar (FJ 59) with his distinguished ancestry and to some extent at first hand with his own success.[6] He said that there might be some expectation that his accomplishments were on the upswing. The king replied: "This is a good proposal, and in many ways it seems to me an even match. It is quite likely that your deeds will continue to grow in the way they have begun, but just now you have not the means for such a distinguished marriage, and for the moment you are a landless man. But because your success may turn out as I expect, I will not reject you indefinitely." After this exchange, Haraldr prepared

to go abroad, as is alluded to in the poem about his campaign east in Wendland and Saxony and all the way west to France, as Illugi attested:

> *49. Opt gekk á frið Frakka
>   (fljótreitt at bý snótar
>   vasa doglingi duglum)
>   dróttinn minn fyr óttu.

"Opt gekk dróttinn minn á frið Frakka fyr óttu: vasa duglum doglingi fljótreitt at
bý snótar."

Often my lord destroyed the peace of the Franks before dawn: the accomplished
king [Sigurðr] did not have an easy journey to the woman's [Brynhildr] dwelling.

From there he went to Lombardy and then to Rome, and after that to Apulia,
where he set out by ship and came to Constantinople and into the emperor's
presence, as Bolverkr says:[7]

> *50. Hart kníði svol svartan   mætr hilmir sá malma
>   snekkju brand fyr landi   Miklagarðs fyr barði
>   skúr (en skrautla báru   morg skriðu beit at borgar
>   skeiðr brynjaðar reiði):   barmfogr háum armi.

"Svol skúr kníði hart svartan snekkju brand fyr landi, en brynjaðar skeiðr báru
skrautla reiði. Mætr hilmir sá malma Miklagarðs fyr barði; morg barmfogr beit
skriðu at háum borgar armi."

The cool breeze forced the black prow of the ship forward along the coast, and the
armored ships proudly bore their tackle. The eminent king saw iron-thatched
Constantinople before the bow; many fair-prowed ships advanced toward the tall
arm of the city.

Here it is said that he sailed with warships and a great company to Constantinople in order to meet with the Byzantine emperor, whose name was Michael
Catalactus.[8] At that time the queen in Constantinople was Zoe en ríka (the
Powerful). The Norwegians were welcomed there. Haraldr immediately entered the emperor's service and called himself Norðbrikt. It was not generally
known that he was of royal blood (FJ 60). On the contrary, he urged everyone
to conceal the fact because foreigners are shunned when they are the progeny
of kings.[9]

A great multitude of Norsemen were already there and were called
Væringjar.[10] There was an Icelander named Már, who was the son of Húnrøðr
and the father of Hafliði Másson.[11] He was a distinguished chieftain. He was
very suspicious about whether everything these foreigners said was true. He
made it a point to speak with Halldórr Snorrason, who was in the company of
the Haraldr who called himself Norðbrikt. Már wanted to speak with Haraldr,
but Haraldr wanted nothing to do with him. Már got nowhere with him. Then
he left Constantinople, thinking it was not unlikely that major events were in
the offing.

One day when Norðbrikt and his men were sitting in the open in three circles,
Queen Zoe approached them and saw how proudly they behaved. She went up

to Norðbrikt and said: "Give me a lock of your hair, Norseman." He said: "Let's make it an even exchange, majesty," he said, "and you give me one of your pubic hairs." People thought that was an amusing remark, though rather bold when addressed to a lady of such standing. She paid no attention and went her way.

There was a man named Erlendr there among the Varangians. His wife had lost her wits, and Erlendr asked Norðbrikt to advise him since he seemed a wise and prudent man. He sought the woman out and spoke to her, asking her to show him her treasures and precious objects and urging her in a reasonable way. She agreed and showed him the items. He asked who had given her the most precious things, and she replied that she did not have much idea of who he was but that she very much liked the looks of the man who had given her these objects. He asked what she had given him as a reward. She replied that she had given him no reward, but she became rather taciturn. "It is not fitting, mistress," he said, "that you should give no reward for such treasures. If you think you have no reward as appropriate as you would like, I will give you a precious object to use as a reward." She agreed to this.

He went away and had a cross (FJ 61) made of gold, then had it blessed. Then he returned to her a second time and gave her the cross, telling her to keep it by her and to tell him in more detail of her situation, and he pressed her in various ways. She said that a man had come to her, so handsome in appearance that she had not seen his equal. She said that he visited her bed at night—"and I have fallen very much in love with him." After that Norðbrikt went away and told Erlendr what the situation was—"We should now keep a lookout to see if he visits her, then seize him if we can."

One evening they saw a man going to her room. He was tall and handsome, and they thought they saw a golden hue on his skin where it was visible. It seemed to them that they would be able to capture him when he left. He got into the woman's bed, and she showed him the cross, saying: "I don't want just to receive gifts from you and make no return. Now I want to make you a present of this precious object"—and she handed him the cross and asked him to take it. At this he was so overcome that he vanished instantly, and she had no idea what had become of him. After that she found herself in a very weakened state.

They kept watch over her so that she would not make any attempt to leave, and they cared for her in the best way they could. Then Norðbrikt said: "I surmise that this person used to be a wicked man and has turned into a serpent lying on a heap of gold. Do you know of any serpent's den in the vicinity?" He was told that there certainly was. "We will go to that place," said Norðbrikt. And so they did. There were some cliffs in the area. They built a great pyre on a cliff, and when the fire blazed high, a great and monstrous serpent's head appeared. But they could not finish the matter and returned to the city as matters stood. But it seemed not unlikely that the pyre had caused the serpent some grief and that he would move his lair.

The next night a resident in the city dreamt that a man came to him and asked for a ship, saying that he would put the price of the hire in the ship's prow. (FJ 62) The man dreamt that he had hired out the ship. The following morning when he awoke, he went to the ship and saw that it had been used recently and that there was a great golden goblet in the prow. From then on the creature caused no more damage, and Erlendr's wife recovered her health. Everyone was much impressed by Norðbrikt's wisdom, and he became popular among the Varangians. Everyone grasped that he was an estimable man in all his accomplishments and counsels.

10. Concerning Norðbrikt's Travels

That same autumn Norðbrikt sailed into the Aegean Sea with a fleet of galleys and all the Varangians. The commander of the Greek army was Gyrgir, a kinsman of Queen Zoe.[1] They sailed far and wide in the Aegean and among the Greek islands, and accomplished many great deeds. In the words of Bǫlverkr:

> *51.   Snjallr rauð í styr stillir
>   stál ok gekk á mála
>   háðisk hvert ár síðan
>   hildr sem sjalfir vilduð.

"Snjallr stillir rauð stál í styr ok gekk á mála; hildr háðisk hvert ár síðan, sem sjalfir vilduð."

The courageous king reddened steel in battle and served as a mercenary; every year thereafter war was waged according to your will.

One time when they were setting up their tents, Norðbrikt and his men took the higher ground. Then the commander Gyrgir arrived on the scene and ordered the Varangians to move their tents.

Norðbrikt replied: "That is not according to law, and it has not been the custom of the Varangians to accommodate the Greeks by moving into a ditch."

Gyrgir said that rank entitled him to pitch his tents first wherever he wished.

To that Norðbrikt replied: "If you are the commander of the Greeks, I am the commander of the Varangians."[2]

They debated the matter without coming to any resolution, and both sides wanted to resort to arms. Then wise men of good will came forward wishing to settle their difficulties. They asked that they be reconciled and not shame or injure the emperor by fighting, since both were the emperor's men. They should rather settle the matter in a way that satisfied both and gave neither the advantage. They asked them to draw lots in order to decide who should (FJ 63) be first to pitch their tents and moor their ships. They agreed to do this.

Lots were now prepared, and each of them marked his lot, then they threw them into Gyrgir's cloaktails. Norðbrikt was to draw the lots and said to Gyrgir: "Let me see what mark you have made so that we do not mark our lots the same way." Gyrgir passed him the lot and did not suspect that there was an ulterior motive. Norðbrikt now marked his lot in exactly the same way as Gyrgir had done, then tossed it into Duke Gyrgir's lap.

Norðbrikt then drew first. When he had picked up one lot, he said to Gyrgir: "This lot will determine who pitches his tents first, rows ahead, rides ahead, anchors first, and has the first choice in all matters." Then he looked at the lot, held it up high, and said, "This is my lot." Then he flung it away far out to sea.

Gyrgir said: "Why didn't you let me see the lot?"

He replied: "If you didn't see the one I picked up, look at the one that is left. I suspect you will find your mark on it." The lot was then inspected, and it bore Gyrgir's mark.

In such encounters it soon became apparent how ambitious and conspicuous Norðbrikt was. In the summer he went abroad. We are told that Norðbrikt arranged things so that his men avoided battle and all the impending dangers; they were always arrayed in the battle line where the peril was expected to be least. He was thus able to avoid losses in his army, but he did not prevent Gyrgir and his men from being exposed. By contrast, when Norðbrikt was alone with his army, he attacked so vigorously that it was a matter of victory or death. It thus turned out that whenever Norðbrikt was in command, he won the victory. But Gyrgir accomplished nothing.

This became evident to Gyrgir's soldiers, and they said that it would be better if Norðbrikt alone were in command of the whole army. They put the blame on Duke Gyrgir and said that nothing was achieved because of him and his corps. He replied that the Varangians would not support him, telling them to go their own way while he proceeded (FJ 64) with his army and accomplished whatever he could or whatever was alloted to him.

After that Norðbrikt went away, and with him went all the Varangians and the Latins.[3] But Gyrgir took the Greek army. Now it became apparent very soon what each was capable of. Norðbrikt always won the victory and took the booty, but Gyrgir returned to Constantinople with his army, except for the young men who wanted to earn fame and fortune. They joined together and went over to Norðbrikt, whom they made their chieftain. He led his army west to Africa and gathered large forces in that territory. According to King Haraldr's account, he captured eighty towns. Some were surrendered to him, but some he overran and burned. In the words of Þjóðólfr:

*52.	Tøgu má tekna segja	áðr herskǫrðuðr harðan
	(tandrauðs) á Serklandi	Hildar leik und skildi
	(ungr hætti sér) átta	Serkjum hættr í sléttri
	(ormtorgs hǫtuðr) borga:	Sikileyju gekk heyja.

"Má segja átta tøgu borga tekna á Serklandi—ungr tandrauðs ormtorgs hǫtuðr hætti sér—áðr herskǫrðuðr, Serkjum hættr, gekk heyja harðan Hildar leik und skildi í sléttri Sikileyju."

I can report that eighty cities were captured in the land of the Saracens—the young enemy of the fire-red snake square [gold, generous king] exposed himself to danger—before the army diminisher [warrior], dangerous to Saracens, went beneath the shield to start the hard game of Hildr [valkyrie, battle] in level Sicily.

Norðbrikt spent many years in Africa and acquired much gold and many treasures.[4] All the money that he did not need for his military expenditures he sent with his confidential messengers north to Kiev for safekeeping with King Yaroslav. Such a huge amount of money was collected that it could not be weighed. That was not unlikely since he was raiding that part of the world that had virtually the greatest store of gold and treasures. It was not the case that he fought with cowherds, for he said himself that he fought against the king in Africa and won the victory, so that he took possession of a great part of the realm. After that he returned to Constantinople with great distinction. There he remained for a time. (FJ 65)

11. Concerning a Declaration of War

We are told next that Emperor Michael learned of a declaration of war. Gyrgir said to the emperor: "Now we should let the Varangians prove themselves. Many people suspect that you are dealing with a man of royal blood, but you know that it is not customary here for royal persons to enter paid service."[1] The king said: "Your suspicion has not been proved yet, but it is certain that this man surpasses others both in wisdom and prowess. Men like him are best suited to defend our land. For that reason it is a good idea that they should prove themselves."

The Varangians now met together, and Haraldr told them that he strongly suspected that "people will be taking a close look at us here in Constantinople. They will be guessing at our identity and will care little whether we are used as battle fodder or are otherwise imperiled. I suggest now that we make a vow to Saint Óláfr for victory and build a church here in his honor and to the glory of God."[2] They all made a formal agreement to this effect. Then in the name of Saint Óláfr they marched against the heathens.

The heathens had a number of kings commanding their army. One was blind, but he was the wisest of them. They had wheels under their chariots and intended to charge the enemy equipped in this way. But when they launched their charge against the Varangians, they all got tangled. By contrast, the blind king miraculously saw a man riding a white horse before the Varangian army, and the heathens stood in such fear of this man that many of the kings fled, while only six remained.[3] It ended with the Varangians winning the victory. After that they returned home in great triumph and honor, and immediately arranged that a worthy church should be built.

But at the insistence of others, the emperor refused to let the church be dedicated. Haraldr had a feast prepared and intended to summon the bishop to dedicate the church. The emperor banned the use of firewood for the preparation of the feast and said that it was hard for him as emperor to maintain his own privileges against the aggressiveness and grand ways of the Varangians. But a way was soon found to arrange the feast (FJ 66) even though the emperor was unwilling. Then Haraldr asked the bishop to proceed with the dedication, but he said that he did not dare go against the emperor. Haraldr replied that he would arrange matters so that the emperor would not forbid it.

Then Haraldr went before the emperor and set forth how wrong it was for him to suppress the project of honoring King Óláfr in return for the miraculous favor he had accorded them and the peace he had bestowed on the emperor's realm. He was able to phrase it in such a way that the emperor himself went with him to the feast, along with the bishop. The feast came off in excellent style. The emperor was astonished that Haraldr had gotten such an abundance of firewood, since he had forbidden him to have any at all. Norðbrikt told the emperor that he had used ship wreckage, brush, and walnuts.[4]

The church was now dedicated, and the emperor gave a magnificent reward for the feast. Then the church was inaugurated and beautifully ornamented with a great bell, which had no equal in Constantinople. But because of the representations of wicked men the king had the clapper removed. They then invoked Saint Óláfr, asking that the clapper be restored to their bell. Óláfr appeared to the emperor in a fearful dream, but the emperor failed to respond. Then he was seized by a violent illness that he could hardly endure. The empress discovered the cause and asked Norðbrikt to come and provide some remedy for the emperor. Norðbrikt came to the emperor immediately and advised him to replace the clapper in Saint Óláfr's church, then make a gift of three things to the church, and go there himself. He was then instructed to honor Saint Óláfr as long as he lived. This the emperor promised to do, and he kept his promise faithfully.

Now both Norðbrikt and Gyrgir set sail again, and it was agreed with the emperor that they should pay him a hundred marks for each ship, but that they should keep anything over and above that.[5] With that they set out on their expedition and came to Sicily. That is a large realm with many sizable towns. The people fled to the towns, where there was no lack of anything the fugitives needed. (FJ 67) The inhabitants thought that they had a secure refuge when they had escaped to the towns.

Norðbrikt and his men now laid siege to a town that was exceptional both in terms of a large population and rich treasures. The town resisted stoutly and was difficult to breach, so that they accomplished nothing.

Then Gyrgir said: "Where the greater remedies won't work, there's no point in trying the lesser ones.[6] This town is not vulnerable and will not fall to our attack. We will have to desist, and I suspect that we will fare better out on the coast, where there is less manpower."

Norðbrikt replied: "It will take a long time to pay our contract with the emperor if we have to scout out every skerry. What will you give me if I can take the town?"

Gyrgir answered, "What is your proposal?"

"Three objects of my choice," said Norðbrikt.

"I agree," replied Gyrgir, and the agreement was sealed and witnessed.

The lay of the land was such that a river ran down a gully by the town. Norðbrikt went there with sixty men, and they were not visible from the town. They had measured the foundation so as to judge how deep they would have to dig down, and they planned to tunnel straight under the main hall. Twenty men began to dig and another twenty to remove the earth. A third group unloaded all the earth in the river. It was only the third group that was visible from the town, and it was not clear what they were doing. They tunneled under the town until they got to the right place, as nearly as they could tell.

Then Norðbrikt said: "Now the tunnel is the size I want. We should do our best and let fortune take its course. Let us dig upward to where we think we can get into some house in the town. But let us not surface before we are all armed and ready. Luck goes to the lucky, as destiny determines.[7] If our break-out goes well, it may be that those who are present will be rather startled and fearful when they see men coming at them out of the earth all of a sudden. Let us also dress in such a way as to keep them guessing, for (FJ 68) I suspect that there are plenty of people who expect creatures other than humans to emerge from the earth." They followed Norðbrikt's advice.

The whole army now armed itself. Everyone donned his helmet except those men who were assigned to finish the last dig up through the earth's surface when everything else was ready. With his wisdom and good planning, Haraldr arranged the breakthrough so masterfully that they emerged in a stone hall in the town, where there were not many men to oppose them. Most of the army went through the tunnel under the town even though they could not all get out simultaneously. When they emerged, Norðbrikt said that they should raise a howl and make the most horrid sound they could. As the dusky helmets started coming out of the earth at them, the men were very much taken aback. It was also rather dark inside. Those who could took to their heels and scattered about the town with cries and shouts of alarm, saying that demons had emerged from the ground and were killing everyone they could find. They claimed that the besiegers were such sorcerers that they summoned devils out of the earth to kill their enemies.

There was now a panic in the town, but when the worst tumult died down and people realized what was going on and what tricks they faced, the best and boldest warriors seized their weapons and defended themselves. But since Norðbrikt and his men were no less ready for battle, the townsmen began to fall like butchered cattle. Those who could save their lives sought to escape. Some surrendered and swore oaths of fealty. But the victors took whatever they wanted in the town.[8]

Then Norðbrikt spoke: "I imagine, Gyrgir, that we will have to travel far and wide before we find such treasure as we have taken in this town, which you were minded to abandon. I wish now to select such items for myself as I desire, as we agreed."

"It is true," said Gyrgir, "that we have won a great prize here, but it would seem to me that it is most honorable for you not to choose your precious objects until we are back in Constantinople."

Norðbrikt said: "I believe I am amply entitled to these riches because this town would still be standing if my advice had not been taken. But what is the view of the chieftains?" They all supported (FJ 69) his case and said that a man who was so valiant well deserved the title of commander.

"It is true that we have gained great booty," said Gyrgir. "I think that we would be well advised to return home as things stand."

Norðbrikt replied: "We still will not be able to pay the emperor a hundred marks for each ship if we accumulate no more wealth than this. We should keep at it longer before we stop, for I have learned where we can expect to find more riches." The whole army agreed with him, and all were greatly impressed by his dealings and the success that he always achieved.

12. Concerning the Raids of Norðbrikt and Jarl Gyrgir

They now besieged another town that was both larger and harder to reduce. Gyrgir spoke: "You will now risk this enterprise beyond your capacity and trust too boldly in the victory you have won. Let us rather explore further and not commit the foolishness of undertaking what we cannot achieve. It is no good to sit down more often than you get up."[1]

Norðbrikt could now see that Gyrgir wanted to depart, and he said: "It is true that this town cannot be taken with the same trick as the last one. But we have not exhausted our hope if we take our time. I will give you the option of leaving and going wherever you wish. Even though we cannot pay the emperor the sum agreed upon, we do have some resources. But the men will not leave because they need the money, and I will not desist as things stand."

"In my opinion," said Gyrgir, "you are not well advised."

"We will see how things turn out," said Norðbrikt. Gyrgir was stuck and could not bring himself to depart with little money or none at all.

There were fair and open fields near the town. In the fields there stood beautiful trees with stout limbs in blossom, like a little forest. The birds with nests always left town and flew there during the day. They flew there for food during the day and flew back in the evening to sleep where they had nests here and there in the thatched roofs of the town. The townspeople thought they were safe since they had strong walls around the town. They told Norðbrikt and his men that they should (FJ 70) make a bold attack because there was much to be had in the way of treasure and precious objects. But they said that they would not make much headway by tunneling under the town or trying to reduce it as they had the previous town. The townspeople addressed them in a haughty tone and treated them with scorn and contempt.

Norðbrikt now spoke to his men: "We should select a few men from each company, but in such a way that the townspeople do not notice the reduction. These men should exchange banter with the townspeople as they have done previous days, and I suspect that they will think your attack does not amount to much. You should expose yourselves to a minimum of danger. There is a pond here close to the town, and you should collect the clay by the lake, which is called 'bitumen,' and you should knead it at night without the knowledge of the townspeople. When it is worked, it will become like mortar, that same mortar with which people generally build towns. Then we will rub the mortar on the trees outside the town, and it will become as hard as rock when it dries. On top of that we will rub wet mortar, and with this device we will bring down a great town. The next phase will be that those of our men who are most familiar]*² with little birds will go to work. It may be that the birds will not find it so easy to detach their feet from the limbs coated with wet clay. And if we can get our hands on the townspeople's little birds, it may be that we can find a way to capture the larger and more substantial birds."

They did as Norðbrikt said, and it worked. The birds stuck fast to the trees when they came for food, and they captured many little birds with this device. Then Norðbrikt said: (FJ 71) "All is well," he said, "and these birds will take part in our capture of the town. Let us now take some resinous and highly flammable wood and ignite a little fire in it by adding sulphur and enclosing it with wax. Then we will attach this load to the backs of the birds in such a way that they are not too weighed down to fly. When night comes on, we will release them all simultaneously, each with its load. It is my guess that they will fly to their habitations and their nests in the town, as they are accustomed." This was done, and the birds flew to their nests and their fledglings.

(U 8) Many of the houses in which the birds made their homes were thatched. It did not take long for the fire to ignite in the feathers, and then in the thatch and the houses themselves. One thing ignited the next, and there was a great conflagration in the town. At the same time, the besiegers were all armed and made a vigorous assault on the town. The townspeople were at a loss to explain the fire and were obliged to defend themselves both against the fire and the armed attack. They were unable to manage both.

The attackers now succeeded in making a great breach in the wall, and before the defenders knew it, they were in the town, and battle had broken out. The slaughter began, and it did not take long before the townsmen lost heart in the face of such odds and surrendered. The same people who had previously addressed Norðbrikt and his men so haughtily were now full of grief and anxiety. Humbly and meekly they beseeched mercy. (FJ 72) The townspeople were so fearful that they thought it unlikely that, with no water at hand, the fire would be extinguished. They therefore surrendered and accepted a truce, and Norðbrikt found the means to extinguish the fire.[3] In the words of Þjóðólfr:

53. Lét (þás lypt vas spjótum) hann hefr fyr sæ sunnan
     liðs hǫfðingi kviðjat   (svá finnask til minni)
     (enn þeirs undan runnu)   opt með oddi keyptan
     ulfs gráð (friðar báðu):   auð (þars leitt vas blauðum).

"Liðs hǫfðingi lét kviðjat ulfs gráð, þás lypt vas spjótum, enn, þeirs undan runnu, báðu friðar. Hann hefr opt keyptan auð með oddi fyr sæ sunnan, þars leitt vas blauðum; svá finnask minni til."

The leader of the army hindered the wolf's hunger when spears were raised, but those who fled pleaded for peace. He often bought wealth with the spear south of the sea where it was uncomfortable for cowards; there are mementoes of that.

In this town they captured much greater riches than in the previous one. Gyrgir said that it was clear they should return home after such a splendid victory and the acquisition of such treasure. He said that the emperor could now expect to get his payment, and that there would be a good share for each of them.

Norðbrikt said: "We are closer now than before, but there is still one town left that it would be great good fortune to capture. It probably boasts greater wealth than the first two put together."

"It seems to me inadvisable," said Gyrgir, "to waste such a victory as we have now gained by investing this third town. There are no trees or woods in the vicinity in which to catch the birds, and there is no chance of tunneling beneath it. Furthermore, a great multitude has gathered here."

Norðbrikt said: "It is true that there is some risk involved, but we should make a concerted effort and see if it will avail." (FJ 73)

Gyrgir was evasive and said that it would not turn out well. Norðbrikt said that he couldn't judge exactly whether the idea would succeed, but he said that he would risk it. Many of his men urged it as well, saying that they would follow his advice. He replied that he inclined that way, too. "But if I am to take this on myself again and devise a plan, I stipulate the same conditions as before." Everyone agreed to that. Then Norðbrikt spoke:

The first thing we will do is to call a halt to such games as are common when men are engaged in a siege. We will set up a tent made of precious material at a distance (U 9) from the other tents, with weathervanes on golden stakes. Every day five or six men should go to this tent and stay for a while. As they leave they should always act more grieved than when they arrive. If you talk or converse with the townspeople, as is customary, I expect that they will ask why you are so dejected and what fair tent it is that is pitched at a distance from the others. You should say that I am sick and am confined to bed there, as indeed I will be.

We will let a week pass in that manner. After that you should make the most dismal faces you can and say that I am dead. Then you should ask for permission to bring the corpse to some church in the town. Say that there will be no shortage of money in connection with the burial, either in the form of gold or precious objects. I suspect that they will give permission, because many people are eager for money. (FJ 74) Then you should ask that sixty men accompany the body into the town, and I imagine that they will not want to allow that. Then you should ask that twelve men be allowed to enter and say that it is not customary that fewer than twelve men should accompany the body of a nobleman. That they will allow. You should construct a coffin, but with no lid on it. Then cover it with the most precious fabric you have and act as if my death causes you great grief. If this is done according to my instructions and they allow twelve men to enter the town with the body, I will be in the coffin.

Then you should carry the coffin on your shoulders with four men as pallbearers and two more carrying flags. Halldórr Snorrason and Úlfr stallari should be in loose robes with chain mail underneath. The army should be fully armed and crowding around when we enter the city gate. It will not be hard to fire up the men who go first, and they will lower the coffin from their shoulders as they enter the gate. Then I will take a chance on how quickly I can get out of the coffin.

When the plan was made, the army took a close look at the town walls and found them hard to breach. There was a duke in command of the town, and the townspeople were full of self-confidence. They challenged the besiegers to attack boldly, since they had a large army. They also gave them to understand that they had heard how inventive they were. But they said that it would take a while to capture the town with small birds, even if they were loaded with shavings. They said they would fend off such tricks. (FJ 75) They then went on to say that it would be courageous to make a more direct attack than in the other two towns. They said that according to their information this was not beyond the power of their chieftains.

When night began to fall, the besiegers made an attack on the town because they could not endure the taunting and jeering of the townspeople, and they were eager to know whether the defenders were as stout and firm as the walls. They made use of all the arts of war that are practiced in this type of warfare. As the army approached the town walls, (U 10) there was no lack of catapults and other projectiles. They saw that the town was so strong that there seemed no hope of reducing it with arms, and *the walls were too thick* to breach. They returned to their tents and huddled around their chieftain as *he had advised*.

Everything now happened according to Norðbrikt's plan and prediction. After they had been there for a week, they *told the townspeople about the death of the chieftain* of the Greek army, and they were very downcast. They asked to give the body burial in one of the town churches and said that they *would make a rich offering*, as was customary for the souls of great men. They also requested funeral processions as Norðbrikt had advised. Those who maintained the churches *in the town* were eager for the gold even if it came from the viking bandits, and everyone offered his church for the chieftain's funeral. They thought that they stood to gain a fortune in gold and other precious objects. They agreed on the size of the funeral procession as Norðbrikt had predicted. Twelve men were to enter the town. (FJ 76)

Then the townspeople went out to meet the procession at the gate in full regalia, with crosses and holy relics. On their side the vikings bore a noble coffin on their shoulders, and it was covered with costly fabric. The men accompanying the body had silken tunics and broad hats to signal mourning, but underneath were helmets and byrnies. When they got to the middle of the town gate, there was an apparent mishap in the procession. They dropped the coffin across the gateway, and at that moment a trumpet sounded near the gate. The army was already fully armed and made a dash for the town, crowding into the gateway. Norðbrikt had acted as a pallbearer, though that is not what he had proposed, and the coffin was empty. He drew his sword, and his men rushed at the gateway, killing many unarmed men. Halldórr Snorrason was wounded by a blow in the face. All twelve were wounded to some extent, mostly by the stones hurled down from the tower above. The duke in the town, who was a distinguished man, had drawn his sword, which was a great treasure. Norðbrikt laid ahold of the sword and twisted it away from the duke, whom he then made his prisoner.

According to the story there was the following exchange of words between Norðbrikt and Halldórr Snorrason. Norðbrikt said that Halldórr should carry the standard into the town ahead of him. Halldórr answered instantly: "May the devil carry the standard ahead of you, coward!"

"That is a mouthful, Halldórr," said Norðbrikt, "but you are valiant all the same."[4]

Norðbrikt asked now whether the duke wished to be beholden to him for his life. He replied by asking: "Who are you? You are certainly of royal blood." (FJ 77)

He told the duke (U 11) the truth in confidence, and the duke accepted his life and land at Norðbrikt's hands. Norðbrikt took possession of all the wealth he desired from this town, but the town itself he relinquished to the duke.[5] He added many places in this land to the rule of the Byzantine Emperor before returning to Constantinople.

He then informed Gyrgir that he wanted the most precious items from the booty, but Gyrgir said that he wished to present them to the emperor. Norðbrikt said that he was fully entitled to have them and that he was not likely to let them go uncontested. He reminded Gyrgir that it was no thanks to him that their campaign had amassed such wealth and produced such great deeds. They then parted, and Gyrgir returned to Constantinople. He came before the emperor and stayed with him at court. But he slandered Norðbrikt, saying that he wanted to appropriate all the money and leave very little for the emperor. He said that it would not be long before Norðbrikt besieged Byzantium if his ambition and arrogance continued in this way. It was said that Queen Zoe had also slandered him grievously to the emperor, claiming that he wanted to be familiar with her niece Maria. She said that the emperor should take stern vengeance, but the people said that it was the queen herself who wanted him. (FJ 78)

13. Haraldr's Journey to Jerusalem

Then Norðbrikt made his way with his whole army from Sicily to Jerusalem, desiring to atone for his transgressions against God.[1] And wherever he went in the territory of Jerusalem, almost all the fortified towns and settlements surrendered to his authority, so great was his good fortune. This is confirmed by Stúfr, who had heard King Haraldr recount these events:[2]

54.   Fór ofrhugi enn øfri   ok með œrnu ríki
        eggdjarfr und sik leggja   óbrunnin kom gunnar
        (fold vas víga valdi   heimil jǫrð und herði
        virk) Jórsali ór Girkjum: (Haralds ǫnd ofar lǫndum).

"Eggdjarfr ofrhugi enn øfri fór ór Girkjum leggja und sik Jórsali; fold vas virk víga valdi. Ok með œrnu ríki kom heimil jǫrð óbrunnin und gunnar herði. Haralds ǫnd ofar lǫndum."

The sword-keen warrior set out from Greece to subjugate Palestine; the country was easy to conquer for the wielder of wars [warrior]. And because of his superior force, the land submitted unburned to the strengthener of battle [warrior]. "Haraldr's spirit above the earth."

The stanza tells how this land came into Haraldr's possession without being wasted or harried. He then went to bathe in the River Jordan, as is the custom among other pilgrims. He contributed to the sepulcher of our Lord and the holy cross and other holy relics in Jerusalem. He gave so much money in gold that no one can calculate the amount. At that time he secured the route all the way to the River Jordan and killed the robbers and other brigands, as is told in this stanza:[3]

55.   Stóðu ráð af reiði   enn fyr afgǫrð sanna
        (rann þat svikamǫnnum)   (illa gat frá stilli)
        Egða grams á ýmsum   þjóð fekk vísan váða
        (orð) Jórðánar borðum: (vist of aldr með Kristi).

(FJ 79; U 12)

"Ráð Egða grams stóðu af reiði á ýmsum Jórðánar borðum; þat orð rann svikamǫnnum. Enn þjóð fekk vísan váða fyr afgǫrð sanna; illa gat frá stilli. Vist of aldr með Kristi."

The justice of the ruler of the Egðir [people of Agder] prevailed in wrath on both banks of the River Jordan; the news of that put an end to the traitors. And people got just punishment for their proven crimes; the king made them suffer sorely. "Reside forever with Christ."

He then returned to Constantinople and continued to use the same name. Many people became envious of him, Gyrgir and the empress at first, then others as well.[4] Norðbrikt and the maiden Maria continued to meet often. One time when they were in a chamber jutting over the sea, the emperor learned of it and was advised to go and discover Norðbrikt's treachery for himself. But Maria realized what was afoot and had Norðbrikt lower himself hastily from the chamber to the water below. When the emperor arrived, he did not find Norðbrikt with her, and she said she knew nothing about him. The fact that the emperor did not find him there stood him in good stead against those who were slandering him. The emperor thought that he was now exonerated and that his accusers had lied.[5]

Next the emperor was given to understand that Norðbrikt was not a faithful guard, but the emperor denied the truth of that. Gyrgir said: "Let's make a test, lord. Let us assign armed men to test how he discharges his duties." This was done, and when Norðbrikt became aware of these men, he had them all killed. A great many of the emperor's men succumbed. The emperor now felt that whatever he got from Gyrgir's counsels turned out badly, (FJ 80) and he could not see how things were likely to improve.

At this time Empress Zoe's dislike of Norðbrikt was rekindled. The first charge against him was that he kept the gold that belonged to the Byzantine Emperor and had not made payment according to the law, but had rather taken a larger portion than the emperor sanctioned. They said that during the time that he commanded the Byzantine army the galleys in his command had contributed almost no gold. The second charge brought against him was that Empress Zoe accused Norðbrikt of being familiar with the maiden Maria. Norðbrikt had asked for her hand in marriage but had not been granted it. People who have been in Constantinople within memory of the Varangians state that Zoe herself wanted him.[6]

The slander was so successful that Empress Zoe and Emperor Monomachus [Munac!] seized Norðbrikt and had him bound and brought to a dungeon. As they led him along the street near the dungeon, Norðbrikt thought that he saw his brother Saint Óláfr. That is where Saint Óláfr's Chapel is now located. After that, he was thrown into the dungeon together with two of his men, Úlfr stallari and Halldórr Snorrason. All their weapons were taken away. The dungeons were like vertical caves with the opening on top. There was a great poisonous serpent that slept by the stream running through the cave.[7] The cave was round and (U 13) dug out on one side to form a sort of den. The serpent (FJ 81) fed off the corpses of men who came into conflict with the emperor or his magnates and were then thrown down there. They went through the mud where the corpses of the men who had been fed as morsels to the serpent lay rotting.

They sat down on the corpses. Then Halldórr Snorrason spoke: "This is *not* much of a lodging, but it may get worse later. The serpent will not sleep long, and we should not look forward to his *awakening. What* is the best course for us to follow?"

Haraldr said: "We should invoke my brother Saint Óláfr and ask him to release us."

"That is good advice," said Halldórr. * . . . * They then made their vow, but we are not told what they vowed. Then Haraldr said that they should ready themselves for an attack on the serpent.

"You, Halldórr," he said, "should attack its head. Úlfr is the strongest and should attack the tail, because that is where the strength of serpents resides. I have a little knife and will go at him from the front and strike where it seems best because I have the greatest confidence in my own luck and good fortune in aiming the knife. I expect that if he is wounded, he will toss one or the other of us in the air as he thrashes about."

Then Haraldr prepared himself by taking off his sheepskin cloak and wrapping it around his hand. He had a stick in his leading hand (FJ 82) and his knife in the other. Then he advanced against the serpent and thrust his left hand into its maw, striking immediately with his right hand into the serpent's left flank where he thought the knife would penetrate closest to the heart. He plunged the knife in up to the hilt, and it was no easy thing to contend with such a huge and evil creature with such a small blade. At that moment the serpent awoke and went into contortions. Haraldr let the cloak absorb the poison and at the same time was dashed down on the serpent. It was so powerful that it sometimes tossed two of them in the air simultaneously, but with the luck and aid of King Óláfr and Haraldr's own valor, as well as the support of his followers, the serpent was overcome, and they were able to get the best of it.

The next night a widow came down to the dungeon. It was a high tower open at the top, and was later called Haraldr's dungeon.[8] The woman had two servants with her. She asked whether anyone was alive inside, and they answered, saying that nothing was wrong with them. She asked if they wanted to be rescued, and they said that they were not loath. "I came," she said, "because King Óláfr wishes to save you." They thanked God and Saint Óláfr for deigning to consider them. Úlfr and Halldórr were drawn up first, then lastly Haraldr.

When he got to the top, he questioned the woman closely about her vision. "King Óláfr (U 14) came to me," she said, "without warning. (FJ 83) He told me where you were, and you now have the benefit of his benevolence, as you always will." "What is better and more fitting," said Haraldr, "than that my brother should release me? What words did you exchange?" "He came to me as I slept," she said, "and told me that I would be cured of the illness I suffered, but that I should go on a mission for him. I asked him who he was and where I was supposed to go to rescue the men he had in mind. He said that he did not want his brother to be tormented in southern lands, even though his designs were not always agreeable to him. Now I have told you of my vision, and after that I awoke and found that I was healed. Then I came here, as you can see."

Haraldr thanked her warmly for her help, and they parted. She went home, but Haraldr and his men went to the Varangians immediately. This was during the night. The Varangians greeted them all joyfully, and Haraldr bade them stand up and arm themselves. This they did. Then they went to the sleeping quarters, where the emperor was asleep, and broke in. They seized him and ended up by putting out both his eyes. In the words of Þórarinn:

> 56.   Náði gørr enn glóðum
>   (Gríklands) jǫfurr handa
>   (stólþengill gekk strǫngu
>   steinblindr aðalmeini).

"Jǫfurr náði enn gørr glóðum handa; Gríklands stólþengill gekk steinblindr strǫngu aðalmeini."

The king gained even more embers of the hands [gold]; the Greek emperor went stone blind from the great injury.

According to Þjóðólfr:

> 57.   Stólþengils bað stinga   lagði allvaldr Egða
>   (styrjǫld vas þá byrjuð) (FJ 84) austr á bragning hraustan
>   eyðir augu bæði   gráligt mark en Girkja
>   út heiðingja sútar: gǫtu illa fór stillir.

"Eyðir heiðingja sútar bað stinga út bæði augu stólþengils; styrjǫld vas þá byrjuð. Allvaldr Egða lagði austr gráligt mark á hraustan bragning, en Girkja stillir fór illa gǫtu."

The destroyer of wolves' distress [warrior] ordered both eyes of the emperor to be put out; then battle erupted. The ruler of the Egðir [people of Agder] put a terrible mark on the brave lord in the east, and the emperor of the Greeks had an ill fate.

In these two poems [*drápur*] and many others about Haraldr, there is mention of this deed, and there is no need to waste words on the fact that he blinded the Byzantine Emperor himself. Some count or duke could have been named in this context if that had seemed closer to the truth, but all of the poems about Haraldr coincide on this point.[9]

That same night Haraldr seized the hall in which the maiden Maria resided, and they took her away with them. Then they took two galleys and rowed out into Sæviðarsund (the Golden Horn), but there were iron chains across the strait.[10] Haraldr said: "Men on both galleys should now be assigned to the oars, but all the men who are not needed for rowing should each take a sleeping roll or other weight in his arms and run to the stern of the ships to see if they will run up onto the chains." They did so, and the ships did run (U 15) up on the chains, but as soon as the impetus was arrested and they came to a standstill, Haraldr said: "Now everyone should run forward to the prow and hold onto their weights." This device had the effect of pitching Haraldr's galley forward over the iron chains, but the other galley was suspended on the chain and broke in two.[11] A great many men were lost in the strait, though some were rescued.

Thus Haraldr escaped from Constantinople and out into the Black Sea.
(FJ 85) But before he set sail, he put the maiden Maria on shore and provided
her with a good escort back to Constantinople.[12] He bade her tell Empress Zoe
that she had departed in Haraldr's company, then ask her how great her power
over him was and who had bested the other. He said that it was not clear to him
that the empress had prevented him from taking the maiden away any time he
wanted. Then they parted, and Haraldr sailed north across the Black Sea.
From there he went west to Kiev. During this journey Haraldr composed his
jesting verses ("gamanvísur"), sixteen stanzas in all, with the same ending in
most, though only a few are recorded here. Here is one of them:

58. Sneið fyr Sikiley víða   vættik miðr at motti
     súð (várum þá prúðir)   myni enn þinig nenna.
     brúnn skreið vel til vánar   Þó lætr Gerðr í Gǫrðum
     vengis hjǫrtr und drengjum: gollhrings við mér skolla.

"Súð sneið víða fyr Sikiley: várum þá prúðir; brúnn vengis hjǫrtr skreið vel til vánar
und drengjum. Vættik miðr, at motti myni enn nenna þinig. Þó lætr Gerðr
gollhrings í Gǫrðum skolla við mér."

The ship sailed far and wide around Sicily: we were proud then; the dark stag of
the ship cabin [ship] glided beneath the crew as ever. I hardly think a sluggish man
will ever travel thither. Yet Gerðr of the gold ring [woman] in Russia ridicules me.

It refers to Elisabeth, the daughter of King Yaroslav, whom he had wooed as
has already been mentioned. He also composed the following stanzas:

59. Fundr vas þess at Þrœndir   skilðumk ungr við ungan
     þeir hǫfðu lið meira   allvalld í styr fallinn.
     varð (sús vér of gerðum)   Þó lætr Gerðr í Gǫrðum
     víst errilig snerra: gollhrings við mér skolla. (FJ 86)

"Fundr vas þess, at þeir Þrœndir hǫfðu meira lið; víst varð errilig snerra, sús vér of
gerðum. Skilðumk ungr við ungan allvald fallinn í styr. Þó lætr Gerðr gollhrings í
Gǫrðum skolla við mér."

The meeting was such that the Þrœndir [people of Trøndelag] had more troops;
the fight we had was truly fierce. As a youth, I parted from the young king, who was
killed in battle. Yet Gerðr of the gold ring [woman] in Russia ridicules me.

60. Senn jósum vér svanni   vættik miðr at motti
     sextán (þás brim fexti)   myni enn þinig nenna.
     (dreif á hlaðna húfa   Þó lætr Gerðr í Gǫrðum
     húm) í fjórum rúmum: gollhrings við mér skolla.

"Senn jósum vér, svanni, sextán í fjórum rúmum, þás brim fexti; húm dreif á
hlaðna húfa. Vættik miðr, at motti myni enn nenna þinig. Þó lætr Gerðr gollhrings
í Gǫrðum skolla við mér."

We bailed, woman, sixteen at a time in four rowing stations when breakers roared;
sea spray battered the loaded ship sides. I hardly think a sluggish man will ever
travel thither. Yet Gerðr of the gold ring [woman] in Russia ridicules me.

61. Íþróttir kannk átta   skríða kannk á skíðum
    Yggs fetk líð at smíða   skýtk ok rœk svát nýtir
    fœrr emk hvasst á hesti   hvártveggja kannk hyggja
    hefk sund numit stundum: harpslátt ok bragþáttu. (U 16)

"Kannk átta íþróttir: fetk at smíða Yggs líð; emk hvasst fœrr á hesti; hefk numit sund stundum. Kannk skríða á skíðum; skýtk ok rœk svát nýtir; kannk hyggja hvártveggja harpslátt ok bragþáttu."

I have eight accomplishments: I know how to forge Yggr's [Óðinn] wine [skaldic poetry]; I am a swift horseman; on occasion I have practiced swimming. I can glide on skis; I shoot and row well enough; I have command of both harp playing and poetry.

62. Fœddr vas ek þars alma   vítt hef ek (sízt ýttum)
    Upplendingar bendu   eygarð skotit barði.
    nú lætk við sker skolla   Þó lætr Gerðr í Gǫrðum
    skeiðr búmǫnnum leiðar: gollhrings við mér skolla.

"Fœddr vas ek, þars Upplendingar bendu alma; nú lætk skeiðr, leiðar búmǫnnum, skolla við sker. Vítt hef ek skotit eygarð barði, sízt ýttum. Þó lætr Gerðr gollhrings í Gǫrðum skolla við mér."

I was born where the Upplendingar [people of Opplandene] bent the bows; now I let my fleet, loathed by farmers, float among the skerries. Far and wide I have steered my ship across the island enclosure [sea] since we set out. Yet Gerðr of the gold ring [woman] in Russia ridicules me.

63. Oss munat ekkja kenna   ruddumk umb með oddi
    ung né mær at værim   eru merki þar verka.
    (þars gerðum svip sverða)   Þó lætr Gerðr í Gǫrðum
    síð í borg of morgun: gollhrings við mér skolla.

"Oss munat ekkja né ung mær kenna, at værim síð í borg of morgun, þars gerðum svip sverða. Ruddumk umb með oddi; þar eru merki verka. Þó lætr Gerðr í Gǫrðum skolla við mér."

No widow or young woman will fault us for being late in the town in the morning, when we made a swinging of swords [battle]. I cleared a path with the spear point; there is testimony of my deeds there. Yet Gerðr of the gold ring [woman] in Russia ridicules me.

Haraldr now arrived in Kiev at the court of King Yaroslav. He got a good reception and took possession (FJ 87) of the great treasure in gold that he had sent home from Byzantium. He brought up the marriage question to the king, saying that he had now acquired the necessary wealth, not to mention a certain reputation for great deeds. The king replied that he would not keep him waiting any longer and would now fulfill his wish. Then King Yaroslav married his daughter Elisabeth to Haraldr, and the Norsemen called her Ellisif, as Stúfr says:[13]

64.   Mægð gat ǫðlingr eiga
       ógnar mildr (þás vildi)
       golls tók gauta spjalli
       gnótt ok bragnings dóttur.

"Ógnar mildr ǫðlingr gat eiga mægð, þás vildi; gauta spjalli tók gnótt golls ok bragnings dóttur."

The fear-inspiring prince got the marriage he desired; the friend of the people gained plenty of gold and the king's daughter.

In the spring Haraldr set sail from the East and told King Yaroslav that he wanted to meet his kinsman King Magnús to see if he would give him a share of the realm, since he himself ruled over two kingdoms. He said that it might well be fitting for Magnús to honor such a close kinsman. The king, supported by the queen, urged him by all means to be gentle in his dealings with King Magnús. They said that it was of the greatest importance to them that he should be as faithful and supportive to him as possible, both in counsel and arms. Haraldr now traveled west from Kiev and sailed a single ship to Sweden. According to Valgarðr:

65.   Skauzt und farm enn frízta   stýrðir hvatt í hǫrðu
       (frami veitisk þér) beiti   hugdyggr jǫfurr glyggvi
       (farðir goll ór Gǫrðum   sátt (þars snædrif létti)
       grunlaust) Haraldr (austan):   Sigtún (en skip hnigði).
                        (FJ 88)

"Haraldr, skauzt beiti und farm enn frízta; farðir grunlaust goll austan ór Gǫrðum: frami veitisk þér. Hugdyggr jǫfurr, stýrðir hvatt í hǫrðu glyggvi, en skip hnigði; sátt Sigtún, þars snædrif létti."

Haraldr, you launched a ship under the most precious cargo; under no suspicion, you brought gold from Russia in the east: you are blessed with success. Valiant king, you steered bravely in the fierce storm and the ship pitched; you sighted Sigtún [Sigtuna] when the snowstorm eased.

There he met with Jarl Sveinn, who had fled from King Magnús in Denmark. (U 17) *Sveinn proposed* that they should join forces in light of the common issue that their birth entitled them to the realms that King Magnús ruled. He claimed kinship with Haraldr since he was related to Haraldr's wife Ellisif, the daughter of Yaroslav and Ingigerðr, who was the daughter of Óláfr. Óláfr's sister was Ástríðr, Sveinn's mother, because Sigríðr en stórráða was the mother of both King Óláfr and Ástríðr.[14] Such was the gist of Sveinn's message to Haraldr. He replied to the effect that he did not want to reject Sveinn's friendship but that he first wanted to meet with his kinsman King Magnús before opposing him or joining his enemies. Haraldr then went to Denmark, as is told in the following stanza:

66.   Eik slǫng und þér yngvi   hýnd bar rif (þars renndi
       ógnblíðr í haf síðan   rétt á stag fyr slétta)

(rétt vas yðr of ætlat   skeið (en skelkðuð brúðir)
óðal) frá Svíþjóðu: (Skáney) (Dǫnum nánar). (FJ 89)

"Ógnblíðr yngvi, eik slǫng síðan und þér í haf frá Svíþjóðu; rétt óðal vas of ætlat yðr. Skeið bar hýnd rif, þars renndi rétt á stag fyr slétta Skáney, en skelkðuð brúðir, Dǫnum nánar."

Battle-rejoicing king, then the ship set out to sea beneath you from Sweden; your due inheritance was awaiting you. The ship carried a sail hoisted high, where it scudded swiftly past flat Skáney [Skåne, Scania], and you scared women related to the Danes.

14. Concerning King Magnús's Meeting with Haraldr

Now the story picks up at the point where it left off, when King Magnús and his uncle Haraldr met in Denmark. Some of the wisest men were assembled and took counsel. Haraldr asked how King Magnús might wish to divide the realm between them. King Magnús gave his kinsman a friendly response and said that he would follow the advice of his magnates and the wishes of his countrymen. Then the magnates were called into session, and King Magnús informed them of Haraldr's request. Einarr þambarskelfir was the first of the magnates to reply: "You were a long way off, Haraldr, when we won the land from the clan of Knútr, and we have no desire to be divided up between chieftains. It has been our custom to serve under one at a time, and that is the way it will remain as long as King Magnús lives and rules."

All the magnates fell in with this speech in their replies, though each modulated his words in his own way. But the upshot was that they wanted to have King Magnús in sole command of the realm, and Haraldr departed with diminished honor. He returned and arranged a meeting with Jarl Sveinn Úlfsson. They now took counsel and joined forces in such a way that Haraldr claimed Norway and Sveinn Denmark. It was determined that they would cooperate in wresting both lands from King Magnús.[1] They gathered ships and troops all over Zealand and harried far and wide, burning farms and capturing a large number of prisoners. In the words of Valgarðr:

67.   Haraldr gǫrva lézt herjat   gekk á Fjón (en fekkat)
       (hnyggr andskotum tyggi) (FJ 90)   fjǫlmennr konungr (hjǫlmum)
       (hvatt rann vargr at vitja   (brast ríkula ristin
       valfalls) Selund alla: (U 18)   rít) (erfiði lítit).

"Haraldr, lézt gǫrva herjat alla Selund; hnyggr andskotum, tyggi; vargr rann hvatt at vitja valfalls. Konungr gekk fjǫlmennr á Fjón, en fekkat hjǫlmum lítit erfiði; ríkula ristin rít brast."

Haraldr, you thoroughly sacked all Selund [Sjælland, Zealand]; lord, you crush your enemies; the wolf ran swiftly to seek slaughter. The king advanced with a great

host in Fjón [Fyn] and gave helmets no little hardship to endure; the richly en-
graved shield split.

68.   Brann í bœ fyr sunnan   lágu landsmenn gnógir
      bjartr eldr Hróiskeldu   ló hel sumum frelsi
      ronn lét ræsir nenninn   drósk harmvesalt hýski
      reykvell ofan fella: hljótt til skógs á flótta.

"Bjartr eldr brann í bœ fyr sunnan Hróiskeldu; nenninn ræsir lét reykvell ronn
fella ofan. Gnógir landsmenn lágu; hel ló sumum frelsi; harmvesalt hýski drósk
hljótt til skógs á flótta."

Bright fire burned in the borough south of Hróiskelda [Roskilde]; the crafty king
let smoldering buildings crumble. Plenty of people had fallen; death deprived
some of their freedom; grief-stricken households fled silently to the forest.

69.   Dvoldu daprt of skilða   láss helt líki drósar
      (drifu þeirs eptir lifðu)   leið fyr yðr til skeiða
      ferð (en fengin urðu   (bitu fíkula fjotrar)
      fogr sprund) (Danir undan):   fljóð mart (horundbjarta).

"Dvoldu ferð, daprt of skilða; Danir, þeirs eptir lifðu, drifu undan, en fogr sprund
urðu fengin. Láss helt líki drósar; mart fljóð leið fyr yðr til skeiða; fjotrar bitu fíkula
horundbjarta."

They delayed the pitifully scattered company; those Danes who were still alive,
fled, but fair women were captured. A lock secured the woman's body; many a
maiden went before you to the ships; fetters bit greedily into the fair-fleshed one.

When Haraldr and Sveinn had accomplished what we have now told, King
Magnús and his friends learned that they were bent on attacking him. He now
thought that they had been ill advised when they counseled him to dismiss
Haraldr. He said that this would be a constant danger to the realm. He decided
to send a secret letter (FJ 91) to Haraldr, saying that it was King Magnús's wish
that they should declare a truce and meet to settle their differences. When the
envoys came to Haraldr with this message, he was agreeable and pondered how
he could detach himself from his alliance with Sveinn without being accused
of perfidy.

One morning when Haraldr was lying on the ship's upper deck, an arrrow
hit the footboard of his bunk, then another followed. (Haraldr himself was lying out by the gunwale, but there was a wooden dummy in his bunk, draped in
precious bedclothes.) At that Haraldr leapt to his feet and said: "There you can
see the treachery of the Danes. That was meant for me. We had better take
measures to protect ourselves because they are unlikely to be faithful in their
dealings with me after they have betrayed King Magnús."

Early in the morning he convened a thingmeeting and said that the treachery contrived by Jarl Sveinn was manifest—"and that will mean the end of our
alliance. I am not likely to have the requisite luck for it, considering that he

swore an oath of fidelity to King Magnús and broke it." Jarl Sveinn learned of Haraldr's words and said that he had made a false charge against him—"he is likely to have thought up this plan himself, and there is no need to ascribe it to others, but it is a serious accusation that I was not true to my oath to King Magnús, though I doubt that will occur often. It seemed to me that there was some justification in light of my heritage, which was occupied by foreign chieftains while I got nothing."

He sent word by the Norwegians that Haraldr accused him of being deceitful in this matter, and he said it was not a daily occurrence that (FJ 92) he could be charged with treachery. He informed Haraldr that, in (U 19) his opinion, the plan was of his own making and that Haraldr had demonstrated his fickleness in this matter since he was at the bottom of it. With that they separated their forces, and Haraldr sailed the outer course north to Norway, as Valgarðr states:[2]

70.   Inn vas í (sem brynni)   skeið bar skolpt enn rauða
        iðglíkt séa miðjan   skein af golli hreinu
        (eldr) (þars yðrum helduð)   dreki fór dagleið mikla
        orms munn (skipum sunnan):   dúfu braut und húfi.

"Vas iðglíkt séa inn í miðjan orms munn, sem eldr brynni, þars helduð yðrum skipum sunnan. Skeið bar skolpt enn rauða; skein af hreinu golli; dreki fór dagleið mikla; dúfu braut und húfi."

It was like looking into the middle of a dragon's mouth the way fire burned when you steered your ships from the south. The ship carried its red head; it glowed from the pure gold; the dragon ship sailed a long day's journey; the wave broke beneath its bottom.

71.   Lauðr vas lagt í beðja   ræðr (en ræsir œðri
        (lék sollit haf golli)   rístr aldri sæ kaldan)
        enn herskipum hrannir   (sveit tér sínum dróttni
        hǫfuð ógurlig þógu: snjǫll) Nóregi ǫllum.

"Lauðr vas lagt í beðja; sollit haf lék golli, enn hrannir þógu ógurlig hǫfuð herskipum. Ræðr ǫllum Nóregi, en ræsir œðri rístr aldri kaldan sæ; snjǫll sveit tér sínum dróttni."

Foam formed long breakers; the swollen sea played with the gold, and the waves washed the horrible heads of the warships. You rule all Norway, and no nobler king will ever cleave the cold sea; the valiant company supports their lord.

Reference is made here to how Haraldr returned to Norway from abroad and how he came to power.

When he came east to Vík, he left his ships behind and went overland to his ancestral estates in Upplǫnd, where he demanded his ancestral title (FJ 93), asking that the farmers call him "king," as his ancestors had been titled. But, given the power of King Magnús, no one had the audacity to call anyone else king as long as Magnús lived. Haraldr then went north to Guðbrandsdalr

(Gudbrandsdalen), where he convened a thingmeeting and asked for the royal title. There was one man among the landowners who consented, and that was Þórir at Steig, who later became a great chieftain. Þórir was fifteen years old when he gave Haraldr the royal title. Haraldr presented him with a maple bowl girded about in silver and with a handle of gilded silver. The bowl itself was filled with pure silver.[3] He also gave him two gold rings, worth a mark taken together, and his cloak. The cloak was dark purple.[4] At the same time he promised him great honors if he became the ruler of the country. Haraldr then traveled around Upplǫnd with an armed following and was titled king by the landowners.

Jarl Sveinn campaigned far and wide among the Danish islands.[5] The matters that we have related were reported to King Magnús. With the advice of his chieftains, he headed his fleet north to Norway. He wished to meet with King Haraldr and ascertain what he wanted, and whether he wished to be reconciled with him or to stand in opposition to him and take up arms. King Magnús wanted, in the first instance, to defend that land which was his ancestral property. He arrived in Vík and gathered all the information on what his kinsman Haraldr was about. (U 20) Haraldr came south to meet him with armed forces. At that point friends and kinsmen on both sides interceded and (FJ 94) offered mediation. The upshot was that the kinsmen were to meet with a truce in effect.

A splendid feast was arranged at a place called Skjaldarakr (Åker, Vang).[6] King Magnús was to be the host for three days and entertain King Haraldr with sixty of his men. The first day of Magnús's entertainment, when the tables had been removed, King Magnús left the hall. A little later he came back, accompanied by men who walked in front and behind him with great burdens. King Haraldr's men occupied the facing benches. King Magnús went up to Haraldr's outermost man and gave him a good sword, and a shield to the next, then a tunic, then clothing, or gold or weapons. Thus he proceeded inward along the benches and presented each man with a gift of increasing value according to the rank of the recipient.

Then he came before his kinsman King Haraldr and had two handsome reed sprigs in his hand. He said: "Kinsman, which reed do you *wish* as a gift from me?"

Haraldr said: "The one that is closer to me, lord."

Then King Magnús said: "With this reed sprig I give you half of *the realm* of Norway with all the taxes and dues and all properties. I declare that you will be king everywhere in Norway with the same rights that I have. When we are together, I will have precedence in greeting, service, and seating. If three men of noble rank are present, I will occupy the center. The royal mooring and quay will be mine. You will support and strengthen my power in recognition of the fact that I have raised you to a position in Norway that I thought no one would occupy as long as I remained in this life."

Then King Haraldr stood up (FJ 95) and thanked his kinsman warmly for this noble gift. They all sat together in good cheer. At the expiration *of three days* King Haraldr prepared a feast with his whole retinue. He invited King Magnús with sixty men and entertained him with great splendor. *On the first day* of the feast Haraldr chose gifts for all of King Magnús's men who were present, and there were many rare objects presented. When everyone had received a gift except the king alone, Haraldr had two chairs set out. He occupied one and asked King Magnús to take the other. He did so and sat down. Then chests both large and numerous were brought into the hall. A cloth was spread over the straw, and King Haraldr ordered that the treasures be opened.[7]

Then he addressed King Magnús: "The other day you conferred a great realm on me, which you had won from your enemies and mine with great honor. You took me as coregent, and that was a generous gesture even though you had more than enough at your disposal. Now we must look at the other side. I have been abroad and in some peril (U 21) in the process of accumulating this gold. I will now divide the whole amount into two halves, and you, kinsman, will take possession of half my gold, since you wished me to have half your land."

King Haraldr now had the gold heaped up and scales brought out, and they divided the treasure between them.[8] Everyone who observed this thought it was a great miracle that so much gold had been collected in one place in the north. But this was in fact the treasure of Byzantium, where everyone says (FJ 96) that there are houses full of ruddy gold.

The two kings were now in a state of high spirits. Then there surfaced a goblet of gold as big as a man's head. King Haraldr picked up the piece and said to King Magnús: "Kinsman, where is the gold with which you could compensate this vessel?"

King Magnús replied: "We have been so involved in war that we have spent all the gold and almost all the silver that we took in land taxes and had in our keeping. There is no gold left but this ring that I have on my arm," and he took the ring from his arm and handed it to King Haraldr.

He looked at it and said: "That doesn't amount to much gold for a man with two kingdoms, and some people will question whether you are even the owner of this ring."

King Magnús replied gravely: "If this ring is not my rightful property, then I don't know what rightful property I have, for King Óláfr gave me the ring when we last parted."

"That is the truth, lord. King Óláfr did give you the ring, but he took the same ring from my father for little cause. It was no pleasure to be a petty king in this country when your father was at the height of his power."[9] The conversation ended there.

They concluded the feast by having twelve of the most powerful men in each retinue swear oaths of reconciliation.[10] They now parted on friendly terms and ruled the realm that winter. They both stayed in Norway, each with his own retinue. This is the way it was told by Þorgils, a prudent man, and he said that he had been told the story by Guðríðr, the daughter of (FJ 97) Guthormr, the son of Steigar-Þórir,[11] He said that he had seen the maple bowl and the cloak that King Haraldr had given Þórir. The latter had by then been cut into an altar cloth. The skald Bǫlverkr confirms this matter:

72.   Heimil varð (es heyrðak)   endisk ykkar frænda
      hoddstríðir þér síðan   allfriðliga á miðli
      grœn (es goll bautt hánum)   sætt (en síðan vætti
      grund es Magnús funduð: Sveinn rómǫldu einnar).

"Hoddstríðir, grœn grund varð þér síðan heimil, es heyrðak, es funduð Magnús, es bautt hánum goll. Sætt endisk allfriðliga á miðli ykkar frænda, en síðan vætti Sveinn rómǫldu einnar."

Hoard enemy [generous king], the green land later came into your hands, I heard, when you met Magnús and gave him gold. The accord between you kinsmen was kept peacefully, but from then on, Sveinn could only await war.

When winter and summer had passed, it is told that the following autumn it chanced that King Magnús and King Haraldr (U 22) were sailing with their retinues westward from Vík and were lying at anchor in a harbor. The following day King Haraldr was ready to set sail first, but King Magnús and his men were not ready yet. King Haraldr sailed ahead, and when they came to the anchorage, King Haraldr anchored in the royal mooring. King Magnús sailed later in the day, and when he reached the harbor, King Haraldr and his retainers had already raised their tents on the ship. King Magnús's men saw that King Haraldr had anchored in the royal mooring, and they told King Magnús. When they had furled their sail, the king said: "Man the oars along the gunwales, and those who are not needed for rowing should break out their weapons. If they do not want to (FJ 98) vacate the mooring for us, we will fight." They did as he said.

King Haraldr was now told that King Magnús was rowing at them fully armed, with shields poised and exhibiting no peaceful demeanor. King Haraldr said: "Cut the hawser and take the ship out of the mooring—my kinsman is angry." They immediately steered the ship out of the mooring, and King Magnús took possession of it. When both had secured their ships, King Haraldr went aboard King Magnús's ship with a few men. King Magnús bade him welcome. "We thought," said Haraldr, "that we were among friends, but a few moments ago we began to have doubts about your intentions. It is true what people say, that youth is impetuous, and I am willing to believe, kinsman, that this was youthfulness."

"This was proof of ancestry, not youthfulness," said King Magnús. "I am able to remember what I gave you and what I withheld. If this little matter had been subtracted from my honor, something else would have followed it quickly. I wish to honor fully the agreement we made and acknowledge everything I gave you, but I also wish to have from you everything that is my due."

King Haraldr arose and replied: "It is an old saw that the wiser man should yield." He then departed and went to his ship. (FJ 99)

In such dealings between the kings it turned out to be difficult to please both of them. King Magnús's men considered that he was in the right, though the less discerning claimed that Haraldr had been rather shamed in this incident. Haraldr's men said that the agreement was to the effect that King Magnús should have the mooring if they both arrived simultaneously but that Haraldr was not obliged to move off if he had come first. They said that Haraldr had behaved well and wisely in this matter. Others, who were ill disposed, considered that King Magnús wanted to break the agreement by wronging and dishonoring his kinsman King Haraldr. Such differences were quickly circulated among the men, (U 23) and there were other problems that created dissension between the two kinsmen. They now ruled the land in the winter, and there was peace and great prosperity in the country with respect to plentiful harvests and other matters.

15. *The Slandering of Þorkell*

There was a man named Þorkell dyðrill, one of King Magnús's stewards.[1] He was slandered to the king and stood accused of not having paid all of the land taxes that he owed. King Magnús went there on his tour of inspection without notice. He was accompanied by a large body of men, and Þorkell did not expect him. The king acted as if he wanted Þorkell to fail in his obligation of hospitality, but such was not the case. Þorkell (FJ 100) gave the king an excellent reception, and the feast proceeded splendidly.

The king was taciturn, and one day when the tables had been cleared away, Þorkell went before him and said: "Sire, would it amuse you to slaughter oxen or goats? I ask you because we need meat for the feast."

The king replied, "Why not?"

A few minutes later Þorkell came before the king leading a goat. The king stood up and brought his sword down on the goat's neck, but it did not penetrate very far. People nonetheless thought they were witnessing a prodigy because some silver pieces tumbled out of the goat.

The king became furious at the sight, saying: "It is clear, Þorkell, that you want to dishonor me in both small matters and large. You have done this to mock me."

Þorkell replied: "I did not wish, sire, that the evil which people tell you about me should be borne out, namely that I betray you. By this time I have been attached to a number of kings and have served them to the best of my ability, first King Óláfr Tryggvason, whom I loved above all men. Then I was in the service of your father, and he would not suspect me of betraying his son. Sire, when the rule of Álfífa overtook us, that wicked age in which every man's money was threatened, I was afraid that I would not be able to protect the king's possessions in my keeping, knowing that they were rightfully yours. I then resorted to this plan and filled goatskins with silver. In this way I was able to safeguard it so that I kept possession of the money. And now you should take your land taxes into your keeping, sire. I do not believe that I have pocketed any of them." (FJ 101)

The king and the other men saw that it amounted to a great deal of money and that he had managed it manfully, as was to be expected of him. The king now gave him his thanks and said that he did not wish him to abandon his office. He said that it was unlikely that another would perform as well. Thus they were reconciled. The king could tell that Þorkell had been slandered and falsely accused. Þorkell was an old man at the time of these events. (U 24)

16. Concerning King Magnús

It happened once that a tall man somewhat up in years came before King Magnús and asked for some money, since the king was known to be a very generous man.

"What is the nature of my obligation to you?" asked the king.

"You owe me very little aside from your kingdom, sire," said the man. The king ordered that half a mark be weighed out and given to him.[1]

Then the man said: "That is a good gift, sire, though on Hlýrskógsheiðr I thought it might amount to more."

The king said, "Are you the man who gave me the advice?" He said that he was.

The king continued: "Accept this ring," and he took the ring from his arm to give to him, but the man replied: "That is a kingly gift, sire, but necessity does not compel me to accept it."[2]

He drew three excellent rings from his arm, saying: "I wish, sire, that you would accept (FJ 102) these rings from me and let me reward you for accepting my advice so kindly and humbly, though it was proffered somewhat candidly. I was on viking expeditions for a long time with your father, and I was as close to him as I am to myself.[3] I often heard your name, and I was eager to know how much you took after him. I wanted to be in your circle of friends, together with my sons. But I have no shortage of money."

The king listened to him kindly and offered his friendship, saying that he was very deserving of it. They parted courteously and on good terms, as was to be expected.

17. How King Magnús Bestowed a Jarldom on Ormr

A mark of King Magnús's good fortune and benevolence is that one time when he was locked in battle with King Sveinn, Sveinn was so hard pressed that he leapt from his ship onto the ship of one of King Magnús's chieftains named

Ormr. He was the son of Ingibjǫrg, daughter of Hákon jarl.[1] Sveinn asked Ormr to spare him, and Ormr agreed.

King Magnús was soon informed of that, as might be expected, and the king asked Ormr how it had come about. He answered: "Sire, that was my second greatest stroke of good fortune. The first was to help you when it was needed, and this was the second."

The king said: "Did it not occur to you that you might incur my displeasure?"

"I did not anticipate that, sire," he said.

"Now I will reward you," said (FJ 103) the king, "as seems fit to me." He gave him a jarldom and said that he was an excellent fellow. This is told to show how unlike other men the king was in making such a fine demonstration and judging that the quality of the man was more important than the enmity that separated them.[2] (U 25)

18. On the Dispute between the Kings

We are told that King Magnús was kind to all the men who were submissive to him but was ferocious toward those who resisted him.[1] There was a man named Þrándr from Upplǫnd (Opplandene).[2] He was a kinsman of Kálfr Árnason, a handsome and wealthy man. King Magnús made his rounds of Upplǫnd and convened thingmeetings at many places. At these meetings he said that he wished to forgive everyone for the grievous matter concerning his father as long as they would now take his part with devotion and steadfastness.

The story has it that Þrándr stood up at the thingmeeting and answered the king in the following words: "Sire," he said, "we are aware that our kinsmen were hostile to your kinsmen, but we were not present at the momentous events that inspired your hatred, to wit the death of your father. I was not in the country at the time. But we wish to treat you well. There is, however, one matter in which I would like to make proof of your affability, and that is to exchange cloaks with you." The king said that he would gladly do so. The cloak that the king received from him (FJ 104) was made of precious fabric. They also exchanged weapons at Þrándr's request, and the difference in value was no less.[3]

Then Þrándr invited the king to a feast, and he was most receptive to the invitation. The king was well entertained by Þrándr. When some time had passed after the feast, King Haraldr learned of the matter. He thought that Þrándr had made a hasty resolution and had demonstrated that he was more eager to honor King Magnús than himself. He was not pleased and took a great dislike to Þrándr.

There was a man named Sveinn gerzki (the Russian). He had arrived with Haraldr and had received a certain fief from him. He was prepared to do whatever Haraldr wanted and was a man of parts. King Haraldr sent Sveinn to

Upplǫnd with eleven men. They were all dressed in dark clothes[4] and gave themselves out as monks. They arrived at Þrándr's farm early in the morning. There were men in the fields in three different places. Sveinn asked the men whom he encountered first whether Þrándr was at home. They said he was not. Then they went up to another group of field workers. Sveinn asked the same question and got the same answer as before.

Then Sveinn spoke to his men: "This is a strange business. They all say the same thing, but I have the feeling that they are not telling the truth. We will press the question a little further with these men."

These men were father and son. They took the younger man and beat him until they conceded that Þrándr was at home. It happened, as they were beating the workers (FJ 105), that Þrándr's foster brother Sigurðr went out and saw what was happening. He went in again and told Þrándr that there were some men in monk's habit beating a field worker.

"They're probably asking about holy places," said Þrándr.

"That may be," said Sigurðr, "but these monks seem to have peculiar ways." (U 26)

"It could also be that they are spies," said Þrándr, "and let's make a test. They will be coming to the building soon, and if they are monks, they will come to the outbuilding and ask for alms. I will invite them to come in and wait until the morning is a little more advanced. But if they are spies, they will not want to do that and will break in. But I have an underground house here and will take refuge there. One end of it is in the main hall. You should stand behind the door, and I suspect that they will go in one after the other as they are lined up. If that happens, you should duck out and close the door. Then I will come in, and it may turn out that we will have them just as much in our power as they have us in theirs."

It turned out as Þrándr guessed.[5] They came to the house and stopped off at the outbuilding to beg alms. When Þrándr and his men were slow to open the door, they tested the lock a little. Then Sveinn said that they would break the door down if it were not opened. "These monks don't hold back," said Þrándr, "and we should rather open the door than let it be broken down."

Sveinn lined up his men to enter and told some to stay outside, but his words were in vain and everybody rushed in. (FJ 106) Sigurðr darted by them and closed the door. Then Þrándr arrived on the scene, and Sveinn and his men were at his mercy. Þrándr had the whole band soundly beaten and gave them their just deserts. They then departed, but Þrándr kept Sveinn with him and treated him well, though he was rather taciturn and thought the hospitality worse than it actually was.

King Haraldr learned of this and was mightily displeased. King Magnús also learned of it and was delighted with Þrándr's resourcefulness. He set out for Upplǫnd with a large following. They arrived in some woods near Þrándr's farm and halted there to see what Þrándr would do. Þrándr was now told that a large body of men was in the area—"and we think it may be King Haraldr."

Þrándr immediately gathered men and sent word to all the nearby settlements. He was so popular among the farmers that everyone was ready to come to his aid. A large and well-armed group assembled, and King Magnús was told that Þrándr had a great multitude armed as if for battle.

Then the king said: "I understand the situation. Some people should go to the farm and say that we come in peace." When Þrándr and his men realized what was afoot, they threw down their weapons on the spot and went out to meet King Magnús joyfully. A feast was prepared for the king. (FJ 107)

The king told Þrándr that King Haraldr was greatly displeased with him and that he was unlikely to be able to maintain his position. He invited him to join his retinue and offered to make arrangements for his land. The offer was accepted, and Þrándr (U 27) joined King Magnús and stayed with him. King Haraldr bided his time, hoping to get at him, but no opportunity was readily available.

When spring came, King Magnús told Þrándr that he found it doubtful whether he could protect him from Haraldr in Norway. "I have now had a ship prepared for you in secret and I want you to sail out to Greenland." This plan was adopted, and the king kept such close watch over him that he himself accompanied Þrándr to the ship and parted with him only when he set sail.

When Þrándr and his men reached the offshore islands after just taking leave of King Magnús, King Haraldr was waiting. He closed on them and joined battle. At this moment King Magnús reflected that he might have taken too early a leave of Þrándr. He realized that in dealing with his kinsman Haraldr he was dealing with a shrewd opponent. He sailed back and saw that a fight had broken out. He ordered his men to bend to the oars and intended to come to Þrándr's assistance. When Haraldr saw King Magnús rowing at them, he broke off and the battle was parted. Þrándr now left Norway according to plan and went to Greenland, where he spent a few years. Both kings remained in Norway and had not a few differences, as is often heard when stories are told about them. (FJ 108)

19. Concerning the Kings

We are told that the farmers now felt that King Haraldr was rather forceful in exacting taxes and land dues, and they found it a heavy burden. Everyone was fonder of King Magnús and preferred to pay him. At a thingmeeting there was a lot of talk about it. King Haraldr was present and claimed these payments as his right. Einarr þambarskelfir learned of this and said to King Magnús: "You will have difficulty securing the realm against King Haraldr." He reported his levies of money and men.

The king attributed it to rumor and the ill will of enemies that Haraldr should stand accused of appropriating more than was rightfully his.[1] Einarr said: "I will inquire how matters stand."

When the thingmeeting was convened, as mentioned above, Einarr came with sixty men. He had been staying with a certain rich widow named Ingibjǫrg, and she provided him with the retainers.

An old man named Tóki stood up at the meeting and said: "We have heard," he said, "that if a man asks for the royal title and there is already a king in the country, who has been accepted at the Eyrarþing, that prior king has the greater authority over us, his people.[2] I request that we should all await the words of King Magnús and honor him in every way."

Einarr stood up and thanked him for his words, as well as all the farmers who had assembled and wished to accord King Magnús the greatest honor. Then King Haraldr spoke: "You are high and mighty (U 28) now, Einarr, and now as always you are making your opposition to me clear. It will be a fine (FJ 109) day when pride takes a fall. By as much as you are now a head taller than everyone else, you will soon be a head shorter." With that, the thingmeeting was disbanded.

We are now told that the two kings, Magnús and Haraldr, were both present at a feast hosted by a man named Áslákr. King Magnús and some of his men sat on one bench and King Haraldr on the other. King Magnús's brother Þórir sat opposite King Haraldr. Þórir was taciturn and not deft with words. King Haraldr thought it a dishonor to sit across from him at a drinking party and aimed the following ditty at him:

73.   Þegi þú Þórir   þegn est ógegn
       heyrðak at héti   Hvinngestr faðir þinn.

Be quiet, Þórir, you're a quarrelsome man; I heard that your father was called Hvinngestr [Thief-guest].

Þórir was a proud man and did not think much of the ditty.[3] He was greatly angered, but had no words for an answer. That affected him deeply, and he became morose.

One day the brothers Magnús and Þórir met, and the king asked: "Why are you so quiet and morose, brother?" Þórir told him what had happened and said that he was irked by Haraldr's sarcasm and scorn, but that he had no words in response. The king said: "I have a remedy. Recite the following if he mocks you": (FJ 110)

74.   Gerði eigi sá   garð of hestreðr
       sem Sigurðr sýr   sá vas þinn faðir.

He never sheathed the phallus of a horse like Sigurðr sýr [Sow]: he was your father.

The next morning when Þórir and King Haraldr met, the king mocked him in the accustomed way. This time Þórir was not silent and recited the verses that had been taught to him. King Haraldr reacted furiously and drew his sword to strike at Þórir, but King Magnús ran up and told them to desist. He suspected that it would not do to let Þórir sit across from Haraldr any longer, and he moved him to the seat closest to his own.

Next there is mention of the kings' dispute,[4] into which Einarr inquired at the thingmeeting, and the rumor that circulated to the effect that Haraldr was more grasping than the agreements prescribed. Testimony was taken, and we are told that their host Áslákr testified on King Haraldr's behalf.

When King Magnús heard that, he said: "If it were up to me, I would wish an ill outcome for those who bear false witness against me." They then parted for the time being. (FJ 111; U 29)

20. Concerning Þorsteinn Hallsson

We are told that at one time Þorsteinn Hallsson came back from a trading voyage to Dublin, which had been undertaken without the approval or leave of the king. Nor had they paid the landing tax that the steward was entitled to collect.[1] He had in fact demanded it, but Þorsteinn maintained that he was not obligated to pay it because he was the king's retainer and thought that he was also privileged to suspend the payment for the fifteen men who were with him. For this reason the matter had not been pressed.

He sailed out to his farm in Iceland during the summer. The king learned of the whole affair and said that he would have waived the landing tax for Þorsteinn himself but not for his men. He said that he did not remember promising any such thing. But he said that it was a more serious matter that he had undertaken the trading voyage to Dublin without having the king's leave, and for that reason King Magnús outlawed Þorsteinn and said that he would discourage all others from breaking the law, no matter how important they were.

The next summer Þorsteinn came to Norway and had with him some excellent stud horses. They arrived in the north in Þrándheimr. People kept away from Þorsteinn because of the king's prohibition. (FJ 112) He always sat in a separate room with his men. The stud horses were pastured above the town at Íluvellir (Ilevolden), and Þorsteinn went there to see them. Einarr þambarskelfir and his son Eindriði were there, and one day Einarr went through the town and out to Íluvellir. He looked over the horses and praised them greatly. When they were ready to leave and were talking about who might be the owner of the horses, Þorsteinn came up and greeted Einarr. He asked him what he thought of the horses, and he answered that he liked the look of them.

"Then I want you to have them," said Þorsteinn, but Einarr declined to accept them.[2]

"I know," said Þorsteinn, "that you are not averse to gifts from people like me."

"That's true," said Einarr, "but you are in a very vulnerable situation, and we take that into consideration."

"That's how it will have to be," said Þorsteinn. Then they parted.

A little later Eindriði went to see the horses. He praised them enthusiastically and asked who the owner might be. He said that he had never seen finer
horses. Þorsteinn came up and greeted him. He said that he would be glad
to have him accept the horses. Eindriði did so and thanked him for the gift.
Then they parted. When Eindriði met with his father, Einarr said that he would
have given a lot to prevent him from accepting the horses. Eindriði said that
he didn't see it that way and that Þorsteinn was a good man to deal with. Einarr
said: "You are not very clear about the forcefulness of my foster son King
Magnús if you think it is easy to be reconciled with him. But perhaps you will
manage it." (FJ 113)

Eindriði invited Þorsteinn to stay with him. He went to his home and was
given the seat next to Eindriði. During the winter he was well entertained. But
King Magnús was displeased. (U 30) People told him that it was not honorable
that they should entertain outlaws who were in royal disfavor in light of the fact
that he had put father and son in command of all Þrándheimr. The king replied monosyllabically. The report has it that Einarr was less than cordial toward Þorsteinn during the winter.[3] He said that Eindriði would offer a good
settlement for him, and he said that it was now none of his concern.

Einarr and Eindriði always celebrated Christmas with King Magnús, and
Eindriði told his father that he would do so as usual. "So you say," said Einarr,
"but I will stay at home, and it would seem to me wiser if you did the same."

Eindriði nonetheless prepared to set out, and Þorsteinn went *with him*.
They had ten companions and came to a little farm, where they stayed the
night. In the morning Þorsteinn took a look outside and *came back in*. He
told Eindriði that there were men riding up to the yard—"and it looks like
your father."

That was the case. Einarr arrived and spoke to Eindriði: "It is a strange idea
to visit King Magnús and (FJ 114) take Þorsteinn with you. You should rather
go back to Gimsar (Gimsan), and I will meet with the king. It will take all my
effort to arrange a settlement, and I know you and the king well enough to realize that you will not frame your words in a helpful way. That won't make it
easier for me later on."

They proceeded in this way. Eindriði went home, and Einarr went on to
town [Niðaróss]. The king gave him a kind reception, and they talked over
many matters. Einarr sat next to the king. On the fourth day of Christmas he
brought up the question of Þorsteinn with the king and said that he wished to
facilitate a reconciliation. He said that Þorsteinn was a good man to have in
one's ranks and that he would not be stinting in his offers.

The king said: "This is not something I wish to talk about."

"I am very reluctant to incur your wrath," replied Einarr. He dropped the
subject, and the king cheered up right away when they spoke of other things.

Time now passed until the eighth day of Christmas, and Einarr brought up the subject again. The result was the same as before. When the thirteenth day of Christmas came around, Einarr asked the king to accept a reconciliation— "and I have some reason to believe that you will honor my request."

The king answered: "This is not a matter I will discuss," he said, "and it seems to me strange that you would entertain a man who is in my disfavor."

"I thought," said Einarr, "that you would grant my request on behalf of one man, and we are eager to honor you in every way. I believe we (FJ 115) have always done so. This matter is more of Eindriði's making than mine, but I think that the cost will be very high before he is killed. I am in a difficult position, sire, when you and my son are at odds and you are not willing to accept a monetary compensation for Þorsteinn and would rather take up arms against my son. I will not bear arms against you, but I think that you do not have much recollection of the time I went east to Russia to bring you home and bolstered your rule and became your foster father. I spend every moment thinking of how I can increase your honor, (U 31) but now I will go abroad and not stand at your side any longer. Some people may think that you are not gaining a great deal in all of this."

Einarr jumped up in anger and headed out of the hall. The king arose and went after him. He put his arm on Einarr's shoulder and said: "Be welcome in our affection here," he said. "Our friendship will never be sundered. Be at peace with the man as you like." Einarr was now pacified, and Þorsteinn was reconciled to the king. (FJ 116)

21. Concerning the Kings

It is told that at one time both kings were sitting at table in the hall when Arnórr jarlaskald arrived. He had composed a poem about each of them. As the skald was tarring his ship, the kings' messengers came to him and asked him to present his poems. He went immediately, without washing the tar off.[1]

When he came to the hall, he said to the doorkeepers, "Make way for the kings' skald." Then he went in before King Magnús and King Haraldr, saying: "Hail to both monarchs."

Then King Haraldr said: "Which of us will hear his poem first?"

"The younger," he said.

The king asked, "Why the younger first?"

"Sire," he said, "we are told that youth is impatient." It seemed to both of them that it was more honorable to be addressed first.[2]

Now the skald began his recital and made mention first of the jarls overseas in the west. Then he narrated his own travels, and when it got to that point, King Haraldr said to King Magnús: "What is the point of listening to this poem when he talks of his own travels and the jarls in the west?"

King Magnús said: "Let us be patient, kinsman. I suspect that before it is over, you will think that enough has been made of my praises." Then the skald recited the following:

75. Magnús hlýð til máttigs óðar   haukr réttr est þú Hǫrða dróttinn
      mangi veit ek fremra annan   hverr gramr es þér stóru verri
      yppa ráðumk yðru kappi   meiri verði þinn an þeira
      Jóta gramr í kvæði fljótu: þrifnuðr allr unz himinn rifnar.

                                                                                          (FJ 117)

"Magnús, hlýð til máttigs óðar; veit ek mangi annan fremra; ráðumk yppa yðru kappi, Jóta gramr, í fljótu kvæði. Haukr réttr est þú, Hǫrða dróttinn; hverr gramr es stóru verri þér; verði allr þrifnuðr þinn meiri an þeira, unz himinn rifnar."

Magnús, listen to the powerful poem; I know no man more prominent; I shall praise your courage, king of the Jótar [people of Jylland, Jutland], in swift verse. You are a true hawk, lord of the Hǫrðar [people of Hordaland]; every king is far inferior to you; may your prosperity increase more than theirs until heaven bursts asunder.

King Haraldr interjected: "Praise this king however you wish," he said, "but do not speak ill of other kings." Now the skald kept reciting, and the poem included these stanzas:

76. Ótti kunnuð elgjum hætta   glíkan berr þik hvǫssum hauki
      œðiveðrs á skelfðan grœði   hollvinr minn í lypting innan
      fengins golls eða fœðið ella   (aldri skríðr und fylki frægra
      flestan aldr und drifnu tjaldi: farligt eiki) Visundr snarla. (U 32)

"Ótti fengins golls, kunnuð hætta elgjum œðiveðrs á skelfðan grœði, eða fœðið ella flestan aldr und drifnu tjaldi. Visundr berr þik snarla, hollvinr minn, glíkan hvǫssum hauki í lypting innan; aldri skríðr farligt eiki und frægra fylki."

Terror of captured gold [generous king], you know how to risk the moose of abundant wind [ships] on the rough sea and otherwise you spend most of your life beneath the windswept awning. Visundr [bison] carries you, my dear friend, swiftly on the raised stern like a keen hawk; never will a splendid ship glide beneath a more glorious king.

77. Eigi létuð jǫfra bági   hlunna es sem rǫðull renni
      yðru nafni mannkyn hafna   reiðar búningr upp í heiði
      hvártki flýr þú hlenna þreytir   (hrósak því es herskip glæsir
      hyr né malm í broddi styrjar: hlenna dolgr) eða vitar brenni.

"Jǫfra bági, létuð eigi mannkyn hafna yðru nafni; hlenna þreytir, þú flýr hvártki hyr né malm í broddi styrjar. Hlunna reiðar búningr es, sem rǫðull renni upp í heiði, eða vitar brenni; hrósak því, es hlenna dolgr glæsir herskip."

Enemy of kings, you did not let mankind forget your name; tester of thieves [righteous king], you flee neither fire nor iron at the battle front. The rigging of the chariot of the ship rollers [ship] is like the sun rising on the clear sky or beacons burning; I praise the fact that the enemy of thieves [righteous king] outfits his warships splendidly.

Then King Haraldr said: "This man really has the wind under his wings, and I hardly know where it will end."

78.   Mǫnnum lízk es mildingr rennir   eyðendr fregnk at elska þjóðir
        Meita hlíðir sævar skíði   (inndrótt þín es hǫfð at minnum)
        unnar jafnt sem ásamt renni   grœði lostins guði et næsta
        engla fylki himna þengils: geima Vals í þessum heimi.

(FJ 118)

"Mǫnnum lízk, es mildingr rennir Meita hlíðir sævar skíði, jafnt sem engla fylki himna þengils renni unnar ásamt. Fregnk, at þjóðir elska eyðendr grœði lostins geima Vals et næsta guði í þessum heimi; inndrótt þín es hǫfð at minnum."

When the generous king lets the ski of the sea [ship] skim the slopes of Meiti [sea king, waves], it appears to men as if the host of angels of the heavenly lord flitted together across the waves. I hear that people love that destroyer of the wave-battered Valr [horse] of the sea [ship, sea king] next to God in this world; your retinue will always be remembered.

When the poem was finished, the skald began Haraldr's poem. It was called the "Blágagladrápa," or the black goose panegyric, and it was a good poem. When the poem was finished, King Haraldr was asked whether he thought his was the better poem, but he said: "I can see the difference between the poems. Mine will be soon forgotten and no one will be able to recite it, but the poem composed about King Magnús will be recited as long as the North is peopled."[3]

King Haraldr gave the skald a spear inlaid with gold,[4] and King Magnús began by giving him a gold ring. Then he went out along the hall with the gold ring drawn over the neck of the spear and said: "I will raise both royal gifts on high."

King Haraldr said: "That fellow was rather long-winded."[5] The skald had promised King Haraldr to compose a memorial poem for him in the event that he survived him. King Magnús later gave him a trading vessel with a full cargo and became his close friend.

22. The Good Counsels of King Haraldr

It befell the son of a distinguished woman that he lost his memory, almost as if he had gone out of this mind. His mother came to King Haraldr and asked him for advice. He said, "Go to King Magnús. There is no better source of advice in the land, and whatever he suggests will be beneficial and efficacious."

She went to King Magnús (FJ 119) and asked for some good advice. He said, "Have you gone to King Haraldr?"

"I went to him," she said, "and he sent me to you," and she reported their conversation. King Magnús replied: "No one is wiser than King Haraldr in this land, and he will know the solution if he is willing to provide it."

Then she went to see King Haraldr a second time and told of her conversation (U 33) with King Magnús. Haraldr said: "I will suggest something. I think I know what your son suffers from. He has lost the capacity to dream, and that does no one any good. It is not our nature not to dream without suffering some injury. Go to the place where King Magnús has bathed and have the boy sip from the basin. Then make him chant, and even if he gets sleepy or begins to yawn, do not let him sleep. After that go to the place where the king has rested and let him sleep there. It is not unlikely that he will then recover his dreams."

She did everything she was told, and the boy slept for a while. When he awoke, he laughed and said: "I dreamed, mother, that the two kings Magnús and Haraldr came to me, and both whispered to me, each in one ear. King Magnús said this: 'Be the best you can,' he said. King Haraldr said: 'Learn and retain as best you can.' This boy turned out to be an outstanding man, and King Haraldr's cure worked for him. King Magnús composed this stanza:

79.   Margr kveðr sér at sorgum   enn ef einhver bannar
      sverðrjóðr alin verða (FJ 120)   Eldgefn fyr mér svefna
      (uggik allítt seggja   víst veldr siklings systir
      ótta) búkarls dóttur: svinn andvǫku minni.

"Margr sverðrjóðr kveðr búkarls dóttur verða alin sér at sorgum; uggik allítt seggja ótta. Enn, ef einhver Eldgefn bannar svefna fyr mér, veldr svinn siklings systir víst andvǫku minni."

Many a sword reddener [warrior] claims that the farmer's daughter causes him grief; I care very little for men's fears. Yet, if a certain fire-Gefn [goddess; woman] deprives me of my sleep, it is certainly the sagacious sister of the king who causes my unrest.

23. Concerning King Magnús and Margrét

There was a distinguished district chieftain named Þrándr living to the east in Vík. His estate was called At Stokkar.[1] He had a daughter named Margrét. She was a highly intelligent woman, and very beautiful. Word of her outstanding qualities spread far and wide.[2]

There was a man named Sigurðr, nicknamed "king's kin." He was installed as a steward not far from where Þrándr lived. He was a handsome man and closely related to King Magnús. It is reported that one autumn there was a well-attended feast at Þrándr's residence, and many of the landholders came together there. It was Þrándr's habit to consult his daughter on practically all matters.

One day, as the feast was in progress, people were standing outside in the fields, where there was a good view, and were playing various games. As the day declined, they saw a ship splendidly adorned with dragons' heads and weather-vanes, with shields ranged stem to stern. As it approached, they saw that it was manned by valiant men rowing with an even stroke. There was a lot of specu-lation about who they might be.

Þrándr went to his daughter and told her the news—"we have no reason to expect King Magnús, (U 34) but these look to be noble men."

She replied: "It is still unlikely," she said, "that it will be King Magnús, and we may be very grateful (FJ 121) if some time passes before he visits us."[3]

Þrándr said: "Why do you say that? Everyone loves him, and we will make him very welcome."

"That is your view," she said, "but I still have a feeling that tells me that it would be better for him not to come."

The ship came into the anchorage, and men went down to meet it. It turned out to be King Magnús. People streamed back to the residence, and a great re-ception was prepared. The king was in a good mood and the chieftain treated him with perfect hospitality. When the women entered the hall, Margrét went first but did not greet the king. He asked Þrándr who the fair woman was who preceded the others. Þrándr said it was his daughter. The king said: "And still she does not want to greet us. She must certainly be well bred, and she is a beautiful woman to boot. I wish to spend the night with her."

"That does not befit your honor, sire," said Þrándr.

"This is nonetheless the way it will be," said the king.

Þrándr told his daughter about the king's intention, and she said that it did not take her by surprise. "I know," she said, "that the king only has in mind what is contrary to my wishes, and it is difficult to love him first and then lose him immediately."[4]

Þrándr repeated her words to King Magnús, and he replied: "I am not gen-erally reputed to be a scoundrel, and this can be done in a way that turns to her advantage. But there is no fitting alternative to my deciding this matter."

When Þrándr saw how matters stood, he had a chamber carefully prepared and a bed made. She was brought there and was to occupy the chamber alone. She was very downcast. The construction was such that there were two doors to the room (FJ 122). As she lay there, she heard someone crave admission twice at one of the doors. The third time the door was opened. A man entered wearing a hood and asked whether anybody was there. She said not a word. The man then made his way to the bed and took ahold of her, saying: "Do you think you are in a difficult position with respect to the king?"

"It is most certainly not to my liking," she said.

"Do you want to make a bargain with me if I can arrange it that the king refrains from what displeases you? If so, you must entrust yourself to me."

"I think that is preferable," she said.

"So be it," he replied. He then touched her breast and marked her for himself, and she felt a cold shiver go through her. He said: "When the king lies down next to you, say that you have been with his kinsman Sigurðr, and let us see how that affects him. I will see to it that nothing more is needed."

The man went away after that, and the king arrived a little later. When he had gotten into bed with her, he told his men to leave and turned toward her with winning words. (U 35) He said that he would do much to honor her if she would favor him.

She replied: "There is no little peril involved since you are such a noble and distinguished man. You should know that I have been with your kinsman Sigurðr."[5]

The king responded angrily and jumped to his feet: "Then it is not fitting that I should lie in this bed." He went out and proceeded to the room where Þrándr was sleeping. He knocked on the door. Þrándr opened it and saw immediately that the king was very angry. (FJ 123)

He asked what the trouble was. "I am most eager," said the king, "to have Sigurðr brought here." Þrándr immediately provided men for the purpose, and the king gave them instructions to tell him that he was to make the trip whether he wanted or not.

The messengers set out and arrived at Sigurðr's residence. They asked him to get ready as quickly as possible and come with them. They gave him the king's message uncut. He said that he would go and that he expected any trip for the purpose of seeing such a kinsman of his as the king would turn out to be a good one. Sigurðr went with them and met with the king. Magnús was very angry and asked what meetings he might have had with Margrét.

Sigurðr said: "I have attended Þrándr's feasts, sire," he said, "and I have seen her, but have not talked to her very much. I am, however, prepared to swear that I have had no commerce with her."

The king then had Margrét summoned and questioned her closely about what had happened. She now told of the man's visit, his advice, and the mark he left. The king said: "Let me see the mark." She did so, and when the king saw the mark on her breast, it looked to be in the shape (FJ 124) of a silver penny.

Then the king said: "It turns out," he said, "that my father does not wish me to lie with this woman. The man who visited her was my father. I reacted so strongly and resolved the matter so quickly because God and Saint Óláfr were opposed. And now, Sigurðr, you shall have this match, and my friendship with it."

The matter was concluded as the king prescribed, and Margrét was married to Sigurðr. He became a powerful figure and an excellent man. She was also deemed to be an outstandingly intelligent woman and was distinguished in many other ways. The king departed when the feast was over and continued on his business. That is the end of this tale.

24. *Concerning Hreiðarr heimski*

There was a man named Þórðr. He was the son of Þorgrímr, who was the son of the Hreiðarr whom Glúmr killed.[1] Þórðr was a small man in stature and handsome. He had a brother named Hreiðarr, who was an ugly man and had scarcely the wits to take care of himself. (U 36) He was swift of foot and very strong, with an easygoing disposition. He was always at home, but Þórðr traveled abroad. He was King Magnús's retainer and was well thought of.

Once when Þórðr was readying his ship in Eyjafjǫrðr, his brother turned up. When Þórðr saw him, he asked him why he had come. Hreiðarr said: "I would not be here if I did not have business."

"What is it you want?" asked Þórðr.

"I want to go abroad," replied Hreiðarr.

Þórðr said: "I don't think this voyage is the right thing for you. I would rather offer you the whole of our paternal inheritance, and that amounts to twice as much money as I have invested in my trade."

Hreiðarr said: "My wits aren't worth much," he said, "if I accept this disproportionate share of the money and am obliged to sacrifice myself by losing your protection. Everybody will set about cheating me out of our money since I have no management skills (FJ 125) that will avail. Your part will be no easier if I come to blows with men or am otherwise embroiled with those who are after my money and try to steal it away from me. It might turn out that I am beaten or wounded because of my actions. It is also true that it will be hard to hold me back if I really want to make the voyage."

"That may well be," said Þórðr, "but don't tell anybody else about the voyage." He promised not to.[2]

As soon as the brothers parted, Hreiðarr started to tell anyone who would listen that he was about to go abroad with his brother. Everybody criticized Þórðr for taking a fool with him, but they sailed when they had made their preparations. The voyage went smoothly, and they put in at Bjǫrgvin (Bergen). Þórðr immediately asked about the king's whereabouts and was told that he was in town, having arrived a short time before. He did not want to be troubled[3] the same day since he had just arrived and needed to rest.

People could see right away that Hreiðarr stood out among other men. He was tall and ugly and not very loquacious when he met others. Early in the morning, before the others awoke, Hreiðarr got up and called out: "Wake up, brother. The slug-a-bed is slow to learn. I'm onto something and have just heard a strange sound."

"What did it sound like?" asked Þórðr.

"Like a living creature," said Hreiðarr, "and it made a loud roar, but I have no idea what the sound was."

"Don't make such a fuss," said Þórðr, "it must have been a trumpet blast."

"What does it mean?" asked Hreiðarr.

Þórðr replied: "A trumpet always signals a meeting or a ship levy."

"What kind of a meeting?" asked Hreiðarr.

"It is a forum for discussing difficult issues," said Þórðr, "and for any business the king judges should be brought to the attention of the people."

"Will the king be at the meeting?" asked Hreiðarr.

"I am certain he will be," said Þórðr.

"Then I must go there," said Hreiðarr, "because I want to be the first on hand where *I can see the greatest number of men* gathered together."

"That makes for a real difference between us," (FJ 126) said Þórðr, "because the less you get into crowds, the better off you seem to me (U 37), and I *have no intention of going."

"That's no way* to speak," said Hreiðarr. "We should go together. It will not turn out better for you if I go alone, and you're not going to talk me out of *this trip*."

Hreiðarr ran off, and Þórðr could see now that he had to go. He went after him, but Hreiðarr went at top speed and put a lot of distance between them. When Hreiðarr saw that Þórðr was lagging behind, he said: "It's a disadvantage to be small and have almost no strength, but you could at least have had speed, though I can see that you did not get much. It wouldn't be bad for you to be less good-looking, if only you could keep up with other men."

Þórðr said: "I don't know that your strength is any less of a disadvantage to you than my lack of strength is to me."

"Let's put it to the test by arm-wrestling, brother," said Hreiðarr. They did so and kept at it for a while until Þórðr's hand began to go numb and he let go. He thought it would not improve their relations to go on with Hreiðarr's tomfoolery.

Hreiðarr rushed off now and did not stop until he got to the top of a hill. He made big eyes when he saw the great crowd of men at the meeting. When Þórðr caught up with him, he said: "Let's go together, brother," and so they did. At the thingmeeting a lot of people recognized Þórðr and gave him a warm welcome. The king got wind of it, and Þórðr approached the king and greeted him. The king gave him a friendly reception.

The two brothers got separated as soon as they arrived at the thingmeeting, and Hreiðarr was pushed and pulled around quite a lot. He chattered away and laughed a lot, and that made it all the more fun to roughhouse with him. But it soon turned into hard going.

The king asked Þórðr for news, then asked who in his company should be received at court (FJ 127). "My brother has come with me," said Þórðr.

"He is likely to be an excellent man if he is like you," said the king.

Þórðr said, "He's not like me."

To this the king replied: "He may still be a good fellow. In what way are the two of you most unlike?"

Þórðr said: "He is a big man, ugly, and rather unsightly.[4] He is strong and has a good disposition."

The king said: "He may yet have many good qualities."

Þórðr replied: "He wasn't reputed to be very bright when he was young."

"I would rather judge by his present state," said the king—"can he take care of himself?"

"Not really," answered Þórðr.

The king asked: "Why did you take him abroad?"

"He and I are equal owners in our estate, but he makes no use of the money and has not taken a division of the property. The only thing he asked was to go abroad with me. It did not seem right to deny him this one thing when he leaves me in charge of many others. It also seemed to me likely that you might bring him good luck if he came to see you."

"I would like to see him," said the king.

"So be it," Þórðr replied, "but he has been (U 38) chased off somewhere just now." The king then sent for him.

When Hreiðarr heard that the king wanted to meet him, he went about with his head in the clouds and nearly stumbled over anything in his way, not knowing what to make of the idea that the king would ask to see him. He was dressed in ankle breeches[5] and had a gray cloak on. When he came before the king, he fell to his knee and greeted him devotedly. The king responded laughingly and said: "If you have something to tell me, say it quickly because there are others waiting to speak to me."

Hreiðarr answered: "The matter I have in mind is very pressing—I would like to inspect you, sire."

"How do you like what you see?" asked the king.

"Very much," replied Hreiðarr, "but I don't think that I yet have a clear enough view of you."

"How shall we go about that?" (FJ 128) asked the king—"Do you want me to stand up?"

"I would like that," he replied.

When the king had stood up, he said: "That ought to give you a clear enough view of me."

"Not quite clear enough," said Hreiðarr, "though better than before."

"Do you want me to take off my cloak?" asked the king.

"Indeed I do," said Hreiðarr.

The king replied: "We should have a little talk about this beforehand. You Icelanders are a sly lot,[6] and I don't know whether this is intended as a mockery. I wish to stipulate that none is intended."

Hreiðarr replied: "Sire, no one would dare to mock or deceive you."

The king now took off his cloak and said: "Look at me as closely as you wish."

"So I shall," said Hreiðarr. He circled around the king and kept mumbling the same thing. "Really splendid, really splendid," he said.[7]

The king asked: "Have you seen enough of me now?"

"Yes indeed," he said.

"Then what is your opinion of me?" asked the king.

Hreiðarr replied: "My brother Þórðr has not exaggerated all the good qualities he has ascribed to you."

The king asked: "Do you have any criticism of what you see—anything that is not generally known?"

"I don't wish to criticize," he said, "nor am I able, for anyone would wish to be in your shoes if he had the choice."

"You're going all out," said the king.

Hreiðarr answered: "It's dangerous for others to make compliments," he said, "if my opinion of you isn't true as stated."[8]

The king said: "Find something to criticize even if it's insignificant."

"The closest I can come, sire, is that one eye is a little higher than the other."[9]

"Just one other person discovered that," said the king, "and that was my kinsman Haraldr. And now we will even the score," said the king. "It is your turn to stand up and take your cloak off so that I can inspect you." (FJ 129)

Hreiðarr threw off his cloak and revealed dirty hands. He had big, ugly hands, indifferently cared for. The king (U 39) looked at him closely.

Then Hreiðarr said: "Sire," he asked, "what do you find to criticize in me?"

The king replied: "I don't think there's an uglier man in Christendom than you are."

"That's what people say," said Hreiðarr, "but is there anything about me that in your view is to my advantage?"

The king said: "Your brother Þórðr told me that you had a good disposition."

"That is true," said Hreiðarr, "and I think that it is a pity that it is so."

"You will nonetheless be capable of anger," said the king.

"Bless you for saying so," said Hreiðarr, "but how long will it take?"

"I don't know exactly," said the king, "but I rather imagine it will be this winter."[10]

"An excellent prophecy," said Hreiðarr.

The king asked whether Hreiðarr was good with his hands. Hreiðarr said: "I can't tell because I've never tried."

"It doesn't seem unlikely all the same," said the king.

"That's welcome news," said Hreiðarr, "and it is likely to be as you say, but I seem to need a winter's lodging."

The king replied: "You are in my care, but I think you would be lodged better where there are fewer people."

"That is so," said Hreiðarr, "but there are never so few people that word of what is said doesn't get around, especially if it seems amusing. I'm not cautious in my speech, and a lot of words slip out. It might happen that people are angered at my words and mock me and make too much of what I have said in jest. It seems to me wiser to be near someone who cares for me, like my brother Þórðr, even if there are a lot of people present, rather than to be where there are few people and none to take a hand on my behalf."

The king said: "The choice is up to you—both you and your brother should stay at court if that is your preference." (FJ 130)

Hreiðarr ran off as soon as he heard the king's words and told anyone who would listen that his visit with the king had turned out extremely well. In particular, he told his brother Þórðr that the king had granted him leave to stay at court.

Þórðr said: "Provide yourself with proper clothes and weapons. Nothing less would be fitting, and we have the means to afford them. Many men respond well to fine clothes, and it is harder to meet the standard at the king's court than elsewhere. It is important not to become the object of the courtiers' mockery."

Hreiðarr said: "You're not close to the mark if you think that I am going to dress up in fine clothes."

Þórðr replied: "Let's take a measure of homespun then."

"That's better," said Hreiðarr.

It was done as Þórðr suggested, and Hreiðarr was amenable. He now wore clothes of homespun and cleaned himself up so that he seemed to be quite a different person. He still appeared to be ill-favored, but quite strapping.[11]

Hreiðarr's nature was nonetheless such that when he and Þórðr were at court, he was at first subject to a lot of rallying by the courtiers. *They found many* ways to tease him (U 40) and discovered that he was voluble no matter what. They had a lot of fun at his expense, *but he* always laughed cheerfully at what they said and was so full of jest that he outdid all of them, both with respect to volubility and most particularly *tests of strength* because he was strong. When they realized that he was not vulnerable, the courtiers gave up*. . . .*

At that time both King Magnús and King Haraldr were ruling the land. There had been some trouble *between the kings because* one of King Magnús's retainers had killed a retainer of Haraldr's, and a meeting had been arranged for the kings to *meet*[12] in order to settle the matter.

When Hreiðarr heard (FJ 131) that King Magnús was going to meet with King Haraldr, he went to see King Magnús and said: "There is something I would like to ask you."

"What is it?" asked the king.

Hreiðarr said: "To go to the mediation meeting. I am not widely traveled, and I am very curious to see two kings in the same place at the same time."

The king replied: "It is true that you are not widely traveled, but I will not grant you this journey because you are not fit to fall into the hands of King Haraldr's men. Harm might come of it either for you or for others. I fear that you might succumb to the anger you long for, and I think it would be best to avoid that."

Hreiðarr said: "That's what I wanted to hear, and I will certainly go if there is a prospect of anger."

The king asked: "Will you go even if I do not allow it?"

Hreiðarr answered: "I will go all the same."

"Do you think that dealing with me is the same as dealing with your brother Þórðr?—With him you always get your way."

Hreiðarr said: "It will be all the better to deal with you because you are wiser than he is."

The king could see now that he would go even if he forbade it or excluded him from his company. He thought it no better if he came in different company, and it seemed to him doubtful how well it would sit with Hreiðarr if he alone chose to decide the matter. He therefore preferred to permit Hreiðarr to come with him. He was given a horse to ride, and as soon as they set out, he rode off at a great pace. He exercised no control so that his horse collapsed from exhaustion.

When the king was informed of this, he said: "That's a lucky break. Let Hreiðarr go home and not make the trip."

Hreiðarr said: "It won't stop me just because my horse collapsed. My speed isn't to much avail if I can't keep up with you."

They continued on their way, and many of them rode next to him (FJ 132) and thought it good sport to test his speed, considering how unashamedly[13] he vaunted his own powers. But it turned out that he wore down every horse that came forward.[14] He said that he didn't (U 41) deserve to come to the meeting if he couldn't keep up with them. For that reason, many of the men dismounted.

When they came to the place where the kings were to meet, King Magnús spoke to Hreiðarr: "Do what I say and stick close by me. Don't leave my side. I am not very reassured about what may happen when King Haraldr's men catch sight of you."

Hreiðarr said that he would do as the king said—"the closer I am to you, the better I feel."

Then the kings met and began their discussions. King Haraldr's men saw that Hreiðarr was there. They had heard tell of him and thought this was a real opportunity. As the kings were discussing, Hreiðarr joined Haraldr's men, and they took him off to a nearby woods. They tugged at his clothing and pushed him about. Sometimes he flew about like a wisp of straw and sometimes he stood like a stone wall so that they bounced off him.[15]

But soon it got to the point where the sport was rather rough. They began to use their ax handles and scabbards. The studs in the metal scabbard tips caught him in the head and left scratches.[16] But he still acted as if it were rollicking fun and laughed the whole time. When that had gone on for a while, their sport wasn't taking any turn for the better.

Hreiðarr said: "Now we've had some good fun, and it's time to stop because I am tiring of it. Let's go to your king, whom I am eager to see."

"That will never happen," they said. "You are too great a troublemaker to see our king, and we would rather send you to the devil." He was not much pleased by the prospect and had the feeling that they (FJ 133) would do what they said.

At this point his resentment was kindled and he became angry. He seized the man who was most aggressive and was giving him the roughest treatment. Swinging him into the air, he thrust him down on his head so that his skull split and he died. They suddenly thought that his strength was superhuman and fled from the fray.

They went and told King Haraldr that one of his retainers had been slain. The king said: "Kill the man who did it."

"That's easier said than done," they said, "because he is already gone."

Hreiðarr now met up with King Magnús. The king asked: "Have you found out what it is like to get angry?"

"Yes," he said, "now I know."

"How did it feel?" asked the king. "I had the impression that you were curious to know."

Hreiðarr said: "I didn't like it because I felt like killing all of them."

The king said: "It always seemed to me that your anger would be dangerous. I will now send you to my district chieftain Eyvindr in Upplǫnd so that he can protect you from King Haraldr, because I have no confidence that you can be protected as long as you are with (U 42) my retinue, given the fact that Haraldr and I are in frequent contact. My kinsman is resourceful and difficult to fend off. You should come back to me when I send for you."

Now Hreiðarr took his leave and went to Upplǫnd. Eyvindr received him as the king instructed.

The kings had now concluded the matter on which they differed and had reached a settlement, but they could not agree on Hreiðarr's case. King Magnús thought that Haraldr's men had forfeited any compensation and were responsible for any breaches of the law. He thought that Haraldr's retainer had fallen without title to indemnity. But King Haraldr demanded compensation for his retainer, and they parted with no resolution.

It did not take long before King Haraldr learned where Hreiðarr was in seclusion. He set out and came to Eyvindr's residence in Upplǫnd (FJ 134) with a company of sixty men. He arrived in the early morning and hoped to catch people by surprise, but that was not the way it turned out, because Eyvindr was expecting him and was never unprepared. He had secretly summoned men, and they were in the woods close to his residence. Eyvindr was to signal them if King Haraldr came and he needed reinforcement.

We are told that at one time prior to Haraldr's arrival Hreiðarr had asked Eyvindr for some silver and gold. "Are you a skilled craftsman?" asked Eyvindr.

Hreiðarr said: "King Magnús told me I was, but I have no way of knowing because I have never tried it. But he is likely to have said what he was sure of, and for that reason I believe him."

Eyvindr said: "You are a strange man, but I will give you the wherewithal. You should return the silver to me if your work fails, but otherwise keep it for yourself."

Hreiðarr was locked in a house and began his smithying. Before his job was finished, King Haraldr arrived, but as I have already indicated,[17] Eyvindr was by no means unprepared. He accorded the king a good reception, and as they sat at drink, the king asked if Hreiðarr was there: "You will earn my friendship if you turn the man over to me."

Eyvindr said: "He is not here just now."

"I know that he is," said the king, "and you need not conceal him."

Eyvindr said: "Even if that were the case, I would not make such an invidious distinction between you and King Magnús that I would turn over to you a man he wishes to shelter." With that he left the hall.

As he emerged, Hreiðarr was pounding at the door and saying that he wanted to get out.

"Keep quiet," said Eyvindr. "King Haraldr has arrived and wants to kill you."

Hreiðarr pounded away (FJ 135) all the same and said that he wanted to meet the king. Eyvindr could see that he was going to break down the door, so he went to unlock it, saying: "The devil take you if you intend to get yourself killed."

Hreiðarr went (U 43) into the hall and approached the king. He greeted him and said: "Sire, release me from your wrath, for I can be serviceable to you in many ways. I can accomplish what you wish to have done even if it is no great test of manhood or anything else. I will not be hesitant about any mission on which you want to send me. Here is an object of some value that I wish to give you." He put it on the table before him, and it was a pig made of gilded silver.

When the king looked at the pig, he said: "You are such an accomplished craftsman that I have hardly ever seen better workmanship." It was passed around among the men. The king said that he would grant him reconciliation—"You are a good man to send on dangerous missions. As far as I can see you are strong and undaunted."

At this point, the pig circulated back to the king. He picked it up and took an even closer look at the handiwork. He saw that there were teats on it and that it was a sow. He realized that it had been made as a mockery and threw it down, saying, "Go to the devil! Up and kill him!"[18] But Hreiðarr gathered up the pig and ran out. He left immediately and came to King Magnús's court, where he told the king what had happened.

In the meantime Haraldr's men had gotten up with the intention of killing him, but when they got outside, Eyvindr was there with a large body of men so that they could not press their pursuit of Hreiðarr. The king and Eyvindr parted on these terms, and the king was not pleased.

When King Magnús and Hreiðarr met, the king asked what had happened. Hreiðarr told him *and showed the king* the pig. When the king saw it, he said: "That is an exceedingly skilled piece of workmanship, but my kinsman Haraldr has avenged much lesser mockeries than this. (FJ 136) You are not at all lacking in boldness and are rather ingenious to boot."

Hreiðarr now spent some time with King Magnús. One time he came to speak with him and said: "I wish you to grant me what I am about to request."

"What is it?" asked the king.

"To listen to a poem that I have composed about you, sire," said Hreiðarr.

"Why not?" said the king.

Hreiðarr began to recite, and it was a very strange production, strangest at first but better as it progressed.[19]

When the poem was finished, the king said: "That strikes me as a strange composition, but not bad as you got to the end. The performance is probably in line with your own life. It began in an odd and outlandish way but will get better and better as time goes on.[20] That will also determine my choice of your poet's reward. There is an island here off the Norwegian coast that I wish to present to you. It has good grazing and is good land, though it is small."

Hreiðarr said: "With that I will link Norway and Iceland."[21]

The king said: "I am not sure how that will work out, but I do know that many (U 44) men will be eager to buy the island from you and give you money for it. I think it would be wiser if I redeemed it myself so that it does not become a bone of contention between you and those who wish to buy it. Furthermore, your stay in Norway should be very brief because I can *see what King Haraldr has in store for you if you remain* in Norway for a long time and let him carry out the designs he has in mind."

King Magnús now gave him silver for the island because he did not want to risk his presence there. Hreiðarr went out to Iceland and dwelled in the north in Svarfaðardalr, where he became a great man.[22] His life went much according to King Magnús's prediction, to the effect that it would turn out better and better as time went on. Those oddities (FJ 137) to which he was given in the early part of his life he succeeded in turning to great advantage. He grew old in Svarfaðardalr, and many men are descended from him. Here the tale ends.

25. How the Kings Harried and How the King's Mother Granted a Captive His Life

When King Magnús and King Haraldr had both ruled the land together for two years, they assembled their army for a campaign south in Denmark and called up their naval forces in Norway. That was a year after the fall of Jarl Rǫgnvaldr Brúsason to the west in Orkney.[1] The kings sailed south with their army to Denmark and intended to do battle with Sveinn Úlfsson, who had spent the winter in Denmark. There was a man named Þorgils Birnuson, who ruled almost a third of Denmark.[2] As the kings proceeded, there was always a good distance between their fleets at night.

When they arrived in Denmark, King Magnús and his men made a landing one day where the king had the greatest suspicion about the loyalty of the

population. They killed a number of men and captured others, who were led
away in fetters. It was not very late in the day when they came down to their
ships with twelve captives. King Haraldr had not yet arrived. They went inland
again, and the king left specific directions not to release these men.

When the king and his men had gone up into the country, the king's mother
asked the captives who they were—"and who is that worthy man," she asked,
"who looks to me (FJ 138) to be your leader?" He said nothing. She asked then
if he wanted to have his life spared.

"I am not inclined that way," he said.

"Why is that?" she asked.

"There are two reasons," he said. "The first is that I will not be loyal to the
king, and the second is that there is no better man than the king to put an end
to my life. That is fitting because I have always been opposed to him.[3] Furthermore, not many people will miss me other than my young wife, for whom
I will be a loss."

She said: "I can see that you are a distinguished man, and your life will be
spared."

He replied: "I am most willing to owe you my life, but the king will not be
pleased by this move. I am greatly indebted (U 45) to your majesty for your
benevolence, and you should count on Þorkell geysir as a faithful friend if you
ever need him."

The twelve men departed and went on their way. When the king came back
and realized what had happened, he was furious and declared it an outrage
that she should contravene his order—"Do you think that you know better or
are more in charge than I am?"

She said: "My intention in this matter was no worse than yours, whatever
other cases entail. I think that there will be a time when this does [not] seem
like the wrong decision."[4]

The king said: "Many people owe a great deal to their fathers, and none
more than I in most matters, but he did not choose a good mother for me."

She said: "You should not quarrel with him on this account because he could
have made a lesser choice, but you should rather honor me more for the father I chose for you.[5] (FJ 139) There is no point in going after these men now
because they are all clean away."

The kings continued their campaign. It is reported that they made still another landing and led many men down to the shore in fetters. During this
landing they confiscated a great deal of money from many men who had submitted to King Sveinn Úlfsson. King Haraldr was present this time.

King Magnús spoke to his mother in secret: "Because I spoke to you harshly
last time, when you released captives from their fetters, I will now make repa-
rations. It will be your reward to ask me for the release of the highest ranking
of these captives publicly so that all can hear."

"Why should I repeat this procedure with your enemies," she asked, "since
you were so ill satisfied when I released the others?"

"Because it is not destined that you will have the advantage of my presence much longer. It will then be to your advantage to look for assistance where some has been given, because you will not be able to have much trust in King Haraldr's protection when I am gone."[6]

She now spoke up so that everyone could hear and said: "For my sake, sire, spare this distinguished man's life."

The king said: "You shall have your request, mother."

The man was released. He then went before the king and thanked him for his life. He also spoke to the king's mother and said that if she ever needed his aid, though the prospect seemed unlikely, she should appeal to Þorgils, a kinsman of Sveinn Úlfsson, like an old friend.[7] Then he departed.

We are told next that the kings were with their forces in the vicinity of a thick forest. A man rode (FJ 140) out of the forest in knightly accouterment and put his horse through elegant paces. He was dressed in rich gold and precious fabrics. He was of very courtly appearance and skilled in many exercises. King Magnús's men saw how he pranced, and when he had done so for a (U 46) while, he turned to the troops and said: "I have misused King Magnús, and King Haraldr has misused me.[8] King Magnús and King Haraldr are very different kings." He then rode off into the forest and vanished.

King Magnús was convinced that this was King Sveinn and said: "Sveinn is a diamond," he said. "If he had troops as valiant as he is himself, he would be victorious more often." Now we are told that Sveinn fled the country and went to Sweden. In the meantime the kings convened thingmeetings throughout the summer and thus expanded King Magnús's realm.

26. *[King Magnús Dies]*

When King Magnús was in Jutland, matters took a turn that made for important developments. One morning as the king lay in the ship's castle in an exhausted state, he threw off the covers and practically steamed from a hot sweat. Einarr þambarskelfir was with him and said: "Are you sick, lord?"

"I am not very sick yet, foster father," said the king.

"It will grieve us greatly," said Einarr, "if anything should befall you, and it would be an irreparable loss to your friends."

"Foster father," he said, "have a bed made for me out by the gunwale, where it will be cooler and more comfortable." That was done, and when the king was brought there, he was barely able to speak: "It doesn't help—take me back to where I was."

They did so, and Einarr said: "Tell your friends what they need to hear, sire, (FJ 141) and give us good counsel. It may be that we do not have long to talk."

"So I shall, friend," said the king, "and it seems very likely that this illness will end our companionship."

At that moment King Haraldr arrived and asked: "Are you ill, sire?"

King Magnús replied: "Yes, I am ill, kinsman, and *I wish* to request that you be a friend to my friends."

"It is fitting that I do that for you," said Haraldr, "but they are quite self-sufficient and look rather askance *at me*."

Then Einarr said: "This is not a useful discussion, and he has presumably made up his mind no matter what he promises."

King Haraldr said: "Is it not most fitting, and therefore my first reponsibility, to be a friend to *my* friends?"

Einarr said: "Say rather, *your majesty*, what is more important for the welfare of the kingdom."

Then King Magnús said: "It is my advice, kinsman Haraldr, that you return to *your ancestral lands in Norway to protect and govern them in the best possible way but do not aspire to rule here in Denmark, for it was my agreement with Hǫrðaknútr that Denmark should not pass from me to my family, should it come into my possession, and similarly with Norway should it pass into his possession. Let King Sveinn have Denmark and hold it in peace. I wish now to surrender that realm and the claim I have had to it."

Then King Haraldr said: "I believe I am entitled to inherit Denmark as well as Norway after you, should we lose you."

"That is not the case, sir," said (FJ 142) King Magnús. "But I understand now," he said, "that my words will not avail much, even though it is clear that you are not destined to be king over Denmark, however little account you wish to take of my advice."[1]

Then King Haraldr asked: "How much is left of the gold that I brought to Norway and half of which I gave into your possession?"

Magnús said: "Look over the tables here, kinsman," he said—"at them are seated men who are excellent and highly esteemed. To these men I have given gold and received in exchange for that gold their affection and devotion. And surely the loyalty and valor of a good man is better than a heap of money."

Then King Haraldr went away. Einarr said: "Sire, do you have any good counsel for your kinsman Þórir? I don't think that your uncle King Haraldr will pay him much heed if he seeks his favor."

Þórir then joined them, together with a man named Refr. As soon as he recognized them, King Magnús addressed them as follows: "Leave the ship and go into the forest that is nearby. It will not be long before the local residents report my death. You should then make your way quickly to King Sveinn and ask him in my name to receive you, Þórir, in the same way that he would wish that I should receive his brother if he came to me on his dying day. Do not tell him at first of my death but rather of my illness."[2]

Þórir was unable to speak to the king because of the grief he felt. Then King Magnús said: "Give the king my greetings and tell him in addition that I abandon any claim I may have to this realm and that I wish him to prosper in it, for I believe he has the most legitimate claim and that justice is served if it belongs to him." Then Þórir and his men went into the forest and waited to see what would happen.

Sometime later Þorsteinn Hallsson came to King Magnús. He was newly arrived from a journey south to Rome. At that point King Magnús had distributed such money as he possessed to most of his men. Þorsteinn said: "Our meeting will not be as joyful as I thought a while ago. I will not ask you for money, but I request that you give me your name."

The king answered: (FJ 143) "For many reasons you deserve only the best from me, Þorsteinn, and you yourself are an estimable man. I am content that you should have my name to give to your son. But even if I have been a king of no great account, it is nonetheless something of a presumption for nonnoble men to name their children after me. Nonetheless, since you ask for this earnestly and I can see that it matters to you, I will assuredly grant it to you. Still, I have a foreboding that there will be both nobility and grief attached to this name."[3]

A little later, before the king died, he fell asleep for a while. King Haraldr was there by his bed. As he slept, his mouth fell open and people thought they could see a fish swim out of the king's mouth, and it was the color of gold. Then the fish wanted to get back into his mouth, but was unable to do so and made for the mouth of King Haraldr, who was sitting close to the king.[4] It struck the onlookers that it then had a dark complexion. Then King Magnús woke up and was told of this. He said: "This signifies that I do not have long to live, and some people may feel that the counsels of my kinsman King Haraldr are colder and darker than my own."

Then he gave King Haraldr specifically the kingdom of Norway, but Haraldr did not say much. Afterward the priests came and performed solemn rites. The king said to his page: "Have I given you any token?"

"Not as yet," he said. The king then handed him a knife and belt,[5] and both were treasures, as might be expected considering the man who had owned and worn them. As the boy took the treasures, he looked at the king, who expired at that very moment. The boy took it so much to heart and was so overwhelmed that he lost consciousness. When he recovered his senses, the precious objects were gone in the tumult and he never saw them again.

The death of King Magnús occurred three nights before the feast of Simon and Jude.[6] The trumpets sounded throughout the army. Þórir and his men heard them in the forest where they were hiding, and they were now certain that King Magnús had died. At the same time they heard voices near them in the forest, and words to this effect: "They were here (FJ 144) just now." The next thing they knew, arrows were flying into the woods in their direction, but they took to their heels and escaped. "I take it that these are sweet greetings to me from King Haraldr," said Þórir, "whether he dispatched them himself or let others do it. He probably noticed our departure and that we took refuge here."

They then proceeded on their way until they reached King Sveinn, who had not yet left Denmark. They found him by the Helgeå.[7] He had already mounted his horse and intended to abandon the realm. Þórir was so overwhelmed with grief that he could not address the king, but he could see that they were the bearers of urgent tidings and said: "What news do you have to tell me?"

Then Þórir's companion Refr said: "Sire, he must report the death of King Magnús." They told of the king's words and his request for asylum for his brother Þórir, and he described to the king the grief and loss that he had suffered through the death of King Magnús.

King Sveinn replied: "This is momentous news. You, Þórir, will be welcome here with me, and I will accord you great honor because I believe that King Magnús would have done the same for my brother."

Þórir spent some time with King Sveinn and was duly honored as the king had promised, but he could not thrive in his grief and did not live long.

After King Magnús's death, his mother went to Þorkell geysa.[8] He gave her a good reception and put whatever he had at her disposal. She stayed with him for a time, but when Christmas approached, she became downcast. "Why are you so dejected?" he asked. "We will do everything we possibly can for you. Tell me what it is that you need."

"You have the very best intentions," she said, "but I am thinking back to the Christmases when I could sit by my son. It grieves me now to celebrate Christmas with commoners."[9]

"It is understandable that you should feel this way," he said, "and if you have it in mind to be with the king, I will accompany you there. I know for a certainty that he will receive you well." (FJ 145)

She accepted that, and Þorkell took her to the king. King Sveinn gave her an excellent reception, and she took up residence with him. We are told that she gave King Sveinn a precious plate worked in gold.[10]

Returning to the story, we can report that with the death of King Magnús there was a great falling off in both Denmark and Norway. His death was a grievous loss to everyone, especially since he was survived by only one daughter. She was then no more than a child, and her name was Ragnhildr.

27. Haraldr's Thingmeeting

After these momentous events King Haraldr summoned a thingmeeting with his army and told his men that he intended to go to the Vébjǫrg (Viborg) Thing with his whole army and have himself declared king of all Denmark. He would then subject the whole realm to his dominion, since after the death of King Magnús he considered Denmark to be just as much his inheritance as Norway. He bade the army prepare itself and declared that if they conquered the land, the Norwegians would forever after be the lords of the Danes.

Then Einarr þambarskelfir stated that it was much more fitting to bring the body of his foster son King Magnús north to Norway for burial and return him to his father Saint Óláfr than to go to war abroad and covet the realms and possessions of other kings for no good reason.[1] He concluded his speech by saying that he would rather serve King Magnús in death than any other king alive. They then took King Magnús's body and laid it out splendidly among his possessions on the upper deck of the royal ship. With that all the Þrœndir and most of the Norwegians prepared to accompany Einarr and King Magnús's body home to Norway. The levy thus disbanded, and King Haraldr saw no alternative but to return to Norway first and take possession of the realm that had been given him there and to which his birth entitled him. He would then be able to gather forces as he liked. Thus he returned with the whole army, and the land swore fealty to King Haraldr at the Borgarþing through the delegation of representatives.[2] (FJ 146) From there he proceeded north to the thingsites, and many of the people submitted to him.

28. King Magnús's Funeral Voyage

Einarr set sail with King Magnús's body, accompanied by all the men of Þrœndalǫg. When they came to Sámsey (Samsø) and anchored in the harbor where King Magnús had always anchored off that island in earlier days, a poor blind man was present, whom King Magnús had always remembered with a gift of money. In the evening he became aware that a host of ships had arrived at the island. He went down to the harbor and inquired: "Who is the ranking man in the fleet?"

Einarr answered: "King Magnús, son of Óláfr."

The blind man said: "Will the king remember my destitution as he always has before?"

Einarr said: "The matter does not stand as you think, brother. The king is now dead."

The poor man was overcome, and for a long time he could not utter a word in his grief. But when his grief receded, he said: "Of what mind are you, Einarr? Will you remember my poverty as the king used to do because of your generosity and my own need, or will this attentiveness come to an end?"

Einarr said that he would most certainly remember him for the sake of God. He then determined what should be given to him from each company and the provisions of each ship. It turned out to be a most ample supply, and Einarr had it sent to him.

The blind man said: "Now once again you have demonstrated your generosity, Einarr, and this help goes a long way, but I ask you whether there is some little thing King Magnús had in his possession that you might give me as consolation."

Einarr said: "The king parted with us by giving us many precious objects, such as gold and raiment. I hardly know what is left." He reached into his purse and found a little ring. He asked that it be given to the man and said: "I do not see that my foster son Magnús and I will make better use of this little piece of gold that he gave me long ago. Add it to your possessions."

He was touched to the heart and held the gold up (FJ 147) before his eyes as the tears ran down his cheeks and onto the gold. He said: "I had a hopeful feeling that if I met with King Magnús again, something good would come of it,[1] and so it has turned out. You have given me much help with your contribution, and now the king, with the help of God, has given me the sight of both eyes.[2] For I was completely blind before and now do not need the help of other men. I can earn my keep if God allows me to preserve my health." All the king's close friends were filled with joy, and they all praised God, whether he granted this for King Magnús's own merit or for his father Saint Óláfr. But they all thought that it would avail.

Then Einarr and his men went north to Niðaróss. Concerning their journey the following was composed:

*80. Nú fara heim í húmi   ǫld hefr illa haldit
      herkunn fyr lǫg sunnan   (esa stríðvana síðan)
      daprar skeiðr með dauðan   (hulit hafa hirðmenn skylja
      dýrnenninn gram þenna: hǫfuð) (þess's fremstr vas jǫfra).

"Nú fara daprar skeiðr heim í húmi fyr herkunn lǫg sunnan með þenna dauðan, dýrnenninn gram. Qld hefr haldit illa; esa stríðvana síðan; hirðmenn skylja, þess's vas fremstr jǫfra, hafa hulit hǫfuð."

Now the drooping ships sail home in the dusk north past well-known districts with this dead, powerful king. People are sorely grieved; there will be no lack of sorrow later; the retainers of that lord, who was the foremost of kings, have covered their heads [in mourning].

The body was received by all the people, and the bells rang throughout the town. Everything was conducted in all solemnity, though with great grief. The body was buried at Christ Church outside the choir,[3] but now it is within the choir and outside the archbishop's chamber. Many brave and valiant men wept over his grave. In the words of Oddr kikinaskald:[4]

*81. Felldu menn (þás mildan)   deildisk hugr (svá at heldu
      mǫrg tár (í grǫf báru)   húskarlar grams varla)
      (þung byrðr vas sú) (þengil)   siklings þjóð en síðan
      (þeim es hann gaf seima):   sat opt hnipin (vatni). (FJ 148)

"Menn felldu mǫrg tár, þás báru mildan þengil í grǫf: sú vas þung byrðr þeim, es hann gaf seima. Deildisk hugr, svát húskarlar grams varla heldu vatni, en síðan sat siklings þjóð opt hnipin."

Men shed many tears when they carried the generous king to the grave: it was a heavy burden to those whom he gave gold. The mind was mournful, so that the

king's liegemen could hardly keep from weeping, and often thereafter the lord's
men sat grieving.

*82.　Mák síz Magnúss ævi　　　　hvarflak hvers manns þurfi
　　　móðfíkins þraut góða　　　　harmr strangr fær mér angrat
　　　(Odd hafa stríð of staddan)　　(þjóðs at dǫgling dauðan
　　　stillis harðla illa:　　　　　　dǫpr) því fǫrum aprir.

"Mák harðla illa, síz góða ævi Magnúss, móðfíkins stillis, þraut: stríð hafa Odd of
staddan. Hvarflak þurfi hvers manns; strangr harmr fær mér angrat; þjóðs dǫpr at
dǫgling dauðan: því fǫrum aprir."

I have been sorely grieved since the good life of Magnús, the ambitious king, came
to a close: Oddr is overcome by sorrow. I roam around in need of company; hard
grief has beset me; men mourn the dead king: therefore I am downcast.

These events provoked the grief of many a man in all of Norway. Everyone
agreed that no man had been more beloved by all the people than King
Magnús. Here his story comes to an end.

29. Haraldr's Thingmeeting

When King Haraldr returned north to Þrándheimr, he convened the Eyrarþing, and all Norway swore fealty to him at that meeting.[1] From then on, he was
sole monarch over the whole land.

All agree, as was mentioned above, that King Sveinn learned of King
Magnús's death when he was in Skáney (Skåne, Scania) by the Helgeå. It was
there that he spoke the words we reported. In addition, he said that when King
Magnús died, he would either acquire all of Denmark or else die on his native
soil. He then mounted his horse and headed back to Denmark. Troops gathered to support him, and he subjected the whole land to his rule. Early in the
winter he went south in Jutland and convened the Vébjǫrg (Viborg) assembly.
Here the royal title was conferred on him anew according to the wishes of all
the Danes. Þorkell geysa invested him with the royal title, and the Danes
claimed that the title filled the Norwegians with fear. The Danes made such a
mockery that they cut anchors from cheese and said that they were quite firm
enough for the ships with which King Haraldr intended to conquer Denmark,
and with that they intended to deride and ridicule the Norwegians.

30. [Halldórs þáttr Snorrasonar][1]

[Halldórr Snorrason had been abroad in Constantinople with Haraldr, as
has been related, and he came to Norway with him from the east in Russia.

He enjoyed great honor and recognition from King Haraldr at that time, and he stayed with the king during the winter when he resided in Kaupangr (Trondheim).[2]

When the winter passed and spring was at hand, the merchants made preparations for their trading voyages early because there had been little or no shipping from Norway owing to the state of war and the fear that had prevailed between Norway and Denmark. But as spring wore on, King Haraldr noticed that Halldórr Snorrason became very dejected.

One day the king asked him what was on his mind. Halldórr replied: "I am eager to go to Iceland, lord."

"Many others must have been more homesick than you," said the king. "But what is the state of your cargo, and how is your money invested?"

"The investment is easy," he answered, "because I have nothing but the clothes on my back."

"That's not much of a reward for long service and many perils. I will give you a ship and cargo so that your father will see that you have not served me for nothing." Halldórr thanked the king for his gift.

A few days later Halldórr met up with the king, who asked how much crew he had hired. He replied: "All the trade hands have hired on already so that I have no one left to hire. I therefore think that the ship you gave me will have to remain where it is."

"Then it doesn't amount to a token of much friendship," said the king, "and let us wait to see how to solve the matter of a crew."

The next day the trumpet was sounded in the town to summon a meeting, and it was announced that the king wished to speak to the townspeople and the merchants. The king arrived at the meeting late and had a look of concern when he came. "We have heard," he said, "that war has broken out in the eastern part of our realm, but on no account will we surrender our lands. For that reason we forbid the sailing of any ship until I have taken what I wish with respect to men and provisions. The only exception is a small merchantman owned by Halldórr Snorrason, which is cleared for Iceland. This may seem to you rather harsh since you have prepared to set sail, but we are compelled to such measures. It would seem better to us that things settle down so that each may choose to go any way he wishes." After that the meeting dispersed.

A little later Halldórr sought out the king, who asked him how his preparations were proceeding and whether he had gotten some crew. Halldórr replied: "I have hired quite a number because now many more are applying to me than I can accommodate. People are besieging me and practically knocking my doors down so that I have no relief from appeals either night or day."

The king said: "Keep the crew members you have hired, and let us see what will happen."

The next day the trumpet was sounded and it was announced that the king wished to speak with the merchants again. This time the king was not late for the meeting. He was among the first to arrive and had a serene look on his face. He stood up and spoke: "There is good news to report. What you heard the other day about war is nothing but nonsense and lies. We now grant every ship permission to sail wherever you wish. Return in the fall and bring us valuables, in return for which you will receive our friendship and recompense."[3]

All the merchants who were present were delighted and thanked him as the best of kings. Halldórr went to Iceland that summer and spent the winter with his father. He sailed again in the summer and returned to King Haraldr's retinue, but we are told that Halldórr was not as devoted to the king as before and stayed up evenings after the king had gone to bed.

There was a man named Þórir englandsfari (Englandfarer). He was a great merchant and had long been in commerce with various lands, bringing the king valuables. Þórir was King Haraldr's retainer and was now very old. He entered conversation with the king and said: "I am an old man, as you know, and much depleted. I do not think I am able to observe the customs of the retinue with respect to drink and the other matters that go along with it. It will now be necessary to find a replacement, though it is best and pleasantest to stay with you."

"There is an easy answer, friend," replied the king. "Stay in the retinue and drink no more than you wish, with my permission."

There was a man from Upplǫnd named Bárðr. He was a good fellow and not up in years. He was in King Haraldr's service and great affection. Bárðr, Þórir, and Halldórr were table companions. One evening, at the moment the king went by where they were sitting and drinking, Halldórr passed the drinking horn. It was a large horn and quite transparent. It was easy to see that he had drunk a good half before passing it to Þórir, but Þórir took his time drinking it off. The king said: "It takes years to test men, Halldórr, since I now see that you cheat old men at drinking and run to whores late at night rather than accompanying your king."[4]

Halldórr said not a word, but Bárðr could tell that he disliked the king's remark. Bárðr went to the king early in the morning. "You're an early bird, Bárðr," said the king.

"I have come to reproach you, sire," said Bárðr. "You spoke ill and unjustly to your friend Halldórr last night when you accused him of drinking like a weakling, because that was Þórir's drinking horn and he had drunk his fill]* (U 46) and would have returned it to the keg if Halldórr had not drunk it for him. It was also a great lie when you said that he visited whores. (U 47) But people would prefer (FJ 149) that he be more devoted in his service to you." The king said that they would arrange this matter between them when he met with Halldórr.

Bárðr met with Halldórr and told him of the king's accommodating words. He said it was clear that he should not be affected by the king's comments. Bárðr did his best to promote conciliation. The Christmas season was approaching, and the king and Halldórr were not on very agreeable terms. When Christmas was at hand, the fines for breaches of decorum were announced, as was the custom. One morning the timing of the bells was changed, by arrangement with the pages. A great many men were fined, and they settled down in the straw and set about drinking the penalty libations.[5]

Halldórr sat in his customary seat, but they brought him the drink all the same. He said he would not drink, and they told the king. "That cannot be true," said the king. "He will surely drink if I bring him the libation." Then he took the penalty horn and went over to Halldórr, who stood up to meet him. The king asked him to drink.

Halldórr said: "I do not consider myself penalized even though it is your trick to set the bells ringing for the sole purpose of fining people."

The king said: "You will have to drink the penalty draughts just like everyone else."

"It may be, sire," said Halldórr, "that you can get me to drink, but I can tell you that Sigurðr sýr could not have forced Snorri goði (the Priest)."[6] With that, he reached for the horn and drank it down. But the king was greatly angered and went to his seat.

When the eighth day of Christmas came around, the men were given their military pay. It was called Haraldr's coin and consisted more of copper than of silver, at most half silver. When Halldórr took his pay, he laid the silver on his coattail and looked at it. It did not look pure. He swept it (FJ 150) down with one hand, and it all landed in the straw. Bárðr spoke up, saying that this was unbecoming conduct: "The king will feel dishonored and will think that you have wronged him with respect to the pay."

"It is of no account," said Halldórr, "and there is not much at stake."[7]

Now we are told that they readied their ships after Christmas. The king intended to sail south along the coast, and when he was on the point of departure, Halldórr had made no preparations. Bárðr asked: "Why are you not readying yourself, Halldórr?"

"I have no wish to," he said, "and I have no intention of sailing. I can see that the king does not value my service."

Bárðr said: "He will surely wish you to make the journey with him."

Bárðr then went to the king and told him that Halldórr was not preparing for the journey: "You will find that there is a real deficiency in the prow of your ship if he is missing."

The king said: "Tell him that I wish him to accompany me and say that the recent friction between us is not serious." Bárðr met with Halldórr and told him that the king did not for any reason wish to lose his service. The result was that Halldórr went after all.

The king and his company sailed south along the coast. (U 48) One night as the ship was sailing its course, Halldórr said to the helmsman: "Change course."

The king said to the helmsman: "Keep a straight course."

Halldórr said a second time: "Change course."

The king repeated his command.

Halldórr said: "You are headed right for a skerry," and then it happened. It tore the bottom out of the ship, and they had to reach land on other ships. Then a tent was set up on land, and the ship was repaired. Bárðr woke up to find Halldórr tying up his sleeping roll. Bárðr asked him what he had in mind, and Halldórr said that he would go on board a merchant ship that lay nearby: "It may be that our paths will now part. I have had enough, and I do not want the king to ruin more ships or other prized possessions in order to humiliate me and make my lot (FJ 151) worse than before." "Wait a little longer so that I can talk to the king," said Bárðr.

When he arrived, the king said: "You're out early, Bárðr."

"There is a need, sire. Halldórr is about to depart and feels that you have been ungracious to him. It is a little difficult to figure out the two of you. He intends to make off and set sail for Iceland with his gear, but that is not a proper parting of the ways. I think you will hardly find another man as dependable as he is."

The king said that they could still be reconciled and that he would not take offense at this.

Bárðr met with Halldórr and reported the king's friendly words.

Halldórr said: "Why should I serve him any longer when I don't even get my pay in genuine currency?"

Bárðr said: "That is not a matter you should speak of. What is good enough for the sons of Norway's magnates should be good enough for you. You did not proceed with moderation the last time when you threw the king's silver into the straw and spoiled it. You must surely know that the king felt dishonored by that act."

Halldórr said: "I am not aware that my service has ever been so deprecated as in the king's compensation."

"That is true," said Bárðr, "but be patient. I want to meet the king one more time." And so he did.

When Bárðr met the king, he said: "Give Halldórr his pay in pure silver. That is what he deserves."

The king said: "Don't you think it is presumptuous to ask that Halldórr be paid differently from the sons of our magnates—considering his disgraceful treatment of our payment last time?"

Bárðr said: "What must be considered, sire, is that his valor is worth much more, as well as your long-standing friendship, and not least of all your own generosity. You know Halldórr's disposition and his stubbornness, and it is honorable for you to honor him."

The king said: "Give him the silver." And so it was done.

Bárðr went to Halldórr and brought him twelve ounces of pure (FJ 152) silver, saying: "Can't you see that you get whatever you demand of the king? He wishes you to have whatever you think you need."

Halldórr said: "I will stipulate that I shall (U 49) no longer be on board the king's ship. If he still wishes to have my service, I want to have a ship under my command and in my possession."

Bárðr said: "It is not fitting that any magnate should surrender his ship to you, and you are too demanding." Halldórr said that he would not agree under any other conditions.

Bárðr told the king what request Halldórr had made: "And if the crew of this ship is as dependable as the captain, you will be well off."

The king said: "Although this request seems very forward, I will fall in with it."

A magnate named Sveinn from Lyrgja was in command of a ship, and the king had him summoned. "It is well known to you," said the king, "that you are a man of great ancestry. For that reason I wish you to be on my ship, and I will put another man in command of your ship. You are a wise man, and I have special need of you in my councils."

He replied: "In the past you have been accustomed to consult other men more than me, and I am not well qualified. Whom do you have in mind for the ship?"

"Halldórr Snorrason will command it," said the king.

Sveinn said: "It did not cross my mind that you would choose an Icelander and demote me from command."

The king said: "His ancestry in Iceland is no worse than yours is in Norway, and not that much time has elapsed since those who now live in Iceland were Norwegians themselves."[8] It was done as the king wished, and Halldórr was given the ship. Then they traveled east to Ósló (Oslo) and received the hospitality due the king.[9]

We are told that one day when the king and his men were sitting at drink and Halldórr was present in the king's hall, the men who were charged to guard his ship came to him thoroughly drenched and said that Sveinn and his men had seized the ship and thrown them overboard. Halldórr stood up and went before the king. He asked him whether it was in fact (FJ 153) his ship and whether the king intended to keep his word. The king said that he would indeed keep it. He then summoned his retinue to take *six ships* and accompany Halldórr. Each ship had a triple crew. They set out in pursuit of Sveinn, but *he fled to the coast* and immediately ran up onto the shore. Halldórr and his men took possession of the ship and returned to the king.

When the feast was *concluded, the king proceeded* north along the coast, arriving in Þrándheimr at the end of summer. Sveinn from Lyrgja sent word to the king that he was ready to *abandon his claim to the ship* and leave it to the king's discretion to mediate between him and Halldórr as he wished, although he would prefer to purchase the ship if the king were willing. When the king understood that Sveinn was leaving the matter entirely to his judgment, he wished to settle things to the satisfaction of both. He bought the ship from Halldórr and wished him to have a proper price, while Sveinn should have the ship. The king made the purchase, and Halldórr received the price. It was paid in full, except for half a mark of gold that remained (U 50) unpaid. Halldórr did not press the issue, and the money was not paid. And so it remained throughout the winter.

When spring came, Halldórr told the king that he wanted to go to Iceland for the summer and that it was a good moment to pay the balance of the ship purchase, but the king was hard to pin down on the matter of the debt. He did not like being dunned, but he did not forbid Halldórr to make the voyage. He readied his ship in the spring in the River Nið and stood off Brattaeyrr. When they were fully prepared and the breeze was favorable, Halldórr went up to town with a few men late in the evening. He was armed. They went to the place where the king and queen slept. His companions stood below the loft while he went in with his weapons at the ready. He caused some noise and commotion, which roused them. The king asked who was breaking in on them at night.

"It is Halldórr, who is ready to set sail (FJ 154) and has a favoring breeze. Now is the time to make the payment."

"That cannot be done on the spur of the moment," said the king, "and I will pay out the money tomorrow."

"I want it now," said Halldórr, "and I don't intend to leave with unfinished business. I know your temper only too well, and I know just how much you will like the way I go about it and how I dun you. No matter what you say now, I will have no trust in you in the future. There is little prospect that we will meet often enough so that I will ever have the upper hand again, and I intend to make the most of this opportunity. I see that the queen has a ring of about the right size on her arm. Give it to me."

The king said: "We will have to call for scales and weigh the ring."

"No need," said Halldórr. "I will take it as my payment, and you are not going to get the best of me with trickery this time. Hand it over now."

The queen said: "Don't you see that he is standing over you with murder in his heart?" Then she took the ring and gave it to Halldórr.

He accepted it and thanked them for the payment, then bade them farewell —"and this will be our parting." He went out and told his companions to run to the ship as quickly as possible—"because I am loath to spend much time in town." They did so and boarded the ship. Some hoisted the sail, some tended to the ship's boat, some raised the anchor, and everyone pitched in as best they could.

By the time they set sail, there was plenty of trumpeting in the town. The last thing they saw was three longships under way and headed for them, but they pulled away from them and headed out to sea. There they lost sight of each other, and Halldórr had a fair passage to Iceland. But the king's men turned back when they saw that Halldórr was drawing away to sea.

Some years later, King Haraldr sent word to Halldórr Snorrason to join him once again. He said that his honor would never be greater than if he would agree to the trip.[10] But Halldórr said that he would never join the king again and that they would now have to be content with the status quo. "I see clearly," he said (FJ 155), "that the gallows are waiting for me in Norway if I go there. I know his temper and I do not trust him."[11] (U 51)

When King Haraldr was much advanced in age, we are told that he sent word to Halldórr to send him some foxskins. He wanted to make a bedcover of them because the king was at an age when he needed warmth. When the king's message reached him, it is said that the first words that escaped him were: "The old cock is drooping now."[12] But he sent him the skins. They never saw each other again after they parted in Þrándheimr, though that parting was not of the friendliest. There is now no further mention of Halldórr.[13]

31. *[King Haraldr's Campaign in Denmark]*

The summer after King Magnús's death King Haraldr called out the Norwegian levy both with respect to troops and provisions.[1] He said that he was inclined to test whether he could fasten his anchor off Denmark that summer. He addressed his men, telling them to press the attack all the harder because they would not have to dispute the booty. He said that for his part he would be well content if they paid him a few weights of pure silver, especially since he could raid the shores to provision the army. He said that he did not mind if they put their hearts in the work in order to avenge the mockery of the Danes. The whole army was eager to have the Danes pay a proper price.

They now sailed south to Jutland, and the king harried there in the summer and burned the land far and wide. The people fled left and right and always avoided the Norwegian army. King Haraldr put into Goðnarfjǫrðr (Randersfjord), at which time we are told that he recited the following stanza (FJ 156):

83. Látum vér (meðan lirlar   sumar annat skalk sunnar
     líneik veri sínum)   (segik eina spá) fleini
     (Gerðr) í Goðnarfirði   (vér aukum kaf króki)
     (galdrs) akkerum haldit: kaldnets furu halda.

"Látum vér akkerum haldit í Goðnarfirði, meðan líneik, Gerðr galdrs, lirlar veri sínum. Annat sumar skalk halda kaldnets furu fleini sunnar; segik eina spá; vér aukum króki kaf."

Let us ride at anchor in Goðnarfjǫrðr [Randersfjord] while the linen oak [woman],

Gerðr of the incantation [woman], sings her husband to sleep. Next summer, I'll let the fir tree of the cold trawl net [ship] ride at the anchor hook even farther south; that I predict; we'll plunge the hook deeper.

The skald Bǫlverkr confirms that the summer after King Magnús's death, Haraldr made this expedition from Norway:

84. Leiðangr bjótt af láði   skokkr lá dýrr á døkkri
    (lǫgr gekk of skip) fǫgru   (Danir váru þá) báru
    (gjalfrstóðum reist grœði   (skeiðr sá herr fyr hauðri
    glæstum) ár et næsta: hlaðnar) (illa staðnir). (U 52)

"Bjótt leiðangr af fǫgru láði ár et næsta; lǫgr gekk of skip; reist grœði glæstum gjalfrstóðum. Dýrr skokkr lá á døkkri báru; Danir váru þá illa staðnir; herr sá hlaðnar skeiðr fyr hauðri."

The next year you summoned the levy from the fair land; water swept over the ships; with the splendid wave steeds [ships] you furrowed the sea. The precious bottom board rested on the dark wave; then bad luck befell the Danes; people saw loaded ships off the shore.

The story relates that a lookout who had spotted King Haraldr's fleet addressed Þorkell geysa's daughters in these terms: "You were much engaged in mocking and ridiculing King Haraldr. You said that King Haraldr would not come to Denmark. But who is it you think has now come?" They knew nothing about the arrival of the army and said they had no idea about Haraldr's whereabouts.

When King Haraldr and his men went ashore, the king said: "I have learned that not far from here can be found the residence of Þorkell geysa, the man who gave Sveinn (FJ 157) the royal title and became our greatest enemy. He is the wealthiest man in this country, and it seems to me only fitting for him to know that Norwegians have arrived. His daughters can find out whether our anchors are made of cheese or whether they turn out to be a little firmer. Attack boldly," he said, "because we will collect more riches here in this one place than all over Jutland."

They set out and came to Þorkell's residence, which they promptly set on fire. When the people inside perceived that the fire was spreading, they asked for a truce and free exit. King Haraldr said: "Though Geysa's daughters deserve to burn inside the house here, I think it proper that you should rather test whether Norwegian flukes can fasten on Danish trunks."[2] King Haraldr now burned Þorkell geysa's residence, and his daughters were led down to the ships in fetters. Then the following stanza was recited:

85. Skáru jast ór osti   nú sér mǫrg í morgun
    eybaugs Dana meyjar   mær (hlær at því færi)
    (þat of angraði þengil   ernan krók ór jarni
    þing) akkerishringa: allvalds skipum halda.

"Eybaugs Dana meyjar skáru akkerishringa ór jast osti; þat þing of angraði þengil.

Nú sér mǫrg mær í morgun ernan krók ór jarni halda allvalds skipum; færi hlær
at því."

The girls of the Danes of the isle ring [ocean, coastal Danes] carved anchor rings
from the yeast cheese; that object angered the king. Now this morning many a
maiden sees a strong hook of iron holding the lord's ships; not many laugh
at that.

Þorkell geysa met with King Haraldr and asked for mercy. He offered money
in compensation for all the breaches of friendship that he had committed
against the king.

King Haraldr (FJ 158) replied: "It is a great folly to mock and ridicule chieftains as you have done to us. It is now fitting that you should experience what
we are capable of, but far more grievous is your opposition and enmity toward
me, and the presumption you committed in giving Sveinn the royal title."

"I wish," said Þorkell, "to leave my case to your discretion."

The king replied: "Because it does not seem worthy of a king to kill your
daughters for their mockery, even though they have done everything to deserve it, and because you surrender yourself to my discretion, I will accept
compensation from you. You shall make payment in money, and it will not be
a small amount. I am not going to let you off lightly." (U 53)

Þorkell said that he was very willing, and he redeemed his daughters with a
huge amount of money, thus indemnifying himself as well, though history fails
to relate the exact amount. The skald Grani recited the following:[3]

86. Lét aldrigi úti   Fila dróttinn rak flótta
     ósvífr Kraka drífu   fjanda grams til strandar
     Hlǫkk í harða þjokkum   auð varð út at reiða
     Hornskógi brá þorna: allskjótt faðir dóttur.

"Ósvífr lét aldrigi Kraka drífu Hlǫkk þorna brá úti í harða þjokkum Hornskógi. Fila
dróttinn rak flótta fjanda grams til strandar; faðir varð allskjótt at reiða út auð
dóttur."

The reckless one never gave the brow of Hlǫkk [valkyrie] of Kraki's drift [gold,
woman] a chance to dry in the very dense Hornskógr [Hornslet, Jylland (Jutland)]. The lord of the Filar [people of Fjaler] chased the fleeing army of his
enemy down to the beach; at once, the father had to pay out the riches of his
daughter.

And again:

87. Dǫglingr fekk at drekka   ætt spornaði arnar
     danskt blóð ara jóði   allvítt við valfalli
     (hríð hykk hilmi gerðu)   (hold át vargr sem vildi)
     Hugins jól (við nes Þjólar):   (vel njóti þess) (Jóta). (FJ 159)

"Dǫglingr fekk ara jóði danskt blóð, Hugins jól, at drekka; hykk hilmi gerðu hríð
við Þjólarnes. Ætt arnar spornaði allvítt við valfalli; vargr át hold Jóta, sem vildi: vel
njóti þess!"

The king gave the brood of eagles Danish blood, Huginn's [raven] banquet [blood], to drink; I heard the lord waged war by Þjólarnes. Far and wide the eagle's kin stalked over the corpses of the fallen; the wolf ate the flesh of the Jótar [people of Jylland, Jutland] as he pleased, may he enjoy that!

These were the terms on which King Haraldr and Þorkell geysa parted.

The king harried all that summer in Denmark and collected an enormous amount of money. He was not in Norway during the summer, but he returned during the fall, telling his men that the campaign had turned out well, rather better than if they had sat idly in Norway—"and it may mean that people will think in terms of paying some taxes. It should cheer you that you may get a good part of the money. As for me, I am content with both the money and the prospect that the Danes will not be unafraid of us."

The king spent the winter quietly in Norway. In the summer he announced an expedition to Denmark. He said that he expected to get the best of them again: "That land will not remain in peace this summer. King Sveinn's defeats began as you best know," he said, "when you consider how faithfully he kept his promises to King Magnús. His record of defeat will continue as it began. We Norwegians should also remember how we had to knuckle under to the arrogance and aggression of the Danes when they had the upper hand in Norway in the days of Sveinn Álfífuson, and we should take revenge if the opportunity presents itself. It is clear that you hate them, and your deeds should match your feelings."

The king now went south to Denmark and harried the Danes, inflicting great damage on them. He conducted a hard campaign and (FJ 160) met no opposition. He took a great deal of booty and continued to do so throughout the summer, but the Danes fled before his army whenever they could. No one taunted the Norwegians and incited them to misdeeds any longer since they felt that they had gotten a sufficient sample already.

King Haraldr (U 54) and his men sailed home in the autumn with their ships laden with booty. The king said that this money would be enough to provide a lot of good fellows in Norway with pocket change, though it did not represent much of a reduction for the Danes. "But it may still be a little reminder to them that the king of the Norwegians lives, and it seems unlikely that King Sveinn would pay greater tribute in half a year." There was no meeting between the kings Haraldr and Sveinn during the summer. King Haraldr spent the winter in Norway, but in the summer he returned to Denmark and did so summer after summer to harry in Denmark. He performed many great deeds far and wide in King Sveinn's realm and made it a war zone, as Stúfr said:

> 88. Autt varð Falstr at fréttum
> fekk drótt mikinn ótta
> gœddr vas hrafn en hræddir
> hvert ár Danir váru.

"Falstr varð autt at fréttum; drótt fekk mikinn ótta; hrafn vas gœddr, en Danir váru hræddir hvert ár."

Falstr [Falster] was laid waste, we were told; people were terrified; the raven was fed, and the Danes were frightened every year.

But King Sveinn still remained in Denmark. He undertook nothing in the winters, but had his fleet out in the summer. He threatened to invade Norway with the Danish army and to wreak no less havoc there than Haraldr wreaked in Denmark. King Sveinn, with the advice of his chieftains and countrymen, sent men north to Norway in the winter to meet with King Haraldr. They wanted to take counsel on how the disaster of King Haraldr's harrying could be alleviated as swiftly as possible.

The envoys came to (FJ 161) King Haraldr and told him of their mission from King Sveinn and all the Danish chieftains. They asked that Haraldr should bring his army from the north, while King Sveinn brought his from the south so that they could meet at the Gautelfr (Götaälv) and fight it out there in order to settle the territorial dispute. King Haraldr said: "That is a valorous offer on the part of King Sveinn and the Danes, and I think it would be best, if this encounter takes place, to have the Danes remember it. That is what I desire. You should take the message to King Sveinn and the Danes that I will come to the encounter."

Sveinn's men now returned, and both sides prepared their ships during the winter. In the summer they called up their troops. At that time Þorleikr fagri came from Iceland and composed a poem on King Sveinn.[4] When he arrived in Norway, he learned that King Haraldr had gone south to the Elfr (Götaälv) to meet King Sveinn. He recited the following:

89. Ván erumk vísa kœnum   þó má enn hvárr annan
     vígs á Rakna stígu   ǫndu nemr eða lǫndum
     ǫrr í odda snerru   (lítt hyggr Sveinn á sáttir
     Innþrœnda lið finni: sjaldfestar) guð valda. (U 55)

"Ván vígs erumk kœnum vísa á Rakna stígu, ǫrr finni Innþrœnda lið í odda snerru. Þó má enn guð valda, hvárr annan nemr ǫndu eða lǫndum: lítt hyggr Sveinn á sjaldfestar sáttir."

I expect war will await the courageous king on Rakni's [sea king] path [sea] and that the brave one will meet the band of the Innþrœndir [people from the inner districts of Trøndelag] in the shower of spears [battle]. Yet God will decide which of the two will deprive the other of life or lands: Sveinn cares little for shaky agreements.

90. Fœrir reiðr (sás rauða   en lauks of sæ sœkja
     rǫnd hefr opt fyr lǫndum)   Sveins fagrdrifin steini
     breið á Buðla slóðir   glæsidýr (þess's geira)
     borðraukn Haraldr norðan: gullmunnuð (rýðr) sunnan. (FJ 162)

"Haraldr, sás hefr opt rauða rǫnd fyr lǫndum, fœrir reiðr breið borðraukn norðan á Buðla slóðir. En gullmunnuð lauks glæsidýr Sveins, þess's rýðr geira, sœkja sunnan of sæ, fagrdrifin steini."

Haraldr, who frequently hoists the red shield off the shores, fiercely steers the broad board steeds [ships] from the north on Buðli's [sea king] paths [sea]. But the splendid gold-mouthed mast beasts [ships] of Sveinn, who reddens spears, set out to sea from the south, wondrously colored.

Now King Haraldr came with his army to the appointed meeting of the kings, but Sveinn lay with his fleet to the south off Zealand. Then King Haraldr said:

> 91.　Logit hefr Baldr at Baldri

Þjóðólfr composed the following:

> brynþings fetilstinga
> linns (sás land á sunnar)
> láðbrjótr (fyrir ráða):
> þós sjá Njǫrðr enn nørðri
> (norðr) glymhríðar borða
> (gramr est frœkn) ok fremri
> fastmálari hála.

"Baldr brynþings hefr logit at Baldri fetilstinga; linns láðbrjótr, sás á land sunnar ráða fyrir. Þós sjá Njǫrðr glymhríðar borða enn nørðri hála fastmálari ok fremri: norðr gramr, est frœkn!"

Baldr of the byrnie assembly [battle, warrior: Sveinn] has lied to Baldr of the baldric stick [sword, warrior: Haraldr]; the cleaver of the snake's land [gold, generous king: Sveinn], who has a country to rule farther south. Yet that more northerly Njǫrðr of the boards of the din storm [battle, shields, warrior: Haraldr] is far more reliable and distinguished: northern king, you are courageous!

Then King Haraldr said: "It is true, skald," he said, "that King Sveinn has not kept his appointment with me. It may be that the Danes think it is pleasanter to herd pigs in the forest than to do battle with us.[5] Since they have not come here, we will visit them in their realm and give them the same treatment as before, or maybe a little worse." King Haraldr then organized his forces. He let the militia go home and proceeded with his retinue, his magnates, and the elite troops. Of the people's army, he took only those who lived closest to the south coast. He turned south to Jutland south of Vendilskagi (Skagen), and he marched all through Þjóð (Thy) (FJ 163) burning and killing, as Stúfr said:[6]

> 92.　Flýðu þeir á Þjóðu
> þengils fund af stundu
> stórt réð hugprútt hjarta.
> Haralds ǫnd ofar lǫndum.

"Þeir á Þjóðu flýðu þengils fund af stundu; hugprútt hjarta réð stórt. Haralds ǫnd ofar lǫndum."

The people at Þjóð [Thy] soon fled the king's coming; the proud heart prevailed. "Haraldr's spirit above the lands."

They now harried as as if their previous attack had been mere play, and they took immense booty. Then King Haraldr said: "I would like the Danes to have

a long memory of our visit and reflect on our prowess in attacking them (U 56)
and meting out the harshest treatment we can. We have now taken more booty
than in a whole series of earlier summers, but I wish now to go south to Heiðabýr (Hedeby). It would be quite an accomplishment to penetrate that far and
wreak some devastation."

They then got under way with the army and harried with fire and steel wherever they went. They marched fearlessly, and the Danes fled as best they could
to King Sveinn. They made complaint to him, citing the damage done to them
and the grievous treatment they had suffered. King Haraldr now arrived at
Heiðabýr (Hedeby) with his army. They descended on the town like a whirl-
wind, seizing great and numerous treasures, for almost all the wealthiest
people of the land had come there, as well as the wives of powerful men. Almost all the fame and resources of Denmark were concentrated in that one
spot.[7] They *seized* everything they wanted, both women and money.[8] Then
King Haraldr said: "Even though the Danes opposed my being their king, they
do not do much to prevent their women and money from falling into the
hands of the Norwegians." (FJ 164)

When they had plundered the town and taken what they wanted, they
burned it down completely. Haraldr's men composed the following:

93.   Brenndr vas upp með endum   váns at vinnim Sveini
      allr (en þat má kalla   (vask í nótt fyr óttu)
      hraustligt bragð) (es hugðak)   (gaus hár logi ór húsum)
      Heiðabœr af reiði: harm (á borgar armi).

"Allr Heiðabœr vas brenndr upp með endum af reiði, en þat má kalla hraustligt
bragð, es hugðak. Váns, at vinnim Sveini harm; vask í nótt fyr óttu á borgar armi;
gaus hár logi ór húsum."

In wrath, all Heiðabœr [Hedeby] was wasted with fire, and that one can call a
valiant deed, I believe. I expect we will do damage to Sveinn; last night before dawn
I stood on the rampart of the stronghold; the high flame gushed from the houses.

Þorleikr fagri also took note of the event in his poem (*flokkr*):

94.   Hvé hefr til Heiðabýjar   þás til þengils bœjar
      heiptgjarn konungr árnat   þarflaust Haraldr austan
      Folkrǫgnir getr fregna   ár (þats án of væri)
      fylkis sveit hinns veitat: endr byrskíðum renndi.

"Folkrǫgnir, hinns veitat, getr fregna fylkis sveit, hvé heiptgjarn konungr hefr
árnat til Heiðabýjar, þás Haraldr renndi endr byrskíðum þarflaust austan til
þengils bœjar ár, þats án of væri."

That battle-Rǫgnir [Óðinn, warrior] who does not know asks the leader's men how
the war-eager king traveled to Heiðabýr [Hedeby] when once, without cause, Haraldr sent the skis of fair wind [ships] west to the lord's town, that year, that never
should have been.

King Haraldr and his men now went back north with their booty. They had
sixty ships, large and heavily laden with the plunder they had taken during the

summer. As they sailed north off Þjóð (Thy), King Sveinn, at the head of a great army, marched out toward them and called aloud to King Haraldr: "Now is the time," he said, "to make for land and do battle. To my mind you will not have to slander us any longer because we fail to meet in battle, even though it is a little later in the summer than the appointed time. (FJ 165) It would be a bold move on the part of the Norwegians, since they feel superior to the Danes in every circumstance, to go ashore and do battle with them. It will be rather more to your (U 57) credit, even if their king is not all-powerful, to do battle against him rather than to seize people's calves and kids and valuables as you have done hitherto in Denmark."

King Haraldr said: "I think most people know that we have done more than fight with mere farmers. We were scheduled to meet at the Gautelfr (Götaälv), as you suggested, and that was a plan worthy of a king, but we thought it unseemly to break that appointment after a great army had gathered. It was not chieftainly of you to deal in deceit and expose yourself to the reproaches of many men. And it was a fitting revenge against the Danes when we occupied their land. It seems likely to me that if they had come near enough to us for an armed encounter, we would have given them a crushing reception. But it was easier for them to afford no protection either for their possessions or their women. But, to land here, as you request, and do battle with the whole Danish army is not my intention, given that I command no more troops than are here present. But I will meet you in a naval battle if that is your wish, even though the Danes have twice our numbers." This offer of Haraldr's is confirmed by the skald Þjóðólfr:

95. Bauð (sás beztrar tíðar   þó lézk heldr (at heldi
borinn varð und miðgarði)   hvatráðr konungr láði)
ríkri þjóð at rjóða   á byrjar Val berjask
randir Sveinn á landi: bilstyggr Haraldr vilja. (FJ 166)

"Sveinn, sás borinn varð beztrar tíðar und miðgarði, bauð ríkri þjóð at rjóða randir á landi. Þó lézk bilstyggr Haraldr heldr vilja berjask á byrjar Val, at hvatráðr konungr heldi láði."

Sveinn, who was born at the luckiest time on earth, bade the powerful troops redden the shields ashore. Yet the impatient Haraldr said he preferred to fight on the Valr [horse] of fair wind [ship], because the resourceful king [Sveinn] held sway on land.

King Haraldr now sailed north, and they turned east toward the Limafjǫrðr (Limfjord), chiefly because they were driven off course by the wind.[9] But they kept harrying everywhere they went. Then the breeze failed them, and they began to row north. During the night they anchored off Sámsey (Samsø), and first thing in the morning they awoke at dawn and saw that a great fog lay over the whole island. A little later, they looked the other way out to sea and saw something that looked like fires burning.

King Haraldr was told, and he said: "Take down the ship tents as quickly as possible and head north at the oars. I am quite sure," he said, "that an army is upon us. The fog lies along the shore, but out to sea the sun is probably shining brightly, and the reflection that looks like fire is probably from a royal ship with the morning sun glancing off gold."

It was again just as the king said, and King Sveinn had arrived with an enormous army. When he saw the Norwegian forces, he urged his men to row after them vigorously: "Bear in mind what you have lost to them and what a humiliation you have to avenge in the loss of life and property. There will be many men here who are looking to recover distinguished women and great wealth. There is likely to be no better opportunity (U 58) than this, and we will be long remembered if we manage to avenge in a short time the shame they have brought upon us." The Danes pulled hard at the oars and had (FJ 167) much swifter ships, which did not lie so low in the water.

The distance between them began to close, and King Haraldr could see that the situation was not tenable. His dragon ship brought up the rear, and he himself was at the helm. He spoke as follows: "We are going to have to look for a way out, because it will not do as things stand. We will cast beams overboard and lay out precious materials and other valuables on them, for there is a great calm for the moment, and the current is such that the beams will drift toward them. My feeling about the Danes is that they will change their course to meet them as soon as they see their treasures afloat on the water."

It was done accordingly, and the king was close to the mark. The moment the Danes saw their possessions drifting on the sea, those who arrived first veered in that direction. That slowed the pursuit, and when King Sveinn came to the spot with his ship, he urged them on: "It is a great shame, considering the size of the Danish force, if we do not now overcome the Norwegians. You seem to have a bad memory for all the ill deeds for which you need to exact vengeance."

The Danes now bent to the oars a second time, and the distance began to close again. King Haraldr could see that the Danish ships were making greater headway: "We must lighten our ships. Pitch the heavy cargo overboard, both malt and wheat, and pour out the ale." This was done, and they proceeded for a while.

Then King Haraldr saw again that the remedy was insufficient and said: "You should take the battlements and empty casks and throw them overboard. The next to go overboard will be captive men, the friends and companions of these Danes, and their wives along with them." It was done as the king ordered, and everything was dumped in the water. (FJ 168) The women and other people clung to the boards, and everything drifted with the current.

When the Danes arrived and saw the people in dire straits and recognized their wives and friends, they headed toward them and wanted to rescue the people at any cost. The fleet thus came to a standstill. It was necessary to cover a broad area in order to pick up the people. The Norwegians pulled away hard to the north, but the Danes tired of rowing. We are told that during the delay the fleets separated. King Haraldr went on to Norway, saying that he hoped not too much time would pass before he met up with King Sveinn so that this could be avenged.

King Sveinn again spoke to his men when he caught up and they were picking the people out of the water. "It is understandable," he said, "that you are helping these people in their need, but you would have taken a much greater haul if you had been as keen as I am. If King Haraldr and I had met this time, the Norwegians would have found out whether the Danes can fight (U 59), but now that our encounter was not meant to be, it is likely that we will be afflicted by this state of war for a long time." On this subject Þorleikr composed the following:

96. Allt of frák hvé elti   fengr varð Þrœnda þengils
     austmenn á veg flausta   (þeir léttu skip fleiri)
     Sveinn (þás siklingr annarr)   allr á éli sollnu
     snarlundaðr (helt undan):   Jótlands hafi fljóta. (FJ 169)

"Allt of frák, hvé snarlundaðr Sveinn elti austmenn á veg flausta, þás siklingr annarr helt undan. Allr fengr Þrœnda þengils varð fljóta á éli sollnu Jótlands hafi; þeir léttu skip fleiri."

I heard it all, how quick-tempered Sveinn pursued the Norwegians on the path of ships [sea] when the other king fled. All the loot of the lord of the Þrœndir [people of Trøndelag] was to float on the hail-swollen sea of Jótland [Jylland, Jutland]; they emptied more ships [of their cargo].

King Sveinn now headed south back to Sámsey. There he encountered seven ships from Vík, farmers and militiamen. When King Sveinn approached them, they asked to be spared, offering money as indemnity and throwing themselves on the king's mercy. King Sveinn replied: "Since the greater victory got away from us, it is only fitting to spare your lives." As Þorleikr said:

97. Sætt buðu seggja dróttni   ok snarráðir síðan
     siklings vinir mikla   sókn (es orðum tókusk)
     svǫfðu hjaldr (þeirs hǫfðu)   (ǫnd vas ýta kindum
     hugstinnir (lið minna):   ófǫl) búendr dvǫlðu.

"Siklings vinir buðu seggja dróttni sætt mikla; hugstinnir, þeirs hǫfðu lið minna, svǫfðu hjaldr. Ok snarráðir búendr dvǫlðu síðan sókn, es orðum tókusk; ǫnd vas ýta kindum ófǫl."

The king's [Haraldr] friends offered the lord of men [Sveinn] a mighty settlement; the fierce-hearted ones, who were outnumbered, put an end to the fight. And the quick-witted farmers later suspended the battle when the parley began; life was precious to the progeny of men.

Many urged the king to kill them and said that many Norwegians should pay for what Haraldr had done. The king said: "It doesn't seem right that I should be so little fortunate in battle and yet kill men who throw themselves on my mercy. That will not be what I choose to do," he said. The farmers now went in peace, and no[10] *[mention is made of money payments, though all the men were granted their lives by King Sveinn. He remained at home in Denmark that winter without undertaking anything.

32. Concerning King Haraldr

King Haraldr was a powerful man and a firm ruler in Norway. He had a profound intelligence, and it is the opinion of well-informed (FJ 170) men that no one in all the northern lands was more penetrating than King Haraldr. He was the most resourceful of men so that he was never without a remedy. He was physically powerful and superior to everyone in arms. He was a valiant warrior and very successful in his accomplishments, as has been recounted at length. But by far the greatest number of his deeds have not been told. That can be explained chiefly from our lack of information and our reluctance to write down unattested tales even if we have heard some stories, for it seems better to us that our account should be supplemented in the future instead of our being obliged to retract this version.[1] A great narrative of King Haraldr is recorded in the poems composed during his lifetime, and they were recited to him by those who composed them. King Haraldr was a great friend to them because he appreciated their praise, being, as he was, the greatest chieftain in the world.[2]

But there is still more to tell of his deeds. Of all the Norwegian kings, he was best disposed toward the Icelanders. When there was a great famine in Iceland, King Haraldr sent four ships laden with flour and stipulated that a *skippund*[3] should not cost more than three marks' worth of homespun. He allowed all the poor people to go abroad if they could get an ocean passage, and a great number of poor people did indeed go abroad. From that time on, the country returned to prosperity and conditions improved, though they had previously reached rock bottom because of the famine that prevailed.

King Haraldr sent a bell to Iceland for the same church for which Saint Óláfr had supplied the timber, together with another bell. That church was built on Þingvellir, where the parliament meets.[4] Such treasures were in the possession of his men in Iceland and, in addition, many great gifts presented to those who visited him. King Haraldr appointed the Icelander Úlfr Óspaksson his marshal and thereby accorded him the greatest honor. He chose for him a worthy wife in the person of Jórunn, the daughter of Þorbergr Árnason. King Haraldr had himself married Þorbergr's daughter Þóra, Jórunn's sister. Úlfr stallari had important progeny in Norway. His son was named Jón, who was the father of Hímaldi, the father (FJ 171) of Archbishop Eysteinn.[5] King Haraldr had two sons by Þorbergr's daughter Þóra. The older was named Magnús, the younger Óláfr.

King Haraldr had the Church of Saint Mary built north in Niðaróss, and the altar stood where the steps can now be seen by Christ Church.[6] He established generous prebends and promoted the Niðaróss market greatly. In his day the Arnmœðlingar were the greatest magnates in Norway because of their relationship by marriage to the king.[7] The king also relied on them chiefly in all the matters that concerned him.

33. Concerning the Disagreement between the King and Einarr þambarskelfir

King Haraldr fell out with Einarr þambarskelfir because Einarr wished to be as powerful as the king in Þrœndalǫg. He never came to town when King Haraldr was present without having a great following. The king could hardly conclude his business because of the overwhelming authority Einarr exercised. Einarr committed the presumption in town of taking a known thief from the public assembly so that the king was not able to make judgment, even though he too was present at the assembly.[1] King Haraldr recited the following in the hearing of some men:

> *98.   Rjóðandi mun ráða
>   randabliks ór landi
>   oss (nema Einarr kyssi
>   øxar munn enn þunna).

"Rjóðandi randabliks mun ráða oss ór landi, nema Einarr kyssi øxar munn enn þunna."

The reddener of the rims' flash [sword, warrior] may drive me from the country, unless Einarr kisses the thin mouth of the ax.

We are told that King Haraldr recited this stanza as he was looking out through some latticework and saw Einarr proceeding down the main street with a following numbering no more nor less than five hundred men.[2]

> *99.   Hér sék upp enn ǫrva   fullafli bíðr fyllar
>   Einar (þanns kann skeina   (finnk opt at drífr minna)
>   þjalfa) þambarskelfi   hilmis stóls (á hæla
>   (þangs) fjǫlmennan ganga: húskarla lið jarli). (FJ 172)

"Hér sék enn ǫrva Einar þambarskelfi, þanns kann skeina þjalfa þangs, ganga upp fjǫlmennan. Fullafli bíðr fyllar hilmis stóls: finnk opt, at minna húskarla lið drífr á hæla jarli."

Here I see the undaunted Einarr þambarskelfir, who knows how to cleave the enclosure of seaweed [ocean], walk along with many men. The mighty chieftain expects to occupy the royal throne: I often find that a lesser host of liegemen follows at the heels of a jarl.

This was the sort of difference that divided the king and Einarr.

34. Concerning an Icelander

We are told that there once came a man from Iceland, who, it is reported, was poor and was a native of the northern districts. He kept watch on their ship at night, and when the men had fallen asleep, he observed up toward Gaulardalr on Gaularáss that two men had gone there in secret with digging tools and were digging in the earth.[1] He thought that they were searching for treasure. He left the ship and came up to them unobserved and saw that they had brought a chest to the surface. He suspected that it was full of gold and silver.

He spoke to the one who seemed to be in charge, a man named Þorfinnr, suggesting that they make some payment to him and promising that he would conceal their discovery. "I stipulate three marks of weighed silver," he said, "and if I should be in need again later, you should give me the same amount, because you have found a sum of money large enough to make many a man's fortune." Þorfinnr accepted the condition and gave him what he asked for.

Then the Icelander saw that there were runes on the chest to the effect that Hákon jarl was the owner of the money and had hidden it himself.[2] It struck the Icelander that Hákon's heirs were now the rightful owners. On top of the chest lay a thick gold ring and a golden torque. With this they parted. The Icelander went to the ship with his share and said not a word about the matter.

But Þorfinnr had become such a rich man in so short a time that he hardly knew what he had. He was now called Þorfinnr kaupmaðr (the Merchant) or Þorfinnr enn auðgi (the Rich). He invested in practically every merchant enterprise and equipped himself splendidly with weapons and clothes. People began to talk about him a lot, and they did not quite fathom that his finances should mount up so rapidly. But the Icelander did not fare well with his money and lost all of it.

Some summers later he looked up Þorfinnr and asked him for the money they had agreed on. (FJ 173) Þorfinnr pretended he knew nothing about this and said that he had no claim on him. They then parted for the moment. Sometime later the Icelander went to Einarr þambarskelfir and asked for help, saying that he was without means. Einarr took him under his care. He determined to reward Einarr by telling him of the treasure-trove, and he thought it not unlikely that he would consider that he had some claim to money belonging to his kinsman Hákon Hlaðajarl. But he put it off and made no mention of it to Einarr.

Now winter passed, and it turned summer without his remembering to say anything. When people began to prepare for their voyages in the spring, Einarr asked the Icelander what he planned to do, and he said he was eager to journey out to Iceland. "That is the best plan for you," said Einarr. "I have a little money I wish to give you so that you can buy some necessities. I will have them brought to the ship. There is a chest with some goods in it, and I will give you provisions." Then they parted and the Icelander went his way without mentioning the treasure. He went to town and met up with King Haraldr.

One day when people were leaving church, the king asked: "Who is that elegantly dressed man going down the street?" He was told that it was Þorfinnr kaupmaðr. The king said: "It is a strange business when such men accumulate so much money in so short a time and become rich as Croesus. I can remember a short time ago when he was almost penniless. It's an odd thing if there is no foul play involved. Bring him to me—I want to speak with him."

This was done, and when he came before King Haraldr, the king asked: "Where did the money come from that you have accumulated so quickly?" He was slow in answering but hit on one thing and another that turned a profit. "No," said the king, "there is nothing in what you say. Now you have two options, to tell the truth voluntarily, or else you will be forced to speak by torture." He told the truth voluntarily, and when the king knew truly the cause of his wealth, he confiscated the money and took it into his own possession, even what was invested in merchant enterprises. Even at that he said that he was treating Þorfinnr (FJ 174) better than he deserved by not killing him when he was found in possession of the king's money. The king gave him some means, and he went abroad.

It now occurred to the Icelander that he had been silent about the treasure long enough. He went to Einarr and told him the whole story. Einarr said: "It would have been better for you and all of us if we had succeeded in getting the money before King Haraldr. It is now no easy thing to contend with him, but we had an advantage in dealing with Þorfinnr, and things would have turned out better for him than they did. You don't bring much luck, though you seemed promising at first. Even so, I will give you some silver again, and you should head for Iceland as soon as possible and not return to Norway as long as King Haraldr is in power." With that they parted.

A little later Einarr went to town with a great following of kinsmen and friends. When he arrived in town, he proceeded to the place where King Haraldr was at church. As the king was leaving the church, Einarr met and greeted him. The king returned his greeting. Then Einarr asked if he had taken possession of the money that Þorfinnr enn auðgi had kept. The king confirmed that he had and added that it was the law of the land that the king should appropriate any valuables found in the earth.[3] Einarr said that was true of unidentified valuables—"but I have evidence both in the form of runes and particular objects that this wealth was in the possession of my kinsman Hákon jarl. I believe that I, along with my wife Bergljót, Hákon's daughter, have title to this inheritance as well as anything else left by Hákon. And if you do not wish to release the money," he said, "we will not neglect to press the claim, but you may oppose me if that seems a better choice."

King Haraldr replied: "You are powerful indeed, Einarr, if you rule the land rather than me even though I have the title."

"Not at all," he said, "you are the ruler of your country, but I will not endure breaches of the law by anyone."[4]

Reasonable men now intervened to ensure that it got no worse. They parted for the moment. The case was now allowed to rest for a while, and as time went on, tempers settled and became calmer with the good offices (FJ 175) of those who were friendly to both the king and Einarr and wanted to do their best to reconcile them.

35. Concerning King Haraldr's Wise Counsels

It is said that at one time King Haraldr succeeded in capturing two Danes who had King Sveinn's seal in their possession. Then he had a letter addressed to the magnates and all the chieftains in the land and affixed King Sveinn's seal to the letters. He suborned the Danes to take these letters to the chieftains claiming to be the messengers of King Sveinn of Denmark. They were also given large amounts of money to give the chieftains in return for supporting him if he came to Norway. After that they set out, according to the king's directives, with King Sveinn's letters and seal. Wherever they went, they said in secret that they were King Sveinn's messengers, as their letters attested. They traveled far and wide and got very differing receptions, though the men they visited are not all named.

It is told that they came to Einarr þambarskelfir and showed him the letters and the money that he was offered. He said: "It is well known that King Haraldr is not my friend, but King Sveinn is always well disposed toward me. I will certainly be his friend, and you should tell him so. But if he should come to Norway and invade King Haraldr's land and harry in his realm, I will oppose him with all my strength and support King Haraldr as best I can. No matter how things turn out for King Haraldr and me, I will not betray him or detach his land from him."[1]

With that they departed and came to Þórir at Steig. They went before him and showed him the money and presented the letters. Þórir said: "King Sveinn always treats us in a friendly and benevolent way, and in my opinion it may be that this practice will not diminish at such time as we reciprocate." Þórir took the money in his keeping, and the messengers continued on their way.

Then they came to (FJ 176) a man named Høgni, the son of Langbjǫrn and a very wealthy and accomplished man.[2] They showed him the letters and the money. He said: "It seems likely that Sveinn does not know much about me since I am just a farmer, but my response is as follows. If King Sveinn comes to this country with his army, no farmer's son will be harder on him than I will."

They departed as things stood and returned to King Haraldr. He welcomed them and quizzed them closely on what had happened in each place. They told him. "What words did you exchange with that warrior Einarr at Gimsar?" The messengers repeated Einarr's words to him. The king said: "It was quite to be expected of him that he would speak boldly and with no affection for me. How did you fare with Steigar-Þórir?" They told him that he had accepted the money but had spoken only well of both kings. King Haraldr said: "He is the hardest to fathom. We have conferred great benefits on him, and he on us. But how did you fare with Hǫgni?" asked the king. They told him what words had been spoken, that he had said that no man would be more opposed to King Sveinn should he make an armed invasion of Norway. Then King Haraldr said: "That man has the makings of a district chieftain."

We are told that King Haraldr made the rounds soon after that and had a good idea of where his friends and enemies were located. He fined those who were guilty of betraying him and killed some of them. Then the king went to see Þórir and intended to catch him unawares. But it happened that there was a man in the king's retinue who was a friend of Þórir's. He stole away from the king's following and told Þórir that the king was headed for his residence and was very angry at him. He told him how matters stood and what penalties had been inflicted on the men who had accepted the money.

Þórir immediately took his horse and rode toward the king, bringing with him all the money he had received. When they met, Þórir welcomed the king warmly and said: "A feast is prepared at my home, sire, and I would be greatly indebted if you would attend. (FJ 177) I wish to tell you too that there have been men from the south, from Denmark, dispatched by King Sveinn and bringing letters and some money, which they offered on his behalf. It occurred to me to accept the money because it seemed better that you should have it rather than the Danes. And here it is." With that he handed him the purse.

"That is well done," said the king.

"It has come about, lord," he said, "that some of my men in the area are at each other's throats, and I am obliged to go and reconcile them if you permit. I will then join you in the evening." Then he slapped his horse and rode off.

The king went to the feast and found that there were not many men present. Þórir did not come home. The king said: "The devil take the sly fellow. There is a man whose mind is completely opaque. It is hard to tell now what he is up to, but we are not going to catch him for the time being. I suspect it will be hard to figure out which way he will go, given his trickiness and deceit." The king now left the feast without meeting Þórir.[3]

Then he came to Hǫgni's farm and was entertained there. The king was in high spirits and said that Hǫgni's well-intentioned words had been reported to him. He said that they would stand him in good stead and that he would appoint him as a district chieftain. Hǫgni replied: "I wish to accept your friendship with thanks, lord, and I will serve you in any way I can. But I do not wish to have the title of district chieftain because I know what the chieftains will say when they meet: 'There sits Hǫgni, the least of the chieftains, a farmer by lineage.' It would not serve to honor me but to make me an object of scorn and ridicule.[4] I would rather be the greatest among the farmers, so that when people assemble, they may say that Hǫgni is the first among them. That reputation will be much more positive and much more to my liking. But I will happily accept any honor or distinction you wish to confer on me, sire, though I am only a farmer." The king said that these were worthy and impressive words he had spoken, and they parted on very affectionate terms.[5]* (FJ 178)

We are now told that at one time King Haraldr invited Einarr þambarskelfir to a feast and held out the promise of friendly relations. The king gave him a good reception and placed him on the seat next to him. In the evening when they had eaten, the tables were removed and the king and Einarr with their confidants remained at drink. They sat on straw with cushions behind them. The king and Einarr began to converse and entertain each other. The king told of some of his exploits abroad and noticed that Einarr was not paying attention and was dozing off.[6] Einarr was a very old man at that time. When the king realized that Einarr was not paying attention and (U 60) seemed to be belittling the story, he considered that both at present and at other times in their dealings Einarr wished to pay him no heed, despite the fact that he had now softened his disposition and initiated friendly relations. The men had drunk deeply by now, and Einarr was almost asleep. He sat leaning up against a cushion. The king leaned over and whispered to his kinsman Grjótgarðr: "Take some straw," he said, "weave it together, and give him a good poke, saying 'Let's go, Einarr.'" Grjótgarðr did so and [Einarr] took a firm hold and let go a fart. The king went his way.[7]

When Einarr learned what (FJ 179) had happened, he was very angry and returned home that same night. The following morning he came to town with a large body of men and went straight to the loft in which Grjótgarðr slept. They drew their weapons, and the upshot was that they killed Grjótgarðr. The king was most displeased about what had happened to his kinsman, and the relations between Einarr and the king once more became very strained. The king did not seek compensation, and Einarr offered none, though he intended to pay up if the king pressed the case. But it seemed to the king that Einarr should make the first offer, so that they were at loggerheads.

Their friends now intervened and wished to reconcile them. The matter progressed to the point that Einarr went to town with a large following and intended to offer the king a settlement. The king suggested that they should talk the matter over, and the plan was for Einarr to go to the king's chambers for the discussion. The chambers were down by the River Nið, where the hall now stands. Einarr went to the building and entered it, saying, "It's hard to see in the king's quarters." Einarr told his son Eindriði to stand in the antechamber, thinking that the king would not attack him if his son remained behind.

When Einarr entered the room, the men who were there set upon him with their weapons. Einarr plunged ahead to where the king was and struck at him without inflicting a wound because he was encased in two byrnies. Einarr said: "The king's dogs (FJ 180) have sharp fangs." When Eindriði heard that, he could not be restrained and ran in. The man who killed him was named Árni. That was the end of Einarr and his son Eindriði, who was a most valiant and accomplished man.

Thus the hatred and enmity that King Haraldr had long contained and suppressed finally brought about Einarr's death.[8] As has been previously referred to in this story, there were many forebodings of what was to happen before it ended in this way. At this time, the magnates of Norway were so reckless that as soon as they were displeased with the king about something, they headed south for Denmark to King Sveinn. He made great men of them there in Denmark. To some he gave gold and to some other honors, as Þjóðólfr states: (U 61)

> 100. [Frán hefr sveit við Sveini
>   sinni skipt til minna]
>   Dáð ok dróttni góðum
>   drengspell es þat lengi.

"Frán sveit hefr skipt sinni dáð ok góðum dróttni við Sveini til minna; drengspell es þat lengi."

The keen company has altered their courage and exchanged their good king for Sveinn at a loss to themselves; that disgrace will be long remembered.

At that time Finnr Árnason left the country and went south to Denmark. King Sveinn gave him a jarldom and a great fief.

36. How Auðunn from the Westfjords Brought King Sveinn a Bear

There was a man named Auðunn, a native of the Westfjords and a man of few resources. He sailed abroad from the Westfjords with the support of a good farmer named Þorsteinn and the ship captain Þórir, who had been lodged by Þorsteinn during the winter. Auðunn was part of the household too and worked for Þórir. In compensation he was given the passage abroad and Þórir's help. Auðunn left most of his money (FJ 181) for his mother before he went abroad. It was calculated as a subsistence for three years.

Now they set sail and had a smooth passage. Auðunn spent the following winter with the captain Þórir, whose residence was in Mœrr (Møre). The next summer they sailed out to Greenland and spent the winter there. We are told that Auðunn bought a bear there, a great treasure, for which he paid everything that he owned.[1] The following summer they returned to Norway and had a good passage. Auðunn had his bear with him and intended to travel south to Denmark to meet with King Sveinn and give him the bear. When he arrived in the south of Norway where King Haraldr was located, he left the ship leading the bear and took lodging.

King Haraldr very soon got the news that there was a newly arrived bear in the possession of an Icelander, a great treasure. The king immediately sent men for him, and when Auðunn appeared before the king, he greeted the king courteously. The king responded graciously and asked:

"Do you have a great treasure in the form of a bear?"

He said that he did have a certain animal.

The king asked: "Do you wish to sell me the bear at the same price for which you bought it?"

"No, sire," he said, "that is not my wish."

"Do you wish then," asked the king, "that I should give you double the value? That would be more appropriate if you have given everything you own for it."

"That is not my wish, sire," he said.

The king said: "Is it your intention to give it to me then?"

"No, sire," he said.

The king asked: "What then do you intend to do with it?"

He replied: "I wish to travel to Denmark and give it to King Sveinn."

King Haraldr asked: "Are you such a foolish man that you have not heard of the war being waged between these two countries? Or do you think that your good fortune is such that you can travel freely with treasures where others can hardly get off unscathed, though it is a matter of life and death?" (U 62)

Auðunn said: (FJ 182) "Sire, that is a matter for you to decide, but I cannot alter what I have already said."

The king replied: "Why shouldn't you proceed on your way as you choose, but come to me when you return and tell me how King Sveinn rewarded you for the beast. You may turn out to be a lucky man."

"This I promise," said Auðunn.

He now proceeded south along the coast and east to Vík and then to Denmark. At that point his last penny had been spent, and he was obliged to beg food both for himself and the bear. He came to the residence of King Sveinn's steward, a man named Áki, and he asked him for food both for himself and his animal.

"It is my intention," he said, "to give the animal to King Sveinn."

Áki said that he would sell him provisions if he wished.

Auðunn said that he had no money with which to pay, "but I wish I could manage it," he said, "so that I can bring the animal to the king."

"I will give you the provisions you need to get to the king, but in exchange I wish to have half the animal.[2] You should consider that it may die during the journey since you need ample provisions and have used up all your money. It may turn out then that you have no fraction of the animal at all."

As Auðunn thought about this, it struck him that there was some truth in what the steward said. They therefore agreed on his selling half the animal to Áki with the understanding that the king would make a total evaluation. It was settled that they would both go to meet the king.

They did so and made their way into the king's presence. As they stood before his table the king reflected on who this man, whom he did not recognize, might be.

Then he asked Auðunn: "Who are you?"

Auðunn replied: "I am an Icelander, sire, recently come from abroad in

Greenland, then Norway. It was my intention to bring you this bear. I bought it with everything (FJ 183) I owned, but I have encountered great difficulties. I now own only half of the animal." Then he told the king of his dealings with his steward Áki.

The king asked: "Is what he says true, Áki?"

"It is true," he said.

The king went on: "Did you, someone whom I have raised to a high position, think it correct to obstruct and interfere with a man who wished to bring me a treasure after giving all his possessions for it and after King Haraldr, who is our enemy, saw fit to let him proceed in peace? Consider how proper that was on your part. You deserve to be killed, but I will not do it. Rather, you shall go into exile immediately and never appear before me again. But to you, Auðunn, I am indebted as if you had given me the whole animal, and I wish you to stay with me." He accepted and stayed with King Sveinn for a while.

When some time had passed, Auðunn said to the king: "I wish to depart now, sire."

The king was not quick to respond. "What is it you want," he asked, "if you do not want to stay with me?"

"I wish to go to (U 63) Rome," said Auðunn.

"If you had not chosen such a worthy option," said the king, "I would have resented your wish to depart."

The king now gave him a large amount of silver, and he traveled south with the pilgrims to Rome under the king's auspices. He told Auðunn to come to him when he returned.[3]

He now proceeded on his way until he came to Rome, and when he had stayed for such time as he wished, he returned. He then fell very ill and became terribly emaciated. All the money that the king had given him for the journey was used up, and he was obliged to take up the beggar's staff and beg for food. He became bald and altogether wretched. He returned to Denmark at (FJ 184) Easter and came to the place where the king was in residence. But he did not dare to show himself and lurked in a wing of the church, thinking to meet the king when he went to vespers. When he saw the king and his splendid retinue, he did not dare to reveal himself, and when the king went to drink in his hall, Auðunn ate outside as is the custom among pilgrims to Rome as long as they have not cast off their staffs and scrips. In the evening, as the king was going to vespers, Auðunn thought to meet him, but no matter how apprehensive he had been before, he now felt a great deal more apprehensive because the retainers were drunk.

When they returned, the king caught a glimpse of a man and had the feeling that he did not have the courage to approach him. As the retinue entered the hall, the king stepped aside and said: "Let the man who wishes to see me step forward, and," pointing him out, "I suspect that you there are the man."

Then Auðunn went forward and fell on his knees before the king, and the king scarcely recognized him. As soon as the king realized who he was, he took him by the hand and made him welcome—"but you have undergone a great change since we last saw each other." He led him in, and when the retinue saw him, they laughed at him. But the king said: "You have no need to laugh at him, for he has seen to the condition of his soul better than you have." Then the king had a bath prepared for him and gave him clothes. Auðunn remained with him as his guest.

We are told that during the spring the king invited Auðunn to prolong his stay, saying that he would make him a page and maintain him in good standing. Auðunn responded: "God's thanks, sire, for all the honor you wish to accord me, but I have it in mind to go to Iceland."

The king said: "That seems to me (FJ 185) to be a curious choice."

Auðunn said: "I cannot endure the thought, *lord*," he said, "that I should enjoy such honor with you while my mother treads the beggar's path out in Iceland, for the provision that I laid aside before I left Iceland is now exhausted."

The king said: "Well spoken," he said, "and those are manly sentiments. I judge you to be favored by fortune. You provide the only reason (U 64) for your departure that does not displease me. Be my guest now until the ships are ready to sail." He agreed to do this.

One day, when the spring was somewhat advanced, King Sveinn went down to the quays as the men had begun to ready their ships for voyages to various Baltic countries or Saxony or Sweden or Norway. A group including Auðunn came to a fair vessel that was being readied. The king asked: "How do you like that ship, Auðunn?"

He said, "I like it, sire."

The king said: "I wish to give you this ship as a reward for the bear." Auðunn thanked him to the best of his ability.

When the time came and the ship was ready to sail, the king said to Auðunn: "If you wish to depart, I will not detain you, but I have learned that harbors are few and far between in your country and there are long stretches of inaccessible coast perilous for ships. If you should wreck your ship and lose your money, there would be no way to tell that you met with King Sveinn and gave him a treasure." Then the king gave him a pouch full of silver—"that will ensure that you are not altogether penniless if you wreck your ship but still manage to hold onto this. But it may still be," said the king, "that you will lose this money. Then it will be of little profit to you that you met up with King Sveinn and gave him a treasure."

Then the king drew a ring from his arm and gave it to Auðunn and said: "Even if you have the bad luck to wreck your ship and lose your money, you will not be penniless if you make it to shore because many people can hold onto their gold (FJ 186) in shipwrecks. If you have the ring, it will still be apparent that you met King Sveinn. But I wish to advise you," he said, "that you should not give the ring away unless there is some outstanding man to whom you are greatly indebted. Then you should give him the ring because it is fitting for noble men to accept gifts. And now I bid you farewell."

Auðunn set sail and came to Norway. He brought his cargo ashore, and that required more labor than the last time he was in Norway. He then went to meet with King Haraldr, wishing to fulfill the promise he had made before sailing to Denmark. He greeted the king and was well received. "Sit down," he said, "and drink with us." He did so. Then King Haraldr asked: "How did King Sveinn reward you for the animal?"

Auðunn replied, "By accepting it, sire."

The king said: "That is a reward I would have given you. What else did he give you?"

Auðunn said, "He gave me silver for a pilgrimage to Rome."

King Haraldr said: "King Sveinn gives many people silver for pilgrimages or other causes, even if they don't bring him treasures. What else did he do?"

"He offered to make me his page," said Auðunn, "and to confer great honor on me."

"That was well done," said the (U 65) king, "but he probably did still more."

Auðunn said: "He gave me a trading vessel with a full cargo most suited for Norway."

"That was magnificent," said the king, "but I would also have given you that reward. Did he give you anything else?"

Auðunn said, "He gave me a pouch full of silver and said that I would not be penniless if I held onto it even though the ship was wrecked off Iceland."

The king said: "That was a splendid gesture, and I would not have done the same. I would have considered it a full reward if I had given you the ship. Did he give you anything else?"

"He certainly did," said Auðunn. "He gave me this ring that I have on my arm, saying (FJ 187) that it might happen that I lost all the money. He said that I would then not be penniless if I had the ring, and he told me not to bestow it unless I was so indebted to some noble man that I wished to give it to him. And now I have found that man, because you had the option to take the animal from me, as well as my life. But you gave me leave to travel in peace, as others could not."

The king accepted the gift kindly and gave Auðunn good gifts in exchange before they parted. Auðunn invested the money in goods for Iceland and left for Iceland that same summer. He was judged to be a man of great good fortune. Þorsteinn Gyðuson was descended from this Auðunn.[4]

37. Concerning King Haraldr and the Upplanders

It happened that at this time King Haraldr had a falling out with the Upplanders. They considered that Saint Óláfr had given them a number of legal advantages over other men with respect to taxes and the levy and many questions of governance, compared to the practices elsewhere among the farmers of Norway. They believed that King Óláfr had given them these forms of autonomy after the Battle of Nesjar because the Upplanders had come to his aid when he won all of Norway from Jarl Sveinn Hákonarson.[1] It was then that Jarl Sveinn fled the land.

This opinion did not please King Haraldr, and he wanted all Norwegians to have the same law. In the words of the skald Þjóðólfr: (FJ 188)

> 101. Létu lystir sleitu   ok því ráði þjóða
>   landkarlar gram varla   þeim brutu troll es ollu
>   (gerði ǫld) á jǫrðu   hæls í hleypikjóla
>   (ódœmi) lǫg sœma: hrís andskotum vísa.

"Landkarlar, lystir sleitu, létu gram varla sœma lǫg á jǫrðu; ǫld gerði ódœmi. Ok troll brutu hrís í hæls hleypikjóla þeim andskotum vísa, es ollu því ráði þjóða."

The farmers, longing for a quarrel, hardly let the king uphold the laws in the land; the people committed an act unheard of. And trolls broke twigs in the running keels of the heel [shoes] of those enemies of the king who urged that counsel for the people.

King Haraldr marched against them into Raumaríki (Romerike) and harried and burned far and wide, as Þjóðólfr said: (U 66)

> 102. Tók Holmbúa hneykir   eldr vas gǫrr at gjaldi
>   harðan taum við Rauma   gramr réð en þá téði
>   þar hygg'k fast ens frægsta   hár í hóf at fœra
>   fylking Haralds gingu: hrótgarmr búendr arma.

"Holmbúa hneykir tók harðan taum við Rauma; þar hygg'k fylking ens frægsta Haralds gingu fast. Eldr vas gǫrr at gjaldi; gramr réð, en þá téði hár hrótgarmr at fœra arma búendr í hóf."

The conqueror of the islanders [the Danes] governed the Raumar [people of Romerike] with a tight rein; I know that the troops of most famous Haraldr harried fiercely there. Fire was set as reprisal at the king's command, and then the tall roof-Garmr [dog, fire] brought the poor farmers to reason.

From there he marched up to Hringaríki (Ringerike), where he burned farms. Þjóðólfr also reports how they submitted to him and were bent to his service. In his words:

> 103. Lífs báðu sér lýðir   lýtr folkstara feiti
>   logi þingaði Hringum   (fátt es til nema játta
>   nauðgan dóm áðr næði   þat sem þá vill gotnum)
>   niðrfall Háalfs galla: þjóð ǫll (konungr bjóða). (FJ 189)

"Lýðir báðu sér lífs; logi þingaði Hringum nauðgan dóm, áðr niðrfall Háalfs galla næði [Hringum]. Ǫll þjóð lýtr folkstara feiti; fátt es til, nema játta þat, sem konungr þá vill bjóða gotnum."

People pleaded for their life; the flame pronounced a forced verdict on the Hringar [people of Ringerike] before the extinction by Hálfr's [legendary king]

destruction [fire] reached [them]. All men submit to the fattener of the fight starling [bird of prey, warrior]; there are few options but to consent to that which the
king then wants to command the people.

After that the farmers gave in and maintained the laws at the king's behest
and obeyed all his commands. For his part, he stopped burning their farms.

After their difficulties had been settled, King Haraldr made a circuit of feasts
in Upplǫnd, and we are told that he stayed with a man named Árni. He was a
wealthy man, and at that time all the provinces were at peace. Árni said that it
was a great joy to all that the king was at peace and in the affection of his
friends.

There was a man named Úlfr auðgi (the Wealthy). He owned fourteen or
fifteen farms. His wife asked him to invite the king to a feast and said that it
would be a more appealing prospect than to be plundered by the king. Úlfr
said that he was not eager to invite the king and that the king was more interested in his wealth than seemed to him fitting. But because of his affection for
his wife, he went to invite the king while he was feasting with Árni. The king
told Úlfr that he would come.

Úlfr now prepared the feast, and when the king left Árni's residence, he was
true to his promise and visited Úlfr auðgi. The provision that had been made
was splendid; the table setting, the drink, and the adornment of the hall were
resplendent and costly. (FJ 190) One time, when the men had sat down at the
feast, the king spoke up and said: "It is fitting," he said, "that we should provide some entertainment for this feast." Everyone said that it would honor and
adorn the feast greatly if such a man were to provide entertainment. (U 67)

The king said: "In that case, I will tell a little story. The story begins with a
son of Haraldr hárfagri named Sigurðr hrísi. Sigurðr had a son named Hálfdan. A jarl of his was also named Hálfdan. The king and Hálfdan jarl were foster brothers of the same age and good friends. One of the king's thralls was
named Álmsteinn, also of the same age. The king's men and the jarl were in
the habit of getting together for games. As years passed, King Haraldr became
ill, and he had an intimation that the illness would be the death of him. He
arranged to have the jarl govern the realm together with his son Hálfdan. He
said that because of their lifelong friendship he expected that the jarl would
be the most faithful support to his son. Then the king died.

"The jarl became a powerful supporter of King Hálfdan and gathered land
taxes for him. Álmsteinn, who became King Hálfdan's thrall, was a big, handsome man and was more accomplished than any of the king's other thralls.
There is no information on his genealogy. Álmsteinn offered to collect the
land taxes for three summers, and since he was known to be an energetic man
and virtually a foster brother of King Sigurðr, the father of King Hálfdan, and
the jarl, the decision was made to have him collect the land taxes. But as things
turned out, not much of the money (FJ 191) got to King Hálfdan.

"At this time the jarl died, but Álmsteinn circulated the money to various countries, increasing it and finally taking possession of it.[2] He recruited men with gifts of money, and when he learned of the jarl's death, he returned to Norway and came with an armed following to Hálfdan's residence during the night and set it on fire. The jarl had left a son behind, and he was inside with Hálfdan. When those inside became aware of the fire and realized that it was of human origin, the sons of the king and the jarl escaped into an underground hideout that gave onto the woods, into which they fled.

"They now spent some time in the wilderness. They eventually made their way to Sweden, where they appealed to Hákon jarl for leave to stay at the court. The jarl stared at them, agreeing to provide food but without according them any honor. They spent three years with the jarl, but back in Norway Álmsteinn burned the residence and assumed that he had burned the king's son and the jarl's son with it.

"After that Álmsteinn seized the realm and made himself king. No one offered any resistance, but no one was pleased to live under his rule. He abducted respectable women and kept them in his bed for whatever period of time pleased him and fathered children with them. Now that the boys had spent three years in Sweden with Hákon jarl, they decided to depart and went before the jarl to thank him for his provision of food. He (U 68) said: 'It amounts to very little, Hálfdan, but in fact I knew exactly who you were when you arrived here. But I paid little attention to you so that word would not circulate (FJ 192) that you were still alive and so that you could regain your land. I will now give you three hundred men in the hope that you may catch them unprepared and take revenge against that wicked Álmsteinn.'

"They set out with this body of men and returned to Norway. There was no hint of their arrival, and they came to Álmsteinn's residence unexpectedly and set it afire. The members of the household were allowed to leave. Álmsteinn asked for free exit, but Hálfdan said that it was fitting for him to have the same judgment that had been meant for him. 'But because,' he said, 'we are not equals, I will give you the choice of returning to your nature and being a slave the rest of your life, along with all who may be your descendants.' That was Álmsteinn's choice, and Hálfdan gave him a coarse white tunic to signal his slave status.[3]

"After this a thingmeeting was convened, and Hálfdan assumed the royal title along with his realm. Everyone welcomed this change and thought that the previous state had been wretched. The thrall Álmsteinn had many children, and I believe, Úlfr," said the king, "that your ancestry is such that Álmsteinn is your grandfather. I, on the other hand, am the grandson of King Hálfdan. You and your kinsmen have siphoned off royal property, as is evident here in the drinking vessels and other precious items. Now, Úlfr," said King Haraldr, "you will take the white tunic that my grandfather Hálfdan gave your grandfather Álmsteinn and with it your hereditary title. You shall be a slave forever after, for that was stipulated, as I have already mentioned, when Hálfdan arranged that your grandfather should take the tunic. At that time the mothers of his children came to the meeting and all his children were clad in this sort (FJ 193) of garment. And so it was to be for all those who descended from them." Now King Haraldr had the white tunic brought before Úlfr and recited the following:

104.   Kennir kyrtil þenna   bǫrn ok allt þats árnar
        kú átt skjǫldungi gjalda   átt skjǫldungi gjalda
        ok alvaxinn oxa   svín ok aligás eina
        átt skjǫldungi gjalda: átt skjǫldungi at gjalda.

  Do you know this kirtle? You must yield a cow to the king, and a full-grown ox you must yield to the king. Your children and all you acquire, you must yield to the king; a pig and a tame goose you must yield to the king.

To that the king added the following couplet:

      Margar eru manna vélar
      mosa átt ok skjǫldungi at gjalda. (U 69)

  Many are the deceits of men: moss, you must also yield to the king.

"Now take this tunic that I offered you and which your kinsmen have had, and with the same title and honor they had."

Úlfr found the king's wit bitter but hardly dared do other than to accept the tunic. His wife and her kinsmen intervened and asked him not to take it no matter what happened. Then his wife went before the king with a following of relatives and asked that Úlfr be forgiven and not be dishonored in this way. The end of it was that the king yielded to their plea and granted Úlfr one of the fifteen farms he had owned and did not force him into slavery. But the king confiscated all his drinking vessels and other valuables (FJ 194) and took over all his other farms, aside from the single one that he granted him. After this feast the king went to Niðaróss and resided there.

38. Concerning King Haraldr and Brandr ǫrvi (the Open-Handed)

Now we are told that one summer Brandr ǫrvi came to town. He was the son of Vermundr in Vatnsfjǫrðr and a very popular and generous man. The skald Þjóðólfr had often told the king how distinguished and accomplished a man Brandr was. Þjóðólfr had even told him that it was not clear that any other man was better suited to be king of Iceland because of his generosity and outstanding personal qualities, and he gave the king many examples of his generosity.[1]

The king said: "I am now going to test that. Go out to him and ask him to give me his cloak." Þjóðólfr went away and entered the chamber where Brandr was to be found. He was standing in the middle of the floor and was measuring linen. He was dressed in a fine tunic and had a fine cloak over it, with the fastening cord pushed back on his head.[2] He had a gold-inlaid ax under his arm.

Þjóðólfr said: "The king wishes to have your cloak." Brandr continued his work and said nothing, but he let the cloak slide off. Þjóðólfr picked it up and brought it to the king. The king asked what had passed between them, and Þjóðólfr said that Brandr had not spoken a word. Then he related what he was doing and how he was dressed.

The king said: "That man is certainly self-important. He must believe that he is high and mighty since he feels no need to say anything. Go to him again and say that I would like a gift of his gold-inlaid ax."

Þjóðólfr said (FJ 195): "I am not very keen to go again, sire, because I am not certain whether he will honor your request."

"You have constantly raised the topic of Brandr, both now and earlier," said the king, "and you will do as I say and ask for the gift of his gold-inlaid ax. I will not believe that he is generous unless he gives it to me."

Þjóðólfr now went to see Brandr and said that the king wanted a gift of the ax. (U 70) He held out the ax without saying a word. Þjóðólfr brought the ax to the king and described the scene. The king said: "It is becoming increasingly apparent that this man is more generous than others, and the cost is going up. Go once again and say that I wish to have the tunic that he is standing in."

Þjóðólfr said: "It is not fitting that I should go again."

The king replied: "You will most certainly go."

He went to Brandr's chamber and said that the king wished to have the tunic. Brandr then stopped his work and pulled off the tunic without saying a word. He detached one sleeve and threw down the tunic, keeping the sleeve. Þjóðólfr picked it up and went to the king to show him the tunic.[3] The king looked at it and said: "This man is both wise and self-assertive. It is clear to me why he detached one sleeve. It seems to him that I have only one arm, and that one made only to receive and never to give. Go now and bring him here."[4] That was done, and Brandr came into the presence of the king and was accorded fitting honor and given valuable gifts. Haraldr acted in this way so as to test him.

39. Concerning King Haraldr

There was a wealthy man named Halldórr, a friend of King Haraldr's. His daughter was named Ingibjǫrg, a wise and fair woman who had friendly relations with the king. The king was often entertained there, and he and Ingibjǫrg had much to talk about. She was conversant and knowledgeable about many things. (FJ 196)

One autumn we are told that she became very ill. Her belly swelled and she had terrible spells of fever and thirst. She didn't care to say much about it in public, but there was much speculation. Some people thought that the king was responsible for her state, but it got to the point where it seemed to amount to more than could be explained by human agency, and her illness was accompanied by great pain.

Word was now sent to the king asking him to offer good counsel. He came and looked at her condition, then spoke with her father Halldórr: "I am obliged to return to the queen. She is ill and is scheduled to give birth, but it is a perilous matter. As for your daughter's illness, I judge it to be serious. It seems most likely that she drank from some spring, but this area is much infested by worms, and I think she may have swallowed some little worm that has grown in her belly. My presence is of no importance here, but I will advise you how to treat this illness. What seems to me best is the following, though it involves considerable risk:

> You should withhold drink from her. She will find that hard to bear, but you should pay no attention. Then take her to a waterfall, plunging off some cliff (U 71), and stem the flow at the top of the falls just enough so that there is only a constant drip, but let the stream fall from the cliff nearby so that it is clearly audible. (FJ 197) Then spread out a piece of homespun and let her lie on it as comfortably as possible. Arrange things so that the creature in her experiences the greatest possible thirst. Place her where it drips little by little into her mouth, and make sure that she gets nothing to drink. You, Halldórr, should stand close by with some sharp weapon, and if everything goes as I suspect and the creature in her goes after water, be on your guard when it comes to her mouth and do not let it see you. Take very good care that you do not attack it before the forequarters and the heart are out because of the poison in the upper body, but it makes no difference whether she digests the lower body of the worm. Pay no attention if she cries out because this remedy will serve if it is carried out correctly, but fortune and the intercession of Saint Óláfr will decide the issue. Call on him for his aid and use the treatment I have described."[1]

After this the king departed. Halldórr followed the directions and brought her to the foot of a cliff where he carried out all the measures as he had been instructed. She complained bitterly and said that she would never have believed that her father would wish to torment her in this way—"and it may be that King Haraldr's cruelty is in evidence." They pretended to hear nothing, whatever she said or however she moaned, and there dripped just enough water into her mouth so that she felt the maximum thirst. Halldórr stood close by with a drawn sword, but he concealed himself.

Two men were dispatched to manage the waterfall, and they did exactly as they were told at the top of the cliff. Then (FJ 198) Halldórr saw that a snout was coming out of her mouth and peered about and went back in. A little later it came out again and showed a little more of itself and peered around, eager to get to the water. But it was still not a good target and crept back in. Then it came out a third time, and Halldórr saw that the upper body was exposed. He called on Saint Ólafr again, got ready, and sliced the worm in two. The front part fell out and the back part slid back in.

In the process she had become so weak that she seemed on the point of death. They brought her home gently, and she recovered little by little though she was weak for a long time. She was in a state of terror and suffered gravely from it. They sent for the king, who came to see her. At first she did not want to speak to him, and when the king learned that, he asked why she was unwilling. She finally gave the reason and said that he had shown great cruelty in his remedy. The king said (U 72) that this would not prove to be the case and that she had been possessed by a creature that was difficult to appease.

The king now spoke to her father: "You should pray for her now," he said. "She should sing 'Beati Immaculati' and seven psalms, and especially the mass of the Virgin Mary." [2] And after these prayers she recovered completely and was known as the best match in Norway. A district chieftain appeared to woo her. He was both young and fair, and her father inclined very much toward the match. He sent word to the king about his wishes, but the king replied that (FJ 199) he did not wish her to marry. Halldórr said it was fitting that he should have a major role in the decision.

The king now met with the district chieftain who had asked for her hand and they discussed the matter. The chieftain said that many believed that he was attached to her and therefore made her unavailable to others. The king said that it would benefit no one to marry her and he promised to be the chieftain's friend if he would abandon the idea. He said that his plans for her remained to be revealed. When this business was concluded, the king sent her to a nunnery, and there she lived out her days with a good life. [3]

40. Concerning the Storytelling of an Icelander

It happened one summer that an Icelander, who was young and nimble, came to the king and asked for hospitality. The king asked him if he had any sort of learning, and he said that he could tell stories. [1] The king said that he would receive him, but that he was obligated to provide entertainment any time he asked. He did so and became popular among the retainers. They gave him clothes, and the king presented him with weapons. Time now passed until Christmas came around.

Then the Icelander became downcast, and the king asked what the cause was. He said that it was his own moodiness. "That isn't it," said the king, "and I will make a surmise. I will guess that you have now exhausted your store of tales. You have entertained us this winter as is most fitting, (FJ 200) and now you are probably distressed that the supply runs out just at Christmas."

"You are right as usual," he said. "I have only one story left and I do not dare to tell it here because it is the story of your foreign adventures."

The king said: "That is the story I would most like to hear. You should now call a halt to your storytelling until Christmas since everyone is preoccupied with preparations, but on Christmas day you should begin on this story and tell a bit of it. I will see to it that the tale and the duration of the Christmas holidays are coterminous. There are big drinking parties at Christmas and the attention span of the listeners is short. While you are telling the story, I will give no indication of whether I am pleased (U 73) or not."

Thus it came about that the Icelander told the story. He began on Christmas and carried on for a while, but soon the king asked him to stop. The retainers began to drink and comment that it was a temerity for the Icelander to tell this story and to wonder how the king would react. Some thought that he told the story well, but others were less impressed.

The holidays advanced. The king paid close attention to the timing and with his forethought contrived that the story was concluded as the holidays came to an end. On the thirteenth day, when the story had been finished earlier in the day, the king said: "Aren't you curious to know, Icelander," he asked, "what I think of the story?"

"I am afraid to ask, sire," he said.

The king said: "I am very pleased with it. It is perfectly faithful to the actual events. Who taught you the story?"

He replied: "It was my custom out in Iceland to go to the thingmeeting every summer, and every summer I learned something of the story from Halldórr Snorrason."

"Then it is not surprising," said the king, "that you know the story well, and it will turn out to your benefit. You are welcome to stay with me whenever you wish." The king gave him a good stake and he became a prosperous man. (FJ 201)

41. Concerning Þorvarðr krákunef's Gift of a Sail to King Haraldr

There was a man named Þorvarðr krákunef from the Westfjords. He was a wealthy man and an excellent fellow. He sailed to various countries and was held in high esteem wherever he went. One summer he arrived with his ship in Niðaróss. King Haraldr was there in town together with his kinsman Eysteinn orri, the son of Þorbergr and the grandson of Árni.[1] He was a very valiant man and much honored by the king.

Þorvarðr unloaded his ship and rented lodgings.[2] Then he went to see King Haraldr where he was at drink. When he arrived at the hall, the king was outside and as he was about to enter, Þorvarðr said: "Greetings, sire, there is a sail down on my ship that I wish you to have."

The king frowned and said: "Once before I accepted a sail from you Icelanders and it almost turned out to be a disaster for me.[3] It split on the high seas, and I have no intention of accepting another."

Eysteinn said: "Go and look at it, sire. You may like it. There are a lot of gifts that are likely to do you less honor than the one he has in mind for you."

The king said: "I will keep my counsel, and you should keep yours." Then he entered the hall and refused to listen.

Þorvarðr next asked Eysteinn to accept the sail. "Come with me," he said. Eysteinn did so and thought that he had never seen such a (U 74) treasure of a sail. He gave warm thanks for it and invited Þorvarðr to come to his (FJ 202) estate at Gizki (Giske) in Norðmœrr and spend the winter with him.

The winter was uneventful. When spring came, Þorvarðr readied his ship and sailed south, heading out to sea at Sólskel (Solskelsøya). One day they saw a ship bearing down at full speed and manned from stem to stern. A handsome and splendidly attired man stood in the prow wearing a fine tunic. He asked if Þorvarðr was there. He identified himself and greeted Eysteinn warmly. Eysteinn said: "You took your time in visiting me, but come aboard now with as many men as you wish because the winds are not propitious for your voyage just now." He did so and rowed with a few men to the island of Gizki. There they found a good reception and a feast prepared.

There were large, well-built houses on the estate. When the evening and night passed and dawn broke, Þorvarðr awoke and saw that Eysteinn was already up. He said: "The winds are still not favorable for sailing. Stay with us today and let me forecast the weather for you. You should wait for the right breezes."

During the day, as they drank and made merry, Eysteinn said: "Because you left your ship to come with me, I ask you to accept this tunic." It was ornamented with lace and cut from a precious material. Þorvarðr thanked him for the gift. Eysteinn said: "It is not a reward for the sail."

They sat together during the day and there was no lack of good drink. The next morning Eysteinn said to Þorvarðr: "You should not go anywhere today because the wind is not favorable."

Þorvarðr replied: "I leave that to you." And now the drinking and festivities rose to a new pitch. Then Eysteinn had a cloak brought out. It was all of gray fur, richly adorned, and with a fine mantle over it.

Then Eysteinn said: (FJ 203) "You shall have this cloak, and now the sail has been rewarded, for this cloak is superior to all other cloaks, just as the sail outdoes all other sails." Þorvarðr gave warm thanks for the gift.

The night passed, and early in the morning Þorvarðr was awakened. Eysteinn was there and said: "Now I will no longer delay you because the wind is right." They ate and drank before leaving.

Then Eysteinn said: "It was not fated that the king should accept the sail from you, but I think that if he had accepted it, he would have rewarded it in the same way I have.[4] But you still have no compensation for the fact that it was not the king who gave you the reward. Though I am less noble than the king, I am not content to leave it at that, and for the discrepancy in our standing you shall have this gold ring." He drew it off his arm. Þorvarðr thanked him for the ring. Then they went to their ship. They had a favorable wind and a good passage to Iceland, where Þorvarðr became a man of high standing.

In the summer, as King Haraldr and Eysteinn were sailing along the coast (U 75) and Eysteinn was gaining speed out ahead, the king asked: "Where did you get that fine sail?"

Eysteinn said: "It is the sail that you refused to accept, sire."

The king said: "I never saw a better sail, and I have turned down a good thing."

Eysteinn said: "Do you want to kiss between the sheets, sire?"[5]

The king laughed and said, "Why not?" He then went up next to the mast.

Eysteinn said: "Don't be silly and take the sail if you wish. It is good that you should know what it is that you (FJ 204) refused." The king thanked him and raised the sail on his ship. The king's sail could not be rivaled in racing, for it was a large ship but nonetheless thought to be a great miracle of construction.

42. Concerning King Haraldr and Hákon

The most important development in Norway was that King Haraldr called out the levy and sailed with his army south to Denmark to harry. He lay anchored south off Halland in Lófufjǫrðr (Laholmsbukten) after having harried in a large part of Halland. He had 150 ships, and the king was of the opinion that he would fare better than in the Sea of Jutland (Kattegat).[1] The Danes had not been able to boast often about chasing the king and the Norwegians. He said that they had had to compensate for that by chasing after their own possessions.

As King Haraldr and his men now lay at anchor in Lófufjǫrðr, they were taken by surprise by King Sveinn coming at them from the sea with an enormous army. He had 300 longships, and the Danes caught the Norwegians in the fjord.[2] They closed in from the sea before King Haraldr realized it. The king's army was numerous and low on water, but it was unsafe to venture into the country because of the hostile population. King Sveinn intended to starve them for a while.

There was an island nearby in the fjord. No one knew of any water on it, but the king gave orders to look for a live snake on the island. They succeeded in finding one, and the king ordered that it be dehydrated by the fire so that it became as thirsty as possible—"and it may be," he said, "that the snake knows of some water (FJ 205) on the island even if we do not. It would not be able to sustain itself here unless it knew of water."

Now the king said that a long thread should be tied to the snake's tail and that it should be allowed to go wherever it wished. But a man was to follow it and hold onto the thread. The snake went straight to the place where it knew there was water, though the water was hidden, and thus with the aid of the king's resourcefulness water was found. The device was preserved in memory because it seemed wise and ingenious.[3] They now brought as much water as they needed for the ships. (U 76)

There was a man named Ívarr hvíti (the White). He had been one of Saint Óláfr's district chieftains, an important man, quarrelsome and somewhat fickle. He was once in attendance with King Óláfr at a feast. One day Sigvatr the skald had recited a poem in honor of King Óláfr, and the poem was much praised. But Ívarr said to Sigvatr that there was good reason to honor the distinguished men and not just the king—"Because it might turn out that the king gets tired of giving you gifts as you go on reciting for him." Sigvatr said that Ívarr was a good man to compose poetry about for various reasons, and when Ívarr left, Sigvatr asked the king a little later for leave to visit him. The king said: "The honor that I accord you should be quite sufficient, and there is less honor in receiving gifts from district chieftains. But it is up to you, although some people say that Ívarr is not completely reliable."

Sigvatr went east to Vík to Ívarr's residence and greeted him. Ívarr was rather taciturn and gave no indication of pleasure. Sigvatr said that he had composed a poem about him (FJ 206) and that he had come to recite it. Ívarr said: "That's what you skalds always do when the king gets tired of your bawling. Then you go off and try to bilk the farmers." Sigvatr recited a stanza:

105. Eigi sátuð ítrum   þérs (alls hann réð hlýða
       Ívarr meginfjarri   hróðr sinn) lofi þínu
       (orð þás ossum fœrðak)   (hljóðs hefk beitt á báða
       (at sóttisk lof) (dróttni):   bekki) vant at hnekkja.

"Ívarr, eigi sátuð meginfjarri ítrum, þás fœrðak orð ossum dróttni; lof sóttisk at. Þérs vant at hnekkja lofi þínu, alls hann réð hlýða hróðr sinn; hefk beitt hljóðs á báða bekki."

Ívarr, you did not sit very far from the splendid one when I brought my words to our lord; the praise was powerful. You can hardly refuse your praise, when he listened to his poem; I have asked for a hearing from both benches.

Then Ívarr said: "What you say is true, and I will indeed listen." Sigvatr recited the poem and received a good reward. Afterward he returned to the king.[4]

This Ívarr had a son named Hákon.[5] He was a very handsome and accomplished man. He went on harrying expeditions in his youth and performed many great deeds. Ketill of Hringunes (Ringnes) and Finnr Árnason had joined forces in harrying.[6] Hákon sought them out, and they spent several summers together. None of them was bolder than Hákon.

They arrived in Denmark at the same time that King Haraldr was there and intended to do battle against King Sveinn. Hákon told his men that a battle between the kings was in the offing and that it seemed likely to be decisive. "The situation is this," said Hákon: "King Sveinn is popular and our king is not, but I am more inclined to help him." Finnr said that he would join King Sveinn, but Hákon's warriors told him to make the decision for them. (FJ 207) There were (U 77) ten ships in his command. He went now to meet with King Haraldr and offered him his aid. The king thanked him and said that he had heard of his valor.

King Haraldr now gathered his whole force and spoke as follows: "King Sveinn has met up with us, as you know, and even though he has a great following, he still has smaller ships than we have, and I surmise that his troops are less reliable. We have harried far and wide and seized great treasure, but consider what sort of fame it is we have won—none at all except for trifling coastal raids. There is no glory when we have not encountered the king. It would be worth more if we could gain victory and honor and conquer the land. I will owe you thanks if you will tell me whether it is to your liking to give battle, but you are free to sail away if you do not wish to fight."

Hákon said: "I have not been in your service before now, sire, but I wish to fight on your side. I wish that my ships be free and not chained together in the attack."[7] Skjálgr Erlingsson was also in the king's following. Þórólfr mostrarskegg was there in the company of the king's son Magnús, and Úlfr stallari as well.[8] They were all captains, together with many other distinguished men.

The king was in good spirits and said: "I dreamed last night that I had an encounter with King Sveinn and we both had ahold of the same hank and were tugging at it. He pulled the hank away from me." People had different interpretations of the king's dream, and most of them judged that King Sveinn would win the contest.

"It may be, sire," said Hákon, "that they are right, but it seems more likely to me that King Sveinn will get the worst of it."

"It seems more likely to me," said the king, "that this is the better solution." Then the king drew his sword and struck the air three (FJ 208) times in the direction of the enemy.

"What does that mean?" asked Hákon.

The king replied: "It is called a victory beacon in foreign lands when the king signals his wrath in this way."[9]

King Haraldr now urged his men forward again and said that it was nonetheless overwhelming odds to fight an army of twice their size—"or would you rather retreat?" They all left the decision to him but said that the odds seemed almost insurmountable.

"I can see now," said the king, "that you wish to hear my view, and so it shall be. We have such a fair and numerous force that we will flee under no

circumstances. We should rather die, stacked one upon another." In the words
of Steinn Herdísarson, who was on Úlfr stallari's ship:

106. Sagði hitt (es hugði)   heldr kvað hvern várn skyldu
      hauklundr (vesa mundu)   hilmir frægr an vægja
      þar kvað þengill eirar   (menn brutu upp) of annan
      þrotna ván frá hánum: (ǫll vápn) þveran falla. (U 78)

"Hauklundr sagði hitt, es hugði vesa mundu: þengill kvað þar þrotna ván eirar frá
hánum. Frægr hilmir kvað hvern várn skyldu falla of annan þveran heldr an vægja;
menn brutu upp ǫll vápn."

The hawk-minded one said what he thought likely to happen: the king claimed
there was scant hope of mercy from him. The famous lord said each of us
should fall crosswise upon the other rather than surrender; the warriors readied
all weapons.

He also recited this stanza on the size of the opposing forces:

107. Hætti hersa dróttinn   næst vas þats réð rísta (FJ 209)
      hugstrangr (skipa langra   reiðr atseti Hleiðrar
      hinns við halft beið annat   þangs láð mǫrum þangat
      hundrað Dana fundar):   þrimr hundruðum sunda.

"Hætti hugstrangr hersa dróttinn, hinns beið Dana fundar við halft annat hundrað
langra skipa. Næst vas, þats reiðr atseti Hleiðrar réð rísta þangs láð þangat þrimr
hundruðum mǫrum sunda."

The brave-hearted lord of nobles [Haraldr] put himself at risk, he who awaited the
Danes with a hundred and fifty longships. Next, the furious lord of Hleiðr [Lejre:
Sveinn] furrowed the kelp's land [sea] thither with three hundred steeds of the sea
[ships].

Then King Haraldr had the trumpets blown to signal the advance and
headed for the ships of King Sveinn. He had his own ship lead the advance.
Then Úlfr stallari called out to his men: "Bring our ship forward next to the
king's," as is recorded here:

108. Hét á oss (þás úti)   vel bað skip með skylja
      Ulfr (hákesjur skulfu)   skeljeggjaðr framm leggja
      (róðr vas greiddr á grœði)   sitt (en seggir játtu)
      grams stallari alla: snjalls landreka spjalli.

"Ulfr, grams stallari, hét á oss alla, þás hákesjur skulfu úti; róðr vas greiddr á grœði.
Skeljeggaðr spjalli snjalls landreka bað leggja skip sitt vel framm með skylja, en
seggir játtu."

Ulfr, the king's marshal, incited us all, when the long spears quivered out at sea;
the rowing was accelerated on the ocean. The keen companion of the brave conqueror commanded that his ship should advance briskly alongside the king's, and
his men concurred.

Now King Haraldr had the prows of his ships chained together, and the
Danes rowed out while the trumpets blared to urge the men on. The Danes
thought that the Norwegians were at their mercy this time. It was the evening

before Saint Lawrence's Day, and it was late in the evening before battle was joined.[10] They fought during the night. King Haraldr stood amidships and shot from there with his bow. In the words of Þjóðólfr:

> 109. Alm dró upplenzkr hilmir
> alla nótt enn snjalli
> hremsur lét á hvítar
> hlífr oddviti drífa. (FJ 210)

"Upplenzkr hilmir enn snjalli dró alm alla nótt; oddviti lét hremsur drífa á hvítar hlífr."

The brave king from Upplǫnd [Opplandene] bent his bow all night long; the war leader let arrows rain on white shields.

The battle became fierce. King Sveinn brought his squadron forward and ranged his ship against King Haraldr's. Finnr Árnason was also among them, and his ship was parallel with King Sveinn's and lent him assistance. King Sveinn now urged his men on, reminding them how much destruction King Haraldr had wreaked in their realm and how they had suffered from the hostile campaigning of the Norwegians and what dishonor had been done them: "Let it be said that we advance bravely. There are many noble men and excellent fighters in our company, and let us now settle the issue between us so that we can remain at peace and guard our honor."

The battle now became very intense, and what with the din of weapons and the shouts of men there was an enormous tumult. Hákon placed his ship in the forefront and sought to earn great distinction. (U 79) King Haraldr's men did not have less of a battle line than King Sveinn because their ships were larger. But Hákon's ships, being unattached, had free range and ran among the ships attacking on both port and starboard. His followers were also armed to the best advantage. Hákon had been on viking raids beforehand and had toughened his crews.

We are told that the battle took place not far from the land. Skjálgr Erlingsson's ship was stranded, and he and all his men were immediately killed by the land forces that King Sveinn had not been able to embark on his ships. Men now fell thick along the gunwales, and a lot happened in a short time. The battle was skewed in a way the Danes had not expected, and the Norwegians stood in dense ranks around King Haraldr, fighting fiercely. In the words of Steinn (FJ 211):

> 110. Undrs ef eigi fundu   hvar herskildi heldu
> ǫrmóts viðir gǫrva   (hrafn fekk gnótt í óttu
> (bǫrðumk vér) (þeirs vǫrðu   nás fyr Nizar ósi)
> víða grund) of síðir: Norðmenn Harald forðum.

"Undrs, ef ǫrmóts viðir, þeirs vǫrðu víða grund, eigi fundu gǫrva of síðir— bǫrðumk vér—, hvar Norðmenn heldu Harald forðum herskildi: hrafn fekk gnótt nás í óttu fyr Nizar ósi."

It is a marvel if the trees of the arrow meeting [battle, warriors], those who defended the wide land, finally did not learn fully—we fought—where the Norwegians of old protected Haraldr with the war shield: the raven got plenty of corpses at dawn by the mouth of the River Niz [Niså].

The casualties began to mount on the Danish side. Many fell and some fled. The next thing that happened was that the Norwegians boarded the king's own ship and cleared it along the gunwales. As Þjóðólfr said:

111. Flest vas hirð (sús hraustum
       [hrafns fœði vel tœði)
       dauð (áðr dǫglingr næði)
       (døkks) (á land at støkkva).]

"Flest hirð, sús tœði vel hraustum fœði døkks hrafns, vas dauð, áðr dǫglingr næði at støkkva á land."

Most of the retainers, who served the fearless feeder of the dark raven [bird of prey, war king] so well, were dead before the king could escape ashore.

We are told that King Sveinn fled onto land in a boat that lay near the main deck. In this confusion the Danes detached their ships and disengaged. The sooner they got away, the happier they were, but they left seventy Danish vessels behind that had been cleared. In the words of Þjóðólfr:

112. Sogns kváðu gram gegnan
       glæst sjau tigu et næsta
       senn á svipstund einni
       Sveins þjóðar skip hrjóða.

"Kváðu gegnan gram Sogns hrjóða et næsta sjau tigu glæst skip Sveins þjóðar senn á svipstund einni."

They said that the clever king of Sogn then, in one moment, cleared seventy of the adorned ships of Sveinn's men.

Arnórr recited the following:

113. Hjalmáru lét heyra   naðrs borð skriðu norðan
       hizigs rauð fyr Nizi   nýs at allvalds fýsi
       tyggi tyrfings eggjar   hlaut til Hallands skjóta
       tvær (áðr mannfall væri): (FJ 212)   hrafnþarfr konungr stafni. (U 80)

"Tyggi lét hjalmáru heyra, 's rauð tvær tyrfings eggjar hizig fyr Nizi, áðr mannfall væri. Nýs naðrs borð skriðu norðan at allvalds fýsi; hrafnþarfr konungr hlaut skjóta stafni til Hallands."

The king let the helmet servants [warriors] hear that he reddened both edges of the sword yonder by the River Niz [Niså] before the slaughter began. The boards of the new snake [ship boards] slid from the north at the ruler's behest; the raven-appeasing king set the prow toward Halland.

114. Hrauð (sás hvergi flýði)   skjaldborg raufsk (en skúfar)
       heiðmærr Dana skeiðir   (skaut hoddglǫtuðr oddum
       glaðr und golli roðnum   bragna brynjur gegnum
       (geirjalm) konungr hjalmi: buðlungr) (of ná sungu).

"Heiðmærr konungr, sás hvergi flýði geirjalm, hrauð glaðr Dana skeiðir und golli roðnum hjalmi. Skjaldborg raufsk, en skúfar sungu of ná; hoddglǫtuðr, buðlungr, skaut oddum gegnum bragna brynjur."

The illustrious king, who never fled a spear crash [battle], happily cleared the Danish ships beneath his golden helmet. The shield wall broke and swords sang over corpses; with arrows the treasure breaker [generous king], the king, pierced the byrnies of warriors.

He also told what pressure King Sveinn was under before he fled:

115.　Gekkat Sveinn af snekkju　　　farskostr hlaut at fljóta
　　　　saklaust enn forhrausti　　　　fljótmælts vinar Jóta
　　　　(malmr kom harðr við hjalma)　(áðr an ǫðlingr flýði)
　　　　(hugi minn es þat) sinni:　　　auðr (frá verðung dauðri).

"Sveinn enn forhrausti gekkat saklaust af snekkju sinni; hugi minn es þat; harðr malmr kom við hjalma. Farskostr fljótmælts vinar Jóta hlaut at fljóta auðr, áðr an ǫðlingr flýði frá verðung dauðri."

Fearless Sveinn did not leave his ship without cause, that is my opinion; hard steel clashed against helmets. The ship of the eloquent friend of the Jótar [people of Jylland, Jutland] was to float empty before the king fled from the dead company.

The Danish forces were now routed, and the Norwegians pursued them and bore in mind how the Danes had forced them to row in the Sea of Jutland. They pursued them into the open sea, and the casualties were so great that no one can tally them, and they were mostly among the Danes. Finnr Árnason and Hákon had separated when Hákon went to the aid (FJ 213) of King Haraldr. Jarl Finnr was now captured by King Haraldr's men. At that time he was almost blind. He sat down on his deck when the rout began, and there he was captured and brought before King Haraldr. It is said that King Sveinn had six jarls with him in the battle, as is referred to here:

116.　Sveinn át sigr at launa　　　varð (sás vildit forða)
　　　　sex þeim (es hvǫt vexa)　　　vígbjartr (snǫru hjarta)
　　　　innan eina gunni　　　　　　í fylkingu fenginn
　　　　(ǫrleiks) Dana jǫrlum:　　　Fiðr Árnason miðri.

"Sveinn át at launa sigr þeim sex Dana jǫrlum, es vexa hvǫt ǫrleiks, innan eina gunni. Vígbjartr Fiðr Árnason, sás vildit forða snǫru hjarta, varð fenginn í miðri fylkingu."

Sveinn cannot thank those six Danish jarls, who increase the incitement of arrow play [battle], for success in this one battle. Battle-keen Finnr Árnason, refusing to save his brave heart, was captured in the midst of the army.

The jarl was now placed amidships before King Haraldr. The king was very cheerful and said: "This time we have met here, Finnr, though the last time was in Norway. Tell me, did the Danish troops not stand firm for you? It is hard on the Norwegians to have to drag you around blind just to keep you alive."

　　The jarl said: "There are a lot of things that are hard on the Norwegians, and most of all the work you give them."

"Do you wish to be spared," said the king, "even though you hardly deserve it?"

"Not by a dog like you," said the jarl.

"Are you saying that you want your kinsman Magnús to spare you?" asked the king. The king's son Magnús was in command of a ship but was still very young.

Then the jarl asked: "What sort of reprieve can that whelp manage?"

The king found it amusing (U 81) to tease the jarl and asked: "Will you accept a reprieve from your kinswoman Þóra?"

Then the jarl asked: "Is she here?"

"Here she is," (FJ 214) said the king.

Then Finnr made a vicious comment that was later remembered because it indicates that he was so angry that he could not control his words: "No wonder you bit so well since you have the mare looking on."[11] Finnr was now given a reprieve even though he would not accept it, and King Haraldr kept him in his company for a time.

King Sveinn fled into the interior with a single companion. As the sun rose in the morning, they came to a little cottage, because the Norwegians were searching the village and the larger farms. An old woman was there and asked who they were. The king's companion did the talking and told the woman: "We are beggars and need your charity."

The woman said: "You don't look promising," she said, "and I suspect that you have tidings to tell.[12] Could it be that the kings have done battle tonight, or what was the meaning of the din and tumult that I heard during the night and that gave us no respite?"

"I imagine that the kings may have fought," he said.

Then the woman asked: "Who got the better of it?"

He said: "The Norwegians got the better of it."

Once more the woman asked: "Has our king been killed?"

"He got away," he said.

At that point the woman spoke a very foolish word: "Woe to us—we are miserably provided for since our king is both halt and cowardly."[13]

Then the man who had previously said less spoke up: "I suspect, old woman, that the king is not cowardly but neither is he very fortunate in battle."

In the morning before they ate breakfast,[14] the woman gave them a wash basin, and the guest who had entered second washed first, then took the towel and dried himself on the middle of it. The woman grabbed it away from him and said: "Use the end of the towel (FJ 215) and don't make the whole thing wet."

The tall man said: "It may well be, *woman*," he said, "God willing, that we will enjoy enough honor to sanction using the middle of the towel."

This tale is only for the fun of it and worth telling only because it illustrates wisdom and witlessness. Moreover, when the exchange of words between King Haraldr and Finnr jarl was told, the man who had the power showed mercy, and there was honor in that action and no lack of authority. But the jarl showed how fearless he was. He was unable to do otherwise than to speak what was on his mind, and in that he demonstrated loyalty. He spoke only well of King Sveinn since he had been in his service, but he spoke angrily to King Haraldr, whom he had opposed. (U 82) But King Haraldr treated what he had to say like so many childish words, and that has been the view of everyone ever after.

Hákon Ívarsson distinguished himself and had great success. He had placed his ship next to the king's ship, and no one was bolder than he. His prowess was much praised, and he earned great honor and distinction because he was eager for fame. Now King Haraldr said: "Let us guard our victory carefully so that they do not get the better of us in the future, and let us return home with honor."

During the night, while Haraldr and his men were asleep, two ships left the royal fleet in secret. One was Þórólfr mostrarskegg's ship, the other belonged to Prince Magnús. They made for land and beached their ships, thinking to gain fame and (FJ 216) distinction. They were met by the Danish army, and a battle broke out. In it they were overwhelmed by superior numbers and many of them were killed. Þórólfr escaped with Prince Magnús and carried him in a tunic all the way to Vík.[15]

Back in the main army King Haraldr missed them. He waited for them for a time, but they did not return. The battle had ended with King Haraldr's having captured King Sveinn's ships, mostly as booty, and all the possessions that were on them. They found a reliquary with the relics of Saint Vincent on the deck of King Sveinn's ship and took it with them.[16]

At that point the king did not wish to wait any longer for his son Magnús and the others, thinking it not unlikely that they had been killed. They sailed away with their captured goods and arrived in Vík. There Haraldr had *tents* erected and fires built on the shore, and the king circulated among the fires to inspect the wounds. Then Þórólfr mostrarskegg arrived on foot carrying Magnús on his back. When the king saw that he was alive, he was relieved and happy, but he said that the victory had been spoiled by their heedlessness. He said that what the three of them had undertaken was reckless and had accordingly turned out badly.[17]

The men bandaged their wounds and talked about who had shown the greatest prowess in battle, and the general opinion was that everyone would have wished to have Hákon's name. But King Haraldr said: "Despite that we have won the victory on occasions when Hákon was not present."

Þórólfr was very fatigued and worn down from walking. The king took note of that and asked whether the Danes had (FJ 217) surrendered to them—"or did you think that they would not dare to meet you in an armed encounter? It was not prudent to leave us and venture onto land with a small force. You might well have been content with the victory that we all won together. This alone has diminished our honor, but there is nothing to do about it."

King Haraldr gave the men warm thanks for their support. In particular, he invited Hákon to come join him during the winter (U 83) at Christmastime, saying that he might then expect to receive his reward for his support: "I stand in debt to many men here, but most of all to you." Hákon thanked him for the invitation and promised to come. During the winter he attended to his farms there in Vík, but the king sailed north along the coast until he arrived at home.

In the winter, toward Christmas, Hákon went north to visit the king. We are told that the king himself went out to meet him and received him with great honor. He seated Hákon at his side, and they had long conversations. At that time Ragnhildr, the daughter of King Magnús the Good, was at Haraldr's court. She was the fairest and wisest of women.

One time, during the Christmas holidays, King Haraldr asked Hákon: "What are your plans for the spring?"

"It is my intention, sire," he said, "to go on a viking expedition."

The king said: "That involves a heavy moral responsibility and is not fitting for Christians. In the days of heathendom it was well enough, when people knew nothing of God, but now it is a great offense against Christianity because it pits Christians against Christians."[18]

Hákon replied: "It seems to me very boring to stay at home in Norway, sire, and I need a great deal of money because I have a large following."

The king said: "Why don't you marry?"

"Because, sire," said Hákon, "I know that the daughters of noble men will not hold me (FJ 218) in much esteem, and I do not want to marry just any chieftain's daughter."

The king said: "It might come about that I reward you for your support with the best match in Norway, and that is King Magnús's daughter Ragnhildr. There are many kings who are not as valorous as you are."

"Do not mock me, sire," he said. "You are aiming too high. You should rather marry me to a jarl's daughter who is your kinswoman and will bring me wealth, because I will be in great need of money if I cannot acquire it by harrying and am forced to give up the practice."

The king said: "It is not clear to me that you will gain more wealth with any other woman, and I will place the matter before her if you wish."

Hákon replied: "There is no marriage I would desire more, and it will be a good thing if your discussion succeeds. The disposition of her wealth remains up to you."

Now the king met with her promptly and explained to her Hákon's distinction and bravery, saying what a valiant man he was.

She replied: "I have no doubt that Hákon has many good qualities."

The king said: "I believe it would be a good match if the two of you married, because you are both outstanding people."

The princess replied: "Such may be your view, sire, but my father would not have imagined that I would be married to a man of nonnoble birth."

The king said: "It is in my power to confer a noble title on him, and it is only the title that he lacks. But (FJ 219) it is fitting for you not to heed only your own wishes but to follow the advice of your relatives."

She (U 84) replied: "If you are determined to marry me to a man who is not of royal or noble blood, I do not know a better man than he is."

The king said: "I will arrange it, kinswoman, so that you will have a jarl as husband."

She replied: "I will not yet thank you for that title, sire, assuming that there will be time enough for that later."[19]

The king now reported their conversation to Hákon and said that she had not been totally opposed to the idea.

Hákon said: "This should not be said in jest and mockery, sire, because I have not earned this reward from you."

The king replied: "Such is not the case, for it is up to me to determine what your rank will be."

Now Hákon reflected on the situation and surmised that what the king said was true and that he had discussed the matter with her as he said. He asked now what words had passed between the king and the princess.

"I put your situation to her," said the king, "explaining your accomplishments and success and how valiant you are. She said that she would not be married to a man of nonnoble blood if her father were alive, and I said it was in my power to make you noble and give you a jarldom."

Hákon said: "If I am so fortunate as to win her hand, it would be appropriate for you to provide the title so that she should not suffer the dishonor of marrying a commoner, for that would not be fitting for her."

Then she was betrothed to Hákon with the promise of the king's friendship, but it was done with the stipulation that the king made the firm promise (FJ 220) of a jarldom for Hákon. With that stipulation she gave her assent, and after Christmas their marriage was celebrated at the king's residence.

When the ceremony was concluded, Hákon returned east to Vík with his wife. She grew to love him, but they were not entirely of one mind in other respects, though she said that she would be content if he were a jarl.

Time passed until Christmas of the next year. Then Hákon went to see the king, thinking that he should inquire into the jarldom that the king had promised. The king gave him a good reception and asked why the princess, his wife, was not with him. Hákon said that such was her wish, and before they parted, he brought up the matter of the jarl's title and the authority it conferred as part of her dowry, as had been promised.

The king countered by asking: "Was your father Ívarr a jarl, or any of his ancestors? But it is clear," said the king, "that you are an improvement on your father."

Now Hákon could see how the land lay and that the title of nobility was being revoked. He took up his weapons and prepared to depart. Before leaving he said: "What is your intention with respect to your gift of a jarldom and the lands that we were to receive from you? It is not proper that she should forego her honor and that she should be disgraced because of me, and it is fitting for a king to keep his word." (U 85)

"The truth is, Hákon," said King Haraldr, "that there is no need to conceal from you that nothing will come of your jarldom."

Hákon now returned home to Vík with nothing more accomplished. The princess went out to meet him, and spoke laughingly: "Greetings, my jarl," she said.

He replied: "I am not a jarl, and if you feel that you have been deceived because of me, (FJ 221) take all my money and possessions and I will depart."

"That is not my wish for the moment, but the king is reneging as I suspected."

During the winter they were on less than good terms, and when spring came, Hákon said to the princess: "I will now inform you of my plans. I have acquired six longships and a numerous following, and I will go abroad never to return, for I do not wish you to suffer dishonor on my account."

She replied: "It is no favor to me that you should depart, and our differences do not stem from any lack of love for you. Nor do I have anything to reproach you for. You may take charge of any move, but I have no desire to occupy your lands if you yourself are gone, even though you make the offer."

They now agreed that he would sell the lands for cash, and they prepared to depart with a great deal of money and the six longships. Before they departed, Hákon arranged to kill the king's steward and confiscate all his property.[20] They then sailed off with all their goods.

The king was told of his steward's killing together with the ensuing losses. The king said: "This is indeed a great loss, but we have suffered a greater loss in the person of the valiant man Hákon, who has lost his mind. I regret deeply that King Magnús's daughter is married to him."

We are told that the king now seized the lands that had been in Hákon's possession even though they had been sold. He took rent and taxes for them. But Hákon had not been gone for long before he returned and killed the men to whom the king had assigned the task of guarding the land. Then he set fire to the farms and reduced them to ashes.

After that he and Ragnhildr set sail, and she asked (FJ 222) what he intended to do during the summer. "It is my intention," he said, "to go on a viking expedition."

"That is not my wish," she said, "for you have only one man's life, despite your being a great warrior, but I am lost if anything happens to you. It is likely that the vikings will take me to their beds, and that is not fitting because of my lineage.[21] It is my advice that you should rather go to meet with King Sveinn, who is an excellent man. Take this gold ring that my father gave me and show it to King Sveinn. Because King Sveinn did not hold to his agreement with my father, he takes a benevolent view of my father's kinsmen (U 86) and honors them all greatly."

Hákon said: "I can expect nothing of King Sveinn considering how our meeting at Niz ended, but you do not have much of a husband if I should be intimidated and shrink from meeting King Sveinn."[22]

They now sailed for Denmark, and Hákon proceeded with a few men and brought greetings to King Sveinn.

The king said: "Why have you come here after the great injury you have done us?"

"Sire," said Hákon, "the princess Ragnhildr sent me to you with this ring"— and he showed him the ring. Then he told him all about his dealings with Haraldr.

King Sveinn said: "The king did not do well or fittingly to marry his kinswoman to such a lowly man as you. But she is welcome to stay with me, although she will not be fully honored if you are not with her. For her sake and the sake of King Magnús I will give you three choices, all of which seem favorable, though it is not likely that you would have stayed alive if I had gotten my hands on you without your having the benefit of one of them. The first choice is that I will invite you to stay with me with a following of eleven men on condition that you stay with your wife but that your men be lodged elsewhere. Then there is (FJ 223) the choice to receive three farms from me as a gift, but with the obligation to defend my land. The third choice is to go out against my nephew Ásmundr Bjarnarson, who is campaigning against me and demanding the province of Halland. Bring him to me, and if you can accomplish this, I will appoint you jarl of Halland. Even if you choose not to do this and have no compact with me, I wish you to be in peace here for the sake of the princess."

Hákon said: "What you say is only too true, sire, namely that the princess would be ill matched if I did not dare to do battle with Ásmundr. But if I succumb, sire, you will arrange an honorable marriage for her, even if it is not of the most distinguished."

The king said: "I will provide armed troops for your mission."

"No," said Hákon, "then the Danes will say that I had the advantage of their winning the victory, and I dislike that idea. Therefore only my men should be engaged."

The dispute between Ásmundr and King Sveinn began when Swegn Godwinson killed Ásmundr's father Bjǫrn in King Knútr's retinue west in England. King Sveinn Úlfsson had raised Ásmundr and given him three ships so that he could avenge his father. King Harold [Godwinson] was then king of England, but his brother Swegn had died. Ásmundr determined to harry against the Danes and was captured three times and brought before King Sveinn, but each time he spared his life and let him depart in peace. But for all that, he never ceased to ravage his realm. (U 87)

The story now picks up at the point where the princess Ragnhildr went to

King Sveinn, who received her with open arms. She and Hákon stayed there (FJ 224) until he left to confront Ásmundr. He readied six ships for the expedition and then set sail with this force. He inquired into Ásmundr's whereabouts and learned where he was and that he had ten ships. We are told that they met in the mouth of the River Slé (Schlien), and before the ships collided in battle, Ásmundr said: "A man who is promised a jarldom has good reason to advance boldly, but King Sveinn was mistaken to make such a promise, and he did not remember the Battle of Niz very well."

Hákon said: "It is true, Ásmundr, that I was at the River Niz with King Haraldr, and I was not wrong to support my king. It is worse that you constantly seek to undo your lord and kinsman King Sveinn, but today you will learn to your dismay that we have met, and now I propose to attack you."

The battle began, and it was a hard encounter. Hákon and his forces advanced boldly, and men fell thick along the gunwales, but more on Ásmundr's side. Finally Hákon and his men got to the point of boarding, and Hákon boarded Ásmundr's ship. He struck left and right and advanced to the middle of the ship with his men. Ásmundr's men fell in droves, and eventually Ásmundr was captured by Hákon's men and restrained.

Then Hákon said: "I never hope to bring King Sveinn a more despicable offering than the wicked head you wear, Ásmundr." He rushed at him and laid him low.

After that Hákon and his men went home with their victory and some booty, and at the same time it came to King Sveinn's ears what they had been up to. At that very moment Hákon came before the king and greeted him. But the king flushed red and said: "Take your seat"—but it was said with no expression of pleasure.

Hákon said: (FJ 225) "I seem to detect, sire, that you are less grateful for our victory than I expected, but I believe that this man Ásmundr would not hesitate to plot against your life if he had escaped. For that reason I killed him, and now, sire, I would like to have from you what you promised."

"I do not assume that your action is inspired by any hostility toward me but rather by good will. Nonetheless, as things stand, I cannot be a full friend to you, but you may have that part of my realm that is most subject to attack."

We are told that King Sveinn made him jarl of Halland, and he went there with his men and his wife, with whom he was now once again united in mutual love.

Hákon was a very bold man. He went to Vík and harried when he learned that the king was in northern Norway, and he made a habit of this every summer. (U 88) In the third year after the Battle of Niz, peace was made between King Haraldr and King Sveinn with the counsel of the Norwegians and Danes. The terms were that each one of them should rule his realm freely. From that time on, Haraldr was to have Norway and Sveinn was to have Denmark unencumbered. The harrying expeditions were to cease, and each side was to keep

what fortune had allotted. That peace was to be in effect as long as the kings
lived, as Þjóðólfr stated:

> 117. Fœrði fylkir Hǫrða
>   (friðr namsk ár et þriðja)
>   (rendr bitu stál fyr strǫndu)
>   starf til króks at hvarfi. (FJ 226)

"Fylkir Hǫrða fœrði starf til króks at hvarfi; friðr namsk ár et þriðja; stál bitu rendr
fyr strǫndu."

The king of the Hǫrðar [people of Hordaland] finally brought the fight to a close;
peace commenced the third year; steel bit shields off the coast.

After this peace had been concluded between Denmark and Norway, King
Haraldr began to harry in the realm of the Swedish king Steinkell in Gautland.
King Steinkell went to meet with King Sveinn and asked for his support. King
Sveinn reported the reconciliation that he had concluded with Haraldr: "I do
not want to contravene it," he said. "Furthermore, I did not make much headway in my hostilities with King Haraldr, but I will provide you with some counsel. Hákon Ívarsson is at odds with King Haraldr. He is a conspicuous warrior
and a very bold man. He is now my liegeman. You should give him West Gautland (Västergötland) in exchange for attacking King Haraldr. He is eager for
noble titles, and it would please him greatly if he had a second jarldom. Even
if he dies, you will suffer no loss because he is not your liegeman. But victory
is unlikely if you do not have him on your side."

Messengers were now sent after the jarl, and he presented himself. The matter was placed before him, and he responded by asking: "How is the king disposed? It is a perilous matter to enter battle against King Haraldr, and I will not
resolve to do it unless you forswear your hostility and take me into your full
confidence."

King Sveinn said: "That is something I can agree to, but *I did not foresee
it*." They now agreed that Hákon would assume the mission and be in command but that troops would be provided by King Steinkell's men in both West
and East Gautland (Väster- and Östergötland).

After that, Hákon went home and told Ragnhildr what was afoot. When he
prepared to (FJ 227) set out, she said: "It may now come about that you will
be severely tested, and I will endure it even if you fall in battle against King
Haraldr. There is not much I can do to help you, but I wish to give you this
standard that my father had. It was in his possession when he fought (U 89)
at Skotborg River (Kongeå). It is a standard that King Haraldr would like to
have, though he has not gotten his hands on it yet." It was all embroidered
with gold.[23]

When he was ready, Hákon led his men into Gautland and gathered forces
there. When the troops that had been committed to him were assembled, he
called a meeting and spoke to them: "I ask you," he said, "to fight well if it
comes to an encounter between King Haraldr and me, but the chieftain and

his men should be a breastwork for you, for I do not intend to be intimidated by the threats of King Haraldr. Still, I suspect that this army will not be very large compared to King Haraldr's forces, but you should stand in to the best of your ability, and that should be sufficient. Even though I have a lesser title than King Steinkell, it may be that I will be of no less assistance, for he is used to an easy life, while I am accustomed to battles and hard conditions."

It was as he said, that King Steinkell was a portly man and heavy on his feet. He was much given to drinking parties and not much involved in the business at hand. Though some of his men marched with Jarl Hákon, he himself liked to be left in peace.

King Haraldr learned (FJ 228) of these developments and was delighted. He spent the summer at leisure in Norway, but at the end of summer he readied sixty ships and selected a force with chain mail and helmets. The ships were magnificently outfitted, but he did not announce his intended destination. He sailed from the north along the coast and anchored first at Mǫrs (Moss). After that, the king brought his ships up into Lake Vänern through the Elfr (Götaälv).

When they were close to the shore near the place where Jarl Hákon's forces were, a man left his tent at night, and when he returned, King Haraldr asked him about the weather. He said: "There are thick clouds on the horizon."

"That's fine for the time being," said the king. When the man had looked outside again, the king asked about the weather a second time, and he said that snow was falling.

The king said: "That is just how I would have wished it, so that the Gautar cannot get their cattle away from the raids that we will inflict on them." And now the king asked a third time about the weather. The man said that the weather was turning exceedingly cold.

The king said: "Frost is just what I want."

Turning to Hákon, we can relate that he had assembled troops and was marching against King Haraldr. The jarl came to a certain deep valley and halted his troops on the brow of the hill. He wanted to wait for the king there because he knew that they were now in close proximity. Much of Jarl Hákon's following was in light clothing, as is always the case with the Gautar, though the troops that had accompanied him from Denmark were well equipped with both clothes and weapons. (FJ 229)

There was a man named Þorfinnr (U 90) in the jarl's army, the lawspeaker of the Gautar.[24] He had a horse fattened on grain, and he tethered it to a stake close by as they sat overlooking the valley. Of King Haraldr it can be told that he convened a meeting in the morning and knew the jarl's whereabouts. He spoke to his men at the meeting and told them that the encounter was not far off: "But we should not rush things, because we are well supplied with clothes and weapons. The weather is cold, and even though Hákon is a brave man and his own troops are well equipped, I know that the militia from Gautland will be poorly clothed. They will huddle together and not endure the cold easily."

Then King Haraldr and his men marched until they reached the hill on the other side of the valley. The king said: "Now we will sit down for a while, because we have gotten hot in our armor, and see if the Gautar are feeling the cold. They will have drawn their troops together, and it may be easier for us to fight in less of a sweat, but it is uncertain how well they can stand the cold." They now sat down on the opposite hill all armed and ready for battle.

Þorfinnr the Lawspeaker stood up in Hákon's army: "I must say a few words while the young folk swagger. We have a fair and dependable company of men, and it behooves us not to retreat. But if that should happen, then no farther than to the mound, and at the very most no farther than the brook. We have a brave jarl to fight with." And just as he (FJ 230) said this, the horse jerked up and the stake to which it was tethered flew loose and hit Þorfinnr in the ear. At that he jumped away and said: "That was a vicious shot"—and he immediately took to his heels.

They were now across from each other over the valley. Hákon wanted Haraldr to make the first charge because he thought he would have the advantage of the terrain, but Haraldr left that privilege to Hákon. When they had remained motionless for a time, Hákon could see that some of his troops would not survive the cold. He stood up and spoke: "We will now have to make our move, though I had intended to leave the attack to the king. The advantage of the terrain will now be otherwise than I wished."

He incited his army and advanced down into the valley and up toward King Haraldr. The battle began, and Hákon was true to form, exhibiting prowess along with his elite troops. But the king's forces were both more numerous and better equipped, and there were many casualties among Hákon's men. There were also some who fled. Those Gautar who were left standing resisted for a time, but they suffered heavy losses while they fought. There now remained only those men who had come with Hákon from Denmark, and they fought valiantly. The jarl (U 91) also fought hard and performed many great deeds. Haraldr recognized the standard that was carried before the jarl and was eager to capture it. In the ensuing action the jarl came under such a heavy attack that the standard-bearer fell and the standard was carried off by the king's men. Then the jarl fled into the woods together with those who remained with him. In the words of Þjóðólfr (FJ 231):

118.   Qlds (sús jarli vildi   enn (því illa reyndisk
       ógnteitum lið veita)   aflván þaðan hánum)
       (sterkr olli því stillir)   fyrir lét Hákon horfa
       Steinkels gefin helju: hvat segr hinns þat fegrir.

"Qld Steinkels, sús vildi veita ógnteitum jarli lið, 's gefin helju; sterkr stillir olli því. Enn Hákon lét horfa fyrir, þvít aflván þaðan reyndisk hánum illa, hvat segr, hinns þat fegrir."

Steinkell's men, who wished to help the war-happy jarl, have fallen; the mighty king caused that. But Hákon retreated because his hope of their support was poorly met, whatever anyone says to make the tale look better.

As he fled, Hákon said that the princess would think that he had kept rather a loose hold on King Magnús's standard, which she had given him. King Haraldr now pursued the fugitives, and his men said that Hákon had given a poor return for King Steinkell's jarldom. They said that he did not know his own limitations well enough to realize that he was not strong enough to contend against the king himself. But some said that he was a valiant man and had fought well.

The king had the standard carried before him as soon as it was captured, and he called it a great victory that he had won it. As they were proceeding along a forest path and were least expecting it, a man ran out of the woods across the path and seized the standard with one hand while he thrust his spear at the man carrying it with the other hand. Then he made off into the forest on the other side of the path. They could not lay hands on him, and the man who had been speared succumbed.

Then King Haraldr said: "That will have been Hákon, and not many men could have made such a stroke. It is certain that he will think this coup no less a victory than my victory in the battle. But I would seriously underestimate my kinswoman Ragnhildr's temper if I supposed that it would be easy for him to get into her bed if he had lost the standard, but as things stand, they will make their peace."

They now went to their (FJ 232) ships. The king and part of the army were on board. Another part was on land, along with the scullery boys who had cooking pits on shore. In the evening, while those on land were eating, a poor man all in tatters approached them and begged for food. They gave it to him. He asked whether the king was on land or on board the ship. They said he was on the ship.

"I owe it to you, good men," he said, "to reward you for the food, and I see how it can be done. I know where Hákon jarl and a few of his men are close by, and the king might reward you very well if you succeeded in killing or capturing him. I will tell you the way because I was there a short time ago."

They (U 92) listened to his advice and went with him in large numbers.[25] As he walked, his gait seemed rather decrepit. They took a path deep into the woods, and it seemed to stretch out farther and farther. They wanted to turn back, but he said that it was not far until they found Hákon. Then they came to a place where there was a log across the path. They crossed it and saw some men ahead of them. The poor man was slow in getting over the log, and he told them to give chase to the men they saw, saying that they were Hákon's men. When they had crossed the log, he threw off his rags and leapt onto the log with his sword drawn. He struck with all his might, and they realized that they had met up with Hákon jarl.

Then men rushed at them both from the surrounding woods and the path ahead of them and made an armed attack. They defended themselves but saw that it was an ambush and wanted to retreat. (FJ 233) The log lay in their way and prevented them, and most of them were killed. Some escaped to the ships in a sorry state and told the king of their venture in the morning. He said that the venture had turned out as was to be expected—"for you do not have Hákon's intelligence, and you proceeded incautiously and with little reflection."

The king remained there for a time because he could not free the ships from the ice. The king's men went inland on a regular basis to raid for supplies, and every time they left five or ten of their men behind because the land was swarming with Hákon's ambushes. The next thing that happened was that Hákon circulated a rumor that came to the ears of King Haraldr and his men, to the effect that Hákon jarl had gone to Sweden to recruit a large force and that he and King Steinkell would come there in a short time with a big army. It was rumored that King Sveinn would also block the river mouth with a naval blockade.

King Haraldr believed these rumors and began to hack away the ice around his ships. As they were at this work, somebody said: "No one does his job like Koðrán's Killer."[26]

He was referring to Hallr Ótryggsson, who had killed Koðrán Guðmundarson, and Hallr was there in King Haraldr's army. Þormóðr Eindriðason jumped up and delivered Hallr's death blow because he could not stand to hear the praise of Koðrán's killing. Þormóðr was one degree from being the nephew of Guðmundr Eyjólfsson, Koðrán's father. When the men crowded about and wanted to kill Þormóðr, the ice broke under them and there was a great tumult because many men were on the point of drowning. King Haraldr's son Magnús came to Þormóðr's aid and asked that he be spared. He offered a settlement because Þormóðr (FJ 234) was in his crew, and a reconciliation was reached.

Subsequently, Þormóðr went south to Denmark and from there to Greece and wanted to take imperial service, but the emperor said that he was too small in stature. One day as the emperor was looking through some latticework, he saw a very large bull being led out (U 93), and Þormóðr struck off its head. Then the emperor said that he could probably use his sword to good effect on things other than cattle, and he accepted Þormóðr into his service.

King Haraldr and his men were able to float their ships and sailed out to sea on the Gautelfr (Götaälv), from where they went north to Norway. Some of Haraldr's men succumbed as they sailed down the river because the Gautar shot at them. But Jarl Hákon was reputed to be a very outstanding man. His daughter was named Sunnifa and his son Hákon, who was married to the daughter of King Sveinn Úlfsson. Their son was Eiríkr Lam, the king of the Danes.[27] Here the story of Jarl Hákon and King Haraldr ends.

43. Sneglu-Halla þáttr

One summer a ship came from Iceland with Sneglu-Halli on board.[1] He was from the north of Iceland and was a skald. He was not very reticent in his speech. They came to Agðanes and sailed into the fjord.[2] Some longships bore down on them, and a man in a red tunic stood on the first warship. He asked: "Who commands the ship, and where were you last winter? Where did you embark, and where have you landed? Where were (FJ 235) you last night?"

Halli said that the captain's name was Sigurðr: "We spent last winter in Iceland and embarked at Gásir.[3] We made our landfall at Hítrar (Hitra) and last night we were at Agðanes."

The man said: "Didn't old Agði screw you?"

Halli replied: "I can't say that he did."

"Was there some reason for that?" asked the man.

"Yes, sir," said Halli, "he was waiting for a better man and was expecting you this evening."[4] It was King Haraldr who exchanged words with Halli.

They now arrived in the town, and Halli went to the king and greeted him: "We would like to be received by you, lord."

The king replied: "It is no place for foreigners and you should find your own lodging, but I will not be stingy with food for you." Halli took up residence there with the retinue. The skald Þjóðólfr was also staying with the king and was considered to be a bit envious toward the men who came to court.

One day when Þjóðólfr was going down the street with the king, they passed an upper chamber and heard some men quarreling, and then they heard a fight break out. The contestants were a tanner and a blacksmith. "Let us not linger," said the king, "but I want you to compose some verse about the quarrel, Þjóðólfr."[5]

He said: "There is no reason for that, lord."

"Do as I say," said the king—"the task is a little more difficult than you think. You must represent them as different characters. Let one of them be the giant Geirrøðr and the other Þórr."[6] Þjóðólfr recited a stanza (U 94):

119. Varp ór þrætu þorpi   hljóðgreipum tók húða
      Þórr smiðbelgja stórra   hrøkkviskafls af afli
      hvápteldingum hǫldnum   glaðr við galdra smiðju
      hafra kjǫts at jǫtni: Geirrøðr síu þeiri. (FJ 236)

"Þórr smiðbelgja stórra varp hvápteldingum ór þrætu þorpi at hǫldnum jǫtni hafra kjǫts. Hljóðgreipum tók glaðr Geirrøðr húða hrøkkviskafls af afli við þeiri síu galdra smiðju."

Þórr of the large forge bellows [blacksmith] threw lip lightnings [insults] from the farmstead of complaint [mouth] at the prosperous giant of goat's flesh [tanner]. With the sound grips [ears], happy Geirrøðr [giant] of the hides' wrinkling breaker [hide scraper, tanner] vigorously received that cinder of the smithy of incantations [mouth, insult].

The king said: "That is a good stanza and well composed. Now make another one, and let one of the characters be Sigurðr Fáfnisbani and the other Fáfnir, but each should be characterized by his trade." Þjóðólfr recited another stanza:

120. Sigurðr eggjaði sleggju   menn sáusk orm (áðr ynni)
      snák váligrar brákar   ilvegs búinn kilju

en skafdreki skinna   (nautaleðrs á naðri
skreið of leista heiði: neflangr konungr tangar).

"Sigurðr sleggju eggjaði snák váligrar brákar, en skafdreki skinna skreið of leista heiði. Menn sáusk orm, búinn ilvegs kilju, áðr neflangr konungr tangar ynni á naðri nautaleðrs."

Sigurðr of the sledge hammer [blacksmith] taunted the snake of the dangerous tanning tool [tanner], and the carving dragon of hides [tanner] slid across the heath of the stocking feet [floor]. People feared the worm, clad in the cover of the foot path [foot, shoe, tanner], before the long-nosed king of tongs [blacksmith] attacked the snake of cattle leather [tanner].

The king said: "You are a good skald, Þjóðólfr"—and he gave him a finger ring. In the evening the people talked about the stanzas, and the retainers said that Halli would not be able to compose such stanzas. He said: "I am not as good a skald as Þjóðólfr, least of all when I am not present."

There was a man at Haraldr's court named Túta, a Frisian, and he was distinctive for being as short and plump as a dwarf. One evening the king gave him his weapons and his byrnie Emma, and a helmet and sword, and told him to parade before the retinue in the drinking hall, where men were sitting at table. He came in wearing this get-up and looking very strange, and people laughed at him. Then the king said: "The man who will compose a stanza about him on the spot will get this knife and belt from me." They were precious items. Then a man recited from the benches, and it was Halli:

121. Fœrðr sýndisk mér frændi   flœrat eld í ári
      Frísa kyns í brynju (FJ 237)   úthlaupi vanr Túta
      gengr með hirð í hringum   sék á síðu leika
      hjalmfaldinn kurfaldi: sverð rúghleifa skerði.

"Frændi Frísa kyns sýndisk mér fœrðr í brynju; hjalmfaldinn kurfaldi gengr með hirð í hringum. Túta, vanr úthlaupi, flœrat eld í ári; sék sverð leika á síðu rúghleifa skerði."

The kinsman of the Frisians appeared before me dressed in a coat of mail; in a ring byrnie, the helmet-clad dwarf prances among the retinue. Túta, accustomed to furtive raids, is unwilling to flee the kitchen fire in the morning; I see a sword dangling by the side of the cleaver of rye loaves.

"That is well turned," said the king, and sent him the gift. Þjóðólfr was not pleased.

Sometime later the king was walking down the street with his retinue. Halli was in the group, and when it was least expected, he ran off ahead of them. The king asked:[7]

"Where, Halli, are you headed?" (U 95)

He replied:

"Hard ahead to buy curds."

The king rejoined:

"Gruel is what you'll grab for."

Halli answered:

"Greasy gruel is good food."

Then he ran into a courtyard off the street where a woman had a kettle on the fire with gruel in it.[8] He took the kettle down and went out with it. Then he sat down by the house and ate the gruel.

When the king missed him in the group, he said: "This is a bad sign—Halli has run off. Let's go and look for him."

They split up into two groups of six and found him where he was spooning gruel. Then the king spoke to him sternly: "What was the point of leaving Iceland to visit great men just to make a spectacle of yourself?"

"Don't be angry, lord," said Halli. "I want (FJ 238) my pleasure where I can lay hands on it, and in the evening I never see you turning down good dishes."

The king departed, and Halli stood up and threw down the kettle so that the handle clattered. Then Halli recited the following:

> 123.   Haddan skall en Halli
> hlaut offylli grautar
> hornspánu kveðk hánum
> hlýða betr an prýði.

"Haddan skall, en Halli hlaut offylli grautar; kveðk hornspánu hlýða hánum betr an prýði."

The handle clattered and Halli was stuffed with gruel; I say that horn spoons become him better than tokens of honor.

The king was angry with Halli, and Þjóðólfr thought that his prank was ridiculous. In the evening the king had a trough of gruel set before Halli and told him to eat from it. Halli said he would eat the gruel and that it was delicious. He ate away and stopped when he thought it was time. The king told him to keep eating.

"No, sire," said Halli, "that I will not do. You can kill me if you wish, but I will not eat myself to death."

In the evening the king had a roast pig taken from his table and gave it to Túta, saying: "Take this to Halli and tell him to compose a stanza before you get to his place. Deliver that message when you get halfway across the floor, and if he does not get the stanza finished, it will cost him his life."

Túta said: "Lord, I am reluctant to do this."

The king (U 96) said: "I hope you like the stanza, and that you will be able to hear it clearly."

Then he took the pig, went halfway across the floor, and said: "Compose a stanza, skald, by the king's command, and do it as if your life depended on it." When Túta arrived at Halli's place, he reached out for the pig and recited a stanza:

> 124.   Grís þá greppr at ræsi   runa síður lítk rauðar
> gruntrauðustum dauðan (FJ 239)   ræðk skjótgǫru kvæði
> Njǫrðr sér bǫrg á borði   rana hefr seggr á svíni
> bauglands fyr sér standa: (send heill konungr) brenndan.

"Greppr þá dauðan grís at gruntrauðustum ræsi; Njǫrðr bauglands sér bǫrg standa
fyr sér á borði. Lítk rauðar runa síður; ræðk skjótgǫru kvæði; seggr hefr brenndan
rana á svíni; send heill, konungr!"

The poet got a dead pig from the most commendable king; Njǫrðr of the ring land
[shield, warrior] sees a boar standing before him on the table. I see the red sides
of the pig; I produce a quickly composed poem; a man has singed the snout of the
swine; thanks for the helping, lord!

Then the king said: "The case against you is dismissed, Halli—your stanza is
excellent."

Halli now stayed at the court and was well treated. On Christmas Eve he went
before the king and greeted him. The king gave him a good reception. Halli
said: "Sire, I have composed a poem about you, and I wish you to listen."

The king asked: "Have you had any practice in composing poems?"

He replied: "No, sire."

The king said: "Some people may feel that you are biting off a big piece for
your first effort, considering the skalds who have celebrated me. How do you
think we should proceed, Þjóðólfr?"

He answered: "I am not in a position to advise you, lord," he said, "but it is
more likely that I could give Halli some good advice."

The king asked: "What advice?"

Þjóðólfr said: "That he not lie to you."

The king asked again: "What lies is he telling?"

"That he has not composed a poem before, sire. I believe he has."

"What poem?" asked the king.

Þjóðólfr replied: "It is called the 'Bessie Verses' and is about the cows he
used to tend out in Iceland."

The king asked: "Is what he says true, Halli?"

"It is true," said Halli.

The king said: "Then why did you say that you had composed no poem before mine?"

"Because, sire," said Halli, "I did not expect it to strike people as a model of
poetry if word got around."

"Recite that first," said the king.

Halli said: "There should be more entertainment than that, sire."

"Of what sort?" asked the king.

"Þjóðólfr should recite the 'Ashcan Verses,' which he composed out in
Iceland."

The king asked: "What kind of a poem is it?"

Halli (FJ 240) said: "It was Þjóðólfr's job when he was at home to carry out
the ashes with the other youngsters because he did not seem fit for anything
else. He was obliged to see to it that no fire broke out."

"Is that true, Þjóðólfr?" asked the king.

"It is true," said Þjóðólfr.

The king asked: "Why did you have such a menial job?"

"It happened, sire, because there were a lot of children. I did the work with them and recited the poem to make it seem like a (U 97) game."

"I want to hear both poems," said the king.

They now recited their poems, and when they were through, the king said: "Neither poem is worth much, but the subject matter did not amount to much either. Of the two, yours, Þjóðólfr, is even more trivial."

Then Þjóðólfr said: "Halli has a sharp tongue, but it might be more appropriate for him to avenge his father rather than to make verbal attacks on me."

The king asked: "Is that true, Halli, that you have not avenged your father?"

"It is true, sire," said Halli.

The king asked: "How could you come to Norway with that job unfinished?"

"The reason was, sire," said Halli, "that I was a child at the time he was killed, and my kinsmen were in charge of the case. They settled on my behalf. The name of a truce-breaker does not sit well with us."

The king said: "That is a good answer, and you, Þjóðólfr, seem to have no answer."

"Sire," said Halli, "Þjóðólfr is privileged to talk very freely about such things because I know of no one who has avenged his father more fiercely."

"What is the evidence," asked the king, "that he has carried out the task more effectively than others?"

"The evidence," said Halli, "is that he ate his father's killer."

The king asked: "How can that be?"

"Sire," said Halli, "his father Arnórr lived in northern Iceland. He was a poor man and not well provided with what he needed for a brood of children. (FJ 241) His household lived mostly off the charitable contributions of the district. One autumn the district men had a meeting about the paupers to consider what aid should be given them, and Þjóðólfr's father was at the top of the list. To make a long story short, sire, one man was so generous that he contributed a calf of six months. Þjóðólfr's father went to collect the calf because it seemed important to go to where the greatest help was.[9] He went home leading the calf after him and held it by a long, solid rope. The end of the rope was tied in a loop, and he had put the loop over his head and held it with his hands. When he got to the turf wall outside his house, it was not very high on the outer side but inside there was a deep trench. When he climbed onto the wall and slid down inside, it was higher than he thought, sire, and his feet didn't reach the ground, but on the other side of the wall the calf dug in its hooves. He had not taken care to slip the rope off his neck, and that was the death of him. When the children saw that, they ran up and dragged the calf home, and I suspect, sire," said Halli, "that Þjóðólfr had his share of that calf."

The king said: "That would seem reasonable."

Þjóðólfr jumped up and wanted to strike Halli down, but he was stopped. Then the king said: "I will reconcile you in such a way that it will profit neither of you to injure the other. But you, Þjóðólfr, initiated the dispute (U 98), and that was not called for." After that it was quiet, and Halli presented his poem. It was a good poem and well fashioned. King Haraldr treated Halli well.

We are told that Einarr fluga was expected at the king's court.[10] They were good friends, though there were ups and downs. Einarr was in charge of collecting the Lapp tax on the king's behalf. Before his arrival, one of the retainers said in Halli's hearing that Einarr was a great (FJ 242) chieftain but an inequitable man who never compensated the kinsmen of a man he killed.[11]

Then Halli said: "There is more hope that he will pay compensation for my kinsman if I ask for it."

The retainer replied, saying that he would not pay compensation because he had never paid compensation for anyone. They disputed the point until they placed a wager. The retainer staked a gold ring and Halli his head.

Einarr now arrived at the king's court and the king seated him by his side a week after he came. One evening, when they were drinking after their meal, the king asked how the Lapp journey had turned out.

He said: "The last time we were in the north, sire, we encountered a vessel from Iceland and we charged them with engaging in the Lapp trade without our permission. When they denied it, their words made it clear that they were in fact guilty, and we attacked. They defended themselves, but we did not desist until they were overcome. There was one man there who put up the stiffest resistance, and it would have been a hard victory if there had been many such."

Then Halli went to his seat and was very quiet. The retainer asked what the reason was for his distress. He said that there was ample cause: "I have learned of the death of my kinsman, who was killed by Einarr fluga. It may be that this is the opportunity to seek compensation from him."

The retainer said: "I wish you would not speak of this and let the wager go."

Halli said that he would nonetheless seek compensation.

"That is your decision," said the retainer.

In the morning Halli went to Einarr and said: "Last night you told news of my kinsman's death that concerns me deeply. I wish to know if you are going to pay some compensation."

Einarr replied: "Have you not heard that I pay compensation for no one? I cannot tell by looking at you that compensation is more justified in your case than in another, and as soon as I pay one claim (FJ 243), others will feel entitled."

Halli said: "You might pay an amount that is no great loss for yourself but is still some consolation for me." Einarr told him to be off and say no more about it. With that, he went to his seat.

The retainer asked if he had been willing to pay compensation. Halli said that such was not the case. The retainer replied: "I knew that beforehand, and let us cancel the wager. Do not mention it again."

Halli said: "I will raise the question a second time."

In the morning Halli met with Einarr and brought up the same matter: "I still wish to know," he said, "whether you will compensate me for my kinsman."

Einarr said: "You are persistent, and if you do not get yourself off, you will be killed."

Halli went to his seat. (U 99)

The retainer said: "How did your appeal to Einarr go?"

Halli said that he had gotten threats for compensation.

"That's what I always thought you would get," said the retainer, "and I am still willing to cancel the wager if you will not bring up the matter again."

Halli answered: "You are a gentleman," he said, "but I am going to raise the matter a third time. Then it will seem fully tested to me."[12]

Now Halli went before the king and greeted him: "Greetings, lord," he said.

"Welcome, Halli," said the king—"what do you wish?"

"Sire," said Halli, "I wish to tell you my dream—you are a good interpreter of dreams. I dreamed that I was a different man. I dreamed that I was the skald Þorleifr, and that Einarr fluga was Hákon jarl. I dreamed that I cursed him, and I remembered some of the words when I awoke." Then he went back from the high seat and muttered something so that no one could understand the words, but everyone heard that he mumbled something.[13]

Then the king said: "Do as I ask you, Einarr, and give him some compensation. He will shrink from nothing, and a single ditty that is circulated and remembered is worse for you, considering your rank, than paying compensation. You and I can see what he has in mind (FJ 244), and this is no dream that he has told. He will do what he says, and there are precedents that a curse has worked on men more powerful than you. It will not be forgotten as long as the northern lands are populated. Do this for my sake."

Einarr said: "I will do as you wish, sire. Let him have three marks of silver from my treasurer, who will pay them out."

Then Halli said: "Have thanks. I am now well content." He met the treasurer and told him. The treasurer said that there were four marks in the purse.

"Three marks are what I should have," said Halli.

They now weighed out three marks so that there was no overage, because that was what Halli insisted on. After that he went to Einarr and told him that he had the money.

"Did you take what was in the purse?" asked Einarr.

"Not at all," said Halli. "You will have to find some other capital offense against me rather than to make me the thief of your money. I penetrated your deceit, and this is how we will part." Einarr had planned exactly what Halli said, but things remained quiet and Halli went to his seat.[14]

Then the retainer said: "You have won the wager."

"You should keep your money," said Halli, "because you have dealt with me very decently in this affair. My only reason to contest the matter with you at the outset was to test whether I could get the money from Einarr or not. I never had any kinship with this man that I know of, or with any other man whom Einarr has killed." Then Einarr departed from court.

After that Halli asked the king for permission to go south to Denmark in the summer. The king said that he would give his leave if he would return quickly, but he told him to proceed cautiously because he knew that Einarr fluga (U 100) would have evil designs against him if they met. He said there were few examples that had ended up with Einarr's paying compensation (FJ 245) for killings he committed, and he said that Einarr would be ill content.

In the summer Halli went to Denmark and stayed with a powerful man. An assembly was held with a large attendance. Halli went to the assembly with the chieftain, and when the cases were being discussed, voices became very loud.

The chieftain said: "Anybody who could figure out how to make all these people quiet would be a resourceful man."

Halli replied: "I will manage it so that everyone is silent."

"No," said the chieftain, "that you cannot manage," and it ended with their laying a wager. The chieftain bet a gold ring and Halli staked his life.

The next day when they came to the assembly, there was no less tumult than before, with murmuring and shouting, noisy talk and a general din. When it was least expected, Halli jumped up and called out: "Everyone listen, because this is important. I want to lodge a complaint about a problem. I have lost a whetstone and the whetstone lubricant, and a needle and bag, and everything that goes with the bag and is better to have than to lose."

Then there was silence and consternation, because some thought that the man was mad and some thought he had something to say, and they were curious to hear it, though they thought he had started out rather strangely. But Halli sat down and thought that he had accomplished what he had promised inasmuch as people were listening. Then people left the assembly. Halli won his wager and departed in secret.

Then he journeyed to England and intended to go from there to Norway. When those who intended to go to Norway were ready, Halli went to the king and said that he had composed a poem about him. There was a man named Rauðr with the king, also a skald. When Halli had recited his poem, the king asked Rauðr how good it was. Rauðr said it was good. Then the king (FJ 246) invited Halli to stay with him so that people could learn the poem. "I cannot accept, sire," said Halli, "for I have prepared to depart and cannot delay any longer."

Then the king said: "The reward will be commensurate with the profit we have had from the poem. Sit down now and I will have silver poured on your head. You can keep whatever sticks in your hair." Halli said that he had to go out for a moment to relieve himself. He did so and got some tar, which he dumped on his head and rubbed into his hair as thoroughly as he could. Then he went back into the hall and sat down, saying that he was ready and eager. The king did what he promised and poured silver onto his head. A goodly amount of money stuck to it.[15] But the poem was a fragment that he made up on the spur of the moment.[16] Then Halli went to his ship.

By that time many Germans with heavy cargoes had taken passage, and Halli could not find a (U 101) place. The captains gave him to understand that they were quite willing to take him if he could find a way to get rid of the Germans. There was a captain who was well-disposed to Halli. One night he tossed in his bed and was awakened. They asked him what he had been dreaming. He told his dream and said that he expected a hard passage. He said that an enormous man had appeared to him and recited the following:

125. Hrangs þars hávan þ̨ongul   ljóst es lýsu at gista
      heldk umb (síz fj̨or seldak)   l̨ond ák út fyr str̨ondu
      sýnts at sitk at Ránar   því sitk bleikr í brúki
      sumir ró í búð með humrum: blakir mér þari of hnakka;
                                         blakir mér þari of hnakka. (FJ 247)

"Hrangs, þars heldk umb hávan þ̨ongul, síz seldak fj̨or; sýnts, at sitk at Ránar; sumir ró í búð með humrum. Ljóst es at gista lýsu; ák l̨ond út fyr str̨ondu; því sitk bleikr í brúki; blakir mér þari of hnakka, blakir mér þari of hnakka."

It's noisy where I'm grasping the tall stalk of seaweed, since I lost my life; clearly I'm living at Rán's [sea goddess]; some share their residence with lobsters. It's light when one visits the whiting; I own land off the shore; hence I sit pale in the pile of seaweed; kelp is flapping around my neck, kelp is flapping around my neck.

The stanza did nothing to suggest that they would not have a rough time, and it seemed a miserable prospect to get into such peril, so that many ended by unloading their cargoes and leaving. But Halli went on board and had a perfectly smooth passage to Norway. Then he went to see the king and stayed with him for some time.

44. [The King Encounters a Man in a Boat][1]

One summer, when King Haraldr was sailing along the coast with his squadron, they saw a man fishing in a boat ahead of them. The king was in a good humor and called out to the fisher as his ship sailed by: "Can you make verses?"

"No, sire," he said.

"That won't do," said the king. "Compose something for me."

The man said: "Then you will have to reciprocate."

"I will," said the king.

The fisher declaimed a stanza:

126. Ófúsa drók ýsu   þó mank hitt es hrotta
      áttak fang við l̨ongu   h̨ofðum golli vafðan
      vannk of h̨ofði hennar   dúðum d̨orr í blóði
      hl̨omm (vas þat fyr sk̨ommu): drengs (vas þat fyr lengra).

"Drók ófúsa ýsu; áttak fang við lǫngu; vannk hlǫmm of hǫfði hennar: vas þat fyr skǫmmu. Þó mank hitt, es hǫfðum hrotta golli vafðan; dúðum dǫrr í blóði drengs: vas þat fyr lengra."

I pulled up the reluctant haddock; I wrestled with the ling; I exulted above its head: that was recently. Yet I recall when I owned the gold-wrapped sword; I shook the spears in the warrior's blood: that was longer ago.

The king asked: "Have you spent time with powerful men or been in battle?"

"I expect that I have been with powerful men, lord," he said. "And now compose a counterstanza."

The king recited a stanza: (FJ 248)

127. Hjoggu harða dyggvir   hitt vas fyrr es fjarri
      hirðmenn Dani stirða   fóstrlandi rauðk branda
      sótti ferð á flótta   sverð í Serkja garði
      framm (en þat vas skǫmmu):   sǫng (en þat vas lǫngu). (U 102)

"Harða dyggvir hirðmenn hjoggu stirða Dani; ferð sótti framm á flótta: en þat vas skǫmmu. Hitt vas fyrr, es rauðk branda fjarri fóstrlandi; sverð sǫng í Serkja garði: en þat vas lǫngu."

The loyal retainers slayed relentless Danes; troops rushed forth in flight: and that was recently. Earlier I reddened the blades far from my native land; the sword sang in the stronghold of the Saracens: yet that was long ago.

Then the king said: "Now it is your turn, Þjóðólfr."

Þjóðólfr recited a stanza:

128. Mildingr rauð í móðu   setti niðr á sléttu
      (mót illt vas þar) spjóta   Serklandi gramr merki
      (Dǫnum váru goð) geira   stóð at stillis ráði
      (grǫm) (en þat vas skǫmmu):   stǫng (en þat vas lǫngu).

"Mildingr rauð geira í móðu spjóta; þar vas illt mót; goð váru grǫm Dǫnum: en þat vas skǫmmu. Gramr setti merki niðr á sléttu Serklandi; stǫng stóð at stillis ráði: en þat vas lǫngu."

The generous ruler reddened spears in the river of javelins [blood]; a terrible encounter took place there; the gods were angry with the Danes: and that was recently. The lord planted his standard in the level land of the Saracens; the staff stood at the king's command: yet that was long ago.

The king said: "Listen to the great poet! You said 'grǫm' and 'skǫmm,' and that is not a true rime. A true rime would have been 'hrǫm / skǫm,' but it would make no sense, and you have composed much better verse than this."[2]

Þjóðólfr became angry and said that anybody who could do better was free to do so.

Then the king said to the fisher: "Recite a stanza now."

He replied: "The decision is yours, but it is hard to compose verse after Þjóðólfr and after you went first."

"Take this gold," said the king, and he handed it to him, "and recite a stanza." He took the gold and recited: (FJ 249)

129. Heyr á uppreist orða   saddir ǫrn ok eyddir
      ótvínn konungr mína   ǫrum blámanna fjǫrvi
      gaf mér goll et rauða   gall styrfengins stillis
      gramr (vas þat fyr skǫmmu):   strengr (vas þat fyr lengra).

"Ótvínn konungr, heyr á uppreist orða mína! Gramr gaf mér goll et rauða: vas þat
fyr skǫmmu. Saddir ǫrn ok eyddir ǫrum blámanna fjǫrvi; gall styrfengins stillis
strengr: vas þat fyr lengra."

Unwavering king, hear my improved creation! The lord gave me red gold: that was
recently. You fed the eagle and wasted Africans with arrows; the bowstring of the
battle-eager king twanged: that was longer ago.

The king said: "Þjóðólfr, compose something in return." But Þjóðólfr said he
would not do so. The king said: "It is a fact, Þjóðólfr, that you are a good poet,
but it is also true that you are difficult about it." Then the king declaimed:

130.   Hlautk af hrauðung skjóta   enn fyr England sunnan
       hlýri mær en skýra   óð borð und mér norðan
       súð gekk feld á flœði   ristin skalf í rǫstum
       framm (vas þat fyr skǫmmu):   rǫng (en þat vas lǫngu).

"Hlautk skjóta hlýri af hrauðung, mær en skýra; feld súð gekk framm á flœði: vas
þat fyr skǫmmu. Enn fyr England sunnan óð borð und mér norðan; ristin rǫng
skalf í rǫstum: en þat vas lǫngu."

I launched the ship from the landing, wise woman; the robust vessel advanced on
the ocean: that was recently. But south of England, the ship slid beneath me from
the north; the carved frame quivered in the currents: yet that was long ago.

Then the fisher recited as the king ordered:

131.   Víg lézt Vinða mýgir   enn fyr Serkland sunnan
       virðum kunn of unnin   snarr þengill hjó drengi
       (Þrœndr drifu ríkt und randir)   kunni gramr at gunni
       rǫmm (en þat vas skǫmmu):   gǫng (vas þat fyr lǫngu).

"Vinða mýgir, lézt of unnin rǫmm víg, virðum kunn; Þrœndr drifu ríkt und randir:
en þat vas skǫmmu. Enn snarr þengill hjó drengi fyr Serkland sunnan; gramr
kunni gǫng at gunni: vas þat fyr lǫngu."

Waster of the Wends, you waged furious wars, famous among men; mightily, the
Þrœndir [people of Trøndelag] mustered beneath the shields: yet that was recently. But the ruthless king felled men south of the land of the Saracens; the lord
knew how to advance in battle: that was long ago.

The king said: "These are the best line endings in your verses, and you had
in mind that I would know the ways (FJ 250) of battle. If (U 103) you are a poor
man and in difficulties, come to me and I will make you a gift."

"Sire," he said, "I am in no difficulty, and I went fishing for my own amusement.[3] I was in the army of your brother King Óláfr at Stiklastaðir, and my
name is Þorgils." He then threw off his fisherman's disguise and turned out to
be a very gallant fellow. He joined the king's retinue.

45. [Concerning King Haraldr and a Dear Friend of Tryggvi Óláfsson] [1]

It happened once that King Haraldr came to the place where there had been a battle between Tryggvi, the son of Óláfr Tryggvason, and Sveinn Álfífuson. The king went on shore to relax and met a man who had been with Tryggvi, a dear friend of his. The man became very dispirited when he saw the king.

Haraldr realized that and asked the reason: "I am not aware that I have ever caused you any grief or injury."

"That is true, sire," he said, "but I am always depressed when I see noble men."

The king asked why that was.

He answered: "The last time I was here was with King Tryggvi." He now told the king in detail about the events of the battle and how grieved he was at the thought of how King Tryggvi probably died. He said that he thought he had probably been murdered by a farmer—"and the one I think did it still lives here," he said.

The king said that it was not strange that the world was in such a sorry state when such deeds were done. "And it may be," he said, "that there is some family likeness between me and King Tryggvi." He had the farmer seized and compelled to speak, so that he finally confessed. Then the king had him hanged (FJ 251) on a gallows and thus cleansed the land and avenged the king. He took the man who was so grieved into his retinue.

46. [Concerning Gizurr Ísleifsson] [1]

When Gizurr Ísleifsson came to King Haraldr, the king was told that he was a distinguished man. Then King Haraldr said: "What you tell of him could be made into three men. He could be a viking chieftain, and has the makings for it. Given his temperament, he could be a king, and that would be fitting. The third possibility is a bishop, and that is probably what he will become, and he will be a most outstanding man." (U 104)

47. Concerning Stúfr enn blindi

At that time Stúfr enn blindi (the Blind) came from Iceland, the son of Þórðr kǫttr (the Cat), whom Snorri goði had fostered. Stúfr's father Þórðr was the son of Þórðr Glúmsson and the grandson of Geiri. Þórðr Glúmsson was married to Guðrún Ósvífrsdóttir.[1] Stúfr was blind, a wise man and a good skald. He came to Norway in the days of King Haraldr Sigurðarson and took lodging with a good farmer in Upplǫnd, where he was well treated.

One day when people were outside, they saw a large body of men riding toward the farm. They were handsomely dressed. Then the farmer said: "I am not certain what is afoot. I am not expecting the king, but these men have a royal look about them." They kept a lookout, and (FJ 252) the men arrived at the farm. It turned out that it was in fact the king who was to be welcomed.

When they met, the farmer said: "Our hospitality will not suffice for you, sire."

The king replied: "We will make small demands on you. We are conducting our business around the countryside, and my men will tend to their own horses while I go inside."

The king was in good spirits, and the farmer brought him in and seated him. Then the king said: "Do whatever you wish and be completely at your ease with me."

"I am obliged to take advantage of your permission," said the farmer. He went away, and the king looked down the benches. He caught sight of a large man at the end and asked who he was.

"My name is Stúfr," he said.

"That's not much to go by," said the king, "and whose son are you?"

"I am the cat's son," he said.[2]

"That's the same kind of answer," said the king. "Who is the cat?"

"Guess, sire," said Stúfr, and he laughed.

"Why did you laugh?" asked the king.

Stúfr said: "Guess again."

The king replied: *"It is not easy to guess your mind, but I will guess that you laughed because you were wondering what sow it was that my father was named after."[3]

Stúfr said: "You guessed right, sire."

Then King Haraldr said: "Come closer on the bench and let's talk." He did so, and the king was well pleased with their conversation.

The farmer now returned and said that the king was probably bored.

"That's not the case," said the king, "because your winter lodger is keeping me well entertained, and he should keep me company this evening over drink."

"It will be as you wish," said the farmer. This was the arrangement, and the king talked a lot with Stúfr and found him to be a wise man even though he was blind. (FJ 253)

When it was bedtime, the king asked Stúfr to stay in his house and entertain him. He did so and first recited (U 105) a *flokkr*. When it was finished, the king said: "Recite another"—and he went on with another ten or so *flokkar*. The king asked: "Can you recite anything more than *flokkar*, and who are the poets?"

Stúfr answered: "I know as many *drápur* as the *flokkar* I have now composed and recited. Does your majesty think there is any poetry in these verses?"

"Yes," said the king, "they are certainly well made, and the person who composed them deserves to be called a skald wherever they are recited among discriminating men. And you appear to be a very learned man. But now it is time to sleep."

In the morning, when they were getting ready to leave, Stúfr said: "Will you grant me what I ask, sire?"

King Haraldr said: "Let me hear your request."

"Promise before I tell you," said Stúfr.

"That is not quite my custom," said the king, "even with men to whom I am more obligated than to you, but because of the amusement*[4] and entertainment you have afforded me, I will risk it."

Stúfr said: "The journey I am engaged in will take me east to Vík to claim a certain inheritance, and I wish you to give me a letter with your seal so that I may obtain the money."[5]

"That I will certainly do," said the king.

Then Stúfr asked: "Will you grant me another request?"

The king asked what it was.

"Promise me before I tell you."

The king said: "You are a strange man, and no one has framed requests to me like this before. But I will still risk it."

Stúfr said: "I wish to fashion a poem about you."

The king said: "I think your poem is likely to be good, and I will grant my permission."

Stúfr asked: "Will you grant me a third request?"

The king replied: "What is the request now?"

"Promise first once again, (FJ 254) sire," said Stúfr, "before I tell."

"This time I will not do so," said the king, "and this has gone on long enough. Now tell me what you want."

Stúfr said: "I wish to become your retainer."

The king said: "Now it is a good thing that I did not promise first, because I need the counsel of the retainers.[6] Come to me at court."

Now they parted, and the money was paid out properly to Stúfr according to the king's instructions. After that Stúfr went to see the king and was well received. The king brought the matter up for discussion, and with the agreement of all the retainers Stúfr took service with the king. He composed an obituary poem about him that is called "Stúfr's Drápa," and he remained with the king.

48. Concerning Oddr Ófeigsson

One summer Oddr, the son of Ófeigr and the grandson of Skíði, arrived from Iceland and went north to Finnmark, where he spent the winter.[1] King Haraldr was then reigning in Norway. When they sailed from the north in the spring, Oddr spoke to his shipmates: "There is some danger involved in this voyage," he said, "because no one is supposed to conduct commercial dealings in this area without the king's permission (U 106), or that of the king's administrator. A man has also been appointed to collect the Lapp tribute and administer sanctions.[2] That man is Einarr fluga, and he does not have a lenient nature. Now, I want to know how much you have earned in your dealings with the Lapps." But they did not reveal their dealings.

As they were sailing from the north (FJ 255) and were off Þjótta (Tjøtta), they saw a longship bearing down on them from an island.[3] It was Einarr. When they realized this, Oddr urged his men to make sure that no Lapp treasure was found on them—"if, as I suspect, your dealings with the Lapps have not been entirely legal. Let us gather that money in one place in case the ship is searched." What Oddr suspected turned out to be true, and each man produced what he had acquired. They hid it where Oddr thought best and had finished the work before Einarr reached them.

Einarr and his men laid to next to the ship. There was a breeze that was beginning to pick up and blow hard. Oddr greeted Einarr because they were acquainted, and Einarr said: "You know what is fitting, Oddr, but you have been among the Lapps this winter, and it may be that some of your men have not been so circumspect in dealing with the Lapps. But this is a commission that the king has put in our hands, and we wish to search your ship."

Oddr said that they were free to look over the cargo, and his men unlocked their chests. Einarr and his men went on board and searched without finding any Lapp treasure. Then Einarr said: "These men have (FJ 256) had more foresight than I imagined. At this point I hardly think that I can break into the cargo because the wind is rising and we need to return to our ship."

Then a man who was sitting on the cargo planks said: "First you should look at this bag that I have found and see what is in it." He set about opening it, and Einarr waited.

There was a long cord around the bag that was difficult to untie, and he kept at it for a long time. Einarr told him to hurry up. He said he would and took out another bag and started to work at that. There were a lot of cords around it, and he got all tangled up. Then Einarr said: "You take your time with the task"—but he kept waiting to see if the bag would produce anything incriminating. Then a third bag emerged, and when he finally got that torn open, there was nothing in it but a few rags and things of no consequence.

Then Einarr said: "You wretch, you have delayed and misled us until the island is out of sight."

He returned to his ship because the wind was stiffening, and they could not remain alongside the merchant vessel. With that they parted, and Oddr said: "We have now escaped (FJ 257) Einarr fluga, but it seems to me important that we not meet up with the king."

Einarr immediately sent word to the king to let (U 107) him know what had

happened. When Oddr and his men got south to Mjǫla (Meløy), it happened
that King Haraldr was there.[4] They spotted the merchant vessel, and because
the king was apprised, he said: "This could be a good opportunity. That is
probably Oddr's ship, and it is quite fitting that we should meet. Einarr has
seldom been as duped as he was by Oddr and his crew." The king was in high
dudgeon.

Oddr and his men now anchored at the island, and the king didn't wait for
niceties but went to meet them. Oddr gave the king a good welcome, but the
king was taciturn and angry. He said that Oddr had treated him badly; he said
that he had always given him an honorable reception but that he had traded
with the Lapps without his permission.

Oddr replied: "Sire, we would gladly have made our landfall farther south
than Finnmark, but I knew better than to trade without your permission."

The king said: "I think there are grounds for all of you to be strung up and
hanged on the highest tree. Even though you yourself may not be responsible,
your men look to me as though they have engaged in unlawful trade, and we
wish to search your ship."

"You are free to do so, sire," (FJ 258) said Oddr. This was done, and nothing
was found.

There was a man named Þorsteinn, a kinsman of Þórir hundr.[5] He was a
handsome young man and a good friend of Oddr's. At the time of which we
are speaking he was staying with the king. Þorsteinn stayed behind on the ship
when the king and his men went away. He took Oddr aside in confidence *and
asked whether they were in any way guilty of the charges.[6] He said that the king
was angered and that the case would be pressed hard against them.

Oddr said: "I think we are not clear of the charge. My crew members were at
first involved on their own initiative, though I forbade it, but I ended up giving advice on how the matter might be concealed."

"What have you done with the proceeds?" asked Þorsteinn.

Oddr said that it was all in a leather bag.

Þorsteinn said: "The king will return to do another search. You should take
the bag and place it under the king's seat. The last thing he will think of is that
he is sitting on the very thing he is looking for, but there is some risk involved."

Then Þorsteinn went away, and Oddr did as he advised. The king arrived a
short time later and sat on the seat that had been prepared for him. His men
searched for the money in the chests, and every place that seemed to be a likely
hiding place was broken into, but nothing was found.

The king said: "I am puzzled because there is no reason to think that the
money we are looking for is not on the ship."

Oddr answered: "It's an old proverb, sire, that the man who guesses often
goes astray."[7]

The king and his men now went away, but Þorsteinn stayed behind on the
ship and said to Oddr (U 108): "This trick will not work any longer, and the

king will see through it in a while. You can believe that he will not abandon the search easily. You should now put the money in the furled sail and draw the sail up on the mast because everything on the ship will be broken into, the cargo and everything else."*[8] (FJ 259) Oddr and his men followed Þorsteinn's advice, and he took his leave.

When Þorsteinn caught up with the king, the king asked why he had stayed behind. "I was obliged to, sire," he said, "because I had to fix my leggings." The king was not much pleased.

A little later the king came on board Oddr's ship and said: "There is a possibility that you have set up my seat with the Lapp tribute, and that is the first place we will look. Then we will look everywhere in the ship, and the harder it is for us, the worse it will be for you." Now every place they could think of was searched, and nothing was found.

The king went ashore, and Þorsteinn was not quick to follow him. He said to Oddr: "This won't work for long either, and now nothing else will do but to remove the money from the ship. Move it out to the head of the point, and I will take a different path home from the king. Then it will take longer for him to find out that I have lingered behind. In the evening when the sunlight fades, haul up the anchors and make use of your nautical skill, Oddr. Otherwise the king will press you so hard that there will be no escape. He is a very resourceful and persistent man when he has his mind made up." Oddr said that Þorsteinn had gotten a very poor reward for the help he had given them. Then they parted, and Þorsteinn took his leave.

Oddr and his men (FJ 260) did as he said. They worked at night, but in the morning the king came and searched in the sail, though nothing was found. But after the fact the king always suspected where they had probably hidden it. Oddr spoke up: "Sire, now you can no longer suspect us because every shred of our ship has been combed."

The king said that things were not as he claimed, and that no one had ever tried to practice such deception on him. The king was so angry that no one could make him listen.

The day passed, and when night came, they moved the money back and readied the ship. Toward daybreak a breeze sprang up and pushed them out to sea.

The king awoke early and said: "Now I think I grasp their whole strategy. I surmise that they are not the only ones involved, and I think we can now find what we are looking for on the ship. But I could not accuse them of a capital crime as long as I was just guessing. Let us now proceed with the search."

When they emerged from the tents and looked around, they saw Oddr's sail among the outer islands. The king said: "That will conclude my business with Oddr for the moment, but you, Þorsteinn, know how to help your friends, and you have attached more importance to Oddr than to me. It may be that you are true to your family with respect to treachery."

Þorsteinn replied: "It is no treachery, sire, to keep you from killing Oddr (U 109), who has been a good friend to you, along with many other men on a mere suspicion. I think it is an act of loyalty to save you from such an enormity."

Oddr and his men headed out to sea and found favorable breezes. Then Oddr said to his companions: "Now I will give you an account of what happened and why I acted as I did. I told you not to have more commerce with the Lapps than was legal, but you paid no attention, and when we encountered Einarr, I told you (FJ 261) to treat him honorably and draw out the conversation and contrive delays, because I knew that you were guilty. I asked you to sail while he lingered so as to put the greatest distance between us. When the king was first told that our ship had been sighted, he asked whether it was our ship. But our friend Þorsteinn said that men were fishing out there. 'Good fishing,' said the king, 'as anyone would say who knows you, and that catch belongs to me.' But we have held onto the catch and have escaped. For that we are much indebted to Þorsteinn."[9] Oddr came out to Iceland and went to his farm.

There was a seafaring merchant named Hárekr, a kinsman of Þorsteinn's. He arrived in Miðfjǫrðr. It was a famine year here, but Oddr invited him to stay the winter at his home and sent good stud horses back with him. They were chestnut, with white manes, and were intended for Þorsteinn, whom he described as his savior.

Hárekr sailed to Norway in the summer and met with Þorsteinn, who was still with the king. He brought him the horses and said that Oddr had sent them.

Þorsteinn said: "This is most inopportune, because the matter could otherwise have been concealed, but under these circumstances it will come out. We are now in a tight spot."

Þorsteinn showed the horses to the king and said that Oddr had sent them to him as a gift.

The king said: "I was owed no gifts from Oddr, and he sent the horses to you, not me. You shall keep them."[10] He ordered that Þorsteinn be killed, but people were unwilling. Þorsteinn left the retinue and was no longer the king's friend. (FJ 262)

49. How It Came about That King Haraldr Journeyed to the West

In the twentieth year of King Haraldr Sigurðarson's rule, King Edward the Good (the Confessor) died west in England on the fifth day of Christmas. On the seventh day the English took as their king Harold, the son of Godwin and Gyða, the daughter of Þorgils sprakaleggr and the sister of Jarl Úlfr. Harold was anointed king in London at St. Paul's on the eighth day of Christmas. King Edward had been married to Gyða, the daughter of Godwin and the sister of King Harold. Edward died childless, and with that the English throne was separated from the line of Æthelstan the Good.[1]

Godwin's other son Tostig thought (U 110) that he was no less entitled to rule than his brother Harold. It became apparent that he wanted to stand against his brother for election by all the chieftains of the land. He asked that all the chieftains and all the people should elect the one they wanted, and many people said that Tostig was the wiser man and no less qualified to be king than his brother. But Harold had a better grip on the throne since he had the title and had been placed on the throne and been anointed, even if that had been done rather quickly. Harold also had possession of the palaces and treasures and wished on no account to abandon his claim. As a consequence the whole land had submitted to him, and when the king became aware of his brother's aspirations, he forced him to flee the country.

He went east to Denmark to meet with his kinsman King Sveinn, and he asked him to give him support and troops and reinforce him so that he could (FJ 263) vindicate his honor against his brother Harold. King Sveinn received him well and invited him to stay with him and accept some fief in Denmark. Then Jarl Tostig said: "If you do not wish to lend us some of the power of your realm so that we can recover our honor, rather than see everything slip away we would prefer to support you if you wish to lead an army and conquer England as your uncle King Knútr did. With my aid you will then win the realm or that part of the English realm that favors me."

Then King Sveinn answered: "I am so much inferior to our kinsman Knútr the Old that I can scarcely maintain my land against the Norwegians. Knútr the Old acquired Denmark as his inheritance and England by warfare and good fortune, though for a time it looked as though he might lose his life there. He won Norway without a battle, but we can choose moderation more in line with our modest ambition than with the success of our kinsman Knútr the Old."

Then Tostig answered: "Our kinsmen become our enemies, but their enemies can also be our kin."[2] He took his leave of the Danish king in such a way that both were angered.

He then sailed back, but first went to Norway, where he met with King Haraldr and presented his problem. He offered him his service and alliance. After that the king assembled his wise men and counselors. Both the king and the jarl addressed each other in friendly terms. The king disclosed the wrong done the jarl and how he had been driven from his realm without cause.

The jarl spoke as follows: "I begin my tale, sire," he said, "when Hǫrðaknútr, the son of Knútr the Old, ruled England after his brother Haraldr" (FJ 264). He explained what oaths had been sworn by King Magnús the Good and Hǫrðaknútr, and that King Magnús was Hǫrðaknútr's proper heir, and how King Magnús (U 111) had taken pity on King Edward by not claiming his realm and title in England as well as Denmark. "But who is the proper heir to the realm of King Magnús? None other but you, his uncle King Haraldr. But tell me how you remember the arrangements."

King Haraldr replied: "What you say is true." And he was reminded of what the agreement had always been.

Haraldr considered this conversation carefully, and he discussed it with the jarl over a period of days. To make a long story short, Tostig swore fealty to King Haraldr and promised the king his support and cooperation in a campaign to the west in England. King Haraldr promised him in return that he would rule England and that he would grant him honor in proportion to the territory that he would win in England. But some people relate that Jarl Tostig sent Gunnhildr's son Guthormr to treat with King Haraldr and to offer him Northumbria with binding oaths and to urge him to undertake a campaign in the west.[3] According to this version Guthormr went to Norway and Tostig went south across the sea to Normandy to confer with his relatives.

At the end of winter and toward spring King Haraldr sent word throughout the realm and called out the levy, specifying who should report for duty from each district. Everyone who knows something of these events says that there was never such an elite force gathered (FJ 265) in Norway for any expedition. The news was spoken of in every home, but most often in the king's retinue, and people discussed how King Haraldr might fare in England. Some people tallied up the great deeds that King Haraldr had accomplished in many lands. Others said that England was powerful and populous and boasted an army known as "þingamenn."[4] It was composed of men from various countries, though mostly Norse-speaking. They were supremely confident and were such hard-bitten and aggressive warriors that it was said that the support of one "þingamaðr" was worth no less than that of two of the best Norwegians among King Haraldr's champions. When Úlfr stallari learned of this matter, he recited a stanza:

132. Esat stǫllurum stillis   ef hǫrbrekka hrøkkva
      stafnrúm Haralds jafnan   hrein skulum tveir fyr einum
      (ónauðigr fekk'k auðar)   (ungr kenndak mér) undan
      innan þǫrf at hvarfa: (annat) þingamanni.

"Esat stǫllurum stillis þǫrf at hvarfa jafnan innan stafnrúm Haralds—fekk'k ónauðigr auðar—ef, hrein hǫrbrekka, skulum tveir hrøkkva undan fyr einum þingamanni; ungr kenndak mér annat."

There is no need for the king's marshals always to idle in the prow of Haraldr's ship—I acquired wealth with ease—if, fair flax slope [woman], we should flee two before one English soldier; as a youth, my habits were different.

While preparations for this campaign were under way, Úlfr stallari died. We are told that as King Haraldr left Úlfr's grave, he said the following words, which were a great tribute to Úlfr: "Here lies a man (U 112) most loyal and devoted to his lord." Then Styrkárr was sole "stallari" (marshal), a title that they had previously shared. King Haraldr had two hundred ships and countless supply ships and lesser craft. He appointed his son Magnús to be regent in

Norway, but he took his son Óláfr (FJ 266) with him. Steigar-Þórir did not come because he had had an ominous dream about the king.[5]

It happened when the king stepped into the boat that he weighed it down heavily.[6] Jarl Erlendr was with him and prophesied a bad end to the expedition. King Haraldr sailed first west to Orkney and recruited the aid of Jarl Þorfinnr's sons Páll and Erlendr. There he left his wife Þóra and his daughter María behind.[7] Then King Haraldr turned his fleet south to England, and we are told that when the king was anchored in a harbor, a woman came down from the land and out onto the cliffs by the harbor and recited a stanza:

> 133. Skœð lætr skína rauðan   svipts í svarðar kjapta
>   skjǫld (es dregr at hjaldri)   (svanni) holdi manna
>   brúðr sér Aurnis jóða   (ulfs munn litar innan
>   ófǫr konungs gǫrva: óðlát kona blóði).

"Skœð lætr skína rauðan skjǫld, es dregr at hjaldri; brúðr Aurnis jóða sér gǫrva ófǫr konungs. Svipts holdi manna í svarðar kjapta; svanni, óðlát kona, litar ulfs munn innan blóði."

The trollwoman lets the red shield shine as battle draws near; the bride of Aurnir's [giant] brood [giants, trollwoman] sees the king's destined defeat at hand. Men's flesh is tossed into the hairy jaws; the woman, the raving female, reddens the wolf's mouth within with blood.

Then she disappeared, and people thought it was not a good omen. The next evening a second woman, as far as they could tell, came and recited another stanza:

> 134. Vísts at allvaldr austan   þar á valþiðurr velja
>   eggjask vestr at leggja   (veit œrna sér beitu)
>   mót við marga knútu   steik af stillis haukum
>   (minn snúðr es þat) prúða: stafns (fylgik því jafnan). (FJ 267)

"Vísts, at allvaldr austan eggjask vestr at leggja mót við marga prúða knútu; minn snúðr es þat. Þar á valþiðurr velja steik af stafns haukum stillis; veit sér œrna beitu; fylgik því jafnan."

It is clear the king from the east is being enticed west to join forces with many a famous knuckle [i.e., he will die there]; that is my fortune. There the corpse grouse [bird of prey] can choose food from the foremost of the king's champions; it knows it has ample supplies; I always support that.

Then she ran off. We are also told that during the trip a stanza was recited to King Haraldr in a dream:

> 135. Gramr vá frægr til feigðar   uggik øfst ráð tyggja
>   flestan sigr enn digri   yðr mun feigð of byrjuð
>   hlýtr (ef heima sætir)   trolls gefið fákum fyllar
>   heilagt fall til vallar: fíks (ræðra guð slíku).

"Frægr gramr enn digri vá flestan sigr til feigðar; hlýtr, ef heima sætir, heilagt fall til vallar. Uggik øfst ráð tyggja; yðr mun of byrjuð feigð; gefið fíks trolls fákum fyllar; ræðra guð slíku."

The famous stout king [St. Óláfr] was mostly victorious, yet doomed to die; if you stay home, you will die a holy death on the battlefield. I fear the final state of the king; death will be in store for you; you will provide food for the steeds of the greedy troll [wolves]; God will not cause that.

It is not known who recited this stanza to the king, but it is attributed most often to Saint Óláfr.

King Haraldr made his first landfall so that he landed at a place called Cleveland. The inhabitants all fled. The king took (U 113) hostages and tribute from the country. Then he went south to Scarborough and laid siege to it, but it was difficult to storm and was well defended. They eventually reduced it with fire. He subjected the whole north of England, then sailed south to the Humber and sailed up the Ouse. There the jarls of Northumbria, the sons of Jarl Godwin, Morkere and Waltheof of Huntingdon, marched against him with an enormous army that had been gathered throughout the summer and autumn.[8]

King Haraldr elected to give battle. He landed and drew up his troops on the riverbank, with one wing (FJ 268) toward the river and the other toward the still water of a deep pool. The jarls led their formation with all the rank and file down along the river. The king's standard was close to the river, where his battle array was densest, while it was thinnest by the pool. There too the troops were least reliable, and when the attack was made, that wing gave way. The English launched their attack down along the river, then toward the pool, and they thought that the Norwegians would flee.

King Haraldr led the attack with his troops and joined battle so fiercely that the enemy was split and the local army began to flee. They retreated to a place where there was no armed opposition, in the swampy ground around the pool. Jarl Morkere had followed the standard closest to the pool, and Jarl Waltheof fought the king more toward the river. He fled up along the river, and the troops with him were the only ones to escape. Jarl Morkere fell, and together with him so many men that the pool was full of corpses where the fleeing men had congregated. Some were driven into the water and killed there together with some who jumped into the pool and were speared, so that it was filled with corpses, as Steinn Herdísarson says:

136. Þjóð fórsk mǫrg í móðu   Fila dróttinn rak flótta
    menn drukknuðu sukknir   framr (tók herr á ramri
    drengr lá ár of ungan   rás fyr rǫskum vísa).
    ófár Mǫrukára: Ríklundaðr veit undir. (FJ 269)

"Mǫrg þjóð fórsk í móðu; menn drukknuðu sukknir; ófár drengr lá ár of ungan Mǫrukára. Framr Fila dróttinn rak flótta; herr tók á ramri rás fyr rǫskum vísa. Ríklundaðr veit undir."

Many died in the river; submerged men drowned; soon countless warriors lay dead around young Morkere. The proud lord of the Filir [people of Fjaler] pursued the fleeing enemies; the army rushed madly before the ready king. "Proud-minded knows beneath [the sun]."

He composed the praise poem that includes this stanza for King Haraldr's son Óláfr. It was the evening before Saint Matthew's Day, which fell on a Wednesday.[9] After this battle all the troops in the neighboring districts submitted to King Haraldr, but some fled, as is told in this poem:

137. Ungr vísi lézt Úsu   þeim mun þangatkváma
      allnær búendr falla   þengils vesa Englum
      sótti herr þars hætti   enn sem eptir renni
      hlíftrauðr konungr lífi: iflaust es þá lifðu. (U 114)

"Ungr vísi, lézt búendr falla allnær Úsu; sótti herr, þars hlíftrauðr konungr hætti lífi. Þangatkváma þengils mun iflaust vesa þeim Englum, es þá lifðu, sem enn renni eptir."

Young lord, you let farmers fall close to the River Ouse; the army attacked where the reckless king risked his life. The arrival of that king must undoubtedly appear to those Englishmen who were left alive as if they are still pursued.

And again:

138.   Fellu vítt of vǫllu
        (vargr náði þar bjargask)
        benja regn (en bragna
        blóð víkingar óðu).

"Benja regn fellu vítt of vǫllu, en víkingar óðu bragna blóð; vargr náði þar bjargask."

The rain of wounds [blood] fell far and wide on the fields and the vikings waded in warriors' blood; there the wolf got its fill.

Arnórr also notes what a great and glorious battle this was:

139.   Þung rauð jǫrn á Englum
      . eirlaust (né kømr meira)
        vísi vel nær Úsu
        (valfall of her snjallan).

"Vísi rauð vel eirlaust þung jǫrn á Englum nær Úsu; né kømr meira valfall of her snjallan."

Mercilessly the king reddened heavy weapons on the English near the River Ouse; a greater slaughter will never befall a brave army.

And again: (FJ 270)

140. Fell at fundi stillis   þjóð hykk þaðra náðu
      (framm óðu vé) móða   þúsundum togfúsa
      (ámt fló grjót) á gauta   (spjót flugu) líf at láta
      glóðheitr ofan sveiti: (laus í gumna hausum).

"Glóðheitr sveiti fell ofan á móða gauta at fundi stillis; framm óðu vé; ámt grjót fló. Hykk togfúsa þjóð náðu þaðra at láta líf þúsundum; spjót flugu laus í gumna hausum."

Red-hot blood poured down on weary warriors at the encounter with the king; standards advanced; dark stones flew. I believe battle-eager men lost their lives by the thousands there; spears swarmed [and stuck] in warriors' skulls.

141. Gagn fekk gjǫfvinr Sygna
    (gekk hildr at mun) vildra
    (hinns á hæl fyr mǫnnum
    hreinskjaldaðr fór aldri):

dunðu jarlar undan
(eir fekka lið þeira)
(mannkyn hefr at minnum
morgun þann) til borgar.

"Gjǫfvinr Sygna, hinns hreinskjaldaðr fór aldri á hæl fyr mǫnnum, fekk gagn vild-ra; hildr gekk at mun. Jarlar dunðu undan til borgar; lið þeira fekka eir; mannkyn hefr at minnum morgun þann."

The generous friend of the Sygnir [people of Sogn], who, with the shining shield, never yielded to men, gained a more glorious victory; the battle went as desired. The earls hastened to the stronghold; their men received no mercy; mankind will remember that morning.

These instances all refer to this event.

50. The Treachery against King Haraldr

Now King Haraldr set out to besiege the town of York. The army encamped at Stamford Bridge, and because the king had won such a great victory against such important chieftains and overwhelming odds, the people had become fearful and despaired of resisting. The townspeople resolved to send word to Haraldr. They submitted to him and surrendered the town. On Sunday King Haraldr marched with his troops and his whole army to York and convened a thingmeeting outside the walls. All the most powerful men submitted to King Haraldr and gave him (FJ 271) the sons of noble men as hostages. Jarl Tostig could advise the king in this matter because he was informed as to who the no-blest citizens were.

In the evening they went down to their ships, having won a victory without drawing a sword, and were in high spirits. A thingmeeting was scheduled for the morning in the town. King Haraldr was to make the administrative ap-pointments and give the officers their privileges and authority. But that same evening (U 115) after sunset King Harold Godwinson came to the town from the south with an enormous army, and he rode into the town with the leave and the approval of the townspeople. All the gates and walls were secured and guarded, and no word was to get to the Norwegians. The army spent the night in the town.

On Monday, when King Haraldr Sigurðarson and his troops had eaten their breakfast, he had the trumpets signal the landing. He made his preparations and determined who should march and who should stay behind. He took two men from every company for every one who stayed behind, so that he had two thirds of his army with him. Jarl Tostig readied his company to disembark with King Haraldr, but Haraldr's son Óláfr and Eysteinn orri remained behind to guard the ships. Eysteinn was the son of Þorbrandr and grandson of Árni, and was the man who was most distinguished and closest to King Haraldr of all his district chieftains.[1] King Haraldr had promised him his daughter María when they returned.

The sun shone brightly and the weather was very hot. They therefore left their chain mail behind and marched with shields and helmets and pikes, and they girded on their swords. Many were equipped with bow and arrows, and they were in high spirits, suspecting no hostility. When they arrived in the vicinity of the town, they saw a great cloud of dust kicked up by horses. Then they distinguished fair shields and shining byrnies and realized that a great host (FJ 272) was riding toward them.

King Haraldr immediately brought his army to a halt. He summoned Jarl Tostig and asked him what force this might be marching toward them. The jarl answered and said that it was likely to be a hostile force. "But," he said, "it could also be that these are some of our kinsmen, who wish to join us in kindness and friendship in order to offer us loyalty and support."

The king said: "For the moment we will take no action with respect to the army that is approaching."

They waited accordingly, and the force looked larger the nearer it came and the more clearly they saw. It looked just like gleaming ice. Then the jarl spoke: "Sire, now it is time to find some prudent strategy. There is no longer any doubt that this means hostility, and I suspect it is the king himself and his army."

King Haraldr asked: "What is your advice?"

"The first thing we should do is to return to our ships as quickly as possible in order to collect our troops and weapons. Then we can do battle to the best of our ability, or, alternatively, take cover in our ships so that the mounted horsemen do not overpower us."

The king said: "I have another plan, and that is to put three valiant fellows on our swiftest horses so that they can ride back as quickly as possible and tell the Norwegians of our straits. They will come to our aid quickly. But the English can expect a tough battle from us before we retreat, and we will put up a fierce fight for a time before we succumb."

The jarl said: "It is your decision, sire, in this matter as in others (U 116), and I am no more eager to retreat than anyone else, though I was obliged to say what I thought was most advisable."

King Haraldr set up his standard, which was called "Landeyða" (land-ravager). Friðrekr was the name of the man (FJ 273) who carried the standard. At another place Jarl Tostig set up his standard and marshaled his troops around it. Then King Haraldr said: "When the English ride at you, thrust your spear butts down into the ground and let the spear tips be aimed no higher than a man's middle. Those in the front ranks should also have their spears in the earth and the blades chest high toward the horses riding at them. We will thus oppose them with pikes, but the bowmen should stand at the rear of the formation and protect the flanks.[2] Let us stand fast and not move unless we go forward." In the words of Arnórr:

142. Uppgǫngu bauð yngvi
ítr með helming lítinn
sás á sinni ævi
sásk aldrigi háska:

enn of England sunnan
ǫflugr herr at berjask
fór við fylki dýran
fundusk þeir af stundu.

"Ítr yngvi, sás á sinni ævi aldrigi sásk háska, bauð uppgǫngu með helming lítinn. Enn ǫflugr herr fór sunnan of England at berjask við dýran fylki; fundusk þeir af stundu."

The splendid king, who never in his life shunned danger, bade his small army disembark. But a mighty host marched from the south through England to fight the esteemed lord; they soon met.

143. Olli ofrausn stillis
ormalátrs þvís máttit
stáls í strǫngu éli
stríðir elli bíða:

sás aldrigi aldins
ótams lituðr hramma
viggs í vápna glyggvi
varðrúnar sik sparði.

"Ofrausn stillis olli, þvís ormalátrs stríðir máttit bíða elli í strǫngu éli stáls; lituðr hramma aldins ótams viggs varðrúnar, sás aldrigi sparði sik í vápna glyggvi."

The king's arrogance caused it, that the enemy of the snake lair [gold, generous king] could not bide old age in the strong storm of steel [battle]; that colorer of the claws of the old, untamed steed of the giantess [wolf, warrior] who never spared himself in the wind of weapons [battle].

In the uproar as they awaited the English army Þjóðólfr recited a stanza: (FJ 274)

144. Skalkak frá (þótt fylkir
falli sjalfr til vallar)
(gengr sem guð vill) ungum
grams erfingjum hverfa:

skínna sól á sýnni
(snjallráðs) an þá báða
(Haralds eru haukar gǫrvir
hefnendr) konungsefni.

"Skalkak hverfa frá ungum erfingjum grams, þótt fylkir falli sjalfr til vallar: gengr sem guð vill. Skinna sól á sýnni konungsefni an þá báða; snjallráðs Haralds hefnendr eru haukar gǫrvir."

I shall not forsake the lord's young heirs though the king himself may fall: God's will be done. The sun does not shine on a more promising prince than those two; the avengers of quick-witted Haraldr are true hawks.

When King Haraldr had marshaled his forces, the English army arrived. The vanguard halted and waited for the arrival of the others. King Haraldr Sigurðarson rode at the head of his formation on a black horse with a white blaze on its forehead. He inspected the troops and gave directions wherever he wanted to draw them farther forward. As he was riding, the horse fell under him, and he pitched off it and said: "A fall is good fortune."[3]

Then King Harold Godwinson asked a Norwegian in his retinue: "Did you recognize the tall man who pitched off his horse and had a blue tunic and a handsome helmet on?"

"Sire," he said, "that was Haraldr, the king of the Norwegians."

Then King Harold Godwinson said: "He is a stately and splendid man, but it looks as though his luck may have run out."[4] (U 117)

Then twenty horsemen rode out before the Norwegian formation. They were all clad in chain mail, as were their horses. One of the horsemen asked: "Is Jarl Tostig present?"

He answered: "There's no denying that you will find him here."

Then the horseman said: "King Harold your brother sends you greetings and lets you know that he will give you a truce and all of Northumbria, and he would rather share a third of the whole realm with you than that you should fail to align yourself with him." (FJ 275)

Jarl Tostig replied: "That is a rather better offer than the disgrace and enmity I was offered last fall. If the offer had been what it is now, many a man who will not return home would have saved his life, and that would be better for the English realm. If I accept this offer, what will my brother give King Haraldr of the Norwegians for his trouble?"

The horseman answered: "He did say something about how much of England he would grant him. King Haraldr will have seven feet of sod, or as much more as he needs because he is taller than other men."

Then the jarl said: "Go now and tell my brother King Harold that he should prepare for battle. The Norwegians will have something else to relate than that Jarl Tostig left King Haraldr and joined the army of the enemy when he undertook to do battle for the English realm. We will all make the same choice— to die here with honor or win England in battle." Then the horsemen returned to their lines.

After that King Haraldr Sigurðarson asked Jarl Tostig: "Who was that well-spoken man who addressed you?"

The jarl answered: "That was King Harold Godwinson himself."

Then King Haraldr Sigurðarson said: "This was too long hidden from me, because they were close enough to our forces so that my namesake would not have lived to report the death of our men."

The jarl replied: "I saw, sire, that this chieftain advanced imprudently, and it may have turned out as you say. But he came to offer his brother a truce and a great fief, and I would surely have been called a wicked chieftain if I had awaited old age with the reputation of being my brother's killer. (FJ 276) It is better to suffer death at the hands of your brother than to be responsible for his death."

Then King Haraldr addressed his men: "This was a small man, lads, and yet he stood haughtily in his stirrups." King Haraldr is reported to have recited this stanza:

145. Fram gǫngum vér   í fylkingu
     brynjulausir   und blár eggjar:
     hjalmar skína   hefkat mína
     nú liggr skrúð várt   at skipum niðri. (U 118)

Without byrnies, we advance in battle array beneath blue [sword] edges; helmets shine—I don't have mine [*scil.* byrnie]—now our armor lies down by the ships.

King Haraldr's chain mail was called Emma. It went down to the middle of the leg and was so strong that no weapon could bite into it. His standard was called "Landeyða" (Land-ravager), as I mentioned before,[5] and it had been in many lands, as the name suggests.

Now King Haraldr said: "That stanza I just recited was not well made, and I will make another, better one." Then he recited this stanza:

146. Krjúpum vér fyr vápna   hátt bað mik (þars mœttusk)
     (valteigs) brǫkun eigi   menskorð bera forðum
     (svá bauð Hildr) at hjaldri   (Hlakkar íss ok hausar)
     (haldorð) í bug skjaldar: hjalmstall í gný malma.

"Krjúpum vér eigi í bug skjaldar fyr vápna brǫkun at hjaldri; svá bauð haldorð valteigs Hildr. Menskorð bað mik forðum bera hátt hjalmstall í gný malma, þars Hlakkar íss ok hausar mœttusk."

In battle we do not hide from the crash of weapons in the hollow of the shield; thus the loyal Hildr [valkyrie] of the hawk field [arm, woman] commanded. Earlier, the necklace pole [woman] told me to hold the helmet stem [head] high in the clamor of steel [battle] where Hlǫkk's [valkyrie] ice [sword] and skulls were clashing.

Now the English rode at the Norwegians, and they encountered stiff resistance. The pikes were set in such a way that the horses could not get by them. Both sides fought (FJ 277) with the greatest intensity, and there were few casualties at first. But there was such a large discrepancy in numbers that the English destabilized the Norwegian troops, encircled them, and attacked them from every direction. As happens in such cases, the casualties began to mount on both sides. The formation crumbled and reeled back, and large numbers of King Haraldr's men fell.

When the king realized that the standard was under heavy attack, he gripped his sword with both hands and hewed to left and right. He did not wait for the standard but cleared a path before him, killing many men in the process. Everyone agrees that no more valiant assault, pressed with such daring, has ever been witnessed. Both his arms were bloody, and he went among his enemies almost as if he were cleaving the wind, showing that he feared neither fire nor iron, as Stúfr says:

147. Gekk sem vind (sás vætki)   gramr flýðit sá síðan
     varðandi (fjǫr sparði)   (sœm eru þess of dœmi
     geira regns í gǫgnum   éls und erkistóli)
     glaðr orrostu þaðra: eld né jarn et fellda.

"Glaðr varðandi geira regns, sás vætki sparði fjǫr, gekk sem vind í gǫgnum orrostu þaðra. Sá gramr flýðit síðan eld né jarn et fellda; eru sœm of dœmi þess und éls erkistóli."

There the spirited warden of the spears' rain [battle, warrior], who did not heed his life, went through the battle like the wind. That king afterward fled neither fire nor pure iron; there are fitting proofs of that under the arch-seat of the storm [heaven].

Arnórr says the following in his poem:

148. Hafðit brjóst (né bifðisk   þars til þarfar hersa
         bǫðsnart konungs hjarta)   þat sá menn at skatna
         í hjalmþrimu hilmir   blóðugr hjǫrr ens barra
         hlítstyggr fyr sér lítit: (FJ 278) beit dǫglinga hneitis. (U 119)

"Hlítstyggr hilmir hafðit lítit brjóst fyr sér í hjalmþrimu, né bifðisk bǫðsnart hjarta konungs, þars menn sá þat, at blóðugr hjǫrr ens barra dǫglinga hneitis beit skatna til þarfar hersa."

The imperious lord showed no mean courage in the helmet clash [battle], nor did the battle-brave heart of the king waver where men saw that the bloody sword of the keen conqueror of kings bit warriors for the benefit of nobles.

King Haraldr now received a spear thrust in his throat, and the blood gushed from his mouth. That was his death wound, and he fell to the ground. When this had happened, the English pressed the attack so hard that all the troops who had stood closest to the king fell. The English gave a mighty shout, and when Jarl Tostig realized that the king had fallen, he headed to the place where he saw the standard "Landeyða" and urged his troops on. He ordered that the standard now be carried before him, and fierce fighting was joined once again because all the Norwegians encouraged each other and refused to flee.

Then King Harold Godwinson had it proclaimed loudly that his brother Tostig would be given a truce along with the surviving army, but they shouted in a single voice that they would never accept a truce. They stated that they wished to defeat their enemies or lie dead with their king. In the words of Arnórr jarlaskald:

149. Eigi varð ens œgja   heldr kuru meir ens milda
         auðligr konungs dauði   mildings (an grið vildi)
         hlífðut hlenna sœfi   of folksnaran fylki
         hoddum reknir broddar: falla liðsmenn allir. (FJ 279)

"Eigi varð dauði ens œgja konungs auðligr: hoddum reknir broddar hlífðut hlenna sœfi. Allir liðsmenn ens milda mildings kuru meir heldr falla of folksnaran fylki, an grið vildi."

The death of the dreaded king was ill-fated: the gold-adorned spears did not spare the bane of thieves [rigorous king]. All the followers of the generous lord chose rather to fall around [the body of] the battle-brave king than to accept a truce.

The battle was now engaged again with Jarl Tostig in command of the troops.

During the pause before the armies clashed again, Þjóðólfr composed this stanza:

150.   Qld hefr afráð goldit
     illt (nú kveðk her stilltan)
     bauð þessa fǫr þjóðum
     þarflaust Haraldr austan:

     svá lauk siklings ævi
     snjalls (at vér róm allir)
     (lofðungr fekk ens leyfða
     lífs grand) (í stað vǫndum).

"Qld hefr goldit illt afráð; nú kveðk her stilltan; Haraldr bauð þessa fǫr þjóðum þarflaust austan. Svá lauk snjalls siklings ævi, at vér róm allir í vǫndum stað; lofðungr fekk grand ens leyfða lífs."

People have paid a heavy price; now I declare that the army was deceived; without cause, Haraldr ordered his men to embark on this journey from the east. Thus ended the days of the daring king, so that we all are imperiled; the lord lost his commendable life.

The encounter was hard but of short duration, and the casualties mounted. The Norwegians fell in large numbers. The jarl fought valiantly and stayed by the standard, but before the battle ended, he fell with great fame and glory.

At that moment Eysteinn orri arrived with the troops who had been at the ships, all in chain mail. Now the third battle began, and Eysteinn advanced with King Haraldr's standard "Landeyða." This battle was the fiercest of all the attacks. Many of the English troops fell, and they were on the point of fleeing.

Eysteinn and his men became so incensed that they attacked furiously. On the other hand they were fatigued from having traveled a long distance in chain mail, and there was a hot sun, so that they were nearly overcome by their (U 120) fatigue. They shed their byrnies, as Þorkell hamarskald reported (FJ 280) when he composed a poem about Eysteinn orri.[6] They now fought for a time and resolved that they would either die or gain the victory. But the battle went as might be expected, and the army with the greater numbers had the upper hand. Eysteinn orri fell in the battle, which came to be known as Orri's Battle. There almost all the flower of Norway fell. It was toward the end of the day, and not all the Norwegians remained equally undaunted when all the chieftains and nobles had fallen.[7] Some were still granted a longer life and were able to escape. Styrkárr stallari escaped, a man of great fame. He got away when a man provided him with a horse, and he rode off in the evening.

A wind sprang up and the heat of the day dissipated. He had only a shirt on and was wearing a helmet, and had a naked sword in his hand. When he caught his breath, he began to feel the chill. A fellow with a wagon came toward him, wearing a wide jacket.

Styrkárr said: "Do you want to sell me the jacket, good fellow?"

"Not to you," he said, "you must be a Norwegian—I can tell by your speech."[8]

Then Styrkárr said: "If I am a Norwegian, what of it?"

"I would like to kill you," he said, "but as luck would have it, I have no usable weapon with me."

Styrkárr said: "If you can't kill me, let's see if I can kill you." And he took aim
with his sword and swept off his head. Then he took the jacket, put it on,
jumped on his horse, and rode down to the ships. Arnórr jarlaskald composed
the following about the last battle fought by King Haraldr and his men: (FJ 281)

151. Vítt fór Vǫlsungs heiti
       varð marglofaðr harða
       sás skaut ór Nið nýtla
       norðan herskips borði.

"Vǫlsungs heiti fór vítt; varð harða marglofaðr, sás skaut nýtla herskips borði
norðan ór Nið."

The name of the Vǫlsungr [legendary king] traveled far and wide; he was much acclaimed who so deftly steered the wooden warship southward from the River Nið
[Nidelven].

This too:

152. Myrkts (hverr meira orkar)   ǫrt gat óslætt hjarta
       mér (alls greppr né sérat)   eljunfims und himni
       (harðrs í heimi orðinn   mest hefr mildingr kostat
       hrafngrennir) (þrek jǫfnum):   minni hvers grams vinnur.

"Myrkts mér—alls greppr né sérat—hverr orkar meira jǫfnum þrek: harðr hrafn-
grennir 's orðinn í heimi. Gat ǫrt, óslætt hjarta; mildingr hefr kostat minni mest
vinnur hvers eljunfims grams und himni."

It is obscure to me—because the poet fails to see—who performs with more than
average boldness: the hardened raven feeder [warrior] has fallen in this world. He
had a fierce and brave heart; the generous king has proven the achievements of
any persevering hero beneath heaven to be far inferior [to his own].

And again:

153. Haraldr vissi sik hverjum   hefr afreka ens øfra
       harðgeðr und miðgarði   ættstýrǫndum dýrri
       (dǫglingr réð til dauða   (hnígrat hilmir frægri)
       dýrð slíkri) gram ríkra: (U 121) heilǫg fold (til moldar).

"Harðgeðr Haraldr vissi sik ríkra hverjum gram und miðgarði; dǫglingr réð slíkri
dýrð til dauða. Heilǫg fold ens øfra hefr afreka, ættstýrǫndum dýrri: hnígrat hilmir
frægri til moldar."

Hard-minded Haraldr knew himself to be mightier than any lord in the world; the
king possessed such distinction until his death. The holy land of the higher one
[God, heaven] has the hero, more splendid than other nobles: never will a more
famous king bow to the ground.

51. Óláfr Haraldsson's Return to Norway

After these great events King Haraldr's son Óláfr became commander of the
remaining army and of those who were still alive. He prepared for departure,
and leaving England behind, they put out to sea. (FJ 282) In the autumn they

sailed north to Orkney, where Óláfr spent the winter. It is told that on the same day when King Haraldr fell, his daughter María died to the west in Orkney, and people said that they shared the same life.[1] She was the wisest and fairest of women, and most loyal to her friends. The following summer Óláfr brought the whole army to Norway, as is told by the skald Steinn Herdísarson:

154. Fylkir lét en fljótu   tráðu borðvigg breiðan
       flaust es leið at hausti   brimsgang (skipa langra
       skaut í haf (þars heitir   óðr fell sær of súðir).
       Hrafnseyrr) konungr stafni: Sik beztan gram miklu.

"Fylkir lét en fljótu flaust, es leið at hausti; konungr skaut stafni í haf, þars heitir Hrafnseyrr. Borðvigg tráðu breiðan brimsgang; óðr sær fell of súðir skipa langra. Sik beztan gram miklu."

The lord went on the swift ships when autumn approached; the king set out to sea at a place called Ravenseer. The plank steeds [ships] stepped on the broad wave path [sea]; the raging sea poured over the sides of the longships. "Himself to be the foremost king."

Further:

155. Austr helt Engla þrýstir   glaðr tók herr (þás heðra
       ótvínn liði sínu   hringlestir kom vestan)
       (stóran braut of stýri   allr við oflgum stilli.
       straumsæ) konungr Rauma: Óláfr borinn sólu.

"Ótvínn Engla þrýstir, konungr Rauma, helt liði sínu austr; stóran straumsæ braut of stýri. Allr herr tók glaðr við oflgum stilli, þás hringlestir kom vestan heðra. Óláfr borinn sólu."

The undaunted conqueror of the English, the king of the Raumar [people of Romerike], steered with his army to the east; the heavy sea flow pressed against the helm. All people received the awesome king warmly when the ring wounder [generous king] arrived here from the west. "Óláfr born [beneath] the sun."

That same summer Óláfr succeeded to the throne in Norway with his brother Magnús, and they ruled together for a time before Magnús fell fatally ill. He was ill for some time before he died and was afflicted with what is called ergotism.[2] He had a son (FJ 283) whose name was Hákon and who was fostered in Guðbrandsdalir with Steigar-Þórir. Magnús had ruled over northern Norway and Óláfr over eastern Norway. After the death of King Magnús, Óláfr was sole king over Norway. In the words of Steinn:

156. Heldr (síz hári foldu   mætr hilmir verr malmi
       heiptbráðr jofurr náði)   (mank skjoldungs lof) koldum
       (ætt þreifsk Egða dróttins)   Rauma grund ok rondu.
       ólaust konungr stóli: Ríklundaðr veit undir. (U 122)

"Konungr heldr ólaust stóli, síz heiptbráðr jofurr náði hári foldu: ætt Egða dróttins þreifsk. Mætr hilmir verr Rauma grund koldum malmi ok rondu; mank skjoldungs lof. Ríklundaðr veit undir."

The king holds the throne firmly since the fierce prince took possession of the lofty land [Norway]; the family of the lord of the Egðir [people of Agder: Haraldr] has prospered. The distinguished king defends the land of the Raumar [people of Romerike] with cold steel and shield. I recall the hero's reputation. "Proud-minded knows beneath [the sun]."

Skúli, the son of Jarl Tostig Godwinson, and Ketill krókr from Hálogaland came to Norway with King Óláfr. King Óláfr arranged a good marriage for Ketill and appointed him as a district chieftain in the north. Many distinguished men are descended from Ketill. Skúli was a wise and outstanding man, very handsome and well-spoken. He became a leader in the king's retinue, addressed thingmeetings, and participated in the king's councils. He was called the king's foster father.

King Óláfr offered to give Skúli the district in Norway that suited him best, with all the revenues and land taxes that were in the king's name. Skúli thanked the king warmly for his offer but said that he had other requests: "For," he said, "if there is a new king, it may be that the grant will be revoked. I would rather receive some property near the town in which you reside, sire, and in which you celebrate Christmas."[3] The king granted that and gave him lands to the east near Konungahella, (FJ 284) Ósló, and Túnsberg, and to the north near Niðaróss. These were very nearly the best lands to be found in each of these locations, and they stayed in the possession of his descendants.[4]

The son of Skúli, named King's Foster Father, was Ásólfr, the father of Guthormr at Rein,[5] the father of Bárðr, the father of King Ingi and Skúli jarl. Not long after King Haraldr's fall, Skúli went west to England to ask for the return of King Haraldr's body. It was readily granted to him, and he returned to Norway, where he enjoyed great honor. He now lies buried at Elgisetr because it seemed fitting that he should lie in the church that he himself had constructed.[6] Archbishop Eysteinn had him delivered there to the care of the monks and made great donations. He increased the prosperity of the place greatly with the properties that he himself had donated. During the twelve months that King Haraldr and his son Óláfr were in the west, his son Magnús ruled Norway. He was a very handsome man.

52. The Death of King Harold Godwinson

After the fall of King Haraldr, Harold Godwinson hastened to the south of England with his army because the jarl of Normandy had arrived from the south with a great army and was subduing the land everywhere he went. That jarl was named William, the son of Robert Longspear. Robert was the brother of Emma, the mother of King Edward. William thought he was more in line to receive King Edward's inheritance than Harold, who had renounced his claim to the realm.

This renunciation came about in the following way. When Edward the Good (the Confessor) was king of England and childless (U 123), he sent Robert,

Archbishop of Canterbury, to his kinsman William (FJ 285) in Normandy and wanted to designate him as his successor. Another time he sent Jarl Harold Godwinson on the same mission to William. Harold was the son of Godwin and Gyða, the daughter of Þorgils. He spent some time with William, and people suggested that he had taken a liking to William's wife and that they were much enamored of each other. The jarl was suspicious because of these rumors, and they solved the matter by having Harold betrothed to William's daughter. In this way Harold escaped the suspicion that William harbored against him. In addition, Jarl Harold swore an oath to Jarl William on the reliquary of Odmarus that he would never be opposed to him.[1]

After that Jarl Harold returned to King Edward. He stayed with him and succeeded him on the throne. William therefore thought that he was going against his oath, since King Edward had given William the throne upon his death.[2]

Now the story returns to the moment when William had arrived in England from the south and was subduing the land wherever he went. It is told that before William left home, his wife went out to his horse and asked him not to do battle with King Harold Godwinson. William replied angrily and said that her motives in asking this were not good. He dug his spurs into the horse and one spur struck her in the head and killed her. People reproached him for this action. William answered: "The action is surely reprehensible, but it may be according to her deserts, for she betrayed me." He attached the reliquary of Odmarus to his standard, that same reliquary on which Harold had sworn.

King Harold and William (FJ 286) fought a great battle when they met. That took place twelve months after the fall of King Haraldr Sigurðarson, and the battle went badly for Harold.[3]

He asked: "What is attached to William's standard?"—and he was told. "It may be," said King Harold, "that there is no escape." King Harold Godwinson and his brother Gyrth fell there. William became king and eventually succumbed to illness in Normandy. He was followed on the throne by his son William Rufus, who ruled for fourteen years. He, too, died from illness. Then his brother Henry, the second son of William I, succeeded him as king.

53. The Saga of King Óláfr kyrri (the Quiet)

King Haraldr's son Óláfr was a tall man, and everyone agrees that there has never been seen a fairer man or a man of nobler appearance. He had blond hair, a light complexion, and pleasing eyes, and he was well proportioned. He was taciturn for the most part and not much of a speechmaker, although he was good company over drink. (U 124) He was good-natured toward his friends and moderate in all things.

After the fall of King Haraldr, Sveinn, the king of the Danes, considered that the peace between the Norwegians and the Danes was at an end. He took the view that it was in force only as long as the two kings lived. Armies were gathered in both realms. King Óláfr called out the militia and the naval levy as Steinn recounts:

157. Sín óðul mun Sveini   ætt sinni mun unna
      sóknstrangr í Kaupangi   Áleifr konungr hála
      (þars heilagr gramr hvílir)   (Ulfs þarfat þar arfi)
      (hanns ríkr jofurr) banna: (FJ 287) alls Nóregs (til kalla).

"Sóknstrangr í Kaupangi, þars heilagr gramr hvílir, mun banna Sveini sín óðul; hanns ríkr jofurr. Áleifr konungr mun hála unna ætt sinni alls Nóregs; Ulfs arfi þarfat þar kalla til."

The war-fierce one in Kaupangr [Nidaros], where the holy king rests, will refuse Sveinn his inherited realm; he is a mighty lord. King Óláfr [St. Óláfr] will certainly grant his kin all Norway; Ulfr's heir has no claim there.

Steinn records how King Óláfr marched through the land with troops and warships, in the following stanza:

158. Mætr hilmir ferr malmi
      (mank skjoldungs lof) koldum
      Rauma grund ok rondu.
      Ríklundaðr veit undir.

"Mætr hilmir ferr Rauma grund koldum malmi ok rondu; mank skjoldungs lof. Ríklundaðr veit undir."

The distinguished king goes through the land of the Raumir [people of Romerike] with cold steel and shield; I recall the hero's reputation. "Proud-minded knows beneath [the sun]."

And again:

159. Oll biðr Engla stillir   jorð mun eigi verða
      eggdjarfra lið seggja   auðsótt Fila dróttins
      sund fyr sínu landi   sóknherðir veit sverða
      sóknorr stika dorrum: sik beztan gram miklu.

"Sóknorr Engla stillir biðr lið eggdjarfra seggja stika dorrum oll sund fyr sínu landi. Jorð Fila dróttins mun eigi verða auðsótt; sóknherðir sverða veit sik miklu beztan gram."

The battle-brave subjugator of the English bids the bands of edge-fierce warriors enclose all inlets of his country with spears. The earth of the lord of the Filir [people of Fjaler] will not be easy to conquer; the strengthener of the swords' attack [battle, warrior] knows himself to be the foremost of kings.

And still again:

160. Veitk hvar Óláfr úti   hlaut til hafs fyr útan
      óslækinn rauð mæki   Halland konungr branda
      (deilask mér til mála   (fogr sverð ruðu fyrðar)
      minni) fyrsta sinni: fjolgóðr litat blóði. (FJ 288)

"Veitk, hvar óslækinn Óláfr rauð mæki úti fyrsta sinni: minni deilask mér til mála."

Fjǫlgóðr konungr hlaut branda litat blóði til hafs fyr útan Halland; fyrðar ruðu fǫgr sverð."

I know, where tireless Óláfr for the first time reddened the sword at sea: that memory gives me material for tales. The excellent king colored the blades in blood on the ocean off the coast of Halland; men reddened fair swords.

Further:

161. Gengu danskir drengir   sukku sárir rekkar
     (dynr varð gǫrr) með brynjur   sunnan hafs til grunna
     útanborðs til jarðar   hár varp hausum þeira
     (úrigs malms) ok hjalma: hranngarðr á þrǫm jarðar. (U 125)

"Danskir drengir gengu útanborðs til jarðar með brynjur ok hjalma; dynr úrigs malms varð gǫrr. Sárir rekkar sukku sunnan hafs til grunna; hár hranngarðr varp hausum þeira á þrǫm jarðar."

Danish warriors went overboard and sank to the bottom with byrnies and helmets; there was a din of wet steel [battle]. Wounded warriors sank to the shallows south of the sea; the tall wave enclosure [surf] threw their skulls onto the edge of the earth [shore].

162. Enn at gerva gunni   út fœrðu lið lítlu
     gramr bjósk við styr ramman   lǫng borð fyr Stað norðan
     herskildi bað halda   (tráðu túnvǫll reyðar
     hraustgeðr konungr austan: tveir dǫglingar) meira.

"Enn bjósk gramr við styr ramman at gerva gunni; hraustgeðr konungr bað halda herskildi austan. Lǫng borð fœrðu meira lið út lítlu fyr norðan Stað; tveir dǫglingar tráðu túnvǫll reyðar."

Again the lord prepared for fierce fighting in the endless war; the keen-minded king commanded the war shield to be carried from the east. The longships brought even more troops out to sea a little north of Staðr [Stad]; two nobles stepped on the farmyard of the whale [sea].

King Óláfr now sent a message to King Sveinn with conciliatory proposals. They arranged a meeting at Konungahella, as is customary between kings.[1] King Óláfr informed the king of the Danes that he wished to maintain the sort of peace that his father agreed to with the Danes, without changes. The alternative was the prospect that the Norwegians would again launch an attack, which would make the Danes feel that they had their hands full, even if King Haraldr was no longer alive. On these conditions they again made an agreement between the Danes and the Norwegians, and at the same time King Sveinn betrothed his daughter Ingiríðr to King Óláfr, so that they parted in peace. King Óláfr was given the nickname "kyrri," as Steinn says:

163. Lǫnd vill Þrœnda þengill   hugnar þjóð þats þegna
     (þat líkar vel skǫtnum)   þrályndr til friðmála
     ǫll við œrna snilli   kúgar Engla œgir.
     eggdjarfr í frið leggja: (FJ 289)   Óláfr borinn sólu.

"Eggdjarfr Þrœnda þengill vill leggja ǫll lǫnd í frið við œrna snilli: þat líkar vel skǫtnum. Þjóð hugnar, þats þrályndr Engla œgir kúgar þegna til friðmála. Óláfr borinn sólu."

With his great wisdom, the edge-keen king of the Þrœndir [people of Trøndelag] wishes to establish peace in all lands: that pleases people. Men like it, that the obstinate intimidator of the English forces people to peace talks. "Óláfr born [beneath] the sun."

This peace between the two countries remained in force for a long time.

King Óláfr and all his men now enjoyed the sort of tranquility and ease that had not been seen in Norway for many years. The land prospered greatly, became wealthy, and overflowed with plenty. A trading town was established in Norway that was more magnificent than any previous one, with the exception of the center at Niðaróss.[2] That town was called Bjǫrgvin. It soon became the seat of wealthy men, and it had the greatest contact with foreign lands. There were drinking parties and taverns to a much greater extent than before. People wore court breeches laced to the leg, and some fastened gold rings around their legs.[3]

It was an ancient custom in Norway, as in Denmark and Sweden, that where there were great royal residences and feast halls the king's high seat was on the bench that faced the sun.[4] The queen sat on the king's left, and that seat was called the "second seat." The seat that was closest to the "second seat," on both the men's and women's side, was considered the most honorable. The seat that was farthest out and closest to the door was the least honorable.

The most distinguished man, who was old and wise and titled "king's counselor," because kings had long been in the habit of keeping wise elders by their side in order to learn the old customs and ways of their ancestors—this man was to sit on the lesser bench opposite (U 126) the king, and that seat was called "the lesser second seat." From his right hand extended the women's seats and from his left the men's seats. It was the custom of chieftains to carry beer across the central hearth and drink to their opposites, and it was considered the greatest honor to be (FJ 290) pledged by the king. To show that this is the truth, we note that Arnórr jarlaskald composed the following:

164.   Hétk (þás hvern vetr sátum)
        hrafns verðgjafa jafnan
        (líð drakk gramr á góðar)
        (gagnvert) (skipa sagnir).

"Hétk hrafns verðgjafa jafnan, þás hvern vetr sátum gagnvert; gramr drakk líð á góðar skipa sagnir."

I always drank to the furnisher of the raven's food [corpses, warrior] when every winter we sat opposite each other; the chieftain toasted the worthy ship crew with wine.

King Óláfr had a daïs constructed in his banquet halls and placed his high seat at the center of the cross bench, lining up the servants and pages before him. He had a candle held before each nobleman who sat at his table. He had servants stand by as many can*dles as* there were noblemen. He had marshal's seats erected and assigned his marshals and counselors to them. King Óláfr took one hundred *men into his service, and they* were his retainers. The old laws prescribed that the king should have sixty retainers. He also had sixty "guests," whereas earlier kings had had thirty, and sixty other men at table who were beneficiaries of his hospitality but were not in his official retinue. They were held in less esteem. They carried out all the tasks that the king or his stewards required and made purchases, and they were obligated to perform the king's work.

The farmers asked the king why he maintained a larger retinue than previous kings had, but he replied to the effect that he was so much less forceful than his father that he could not maintain peace and rule the kingdom better with two hundred men than King Haraldr could with ninety or a hundred. King Óláfr spent a long time to the east in Ranríki (Bohuslän), on a rich estate called Haukstaðir. He married his sister Ingigerðr to Óláfr, the son of the Danish king Sveinn. Óláfr reigned in Denmark after his brother Saint Knútr.[5] (FJ 291)

King Óláfr had a son by his concubine Þóra, the daughter of Árni lági. His name was Magnús, nicknamed Magnús berfœttr (Bareleg),[6] and during his lifetime some people called him Styrjaldar (Battle-Age)–Magnús. He was a most handsome man in appearance, not taking into account his father Óláfr, and a very tall man. The height of the three kinsmen King Haraldr, King Óláfr, and King Magnús berfœttr was marked on Saint Mary's Church, which King Haraldr had built north in Kaupangr.[7] A cross was chiseled on the stone wall by the door high enough for King Haraldr to kiss, a second one for King Óláfr, and a third for King Magnús, which was much the lowest, but the distance was equal between them. King Magnús was a very courtly man. (U 127)

In the days of King Óláfr there were good harvests in Norway and great abundance.[8] From the time of King Haraldr hárfagri there had never been such plenty in the lifetime of any king, or such peace and contentment. King Óláfr was lenient with respect to many matters that his father King Haraldr had initiated aggressively and pursued in the same spirit. He was generous with gold and silver, precious objects and treasures, but he kept a firm grip on the realm. His wisdom was chiefly responsible for this, and his knowledge of what was right and proper for royalty. Many good and kingly works are credited to him. He built a stone church in the bishopric of Niðaróss over the body of his kinsman Saint Óláfr and completed the construction. That is indicative of his goodness and his devotion to the people.

These qualities may also be seen in the words that he spoke one day at the Great Guild.[9] He was cheerful and in good spirits, and people were moved to say: "Sire, it is a joy to us to see that you are in such high spirits." He replied: "I can indeed be cheerful when I see (FJ 292) my people in freedom and happiness and when I sit in a company dedicated to my kinsman Saint Óláfr. In the days of my father this people was in great fear and trembling, and many hid their gold and treasures, but now I see what you possess shining on you, and your freedom is my joy." There was such a peace during his reign that it secured his people and himself abroad as well. Notwithstanding, his rule inspired great dread, although he himself was amenable and accommodating, as the skald remarked:

> 165.   Varði ógnarorðum
>   Áleifr ok friðmálum
>   jǫrð svát engi þorði
>   allvalda til kalla.

"Áleifr varði jǫrð ógnarorðum ok friðmálum, svát engi allvalda þorði kalla til."

Óláfr defended his territory with words of threat and truces, so that no king dared to lay claim to it.

During his reign there was a change of kings in Denmark, and King Óláfr was a great friend of the Danish king Knútr. He set out to confer with him, and they met to the east at the Elfr (Götaälv), where it had been customary to convene the meetings of kings. King Knútr broached the plan of campaigning west in England, considering what they had to avenge there, first and foremost King Óláfr but the Danish king as well. "Now choose," he said, "whether you want me to give you sixty ships so that you can lead the enterprise or whether I should be the leader and you should give me sixty ships."

King Óláfr replied: "King Knútr," he said, "the matter you bring up is to my liking, but we two have differing qualifications. You and your kinsmen, such as Knútr the Great, have had the good fortune to win England with honor and great success, and that success may run in your family. But when my father King Haraldr (U 128) went west on such a mission, he lost his life. He set out with the flower of Norway and (FJ 293) an army that has never been matched in our country. And at the behest of a leader such as King Haraldr was, both in wisdom and good fortune, the expedition was splendidly prepared in every respect. And yet it turned out as you well know. Now I can judge my own lack of prowess and see how little capable I am of leading this expedition. For that reason I will choose you for the task and let you set out with my support."[10]

Then he gave King Knútr sixty large ships splendidly equipped and with reliable crews. He had them commanded by his leaders and district chieftains. It is reported that he had made a grand contribution with such a force, and it is told in the saga of King Knútr[11] that the Norwegians were the only ones not to abandon the naval rendezvous ahead of time. But the Danes fled. The king gave the Norwegians great credit for this and granted them permission to trade wherever they wished. He sent the Norwegian king precious gifts in return for his support, but he signaled his wrath toward the Danes with fines.

54. Concerning King Óláfr and the Kráku-karl (Crow Man)

It happened once, when King Óláfr's men had collected the king's land taxes, that the king asked where they had received the best hospitality. They told of a particular district that seemed to them to take pride of place. The king asked: "What was it that seemed better about this place than other places?"

"Sire," they said, "there is an old farmer there who is wonderfully knowledgeable. We asked him about many things, and he knew the answers. It was a great delight to talk with him. We imagine that he can even understand the speech of birds."

The king replied: "That is great nonsense, and I don't believe a word of it."

One time when the king was sailing along the coast (FJ 294) past some narrows, he asked what the local settlement was. They answered: "Sire, this is the district in which we told you we were so well received."

The king asked: "What house is this that stands up above the narrows?"

They answered: "That house belongs to the wise man we told you about." Then they saw a horse by the house.

The king said: "Go and kill the horse."

They answered: "We wish to do him no harm, because he does not deserve that from us."

"It is up to me to decide the matter," said the king. "Chop off the horse's head and make sure that no blood falls on the ground. Then bring the head out to the ship and go after the farmer. Do not tell him what you have done to the horse, and it will cost you your lives if you disobey me. Tell the fellow that I wish to meet him."

Then they went ashore and did as the king had instructed them. They gave the man his message (U 129), and he went to meet him. The king asked the farmer: "Who owns the land that you live on?"

He answered: "You own it, sire, and you collect the rent."

The king said: "Show us the route along the coast, because you are probably familiar with it."

He did so, and as they rowed, a crow flew by the ship and cawed ominously. The farmer looked in its direction, and the king asked: "Do you make anything of this cawing?"

"It's not usual," said the farmer.

At that moment another crow flew over the ship and screamed. Then the farmer stopped rowing, and the oar lay loose in his hand. The king said: "You seemed to be paying a lot of attention to what this crow is saying."

The farmer replied: "Sire, I am now beginning to get the meaning."

Then a crow flew by for the third time, with a terrible din, and brushed by the boat as it flew. The farmer stood and faced it, and it screamed directly at him. The farmer paid his rowing no heed.

The king asked: "What does it say now, farmer?" (FJ 295)

He replied: "I am not likely to know."

"Tell us now," said the king.

The farmer replied:

166.   Segr vetrgǫmul   veit ekki sú
       ok tvévetr segr   trúik eigi at heldr

en þrévetr segr   þykkira mér glíkligt
kveðr mik róa   á merar hǫfði
en þik konungr   þjóf míns fíar.

The one-year old [crow] says—it doesn't know—and the two-year old says—I
don't believe it either—but the three-year old says—it seems unlikely to me—:
it claims I'm rocking on a mare's head, and that you, king, are the thief of my
property.

The king exclaimed: "What now, farmer! Are you calling me a thief? That is
no way to address me."

"It is true, sire," said the farmer, "that it is not proper, but it looks as though
you have played some trick on me."

"That is the truth, farmer, and I did it to amuse myself, but I will give you a
reward." He gave him good gifts and forgave the land taxes for the land he
lived on. With that they parted, and the farmer went home.[1] There are many
examples reported on how generous King Óláfr was in his gifts of money. He
also bestowed all sorts of treasures, as the skald Steinn mentions:

167. Gefr ættstuðill jǫfra   þjóð nýtr Óláfs auðar
      ǫrr ok steinda knǫrru   annarr konungr mǫnnum
      (hann vill hnøggvi sinnar)   séðu hverr slíkt fé reiðir.
      hábrynjuð skip (synja):   Sik beztan gram miklu. (U 130)

"Ǫrr ættstuðill jǫfra gefr hábrynjuð skip ok steinda knǫrru: hann vill synja
hnøggvi sinnar. Þjóð nýtr Óláfs auðar; séðu, hverr annarr konungr reiðir slíkt fé
mǫnnum. Sik beztan gram miklu."

The liberal pillar of royal lineage gives out armored warships and painted mer-
chantmen: he wishes to repudiate his parsimony. People enjoy Óláfr's wealth; look,
what other king gives men such gifts! "Himself to be the foremost."

And again: (FJ 296)

168. Herþengill gleðr hringum   Norðmǫnnum gefr nenninn
      hoddǫrr (sás rýðr odda)   Nóregs konungr stórum
      bekksagnir (lætr bragna   ǫrr es Engla þverrir.
      bragningr gjǫfum fagna):   Óláfr borinn sólu.

"Hoddǫrr herþengill, sás rýðr odda, gleðr bekksagnir hringum; bragningr lætr
bragna fagna gjǫfum. Nenninn Nóregs konungr gefr Norðmǫnnum stórum; ǫrr es
Engla þverrir. Óláfr borinn sólu."

The treasure-generous war leader, who reddens spears, gladdens his retinue with
rings; the king lets his companions enjoy the gifts. The crafty king of Norway rewards the Norwegians lavishly; the diminisher of the English is open-handed.
"Óláfr born [beneath] the sun."

169. Hilmir gefr ok hjalma   dyggr lætr þungar þiggja
      (hirð) (svát enskis virðir)   þengill af sér drengi
      (konungs prýða þau klæði)   (vás launar svá vísi
      kynstórr firum brynjur: verðung) Háars gerðar.

"Kynstórr hilmir gefr firum brynjur ok hjalma, svát enskis virðir; þau klæði prýða hirð konungs. Dyggr þengill lætr drengi þiggja af sér þungar Háars gerðar: svá launar vísi verðung vás."

The high-born hero gives men byrnies and helmets unguardedly; those clothes adorn the king's retinue. The reliable lord let his men receive from him the heavy garments of Hárr [Óðinn, armor]: thus the king rewards his retainers for hardship.

170. Óláfr gefr (svát jǫfra   grams es heiðum himni
     alls engi má snjallra)   (hanns fremstr konungmanna)
     hǫggvit goll til hylli   (spyr hverr glíkt mun gerva)
     hildinga konr mildi: gjǫflund borin undir.

"Óláfr, mildi hildinga konr, gefr hǫggvit goll til hylli, svát alls engi snjallra jǫfra má. Gjǫflund grams es borin undir heiðum himni; hanns fremstr konungmanna; spyr, hverr glíkt mun gerva!"

Óláfr, the bountiful kinsman of kings, bestows cleft gold as commendation, as no other undaunted king can. The lord's generosity is famous beneath the clear sky; he is the foremost of kings; just ask, who else could match his behavior!

King Óláfr became mortally ill to the east in Vík at Haukstaðir.[2] His body was moved north to Þrándheimr and buried in Christ Church. He had reigned over Norway for twenty-seven years when he died. (FJ 297)

55. The Saga of King Magnús berfœttr

Two kings were now installed in Norway. Magnús, the son of King Óláfr, ruled in the east, but the Þrœndir took as their king Hákon, the son of Magnús and grandson of Haraldr. Hákon had originally been fostered by Sveinki Steinarsson to the east in Vík, and later by Steigar-Þórir. He was called Hákon "Foster Son to Þórir," and was very popular with the farmers. King Hákon had traveled to Permia and campaigned there victoriously.[1] He did much to improve the rights of the Þrœndir, and they were his most eager supporters.

King Magnús stayed in the east in Vík for a long time. Each king had his own district chieftains, and their supporters contested a number of things with one another. But the kings were at peace and were rarely in the same place. One winter they were both in Niðaróss. Magnús stayed in the royal residence and Hákon stayed in Skúlagarðr below Saint Clement's Church.[2] Hákon celebrated Christmas there, and on that Christmas he forgave the farmers their Christmas contributions and all their land taxes in Þrándheimr.[3] He made this provision for the Þrœndir but also for all the Upplendingar in the east who accepted him as king, and he improved the lot of the farmers in many ways in return for their acknowledging his royal title.[4] (U 131)

For this reason King Magnús became angered, since he thought he was getting less land and revenue than his father and uncle had had. He thought that his property was being given away, no less than Hákon's, to benefit the recipients. In this respect he thought he was being dishonored and mistreated by his kinsman in consultation with Steigar-Þórir. On the other hand, King Hákon and Þórir were very apprehensive about how King Magnús would react because he maintained seven longships throughout the winter in ice-free water by the town. (FJ 298)

In the spring around Candlemas he sailed away in the dark of night with the ship awnings in place and concealed lights.[5] He sailed to Hefring (Høvringen) and stayed there during the night.[6] They built great fires up on the land, and that made Hákon and his retainers in the town fear that treachery was afoot. He had trumpets sounded for an assembly at Eyrar, and all the townsmen gathered and remained there during the night.

In the morning when the sun came up and King Magnús saw the townsmen on Eyrar, he sailed out of the fjord and south to the legislative district of Gulaþingslǫg. King Hákon thanked the men for the assistance they had lent him. Then he set out east to Vík, but first he convened an assembly in the town. The king sat on his horse at the assembly and spoke: "Everyone who can hear me should be assured that if I return to this town, I will reward each according to his birth and service. I promise all the townsmen my friendship. But I have some suspicions about the intentions of my kinsman King Magnús and am not certain how things will turn out." In return, everyone promised his friendship if it were needed, and all the people followed him out to Steinbjǫrg and he headed into the mountains.[7] It is reported that one day he pursued a ptarmigan for a long time, and it kept flying out of reach. During this ride he became ill, and that illness was fatal. He died there in the mountains.

Two weeks later they returned to the town with his body. They went out to meet his body and wept, for almost everyone loved him dearly. His body was buried at Christ Church. The two kinsmen had ruled the land for not all of two years when King Hákon died. After his death, the Þrœndir took Sveinn, the son of Haraldr flettir (Despoiler), as their king. Many men accepted this counsel, but the leader was (FJ 299) Steigar-Þórir, together with Egill Áskelsson.[8] Skjálgr of Jaðarr and most of the Þrœndir agreed and prepared to defend their land against King Magnús, as Þorkell hamarskald indicates: (U 132)

171. Vítt dró sínar sveitir   snǫrp frák á (þvís urpu)
       saman stórhugaðr Þórir   endr Skjalgs vinum (lendir
       (heldr várut þau hǫlðum   menn við morðvals brynni)
       haglig ráð) með Agli: mein (of afl sér steini).

"Stórhugaðr Þórir dró vítt saman sínar sveitir með Agli; þau ráð várut hǫlðum heldr haglig. Frák endr snǫrp mein Skjalgs vinum á því, 's lendir menn urpu steini of afl sér við morðvals brynni."

With Egill, ambitious Þórir gathered his troops far and wide; those preparations were not quite comfortable for the men. I heard that Skjalgr's friends formerly received great harm when the district chieftains lifted too heavy a stone against the feeder of the strife falcon [bird of prey, warrior: Magnús].

Þórir overran both Norðmœrr and Sunnmœrr and large areas around Þrándheimr, killing some and plundering others who did not want to submit and wreaking havoc far and wide. When King Magnús learned of this, he gathered troops and ships. Then he traveled north against Þórir and his followers with a great host. Gísl Illugason, who was then with the king, spoke as follows:[9]

172. Ungr framði sik   þars alendr vildu
       lofsælan gram   landi ræna
       imðar faxa   en jǫfurr sótti
       Báleygs viðu   með blám hjǫrvi.

The youth excelled when the feeders of the giantess's steed [wolf, warriors] wished to rob the famous lord of his land; but the king attacked Báleygr's [Óðinn] trees [warriors] with the black sword.

In the following stanza he notes that King Magnús set out against them with his army from the east in Ósló: (FJ 300)

173. Ýtti ór Ósló   til Egils fundar
       lofðungr liði   lands at krefja:
       fylgðu ræsi   ok Rygir sunnan
       linns láðgefendr   ór lǫgum tvennum.

The king set out with his men from Ósló [Oslo] to meet with Egill and reclaim his country; dispensers of the snake's land [gold, high-born men] from two law districts as well as the Rygir [people from Rogaland] accompanied the lord from the south.

And again:

174. Séa knátti þá   siklings flota
       vel vígligan   ok vanan sigri:
       es fyr Yrjar   í aga miklum
       óþrotligt lið   árar kníði.

Then one could see the king's fleet, war-equipped and wont to conquer: when the indefatigable crew smote the oars in heavy seas off the coast of Yrjar [Ørland].

King Magnús and his men went ashore inside Ǫrvahamrar and the king convened an assembly.[10] He told the men at the assembly that an army was marching against them, harrying as it went in his own realm. He said that they had taken a leader who was not born to the title in Norway.[11] He urged his men to rid themselves of this rabble, and wherever people had submitted to them he urged them to waste with fire (U 133) and kill whomever they could:

What greater shame and dishonor could be inflicted on a king whose birth entitles him to rule than what they have done to me? They have taken a man of no royal birth and poor lineage to rule. That is the sort of man he is. As long as our kinsman Hákon was alive, there was some excuse for their giving him the power to rule, and we let that pass, but this is dishonorable. I do not deserve the title of king

(FJ 301) if I do not block this aggression, and I will not much resemble my kinsmen. *You* would do well to assist me in this, and all just and right-minded men
will approve it.

Everyone applauded the king's speech. Thus *says Gísl Illugason*:
175.   Átti hilmir   húsþing við sæ
       þat vas fyr innan   Qrvahamra:
       bjósk at brenna   en búendr flýðu
       stórráðr konungr   af Staði útan.

The lord convened an assembly by the sea; that was on the inner side of Qrvahamrar; the imperious king proposed to waste the land with fire, and the farmers
fled out from Staðr [Stadsbygd].

176.   Hyrr sveimaði   hallir þurru
       gekk hár logi   of heruð þeira:
       séa knátti þar   es salir fellu
       landráð konungs   of liði Þóris.

Fire spread, halls crumbled; the high flame rushed through their counties; there
one could see the king's justice as houses collapsed around Þórir's crew.

   When King Magnús made the preparations described here and carried out
such retaliations against them, Haraldr [*recte* Sveinn] [12] and his men learned of
it and withdrew to the north. In the words of Gísl:
177.   Raufsk við róstu   rymr varð í her
       helmingr Egils   við Hlaðir útan:
       máttut hersar   við Haða dróttni
       láðgǫfguðum   landi ráða. (FJ 302)

Egill's army scattered in the skirmish out by Hlaðir [Lade]; the noise of battle resounded throughout the army; the nobles could not hold the country against the
land-endowed lord of the Haðir [people of Hadeland].

   We are told that before King Magnús marched against them, he sent Sigurðr
ullstrengr and many other of his friends against Þórir [Steigar-Þórir]. [13] They
cut up the levy arrow and sent it around the country to gather troops against
Þórir. All the troops assembled at Vigg (Viggja).

   Þórir and Sveinn learned of that and marched their troops against Sigurðr
and his men, saying that they would not yield before King Magnús's chieftains.
Þórir and his followers did battle against Sigurðr, with great loss of life. They
were able to board his ships and had the upper hand that time, inflicting heavy
casualties. But Sigurðr ullstrengr managed to escape and return to King Magnús. Þórir and his men proceeded to the town and turned their fleet in the fjord.
When they were ready to sail out of the fjord, they anchored at Hefring. (U 134)

   King Magnús then arrived at the mouth of the fjord with a large force. Þórir
and his men immediately moved their ships across to the Vagnvík (Vanvikan)
shore. [14] They abandoned their ships and went down into Þexdalr (Teksdal) to
Seljuhverfi (Jøssund sogn, Sørtrøndelag). Þórir was carried across the moun-

tains on a stretcher because he was decrepit with age at the time of these events. Then they located and gathered ships. Þórir owned his own ship, which was large and well built. They set sail north to Hálogaland.

But King Magnús pursued them northward and caught up with them in the Harmr fjord (Velfjorden).[15] There they caught sight of each other. King Magnús had much the larger force. Þórir and his men made for land at Seljutún, thinking that they had reached the mainland. But it was an island called Vambahólmr (Vomma near Tjøtta).[16] Before King Magnús attacked them, Þórir's men proclaimed: "Where has a better ship been seen? Presumably no fairer ship has been constructed since Ormr enn langi (The Long Serpent) was built.[17] This ship is also manned by valiant fellows, from whom a stout defense can be expected."

But when King Magnús's forces attacked them, Þórir's men proved to be worthless, and they fled from him. Then Þórir said: "It may be that our (FJ 303) ship is no less well manned than Ormr enn langi, but I think more men fell in that encounter and more men flee in this one."[18] In that he was close to the mark, because it got to the point where, of the whole force, only two remained on the ship, Þórir and Egill.

Then Þórir said to Egill: "Flee, kinsman. It would be a great pity to lose you, considering what an excellent and valiant man you are."

He replied: "You don't have too numerous a company with you if I alone stand by you, and I doubt that your daughter would suspect me of abandoning you."

Now they realized that they had come to shore at a place encircled by water and that they had missed the mainland, but there was nothing to be done. Sveinn Haraldsson got by King Magnús with a single ship, but all the rest of the troops fled, though large numbers surrendered to the king.

When the ships closed, and before Þórir was captured, Sigurðr ullstrengr called out to him: "How is your health, Þórir?"

He replied: "Hale of hand, but halt of foot." The following stanza was composed:

178. Spurði Ullstrengr orði   lundr kvazk heill at hǫndum
      (at renndusk skip hvatla)   hjǫrs (frágum þat gǫrva)
      (sverð bitu snarpa fyrða   (gerðisk glamm á borði
      slætt) hvé Þórir mætti: grjóts) en hrumr at fótum.

"Ullstrengr spurði orði, hvé Þórir mætti; skip renndusk at hvatla; sverð bitu snarpa fyrða slætt. Lundr hjǫrs kvazk heill at hǫndum en hrumr at fótum; frágum þat gǫrva; glamm grjóts gerðisk á borði."

Ullstrengr asked how Þórir was faring; the ships closed quickly; the swords bit keen warriors bluntly. The wood of the sword [warrior] said he was hale of hand but halt of foot; I certainly heard that; the crash of stones resounded against the ship side.

Now Þórir and Egill were captured. Sigurðr said: "You are a fat catch, Þórir."

"My food and drink account for that," said Þórir.

Then Þórir was led up onto the land, and with him Egill of Forland, who was a very fine (U 135) gentleman (FJ 304) and the most valiant of men. There on Vambahólmr a gallows was erected, and when Þórir saw the gallows and death staring him in the face with only two of them remaining, he said grinning:

179.   Várum félagar fjórir
         forðum (einn við stýri).

Formerly we were four companions, one at the helm.

People who had suffered a lot of injury from Þórir said many harsh words to him. Some had had their cattle slaughtered, some their houses burned, some had had their friends and kinsmen plundered. We are told that when Þórir was led to the gallows and stumbled to one side or the other because he was unsure on his feet, Viðkunnr Jónsson said: "Hard astarboard, Þórir," he said, "hard aport." [19] Viðkunnr said this because Þórir had burned his farm on Bjarkey (Bjarkøy) and a good ship that he owned. When the ship was in flames, Þórir had said: "Steer more to starboard, Viðkunnr, more to port." Viðkunnr had fled with his father Jón. About this burning the following was recited:

180.   Breðr í Bjarkey miðri   Jóan mun eigi frýja
         ból (þats ek veit gólast)   elds né ráns es kveldar
         téra þarft af Þóri   (svíðr bjartr logi breiðan
         (þýtr vandar bǫl) standa: bý) (leggr reyk til skýja).

"Ból, þats ek veit gólast, breðr í Bjarkey miðri; téra þarft standa af Þóri; þýtr vandar bǫl. Jóan mun eigi frýja elds né ráns, es kveldar; bjartr logi svíðr breiðan bý; leggr reyk til skýja."

The farm that I find the best burns in the middle of Bjarkey [Bjarkøy]; nothing good will be gained from Þórir; the harm of the twig [fire] roars. At eventide, Jóan will not have to complain about a lack of fire or plunder; the bright flame scorches the broad farmstead; smoke swirls toward the clouds.

When Þórir was led under the gallows, he said: "Ill counsels, ill outcomes." And when the crossbeam was raised and the noose was around Þórir's neck, he was so heavy that his neck was severed, and that is the way he ended his life.

Then Egill was led to the gallows, where the king's thralls were to hang him. Egill said to the thralls (FJ 305): "Your hanging me does not mean that there is a single one of you who does not deserve it more." In the words of Þorkell hamarskald:

181.   Orð frák Agli verða   hvern þeira kvað hæra
         unnar dags á munni   (hjaldrbliks) an sik miklu
         Sól við siklings þræla   (beið ofmikit eyðir
         satt einarðar latta: angr) makligra at hanga.

"Unnar dags Sól, frák satt orð verða Agli á munni við siklings þræla, einarðar latta. Kvað hvern þeira miklu makligra at hanga hæra an sik; hjaldrbliks eyðir beið ofmikit angr."

Sól [goddess] of the wave's light [gold, woman], I heard that a word of truth was spoken by Egill to the king's treacherous slaves. He said each of them by right should hang higher than he himself; the destroyer of the battle flame [sword, warrior] suffered too terrible an injury.

Then Egill said: "I imagine that people are looking forward to watching me dance on the gallows today." He was dressed in a particolored tunic.

The answer he got was: "Don't you think you can control how you will face death?"

"You will see how well I can control it," he said (U 136).

Then a noose was put around his neck, and when he was raised, he pressed one foot against the other and never moved. And there he died.[20]

Everyone grieved that such an excellent man should perish in this way. King Magnús sat nearby as they were hanged, and he was so angry that none of his men had the courage to ask for the life of either Þórir or Egill. As Egill hung there, King Magnús said: "Your friends were no help to you in your need." That suggested to people that the king would have liked to be asked for Egill's life.

After these events King Magnús went back to Þrándheimr and inflicted penalties on many men, but they threw themselves on his mercy, as Gísl says:

182.   Sættisk síðan   siðr batnaði
         hugfullr konungr   við hatendr sína:
         þann gaf brǫgnum (FJ 306)   es búendr áttu
         rétt ráðspakir   rœkðum launa.

Then the courageous king got reconciled with his enemies; conditions improved; he gave men those privileges which the resourceful farmers were to repay with loyalty.

183.   Gramr vann gǫrvan   en glatat þjófum
         kaupmǫnnum frið   þanns konungr bœtti:
         svát í elfi   øxum hlýddi
         flaust fagrbúin   í fjǫru skorða.

The peace for merchants, which the king had improved, he now completed, and he executed thieves, so that with axes one could buttress the splendidly equipped ships on the shores of the river.

Sveinn Haraldsson fled south to Denmark. He remained there until he became reconciled with King Eysteinn Magnússon. King Eysteinn made him an officer of the court and treated him with kindness and affection. After the events that have been related here, King Magnús was sole ruler of Norway.

56. Concerning King Magnús and Sveinki Steinarsson

After the death of Steigar-Þórir all the great men surrendered themselves to King Magnús's discretion. There was a man named Sveinki, the son of Steinarr. He lived in the east by the Elfr (Götaälv) and was a very tough and powerful man. He had not yet surrendered to King Magnús because he was very devoted to King Hákon and had a difficult time getting his mind off his death.

King Magnús summoned Sigurðr ullstrengr and said that he wanted to send him east to Vík to remove Sveinki from the king's lands: "He has not yet

submitted to us or accorded us any honor, and I wish that (FJ 307) all chieftains in my realm should be submissive to me, or else leave their lands. There
are other chieftains to the east in Vík (U 137), Sveinn bryggjufótr, Dagr Eilífsson, and Kolbeinn klakka. They will act for me and give you the support you
need in serving law and justice."

Sigurðr said: "I didn't expect to hear of any chieftain in Norway, apart from
us, against whom it would be necessary to marshal three other chieftains."

The king replied: "I would not resort to this, Sigurðr ullstrengr, unless it
were necessary."

Now Sigurðr prepared to set sail and took one ship east to Vík. There he
summoned the district chieftains and then convened a thingmeeting in Vík, to
which the men from the region around the Elfr were also summoned. There
was a very numerous attendance, and the district chieftains who were previously mentioned also joined Sigurðr. They told him that Sveinki would prove
to be a handful because he had a great deal of authority and support. They
advised him to use gentle words in approaching him, saying that it was only fitting to proceed diplomatically in bringing his instructions before such a powerful man.

Sigurðr said that Sveinki was indeed powerful if the three of them, with his
own assistance, could not make justice prevail against him. He said that it
would not seem unreasonable to raise this matter. They answered, saying that
they certainly wished to support the king's claim as presented to Sigurðr, but
they said that Sveinki would prove to be a mighty man.

Sveinki let people wait for a time. Then a company of men was sighted, and
it looked like gleaming ice because they were so well equipped with weapons
and chain mail.[1] Sveinki and his men arrived at the thingmeeting and sat in a
circle, five hundred strong.

Now Sigurðr rose and delivered the king's message, saying: "King Magnús
sends God's greeting and his own to God's friends and his, particularly to all
the district chieftains and the leading landholders, and beyond that to all
the people. (FJ 308) He sends fair words and promises of friendship to all who
will acknowledge him. You will have learned that the king has cleansed the
land of the bandits who have caused great injury to the farmers of this country. Would that God might put an end to the arrogance of those who have gone
to the unheard-of length of setting up a chieftain, not privileged by birth to
rule, against King Magnús.[2] That attempt concluded as might be expected,
and now the king wishes to show kindness to all men who agree to serve him.
He is prepared to lead and defend all Norwegians, great and small. In exchange he wishes to have good service and fitting obedience from his countrymen. It is clear that his words should be well received by all, considering the
great good he is able to do you. This is the good treatment he wishes to accord
everyone who makes himself worthy of it."

Then a man from the Elfr rose. He was tall and powerfully built. He wore a fur cloak, had a cudgel on his shoulder, and a broad Danish hood on his head. That man began to speak: "'There's no lack of an oar-handle,' (U 138) said the fox, and dragged the shell along the ice."[3] He then sat down and said not another word.

After a while Sigurðr got up and began to speak: "There is little discernment or appreciation of the king's words among the men of Elfr, and not much demonstration of friendship. That is up to each individual, but to make the king's message clearer, he requires his proper land taxes from the leaders as well as the lesser men, and he requires the naval contributions to which the district chieftains are obligated and the other honors that you are obligated to show his deputies. Now every man should reflect on how he has conducted himself, whether he has chosen out of respect for himself to consider what is fitting and whether he should not give the king the benefit of the law if he has previously been wanting in this regard. He should also bear in mind (FJ 309) what happened to those who opposed the king a short time ago." Then he sat down.

The same man as before rose, threw back the hood a bit and said: "'There's a whiff of snow, lads,' said the Lapps. They had snowshoes for sale."[4] Then he sat down.

A bit later Sigurðr got up, after consulting with the district chieftains and deciding that it was no longer necessary to honeycoat the king's frank message. But they urged him to phrase it diplomatically, saying that the man would prove to be overbearing, as can happen under such circumstances. Sigurðr said that he would put it off no longer. He got up in high dudgeon, threw off a dark cloak that he was wearing, and was dressed in a fine tunic. He said: "Now everyone should save himself. There is no longer any need to disguise matters or manicure my words. It is now evident in what esteem we are held. That can be endured, but it is worse that the king is given a disgraceful reply. However, it is true, as they say, that everyone knows his own worth. There is a man named Sveinki Steinarsson who lives to the east by the Elfr and has long usurped the king's taxes. He covers himself with a large following and great pomp, but I think it likely that the king will want to maintain his authority. The king now wishes to have justice and his own property, and the alternative for Sveinki is to be banished. We are not going to be intimidated by taunts or reply to them, and he will find his equal even if he has no respect for our words. But it would be better for him to mend his words now than later, and not to wait for the humiliation that will follow on his obstinacy."

Then Sveinki rose, threw the hood back, and spoke: "What shameful dogs," he said. "The foxes have fouled our wells. Hear the outrage! What right do you have, sleeveless man (FJ 310) with no coattails, to order me from my land? Two other men, who are related to you, were sent on this mission. One was named Sigurðr ullband (Woolly Yarn) and the other Gilli bakrauf (Arsecleft)—a worse name than most.[5] Wherever they went, they spent one night and thieved.

How dare you banish us? (U 139) You weren't so high and mighty as long as my foster son King Hákon was alive, since you were as timid as a mouse in a trap when you crossed his path. You skulked under cover like a dog on a boat. You were downtrodden like grain in a sack. You were as nervous as a gelded plow ox in the mating pen. You had as much breathing space as an otter in a weir. Look here, you can thank your lucky stars if you escape with your life. Up, men, and let's have at them!"

The only recourse that Sveinn bryggjufótr and the other district chieftains could find was to get Sigurðr on a horse and let him ride into the forest with one other man.[6] The thingmeeting was concluded and Sveinki returned to his estates.

Sigurðr escaped north to Þrándheimr in a sorry frame of mind. He made his way overland with one man and arrived in the presence of King Magnús. He told him what had happened. The king said: "I see that you needed the help of a few of my district chieftains." Sigurðr said that he had never been on such a mission. He said that he was angry and eager to take revenge at any cost, if that were possible, and he incited the king strenuously.

The king said: "The chieftains are too puffed up if they take no account of what is due the king. That was never to their advantage in this country, beginning in the days of Saint Óláfr with respect to his dealings with Erlingr Skjálgsson[7] or when Einarr þambarskelfir wanted to compete in power with my kinsman King Haraldr. It turned out the same way for Steigar-Þórir and Egill. Now these men do not know how to moderate themselves, and it must be said that Sveinki is no less arrogant than he is powerful if he wishes to contend with me." (FJ 311)

The king now readied five ships and sailed south along the coast and east to Vík. There he was officially entertained by his district chieftains and told them that he intended to seek out Sveinki, saying that he alone wished to be king of Norway and that he did not wish the district chieftains to be so obstreperous that his own men should come acropper, as Sigurðr had. They told the king that the man was both powerful and contentious and had an enormous quantity of arms and men.

Now the king and his men left Vík together with the district chieftains Sveinn bryggjufótr, Dagr, and Kolbeinn klakka. They proceeded until they came to Sveinki's residence. Then the district chieftains requested of the king that they be allowed to inquire into the situation, and they went ashore from the ships. They had a suspicion that the woods would be full of armed men. The king told them to do as they pleased but said that he was prepared to launch an attack against the farmers if they did not act with restraint.

When they had disembarked from the ships, they saw Sveinki headed toward them. He had come from his residence with a host of men, and they were well armed. The district chieftains (U 140) raised a white shield, and when Sveinki saw that, he brought his men to a halt.[8] They then met, and Kolbeinn said:

"King Magnús sends you greetings and urges you to be attentive to your own honor and the high office of the king. You should not expect hostilities or make ready to do battle against the king. We wish to offer mediation between you. You are much too wise a man to wish to arm yourself against your duly elected king, whose birth entitles him to the throne, without studying the situation. Such action has never profited anyone."

Sveinki brought his troops to a halt and said that he would not open hostilities against the king. He said that he would wait where he was: "We marched out toward you only to prevent our fields from being trodden down and to counter an attack." They now returned to the king and said that peace and good will could be expected from Sveinki. (FJ 312) They said that his case was entirely in the king's hands.

"It also serves your honor," they said, "to give him the best possible treatment, but he leaves the matter to your judgment."

"My judgment can be arrived at quickly," said the king. "He is to go into exile and never return as long as I rule Norway. And all his property is forfeit."

Kolbeinn said: "Would it not be more honorable, sire, and more to the credit of your reputation, to exile him but allow him to take up residence with prominent men as his wealth enables him? For if we take his lands, he will never return. This would be a fine gesture on your part. Consider the matter, and take your own honor and position into account, along with our words."

The king said: "Let him depart immediately."

Then they met with Sveinki and reported kind words from the king but also that he requested him to leave the country. He should do it to honor the king and compensate for what he had done. "That will enhance both your reputations," they said, "and he will provide an honorable settlement of property. We wish you to consider this."

Then Sveinki replied: "There has been a great change if the king addresses me in peace and decency. But why would I abandon my lands and property? Consider the following," he said: "It is better to fall on one's land than to abandon one's inheritance. Tell the king that Sveinki will not flee so much as a bowshot."

Kolbeinn replied: "That is not a good course, and it is better to acknowledge the honor of an excellent chieftain than to quarrel with so much at stake. An excellent man gets on well wherever he lives, and you will be most honored where men are most powerful, and at the same time retain your property in the face of such a powerful chieftain as the king. Heed our request and consider our long relationship as foster brothers and our perfect friendship. Heed the words of those who are friends to both parties, and listen to our solemn promises. We offer to administer and maintain your property (FJ 313), and we will hold it faithfully in trust. In addition, if you return to your lands as we expect, you will never pay taxes, unless voluntarily. We will stake (U 141) our lives and resources in the interest of arranging this with the king. Do not dismiss this offer, and release men, who are only motivated by good will, from their quandary."

Sveinki was silent for a time. Then he spoke: "You are pursuing these negotiations wisely, but I suspect you may be skewing the king's instructions. Nonetheless, because of the good will you have demonstrated, I will honor your words and leave the country for a year provided that my property will be undiminished when that time expires and you keep your promises. Report my words to the king. I do this for your sake and not the king's, for I find in you true friendship now as before."

Then they rejoined the king and told him that Sveinki left everything to the king's discretion but asked in return that the king accord him honor. "He will be in exile for three years and then return if both of you agree to that. Do this for the sake of your royal title and our entreaty, since everything lies in your discretion. Accept this settlement from him, and we will stake everything on his returning only with your consent."

The king remained silent, then spoke: "You have conducted yourselves worthily in this matter, and for your sake we will do as you request. This you may tell him."

"Those are kingly words," they said.

Then they went to meet with Sveinki and told him the king's gracious words. "We are overjoyed that a settlement is possible. The king asks that three years be stipulated as the term of your exile, but we know that before that term is up he will not be able to dispense with your service in this country. It is therefore clear that you should not reject these terms."

Sveinki replied: "What is better than (FJ 314) not to vex the king with my presence? I leave my goods and chattels in your hands." He led his force back to the residence and immediately departed. He had been prepared for this ahead of time.

Kolbeinn stayed behind and prepared splendid hospitality for the king, pretending that it had been previously arranged by Sveinki. Sveinki rode up into Gautland with as many men as he wished to take with him, and the king was hosted at Sveinki's estate. After that the district chieftains invited him to their residences. He made the circuit of their hospitality and they received him honorably. The king stayed in Vík for some time and was well content with the settlement. Sveinki's lands were designated as royal property and were in the keeping of Kolbeinn. They carried out their commission with the king's honor in mind, but at the same time they took the very best care of Sveinki's property. Then the king returned north along the coast, and peace was restored.

But now the people around the Elfr, left without a chieftain, were beset by ruffians and robbers, who plundered and overran the farmers. The district chieftains sent the king word that the farms in the east were suffering great depredations (U 142) and that the land was being laid waste: "It seems to us clear, lord, that you should let Sveinki stem the tide and drive off these malefactors. Let him be recalled since he is best suited for this task." The king accepted the advice of his district chieftains and sent Sveinki word that he should return to his estates in peace.

When the king's messengers met with Sveinki and told him of the king's words, he replied by saying that he did not know what truth there was in their account. He said that he was suspicious about the idea that he would have been exiled if the king had wanted him to return so soon. Two messages were dispatched to him (FJ 315) by the king, but he did not return. He was in Denmark at that time and did not in fact believe that the king would be serious about it that he should return to his lands.

When King Magnús himself came south to Denmark, he and Sveinki met there. They entered into conversations and were completely reconciled. They discussed matters fully on good terms, and now they both grasped what devoted service the district chieftains had rendered each of them. Sveinki then returned to his lands and became a great bastion for King Magnús's realm. Their friendship and good faith lasted as long as circumstances allowed.[9]

57. Concerning King Magnús's Harrying

King Magnús became a powerful leader as soon as he was sole ruler of Norway. He was imperious and quick to punish disobedience both at home and abroad. He led his army south to Denmark and harried in Halland, where he acquired a great deal of money, some by plundering and some from ransom. In Bjǫrn's words:

> 184. Vítt lét Vǫrsa dróttinn   brenndi buðlungr Þrœnda
>   (varð skjótt rekinn flótti)   (blés kastar hel fasta)
>   (hús sveið Hǫrða ræsir)   (vakði viskdœlsk ekkja)
>   Halland farit brandi: víðs mǫrg heruð síðan.

"Vǫrsa dróttinn lét Halland vítt farit brandi; flótti varð skjótt rekinn; Hǫrða ræsir sveið hús. Buðlungr Þrœnda brenndi víðs mǫrg heruð síðan; kastar hel blés fasta; vakði viskdœlsk ekkja."

With the sword, the king of the Vǫrsar [people of Voss] harried far and wide in Halland; those who fled were followed with haste; the lord of the Hǫrðar [people of Hordaland] torched houses. Then the ruler of the Þrœndir [people of Trøndelag] burned a great many counties; the death of the woodpile [fire] nourished the blaze; the widow from Viskardalr [Viskedal] lay awake.

He also mentions that King Magnús rid the land of pirates and rabble:

> 185. Snarr rauð Sygna harri
>   sverð á úthlaupsferðum (FJ 316)
>   (vítt rann vargr at slíta
>   varma bráð) á Harmi. (U 143)

"Snarr Sygna harri rauð sverð á úthlaupsferðum á Harmi; vargr rann vítt at slíta varma bráð."

The daring lord of the Sygnir [people of Sogn] reddened the sword on the rebels in Harmr [Velfjorden]: the wolf ran far and wide to tear warm flesh.
And again:

> 186. Víkinga lætr vengis
>   vallbaugs hati falla
>   vítt rýðr jǫrn á ýtum
>   Óláfs mǫgr en fǫgru.

"Vengis vallbaugs hati lætr víkinga falla; Óláfs mǫgr rýðr vítt jǫrn en fǫgru á ýtum."
The enemy of the land of the field ring [snake, gold, generous king] lets the vikings fall; far and wide, Óláfr's kinsman reddens fair steel on warriors.

The first stanza says that he burned Viskardalr.[1] That done, he returned to his realm.

Sometime later King Magnús prepared to campaign abroad and took with him many district chieftains and a large army. He crossed the sea westward to Orkney and took the sons of Jarl Erlendr, Magnús and Erlingr, with him. They accompanied him, as Þorkell hamarskald states:

> 187. Vestr lét varga nistir
>   (vann hilmir frið bannat)
>   (hrǫnn brutu hlýr en stinnu)
>   hugprúðr fóru snúðat.

"Hugprúðr varga nistir lét fǫru snúðat vestr; hilmir vann bannat frið; hlýr en stinnu brutu hrǫnn."
The proud-minded feeder of wolves [warrior] embarked on a swift journey to the west; the king debarred the peace; the stiff prows sliced the wave.

After that King Magnús came to the Hebrides and to Lewis. There he harried and took possession of the place. Then he went to Skye, where he slaughtered cattle and took great booty. From that land he took everything that he claimed, as we are told in this stanza:

> 188. Hungrþverrir lét herjat
>   hríðar gagls á Skíði
>   sigrgœðir réð síðan
>   snjallr Manverja falli.

"Hungrþverrir hríðar gagls lét herjat á Skíði; snjallr sigrgœðir réð síðan Manverja falli."
The hunger-diminisher of the goose of battle [bird of prey, warrior] harried in Skye; the fierce victory-increaser [warrior] later caused the fall of the Manxmen.

Then he proceeded to the islands of Tiree and North Uist and harried widely, as is told in this stanza: (FJ 317)

> 189. Ǫrr skjǫldungr fór eldi
>   Ívist (búendr misstu)
>   (róggeisla vann ræsir
>   rauðan) (lífs ok auðar).

"Ǫrr skjǫldungr fór Ívist eldi; búendr misstu lífs ok auðar; ræsir vann róggeisla rauðan."

The warlike king wasted North Uist with fire; farmers lost life and wealth; the ruler reddened the war flash [sword].

Then he came to Iona and went up into the town but spared the place and all the property. People report that he wanted to open the lesser Church of Columcille, but he did not enter it and said that no man should be so bold as to enter that church ever again. The church was locked so that its doors were never again opened.[2]

Then King Magnús took his army out to Mull, where he harried and burned far and wide, as we are told in this stanza: (U 144)

190. Vítt berr snarr á slétta   grœtti Grenlands dróttinn
     Sandey konungr randir   (gekk hátt Skota støkkvir)
     rauk of Íl (þars jóku   (þjóð rann mylsk til mœði)
     allvalds menn á brennur):   meyjar (suðr í eyjar).

"Snarr konungr berr randir vítt á slétta Sandey; rauk of Íl, þars allvalds menn jóku á brennur. Grenlands dróttinn grœtti meyjar; Skota støkkvir gekk hátt; mylsk þjóð rann til mœði suðr í eyjar."

Far and wide the keen king carries the shields on level Sanda; smoke drifted over Islay where the lord's men fueled the fires. The ruler of Grenland grieved women; the banisher of the Scots advanced inland; the men of Mull fled exhausted to the southern isles.

When King Magnús had taken all the northern islands, he brought his army south to Islay and wasted with fire, as previously reported. He harried there for a long time and wasted the land far and wide before the people submitted to him. Gísl also mentions that King Magnús harried in the islands:

191a. Tók á Skíði   en Skotar flýðu
     jǫfra œgir   Ívistar gram. (FJ 318)

The terror of kings [Magnús] captured the lord of North Uist at Skye and the Scots fled.

Lǫgmaðr, the son of King Guðrøðr, ruled over the northern islands. He kept retreating southward before King Magnús's army, then out to sea, and he was unable to mount any resistance. King Magnús captured him with his crew and gave him amnesty. He stayed with the king for some time, as Gísl says:

191b. Hafði fylkir   sás frami téði
     Lǫgmann konung   í liði sínu.

The warlord, aided by courage, kept King Lǫgmaðr in his company.

Bjǫrn composed the following:

192. Hætt vas hvert (þats átti)   nýtr lét nesjum útar
     hvarf (Guðrøðar arfi)   naðrbings tǫpuð finginn
     lǫnd vann lofðungr Þrœnda   Egða gramr (þars umðu)
     Lǫgmanni þar bannat: ungr (véttrima tungur).

"Hvert hvarf, þats Guðrøðar arfi átti, vas hætt: lofðungr Þrœnda vann þar bannat Lǫgmanni lǫnd. Nýtr ungr Egða gramr lét naðrbings tǫpuð finginn útar nesjum, þars véttrima tungur umðu."

Every hiding place of Guðrøðr's heir was hazardous: the lord of the Þrœndir [people of Trøndelag] banished Lǫgmaðr from the lands there. The crafty young king of the Egðir [people of Agder] captured the destroyer of the snake lair [gold, generous king] off the headlands where hilt tongues [swords] wailed.

After that King Magnús headed his fleet south to Kintyre and harried in both lands, up in Scotland and out in Ireland. He performed great deeds in both countries. From there he sailed south to the Isle of Man with his whole army and took the island together with the other islands nearby. After that he led his army south toward Wales and anchored in Menai Strait. There he harried both in Wales and out on Anglesey.

A great army marched against him under the command of two valiant jarls. One was named Hugh enn digri (the Stout) and the other Hugh enn prúði (the Bold). There a great battle was fought. (FJ 319) They closed gunwale to gunwale, and the trumpets sounded. The missiles flew thick and heavy, and many fell. There was a long (U 145), hard battle, and it ended, as has since become famous, when Hugh enn prúði was struck by an arrow. The arrow penetrated the eye so that it came out in the back of the neck. It was called a lucky shot because nothing was exposed on him except the eyes. Most people say that King Magnús loosed the arrow, but there was a man from Hálogaland standing next to him, and they both shot simultaneously. One of the two shot the arrow in question, but Þorkell hamarskald indicates that King Magnús shot the arrow, as is stated here:

> 193. Dunði broddr á brynju   strengs fló hagl á hringa
>   bragningr skaut af magni   hné ferð (en lét verða
>   sveigði allvaldr Egða   Hǫrða gramr í harðri
>   alm (stǫkk blóð á hjalma):   hjarlsókn banat jarli).

"Broddr dunði á brynju; bragningr skaut af magni; allvaldr Egða sveigði alm; stǫkk blóð á hjalma. Strengs hagl fló á hringa; hné ferð, en Hǫrða gramr lét verða banat jarli í harðri hjarlsókn."

The arrow burst on the byrnie; the king shot powerfully; the ruler of the Egðir [people of Agder] bent the bow; blood splattered on helmets. The hail of the bow string [arrows] hit the chain mail; men succumbed, and the king of the Hǫrðar [people of Hordaland] killed the earl in the hard battle for land.

A second arrow struck the nosepiece of the helmet and stuck there. For that reason people have differed over whether the king shot the arrow, since both were close together, and over which arrow followed the other, since both shot simultaneously.[3] After the fall of Hugh enn prúði, Hugh enn digri and all the Welshmen fled. Bjǫrn makes mention of this battle:

> 194. Lifspelli réð Laufa   ǫll hefr Jóta fellir
>   lundr í Ǫngulssundi   eylǫnd farit brandi (FJ 320)
>   (broddr fló) (þars slǫg snuddu)   (vítt liggr dyggs und dróttum
>   (snúðigt) Huga ens prúða: dǫglings grund) of stundir.

"Laufa lundr réð lifspelli Huga ens prúða í Ǫngulssundi; broddr fló snúðigt, þars slǫg snuddu. Jóta fellir hefr farit ǫll eylǫnd brandi of stundir; grund liggr vítt und dróttum dyggs dǫglings."

The log of Laufi [sword, warrior] caused Hugh enn prúði [the bold] to lose his life in Menai Strait; the arrow flew fast where weapons soared. For some time, the slayer of the Jótar [people of Jylland, Jutland] has wasted all the islands with the sword; far and wide the earth is controlled by the retainers of the courageous king. Gísl says the following:

195. Ættlǫndum vann   eyja dróttinn
      folkvǫrðr und sik   fjórum þrungit:
      áðr an hitti   sás hamalt fylkði
      veðrsmiðr Viðurs   valska jarla.

The lord of the isles, the guardian of the people, conquered four ancestral countries before the smith of Viðurr's [Óðinn's] storm [battle, warrior], who marshaled his troops in wedge-shaped array, met the Norman earls.

196. Háðum hildi   með Haralds frænda
      Ǫnguls við ey   innanverða:
      þars af reiði   ríkisvendir
      konungr ok jarlar   kapp sitt brutu.

We waged war with Haraldr's kinsman on the inner side of Anglesey, where, with rage, the royal scepters, the king and the earls, tried their courage.

197. Margan hǫfðu   Magnúss liðar
      bjǫrtum oddi   baugvang skorit:
      varð hertoga   hlíf at springa
      kapps vel skipuð   fyr konungs darri. (U 146)

Magnús's men had splintered many a ring meadow [shield] with the bright spear point; the magnificently equipped shield of the war leader was shattered by the king's spear.

198. Bǫðkennir skaut   báðum hǫndum
      allr vá hilmis   herr prúðliga: (FJ 321)
      stukku af almi   þeims jǫfurr sveigði
      hvítmýlingar   áðr Hugi felli.

The battle-expert shot with both hands; all the king's army fought boldly; white-muzzled arrows flew from the bow that the king bent before Hugh fell.

After this battle King Magnús took all of Anglesey, which is said to be a third of Wales. Then he returned to southeastern Scotland and received an offer of reconciliation from the king of the Scots. The stipulation was that he should not harry in his realm. In return he was to receive all the islands off Scotland separated by a sufficient distance to allow the passage of a ship with a rudder. The settlement was concluded on those terms.

King Magnús now settled his men there and placed these lands under his lordship. And when he sailed back from the south, he anchored off the Mull of Kintyre or by the isthmus. There he had a boat with a rudder portaged across the isthmus while he himself sat on the poopdeck. When the ship had been dragged to the north side, he laid claim to Kintyre, which is a large area, saying that he had passed between it and Scotland with a ruddered ship. But the fleet he sent around the outer peninsula. In this way he acquired Kintyre. The isthmus is so narrow at the top of the peninsula that people frequently portage their boats over it. Kintyre is judged to be a better land than the best island in the Hebrides.

After that King Magnús went north into the islands and followed the inner course along the Scottish coast. He thus took possession of all the outer islands. His men sailed into every fjord and explored every island that was settled. He took possession of them all, even those that were not settled, and he spent the winter in the Hebrides. (FJ 322)

58. Concerning King Magnús

The next summer he sailed north to his realm in Norway, as Gísl reports:

199.　Hǫfðu seggir　　þá vas sókn lokit
　　　heimfǫr þegit　　at hǫfuðsmanni:
　　　landsmenn litu　　of liði gǫfgu
　　　segl sædrifin　　sett við húna.

From their leader, the warriors got leave to return home; then the battle had ended; above the splendid troops, the country folks saw foam-splattered sails secured to the mast tops.

200.　Vágr þrútnaði　　en vefi keyrði
　　　steinóðr á stag　　storðar galli:
　　　braut dýrr dreki　　und Dana skelfi
　　　hrygg í hverri　　hafs glymbrúði. (U 147)

The sea swelled and the raging destroyer of the sapling [storm] made the sails billow; beneath the terror of the Danes [Magnús], the precious dragon broke the back in every roaring bride of the sea [breaker].

201.　Blár ægir skaut　　búnum svíra
　　　gjalfr hljóp í gin　　gollnu hǫfði:
　　　skein af hausum　　sem himins eisa
　　　dǫglings dreka　　djúps valfasti.

The dark sea shoved the adorned neck; the wave leaped into the jaws of the golden head; the flame of the deep [gold] shone from the skulls of the king's dragon like the fire of heaven [sun].

King Magnús had left Erlingr, the son of Jarl Erlendr, in the Orkneys, but his brother Magnús had run away from the king the previous summer and had gone over to the king of the Scots (FJ 323). The bloodhounds had been loosed in the forest, but they had lost the scent immediately.

When King Magnús was in the Orkneys, Malcolm, the king of the Scots, sent his daughter to King Magnús in the Orkneys to effect a reconciliation.[1] King Magnús married her to his son Sigurðr. At that time he was nine years of age, and the girl was five. Then King Magnús appointed his son Sigurðr chieftain over all the western islands and gave him the title of king. He gave him into the charge of his kinsman Jarl Hákon Pálsson as well as Erlingr Erlendsson, with the support of the forces that King Sigurðr had acquired from the realm over which he had been given authority. In this way friendship was established and confirmed between King Magnús and King Malcolm, the father of King David, who ruled in Scotland after his father.

Then King Magnús returned to Norway and spent the following winter to the east in Vík, with a large following. During the winter a man named Giffarðr came to King Magnús and said that he was from Normandy. He offered the king his service and said that he was an accomplished knight. He said that he had learned that the king ruled over a difficult realm and was much in need of good knights for his retinue. The king gave him a good reception and said that such men would be useful to him.[2]

Now it came about that King Magnús prepared to ride up into West Gautland (Västergötland), which he intended to annex. The primary reason that he alleged for his claim and his hostility toward the Gautar was that by right Dalr, Véar (Vedboherred), and Varðynjar (Valboherred) belonged to Norway and had been in the possession of his ancestors.[3] The king marched with large forces, and the West Gautar submitted to him as far as the northern settlements. Then he camped on the frontier and pitched tents, intending to invade and subject the land.

At that time King Ingi Steinkelsson ruled over Sweden and all of Gautland. (FJ 324) He learned of King Magnús's activity, gathered troops, and marched against him with his army. When King Magnús got wind of the fact that Ingi had a great army, he was urged by his chieftains to withdraw, but the king had no wish to do so (U 148) and led his troops forward. He managed things in such a way that he came upon King Ingi and his men the night before they were expected. They met at a place called Voxerni (Fuxerna), and King Magnús marshaled his force for the attack.[4]

Then King Magnús asked where Giffarðr was. The men looked for him, but he could not be found in the army. The king said:

> 202.   Villat flokk várn fylla
> 		falsk riddari enn valski.

Does he not wish to complete our company? Was the Norman knight hiding? Then a skald in the king's retinue went to work and recited a stanza:

> 203. Spurði gramr hvat gerði	framreiðar vas fnauði
> 		Giffarðr (þars lið barðisk)	fulltrauðr á jó rauðum
> 		vér ruðum vápn í dreyra	villat flokk várn fylla
> 		vasat hann kominn þannig:	falsk riddari enn valski.

"Spurði gramr, hvat Giffarðr gerði, þars lið barðisk; vér ruðum vápn í dreyra; vasat hann kominn þannig. Fnauði vas fulltrauðr framreiðar á jó rauðum; villat flokk várn fylla: falsk riddari enn valski."

The king asked what Giffarðr was doing where the army fought; we reddened weapons in blood; he had failed to appear. The coward was quite reluctant to advance on his chestnut steed; he does not wish to complete our company: the Norman knight was hiding.[5]

The battle was joined and caught the Swedes somewhat by surprise because they had scarcely had time to prepare themselves. There were heavy casualties, and it ended with King Ingi's retreating and saving himself by flight. At that moment Giffarðr rode into camp, and there were hard words about him because he had not been at the battle to render King Magnús assistance. He got a bad reputation among the king's men, and he departed (FJ 325) to go west to England.

There is a little tale to tell of him. They had stormy weather in the North Sea, and Giffarðr was little help. He was always leaning over the gunwale while the others bailed. There was an Icelander on board from Húsavík.[6] His name was Eldjárn, and he had come back from Constantinople. Once as Eldjárn went to bail and saw Giffarðr lying there, he recited a stanza:

204.　Hví samir hitt at dúsa　　　　þats satt at býðk byttu
　　　　hirðmanni geðstirðum　　　　(breiðhúfuðum) reiða
　　　　vest nú (þótt kjǫl kosti)　　　　(austrs til hár í hesti
　　　　knár riddari enn hári:　　　　hvaljarðar) Giffarði.

"Hví samir hitt geðstirðum hirðmanni at dúsa? Vest nú knár, riddari enn hári, þótt kjǫl kosti. Þats satt, at býðk Giffarði reiða byttu: austrs til hár í breiðhúfuðum hesti hvaljarðar."

Why is it fitting for an unbending retainer to lie there and rest? Be active now, old knight, although the keel [ship] is sorely tried. It's true that I tell Giffarðr to swing the bucket: the bilge water is too high in the broad-bellied horse of the whale land [sea, ship].

Then they arrived in England. Giffarðr immediately left the ship and went to the nearest town, where he looked up the borough reeve and inquired whether the reeve would help him obtain justice in his dispute with the Norseman. He said that he had been slandered in verse.[7] The reeve was a young man and new to his office. He told Giffarðr that he would look into his case as best he could: "But I am a young man and not accustomed (U 149) to judging cases. There are many details about which I am ignorant, and what I am least qualified to judge is verse. But I will listen all the same. I will convene a meeting, which you should attend."

When the meeting was arranged, Giffarðr reported the reeve's words to Eldjárn, to the effect that he should attend the meeting. They went, and the case was again laid before the reeve. The substance of the case was that the Norseman had slandered Giffarðr, but Eldjárn said it was untrue. He said that he would recite the stanza if the reeve wished. The reeve could then decide. (FJ 326) "Why not hear it?" asked the reeve. "Recite what you composed about Giffarðr." Then Eldjárn recited the following:

205. Frák at flótta rákuð   varð hjalmþrimu herðis
       falsk annat lið manna   hár (þars staddir váruð)
       (þar vas harðr es heyrðak   gangr (þars gauzka drengi
       hernaðr) á Foxerni: Giffarðr í hel barði).

"Frák, at rákuð flótta á Foxerni; falsk annat lið manna; þar vas harðr hernaðr, es heyrðak. Hjalmþrimu herðis gangr varð hár, þars staddir váruð, þars Giffarðr barði gauzka drengi í hel."

I heard you pursued those who fled at Foxerni [Fuxerna]; the other units of the army hid; there was a hard fight there, as I've heard. The success of the strengthener of the helmet crash [battle, warrior] was immense where you stood, when Giffarðr sent Gautish warriors to their death.

Then the reeve said: "I know little about poetry, but I can hear that this is no slander. It means honor and praise for you, Giffarðr, and that is the only judgment I can make."

Giffarðr did not know what to answer. He knew in his heart that this was mockery and not praise,[8] given what the circumstances were, but on no account did he want to reveal to people how he had comported himself at Foxerni (Fuxerna). With that they parted, and Giffarðr was not pleased with the outcome. That is the end of the tale.

After King Magnús and King Ingi had separated on the battlefield, King Magnús threatened to ride east around the lakes to the main district. He sought counsel from his friends and countrymen, thinking that he would have the same following that he had always had in harrying on the mainland. But he wished first to go to Norway himself and return from there with his army. He left two of his chieftains behind in charge of some of the troops to guard what had been won and make whatever further inroads they could in the Swedish king's realm. Finnr Skoptason and Sigurðr ullstrengr were in command of this detachment. They constructed a great fortress with beams and sod, and the king returned to Norway. The skald Þorkell makes mention of this campaign: (FJ 327)

206. Hraustr lét Elfi austar   varð á víg (þars herðar)
       allvaldr saman gjalla   vellmildr konungr (fellu)
       (vitr stillir rauð vǫllu)   (bolr lá gauzkr und gulri
       valskan brand ok randir: grás arnar kló) þrási. (U 150)

"Hraustr allvaldr lét valskan brand ok randir gjalla saman austar Elfi; vitr stillir rauð vǫllu. Vellmildr konungr varð þrási á víg, þars herðar fellu: gauzkr bolr lá und gulri kló grás arnar."

The fearless lord let the French sword crash against shields east of Elfr [Götaälv]; the wise ruler reddened the fields. The generous king was unyielding in the fray where shoulders fell to the ground: the Gautish torso lay beneath the yellow claw of the old eagle.

Gísl Illugason recited the following:

207.   Framðisk síðan   á Svía dróttni
        austr við Elfi   Upplanda gramr:
        liðskelfir tók   ór lǫgum Gauta
        fimmtán heruð   fránni eggju.

Then the lord of Upplǫnd [Opplandene] won honor at the expense of the Swedish king east by Elfr [Gôtaälv]; with the sharp sword, the terror of troops [warrior] took fifteen counties from the law district of the Gautar [people of Gôtaland].

208.   Reið folkhvǫtuðr   fyrst í gǫgnum
        sǫmnuð Svía   sigri hnugginn:
        malmr dreyrugr varð   á meðal hlaupa
        hauss ok herða   hans andskota.

The inciter of fight [warrior] rode first through the defeated ranks of the Swedes; steel became bloody from leaping between the head and shoulders of his enemies.

209.   Hol merki blés   en Huginn gladdisk
        fránn of hǫfði   feðr Sigurðar:
        þann sák fylki   með frama mestan
        snǫrpu sverði   til sigrs vega. (FJ 328)

The billowing standard blew above the head of Sigurðr's father and fierce-eyed Huginn [raven] rejoiced; that king I saw gain victory most gloriously with the sharp sword.

210.   Fylgðak frœknum   sem framast kunnak
        Eysteins fǫður   í Atals drífu:
        opt brák hjǫrvi   með Haralds frænda
        vanr vásfǫrum   þars vega þurfti.

I followed the fierce father of Eysteinn in Atall's [sea king] storm [battle] as best I could; often I, accustomed to hardship, brandished the sword with Haraldr's kinsman where battle was at hand.

Now the Norwegians in their fortress learned that Ingi was gathering forces to attack them, but they thought that laughable because they had prepared well and were confident in their fortress. For that reason they had no fear of the Gautish army. When Ingi's advance was delayed a little beyond the time they had been told, this ditty circulated among them:

211.   Allengi dvelr Ingi
        ofanreið enn þjóbreiði.

Broad-arsed Ingi delays his descent overly long.

But soon after that King Ingi rode down with a huge force against the Norwegians, and because there was no other choice, the Norwegians surrendered to

King Ingi. The king spared their lives and allowed them to keep their weapons, clothes, and horses, but he confiscated all other property.

The Norwegians traveled north to rejoin King Magnús, and they told him what had transpired. King Magnús made ready and set out a second time east to Gautland. He had a great army, and he harried and burned far and wide in the settlements. A Gautish army marched against him eastward toward Foxerni, where the last encounter had taken place.

After that King Magnús returned with his army and had done great damage to the army and the realm of the Gautar by plundering, killing, and burning. He had also suffered heavy losses in his own army during this campaign. (U 151) After that men mediated between the kings (FJ 329) and urged that they should make peace between themselves and their countries.

At that time Eiríkr was king of the Danes.[9] He had the same wish for his own realm. Eiríkr and Ingi sent word to King Magnús and asked that he not covet their realms, and in return they would not disturb the peace of his realm. After that the kings arranged a meeting on the eastern frontier at the Gautelfr (Götaälv). King Magnús came from the north and King Eiríkr of the Danes from the south, while King Ingi of the Swedes came down from Sweden.

When these three kings all stood together in one place, their retainers said, as seemed true enough, that three chieftains of such noble appearance could scarcely be found elsewhere. King Ingi was the eldest, tallest, and stoutest of them and seemed the most imposing. King Eiríkr of the Danes had the fairest and finest appearance. But Magnús, King of Norway, was of all of them much the courtliest and most valiant and martial in appearance. But all of them were tall and powerful. This meeting was arranged with great ceremony because of the hostilities that had prevailed among them.

The kings now met to discuss in private. They were together for no longer than what might be called half a mealtime before they were reconciled and their realms were at peace. Each king was to have his ancestral land undiminished and each was to compensate his countrymen for the damage done to them. The kings were to settle their differences among themselves in a way that was agreeable to all. King Ingi betrothed his daughter Margréta to King Magnús, and she received as her dowry those lands in Gautland which they had disputed. Afterward she was known as Margréta friðkolla (peace-girl). This settlement was reached in much the same way as the one previously arranged between Saint Ólafr and King Ólafr the Swede. (FJ 330)

Now each of the kings returned to his realm in perfect concord. The following stanza is attributed to King Magnús, and it is alleged that he composed it for the emperor's daughter, with whom he was much smitten and with whom he had exchanged messages. Her name was Matilda:[10]

212. Sús ein es mér meinar   sá kennir mér svanni
      Maktildr ok vekr hildi   (sín lǫnd es verr rǫndu)

(már drekkr suðr ór sárum   (sverð bitu Hǫgna hurðir)
sveita) leik ok teiti: hvítjarpr sofa lítit. (U 152)

"Sús ein, Maktildr, es meinar mér leik ok teiti ok vekr hildi; sveita már drekkr suðr
ór sárum. Sá hvítjarpr svanni, es verr sín lǫnd rǫndu, kennir mér sofa lítit; sverð
bitu Hǫgna hurðir."

It is only one, Matilda, who deprives me of fun and pleasure and stirs up strife; in
the south, the seagull of blood [bird of prey] drinks from wounds. That lady with
the light-brown hair, who defends her lands with the shield, teaches me to sleep
but little; swords bit the doors of Hǫgni [legendary king, shields].

And again:

213.   Hvats í heimi betra   þungan berk af þingi
       (hyggr skald af þrá sjaldan)   þann harm es skalk svanna
       (mjǫks langr sás dvelr drengi (skreytask menn á móti)
       dagr) an víf en fǫgru: minn aldrigi finna.

"Hvats í heimi betra an víf en fǫgru? Skald hyggr sjaldan af þrá; mjǫk langr 's dagr,
sás dvelr drengi. Berk þann þungan harm af þingi, es skalk aldrigi finna svanna
minn; skreytask menn á móti."

What's better in this world than fair women? The poet seldom forgets his yearning;
that day is very long that delays men. That heavy care I carry from the assembly,
that I shall never meet my woman; men dress up at the meeting.

It is reported that King Magnús had learned of words spoken by the emperor's
daughter that seemed to indicate that she was well disposed toward him, to wit
that she had said that such a king as Magnús struck her as most honorable. He
then recited this stanza:

214.   Jǫrp mun eigi verpa   annk (þótt eigi finnak
       Armhlín á glæ sínum   opt goðvefjar þoptu)
       orð spyrk gollhrings Gerðar   (viti menn at hykk henni
       góð of skald í hljóði: (FJ 331) hála) rœkðarmálum.

"Jǫrp Armhlín mun eigi verpa sínum [orðum] á glæ: spyrk í hljóði góð orð
gollhrings Gerðar of skald. Annk rœkðarmálum, þótt eigi finnak opt goðvefjar
þoptu; viti menn, at hykk henni hála."

The brown-haired arm-Hlín [goddess, woman] will not have thrown away her
words to no avail: secretly I hear kind words from Gerðr [goddess] of the gold ring
[woman] about the skald. I love those caring words, although I don't often meet
the thwart of precious cloth [woman]; men shall know that I think highly of her.

The skald recited the following about King Magnús at sea: [11]

215.   Vegg blæss veðr of tyggja   mjór skelfr (Magnús stýrir)
       viðr þolir nauð í lauðri   (móð skerr eik at flóði)
       læ tekr klungrs at knýja   (beit verða sæ slíta)
       keip en gelr í reipum: sjautøgr vǫndr und rǫndu.

"Veðr blæss vegg of tyggja; viðr þolir nauð í lauðri; læ klungrs tekr at knýja keip, en
gelr í reipum. Sjautøgr mjór vǫndr skelfr und rǫndu; Magnús stýrir; móð eik skerr
at flóði; beit verða slíta sæ."

The storm fills the sail above the king; the ship board suffers in the spray; the destroyer of bramble [wind] beats against the thole and roars in the mast ropes. Seventy thin oars tremble beneath the shields; Magnús steers; the tired ship slices the water; the boats lacerate the sea.

216. Eggjendr baðat ugga   satt v's at allvaldr átti
     óhlífinn gramr lífi   ógnsnart borit hjarta
     hvégis lét enn ljóti   súð varð í gný grœðis
     landgarðr fyrir barði: geyst farsælu treystask.

"Óhlífinn gramr baðat eggjendr ugga lífi, hvégis enn ljóti landgarðr lét fyrir barði. Satt v's, at allvaldr átti borit ógnsnart hjarta; geyst súð varð treystask farsælu í gný grœðis."

The dauntless king did not ask the warriors to fear for their life, no matter how the hideous land enclosure [sea] howled before the bow. It was true that the king was born with a fearless heart; the swift-moving ship trusted its fortune in the din of the sea.

59. Concerning King Magnús's Death

We are told that after King Magnús had ruled the land for nine years, he again prepared a westward expedition across the sea.[1] The following stanza was recited:

217. Hví launa þér þínir
     þingmæltir dýrlingar
     (vestr bifask rengr í rostum)
     (reyn oss jofurr) hnossir.

"Hví launa þér þínir þingmæltir dýrlingar hnossir? Vestr bifask rengr í rostum: reyn oss, jofurr!"

How do your lovers of splendor [noblemen], so eloquent at assemblies, repay you for your precious gifts? In the west, ship frames tremble in the currents—test us, king!

The king replied: (FJ 332)

218. Auð hefk minn (þanns monnum
     margteitum réðk veita)
     (húf létk kløkkvan klífa
     kolgur) illa folginn. (U 153)

"Hefk auð minn, þanns réðk veita margteitum monnum, illa folginn; létk kløkkvan húf klífa kolgur."

My wealth, which I gave my merry men, I spent unwisely; I let the flexible ship climb the breakers.

On this expedition the king was accompanied by a fair and numerous force. With him were Ogmundr Skoptason, Sigurðr Sigurðarson, Sigurðr ullstrengr,

Dagr Eilífsson, Viðkunnr Jónsson, Sigurðr Hranason, Úlfr Níkolásson, and the
most splendid army from Norway. Serkr from Sogn was present, and Eyvindr
ǫlboli (Beer-Bull), his marshal.[2]

The king sailed first to Orkney and took Erlingr, the son of Jarl Erlendr, and
a great following of men with him. From there he sailed to the Hebrides, then
out to Ireland, where he harried and fought many battles against the Irish. He
was always *victorious*. After that he sailed south to Dublin and laid siege to
the town in order to reduce it. King Magnús then addressed his troops:

It is *well known* to everyone that we have made expeditions westward to these
lands and have always prospered greatly. That may turn out *again to the honor*
of our Norwegian realm.[3] But there is much more to be gained now than before
because this land has great riches, and if we can defeat the Irish, we can readily
imagine what they amount to, in the first place for me, but also for you. Put your
minds to it, for I am eager to have the land, but there is also an abundance of
wealth here, and you will have an equal share in it. Nor is this the only time that
you will stand to be treated generously, but you should do your best as long as this
country boasts such splendor and wealth. The town that we are besieging is the
wealthiest of all, and we have such a fine and reliable force that I think we will succeed. Let us bend our minds to the task to the best of our abilities.

Then Sigurðr (FJ 333) Sigurðarson said:

Sire, everyone is prepared to promote your honor, but we are somewhat apprehensive about what honor is to be had in this country. It is a populous region and
the people are treacherous. We are not certain how well we can guard ourselves
against them. Your kinsman King Haraldr had the experience that people in England at first surrendered to him wherever he went, but it ended with his death.
Your friends would have deemed it best if you had remained quietly in your realm,
considering the advantages that you have.

The king replied: "We will pursue the course we have chosen, and we will succeed excellently as long as we are undaunted."

They then attacked the town, and there was a hard battle. They were finally
able to reduce the town with a number of stratagems, though we are unable to
relate the details.[4] King Magnús placed the town under his authority and appointed his officers to act on his behalf. He himself went up to Connacht and
spent much of the winter there. He joined forces and had amicable relations
with the king who ruled over Connacht, whose name was Muirchertach.[5] King
Magnús now marched far and wide around Ulster harrying and subjecting the
land, so that he was able to take possession of that part of the country. Then in
the summer he set out for Norway, leaving his officers and administrators in
Dublin. His (U 154) fleet lay ready for departure with his whole army embarked, and he intended to sail from there to the northern islands.

King Magnús found that he needed supplies from land, and King Muircher-tach was to send them down from Connacht. He waited for a time, and when the supplies were delayed, he dispatched his men for them. And again it seemed to take these men rather longer than he expected. Then he went ashore himself with the greater part of his army and intended to look for the men who had not returned with (FJ 334) the supplies.

It was the day before Saint Bartholomew's Day,[6] and by the time he found his men, he had penetrated far inland. They came toward him with the supplies they intended to bring him. The king now turned his army around. The coun-tryside that they traversed was dotted with scrub brush, and there were swampy areas. In some places there were deep pools with steppingstones across them. There an Irish army had gathered and got very close before they spotted it be-tween themselves and their ships.

Then the king said: "Prepare yourselves, men, and don't retreat before these breechlings.[7] This is the time to show what brave fellows you are. You may also get the chance to show whether you want to support your king."

He marshaled the troops from the ships under the standard, and there was a great battle. The Irish gathered such great forces that even though many were killed, there were twice as many as at the outset. Eventually the Norwe-gians fell before them, and some fled. King Magnús refused to flee and recited the following stanza:

219. Hvat skulum heimfǫr kvitta   unik (þvít eigi synjar
     hugrs minn í Dyflinni   ingjan gamans þinga)
     enn til Kaupangs kvinna   (œrskan veldr) (þvít írskum
     kømkat austr í hausti: annk betr an mér svanna).

"Hvat skulum heimfǫr kvitta? Minn hugrs í Dyflinni; enn til Kaupangs kvinna kømkat austr í hausti. Unik, þvít eigi synjar ingjan gamans þinga; œrskan veldr, þvít írskum svanna annk betr an mér."

Why should we talk of our homeward journey? My heart is in Dublin; for this fall I shall not return to the women in Kaupangr [Nidaros]. I thrive because the girl does not deny me moments of pleasure; youth causes it, for I love the Irish maiden better than myself.

He kept up the attack and maintained his formation in front of his standard. He thought the men of Upplǫnd would loose their arrows (FJ 335) on the Irish when they crossed the swampy ground, but they chose rather to sling their shields on their backs and run at top speed for their ships.[8]

Then King Magnús called out to Þorgrímr húfa (Hat), saying: "I was a foolish man on the day I outlawed Sigurðr hundr (Dog), but I was much more foolish when I made you a district chieftain. You are taking a cowardly leave of me now, and I will remember it. Sigurðr would not do the same if he were here."

After that, all those in the back ranks also fled across the swamp, but the king himself stood by his standard (U 155) and continued to fight. He thought it would avail because for a long while they slaughtered the Irish like cattle. But when one fell, two came from the surrounding countryside to take his place.

As the troops around the standard began to thin, King Magnús received a spear thrust through both legs. He immediately broke off the spear and threw it away. Then he called out, urging men to fight. He said the wound was of no consequence.

King Magnús was easy to identify. He had a gold helmet on his head, and a shield inscribed with a gold lion, and a sword in his hand called Legbiter. It had an ivory hilt and the grip was bound in gold. It was an exceedingly sharp sword. He had put on a red silken jacket over his shirt, and everyone agreed that they had never seen a more valiant man with such weapons, or a nobler chieftain. A little later King Magnús received a blow from the tip of an Irish ax.[9] It struck him on the neck by the shoulder, and it was his death-blow. The king then fell. Þorkell hamarskald recited the following about this battle:

220.   Uppgǫngu réð yngvi   hátt gall hjǫrr en sótti
       ítr með helming lítinn   (hneit egg við fjǫr seggja)
       áræði hykk áðan   (malmsœkir rauð mæki)
       Eysteins fǫður treystask: (FJ 336)   Magnús í lið gǫgnum.

"Ítr yngvi réð uppgǫngu með helming lítinn; hykk Eysteins fǫður áðan treystask áræði. Hátt gall hjǫrr, en Magnús sótti í gǫgnum lið; egg hneit við fjǫr seggja; malmsœkir rauð mæki."

The splendid king disembarked with a small army; I believe Eysteinn's father earlier put faith in his courage. The sword sang loudly and Magnús advanced through the enemy ranks; the edge jabbed at warriors' bodies; the steel conqueror [warrior] reddened the sword.

Viðkunnr Jónsson had been closest to the king during the day, and so he continued to be, because he felled the man who had given the king his death-blow and cut him in half. Then he took King Magnús's sword Legbiter, but the shield was ruined. Viðkunnr had received three wounds in the battle.

When the king realized that he was mortally wounded, he asked Viðkunnr to make good his escape. "I now expect," he said, "that this will be our parting, but you have stood by me bravely. Bring my greetings to King Sigurðr and all my friends." Then Viðkunnr fled, along with all the other troops that could escape to their ships. Viðkunnr himself said that when he and the others left the king, there were few left on the battlefield to tell the tale. Erlingr, the son of Jarl Erlendr, and Eyvindr Finnsson and many great chieftains fell there with King Magnús.

Viðkunnr and all the men who were fated to escape got to the ships and sailed to Norway. That same autumn they met King Sigurðr in the western islands and brought him to Norway with them. Magnús Erlendsson and Hákon Pálsson were appointed jarls over the Orkneys. Before they left the Orkneys, King (U 156) Sigurðr asked for the details of his father's death. No one could provide them more fully than Viðkunnr Jónsson because he had stood by the king most stoutly and did not flee (FJ 337), as I have indicated,[10] before the king had received his deathblow and had asked on his own initiative that Viðkunnr flee. For that reason Viðkunnr was greatly honored by King Magnús's sons.[11]

Sigurðr left the daughter of King Malcolm of the Scots behind in the west and did not wish to be married to her. He said that he loathed everything that had to do with western chieftains, both in Scotland and Ireland, considering how much he had lost there.

60. The Beginning of the Rule of King Magnús's Sons

After the fall of King Magnús berfœttr his three sons Sigurðr, Eysteinn, and Óláfr were installed as kings. Sigurðr ruled the eastern part of the country and was entitled to official entertainment and the revenue. King Eysteinn ruled the north around Þrándheimr. They both served as regents for King Óláfr and that part of the land that belonged to him, because he was no older than three years when he was named king. The sons of King Magnús were all handsome and magnificent, calm and peaceful in dealing with their subjects. There are many good and admirable things to say about them, but Óláfr was granted too little time, because he did not live more than twelve years after his father's death.

At the outset when all three brothers ruled, King Sigurðr was very impatient to travel abroad to Jerusalem with the support of his brothers and all the foremost men in Norway in order to earn God's mercy and a reputation for valor. He prepared for this journey at great expense. But before he was able to choose as many men as he wished to designate for this voyage, he and his brothers made fast friends with their countrymen and the people at large. They released people from service and impositions, harsh treatment and exactions, which kings and (FJ 338) jarls had imposed on the people, as has been previously related in their stories.[1] The brothers converted slavery into freedom, and that ensured them great popularity among all the people.

61. The Story of King Sigurðr's Adventures

King Sigurðr was ready to set sail from Norway three years after his father's death. He set out and intended to go to Jerusalem. He took with him a select and numerous company, but only men who were themselves intent on making the voyage and giving him support and companionship. (U 157) Many district chieftains and other powerful men readied themselves for this expedition with King Sigurðr, and when the men were prepared, he had a total of sixty ships, as Þórarinn stuttfeldr says:[1]

> 221. Dreif til handa   sem fyrr í for
>   herr framr grami   frétt hǫfðu rétt

hollr hauksnjǫllum	konunga kyn
hvaðanæva svá:[2]	Kraka margspǫkum.

From everywhere, an accomplished army gathered around the king, loyal to the valiant one; just as men rightly have heard that kinsmen of kings of old followed sagacious Kraki [Hrólfr kraki: legendary king].

Before the brothers parted, King Sigurðr said to King Eysteinn: "This expedition is now splendidly equipped, brother, with your aid and support. It is important that we should now conduct ourselves in princely fashion so that the expedition may enhance our fame and the good of our souls."

King Eysteinn replied: "You will distinguish yourself, brother, and are likely to make your mark and achieve great success. In the meantime, I will try to preserve our realm with whatever leadership (FJ 339) I can provide."

Now the brothers parted, and Sigurðr sailed from Hǫrðaland in the autumn and proceeded west to England, where he spent the winter. Þorvaldr blǫnduskald tells the following:[2]

222.	Svá kom fylkis	at skip við skǫp
	framt lið saman	skarfǫgr of lǫg
	margspaks mikit	hreins guðs heðan
	mildingi vilt:	hnigu sex tigir.

The accomplished forces of the sagacious king, dear to their leader, gathered in such numbers that sixty ships, splendidly equipped with shields, set out from here across the sea by the providence of the pure God.

223.	Óðu at Engla	þótti Þrœnda
	ættjǫrðu bǫrð	þar lands sem hvar
	skaplig skipa	yfirmaðr jǫfurr
	skafin vestr of haf:	alls herjar snjallr.

The shapely smooth ship prows headed west across the sea to the ancestral land of the English; there, as everywhere, the audacious king of the Þrœndir [people of Trøndelag] seemed superior to everyone else.

At that time Henry was King of England, the son of William the Bastard, jarl of Rouen.[3] He gave King Sigurðr a good reception, and he spent the winter there with his company, enjoying great honor and hospitality. King Henry was eager to be on friendly terms with King Sigurðr. "Because you have come to visit us," said Henry, "and have devoted yourself to such a good cause, I wish to be of service to you in your labors. You can be expected to need a great deal of money for your equipment and the expedition you have planned." King Sigurðr (U 158) thanked him for his kind promises and splendid (FJ 340) reception and for all the support and honor that he had bestowed on him.

In the spring he set sail for France.[4] The voyage proceeded slowly during the summer, and in the fall they arrived in Compostella. King Sigurðr spent the second winter there and sent his chieftains to parley for peace with the duke who ruled the land. He told them to inform the duke that he had nothing but peaceful intentions toward his men, should the duke give them permission to spend the winter in his realm and supply what they needed, with the understanding that they would be as amenable as possible in their dealings with the local population. That would be a great kindness on the duke's part because they had traveled so far from their own land into foreign parts. He said that he wished to be at peace with him and his men if he would be willing to supply the needed provisions.

The duke gave King Sigurðr's petition a good reception and said he would arrange whatever they needed. These were the terms of their truce: The duke was to establish a food market for the whole winter, while King Sigurðr's army was to be orderly and peaceful, as he had promised. This arrangement did not last longer than to Christmas, when the market was exhausted, and the Norsemen ran low on food as soon as the duke withdrew his patronage, primarily because it was an infertile country and not rich in arable land.

Now King Sigurðr spoke to his men and said: "It strikes me that the duke has not been as good as his word and has broken the agreement. I believe that we are now entitled to be a bit more aggressive in order to provide for our needs. We will have to test our ability, and I suspect that we will find out how good a company I have chosen before this is over. (FJ 341) I suspect too that we will have our courage tested in the process, though our fame will be lasting if we give a good account of ourselves and accomplish something worth telling about.[5] I have a good feeling about my troops, and *things will* turn out well if the leadership is not worse." Everyone applauded his words.

King Sigurðr then marched *with a large force* to the duke's castle, but the duke fled because he did not have many men. King Sigurðr seized *a large amount of food and other booty from the castle* and had it brought to his ships. Then they prepared to leave, and it was the beginning of spring *when he left Compostella* and headed his fleet west for Spain, as Halldórr skvaldri reports in the poem that *he composed about Sigurðr's voyage to Jerusalem*.[6] In that poem he told of the battles that he fought during the voyage, and he began when King Sigurðr had arrived in Spain with his company. There it happened that (U 159) some pirates on the lookout for plunder advanced toward him with a squadron of galleys.

When King Sigurðr realized that, he urged his forces to attack, saying that they stood to gain great fame and fortune if they were victorious. The marauders had seven galleys, ships that were large and almost impregnable. King Sigurðr attacked them with his crews and joined battle. That was the first battle that he fought against the heathens. King Sigurðr was in high spirits as they laid their ships alongside the enemy and said that it was fitting to learn whether the Norsemen could fight or not. It was a hard-fought battle, but King Sigurðr's men were finally able to board the galleys and clear them from stem to stern. Before the battle was over, the pirates found that their encounter with the Norsemen cost them the lives of many men, who were killed or (FJ 342) forced overboard. Anyone who could, fled, and they abandoned the eight galleys in their possession.[7] King Sigurðr and his men took whatever they wanted from them and killed every last man who had not fled. They seized great treasure, as Halldórr said:

224. Náði herr at hrjóða
      (hlaut drengja vinr fengi
      fyrðum hollr) (þars fellat
      fátt lið) galeiðr átta.

"Herr náði at hrjóða átta galeiðr; drengja vinr, fyrðum hollr, hlaut fengi, þars fátt lið fellat."

The army cleared eight galleys; the friend of warriors [Sigurðr], loved by the people, seized loot where not a few men fell.

After that King Sigurðr laid siege to the castle called Sintré (Sintra).[8] It is located in Spain and had been occupied by the heathens. They used it as a stronghold from which to raid the Christians.

Then King Sigurðr addressed his men: "I believe," he said, "that it would advance and strengthen Christendom if we were to reduce this castle, in which the heathens have gathered and from which they make raids and wage war against the Christians. Let us be stout and subdue this castle with the greatest valor."

Then they attacked the castle and fought a hard battle. The men inside defended themselves courageously and *maintained* that this foreign king would not rout them if the natives could not manage it. They thought that they were secure *and had an elite force*, but it turned out that they found their match. The Norsemen broke into the fortress and *captured* the castle and the surviving defenders.

Then the king spoke to them: "The place you *have taken has brought injury to many* a good man, but I think that is at an end. If you will accept the faith, (FJ 343) I will spare your lives, although you deserve to die." They all refused to accept Christianity, and King Sigurðr had them all killed, as Halldórr says: (U 160)

225. Stór ák verk (þaus váru)   gerðisk heldr við Hǫrða
      (Vánar dags) (á Spáni)   hermǫnnum gram berjask
      (prútt vann slǫngvir sóttan   grátt (þeims gǫrva níttu
      Sintré) konungs inna: goðs rétti sér boðnum).

"Ák inna stór verk konungs, þaus váru á Spáni; Vánar dags slǫngvir vann prútt sóttan Sintré. Gerðisk heldr grátt berjask við Hǫrða gram hermǫnnum, þeims gǫrva níttu goðs rétti, boðnum sér."

I must tell the tale of the king's great deeds, those that took place in Spain; the dispenser of Ván's [river] daylight [gold, generous king] courageously captured Sintra. It turned out to be quite perilous to oppose the king of the Hǫrðar [people of Hordaland] for those warriors who refused to accept the proffered laws of God.

After that King Sigurðr and his men departed and proceeded westward along the coast of Spain until they reached the town called Lisbon. That town was half heathen and half Christian. To the west and south of that town lies heathen Spain and that marks the dividing line from Christian Spain.[9] King Sigurðr now consulted with his advisers. He said that it would be a great prize and honor if they captured the town. He said that he had selected his troops with such care, both with respect to intelligence and courage, that he had confidence in the outcome. He said that many of the Christians who lived in the town would be well disposed to them, and he said that he would like to make the town completely Christian if he could. All his men supported his words and attacked the town with great vigor, but those within made ready and encouraged one another to defend the place so that they would not be overrun by foreign chieftains.

A hard battle was joined around the town, and the attack (FJ 344) of the Norsemen was so energetic that they broke the walls with catapults and entered the town. There was a fierce battle within the town, with great loss of life. King Sigurðr was at the head of his troops under his banners. He was highly skilled in warfare. The battle ended with the death of many men, although some surrendered and accepted the Christian faith. King Sigurðr concluded his campaign by taking whatever he wanted from the town.[10] That was King Sigurðr's third battle, as Halldórr says:

226.   Suðr vannt sigr enn þriðja
       snjallr við borg (þás kalla)
       lofðungs kundr (es lenduð)
       (Lizibón) (at fróni).

"Snjallr lofðungs kundr, vannt sigr enn þriðja suðr við borg, þás kalla Lizibón, es lenduð at fróni."

Courageous descendant of the king, you won the third victory south by the city called Lisbon when you reached the shore.

King Sigurðr again proceeded with his troops to a heathen town in Spain called Alkassa (Alcácer do Sal).[11] He told his men that they would try their luck with this town: "I think we have gained strength as we have progressed, and we have already gained much fame and fortune. Let us attack this town bravely." This was the fourth battle that King Sigurðr waged, and he did not desist from the attack until he had taken the town. He killed many heathens in it and took all the treasure in the town, then wasted it, as is told in this stanza: (U 161)

227.   Út frák yðr (þars heitir
       Alkasse) styr hvassan
       folkþeysandi fýsask
       fjórða sinn at vinna.

"Folkþeysandi, frák yðr fýsask fjórða sinn at vinna hvassan styr út, þars heitir Alkasse."

Battle-advancer [warrior], I heard you were eager to engage in fierce fight for the fourth time out by the city called Alcácer do Sal.

And the poet added:

228.   Unnit frák í einni
       eyddri borg til sorgar
       (hitti herr á flótta)
       heiðins vífs (at drífa). (FJ 345)

"Frák unnit í einni eyddri borg til sorgar heiðins vífs; hitti herr at drífa á flótta."
I heard that the heathen woman was caused grief in one wasted city; people were
forced to flee.

From there King Sigurðr sailed to the Straits of Gibraltar and through the
straits. In the vicinity of the straits there are always pirates, and it turned out
once again that a host of heathens attacked King Sigurðr. Here he did battle
for the fifth time, and it was a hard encounter with many casualties among the
heathens. King Sigurðr said that it was all the more incumbent on them to
press the attack and do battle because the heathens were so confident of victory and had initiated battle. They then attacked fiercely, and it ended with
King Sigurðr's carrying off the victory. The heathens who got off with their
lives fled and had little to boast of in this encounter. This is reported by
Halldórr:

229.   Treystuzk egg fyr austan
       (yðr tjóði guð) rjóða
       (náskári fló nýra)
       Nǫrvasund (til unda).

"Treystuzk rjóða egg fyr austan Nǫrvasund: yðr tjóði guð; náskári fló til nýra unda."
You dared to redden the sword edge east of the Straits of Gibraltar: God favored
you; the corpse gull [bird of prey] flew to fresh wounds.

King Sigurðr then continued his voyage and sailed to an island called
Forminterra (Formentera).[12] There a large band of heathens had settled in a
certain cavern and constructed a stone wall across the mouth of the cavern,
thus converting it into a stronghold. There they brought whatever plunder
they acquired. When they arrived at this island and learned of the cavern, the
king said: "In my opinion there has been no greater need of us than here at
this cavern, which has been taken over by bandits and heathens. We must van-
quish this place, where so many enemies (FJ 346) of Christendom have gathered, but I am told that this is a very difficult undertaking. Still we must test
whether our good fortune and courage can accomplish more with God's support than the fortifications of evildoers."

All agreed that they had to confront very superior numbers and that the defenders were well fortified, but the king could not be dissuaded from attacking. King Sigurðr made his landing on the island, and they proceeded to the
cavern. It was located on the edge of a cliff, and it was a steep climb to the stone
wall across the cavern mouth, so that *those in the cavern* had no fear of their
attackers. (U 162) They carried out costly fabrics and other treasures and ex-
hibited them, telling the king of the Norwegians to come and fetch them.

Now King Sigurðr cast about for a solution and took two shipboats, called "barks," ordering that they should be dragged up the cliff, suspended over the cavern mouth, and *made fast with* stout and heavy cables. He manned the boats with bowmen and *lowered them down* the cliff in such a position that those in the cavern could not get at them. From their vantage point in the boats they loosed a *storm of arrows* on the heathens, who had unreliable shields and were frequently wounded by the arrows. Some were even killed. Then they drew back from the wall and into the cavern, but King Sigurðr with his men advanced up the cliff under cover of the wall and broke down the access gates, which the heathens were not defending because they had been forced back toward the cavern by the missiles.

King Sigurðr and his men then entered, and the heathens fled into the interior behind the stone wall that had been built across the entrance. From there they defended themselves. Next, King Sigurðr had large amounts of wood brought to the cavern, where he built a great pyre at the mouth of the cavern and ignited it. As they were beset by smoke and fire, the heathens considered their choices. Some died inside (FJ 347), and some went out to test the hospitality of Norwegian weapons. All of them were either killed or burned. It was here that they collected more plunder than anywhere else on their journey. Concerning this event Halldórr composed the following:

230. Náði folk (þats flýði   lífs bautt enn (þás unnuð)
      ferð skundila undan)   aftíg (gamalt vígi)
      (illr varð hreimr í helli)   (kvǫl beið ǫld í eldi
      heiðit konungr meiða: ósæl) djǫfuls þrælum.

"Konungr náði meiða heiðit folk, þats flýði skundila undan ferð; illr hreimr varð í helli. Bautt enn lífs aftíg djǫfuls þrælum, þás unnuð gamalt vígi; ósæl ǫld beið kvǫl í eldi."

The king maimed the heathen men who hastily fled before the army; there was horrible clamor in the cavern. Again you offered the devil's slaves death when you captured the old stronghold; the luckless people were tormented in the fire.

231. Bǫðstyrkir lézt barka   en í hall at helli
      (bragnings verk á Serkjum   hernenninn fjǫlmennum
      fræg hafa gǫrzk) fyr gýgjar Gǫndlar þings með gengi
      gagnstíg ofan síga: Gnýþróttr neðan sótti.

"Bǫðstyrkir, lézt barka síga ofan fyr gýgjar gagnstíg; bragnings verk á Serkjum hafa gǫrzk fræg. En hernenninn Gǫndlar þings Gnýþróttr sótti neðan í hall at fjǫlmennum helli með gengi."

Battle strengthener [warrior], you let barks be lowered before the pleasure path of the giantess [mountain]; the king's attacks on the Saracens have become famous. But the battle-trim Þróttr [Óðinn] of the din of Gǫndul's [valkyrie] assembly [battle, warrior] advanced with his followers up the cliff toward the fortified cavern.

232.   Bauð gramr guma   þás í reipum
       gunnhagr draga   ramdýr þrama
       byrvarga á bjarg   sigu fyr hellis
       blásvarta tvá: hliðdyrr með lið.

The battle-skilled king bade his men drag two bluish-black wolves of favorable breeze [boats] up on the cliff, when the strong animals of ship rails [boats] were lowered in the ropes with the company before the cavern's gates.

Then King Sigurðr continued his journey and came to an island called Íviza (Ibiza). He spoke as follows: (FJ 348) "I imagine that the news of our victory at the cavern will now have spread far and wide (U 163), as it has before. We will not face greater odds here than elsewhere, and let us make a resolute attack against the heathens on this island. If we show our mettle as before, we will succeed."

There was now a hard battle and great loss of life. The Norwegians pressed hard, trusting as before in the king's valor and honor. This time too the heathens *succumbed*, and King Sigurðr won the victory. Halldórr counted this the seventh battle, as he says:

233.   Margdýrkaðr kom merkir
       morðhjóls skipastóli
       (fúss vas fremðar ræsir
       friðslits) til Ívizu.

"Margdýrkaðr merkir morðhjóls kom skipastóli til Ívizu; fremðar ræsir vas fúss friðslits."

The much-commended colorer of the war wheel [shield, warrior] came with his fleet to Ibiza; the advancer of honor [king] was eager for fight.

After that King Sigurðr brought his forces to *the island that* the Norwegians call Manork (Minorca). That was a populous place, and well defended.[13]

*[After that King Sigurðr sailed to the island of Manork (Minorca), where he waged his eighth battle against the heathens and was victorious. According to Halldórr skvaldri:

F 1.   Knátti enn en átta
       oddhríð vakit síðan
       (Finns rauð gjǫld) á grœnni
       (grams ferð) Manork verða.

"En átta oddhríð knátti enn síðan verða vakit á grœnni Manork; grams ferð rauð Finns gjǫld."

Still later the eighth point storm [battle] was waged on green Minorca; the king's company reddened the Finn's compensation [arrows].

61a. [Roger Became King]

In the spring King Sigurðr arrived in Sicily and remained there for some time. Roger was duke there.[14] He gave the king a good reception and invited him to a feast. King Sigurðr attended with a large following. It was a splendid welcome, and every day of the feast Duke Roger stood at King Sigurðr's table and served. On the seventh day of the feast, when the men had bathed, King Sigurðr took the jarl by the hand and conducted him to the throne, conferring on him the royal title and the right in perpetuity to rule the kingdom of Sicily. Up until that time the realm had been ruled by jarls.

61b. [Concerning King Roger]

King Roger of Sicily was a very powerful monarch. He conquered all of Apulia and subdued a number of large islands in the eastern Mediterranean. He was called Roger the Great. His son was King William of Sicily, who was at war with the Byzantine emperor for a long time. King William had three daughters but no son. He married one daughter to Emperor Henry, the son of Emperor Frederick, who later became emperor in Rome. William's second daughter was married to the Duke of Cyprus, and the third to the pirate overlord Margrit (Berengar Margarito). Emperor Henry killed both of them. The Byzantine Emperor Manuel was also married to a daughter of King Roger of Sicily. Their son was Emperor Kirjalax (Alexios).[15]

61c. [King Sigurðr Sailed to Jerusalem]

In the summer King Sigurðr sailed across the Aegean to Jerusalem and landed at Acre. From there they traveled by land to Jerusalem. When Baldwin, King of Jerusalem, learned that King Sigurðr was to visit the city, he had precious stuffs spread on the road, ever costlier as it approached the city. Then he said: "It is known to you that a famous king from the north will visit us. Many ingenious stratagems and distinguished deeds are attributed to him, and we should give him a good welcome. But we should judge his distinction and wealth in the following way: If he rides straight to the city and takes little notice of these preparations, I will judge that he probably has a good measure of such things in his own realm. But if he leaves the direct road, I will have a lower estimate of his kingly honor."

King Sigurðr now came riding toward the city with great pomp and saw the preparations that had been made. He rode directly onto the carpeting and bade all his men do the same. King Baldwin gave them a good reception and rode out to the River Jordan with King Sigurðr. Einarr Skúlason spoke as follows:

> F 2.   Getk þess's gramr fór vitja   ok leyghati laugask
>   (glyggs) Jórsala byggðar   (leyft ráð vas þat) náði
>   (meðr vitut ǫðling œðra)   hauka fróns í hreinu
>   ógnblíðr (und sal víðum):   hvatr Jórdánar vatni.

"Getk, þess's ógnblíðr gramr fór vitja Jórsala byggðar; meðr vitut ǫðling œðra und

víðum glyggs sal. Ok hvatr leyghati hauka fróns náði laugask í hreinu Jórdánar
vatni; leyft ráð vas þat."

I recount that the war-happy king went to visit Jerusalem; men know no nobler
lord beneath the storm's wide hall [heaven]. And the brisk enemy of the flame of
the hawks' land [arm, gold, generous king] could wash in the pure water of the
River Jordan; that was a commendable deed.

King Sigurðr stayed in Jerusalem for a long time, into the autumn and early
winter. King Baldwin staged a great feast for King Sigurðr and many of his
men. Then King Baldwin gave King Sigurðr many holy relics. On the initiative
of King Baldwin and the Patriarch a piece was taken from the holy cross, and
both swore on a holy relic that this wood was from the holy cross on which God
Himself was tormented. Then that holy relic was given to King Sigurðr with the
stipulation that he and twelve compurgators should swear to promote Christianity with all their might and establish an archbishopric in Norway. The cross
was to be where Saint Óláfr rested, and Sigurðr was to institute the tithe and
pay tithe himself.[16]

61d. [King Sigurðr's Journey to Constantinople]

After that, King Sigurðr made ready and returned to his ships. King Baldwin
prepared his army to march to a city in Syria called Seth (Sidon).[17] It was a heathen city. King Sigurðr [also] marched with his troops to the city. When the two
kings had besieged the city for a short time, the heathens surrendered and the
kings captured the city, leaving their men to plunder it. King Sigurðr gave the
whole city to King Baldwin. Halldórr said the following:

> F 3.   Borg heiðna tókt bræðir
>   benja tíkr af ríki
>   (háðisk hver við prýði
>   hildr) en gaft af mildi.

"Bræðir benja tíkr, tókt heiðna borg af ríki, en gaft af mildi; háðisk hver hildr við
prýði."

Feeder of the bitch of wounds [she-wolf; warrior], powerfully you captured the pagan city and generously you gave it away; every battle was fought nobly.

After that King Sigurðr went to his ships and prepared to leave the kingdom
of Jerusalem. He sailed north to the island of Cyprus and stayed there for some
time. Then he sailed to Greece and landed with his whole force at Engilsnes
(Gallipoli Peninsula). He stayed there for half a month and every day there
was a fresh breeze for a northerly course. But King Sigurðr wanted to wait for
a cross wind so that the sails could be spread from bow to stern on the ships
because all of his sails were covered with precious fabric on both sides to make
sure that neither those forward nor those aft would see what was less sightly on
the sails.[18]

When King Sigurðr sailed along the coast to Constantinople, there was an unbroken succession of villages, towns, castles, and great market centers. Because the sails were mounted lengthwise along the ships, the wind was light, and the ships sailed in close formation, it looked like a single wall of sail to those on shore. There was not a single place along the shore where not everybody turned out as long as the sails could be seen.

Emperor Kirjalax (Alexios) had heard of King Sigurðr and had the gate of Constantinople that is called Gullvarta (the Golden Gate) opened. That is the gate through which the emperor rides when he has been away on campaign for a long time and has won the victory. The emperor had precious fabrics spread on the streets from Gullvarta to Laktjarnir (Blachernai), the emperor's grandest residence.[19] King Sigurðr told his men to ride boldly into the city and pay no attention to all the novelties they saw. They acted accordingly. The emperor had them met with song and dance. In such triumph did King Sigurðr and all his men enter Constantinople. We are told that King Sigurðr had his horse shod with gold before riding into the city and arranged that one shoe would come off on the street and that none of his men should take any notice. When King Sigurðr and his men came to the king's hall, splendid preparations had been made.]*[20]

. . . even if the shoes fell off the horses. They did as he said and the emperor sent out a reception party with song and celebration. Thus King Sigurðr and all his men rode into the city in the midst of this grandeur and then on to the emperor's palace, where everything was prepared for his reception.

62. Concerning the Gifts of Emperor Kirjalax (Alexios I Komnenos)

King Sigurðr's men were now seated in the hall, and the drinking was about to begin. At that moment two of Emperor Kirjalax's messengers entered the hall carrying between them great bags of gold and silver. They said that the emperor had sent this to King Sigurðr. (FJ 349) He did not deign to look at the treasure but told his men to divide it among themselves. The messengers returned and reported to the emperor. He said: "This king must be immensely rich and powerful since he finds no need to take an interest in such gifts or to convey words of acknowledgment."

He then told them to go with large tubs full of gold. They went and came before King Sigurðr again, announcing that the emperor had sent him this money. He replied: "This is a large amount of money. You should divide it among yourselves, men."

The messengers returned and told the emperor. He said: "There are two possible interpretations of this king. Either he is wealthier and more powerful than other kings, or he is not as wise as it becomes a king to be. Go now a third time and take him the reddest gold and fill these tubs to overflowing." And the emperor laid two (U 164) great golden rings on top.

The messengers set out and came before King Sigurðr. They told him that the emperor had sent him this treasure. King Sigurðr stood up, took the rings, and drew them on his arms. Then he made a speech in Greek and thanked the emperor with fair words for his generosity.[1] He courteously distributed the treasure among his men and was greatly honored for this by the emperor. After that it was customary for the emperor and King Sigurðr to occupy the same elevated seating.

King Sigurðr remained there for a time, and once Emperor Kirjalax sent men to ask whether he would rather have six *skippund* of red gold or whether he preferred to have the emperor organize the games that he was accustomed to stage at the hippodrome.[2] King Sigurðr chose the games. The emperor's messengers told King Sigurðr that the games cost the emperor no less than the gold. Then the emperor arranged the games, and when they took place, they went better for the emperor than for the empress, who had the other team. There were contests in every (FJ 350) event, and the emperor's men had better success. The Greeks say that in any year in which the emperor wins more events than the empress, the emperor will win a victory in a military campaign.

Those who have been in Constantinople say that the hippodrome is constructed in such a way that there is a high wall enclosing a field that might be compared with a huge circular homefield.[3] There are tiers along the wall for people to sit on while the games are played on the field. The walls are decorated with all sorts of ancient events. You can find the Æsir, the Volsungs, and the Gjukungs fashioned in copper and iron with such great skill that they seem alive.[4] With this arrangement people have the impression that they are participants in the games. The games are staged with great ingenuity and visual deception so that men look as though they are riding in the air. There are also displays of Greek fire, to some extent with magical effects. In addition, there are all sorts of musical instruments, psalteries, organs, harps, violins, and fiddles, and all sorts of stringed instruments.[5]

63. Concerning King Sigurðr's Feast

One day, sometime later, King Sigurðr was scheduled to arrange a feast for the emperor and ordered his men to make the proper provisions for everything that was needed, according to the customs that were appropriate for powerful men. Then he told his men to go to the wood market in the city, saying that he would need a great deal of wood. They said that every day many loads were brought into the city and that there was no fear of a shortage. But it turned out that the necessary wood was all gone, and they reported that to King Sigurðr. He (U 165) said: "See if you can find some walnuts. They won't be any harder to kindle than (FJ 351) wood."[1] They went and got as many as they needed.

Then the emperor and his confidants arrived, and they all sat down together. There was a great display of hospitality, and the emperor was given princely treatment. When the emperor and empress realized that there was no shortage of anything, she sent men to ascertain what they were using for firewood. They came to a little shed and saw that it was full of walnuts. They told her about the walnuts and that they were used for firewood. She replied: "This king is certainly prodigal and lets nothing stand in the way of his honor, for no wood burns better than this." She had cut off the supply of wood to test King Sigurðr's ingenuity.

We are told that King Sigurðr removed a very ornate dragon-head from the prow of his ship* and placed it on St. Peter's Church. Then he returned to Norway, but before he and the emperor parted in Constantinople, King Sigurðr gave him all his ships. The dragons on the one that the king had commanded were gilded, and his ships were drawn up on the land and put on display in Constantinople for a long time after that. Emperor Kirjalax gave King Sigurðr many horses and gave him an escort throughout his realm. Then King Sigurðr departed from Constantinople, but many of his men stayed behind and entered the emperor's service. There was a wise man in Constantinople who said that King Sigurðr's honor would be shaped like the lion, powerful in the shoulders but tapering toward the hindquarters. He said that his kingship had now reached the zenith of distinction but would later decline.

King Sigurðr then set out from Constantinople through Hungary, Saxony, and Denmark. On this journey King Sigurðr met with the Holy Roman Emperor Lothar in Swabia.[2] The emperor gave him (FJ 352) an excellent reception and provided him with an escort. He established markets for him throughout his realm. When King Sigurðr came to Heiðabýr (Hedeby) in Denmark, he met Nicholas, king of the Danes, there.[3] He prepared a great feast for King Sigurðr and escorted him in person north to Jutland. He gave him a fully equipped ship to take to Norway. In the middle of the summer Jarl Eilífr received him in Schleswig and entertained him splendidly.

And now three years after King Sigurðr departed, all the people could welcome him back in Norway. He was then twenty years of age and had gained great fame because of his voyages and his magnificence. His brother King Eysteinn was a year younger.[4] There are now many places in Norway that are adorned with the treasures that King Sigurðr brought (U 166) back. He made a great and precious donation to the Church of Saint Óláfr.[5] He then traveled through his realm *and was well received*. It is said that no more famous voyage has been undertaken from Norway than the one King Sigurðr *accomplished. The skald* reports how joyful people were when he returned to his country:[6]

234. Herr hauksnǫrum
          harðmóðigr varð.
People were faithful to the proud king.

64. Concerning King Eysteinn

King Eysteinn had not been idle in the land while King Sigurðr was abroad. He built the great hall in Bjǫrgvin, the greatest and most famous wooden building in Norway. *He had Saint Michael's Church constructed* on Norðnes and endowed a monastery, which is the *most magnificent monastery built of stone*. He had the Church of the Apostles constructed in the king's compound in Bjǫrgvin. King Eysteinn had a fortress built at (FJ 353) Agðanes *and a harbor and a church* at Vágar (Vågan) in Hálogaland and provided an endowment. He also constructed a great warship *after the model of* Ormr enn langi. King Eysteinn built the Church of Saint Nicholas at Niðaróss.[1]

He expanded the kingdom by communicating with the wise men of Jämtland and gaining their warm friendship. He honored them with gifts and moved them to thoughts of friendship toward him.[2] Then he circulated the idea of how easy it was for them to get what they needed here in Norway, and how difficult it was to look to the east. They understood that the king spoke in their interest, and each had frequent discussions with the other. They then returned east and obtained the agreement of the people in this matter, and were given sworn oaths. They went back to Norway and placed Jämtland under King Eysteinn's rule with wisdom and affection. That arrangement has since remained firm. Thus King Eysteinn was able to win Jämtland with prudent counsel rather than with hostility and aggression, like some of his ancestors. In this way he made peace with the Jamtar, and in the course of their negotiations all the district chieftains went to meet with King Eysteinn and transferred Jämtland, with its revenues, to him and became his thanes.[3] In return, he promised them his support in the event of hostilities with the king of the Swedes, with the understanding that he was under the same obligation to aid them as the Norwegians or his other thanes. The revenues from that land still belong to the King of Norway.[4]

King Eysteinn also did much to improve the laws of the Norwegians. He was a great supporter of the law and familiarized himself with all the laws in Norway. He was (U 167) a very intelligent man and very handsome in appearance. He was blond, of medium height, eloquent, and outstandingly liberal. (FJ 354) Of all kings, he was the most beloved by his men. He was cheerful and outgoing in his speech. He was married to Ingibjǫrg, the daughter of Steigar-Þórir. Their children were named Guthormr and María, who was married to Guðbrandr, the son of Skafhǫggr.[5]

65. Concerning King Eysteinn and Ívarr

It may be noted in what I am about to tell what an outstanding man King Eysteinn was and how devoted he was to his friends and how accommodating

toward those who stood in his affection, no matter what grief they suffered.[1]
There was a man with King Eysteinn whose name was Ívarr. He was the son of
Ingimundr and an Icelander from an important family.[2] He was a wise man
and a good skald. The king esteemed him greatly and was affectionate toward
him, as will be seen. Ívarr had a brother named Þorfinnr, who also traveled
abroad to meet King Eysteinn. He benefited from the reputation of his brother
in the estimation of *many men*, but he was distressed not to be considered
his brother's equal and to be dependent on his reputation. For that reason he
did not thrive at the king's court and prepared to depart for Iceland. But before the brothers parted, Ívarr asked Þorfinnr to bring Oddný, the daughter of
Jón, word that she should wait for him and not marry. He said that he prized
her above all women.

Then Þorfinnr set sail and had a smooth passage. He made up his mind to
woo Oddný for himself and won her.[3] Sometime later Ívarr also returned and
learned of this. He thought that Þorfinnr had treated him badly. He found no
gratification in Iceland and returned to the king, where he stayed in high esteem as before. Ívarr was now very dispirited, and when the king perceived that,
he invited Ívarr to speak with him and asked why he was so cheerless: "When you
were (FJ 355) here before, you were very entertaining. I do not ask you about
this because I think we have done anything to displease you. You are also a wise
enough man not to have groundless suspicions. Tell me what the trouble is."

Ívarr replied: "I cannot tell you about it, sire."

The king said: "Then I will guess. Are there some men with whom you are
not pleased?"

"No, sire," said Ívarr.

The king asked: "Do you think that you are less honored than you
would wish?"

"No, sire," he said.

"Is there something you have seen in this country that you do not like?"
asked the king.

He said that such was not the case. "The guessing is getting harder," said the
king. (U 168) "Is there something you wish to have at your command?"

He said that there was not.

"Are you mourning the loss of some woman in your country?" asked
the king.

He replied: "That is so, sire."

The king went on: "Do not grieve. As soon as spring is here, you may leave
and I will give you a letter with my seal to deliver to those who are responsible
for making the decision, and I do not expect them to refuse the hand of the
woman when they receive my friendly representations or stern words."

Ívarr answered: "It cannot be."

"This is not possible," said the king, "and I will go even further. Even if another man is married to her, I can still obtain her for you if I wish."

Ívarr said: "The case is more difficult than that, sire. My brother is married to the woman."[4]

Then the king said: "Let us think no more of it. I see another solution. After Christmas I will do my round of official visits and you should accompany me. You will see many elegant women, and if they are not of royal blood, I will give you one."

Ívarr said: "My case is so difficult that whenever I see fair women, I remember the one I have in mind and my grief increases." (FJ 356)

The king said: "Then I will give you a command and property, as I have already offered, and that will serve to distract you."

He replied: "This affords no comfort."

The king said: "Then I will give you money, and you may go on a trading expedition wherever you wish."

He said that he had no such desire.

Then the king said: "The difficulties are mounting, because I have made every effort I can, and only one thing remains, though it amounts to very little compared to what I have already offered you. But I am unable to guess what will help. Every day you should come to me when the tables are removed and if I am not preoccupied with necessary business. Then I will speak with you. We will talk about this woman in any way you wish, and I will take whatever time is needed, for it can happen sometimes that people are relieved of their sorrows when the matter is discussed. And into the bargain I will arrange that you will never leave my presence without a gift."

Ívarr answered: "This is what I would choose, sire, and I thank you for your solicitude."[5]

And now matters were arranged so that whenever the king was not taken up with official business, he would talk to Ívarr about this woman. The device worked, and Ívarr's grief was alleviated more quickly than expected, and he began to cheer up. He recovered the same good disposition and capacity to amuse that he had had before, and he remained with *King* Eysteinn.

66. Concerning the Kings' Genealogies

King Sigurðr was a tall, strong man, distinguished and handsome, with dark hair, a good ruler and bent on enforcing his authority. He maintained the laws well but was not very skilled in the law. He was rather taciturn and (U 169) uncommunicative, and not given to speechmaking at thingmeetings. He was faithful to his word and had a long memory. He was a powerful (FJ 357) *and outstanding king. He was married to M*almfríðr, the daughter of Haraldr Valdimarsson from the east in Kiev. This Valdimarr was the son of *King Yaroslav and* Ingigerðr, the daughter of Óláfr the Swede. Haraldr Valdimarsson's mother was Edith, the daughter of Harold God*winson.

The mother of Queen Ma*lmfríðr was Kristín, the daughter of King Ingi Steinkelsson, king of the Swedes. *Haraldr Valdimarsson's second daughter was Ingibjǫrg, who was married* to King Knútr lávarðr. Their children were King Valdimarr of Denmark and Marg*rét, Kristín*, and Katerín. Margrét was married to Stígr hvítaleðr (White Leather), and their daughter was Kristín, who was married to Karl Sørkvisson, king of the Swedes. Their son was King Sørkvir, the father of King Jón.[1] King Sigurðr jórsalafari (Jerusalem-Farer) and Queen Malmfríðr had a daughter named Kristín. King Sigurðr had a son with his concubine, whose name was Borghildr, the daughter of Óláfr of Dalr. The son's name was Magnús. He was a very handsome man and was raised in his youth north on Bjarkey with Viðkunnr Jónsson.[2] He was thought to be an exceedingly accomplished man.

67. Concerning King Sigurðr's Dream

King Sigurðr became very depressed and would not enter into conversation. He did not linger over drink, and this worried his advisers and friends. They asked King Eysteinn to find some way to ascertain why men who needed to have their cases resolved could get no decisions from him. King Eysteinn replied that it was difficult to approach the king, but in response to their entreaties he agreed.

Once when they were together, King Eysteinn brought the matter up with King Sigurðr and asked what the cause of his depression was. "It grieves many of us, lord, and we would like to know the reason. Have you learned some significant news?" (FJ 358)

King Sigurðr replied: "Not at all."

King Eysteinn asked: "Is it, brother, that you want to travel abroad and extend your power once again as you did before?"

King Sigurðr said that this was not the case. King Eysteinn asked: "Are there men in the country who have become the object of your wrath?"

The king replied that no such thing had happened.

Then King Eysteinn asked: "Have you had a dream that causes you grief?" He affirmed that.

"Then tell me the dream, brother," said King Eysteinn.

King Sigurðr replied: "I will not tell you, lord, unless you interpret what it means, and I will be able to judge clearly whether you are interpreting it correctly or not."

King Eysteinn replied: "Lord, it is a great dilemma on the one hand to suffer your wrath (U 170) if I do not provide a likely interpretation and, on the other hand, that the people should suffer the grief of your cheerlessness. But I will take the risk and see how it turns out. Tell me your dream."

King Sigurðr said: "I dreamed that we three brothers were sitting on a bench

in front of Christ Church in Kaupangr (Niðaróss), and our kinsman Saint
Óláfr went out of the church in royal robes and with a kind and glorious coun-
tenance. He went up to our brother King Óláfr and took his hand and said
gently: 'Come with me, kinsman.' He rose up and entered the church with him
and disappeared from our view. A little later Saint Óláfr came out and approached you, brother, and said that you should go with him, but he was not
as gentle as before. You then went into the church, and I expected that he
would come to me, but it did not happen. Then I was overcome by a great fear
and weakness, and by the illness and melancholy that I have since suffered
from. (FJ 359) At that moment I awoke."

King Eysteinn said: "Lord, I may be inaccurate, but I will at least not be slow
in interpreting this dream. I believe that the bench signifies our realm. When
you saw King Óláfr coming gently toward our brother Óláfr, that means that
he will have the shortest life of us three but has good expectations. He is young
and popular and has not experienced much. Saint Óláfr will intercede for him
with God. And when you saw him approach me less gently, that means that I
will live a few years longer, though I will not grow old. And I too expect his aid.
When he came to me, it means that he will hold his hand over me with God's
mercy, though not with the same fullness as in the case of our brother Óláfr,
for it has come about that I have committed many sins and broken many commandments. But when you thought he was slow in approaching you, I do not
think it signifies your death. It may, however, mean that you will succumb to
some grave illness. And when you felt some darkness and fear envelop you, I
take it to mean that you will live the longest of the three of us and rule this
country longest." Then King Sigurðr answered: "That is a good and wise interpretation, brother, and it is likely to turn out as you say."

68. The Dealings of King Eysteinn and Ingimarr with Ásu-Þórðr

In the days of King Eysteinn and his brothers there came from Iceland a man
whose name was Þórðr. His family was from the East Fjords. He was poor, but
he was an able man, wise, and a good skald. When he came to the town,[1] he
had little (U 171) to defray his expenses. One evening he came to the house
of a woman named Ása. (FJ 360) She was a woman of good family and was
wealthy. She was related to the people on Bjarkey and to Viðkunnr Jónsson.[2]
She took Þórðr in at first for a short time. He was good company and managed
her affairs well, so that he gained favor there and spent the winter. The longer
he stayed, the more the mistress of the house valued him, and people began
to remark that they had a lot to say to each other. Ása was no longer a young
woman.

When spring came, she told Þórðr that she was well satisfied with him: "I will
now give you money for a voyage to England, in which we will coinvest."[3] He

agreed, and the voyage turned out well. He returned in the fall and spent the winter with Ása. This was the arrangement for several summers, and he prospered. He continued to undertake trading voyages, and the longer he stayed and held to this practice, the more he throve, and he was now called Ásu-Þórðr. Her kin found the situation dishonorable and took a dislike to him. He was a handsome man of impressive appearance, and it was commonly rumored that he was involved with Ása. He accumulated a great deal of money and was popular.

It happened once that a man fell into conversation with Þórðr and told him that Viðkunnr Jónsson was expected there—"and I would like you to compose a poem about him if you are so minded, and in doing so you would gain his confidence, because I know that he rather looks down on you. Indeed, most people are not on a level with Ása's kinsmen, and it would be good for you to win his friendship."

Þórðr replied: "Have thanks for your advice. I will do my best to compose a poem."

With that they parted and Þórðr composed the poem. When the time came for Viðkunnr's arrival, he came with a large retinue and took lodgings. One day Þórðr came and greeted Viðkunnr, but he gave a short answer. (FJ 361) Then Þórðr began his poem, and people were quiet while he recited. When he finished, people spoke well of his poem, and Viðkunnr thought it was well made.

He said: "I have had a change of heart, Þórðr, and I will give you a little proof of it." He took a gold ring and gave it to Þórðr, but Þórðr said that he had no need of money and would rather have his friendship as a *reward* for his poem. Viðkunnr promised it to him, and they parted as friends.[4]

Time passed, and one autumn when Þórðr returned from *England* in the west, he drew his ship on shore in the River Nið and removed the ship that already lay in the anchorage below *his house. At that time* King Eysteinn was in the town and many distinguished men with him. Sigurðr Hranason and Viðkunnr Jónsson were present, along with Ingim*arr of Askr*. He was a very powerful district chieftain and a very overbearing man. He had anchored in Þórðr's berth, and *people remarked to Þórðr* that it was not proper that he had removed (U 172) Ingimarr's ship from the anchorage, but *Þórðr paid no attention* to what was said.

When Þórðr and his men unloaded their ship, he could not find the aft or forward tenting. Then he went on board Ingimarr's ship and found a fellow who had made off with the tenting. Þórðr seized him and led him to his house, where he kept him in custody. Then he brought his cargo home.

Ingimarr learned of all this and became very angry. He said that it was a great outrage and went to Þórðr's house with some men to demand that the captive be turned over immediately. Þórðr said that it would not be safe to let an unsentenced thief loose on the town.[5] Ingimarr said that a suet-eating

Icelander like him was not going to condemn his men to death.[6] He said that
the next time he came he would get the man and that Þórðr would never have
had a worse time. He said that he was no district chieftain if (FJ 362) he could
not stand his ground against an Icelandic beggar. Þórðr recited a stanza:

235. Nú tekr ýgr at œgja   trautt munk lausan láta
      ofkúgi mér drjúgum   linnbóls gjafi at sinni
      þinn hefr hǫlðr of hlannat   vísan þjóf (þótt váfi
      hjaldrgegninn mik tjaldi: ván mín und hlut þínum).

"Nú tekr ýgr ofkúgi at œgja mér drjúgum: þinn hǫlðr hefr of hlannat hjaldrgegn-
inn mik tjaldi. Linnbóls gjafi, trautt munk láta lausan vísan þjóf at sinni, þótt ván
mín váfi und hlut þínum."

Now the terrible tyrant begins to threaten me strongly: your man has stolen the
tenting from me, the audacious one. I'm reluctant to release a thief caught red-
handed this time, dispenser of the snake lair [gold, generous man], although my
future rests in your hands.

Ingimarr went away in a rage, and when he had gone, Ása told Þórðr to send
for Viðkunnr because things were not well as they stood. Word reached
Viðkunnr, and he reacted immediately. He arrived at Þórðr's house with unexpected speed and with a large body of men. A little later they heard a great
tumult, and there was Ingimarr with a numerous following. He demanded that
the man be released or he would take him himself. Viðkunnr was charged with
the response and said that it would be best if the matter were submitted to the
"lawmen."[7]

He said that Þórðr had done what was called for and would have been legally
culpable if he had done otherwise. "And we will await the outcome."

"'Dig me in,' said the spade," replied Ingimarr.[8] "It is a major matter if we
are to deal with you, Viðkunnr, and I say that it is a good thing if we district
chieftains contend with each other, and much more fitting than that I should
deal with Þórðr." Then he departed.

Viðkunnr said to his men: "Go now and find Sigurðr Hranason, and tell
him to come here. If he makes some pretext, remind him who helped him
when the Lapps seized his farm." They set out and brought Sigurðr Viðkunnr's
message.

Sigurðr said: "I think it is a good match between Viðkunnr and Ingimarr,
(FJ 363) because each thinks that he is superior to the other." The messengers
remembered Viðkunnr's parting words and repeated them. Then (U 173) Sigurðr said: "It is true that no one helped me as much as Viðkunnr. Let us ready
ourselves and go."

Then they came to Þórðr's residence and soon realized that there was a large
crowd of men in the streets. It was Ingimarr with his retainers, but Viðkunnr's
force had dispersed here and there in the town. When Ingimarr arrived at the
residence, he said: "Now we are prepared to seize the man, Viðkunnr, if he is
not surrendered."

Sigurðr replied: "Let us proceed with forbearance and justice, Ingimarr, for people will wish to safeguard their rights against you even if you are a mighty warrior."

Ingimarr replied: "It is no help for the hare that the hen bears a shield.[9] The stakes are now high if you are both against me and are both district chieftains. But I will come a third time, and I am loath to have you wrest the man away from me." Then he went away and gathered as large a force as he could and assembled many men.

On the other side, Sigurðr sent messengers to King Eysteinn and asked him to come, saying that otherwise a great deal of trouble would break out. "And if the king shows any reluctance, tell him that I was one of the last to part from his father west in Ireland."

The messengers came to the king and reported Sigurðr's words. The king said: "It seems to me that two district chieftains have a sufficient advantage in dealing with Ingimarr, and I cannot see that there is any need for me. They all think they are mighty men."

Then the messengers said: "Sire, who fought hardest for your father at his last battle west in Ireland?"[10]

The king replied: "Sigurðr and Viðkunnr. They may think it important that I come, and so I shall."

The king went to Þórðr's house with a large following of men. A short time later Ingimarr arrived with a large following and said that there was likely to be a confrontation if they did not release the man. (FJ 364).

The king replied: "It is not proper, Ingimarr, to raise such an army in the town over such a minor matter and such an unworthy man. We have no intention of yielding to you."

Ingimarr said: "The affair is becoming serious when the king himself arrives, and we will have to withdraw for the time being."

The king ordered that the thief be taken to the town meeting. This was done, and the stolen tenting was fastened on his back, as is the custom.[11] Then he was judged and hanged, out on Eyrar. The king asked: "What do you think will be the thief's lot in the other world, Ingimarr?"

"A good lot," said Ingimarr.

"No," said the king, "nothing less than hellfire."

Ingimarr replied: "That will not come to pass, but your energy is misspent in favoring this suet-eater though you dare not avenge your father, who was killed in Ireland like a dog gnawing a bone. I think he is the most likely to suffer hellfire."

Then he jumped up, went to his ship, and sailed east to Vík, where he killed one of the king's men. After that he left the country and went south to (U 174) Denmark. King Eysteinn did nothing to impede his journey and took no notice of his foolish words.[12] He let his goodness and intelligence prevail, as was always the case. Þórðr pursued his course and became a notable man in many ways. He was popular, and he and Ása had no lack of wealth. Here the story ends.

69. The Death of King Óláfr Magnússon

In the thirteenth year of their joint rule King Óláfr Magnússon became ill and died.[1] He is buried at Christ Church north in Kaupangr (Niðaróss). He was a very popular man. King Óláfr's mother was Sigríðr, the daughter of Saxi from Vík. Sigríðr was the sister of Kári from Austrátt (Austrått), who was called Kári "King's Brother."[2] He was a powerful and popular man.

Saxi in Vík had another daughter named Þóra. She bore a son *who was named Sigurðr* (FJ 365) and was later alleged to be Magnús's son and was called Sigurðr slembidjákn.[3] Kári "King's Brother" was married to Borghildr, the daughter of Dagr *Eilífsson*. Their son was Sigurðr Austrátt, a district chieftain and the father of Jón, who was married to Sigríðr, the sister of King Ingi Bárðarson.[4]

After the death of King Óláfr the surviving brothers King Sigurðr and King Eysteinn *divided* the land in halves. King Sigurðr ruled the eastern part of the country, and King Eysteinn ruled *the northern part* and resided chiefly in Niðaróss. There was soon some dissension between the kings in the country.

70. *An Account of Legal Dealings between King Sigurðr and King Eysteinn* ("Þinga saga")

*When Jer*usalem-Sigurðr returned to Norway, the three brothers ruled and divided *the country among themselves*. Each kept his own retinue.

King Eysteinn and King Óláfr were most nearly in agreement. *We are told that King Sigurðr was once* being officially entertained north in Þrándheimr at a royal residence. *His kinsman by marriage* Sigurðr Hranason was there and his wife Skjaldvǫr, who was the sister of King Magnús berfœttr. Present as well was a district chieftain named Ívarr, who was identified by his estate and called Ívarr of Fljóðar (Fløan). His wife was named Sigríðr. She was the daughter of Hrani and Sigurðr's sister. She was present at the feast and was the fairest and courtliest of women.[1]

One day when the king was sitting at drink after mealtime and was in good spirits and had in his hand a gold ring, he said: "Here is a ring of high-quality gold and no small dimensions. It is available as a gift to the man who will carry out a mission, the success of which is very important to me." No one replied. Then the king said: "I am not addressing this to men of little consequence (U 175) but rather to the district chieftains, although I cannot be without you, kinsman Sigurðr, in Norway."

Then Ívarr of Fljóðar made a quick reply: "I think (FJ 366) I am not being overhasty in replying, because you have specified a district chieftain for the undertaking, though you exempted Sigurðr. I know of no district chieftain here other than myself, but I am not sure how to understand your mission, especially since it is of great importance. But you will not appeal to no purpose, for I know that you will make good provision, and I will go wherever you wish."

The king said: "It is known to all that my father acquired a large territory in Ireland in the area known as Ulster. Since his death we have had no profit from that realm in fiefs or taxes. I wish to send you west to demand the payment of taxes, and I wish you to set out immediately for Niðaróss and prepare your voyage with all possible speed. I will provide you with both ships and troops and whatever money you yourself determine."

Ívarr said: "I was not prepared for such a rush, but I will not delay."[2]

That same day he left the king and set out for Niðaróss, where he prepared his sea voyage to the west. He had one ship and nearly sixty men, and many valuables and a large requisition from the king's treasury. His voyage was speedy, and he arrived in the west, where he spent the winter in Orkney.

In the early spring he came to Ireland and convened meetings and councils with the people. He presented the king's message and gave the important men good gifts. He asked the people with fair words to honor the king and send him tribute. He explained that the king felt obliged to look to the matter of revenge for his father, and he related what a powerful king he was and how he had conquered far and wide and how well-traveled he was. He said that they could expect the same if they did not respond favorably with payments and honorable delegations. In addition, he promised his own service in persuading the king to make no further demands. He called the tribute (FJ 367) a gift of friendship and not a tax to be rendered to the king. He succeeded in presenting the case so that they agreed to the payment, and it was enormous. He took the money and brought it to Norway.

On the same evening when Ívarr of Fljóðar had taken his leave of the king, the king was in extraordinarily high spirits and stayed up drinking for a long time. Sigurðr Hranason was apt to be sleepy in the evenings and was not fond of nighttime activities and long hours. He asked the king for permission to go to bed. The king told him to do as he pleased, "but you, Skjaldvǫr, should stay up with me and drink." The party went on for a long time, and people gradually dispersed to go to bed.

When Skjaldvǫr and Sigríðr left, the king gave them an escort. Skjaldvǫr was escorted to the quarters where Sigurðr Hranason slept, but Sigríðr was taken alone to the place where the king slept. (U 176) The night passed and the next morning Sigurðr learned what had happened the previous night and was furious. When the king had taken his place in the high seat and the tables were set, Sigurðr Hranason did not come in until a man was sent for him. He went directly to his place and did not greet the king.

Then the king said to him: "You are not proceeding with your customary discretion, Sigurðr. You arrive late and show us no honor."

He replied: "You enjoy great honor and deserve little."

The king said: "Those are ugly words, kinsman. Let us disregard them and be in good spirits."

Sigurðr said: "I cannot disregard the shame and dishonor you have brought on us."[3]

Then the king became angry and said: "You have a bold tongue, thief that you are, to speak to us in this way."

Sigurðr said: "I have not heard myself titled a thief before."

The king replied: "Who is a bigger thief than you are? Every six months you steal no less than sixty (FJ 368) marks from me, since you are charged to collect the Lapp tribute and pay out only half of what is my right. I can assure you," said King Sigurðr, "that you will answer for the discrepancy."[4]

They said no more that day, but Sigurðr could tell that the king was not going to let the matter rest, and he thought he had a poor chance of holding his own against the sort of aggressiveness with which he was faced. Sigurðr then departed because he did not dare to remain. He was unable to control what happened to his sister.

Sigurðr went first to Kaupangr and took lodging there. But he did not stay for long and left Þrándheimr with eleven men, proceeding south along the Norwegian coast and not stopping until he arrived in Vík in the east and met King Eysteinn.

He told him in private everything that had happened. King Eysteinn reproached Sigurðr severely for having spoken so boldly to King Sigurðr and said this was an imprudent way to deal with a man of such rank. But he spoke with him alone for three days and investigated the whole matter. He devised a plan that was later revealed.

Messengers were sent north to meet with Skjaldvǫr and say that King Eysteinn would come north the following spring and try to arrange a reconciliation with King Sigurðr. During that winter Sigurðr was in the north and King Eysteinn in the east. When spring came, King Eysteinn made ready for his trip and arrived in Þrándheimr with his armed company, intending to bring about a settlement between King Sigurðr and Sigurðr Hranason. King Eysteinn made inquiries to determine whether King Sigurðr was in a calmer state of mind, but such was not the case.

King Sigurðr had spent the winter in the north, and the kings met in Kaupangr. They had not spent long in the town before King Sigurðr had a meeting summoned, and at the meeting (FJ 369; U 177) he accused Sigurðr Hranason of having appropriated part of the royal fisc and having collected the Lapp tribute with private greed and contrary to the wishes of those who had rightful possession of it. He said that he had the right to impose the penalty that is proper when the king's property is infringed, and he said that a legal judgment was in order.

Sigurðr Hranason replied to the king's speech as follows: "It is well known that King Magnús berfœttr took his army east to Gautland to raid and carried off great plunder. Then he put his *men in charge*, Sigurðr ullstrengr and many other chieftains, on an island called Valdísey.[5] He himself remained *elsewhere* with some of the forces. I was with him in this campaign and could bring him a reliable report that King Ingi was marching *toward him* with an enormous army so that it was not safe to remain there. He took that to be a friendly service. When that report came, the king *moved* his army to Vík. But Sigurðr ullstrengr and the forces with him were all captured. *King Magnús took the view that* I had saved him. He gave me his sister Skjaldvǫr in marriage and granted me the privilege that I *should have* the Lapp tribute and trade with the Lapps as long as he or his sons ruled Norway. I was to pay the king sixty marks of silver every half year but keep the remainder for myself. I think that I am fully entitled to that money since he granted me the privilege of the Lapp tribute. And I have witnesses to the grant. But what I said to you in the heat of the moment, sire, did not honor you as it should have, and I will offer compensation at your discretion."

King Sigurðr said that he would not accept his offer and persisted in the suit for financial damages.

Then King Eysteinn spoke: "This case that you are bringing against Sigurðr is such, brother, that he should not be prosecuted in a town meeting, because the case is subject to the law of the land and not to the law of Bjarkey.[6] It is well known, brother, that the law of Bjarkey has no jurisdiction in this case." (FJ 370)

King Sigurðr replied: "If it is your wish, King Eysteinn, to oppose a case that concerns you no less than me, I will prepare accordingly."

Then King Sigurðr convened a thingmeeting to assemble in two weeks north on Keflisey [*recte* Kefsisey in Vågan],[7] and he summoned Sigurðr Hranason to defend his case there. Then he left the meeting with his men. King Eysteinn told Sigurðr Hranason to name witnesses that King Sigurðr's case was legally void at the town meeting. He told Sigurðr to travel north to his residence at Steig to assemble as many troops as he could and bring them to the thingmeeting. He went north to Bjarkey and asked Viðkunnr Jónsson for aid. He replied, saying that he wished to be Sigurðr Hranason's friend but that this case was being played out between the kings themselves. He said that he was King Sigurðr's district chieftain (U 178) and that he would support him.

A little later the king sent men to Viðkunnr to tell him to join him with whatever forces he could raise. He did so, and King Sigurðr arrived at the thing first with a very numerous following. When King Eysteinn proceeded north, Sigurðr Hranason came to meet him with a large force, and when they arrived at the thingmeeting, King Eysteinn said: "Now we will marshal our troops as impressively as we can. When the ships have berthed, all the men should march ashore with shields and weapons in tight formation. Only a few men should be left to guard our ships. It strikes me that this will make quite an impression on a lot of farmers who are with King Sigurðr at the thingmeeting, and there is a good chance that they will scatter from the assembly to admire us. Then let us make our way as quickly as possible to the assembly and absorb their followers in our troop. That will make us appear even more numerous."

They acted accordingly and many people came out to gawk at them, while only a few remained behind at the assembly with the king, (FJ 371) apart from his own retinue and Viðkunnr's. King Sigurðr saw that the men were drifting away and said to Viðkunnr: "The truth seems to be that everyone wants to be where Sigurðr Hranason is."

Viðkunnr replied: "That is not the case, sire, and this is a trick devised by King Eysteinn. Our Hálogalanders are merely inquisitive."

Then King Sigurðr presented his case and made the same accusation against Sigurðr Hranason concerning the division of the money. He urged the jurors to decide according to the law. Sigurðr made the same reply and the same offers as before. The king refused his offers and wanted recourse to the law.

Sigurðr Hranason said: "For the sake of our kinship and friendship and the many services I have performed for you, do not press the case. That will only redound to your honor. Do not let evil and envious men slander me, for I have had no more profit from the Lapp tribute than is fitting."

King Sigurðr replied: "I did not expect that you would reward my grant of privilege by taking what is mine and keeping more than was allowed you."

Sigurðr responded: "What people have told you is not true. I have kept only that part which you allowed."

The king replied: "You will not be able to convince me of that."

King Eysteinn arose and spoke: "It is not an easy thing to intervene and make some response to King Sigurðr, but there is a great difference between rendering some assistance in the case and opposing King Sigurðr. This case concerns us both, and because of Sigurðr's need and our kinship, I wish to say a few more words in his support. He considers himself to be guiltless in this matter, brother, and he asks the king to be mindful of a long friendship."

King Sigurðr answered: "It behooves a ruler to punish such breaches."

King Eysteinn replied: "If you wish to adhere to the law and just government, it is best for him to have the benefit (U 179) of his friends. And if you are determined to have legal redress in this case, it is appropriate to look closely at how you observe procedures. It may turn out that your case is rightful." (FJ 372)

Then King Sigurðr said: "This assembly was established by the men of the region, and you said in town that this case was to be prosecuted at a thing-meeting."

King Eysteinn replied: "This assembly was established by lawmen and farmers so that each of them could have the benefit of the law in dealing with each other.[8] But since the accusation is lodged against a district chieftain, it is proper that it be prosecuted at lawthings such as the Þrándarnesþing in this district." The matter was now investigated according to the law, and it appeared to the lawmen that King Eysteinn had interpreted the law correctly.

Then King Sigurðr convened the Þrándarnesthing in two weeks and summoned Sigurðr Hranason to defend himself.[9] After that he went to his ships with all his men. But King Eysteinn and Sigurðr Hranason again named witnesses to attest that this case was quashed at the Kefleyjarþing [recte Kefsiseyjarþing] according to the law. They did this in secret.

King Sigurðr now transferred the case to the Árnarnesþing [MS Arnarheims þings] and intended to prosecute the case there.[10] King Eysteinn also arrived to attend the thing, and when the case was ready to go to the jury, King Eysteinn went before them before the verdict could go against Sigurðr Hranason. Then King Sigurðr asked the lawmen to bring in their judgment, but King Eysteinn responded: "I believe that there will be enough wise men here who are familiar with the laws in Norway that they will know that a district chieftain cannot be outlawed at this thing." And he interpreted the case according to the law so that everyone found the interpretation correct.

Then King Sigurðr spoke: "You are pursuing this case with much energy, but even if it requires more work than I thought to win the case, I will nonetheless persist. I wish to outlaw him in his own region."

King Eysteinn replied: "There is not much in which you will not succeed if you press the matter, considering how many great accomplishments you have to your credit, especially since it can be expected that you will be opposed only by a few insignificant people here. But no one who stands accused in the Frostathing law district, (FJ 373) with the acts having been committed in Hálogaland, can have his case correctly judged here."[11] With that he quashed the case, and they parted in great anger. King Eysteinn and Sigurðr Hranason named witnesses to attest that King Sigurðr's case was quashed.

King Sigurðr now summoned all the district chieftains and their retainers. He called up a large number of militiamen from every district as far as southern Norway, and a great *army* was assembled, and he summoned men northward along the coast. He proceeded north to Hálogaland with the intention of *taking* aggressive enough action to outlaw Sigurðr in his own family stronghold in the north. He summoned all the Háleygjar and Naumdœlir at Þrándarnes. (U 180)

King Eysteinn also assembled a great army and proceeded to the thingmeeting. He said that they should make a martial appearance, arrange their shields in tight *order, hold* their weapons at the ready, and head up on land quickly to show that they were ready for a meeting with King Sigurðr. *They did so* and went to the thingmeeting on the appointed day. Both sides had large followings.

King Sigurðr and his men arrived at the thingmeeting first. When King Eysteinn went to the thing, he asked Sigurðr Hranason: "What offer are you going to make today?"

He said: "I look to you for advice."

The king replied: "Come here and assign me the defense of the case with a handshake and witnesses. We can then say that the case is brought against me and that the litigation is between us brothers. It is more equal that two kings should contest the matter, and let the two of us test *whether the laws can be disallowed*."

Then King Eysteinn went to the thingmeeting with his following. King Sigurðr brought his case against Sigurðr Hranason with the same impetuousness as before, or more. Then King Eysteinn replied to this effect: "It is known to everyone what offer Sigurðr Hranason has made to King Sigurðr. He does not consider the case against him to be valid since he offered to let King Sigurðr determine the settlement and has witnesses that King Magnús granted him the Lapp tribute (FJ 374) on the terms that have since been observed. Those terms dictated that the grant should remain in force as long as his sons ruled Norway. Now as before we wish him to present his witnesses and pay compensation for whatever cannot be witnessed. But if King Sigurðr insists on litigation aimed at a judgment against Sigurðr Hranason, it would still be reasonable to proceed according to the law."

King Sigurðr said that he did indeed wish the case to be pursued to the full extent of the law. He stated that King Magnús could not make the grant for longer than he was king of Norway. "If there is any flaw in the legal procedure, I claim that King Eysteinn is responsible, because the case has now been cited to the thing where King Eysteinn said that the legal issues should be contested."

King Eysteinn replied: "It is certainly true, brother, that I stated your obligation to bring this case against Sigurðr Hranason at the Þrándarnesþing. But if the case is reformulated so that it is contested by the kings themselves, it cannot be lodged with a district thing but must be referred to one or another of the law things, the Frostaþing, Gulaþing, or Heitsefaþing (Eiðsifaþing).[12] This case originated at the Frostaþing, and that is where it must conclude if it is legally tried. For I have taken over the case that should have belonged to Sigurðr, and now it is a case between kings, as you cannot deny."

King Sigurðr said: "Even if it is true that you have taken over this case and are (U 181) opposing me, I will still not let the matter rest." He summoned King Eysteinn to the Frostaþing and then departed. King Eysteinn named witnesses in secret to attest that the case was quashed. Then the time came for the thing to convene in Niðaróss, even though the Frostaþing had been stipulated and that stipulation had to be observed. The summer passed, and King Sigurðr remained in the town. Now the time came for the Frostaþing, though they had to wait for half a year. (FJ 375)

We are told that during the summer while King Sigurðr was in the town and was in conversation with Sigríðr, a man saw a ship approaching and suspected it might be Ívarr of Fljóðar. King Sigurðr sent the priest Einarr Skúlason to find out whether Ívarr had come or not. When he returned and appeared before the king, he recited the following:[13]

236. Þér hefk þengill Mœra   eigis Ívarr bauga
     (þinns vegr mikill) segja   (enn sitt kyrr hjá henni)
     (ert) (svát eigi skortir)   fægirjóðr af Fljóðum
     (allfróðr) sǫgu góða: fingrmjór kominn hingat.

"Þengill Mœra, hefk sǫgu góða segja þér, svát eigi skortir; vegr þinns mikill; ert all-fróðr. Bauga fægirjóðr, eigis fingrmjór Ívarr af Fljóðum kominn hingat: sitt enn kyrr hjá henni."

King of the Mœrir [people of Møre], I have no lack of good tidings to tell you; your glory is great; you are very wise. Colorer of shields, slender-fingered Ívarr of Fljóðar [Fløan] has not arrived: continue to sit undisturbed by her.

That had previously been Ívarr's nickname. That summer Ívarr returned to Norway with a great payment, and that was the end of the matter.

King Eysteinn spent the winter in Þrándheimr, and in the summer both kings sent word to their men, both to the district chieftains and their retainers, telling them to gather forces for the thingmeeting. Their brother King Óláfr was still alive at this time, and he and his men were also summoned. King Eysteinn was already in town (Niðaróss) when it came time for the thingmeeting, and he had his lodging in the royal residence. King Óláfr arrived before King Sigurðr and stayed in a residence close to the Church of Saint Óláfr. King Sigurðr arrived last with a large number of men on his ships, which he sailed into the River Nið. They remained on the tented ships and were in full force.

On the day when the thingmeeting was to be convened, it was announced that the farmers in town and the district men should proceed to the meeting first and set down the courts according to law. (FJ 376) The most important man was Jón Mǫrnefsson, the father of Eindriði, who fell at Sekkr, a district chieftain and a distinguished man.[14] Present with King Óláfr was Sigurðr, the son of Sigurðr of Hvítasteinn, the wisest district chieftain in Norway.[15]

King Eysteinn was the first of the two kings to go to the thingmeeting, which was very fully attended. He immediately urged the district chieftains to adopt his view and support Sigurðr Hranason to the best of their ability. Jón Mǫrnefsson replied and said that it would cause great difficulties to favor one brother over the other, but he said that he was more inclined to support King Eysteinn if that were in line (U 182) with the law.

King Eysteinn replied: "I wish to make no request of you that is contrary to the law, but if I can manage it legally so that you are not obligated to judge the case that is presented today, I wish to have your promise that you will make no judgment contrary to the law in order to accommodate my brother." This was greeted with loud applause.

Then King Óláfr came to the thingmeeting with his following, which was much the smallest. King Sigurðr came last, and almost all his followers were fully armed except that they had no shields. King Sigurðr presented the case against Sigurðr Hranason as he construed it according to the law in consultation with the advice of the counselors who considered it with him. King Eysteinn countered the prosecution. The first order of business was to review at the thingmeeting whether King Magnús could stipulate a matter with such force that it would extend beyond his lifetime or whether his decision would qualify as a proper defense against the charge.

The judges concluded that the king could make provisions for life in his jurisdictions, looking ahead to the next generation, but that such decisions should be publicized at all the lawthings in Norway. Next, inquiry was made into whether Sigurðr Hranason had publicized the grant to be effective beyond the life (FJ 377) of King Magnús and whether there were witnesses to the arrangement. Then King Sigurðr objected that he did not want to sanction laws in Norway that would allow a single king to establish laws beyond his own lifetime. He said that this defense of King Eysteinn's for the concession of the Lapp tribute to Sigurðr Hranason was null and void. King Eysteinn maintained that the king could determine both the beginning and the end of the term.

The matter was resolved in consultation with their advisers to the effect that the kings should draw lots to determine who should have the deciding voice in the future. When the lots were about to be cut and cast, King Eysteinn asked: "*King Óláfr*, with which of us do you wish to agree?" *Óláfr* said that they had long held each other in affection and that he wished to accede to his opinion with respect to laws and governance.

Then King Eysteinn answered: "I recommend that we cut a third lot because Óláfr is no less the son of King Magnús than Sigurðr and I are."

Then King Sigurðr replied: "It is plain that you are looking for any advantage, and you want two votes to my one. But I will not deny King Óláfr any honor or esteem." Then the lots were cast, and King Sigurðr's lot came up so that the decision was his. He then announced the same decision that he had previously desired.

The discussion then turned to whether Sigurðr Hranason had held back money without the leave of the rightful owners. Now *many men joined in* the discussion of what had transpired, but no one other than Bergþórr bokkr (Billygoat) claimed that Sigurðr Hranason was *guilty*. King Sigurðr now asked the judges[16] to render judgment against (U 183) Sigurðr Hranason and said the case was clear. He said that *it would ill* behoove them to announce a verdict that was not to his liking under the prevailing circumstances.

King Eysteinn said that it was entirely *unjust* to convict Sigurðr Hranason of this charge since King Magnús had granted him this privilege in his own name and that of his sons, and no one had abridged it *heretofore*: "I do not know (FJ 378) whether you count my wrath a lesser thing than King Sigurðr's, but I believe that it is of no less concern to me than to him if a judgment is made that seems to me contrary to law, for I think I am somewhat better informed in the law than he is."

Then Jón Mǫrnefsson replied that it did not seem unproblematical to reach a decision but that they would have to fulfill their obligations whether they liked it or not. King Eysteinn replied: "You should wait a little before reaching your decision."

Then he called his witnesses, who had been named to attest that the charge was null and void. Next, he reviewed the case and the evidence that had been brought at the Árnarnesþing to the effect that the charge was null and void. Then the evidence brought forward at the Þrándarnesþing was presented. Finally, he appealed to the judges, wishing to know whether they considered it lawful that prosecutions should be mismanaged in such a way that the same charge was brought over and over again: "I believe that the law states that if the disagreement of the qualified judges is so great that a case is quashed at three or four lawthings and witnesses are named to that effect, then that case should never be brought again, and the judges are obligated to find accordingly."[17]

He then named witnesses enjoining the judges from ruling in the case. Jón Mǫrnefsson replied that, if he was obligated to do so, he would judge the case in the most lawful way, but he said that he would be pleased if the judgment were forestalled in this manner. He also noted that King Eysteinn had stated what the law prescribed.

Then King Sigurðr spoke in great wrath: "It may be that King Eysteinn has quashed this case with his legal machinations, but there remains one instance, and it may be that I am no less adept at convening it than King Eysteinn. That instance will resolve the issue between us if I cannot obtain justice otherwise." He departed from the thingmeeting and went down to his ships with all his company.

King Eysteinn and Óláfr (FJ 379) went to their quarters. When King Eysteinn came into the hall and sat down to drink, he was in high spirits. Some of his friends pointed out what a difference in intelligence there was between the two brothers, and others argued about how the case would end. King Eysteinn asked Sigurðr Hranason how the conclusion suited him and whether he felt that he had been supported. He said that he was extremely pleased and that he had been supported in every respect. He said that he had been supported to the hilt, perhaps even too much. The king was angered and replied: "It is hard to find a man who is sufficiently courageous (U 184) that it is worth giving him full support. I will therefore take less of a hand in this matter than I might otherwise have done."

A little later Sigurðr Hranason got safely away from the drinking hall, and when he emerged, he saw that no one was paying any attention to him. He went away quickly with no cloak but in a fine tunic and dark belted trousers.[18] He carried a large halberd with a shaft long enough so that a standing man could reach to the spear socket.[19] He went directly to King Sigurðr's gangplank. There was a man seated on guard there. He asked for permission to go on board, but the man was slow to respond. Sigurðr said: "You have a choice between two alternatives. Either leave the gangplank or stand up to my spear." He made the more agreeable choice, and Sigurðr went aboard and into the main cabin, where tables were set.

Before anyone was fully aware, he had fallen on his knee and stated that he did not want the brothers to have a falling out over his case. He said that the case had been contentious enough without being pursued further, and he said that he would now rather throw himself on King Sigurðr's mercy. The king replied at the instigation of the chieftains and told Sigurðr that he was free to keep his life.

Many of his men urged the king to give him a good response, and the king finally said: "You are indeed (FJ 380) a distinguished man, Sigurðr, and you have found the solution that is most appropriate for all concerned. Up until now the dangers have been so great that the outcome was clear only to God. But now I will accept a settlement, and you will leave the judgment to me." This was done.

After that the king spoke: "I will not delay the settlement since the matter has already been disputed long enough. I assess a fine of fifteen marks of gold against you, and that amount should be paid up before the end of high mass at Christ Church tomorrow morning. My brothers wished to dishonor me, but I will guard their honor. You should pay me five marks, King Eysteinn five marks, and King Óláfr five marks as well, and you should pay them both before you pay me. The payment should be made in pure gold without exception. I am told that you have become rich in gold from the tribute that belongs to us three kings." He said that there would be no settlement except on these conditions. Sigurðr Hranason thanked the king for granting a settlement, regardless of what amount of gold he might have.

Then he left the king's ship and returned to King Eysteinn to report on what had transpired. The king flushed so that he could have been bled from one finger.[20] He replied: "You have placed us in great peril and given me a poor return for my support. I will have no part in this settlement." Then he left and went to his quarters.

Sigurðr went to his friends and borrowed gold. It amounted to a good five marks of pure gold when he pooled what he had and what he got on loan from others. In the morning at the end of (U 185) matins he went to King Eysteinn and asked him to bring out scales and weigh the money. When that was done, Sigurðr Hranason said: "Now I wish you to accept this money, sire. Call it payment if you wish, or a reward for your support, though it is less than it should be."

The king asked: "What money do you intend to pay King Óláfr and King Sigurðr?"

He replied: "I am beginning (FJ 381) where my greatest obligation lies, regardless of how the rest falls out."

Then King Eysteinn replied: "I suspect that you will have borrowed this money from your friends, and you shall receive it as a gift from me."

Sigurðr thanked the king and then went to find King Óláfr with the same intention of paying him the money. King Óláfr asked him whether he had paid King Eysteinn, and he recounted what had passed between them. Then

King Óláfr replied: "It is now as before that I can devise no better counsel than King Eysteinn, and I wish to give you the money so that they may be reconciled."

Then he went immediately to King Sigurðr, at the moment when the bell rang for high mass at Christ Church. He asked King Sigurðr to have the money weighed, and that was done. It weighed out to a good five marks. Then King Sigurðr asked if his brothers had been paid. He replied that both had been paid. The king rejoined: "It turned out as I suspected that you have become wealthy in gold." Sigurðr then told the whole story of how they had forgiven his payments, saying that this was the gold in question.

The king was silent, then asked: "I wish to stipulate, Sigurðr, that you will be my fast friend even though we brothers have been somewhat at odds. In that case I will make a gift of the money to you."

Then Sigurðr Hranason replied: "It is my wish that you should never be at odds, and I wish only the best for all three brothers. But whatever the cost, even if my life should be at stake, I will never honor any man above King Eysteinn as long as I live."

King Sigurðr replied: "The difference between Eysteinn and me will be greatest if I keep this money, and I will now make a gift of it to you, even though you make no promises in other respects."[21] Sigurðr thanked the king most warmly for all the benefits he had conferred. Then they went to mass.

There were many disputes between the brothers, but peace was maintained (FJ 382) in the land as long as both lived. But after this quarrel there was never again any warmth or kindness or affection between the brothers. People say that there has never been a more distinguished man or ruler in *Norway* than King Sigurðr. But it came to pass at the end of his life that he could scarcely control his temper and mind and succumbed to *severe* illness and disorders.[22] But he has always been reputed to be an outstanding king and a remarkable chieftain because of his exploits and achievements. (U 186)

71. The Contest of the Kings

It happened once that when the two brothers, King Eysteinn and King Sigurðr, were together at a feast, King Sigurðr fell silent and people were unable to engage him in conversation. The host was a friend of King Eysteinn's. He urged King Eysteinn to appeal to King Sigurðr—"because, sire, we find it difficult to frame our words so as to please him. It is true both that he has distinguished himself greatly and that he, as well as all his men, think all other accomplishments to be of little value, even if they were only serving men on the expedition.[1] The wealthy landholders and your friends, sire, are held in contempt by comparison. They strut in precious garments and think they are better than many a brave man."

This seemed true to King Eysteinn, and he spoke to King Sigurðr: "Brother, why are you so downcast? Are you ill? If you are in full health, it is honorable for us to entertain our men."[2]

King Sigurðr replied: "You can be as cheerful as you like, but leave my mood up to me."

King Eysteinn answered: "The decision is yours, lord, but how can it be that you feel disgraced by me? Are we not equal sons of King Magnús? I can tell this by listening to you and seeing your appearance. What seems to you to be the greatest difference between us? Tell me that."

King Sigurðr replied: (FJ 383) "I feel no need to compare our accomplishments."

King Eysteinn said: "If we cannot agree, there are wise men present to judge what we say."

King Sigurðr said: "I believe, King Eysteinn, that I am stronger and a better swimmer."

"That is true," said King Eysteinn, "but I am more skilled and better at board games, and that is worth as much as your strength."

King Sigurðr rejoined: "I believe that common opinion holds that I am no less skilled with weapons than you, and no less good at tourneying."[3]

King Eysteinn replied: "That is true, brother, but I note that men sometimes come to us in need of having their cases resolved. At those times the crowd around me is a little denser when men are unable to get the needed resolution from you."

King Sigurðr said: "To be sure, you are a wise man, King Eysteinn, and many seek you out for counsel. But I hear some say that you sometimes promise what you cannot accomplish and that you do not value your word greatly."

King Eysteinn answered: "It is true, brother, that many seek me out when I cannot help as much as I would wish. I also judge cases on the merits of the evidence. If better evidence comes to light later, I let each man have the benefit of justice, whatever the previous judgment was. But I hear it told that you fulfill your promises (U 187), though your promises are bad more often than not."

King Sigurðr said: "I traveled to the River Jordan by way of Apulia, and I saw no trace of you there. I was victorious in eight battles, and you fought in none of them. I went to the Lord's sepulcher and did not see you there. I entered the river after the example of our Lord and swam across, without finding you there. I tied a knot for you that still awaits you. I took the town of Sidon with the king of Jerusalem and we had no benefit from your support or counsel."[4]

Then King Eysteinn spoke (FJ 384): "Now you have hit the sore spot that I have thought for a long time was ready to bleed. I don't have much to compare with your accomplishments. North in Vágar (Vågan) I established a shelter for fishermen so that poor men could have aid and subsistence.[5] I also had a church built there and established a parsonage. I established a fund for church construction, where the land had been as good as pagan heretofore. Those people will remember that King Eysteinn was in Norway.

"I had a church built on Þrándarnes and endowed it. Those people will also remember that King Eysteinn was in Norway. There was a trail over the Dofra (Dovre) Mountains from Þrándheimr. Men were often exposed there and had difficult journeys. I had hospices built there and endowed them. Those people will remember that King Eysteinn was in Norway. Off Agðanes there was unprotected coastline and no place to put in, so that many ships perished. Now there are harbors and good anchorages, and a church has been constructed. Then I had signal pyres built on the mountains. The people who have the benefit will remember that King Eysteinn was in Norway. Fishermen and merchants, who bring their blessings to this land, will profit from it and the kingdom will have no lack of them.

"I had a hall built in Bjǫrgvin, and the Church of the Apostles and a bridge between them.[6] Later kings will remember this construction. I also built Saint Michael's Church and established a monastery. And I established laws, brother, so that everyone might have justice in his dealings with others. If these laws are maintained, the land will be better governed. I have also brought Jamtaland (Jämtland) into the realm, more with persuasion and wisdom than with aggression. This does not amount to much, but I am not sure that it is less useful or profitable for the people of the nation than your bludgeoning Africans off to the devil and sending them to hell.

"As for your boast of good deeds when you visited the Lord's sepulcher, I think that my merit (FJ 385) was no less when I established a monastery and a church together with it. And with respect to the knot that you tied for me, it seems to me that I could have tied you such a knot that you would never have been king of Norway again. You were penniless when you left the country, and King Óláfr and I dowered you like our sister. You will not take over the country in such a way that I will loose the knot. Now let wise men consider what advantage you have over me. You and your precious followers may realize that there are men who can still compete with you in Norway."[7] (U 188)

72. Concerning Þórarinn stuttfeldr

It happened once when King Sigurðr went from his drinking hall to vespers that his men were in their cups and in high spirits. They were sitting outside the church *singing* the evensong. The singing did not flow smoothly, and the king asked: "What man is that I see by the church *in a short cloak*?" They said that they did not know. The king said:

237. Villir vísdóm allan
    veldr því karl í feldi.

He confuses all wisdom: the man in the cloak causes that.

The man then came forward and said:

238. Hykk at hér megi þekkja   værir mildr ef mæra
    heldr í stuttum feldi   mik vildir þú skikkju

oss (en ek læt þessa   (hvat hafim heldr an tǫtra)
óprýði mér hlýða):   hildingr muni vildri.

"Hykk, at hér megi þekkja oss í heldr stuttum feldi, en ek læt þessa óprýði hlýða
mér. Værir mildr, ef þú vildir mæra mik skikkju muni vildri, hildingr: hvat hafim
heldr an tǫtra."

I know that I'm seen here in quite a short cloak, but I rather like this lack of style.
You would be generous, if you decked me out in a somewhat more desirable cloak,
king: I'd rather wear anything but rags.

Then the king said: "Come to me in the morning when I am at drink."

The night passed. The Icelander, who was later called Þórarinn stuttfeldr
(Short Cloak), came to the drinking hall. (FJ 386) A man was standing outside
with a drinking horn in his hand. He said to the Icelander: "The king said that
you should compose a stanza before entering if you wish to receive some token of friendship from him. Compose it about a man named Hákon Serksson,
who is nicknamed 'mǫrstrútr' (lump of lard), and make mention of that in
the stanza." The man who addressed him was named Árni and nicknamed
'fjǫruskeifr.'[1] Then they entered, and Þórarinn went before the king with his
stanza:

239. Þú vændir mér Þrœnda   lézt at Hákon héti
      þengill (ef stef fengak   hildingr enn fémildi
      frænda Serks at fundi)   (nú samir mér at minnask)
      folkrakkr gefa nakkvat: mǫrstrútr (á þat gǫrva).

"Folkrakkr Þrœnda þengill, þú vændir gefa mér nakkvat, ef fengak stef at fundi
frænda Serks. Hildingr enn fémildi, lézt, at Hákon héti mǫrstrútr; nú samir mér at
minnask gǫrva á þat."

Battle-keen king of the Þrœndir [people of Trøndelag], you promised to give me
something if I composed a poem when I met Serkr's kinsman. Generous king,
you said Hákon was called "mǫrstrútr" [lump of lard]; now it's only proper that I
should remember that perfectly.

The king said: "I never said that, and you must be the victim of a joke. It is
appropriate that Hákon assess the penalty, and go now to his company."

Then Hákon said: "He will be welcome in our company, and I can see how
this came about." He sat the Icelander down among them, and they were in
high spirits. Toward the end of the day it began to go to their heads.

Then Hákon said: "Do you think you owe me some amends?"

He replied: "Indeed I owe you amends."

"Do you not think you were the victim of a trick?" He (U 189) said that
was so.

Hákon said: "Our accounts will be settled if you compose another stanza
about Árni." He said he was prepared to do that, then went *to the place where
Árni was sitting and recited* a stanza:

240. Fullvíða hefr frœðum   ok vannt eina kráku
      Fjǫruskeifr of her veifat   orðvandr á Serklandi

lystr ok leiri kastat   (Skeifr bart Hǫgna húfu
lastsamr ara ens gamla: (FJ 387)   hræddr) varliga brædda.

"Fullvíða hefr Fjǫruskeifr veifat lystr frœðum of her ok lastsamr kastat leiri ara ens gamla. Ok vannt orðvandr varliga brædda eina kráku á Serklandi: Skeifr, hræddr bart Hǫgna húfu."

Gleefully, Fjǫruskeifr has recited his poetry far and wide among people and, eager to blame, he distributed the dung of the ancient eagle [bad poetry]. And, easily offended, in the land of the Saracens you barely managed to feed one crow: Skeifr, you carried Hǫgni's [legendary king] cap [helmet] fearfully.

Árni jumped up and drew his sword and wanted to attack Þórarinn. Hákon told him to stop and keep the peace. He told him that he should *remember that he would be the loser if it came to an open confrontation*. Then Þórarinn went before the king and said that he had composed a praise poem in his honor and asked whether he would listen to it. The king granted permission, and the poem is called "Stuttfeldr's praise poem."

The king asked him what his plans were, and he said that he intended to go south to Rome. The king gave him money and told him to come again when he returned. He said that he would then accord him some honor, but history fails to relate whether they met again.

73. Concerning the Death of *King* Eysteinn

We are told that once when King Sigurðr had come to his throne, King Eysteinn had not taken his seat. Queen Ingibjǫrg Guthormr's *daughter*, King Eysteinn's wife, said to King Sigurðr: "Many and great are the deeds that you have performed in foreign lands, King Sigurðr, and they will be long remembered." He replied with a stanza: [1]

241.   Skjótt bark skjǫld enn hvíta   þat hefk hǫgg of hǫggvit
     (skald biðr at guð valdi)   handvíst á Blálandi
     ár til eggja skúrar   (guð ræðr sókn ok sigri)
     ótrauðr en frá rauðan: svanni þínum manni.

"Skjótt bark ótrauðr skjǫld enn hvíta ár til eggja skúrar, en frá rauðan; skald biðr, at guð valdi. Þat hǫgg hefk handvíst of hǫggvit þínum manni á Blálandi, svanni; guð ræðr sókn ok sigri."

Of old, I incessantly and speedily carried the white shield to the shower of swords [battle], when I carried it back, it was red; the poet wishes that God prevail. That sure blow I struck for your husband in Africa, woman; God determines war and victory.

Six years after the death of King Óláfr it happened that King Eysteinn was at a feast south at Askstaðir.[2] (FJ 388) He fell victim to a sudden illness that cost him his life. His body was moved north to Kaupangr (Niðaróss) and was buried in Christ Church. People say that there was never such a numerous crowd of

mourners at a man's grave in Norway as there was by King Eysteinn's grave, subsequent to the death of King Magnús (U 190) Óláfsson. After that King Sigurðr
was sole king of Norway for the duration of his life.

74. Concerning King Sigurðr and Óttarr

We are told that on Whitsunday King Sigurðr was sitting on his throne with his
friends and a numerous company. People observed that the king was in a sorry
state and ill disposed, and many were apprehensive about what would come of
it. The king rose up and looked out over the people on the benches around
him. He took a precious book that he had brought to Norway, all written in
gold letters. No greater treasure of a book had come to Norway.[1] The queen
was sitting next to him. Then the king said:

> Many things can change during a man's lifetime. When I returned to Norway, I had
> two possessions that I considered most valuable—the book that you see here and
> the queen. Now one seems worse than the other to me, and I seem possessed of the
> very worst things. The queen has no idea about herself, for it appears that goat's
> horns are jutting from her head. The better she used to seem to me, the worse she
> now seems.

Then the king cast the book onto a fire that had been built and struck the
queen a blow in the face. She wept more for the king's disorder than for her
own pain. There was a man standing before the king named Óttarr birtingr, a
landowner's son and a chamberlain in his service. He had dark hair, was small
in stature but manly and courtly. He had a dark complexion but was a fine fellow. He was called "birtingr" because (FJ 389) he was dark.[2] Óttarr ran up and
seized the book that the king had cast on the fire. Holding it, he said:

> It was a different time, sire, when you returned and made a fair and proud ap-
> pearance in Norway, and all your friends ran to receive you eagerly, and all ap-
> proved your kingly station and accorded you the greatest honor. This time, many
> of your friends have gathered and can manifest no joy because of your dejection
> and illness. Favor us, good king, put off your moodiness and gladden your friends.
> All wish to be joyful in your presence. Accept this counsel. First gladden the queen,
> whom you have deeply offended, then all of your other friends.

The king replied: "Who are you to advise me, a lowly cottager's son of no lineage?" He jumped up and drew his sword, as if he were about to cut him down.
Óttarr stood erect and did not so much as wince. The king grasped his sword
with both hands but turned it flat as it came down toward Óttarr's head, then

let it veer off to the side. Then the king was silent, and took his seat. Everyone else was silent, too. But the king looked more amenable than before and said:

> It takes a long time to test the true nature of men. (U 191) Here sat my most distinguished friends, district chieftains, marshals, court officials, and all the best men in the land. But none was so well disposed toward me as this man, who will seem of little account to you. It was Óttarr birtingr who was most devoted to me, for I entered in a rage and wished to ruin my greatest treasure. He saved me from that with one hand and did not fear death. Then he made a fair speech, and he couched his words so as to honor me, without touching on matters that would depress my spirits. He omitted those things that could indeed have been mentioned. But (FJ 390) his words were so well chosen that no man present was so wise that he could have spoken better.
>
> Then I leapt up in anger as if I were about to strike him down, but he showed such courage as to suggest that there was no danger. When I saw that, I averted the deed, which he did not deserve. And now my friends should be informed of the reward that I will give him. Before he was my chamberlain, but now he will be a district chieftain. What is more important is that from now on he will be the most distinguished of my district chieftains. Now go and sit among the district chieftains and cease to be in my service.

Óttarr subsequently became an honorable man and outstanding in many ways.[3]

75. Concerning King Sigurðr and Erlendr

King Sigurðr jórsalafari established his residence and capital in Konungahella. It prospered so greatly as a trade center that none was richer in Norway. The king had a fortress built there of stone and turf with a great moat around it. In that fortress was the king's residence and the Church of the Cross as well, where King Sigurðr placed the holy cross. Before the altar was an altarpiece of gold and silver that he had brought to Norway.[1]

It happened once when King Sigurðr was sailing along the coast with his crew and was anchored in a certain harbor that men went swimming from the king's ship. The best swimmer was a man named Jón, and many praised his skill. The king was lying on deck and was not in a good mood. There were two men with him, Erlendr gapamunnr (Gaping-Mouth) and Einarr Skúlason.[2] When they were least expecting it, the king plunged into the water. He made for Jón and ducked him. When he came to the surface again, the king ducked him a second time, and they were (FJ 391) under water for much longer than the first time. Then the king surfaced and ducked him a third time.

They saw this from the king's ship and said that things were taking a dangerous turn. Einarr said: "It would be a brave deed to help that man and save the king from a misfortune."

Erlendr said: "It is hard to contend with the king, but (U 192) it is true that the man's life is at stake."

Erlendr was a very big and powerful man. He dove off the ship, swam to the king, grabbed him, and plunged him down, then let him up. He plunged him down a second and a third time, letting him up only when he had been down for a long time. Then they swam to shore. People got Jón to shore as well, and he was close to death. He was thumped [on the back][3] for a long time, and people sat by him until he came *to his senses*.

76. Concerning Haraldr gilli

A man had come to King Sigurðr whose name was Haraldr gillicrist.[1] He claimed to be the son of Magnús berfœttr. Hallkell húkr (Hook) had sailed west all the way to the Hebrides, and that man had joined him there with his mother. Haraldr was then in King Sigurðr's retinue but not held in much esteem. He told Erlendr to flee, *saying* that he was an object of the king's wrath. He said that he would not flee but would spend the nights on shore.

There was a man of small lineage on board, closer to Haraldr than anyone. *His name was Loðinn*, but he was quite a vain man. He often said cutting things about Haraldr. He said it was unclear *who he was* and was always nagging at his page.

Now it happened this same evening that Haraldr told the boy to share Loðinn's sleeping bag at night. But when Loðinn realized what had happened, he said that he would not *endure pages occupying his space, and he asked who had told him to make his bed with men of note*. He said that he was doing what Haraldr had told him. Loðinn *chased him out of his sleeping bag. The page went to inform Haraldr. He was angered and rushed out on the ship, not caring whether* he trampled Loðinn's property or not. Loðinn said that he was often *in the habit of dishonoring him. Haraldr said that he got less dishonor than he deserved and struck a blow* on his shoulder and chest. It was a flesh wound (FJ 392) and *people ran to separate them. Haraldr spent the night on shore.

In the morning the king threw off his covers* and asked where Erlendr gapamunnr was. Einarr *Skúlason replied: "We don't know exactly, but how good is the treatment he can expect from you?*"

"I make no promises about that," said the king.

Then Einarr recited a stanza:[2]

242. Erlendr hefir undan   hafa munu heiðar jǫfra
     allvalds gleði haldit   hlíðrœkjanda fríðum

gramr skaltattu gumna   (geta verðr þess fyr gotnum)
gapamunn of þat kunna: galdrs nauðsynjar valdit. (U 193)

"Erlendr hefir haldit undan allvalds gleði: gramr gumna, skaltattu kunna gapamunn of þat. Nauðsynjar munu hafa valdit fríðum hlíðrœkjanda galdrs heiðar
jǫfra; verðr geta þess fyr gotnum."

Erlendr has fled the king's good grace: leader of men, you must not fault "gapamunnr" [Gaping-Mouth] for that. Necessity must have forced the fair tender of
the chant of the kings of the heath's slope [giants, gold, generous man]; I shall tell
people about that.

The king said: "Bring him here." This was done, and when he arrived, the
king said: "How do you feel about your *contest with your king yesterday?"

"Sire," he said, "it was very much in accord with your actions."*

"That is true," said the king, "and I approve it. You showed both affection for
me and courage. I make you a gift of a sword and cloak and will always esteem
you even more highly than before. But what was the racket that I heard on our
ship last night?" He was told.

Then he said: "Summon Haraldr and Loðinn." He asked if they wanted to
leave their case to his discretion, and they agreed.

Then the king said: "I don't have the impression that you are equals, but I
will give Loðinn some amends because he has been in my company, though it
is more proper that he should have no rights. But do not presume again to address honorable men in this way, for it is likely that we will honor such a man
more than a man of no account." Loðinn was obliged to settle for this, but the
king took Haraldr into his retinue among his court officers. (FJ 393)

77. Concerning King Sigurðr and Áslákr hani (Rooster)

It happened once that King Sigurðr was sitting with many distinguished men
in a gloomy frame of mind. One Friday evening the steward asked what food
should be prepared. The king replied: "Why not meat?" People were so afraid
of him that no one dared to contradict him, but everyone was downcast.

The tables were set up, and the platters came in with cooked meat. Everyone was taciturn and grieved because of the king's disorder. But before the
food was blessed, a man named Áslákr hani (Rooster) spoke up. He had been
abroad with the king. He was not a man of great lineage, small in stature, but
bold. When he saw that no one else would contradict the king, he decided to
speak up.

"Sire, what is steaming on the platters before you?"

The king answered: "What would you like it to be, Áslákr hani, and what
does it look like?"

"It looks to me as though I would like it not to be meat."

The king said: "And if it is, Áslákr hani?"

"It is grievous to think," said Áslákr, "that a king who has earned such great honor in the world because of his expedition should have such poor judgment. This is not what you vowed when you came out of the waters of Jordan after bathing in the same water as God Himself. You had a palm sprig in your hand and a cross on your breast, and you did not undertake to eat meat on Friday. If lesser men did this, severe penalties would be in order. Your retinue is not as well manned as it should be if there is no one other than an insignificant man like me to make this point."

The king was silent but did not serve himself, and when some time had passed, he had the meat platters removed and appropriate food (U 194) brought in. As the meal progressed, the king began to recover his spirits and to drink.

People advised Áslákr to make good his escape, but he said he would not: "I do not know how that would help. The fact is that it is a good time to die when I have succeeded in what I wished to do (FJ 394), that is, to save the king from a crime. He has it in his discretion to kill me."

In the evening the king summoned him and asked: "Who incited you, Áslákr, to speak so openly to me in public?"

"Sire," he said, "none other than myself."

The king said: "You probably wish to know what you will get in return for your boldness and what it is that you think you have earned."

He answered: "If you wish to reward me, sire, I will be happy, but if it turns out otherwise, it is up to you."

The king said: "You will receive less of a reward than you deserve. I will give you three farms, though that may seem an unlikely outcome, because you saved me from a great misfortune, a task that should have fallen to my district chieftains, who have much to thank me for." The episode concluded with the king's arriving at the very best resolution.

78. Concerning King Sigurðr

It happened one evening during Christmas that King Sigurðr was sitting in the hall, where the tables were set up. The king said: "Bring me meat."

They answered: "It is not customary in Norway, sire, to eat meat at Christmas."

The king said: "That is the custom I desire." They came in with porpoise on the platters. The king stuck his knife in but did not eat.

Then the king said: "Bring me a woman." They brought a woman into the hall. She had her face covered.

The king put a hand to her head and said: "You are an uncomely woman, but not beyond endurance." Then he looked at her hand and said: "Not a handsome hand and misshapen, but not intolerable." Then he told her to stretch out her foot. He looked at it and said: "A big and monstrous foot, but let it pass." (FJ 395) Then he told her to lift her tunic, and he looked at her legs. "What legs! They are both thick and black. You must be some kind of a whore." He said that he wanted nothing to do with her and told them to take her out.

Toward the end of King Sigurðr's life it happened that he was at a feast in his residence. One morning when he had risen and was dressed, he was so taciturn and gloomy that his friends were fearful that he would have another episode. But the estate steward was wise and resourceful. He addressed the king and asked whether he had learned something that was so serious that it had spoiled his mood, or whether he was dissatisfied with the feast, or whether there was something that could be remedied.

The king said (U 195) that it was none of these things—"but rather that I am musing on a dream I had last night."

"Sire," said the steward, "perhaps it was a good dream, and we would like to hear it."

The king said: "I dreamt I was here in Jaðarr and saw a great, rapidly moving black cloud out at sea. As it approached, it looked like an enormous tree with limbs above and roots in the sea. When it reached the coast, it was stranded and strewn about the shore. Then I seemed to see all of coastal Norway, and in each bay a piece of the tree had washed up. Some pieces were large, others small."

The steward answered: "Sire, it is likely that you will have the best understanding of this dream, and we would like to have you interpret it."

The king said: "The likeliest interpretation seems to be that the dream signifies the arrival of a man in Norway who will settle here, and his progeny will be spread widely but will be of greater or lesser importance."[1]

A little later it was learned that Hallkell húkr had come to Norway bringing Haraldr gilli and his mother with him (FJ 396), as has already been alluded to. Haraldr told his story to the king, and King Sigurðr discussed it with his chieftains. Opinions *varied* greatly, each chieftain speaking for himself, but they deferred to the king. Several were opposed, but the king decided more according to his *own lights than in conforming with the views* of his retainers.

Then King Sigurðr had Haraldr summoned to him and told him that he would not oppose an ordeal to prove his paternity, with the stipulation that he *commit himself to an oath* that, should his paternity be confirmed, he would not lay claim to the throne as long as King Sigurðr and King Magnús lived. That agreement was made.

Haraldr then prepared *for the ordeal, and people say that this was the greatest such ordeal in Norway*. Seven glowing plowshares were laid out *and Haraldr walked over them with bare feet and led by two bishops. As he did so, he called on Saint Columba*. His bed was made by the plowshares.[2]

*Then King Sigurðr's son Magnús said: "He does not tread the plowshares bravely."

The king replied: "That is cruel* and unseemly talk, *because he has borne the test well."

Then Haraldr collapsed on his bed, and after three days the test* was made. His feet were found to be clear of burns. After that *King Sigurðr accepted his kinship, but his son Magnús took a great dislike to Haraldr, and many chieftains* followed his example.

Haraldr was not fluent in *Norse and he stumbled over many words, so that many people ridiculed him*.[3] But King Sigurðr would allow no hint of that when he was present. (U 196)

79. Concerning the Bet between Magnús and Haraldr

It was Haraldr's custom to escort King Sigurðr to bed in the evening. One time they were able to detain him, and they sat *for a long time drinking. Magnús had been sent* a horse from Gautland, a great treasure and very swift. *Those who were present surmised that no horse would be as swift, and* they sought Haraldr's opinion, asking if he knew of any horse as swift. Haraldr answered, saying that nothing was so remarkable that it could not be matched. They doubted that he had ever seen such a good horse. He answered by saying that he had seen many good and swift horses.

They asked: "Have you seen swifter horses?"

He replied that this was not what he had said.

"That's what you said, and we will hold you to it," they insisted.

He replied: "You are very keen on this, and it may be that I have truly seen swifter horses. (FJ 397) And since you make so much of it, I have seen men who are no slower."

They responded: "Could it be that you are no slower than the horse?"

"That's not what I'm saying," he replied.

Then King Magnús[1] said: "That was your claim, and we will make a test and lay a wager. I will stake a gold ring, and you should stake another."

He replied: "I have not become so rich in Norway that it amounts to a gold ring."

Then King Magnús said: "Then bet your life on it."

"That I will not do," he said.

"It will come to the same thing," said Magnús, and with that they concluded their exchange.

In the morning King Sigurðr was told. "It was bound to turn out this way," he said. "Give me the wagered money. You Norwegians are in a sorry state with a mad king ruling you, but I surmise that you would soon give pure gold to have me as king rather than Haraldr and Magnús. One is cruel and the other is a fool."

Now they entered an enclosure to make the test. Haraldr was in stirrup trousers that were baggy around the knees.[2] He wore a short shirt, with a cloak about his shoulders and a stick in his hand. Magnús was also dressed for the occasion. King Sigurðr himself was present together with a great crowd. When they were ready, King Magnús spurred his horse forward and onto the track. But Haraldr was just a bit quicker and kept up the pace. That was the difference when they got to the end of the course.

Then King Sigurðr spoke: "That is a valid test, and Haraldr was not slower."

Then King Magnús said: "Let us make another test." They ran a second race, and Haraldr was ahead by a girth-strap at the end of the race.

King Magnús asked: "Are you holding onto my girth-strap? Concede if you are not up to the race."

Then they readied themselves for a third trial, and everyone could see that there was a space between them and that Magnús (FJ 398; U 197) had jumped into the lead. But Haraldr leapt onto the track with a shout, and you could hardly see his feet touch the ground. At the end of the course he ran out over the enclosure, then turned back to meet Magnús when he reached the end of the course. He said: "Greetings, kinsman." That was the end of it, and King Sigurðr gave King Haraldr the wager.[3]

80. Concerning King Sigurðr and Bishop Magni

Toward the end of King Sigurðr's life his domestic situation changed, with the result that he wanted to abandon the queen and marry a woman named Cecilia, the daughter of a powerful man. He intended to celebrate the wedding in Bjǫrgvin and prepared a great and splendid feast. When Bishop Magni learned of this, he became downcast.

One day the bishop went to the hall and together with him a priest named Sigurðr, who was later bishop in Bjǫrgvin.[1] They came to the hall, and the bishop asked the king to come out. He did so, with a drawn sword. The king welcomed the bishop and invited him to drink. He said that he had other business: "Is it true, sire, that you intend to marry and abandon the queen?"

"That is true, bishop." The king began to swell with anger.

The bishop said: "Why have you decided to do this in our bishopric, sire, and thus disgrace God's law and Holy Church and our bishopric? Now I shall do what I am obligated to do and forbid you to commit this sin, in the name of God, Saint Peter the Apostle, and all the saints."

While he said those words he stood erect with his neck extended as if he were prepared for the king to strike him with his sword. Sigurðr, who later became bishop, related that he seemed to see no more of the heavens than a piece of parchment (FJ 399) because the king was so monstrous in his rage.

Then the king entered the hall, while the bishop went home and was in such good spirits that he greeted every child laughingly and played with his fingers.[2]

Sigurðr said: "You are as cheerful, lord, as if it did not occur to you that the king might visit his anger on you, but it would be better to flee."

Then the bishop said: "It seems to me unlikely that he will do that, but what death would be better than to die for God's holy Christendom and forbid what cannot be sanctioned. I am of good cheer because I have done what I ought."[3]

Then there was a great bustle in the town, and King Sigurðr's men prepared to move great quantities of grain, malt, and honey. The king then went to Stafangr (Stavanger) and prepared his feast. When the resident bishop learned of that, he went to the king and asked if it was true that he intended to marry while the queen was still alive. (U 198)

The king replied: "It is true."

The bishop went on: "If it is true, sire, you may consider how strictly that is forbidden to lesser men. You may well think that such is permissible for you since you have greater power, but it is quite contrary to law, and I cannot imagine why, in our bishopric, you wish to dishonor God's commandments, Holy Church, and our bishopric. Perhaps you wish to endow this church with some great sum of money and thus make recompense to God and my office."

The king said: "Assess the money, but you are very different from Bishop Magni."

Then the king departed. He was no more pleased than with the bishop who had issued an interdiction. Then the king married this woman and loved her greatly.

81. The Death of King Sigurðr

While King Sigurðr was in residence east in Vík, he fell ill. His friends urged him to relinquish his new wife, and she herself wished to depart. As he lay ill, she asked to be released because that would serve them both best. The king said: "It never occurred to me that you would abandon me like the others." He turned from her and flushed red as blood. She departed, and his illness advanced until it became the cause of his death. His body was brought to Ósló and was buried in Saint Hallvarðr's Church. He now lies in the stone wall *out from the south choir*.[1]

82. Concerning Haraldr and Magnús

King Haraldr gilli was a valiant and able man, rather tall and of handsome appearance. The oaths he had sworn with respect to King Magnús remained in force. King Haraldr had also sworn an oath before *being admitted* to the ordeal that he would make no claim to the throne as long as King Magnús lived. Before King Sigurðr died, he *confirmed* his son's oath and *thus ensured* the succession for Magnús and forestalled any danger as long as they were *faithful to their commitments* and oaths. King Magnús was in Túnsberg (Tønsberg) when King Sigurðr died. He was immediately sent word to hasten to Ósló* . . . .[1]

[Three years after the Church of the Holy Cross was dedicated, King Sigurðr fell ill. At that time he was in Ósló. He died there one night after Annunciation (March 25). He was buried at Saint Hallvarðr's Church and was placed in the stone wall outside the choir on the south side. Magnús, King Sigurðr's son, was there in the town. He immediately appropriated all the king's treasury when King Sigurðr died. Sigurðr was king over Norway for twenty-seven years and was forty years old. His reign was good for the people—there was both prosperity and peace.

82a. The Saga of Magnús the Blind and Haraldr gilli (*Heimskringla*)

(Chapter 1) Magnús, King Sigurðr's son, was elevated to the throne in Oslo over all the land, as the people had sworn to King Sigurðr. Many men immediately joined his service, and the district chieftains as well. Magnús was the handsomest of men at that time in Norway. He was imperious and of fierce temper. He was a man of great prowess, but it was chiefly his father's popularity that gained him the people's favor. He was much given to drinking parties, avaricious, disagreeable, and quarrelsome.

Haraldr gilli was affable, cheerful, humorous, gracious, so generous that he withheld nothing from his friends, and so accessible to advice that he allowed others to advise him in any way they wished. That stood his popularity and reputation in good stead. Many powerful men became attached to him not a whit less than to Magnús.

At that time Haraldr was in Túnsberg (Tønsberg) when he learned of the death of his brother King Sigurðr. He immediately held meetings with his friends, and they came to the decision to convene the Haugathing there in the town. At that meeting Haraldr was accepted as king over half the country. The oaths with which he had forfeited his paternal inheritance were considered to have been sworn under duress. Haraldr then established a retinue and appointed district chieftains. Men soon flocked to him no less than to King Magnús. Messengers then passed between them, and so matters stood for a week.

Because Magnús attracted a much smaller force, he saw no alternative but to divide the realm with Haraldr. The division was executed in such a way that each of them was to have half the realm that King Sigurðr had ruled. But King Magnús kept all the ships, tableware, precious objects, and all the liquid assets that King Sigurðr had possessed. He was nonetheless less satisfied with his share. They ruled the land in peace for a time, but they took very different views of the situation.

King Haraldr had a son named Sigurðr with Þóra, the daughter of Guthormr grábarði. King Haraldr married Ingiríðr, Rǫgnvaldr's daughter. He was the son of King Ingi Steinkelsson. King Magnús was married to Kristín, the daughter of

Knútr lávarðr and the sister of the Danish king Valdimarr. Magnús did not become fond of her and sent her south back to Denmark. After that things became more difficult for him, and he was in great disfavor with her kin.

(Chapter 2) When the two kings Magnús and Haraldr had shared the realm for three years, they spent the fourth winter in the north in Kaupangr. Each entertained the other, but their retinues were always at each other's throats. In the spring Magnús took his fleet south along the coast and raised as many troops as he could. He urged his friends to lend him support in removing Haraldr from the throne and giving him whatever portion of the realm he pleased. He represented to them that Haraldr had forsworn the realm. King Magnús secured the agreement of many powerful men to this end.

Haraldr went to Upplǫnd and overland to Vík. He gathered forces when he learned of King Magnús's plans. Wherever they went they wasted each other's lands, and men were killed. King Magnús had much larger forces because he had the whole extent of the land for recruitment. Haraldr was on the east coast of Vík and assembled troops, and each deprived the other of men and resources. In Haraldr's following were Kristrøðr, his brother by the same mother, and many district chieftains, but many more district chieftains were attached to King Magnús.

King Haraldr and his troops were at a place called Fors (Foss) in Ranríki (Bohuslän). From there they went to the coast. On the Eve of Saint Lawrence (August 10) they ate their evening meal at a place called Fyrileif (Färlev). The sentinels were on horseback and kept mounted guard on all sides of the settlement. They sighted King Magnús's troops and observed that they were approaching the settlement. King Magnús had an army of almost six thousand men, and Haraldr had fifteen hundred.

Then the sentinels arrived and brought King Haraldr the news that King Magnús's army had reached the settlement. Haraldr replied: "I wonder what my kinsman King Magnús wants. It does not seem likely that he will want to do battle with us." Then Þjóstólfr Álason spoke up: "Lord, I think you will want to prepare yourself and your troops on the assumption that King Magnús has been gathering forces all summer with the intention of fighting as soon as he meets you."

Then the king rose and addressed his men, urging them to arm themselves: "If it is Magnús's wish to fight, then we too will fight." Then the trumpets were sounded, and King Haraldr's force marched out from the settlement into a field and set up its standards. King Haraldr wore two ring byrnies, but his brother Kristrøðr, who was known as a most valiant man, had none. When King Magnús and his men saw King Haraldr's force, they drew up their formation and extended their wings so far that they thought to encircle the whole of King Haraldr's force. So says Halldórr skvaldri:

> *Hkr* 1. Magnús fekk þar miklu
> (margs gengis naut) lengri

(valr nam vǫll at hylja
varmr) fylkingar arma.

"Magnús fekk þar miklu lengri fylkingar arma; naut margs gengis; varmr valr nam at hylja vǫll."

There Magnús had much more extended wings; he had the advantage of a large force; warm corpses began to cover the field.

(Chapter 3) King Magnús had the holy cross carried before him in the battle. It was a great battle, and hard fought. The king's brother Kristrøðr had attacked the center of King Magnús's formation with his troops and struck left and right, so that men fled on both sides. But there was a certain wealthy land-holder who had been in King Haraldr's force and was stationed behind Krist-røðr. He raised a spear with both hands and thrust it between Kristrøðr's shoulders so that it came out at the chest. Kristrøðr fell there.

Many who were close at hand asked why he had done that wicked deed, and he answered: "Now he can remember that they destroyed my farm this sum-mer, took everything I had there, and forced me to serve in their army. This is what I had in mind for him, should I ever get the opportunity."

After that King Haraldr's army broke, and he himself fled with his forces. Many of his men had fallen. Ingimarr Sveinsson of Askr, a district chieftain in King Haraldr's force, received a mortal wound, and almost sixty retainers fell. King Haraldr fled east to his ships in Vík and then went to Denmark to meet with King Eiríkr eymuni and seek his assistance. They met in Zealand. King Eiríkr gave him a good reception chiefly because they had sworn blood brotherhood. He gave Halland into his charge and presented him with eight longships without tackle.

Then King Haraldr went north through Halland, where troops flocked to him. King Magnús subjected all Norway to his rule after this battle. He granted a pardon to all the men who were wounded and had them healed as if they were his own men, then claimed the whole land. He had the pick of the men in Norway. When they took counsel, Sigurðr Sigurðarson, Þórir Ingiríðarson, and all the wisest men wished to march to Vík and wait to see if Haraldr would come from the south. King Magnús, however, made the decision on his own to go north to Bjǫrgvin and winter there, allowing the army to disperse and the district chieftains to go to their estates.

(Chapter 4) King Haraldr arrived in Konungahella with the troops that had accompanied him from Denmark. They assembled their forces there, both the district chieftains and the townsmen, and they drew up their formations above the town. But King Haraldr went from his ships and dispatched emissaries to the militia, asking them not to bar him from his land by force of arms. He said that he would not ask for more than was his by right, and communications passed back and forth. It ended with the local population's dissolving their troops and submitting to King Haraldr.

Haraldr then gave his own men lands in fief and taxing authority to the district chieftains. He made legal concessions to the men who joined his forces. After that, many people flocked to King Haraldr. Then he went west to Vík and granted truce to everyone except King Magnús's men. Those men he plundered and killed wherever he found them.

When he came west to Sarpsborg, he seized two of King Magnús's district chieftains, Ásbjǫrn and his brother Nereiðr. He gave them the choice that one should be hanged and the other thrown into the waterfall called Sarpr, and he told them to make the choice themselves. Ásbjǫrn chose the waterfall because he was the older and that seemed like the crueler death. And this was the way it was done. In the words of Halldórr skvaldri:

Hkr 2.   Ásbjǫrn varð sás orðum   Nereið lét gramr á grimman
     illa helt of stilli   grandmeið Sigars fjanda
     (gramr fœðir val víða   (húsþinga galt) hengja
     vígs) í Sarp at stíga: (hrannbáls glǫtuðr mála).

"Ásbjǫrn, sás helt illa orðum of stilli, varð at stíga í Sarp; gramr fœðir víða val vígs. Gramr lét hengja Neireið á grimman grandmeið Sigars fjanda; hrannbáls glǫtuðr galt húsþinga mála."

Ásbjǫrn, who failed to measure his words about the king, had to plunge into Sarpr [Sarpsfossen]; far and wide the lord feeds the falcon of carrion [bird of prey]. The king had Nereiðr hanged on the grim harm tree of Sigarr's [legendary king] enemy [Hagbarðr, gallows]; the destroyer of wave fire [gold, generous king] took vengeance for the speeches at the assembly.

After that King Haraldr went north to Túnsberg and was well received there. There too a great force flocked to him.

(Chapter 5) King Magnús was in Bjǫrgvin and learned of what had happened. He then summoned the chieftains who were in the town to council and asked what should be done. Sigurðr Sigurðarson replied: "I can offer good counsel: Take a ship's cutter manned by good fellows and place me or some other district chieftain in charge. Dispatch them to King Haraldr, your kinsman, and offer him reconciliation on terms worked out between you by just men in our land, such that he will have half the realm jointly with you. It seems to me likely, with the intercession of good men, that King Haraldr will accept this offer so that there may be a reconciliation between you."

Then King Magnús replied: "This is not the plan I desire. What good did it do us to win the whole realm last fall if we are now to divest ourselves of half the realm? Devise another counsel."

Sigurðr Sigurðarson replied: "I have the impression that your district chieftains who asked leave to return to their estates last fall are sticking close to home and are in no hurry to join you. You acted in a way quite contrary to my advice when you dispersed the numbers we had at our command because I had the feeling that Haraldr and his men would return to Vík as soon as they learned that there was no one in command there. Now there is another plan available, though not a good one, but it might work. Dispatch your 'guests' (men at arms) with an armed following and have them go to the homes of the district chieftains who will not respond to you in your need and kill them. Give their lands to men you can rely on, although they have not amounted to much before. Let them round up men, bad as well as good, and go east to do battle with Haraldr with whatever force you can raise."

The king replied: "It will be unpopular to have such distinguished men killed and exalt men of little worth. They have often been no more reliable and have administered the land less well. I wish to hear other counsels from you."

Sigurðr answered: "The counsels are now harder to come by since you will neither make peace nor war. Let us then go north to Þrándheimr, where our chief strength resides, and gather as many troops as we can. It may then turn out that the fellows from Elfr (Götaälv) get tired of chasing us."

The king replied: "I do not wish to flee from the men whom we chased last summer. Give me a better plan."

Then Sigurðr stood up and prepared to go away, saying: "I will then give you the advice that I can see you want to hear and is inevitable. Sit tight here in Bjǫrgvin until Haraldr comes with a huge army. Then you will suffer one of two things, death or shame." With that, Sigurðr departed from the council.

(Chapter 6) King Haraldr went west along the coast and had gathered a very large army. That winter was called the "mob winter." Haraldr arrived at Bjǫrgvin on Christmas Eve and put in at Flóruvágar (Florvåg), not wishing to do battle at Christmas because of the holy season. King Magnús made preparations in the town. He had a catapult raised out on Hólmr (Bergenhus) and had chains and wooden barriers constructed and laid across the bay from the king's residence. He had caltrops forged and strewn across Jóansvellir (Engen), and no more than three days were given over to Christmas, during which no work was done. On Twelfth Night King Haraldr had the trumpets sounded to signal the weighing of anchors. Nine hundred men had gathered under King Haraldr's banner during Christmas.

(Chapter 7) King Haraldr vowed that if he won the victory, he would construct a church in honor of Saint Óláfr there in the town at his own expense. King Magnús drew up his troops out by the enclosure at Christ Church, but Haraldr rowed first to Norðnes. When King Magnús and his men saw that, they headed for the town toward the end of the bay.] [2]

... *above the town where Saint Óláfr's Church is now located, which King Haraldr vowed to build if he won the victory. King Magnús returned (U 199) to the town, but his forces were dispersed, and he himself received a wound in the knee. (FJ 401) Almost all of King Magnús's men fled, some into the mountains, some to Nunnusetr, and some over Jóansvellir, where they ran into caltrops.[3] The king and some of his troops took refuge on the ships. He boarded his own ship with a few men, but they were unable to move their ships because of the depleted crews and because the whole bay had been closed off with iron chains. E. [Einarr Skúlason] spoke the following:

243. Luku vág viku
      vara kostr fara
      brýns Bjǫrgynjar
      braut háskrautum.

They closed Bjǫrgyn's [Bergen] bay for a week: it was impossible for the tall ships to speed away.

Sometime after that King Haraldr's men reached the ships, and King Magnús was captured with all his men. Some were killed, and some were seized and kept under guard. Then there were consultations with men of wisdom to decide what to do with King Magnús. With him were his uncle Hákon faukr, a very handsome man, and Ívarr Qzurarson. The outcome was that Magnús was deprived of his throne and could no longer be titled "king." He was turned over to the king's slaves, who maimed him.[4] They put out his eyes, chopped off his feet, and gelded him. Ívarr Qzurarson was also blinded and Hákon faukr was killed.

In this way Magnús fell into King Haraldr's hands and lost his realm. The deed was wicked and not worthy of a king, but it was determined more by his advisers than by the king himself. What followed was no better. King Haraldr had Bishop Reinaldr hanged on the advice of his followers because he did not want to pay the king thirty marks of gold. The bishop preferred to risk his life rather than to impoverish the church's resources with such a payment.[5] (FJ 402)

With this deed the king grieved the hearts and minds of all good men, and it is probable that this crime doomed Norway and all who were implicated and were subject to excommunication and God's wrath. The bishop was strung up out on Hólmr on the king's orders. His body was taken over to Norðnes and buried at Saint Michael's Church. After that King Magnús was moved to Hólmr and assumed the habit of a monk. The great monastery of Hernes was founded for him at Frosta.[6]

King Haraldr was sole king of all Norway that winter. He granted terms to all those who wished to have them and took many into his retinue who had served with King Magnús. In the words of H. [Halldórr]:

244. Nús auðsendir undir
      allr Nóregr þik fallinn
      þín liggr gipt á grœnu
      (guðs ráð es þat) láði. (U 200)

"Auðsendir, nús allr Nóregr fallinn undir þik; þín gipt liggr á grœnu láði: guðs ráð es þat."

Wealth dispenser [generous king], now all Norway has submitted to you; your good luck has settled on the green land: that is God's will.

Einarr Skúlason also composed the following:

245. Alls varð Ellu
      ungr geitunga
      lofaðr lífgjafi
      lands ráðandi.

The young, extolled nourisher of Ella's [Northumbrian king] birds [birds of prey, warrior] became the sole ruler of the country.

Haraldr was now sole monarch in Norway. Einarr Skúlason makes mention of the fact that King Haraldr had been in Denmark and fought two battles there, one at Hveðn (Hven) and the other at Hlésey (Læsø). He was victorious.

246. Ótryggum lét eggjar   áðr (þars ógnar prúðum
     eljunfrár und hári   ulfnistanda) missti
     Hveðn á hǫlðum roðnar   hungr (á hǫnd at ganga)
     hrafns munnlituðr þunnar: (FJ 403)   hræskurðr (Danir urðu).

"Eljunfrár hrafns munnlituðr lét roðnar þunnar eggjar á ótryggum hǫlðum und hári Hveðn, áðr hræskurðr missti hungr, þars Danir urðu at ganga á hǫnd ógnar prúðum ulfnistanda."

The courageous colorer of the raven's mouth [warrior] reddened thin blades on disloyal men beneath lofty Hveðn [Hven] before the corpse cleaver [bird of prey] was satiated, where the Danes were obliged to surrender to the terror-proud wolf feeder [warrior].

247. Átti sókn við sléttan   hús brann upp (en eisur)
     serkrjóðr Háalfs (merki)   ófátt (séa knátti)
     harðr (þars hregg of virðum)   malmr sǫng en hlóð hilmir
     Hléseyjar þrǫm (blésu):   hrækǫst (við ský gnæfa).

"Harðr serkrjóðr Háalfs átti sókn við sléttan Hléseyjar þrǫm, þars hregg blésu merki of virðum. Ófátt hús brann upp, en knátti séa eisur gnæfa við ský; malmr sǫng, en hilmir hlóð hrækǫst."

The hardened colorer of Hálfr's [legendary king] shirt [byrnie, warrior] held battle by the level shore of Hlésey [Læsø] where the storm caused standards to billow above the men. Many a house was consumed by fire, and one could see flames leaping against the clouds; steel sang, and the king stacked a corpse pile.

Halldórr states further:

248. Vann valgrennir   flugu framliga
     viðr ráfiðris   fekk svanbekkjar
     Hveðn hánǫðru   snarr sólþverrir
     hroðit vápnboða: sigr falvigrar.

The feeder of the falcon of the weapon wave [blood, bird of prey, warrior] cleared the tall snake of the mast feather [sail, dragon ship] by Hveðn [Hven]; shafted spears flew densely; the brave diminisher of the sun of the swan bench [sea, gold, generous king] prevailed.

249. Eyddi oddum   líkn gefi læknir
     ey benþeyjar   lofaðr friðrofa
     Hlés helfýsir   heims hafljóma
     hungr gollunga: hár lausnari. (FJ 404)

With the sword points, the death inciter [warrior] destroyed the hunger of the hawks of the wound thaw [blood, birds of prey] at Hlésey [Læsø]: may the esteemed savior of this world, the mighty redeemer, have mercy on the peace disturber of the sea light [gold, generous king].

King Haraldr consorted with Þóra, the daughter of Guthormr grábarði (Greybeard), and brought her to his bed. They had a son named Sigurðr. He also had a son with Queen Ingiríðr. His name was Ingi. One of King Haraldr's daughters was named Birgit, another María. His daughter Birgit was first married to Ingi, the son of Hallsteinn, king of the Swedes, then to Magnús Heinreksson, and last to Birgir brosi (Smile).[7] King Haraldr was the most generous of men.

83. The Gifts of King Haraldr to Bishop Magnús

We are told that during the days of King Haraldr, Magnús Einarsson came from Iceland to be consecrated as bishop. The king gave him an excellent reception and showed him (U 201) much honor. When the bishop was on the point of departure and the ship was ready to sail, the bishop entered the hall where the king was drinking and greeted him respectfully. The king received him well and kindly. The queen sat by the king. Then the king spoke:

"Sir bishop, are you ready to depart?"

"Yes, I am," he replied.

"You did not pick the right time when the tables were set, and now there is no gift as suitable as it should be to bestow on you. What is there to give the bishop?"

The treasurer replied: "The best treasures have already been distributed."

"There is still this drinking vessel," said the king. "It is a thing of value, and I give it to you, bishop." The bishop thanked him for the honor.

Then the queen spoke: "Farewell, and I wish you a good journey, sir bishop."

The king mimicked her, saying: "'I wish you a good journey, sir bishop.' When did you ever hear a distinguished woman address a bishop in this way and give him nothing?"

She replied: "What is there to give, sire?"

"There is the cushion on which you are sitting," said the king. It was brought forth and was cased in a precious fabric, a thing of great value. When the bishop was about to leave, the king (FJ 405) took the cushion on which he was sitting and said: "These have long been a pair."

Then the bishop departed and traveled out to Iceland to assume his office. There was some discussion of what should be done with the drinking vessel that would be most in the king's interest. The bishop sought counsel from his advisers. Some said that it should be sold and the proceeds turned over to the poor. Then the bishop said: "I have a different plan. I will have a chalice made for our church and ensure that he benefit in this way. I would wish that all the saints whose relics are in this holy church might intercede for the king each time mass is sung over the chalice."

That chalice is the largest in the church at Skálaholt. From the precious fabric that covered the cushions given him by king and queen were made robes for the singing before the services in the church. This will illustrate the generosity of King Haraldr.[1]

84. The Story of Sigurðr slembidjákn

There was a man named Sigurðr, the son of Þóra, Saxi's daughter. She claimed that he was the son of Magnús berfœttr, but Magnús's friends and confidants kept this secret because it was problematical, given that Þóra's sister Sigríðr was the mother of King Óláfr, the son of King Magnús.[1]

Sigurðr was fostered in the south by a priest named Albrikt. It appeared to some people that he was the priest's son, as Ívarr Ingimundarson said in the poem that he composed about Sigurðr:[2]

250. Óx í œsku   við Aðalbrikti.

As a youth, he was raised by Aðalbrikt. (U 202)

He was instructed in church learning as a youth. Then the priest sent him to the bishop, who ordained him as a deacon. When he was fully (FJ 406) grown, he was a most valiant man, big and strong. In every accomplishment he was far ahead of his contemporaries or practically anyone else in Norway. As soon as he could determine his own course, he shed his clerical training and went abroad, where he remained a long time. It is told that he stayed in Orkney with *Jarl Haraldr.[3] In the words of Ívarr*:

251. Vas með jarli   afkárlyndum
       vargs verðgjafi   vestr í eyjum:
       unz siklingar   sóknar hvattir
       Fóstra . . .   . . . rufu.

The wolf's food giver [warrior] stayed with the obstinate jarl west in the isles until the chieftains, incited to fight, [killed] Fóstri.

Sigurðr was part of the conspiracy that led to the killing of a distinguished man named Þorkell fóstri.[4] From there he went up *to Scotland to seek out* the king of the Scots. According to Ívarr:

252. Sótti síðan   Sigurðr af eyjum
       dýrr at ráðum   Dávið konung:
       vas með vísa   Vilhjálms bani
       fleinþingasamr   fimm misseri.

Then splendid Sigurðr left the isles to seek King David's counsel; the battle-ready slayer of Vilhjálmr [Sigurðr] stayed five years with the king.

He was well liked by the king and the other chieftains, and he remained there for some time in great honor. As the skald said: (FJ 407)

253. Þótti dýrum   Dáfinns liðum
       engr maðr kominn   œðri þangat:
       bœtti vísi   verðungar lið
       hafði ungr konungr   almanna lof.

It appeared to the glorious men of David that no greater man had ever come there; the ruler rewarded the host of retainers; the young king was unanimously praised. There is also mention of the fact that while Sigurðr was with the king, he was engaged in several battles and was always victorious. In the words of Ívarr:

254.   Ól hertogi   hrafna í fjǫrðum
        skulfu skeyti   í Skota blóði:
        þars fyr jǫfri   austan komnum
        morðáls metendr   merki báru. (U 203)

The leader of the army fed ravens in the fjords; arrows shook in Scottish blood, where the testers of the murder eel [sword, warriors] carried the standard before the king who had arrived from the east.

Again:

255.   Bar Sigurði   sigr at hendi
        ór orrostu   inn frá Stauri.

Victory came to Sigurðr in the battle on the inner side of Point of Stoer.

And again:

256.   Háði hilmir   hervíg fjogur
        skýrstr at ǫllu   í Skota veldi.

The king, most accomplished in all respects, fought four battles in the Scottish realm.

After that Sigurðr traveled abroad. He prepared to set out for Rome and went all the way to Jerusalem and to (FJ 408) the River Jordan. He visited the holy shrines there as is customary for pilgrims. In the words of Ívarr:

257.   Vann Róms gǫtu   ræsir Þrœnda
        fœti farna   sás frama drýgði:
        sótti síðan   ok synðum hrauð
        hers oddviti   helga dóma.

The king of the Þrœndir [people of Trøndelag], who gained glory, went on foot on the road to Rome; then the leader of the army sought the holy shrines and was absolved from his sins.

He also tells of how Sigurðr went to Jerusalem and visited the Lord's sepulcher, thus gaining God's mercy and great worldly honor.

258.   Sótti breiða   borg Jórsala
        ǫrr oddviti   út í lǫndum:
        áðr í vatni   þvís vígði guð
        Sigurðr af sér   synðir þvægi.

The keen war leader sought the wide city of Jerusalem abroad before Sigurðr washed away his sins in that water which God had consecrated.

We are told that five bishops tested his claim and affirmed his paternity.[5] As Ívarr says:

259.   Gerðu skírslu   of skjǫldungs kyn
        fimm byskopar   þeirs framarst þóttu:
        svá bar raunir   at ríks konungs
        þess vas enn mildi Magnús faðir. (FJ 409)

Five bishops, who were deemed most distinguished, participated in the testing of the lord's paternity; the outcome was that generous Magnús was judged to be the father of that mighty king.

Then Sigurðr traveled from Jerusalem through Greece, France, and Saxony, as Ívarr says: (U 204)

260. Létu síðan   súðvigg búin
      œstisk ægir   útan ór Grikjum:
      sótti Frakka   fremðar ræsir
      áðr Saxa sjǫt   Sigurðr kannaði.

Then they readied the steeds of the ship boards [ships] and set out from Greece; the sea raged; the advancer of honor [king] sought the Franks before Sigurðr visited the Saxons' homes.

It is also told in the poem that he then proceeded to the islands (Orkney):

261. Helt snarr konungr   snekkju einni
      vígligr of ver   vestr í eyjar.

The fierce, warlike king steered one ship west across the sea to the isles (Orkney). We are also told that he engaged in trading voyages.

85. Concerning Sigurðr slembir

One winter he was in Iceland with Þorgils Oddason at Saurbœr.[1] Few people knew who he was. In the fall the sheep were herded into the pen for the slaughter. As they were being singled out, one sheep ran up to Sigurðr as if it were looking for help. Sigurðr reached out for it, lifted it out of the pen, and let it run loose up into the hills. He said: "There will be no more appeals for help to me than I can meet."[2]

It also happened in the winter that a woman had taken something. Þorgils was angry and wished to punish her. She ran to Sigurðr for help, and he (FJ 410) placed her next to him on the bench. Þorgils told him to turn over the woman and said what she had done. Sigurðr interceded for her, saying, "Forgive her for her offense, for she has sought my help."

Þorgils said that she should suffer the consequences. When Sigurðr saw that the master of the house did not want to heed his plea, he jumped up and drew his sword, telling him to go ahead and attack. Seeing that he was ready to resort to arms, Þorgils found him very imposing, and he began to suspect who he was. He said that he would refrain from punishing her and let her off.

There were other foreigners with Þorgils, and Sigurðr was the least esteemed. One day when Sigurðr came into the hall, another Norwegian was playing a board game with one of Þorgils's farmhands. He was quite a fop and puffed himself up. The Norwegian called to Sigurðr to advise him on the game because he was familiar with that skill as with others. When he looked at the game, he thought that it was as good as lost.

The man who was playing with the Norwegian had a sore foot, with a toe that was swollen and oozing matter. Sigurðr sat down on a bench and drew a straw along the floor. There were kittens scampering about the floor, and he kept drawing the straw ahead of them until it got to the man's foot. Then (U 205) the kittens ran up and took ahold of the foot. He jumped up with an exclamation, and the board was upset. They now quarreled about who had won. This is told because the victim took the trick to heart.[3]

People did not know that he had clerical training until the Saturday before Easter. Then he blessed the water with the priest. The longer he remained, the more he rose in the estimation of others. During the summer, before he took his leave of Þorgils, Sigurðr said that he should send men who were close to him to Sigurðr slembir. Þorgils asked: "What is your interest in him?" He replied: "I am Sigurðr slembidjákn, King Magnús's son." With that they parted, and Sigurðr sailed abroad. (FJ 411)

86. The Slaying of King Haraldr

At that time King Haraldr was sole king of Norway. It was said that he was not a wise man but not as cruel as his kinsman Magnús Sigurðarson. Sigurðr now arrived in Norway and made his way to King Haraldr in Bjǫrgvin. He placed himself at the king's mercy and delivered his statement. When the king's advisers realized the situation, they said that if Sigurðr were accepted as a ruler, he would prove too much for them, as Magnús had been. At the time things were very quiet, and the district chieftains were in charge of their affairs.[1] They advised the king to seize Sigurðr and kill him. They suggested that the charge against him be that he had participated in the slaying of Þorkell in the western islands.

This plan was adopted. Late one evening some of the king's agents went to where Sigurðr was and took him with them. They took a boat and rowed away from town with him, north to Holdhella (Hella).[2] Sigurðr sat on a chest and considered his situation. He suspected treachery. Two men in the bow guarded him in fetters. When they were cheerfully rowing and were all unsuspecting, Sigurðr said to the men who were guarding him: "Get up with me—I want to go back and bail my boat."[3] They stood up and untied his hands, but his feet were still in fetters.

He gripped them both by the shoulders and plunged them overboard, taking them down with him.[4] They were close to drowning before they were rescued by their companions, who rowed hard to reach them. But Sigurðr surfaced far away and had unfettered himself. He swam to shore before they could reach him and escaped by running because he was very swift of foot. He headed into the hills, and the king's men searched for him all night without finding him. (FJ 412) He took refuge in a mountain crevice and suffered greatly from the cold. He cut a section from the seat of his trousers and pulled it over him, with holes for his arms, and survived for the moment (U 206) that way.[5]

The king's men returned and could make no secret of their mishap. Sigurðr understood now that there was no point in appealing to the king for help. He left the country and went to Denmark. It was his claim, with his friends as witnesses, that he had given proof of his ancestry with the participation of five bishops. But Haraldr's friends said that it should all be viewed as the treachery and falsehood of the Danes.[6]

In the autumn Sigurðr slembidjákn went north to Norway in secret. His friends received him and kept him with them in hiding. He stayed with a certain priest. King Haraldr was in the town (Bergen) at that time, along with many leading men.[7] Queen Ingiríðr was also present. They had a son named Ingi. He was raised by foster parents in the east in Vík. King Haraldr had another son named Sigurðr. His mother was Þóra, Guthormr's daughter. He was fostered to the north in Þrándheimr.[8]

With the aid of his friends Sigurðr now cast about for some way to undermine and kill King Haraldr. He was supported in this plan by his compurgators and those who always sat with him at table and enjoyed great honor.[9] One evening when they were plotting this plan, two men at the king's table spoke up. One said to the king: "Sire, we wish to leave the resolution of our quarrel to you. We have bet a keg of honey on which of us is right. I say that you will sleep with Queen Ingiríðr tonight, but he says that you will sleep with Þóra Guthormr's daughter."

The king answered laughingly, not knowing that this question was inspired by deep deceit. He said that the other man should win the bet, and from this indication they thought they knew where (FJ 413) to find him.

The chief watch was held in the building where most people thought the king and queen slept. The day after Saint Lucy's feast Sigurðr slembir and some of his men put the plan into action.[10] Sigurðr went to the lodging where the king was sleeping, and they began by first killing the guards and breaking down the door. Then they entered with swords drawn. The king had gone to bed after heavy drinking and was fast asleep. He awoke only as they attacked him and said, only half awake: "You have prepared rough treatment for me, Þóra." But she jumped up and said: "They treat you roughly who wish you worse than I do." There King Haraldr lost his life. The men who entered with Sigurðr were Ǫgmundr, the son of Þrándr skagi (Promontory), Kolbjǫrn Þorljótsson from Bataldr, and the Icelander Erlendr.[11]

After that Sigurðr and his men left. He summoned the men who had promised to support him if King Haraldr was killed. They took a ship, had the oars manned, and rowed out across the bay past the king's residence. It was then beginning to dawn. Sigurðr stood up and spoke to the men on the quay, identifying himself as Haraldr's killer. He asked that they (U 207) accept him as their chieftain, as his birth entitled him to be.

Then large numbers arrived from the king's residence, and they were all in agreement. They said that they would never serve a man who had murdered his brother. "But if King Haraldr was not your brother, it is not fitting to call you king, for you have no ancestry among kings."[12] They all proclaimed that the killers should be outlawed and subject to death. Then the king's trumpet was sounded, and all the district chieftains and retainers were assembled. Sigurðr and his men saw that their only chance was to (FJ 414) depart.

He headed north for Hǫrðaland and convened a thingmeeting of the farmers. They submitted to him and gave him the title of king. Then he went inland to Sogn and over the mountains to Firðafylki (Fjordane). Most people responded favorably. But Queen Ingiríðr, the royal retainers, and the district chieftains took counsel. The men of Vík accompanied her east to Vík. She went to her son Ingi, and they accepted him as king at the Borgarþing.[13] At that time he was two years old. Their plan was promoted by Ámundi and Þjóstólfr Álason and many other powerful chieftains.

But the Þrœndir acclaimed Sigurðr Haraldsson as their king. He was four years old at the time. He was confirmed at the Eyrarþing. That move was backed by Óttarr birtingr, Pétr Úlfsson, Guthormr at Rein, Óttarr balli (the Strong), and a host of other men. Almost everyone aligned themselves with one of these brothers, chiefly because their father was alleged to be a saint.[14] The land was given them by oath, with the stipulation that it would submit to none other as long as any of Haraldr's sons lived. In the words of Ívarr the skald:

262. Tóku síðan   Sigurð til landa
       Hǫrðar ok Sygnir   at Harald fallinn:
       svǫrðusk margir   menn á þingi
       buðlungs syni   í bróður stað.

Then the Hǫrðar and the Sygnir [people of Hordaland and Sogn] elected Sigurðr to rule the lands upon Haraldr's death; at the assembly, many men swore that they would be like brothers to the king's son.

Reference is made here to those who accepted Sigurðr slembir as king, as was previously mentioned. Haraldr gilli had been king of Norway for sixteen years and for two years after the Battle of Fyrileif.[15] (FJ 415)

87. Concerning King Sigurðr slembir

Sigurðr slembir proceeded north past Staðr, and when he came to Norðmœrr, letters and seals had already arrived, on the initiative of those men who did not wish to desert Haraldr's sons. He was therefore immediately faced with resistance and the recalcitrance of his enemies. Because he had few troops, they retreated north to Þrándheimr and sought out Magnús Sigurðarson the Blind.

Sigurðr slembir went to Hólmr and took (U 208) his kinsman Magnús out of the monastery by force and against the will of the monks, but most people say that Magnús went willingly and would have accepted any improvement in his condition. Sigurðr expected that this move would increase his following, and that proved to be the case.

King Sigurðr was in town, and there were many powerful men with him.[1] The town was therefore not accessible to Sigurðr slembir. Sigurðr had all his friends with him. They rowed up the river and moored at the king's residence, but they were forced to retreat because all the people opposed them. Sigurðr then departed, expecting support and strength from his own relatives and Magnús's. The expectation was not entirely unjustified.

He departed after Christmas with Magnús and was followed by Bjǫrn Erlingsson, Gunnarr of Gimsar, Halldórr Sigurðarson, Áslákr Hákonarson, the brothers Benedikt and Eiríkr, the retinue that had been with Magnús, and a host of other men. They sailed south along Mœrr and all the way past the Raumsdalr Fjord. There they divided their forces. Sigurðr sailed to the west and Magnús went to Upplǫnd, where he expected that the men would flock to him. He spent the winter and summer there and gathered a great force.

Ingi gathered his army for the encounter, and they met at a place called Mynni (Minne).[2] There was a major battle, and Magnús had the superior forces. It is told that Þjóstólfr Álason carried King Ingi in a sling while the fighting went on (FJ 416), and he followed the standard. He underwent a hard trial of arms and great exertion in the onslaught. People say that it was here that King Ingi was crippled for life so that his back and one leg became crooked. That leg was shorter than the other, and so weak that he could never walk straight as long as he lived.

The casualties mounted against King Magnús. These are the men who fell in the first rank: Þorkell and Halldórr, the sons of Sigurðr, Bjǫrn Erlingsson, Gunnarr of Gimsar, and a great part of King Magnús's retinue before he was willing to flee. In the words of Kolli enn prúði:[3]

263. Unnuð austr fyr Mynni   lǫgðuð ér (en eirar
oddhríð (ok brátt síðan   ǫrr synjaðir brynju)
hilmir fekk und hjalmi   (ungr varðir þú þengill
hrafns verðar lið sverðum):   þitt land) saman randir.

"Unnuð oddhríð austr fyr Mynni, ok brátt síðan, hilmir, fekk lið und hjalmi hrafns verðar sverðum. Lǫgðuð ér saman randir, en ǫrr synjaðir brynju eirar; þengill, ungr varðir þú þitt land."

You fought an arrow storm [battle] east by Mynni [Minne], and soon thereafter, lord, helmeted troops furnished raven's food [corpses] with swords. You let shields clash and, bravely, you refused to spare the byrnie; king, as a youth you defended your country.

And again:

264. Fyrr lá hans (an harri   sundr klauf siklingr Þrœnda
hringmildr þaðan vildi)   sóknfúss of Magnúsi

verðung ǫll á velli.   (þér fekksk hǫlfu hæri)
Vígfimr konungr himni: herskriptr (jǫfurr giptu). (U 209)
"Fyrr lá ǫll verðung hans á velli, an hringmildr harri vildi þaðan. Vígfimr konungr
himni. Sóknfúss siklingr Þrœnda klauf sundr herskriptr of Magnúsi; jǫfurr, fekksk
þér hǫlfu hæri giptu."
His whole retinue lay on the ground before the ring-generous ruler [Magnús]
would retreat. "The battle-skilled king . . . heaven." The war-keen king of the
Þrœndir [people of Trøndelag] cleft the colored shields around Magnús; lord, you
were twice as lucky.

King Magnús fled east to Gautland to Karl Sørkvisson. He was a wise and ambitious man. Wherever they encountered chieftains, King Magnús and his men
said that Norway was free for the taking if any (FJ 417) great leaders had the
stomach for it, now that there was no king in the land and no rule or governance of the district chieftains. "And those who are chosen as advisers by the
district chieftains are torn by envy, so that no one wants the same as another."

Because Karl was eager for power and attentive to these words, he gathered
forces and marched on Vík from the east. Many people submitted to him out
of fear. Þjóstólfr Álason and Ámundi learned of this and marched against him
with the forces they could raise. They had King Ingi with them. They met Karl
and the Gautish army east in Krókaskógr, where they had another battle.[4]
There was great loss of life, but King Ingi was victorious. Many of the Gautar
fell, and the jarl fled east from the forest. King Ingi pursued the fugitives across
the eastern border, and it was a most disgraceful venture for them. In the
words of Kolli:

265. Lýsa munk hvé ljósa   goldit varð (þeims gerðu)
      (laut hrafn í ben Gauta)   glaumherðǫndum sverða
      (ǫrn fylldit sik sjaldan)   (rauns at ríki þínu)
      sárísa rauð vísi: (róg) á Krókaskógi.

"Lýsa munk, hvé vísi rauð ljósa sárísa; laut hrafn í ben Gauta; ǫrn fylldit sik sjaldan.
Varð goldit á Krókaskógi glaumherðǫndum sverða, þeims gerðu róg; rauns at
ríki þínu."
I shall relate how the ruler reddened the shining wound icicles [swords]; the raven
stooped over Gautish wounds; the eagle stuffed itself often. Those strengtheners
of the swords' racket [battle, warriors] who caused dissension, were repaid at
Krókaskógr [Sörbygden]; your power has been proven.

Magnús the Blind went to Denmark to meet with King Eiríkr eimuni.[5] He
was well received. He asked King Eiríkr if he wished to invade Norway with a
Danish army and subdue the country, saying that he would accompany him.
He said that if he came with a great force, no one would dare so much as to
cast a spear at him.

The king called up the levy and sailed north to Norway with two hundred
ships. Magnús the Blind and his men were with the Danish army. (FJ 418)

Eiríkr sailed from the east across Vík and proceeded with moderation and restraint. When they came to Túnsberg, King Ingi was present with an assembly of district chieftains, so that they could not land and renew their water supply. Many of them were killed there.

From there they sailed into Ósló. Þjóstólfr Álason was there. It is told that they wanted to take the reliquary of Saint Hallvarðr out of the town the evening when they became aware that an armed force was approaching. It was shouldered by as many as could get under it, but it was so heavy that they could not bring it farther than out onto the church floor.

In the morning they saw a fleet of vessels sailing in by Hofuðey (Hovedøya). Then four men were able to carry the reliquary out of the town. Þjóstólfr and all his followers left the town with the reliquary, and it was taken up to Fors (Foss) in Raumaríki, where it was left for three months.[6]

Þjóstólfr made (U 210) a stand above the town, and some ran after him and his men. A guardsman of Eiríkr's named Áskell was the swiftest. Þjóstólfr aimed a shot at him. It struck him under the throat and came out at the back of the neck. It seemed a remarkable shot because nothing else was exposed on him.

Þjóstólfr proceeded to Raumaríki and gathered forces at night. But Eiríkr and his men set fire to Saint Hallvarðr's Church and the whole town, and burned everything to the ground. Then Þjóstólfr descended with a great force, and Eiríkr made for open water with his troops. But they could not land anywhere on that side of the fjord because of the local militia gathered there. They left six or seven behind dead wherever they came ashore.

King Ingi was in the Straits of Hornbori together with his foster father Ámundi, the son of Gyrðr and grandson of Logbersi, and a large force.[7] They fought a battle with Eiríkr there, and many of his men fell to Ingi. King Eiríkr fled south to Denmark, and it (FJ 419) was said that there had never been a more disastrous expedition of that size. But it seemed to Eiríkr that Magnús and his men had lied when they said that Norway was ripe for the plucking and that no spear would be cast their way. He said that he would never again be such a friend to them.

88. Concerning King Haraldr's Sons

Now the story turns to the sons of King Haraldr, Ingi and Sigurðr, according to the account of the wise and discriminating man Eiríkr Oddsson. The tale is mostly from the report of the district chieftain Hákon magi, who presided and told of these events when they were first written down. He himself and his sons participated in these expeditions and most of the battles. He knew the men who are named here. He who wrote the story also named several truthful men as sources for the account.[1]

89. Concerning Sigurðr

Sigurðr slembir came to Denmark that summer and fought two battles, one in the Eyrarsund (Øresund) against the Wends and another south at Erri (Ærø).[1] There he cleared eight ships and hanged some of the men. He remained in Germany for some time since he knew there was no support in Norway, mostly because of the opposition of the Þrœndir and the Mœrir. According to Ívarr:

266.　Risu við vísa　　vestan komnum
　　　Þrœndr ok Mœrir　　þeirs þrifum níttu:
　　　brugðusk hǫlðar　　í huga sínum
　　　mennsku mildum　　Magnúss syni. (FJ 420; U 211)

The Þrœndir and the Mœrir [people of Trøndelag and Møre], renouncing their well-being, rose against the ruler who had come from the west; in their mind, men deserted the upright son of Magnús.

He told of the time Sigurðr left Norway and went to Sweden in the following stanzas:

267.　Drifu til reipa　　í rotuveðri
　　　reyndir at risnu　　ræsis þegnar:
　　　urðu seggir　　segls at gæta
　　　þá vas svalt á sæ　　en sumir jósu.

The king's retainers, tested in eminence, ran to the ropes in the roaring rainstorm; some tended the sail and some bailed; then it was cold at sea.

268.　Skók veðrvita　　í vátum byr
　　　golli glæstan　　of grams skipi:
　　　kløkkar urðu　　en konungr stýrði
　　　snekkju sneisar　　of Sigurði.

The gold-plated weathervane shook above the lord's ship in the wet storm; the vessel's thin boards weakened around Sigurðr, and the king steered.

269.　Hratt hvasst skipi　　í hvǫtu veðri
　　　rǫst ríðandi　　rammir straumar:
　　　festu seggir　　snekkju langa
　　　kynstórs jǫfurs　　við Kalmarnes.

The twirling maelstrom, the strong currents, speeded the ship in the biting wind; the crew moored the longship of the noble king by Kalmarnes [the headland of Kalmar].

Then he came to the realm of the king of the Danes and was befriended by many chieftains, and the king himself at first, as is told here (FJ 421):

270.　Sér framliga　　friðar leitaði
　　　ilrjóðr ara　　við Jóta gram.

The colorer of eagles' claws [warrior] successfully sought peace with the king of the Jótar [people of Jylland, Jutland].

Ívarr makes mention of the battle waged at Erri (Ærø), already noted:

271.   Mœtti Vinðum   sás vega þorði
        sókndjarfr Sigurðr   suðr við Erri.

Battle-brave Sigurðr, not afraid to fight, met the Wends south by Erri [Ærø].

And again:

272.   Hrauð ungr konungr   átta snekkjur
        vargr gein of val   Vinða ferðar:
        hné fyr eggju   óþjóðar lið.

The young king cleared eight ships of the Wendish forces; the wolf gaped over the corpses; the army of rabble fell before the sword edge.

He fought another battle at Mœri and killed many Wends, as Ívarr says:[2]

273.   Enn lét aðra   austr fyr Mœri
        gramr geirþorinn   gunni háða:
        neytti vápna   þás Vinðr hnigu
        ǫrr oddviti   ǫðru sinni. (U 212)

The spear-fierce king fought yet another battle east by Mœri [Møre]; the valiant war leader used his weapons for the second time when the Wends fell.

From there he entered the eastern branch of the Elfr (Götaälv) and seized six ships from Þórir hvínantorði and Óláfr, the son of Haraldr kesja, chasing Óláfr onto the shore, as is told here (FJ 422):[3]

274.   Vann í Elfi   þars jǫfurr barðisk
        fall folkstara   til fǫðurleifðar:
        skulfu skeyti   skot mǫgnuðusk
        hnigu hringviðir   hvárratveggju.

He furnished slaughter for the battle starling [bird of prey] at Elfr [Götaälv], where the king defended his paternal property; arrows trembled, shots intensified, sword trees [warriors] fell on both sides.

Þjóstólfr was in Konungahella in order to defend the land. Sigurðr brought his troops there, and they exchanged missiles, but Sigurðr could not land. Men fell on both sides, and many were wounded. Úlfheðinn Sǫxólfsson, a northerner and a warrior in Sigurðr's first rank, fell there.[4] This is mentioned by Ívarr:

275.   Vann leyfðr konungr   af liði Þóris
        þríu skip hroðin   í þeiri fǫr:
        settu undan   Óláfs liðar
        þeirs ór Elfi   eltir váru.

On that expedition, the extolled king cleared three ships from Þórir's fleet; Óláfr's followers, who had been forced to flee from Elfr [Götaälv], rushed away.

When Sigurðr was anchored in a harbor called Portyrja (Portør) off Límgarðssíða and was waylaying ships headed for Vík, which he wrecked or plundered, the men of Túnsberg sent out an expedition and caught him unawares on land as they were dividing their booty.[5] Some of the force came at them from inland, and others stretched their ships across the bay beyond the anchorage. Many of Sigurðr's men fell, including Finnr geit and Áskell Smiðsson.

But Sigurðr escaped onto his ship and rowed out at them. Vatnormr's ship was
closest to him (FJ 423) and gave way, backing off. Sigurðr rowed out to sea and
escaped with one ship. This was *recited*:

> 276.   Varðat vel við styrju
>   Vatnormr í Portyrju.

Vatnormr did not perform well in the battle of Portyrja [Portør].

They sailed out to sea, and since they were sailing with all sheets to the wind,
a crewman perished. His name was *Kolbeinn* Þorláksson from Bataldr. He
perished on the skiff that was tied to the ship. Sigurðr slembir took the outer
course when he got south and spent *the winter in Álaborg (Ålborg)*.[6] (U 213)

90. Concerning King Sigurðr slembir

In the following summer Sigurðr and Magnús both sailed north with seven
ships and made a surprise landfall at Listi (Lista) at night.[1] At the place where
they landed Benteinn Kolbeinsson, one of King Ingi's retainers and a very
valiant man, was in command. They went ashore before dawn undiscovered
and caught the men in their houses, which they intended to set afire. Benteinn
escaped to another house fully armed and intended to defend himself there.

Then Sigurðr asked: "Which of you lads wants to enter and attack Benteinn?
That would be a brave deed." No one was quick to answer. Benteinn heard
what they were saying and replied: "Whoever enters should be prepared for an
armed encounter." It was dark in the house and Benteinn stood by the door
with a drawn sword. He had a shield in hand and a helmet on his head and was
a formidable man.

Sigurðr stood some distance away and saw that no one was eager to enter.
He took a sheepskin cloak that he had with him, stretched it, and wrapped it
around his arm. He drew his sword and headed for the house. He had no
armor and was only in a shirt, with no helmet on his head. He shot into the
house like a bolt, so that he was inside in an instant, launched his attack,
(FJ 424) and delivered a death blow. He came out carrying the head in his
hand and was considered a rather bold man, for none was defter than he, as
the poem recounts:

> 277.   Helt á Lista   lofðungr skipum
>   ǫrr fyr Agðir   austan af Nesjum:
>   hné hersa kyn   herr vas í landi
>   brunnu bygðir   fyr buðlungi.

The valiant lord steered his ships west from Nesjar past Agðir [Agder] to Listi
[Lista]; the descendants of nobles fell; an army was in the country; settlements
were scorched by the king.

> 278.   Dreif til skógar   fyr skjǫldungi
>   landmanna lið   þars logar brunnu:

vǫkðu drengir   með dǫrr roðin
blóð Benteini   áðr bana fengi.

Flocks of countrymen fled before the king to the forest, where fires roared; warriors drew Benteinn's blood with reddened spears before he received his death blow.

They then went to their ships and sailed away. Sigurðr was a big, handsome man with brown hair and a somewhat low forehead. He had blue eyes, regular features, and a bump on his nose. He was adroit and a man of great prowess, the most accomplished of men in every way.

But when King Ingi learned of Benteinn's death, along with his brothers Sigurðr and Gyrðr, the sons of Kolbeinn, the king raised troops in response and joined them himself. He took a ship away from Hákon pungelta, the son of Páll, grandson of Áslákr Erlingsson of Sóli, and nephew of Hákon magi. King Ingi pursued Hákon and all his men into the hills and took everything they owned. They fled up the fjords, Sigurðr storkr, the son (U 214) of Eindriði from Gaulardalr (FJ 425), his brother Eiríkr hæll, and Andréás kelduskítr, the son of Grímr.[2]

But Sigurðr, Magnús the Blind, and Þorleifr skjappa sailed the outer course north to Hálogaland with three ships. Magnús stayed that winter north in Bjarkey with Viðkunnr Jónsson. Sigurðr hid out in Finnmark that winter, and more than twenty men with him. He chopped the stem and stern off his ship and sank them in the inner reaches of Ægisfjǫrðr (Øksfjorden).[3] It is said that he was provisioned by Þorleifr skjappa and Einarr, son of Ǫgmundr of Sandr and Guðrún, the daughter of Einarr and granddaughter of Ari from Hólar [*scil.* Reykjahólar] at Reykjanes.[4] We are told that Sigurðr composed a stanza that winter:

279.   Gótt vas í gamma   vasa þar gamans vant
        þars vér glaðir drukkum   at gamansdrykkju
        ok glaðr grams sonr   þegn gladdi þegn
        gekk meðal bekkja: þar lands sem hvar.

It was pleasant in the turf hut where gladly we drank, and the glad-hearted son of the prince passed between the benches; there was no lack of cheer at the cheerful drinking, retainer delighted retainer, there as everywhere.

The following spring he went south with two ships that the Lapps had constructed for him. There was no nail in them, and they were held together with sinews and used withies instead of brackets to fasten the planks. They were rowed by twelve oarsmen and were so swift that they skimmed over the water.[5] You may have heard the following:

280.   Fátt eitt fylgir   furu háleyskri
        svipar und segli   sinbundit skip.

Not much can keep up with the ship from Hálogaland [Hålogaland]; the sinewbound boat skims forth beneath the sail.

He emerged at Vágar (Vågan), where he seized the priest Sveinn and his two sons and had them all killed.[6] Ívarr recounts this. It was the winter after Benteinn was killed that Sigurðr was in Hálogaland. (FJ 426)

281. Þann vas enn næsta   naðra deyði
      hugfullr konungr   með Háleygjum:
      olli falli   feðga þriggja
      ulfs angrtopuðr   út í Vágum.

That next snakes' slayer [winter] the courageous king stayed with the Háleygjar [people of Hålogaland]; the terminator of the wolf's anguish [hunger, warrior] caused the death of a father and two sons out in Vágar [Vågan].

From there he went to Víkar,[7] and there he captured Vilhjálmr skinnari, the district chieftain, together with another man named Þóraldi keptr, and killed them both. According to Ívarr:

282. Þat vas et næsta   norðr í Vágum
      vápnaskipti   es Vilhjálmr fell.

The next skirmish occurred north in Vágar [Vågan], when Vilhjálmr died.

Then he went south and encountered Styrkárr glæsirófa at Byrða (Børøya), as he was sailing north from Kaupangr (Niðaróss), and killed him.[8] As Ívarr said: (U 215)

283. Mœtti síðan   suðr við Byrðu
      gramr gunnþorinn   Glæsirófu:
      olli stillir   Styrkárs bana
      bar benþiðurr   blóðga vængi.

Then the battle-eager king encountered Glæsirófa south by Byrða [Børøya]; the lord caused Styrkárr's death; the wound grouse [bird of prey] spread bloody wings.

When he came south to Hvalsnes,[9] he met Svína-Grímr and had his right hand cut off. In the words of Ívarr: (FJ 427)

284. Veitti vísi   fyr Valsnesi
      sókn snarpliga   Svínagrími:
      hann lét missa   mildings nefa
      hœgri handar   áðr hjaldr lykisk.

Vigorously, the leader attacked Svínagrímr outside Valsnes; he let the king's nephew lose his right hand before the battle ended.

Then he went south to Mœrr past the mouth of the Þrándheimsfjǫrðr and seized Heðinn harðmagi and Kálfr klingruauga.[10] He let Heðinn off but killed Kálfr. Ívarr recounts that he captured Finnr:

285. Mœtti Finni   fremðargjǫrnum
      ǫrr oddviti   austr á Kvildrum:
      létu nýtan   naddveðrs boða
      Ulfs arfþega   ǫndu týna.

The valiant war leader met ambitious Finnr east at Kvildir [Kville]; they caused the crafty offerer of the spear storm [battle, warrior], Ulfr's heir, to lose his life.

Again:

286. Vann fyr Mœri   mildingr tekinn
      Heðin með hǫndum   ok hans liða:
      hann lét Kalfi   klingruauga
      heldr harðliga   heiptir goldnar.

The king captured Heðinn and his men by Mœri [Møre]; he rewarded Kalfr kling-ruauga [Round-Eye] quite brutally for his belligerence.

Further: (FJ 428)

287.   Herskildi fór   harri Sygna
        allt et ýtra   eyjar ok strandir.

The lord of the Sygnir [people of Sogn] went with the war shield the outer course, beyond islands and shores.

And yet again:

288.   Séa knátti þar   fyr Sigurði
        bitra branda   brynjur hǫggnar:
        skarða skjǫldu   skǫpt blóðroðin
        veðrblásin vé   of vegǫndum. (U 216)

There, before Sigurðr, one could see sharp swords, sundered byrnies, chipped shields, spear shafts reddened in blood, storm-swept standards above the fighting troops.

King Ingi and his foster father Gyrðr learned of Sigurðr's expedition and his doings. They dispatched men in search of him, Jón kúza, the son of Kálfr rangi and the brother of Bishop Ívarr, and a priest named Jón smyrill. They outfitted Hreinninn, the swiftest of ships, with twenty-two rowing stations and sailed south in search of them.[11] It is said that they spotted them but did not attack and returned with no glory.

Sigurðr sailed on until he came to Hǫrðaland, south at Herðla (Herdla).[12] There Einarr, the son of Laxapáll, had his residence. He had gone into Hamarr (Hamar) to the Rogation Days meeting.[13] They seized all his money and a longship with fifteen rowing stations. They also captured his four-year-old son, who was sleeping in the care of a farmhand when they arrived. Some wanted to kill the boy, others wanted to take him with them.

The farmhand addressed them: "There is not much revenge in killing him and not much profit in taking him with you. Besides, he is my son, not Einarr's." They left without taking the boy with them. When Einarr came home, he gave the worker two ounces of gold and said that he would forever be (FJ 429) his friend.

Sigurðr and his men went east to Vík and captured Finnr, the son of Sauða-Úlfr, as he was collecting land dues. They hanged him, then sailed south to Denmark.

91. King Ingi's Letter

The men of Vík and Bjǫrgvin said that it seemed wrong that King Sigurðr would not come to the defense of the land with his brother Ingi. They said that there was a big difference between them when King Ingi and his men exposed themselves to all the danger and engaged in many battles . . . *while King Sigurðr and his friends took no action* north in Kaupangr even though his father's

killers sailed on the main sea lane past the fjord opening at Þrándheimr. Then
King Ingi sent a letter with his seal north to Þrándheimr. The letter was to
the effect that:

King Ingi sends his brother Sigurðr and his counselors, *Sáða-Gyrðr, Qgmundr
sviptir*, Óttarr birtingr, and all his district chieftains as well as his retainers and
housecarles, our friends, the farmers and *tillers* and all the people, rich and
poor, young and old, God's greeting and his own. Our difficulties are known to all
in this *land*, and also our youth, since you are five years old and I am three, so
that we are capable of no initiative unless we have the benefit of our friends and
men of good will. But my friends think that they are in a poor position while your
friends live in ease and tranquility. Now do me the favor of joining me with as many
men as possible, and let us stick together, come what may. Our greatest friends will
be those who do the most to ensure that we remain on good terms and are held in
equal esteem. But should you refuse and fail to come, as you have done before, at
my urgent request, then you should be prepared for me to march against you.
(U 217) God may then decide between (FJ 430) us, for we do not think that we
have the necessary forces to meet this threat as long as you do no more than collect half the revenue in Norway. Fare you well in God's peace.[1]

Then Óttarr birtingr stood up and spoke: "It is King Sigurðr's wish to reply
to his brother King Ingi: May God thank him for his good greeting, his exertion, his many duties, and the manifold perils to which you and your friends
have often been exposed on our behalf. Although some things in King Ingi's
words to his brother Sigurðr seem rather harsh, he has some justification on
several points. I will now speak my mind promptly, if it finds favor with the
king and other men. I advise that you, Sigurðr, march to meet your brother
King Ingi at the first possible moment with whatever troops you can raise. Each
of you should support the other in all matters of mutual interest, and may
Almighty God support you both. And now we wish to hear your words, sire."
     The king was carried to the meeting, and it was Pétr, the son of Sauða-
Úlfr, who carried him. This is what the king said: "All should know that, if the
decision is mine, I will go to meet my brother Ingi at the first opportunity."
Then one after the other spoke to the same effect, as is often done. Both Gyrðr
and Qgmundr and many other district chieftains made long speeches, but it
all amounted to what Óttarr had already said at the outset. Then they journeyed east to Vík to meet the king.

92. Concerning Sigurðr slembir

That same summer Sigurðr slembir and his men came to Norway with thirty
ships in mid-October. Their troops were both Danish and Norwegian, as is indicated here:

289. Fýstisk sunnan   Sigurðr á lesti (FJ 431)
     með lítit lið   lǫnd at sœkja:
     bjósk með hánum   til herfarar
     margs andvani   Magnús konungr.

Finally Sigurðr was eager to travel north with few troops to conquer lands; King
Magnús, much deprived, prepared to join him on the expedition.

290. Helt þrim tøgum   þjóðnýtr konungr
     snekkjum sunnan   við sókn búinn:
     uggðu lýðir   lið Sigurðar
     lék skjǫldr við skjǫld   á skipum vísa.

The benevolent king, ready for battle, steered from the south with thirty warships; people feared Sigurðr's army; shield played against shield on the leader's
ships.

The brothers Ingi and Sigurðr learned of this and sailed against them with
twenty very large ships, as is told here: (U 218)

291. Fóru leyfðir   með liði miklu
     Haralds hróðrsynir   herstefnu til:
     þás at mildum   Magnúss syni
     atróðr á sjá   Ingi knúði.

The honorable, distinguished sons of Haraldr went to battle with a large force
when Ingi hastened the rowing to attack the generous son of Magnús at sea.

They met Sunday after Saint Martin's Day (November 11), which fell on a Saturday, and they fought a battle, as is told here:[1]

292. Hraut í stǫngum   þars hildingar
     við víg vánir   vápna neyttu: (FJ 432)
     friðr slitnaði   frænda á millum
     guðr geisaði   gekk hildr saman.

Standard poles crashed where the kings, experienced in war, wielded their weapons;
peace was broken between the kinsmen, battle raged, the attack commenced.

293. Stunðu seggir   stál roðnuðu
     skaut bjartr konungr   báðum hǫndum:
     hǫrð spjót bitu   benjar svíddu
     herskip hruðusk   hvárratveggju.

Men moaned, swords were reddened, the bright king shot with both hands; hard
spears bit, wounds burned, warships were cleared on both sides.

294. Flugu hundruðum   herstefnu til
     sárgǫgl of sæ   sveita at drekka:
     eyddu oddar   jǫfurs fulltrúum
     morð miklaðisk   þás Magnús fell.

By the hundreds the wound geese [birds of prey] flew across the sea to the battle
to drink blood; swords wasted the king's confidants; the fighting increased when
Magnús fell.

In the very first clash the Danes withdrew with eighteen ships and returned home, as is related here:

295.   Flýðu Jótar   átján skipum
        þeirs Sigurði   sunnan fylgðu:
        raufsk ræsis lið   þás ríkr konungr
        vanr vásfǫrum   vápna neytti.

The Jótar [people of Jylland, Jutland] who had followed Sigurðr from the south fled with eighteen ships; the lord's troops scattered when the mighty king, accustomed to hardship, wielded his weapons.

The ships of Sigurðr and Magnús were then cleared. When Magnús's ship was nearly cleared and he was lying in his bed, (FJ 433) Hreiðarr Grjótgarðsson, who had long been in his company and had been a retainer, picked him up and wanted to leap onto another ship. At that moment Hreiðarr was struck between the shoulders by a spearcast that pierced him. It is told that Magnús was killed by the same cast.

Hreiðarr fell backward onto the deck with Magnús on top of him. Everyone agreed that he had followed his lord well and valiantly, and any man who earns such a reputation should be praised.[2] Loðinn of Línustaðir fell (U 219) there, along with Sigurðr's front-rank warrior Brúsi Þormóðsson, as well as Ívarr Kolbeinsson and Hávarðr fægir. This is told in King Ingi's praise poem:

296.   Rauðri dreif (þás rjúfa   harmar engr (því Ingi
        réð ǫld fyr gram skjǫldu)   átt ráða vel láði)
        mjǫll (áðr Magnús felli   (dǫkk fell drjúgt á skokka)
        morðgjarn) þrumu jarna: dráp Sigvarðar (vápna).

"Rauðri mjǫll þrumu jarna dreif, áðr morðgjarn Magnús felli, þás ǫld réð rjúfa skjǫldu fyr gram. Engr harmar dráp Sigvarðar, þvít átt vel ráða láði, Ingi; dǫkk vápna fell drjúgt á skokka."

The red snowflakes of the roar of steel [battle, blood] drifted before war-eager Magnús fell, when men clove shields before the king. No one mourns the slaying of Sigurðr, because you, Ingi, are entitled to rule the land; the water of weapons [blood] fell densely on the bottom boards.

297.   Syndi sjalfr at landi   ulfs bǫrnum varð arnar
        (snjallr en þú brátt allri)   einkar tíðr í víðu
        (vel of hrósak því) (vísi)   (borð ruðu frægir fyrðar)
        valkǫstr (Munins fǫstu):   fundr Langeyjarsundi.

"Sjalfr valkǫstr syndi at landi, en þú, vísi, brátt snjallr allri Munins fǫstu: vel of hrósak því. Fundr arnar varð ulfs bǫrnum einkar tíðr í víðu Langeyjarsundi; frægir fyrðar ruðu borð."

The very corpse heap floated ashore and you, brave king, concluded the fast of Muninn [raven, hunger]: I truly praise that. The brood of the wolf thoroughly enjoyed the encounter with the eagles in wide Langeyjarsund [Langǫsund]; eminent warriors reddened the ship planks.

When King Magnús the Blind was struck, he said: "That came seven years too late."

The largest part of their forces fell here, because no one who could be caught escaped. (FJ 434) On one island they killed more than sixty men. Two Icelanders were killed, the priest Sigurðr, son of Bergþórr and grandson of Már, and Klémet, the son of Ari and grandson of Einarr.[3] Ívarr skrauthanki, who was the son of Kálfr enn rangi (the Troublesome) and was later bishop north in Þrándheimr, escaped onto the ship of his brother Jón kaða (Hen). He had always served Magnús and escaped onto the ship of his brother Jón kaða. Jón was married to Cecilia, the daughter of Gyrðr Bárðarson, and was there among the troops. There were altogether three who escaped onto Jón's ship. The second was Arnbjǫrn ambi, who was later married to the daughter of Þorsteinn at Auðsholt, and the third was Ívarr dynta, the son of Starri and brother of Helgi Starrason. He was from inner Þrœndalǫg on his mother's side and a very handsome man.[4]

When the enemy became aware of them, they seized their weapons and attacked Jón's group, but he made ready to defend himself, and it looked as though there would be a general conflict. But an agreement was reached with Jón that allowed him to buy off Ívarr and Arnbjǫrn, though the money was later forgiven. Ívarr dynta was led up on shore and executed because Kolbeinn's sons Sigurðr and Gyrðr would accept no money for him, inasmuch as they charged him with having been present at the slaying of their brother.

Ívarr (skrauthanki) later recounted that of everything that had happened to him, he was most overcome when his namesake was led onto shore and under the ax. He embraced them and hoped to see them safe and sound on the other side. Gyríðr, the daughter of Birgir and the sister of Archbishop Jón, said that she had heard Bishop Ívarr tell this.[5]

93. Concerning King Sigurðr slembir

The story now turns to King Sigurðr slembir. His ship began to be boarded, but he defended himself with great valor and inflicted wounds on many men. They advanced toward the midship. In the words of Ívarr (FJ 435; U 220):

298.　　Hrauzk und jǫfri　　austan komnum
　　　　bitu slǫg suðrœn　　snekkja með stǫfnum:
　　　　þás skjǫldungs sonr　　af skipi sínu
　　　　sóknfœrr á sjá　　sunds kostaði.

The warship was cleared from stem to stern beneath the king who had come from the east; southern weapons bit when the battle-crafty king's son, leaping from his ship, tried swimming in the sea.

Then they looked through the fallen men and did not find Sigurðr slembir. They rowed out in their boats to find him. They discovered a man in the water and were about to kill him, but he asked for mercy and said he would reveal where Sigurðr slembir was. They agreed.

Shields, spears, and corpses were scattered over the sea by the ships. The man said: "You can see where there is a red shield afloat; you will find him under it." They rowed to it and captured him, then brought him to shore. He had dived overboard when his ship had been cleared and shed his armor in the water, because he was a powerful swimmer. He had a tinderbox on him, and the tinder was in a walnut shell covered with wax. He had a shield covering him while he swam so that nobody would know whether it was his shield or another, since so many were on the water. They said that they would never have found him if they had not been told. We have told how he kept his tinderbox because it was so ingeniously managed so as not to get wet. Ívarr states:[1]

299.   Varð á vatni   víkingr tekinn
       sás manna vas   mestr fullhugi. (FJ 436)

The viking, who was the most valiant of all men, was captured in the water.

When they reached land, the troops were told that Sigurðr had been captured. The army broke into a loud shout for joy, and when Sigurðr heard that, he said: "Many a wicked man will be overjoyed at my expense today."

Then Þjóstólfr Álason went up to him and said: "How could the son of a slave like you be so bold as to claim to be King Magnús's son?"

He replied: "My father is not to be compared to your father or a slave, for your father amounted to very little compared to mine."

We are told by Hallr, the son of Þorgeirr the physician and grandson of Steinn, and a retainer of King Ingi's who was present at the time, that the king's counselors wanted to kill him immediately.[2] But those who had the greatest grievances to avenge were most in favor of torturing him. Hallr mentioned the sons of Kolbeinn and Pétr Sauða-Úlfsson in this connection. But the greater body of men went away and refused to watch.

Then Pétr bound his arms so tightly that it cut the flesh.

Sigurðr said: "You tie a tight knot, Pétr."

He replied: "You taught me that when you killed my brother Finnr east at Kvildrir (Kville)."

Then they broke his legs with their axheads (U 221), and his arms as well. They scalped him and tore off his clothes, then beat him with walrus-hide whips until there was as little skin left as if he had been flayed alive. People say that he sang the psalter while they tortured him, and he always picked up where he had left off though he lost consciousness intermittently. Then he prayed for his enemies. Ívarr says the following:

300.   Þat telk illa   es jǫfurr skyldi
       kynstórr koma   í kvalar slíkar: (FJ 437)
       tekr Sigurði   síðan engi
       maðr rǫskvari   of meðalkafla.

I declare it a disaster that a highborn king should undergo such torment; no bolder man than Sigurðr will ever grasp a sword hilt.

301. Sǫng saltara   meðan Sigurð pínðu
     jǫfurs óvinir   ýta dróttinn:
     bað fyr brǫgnum   bǫðfrœkn jǫfurr
     þeims vellskata   veittu píslir.

The lord of the people sang the psalter while the king's enemies tortured Sigurðr; the battle-brave king prayed for the men who inflicted torments upon the generous ruler.

When he was no longer among the living, they dragged him to a tree and hung him in it. Ívarr reports:

302. Frák at léti   líf sitt konungr
     þás saltara   sungit hafði:
     vildi ganga   gramr til skriptar
     en því þjóðkonungr   þeygi náði.

I heard that the king gave up his life when he had sung the psalter; the lord wished to be shriven, but the mighty king was not granted that.

After his death everyone agreed, both friend and foe, that no man had been more valorous in every respect than Sigurðr, as far as we know. But he was nonetheless a luckless man. I have reported very few of his words, though not because I have not heard a number of words attributed to him, but Hallr related that he said little and answered only a few though people assailed him verbally. (FJ 438) Hallr also reported that Sigurðr reacted no more than if they had beaten a stock or a stone. He commented that he must have been a remarkable man since he was so brave and stouthearted that he could withstand torture while holding his tongue and showing no sign of pain. Hallr said that his speech was never different from when he sat on the drinking bench among his friends. His voice was no higher or lower, nor did it tremble abnormally. And he was able to speak almost to the point of death.

The priest in charge of the nearby parish had Sigurðr's body brought to the church, though he was a friend of the kings. But they were angered at him for this, and he was obliged to pay compensation. (U 222) They had his body taken away and covered with a heap of rocks. Later, his friends in Denmark recovered his body and had it brought south to Álaborg (Ålborg), where they buried it at Saint Mary's Church. Ketill, the provost who maintained the church, said that Sigurðr was buried there.[3]

Þjóstólfr Álason had King Magnús's body brought to Ósló and buried in Saint Hallvarðr's Church, next to his father. They brought Loðinn saupruðr to Túnsberg and buried all the other bodies there. Then they departed, having won a great victory. Bǫðvarr halti commemorates this in a praise poem that he composed about King Sigurðr, son of Haraldr:[4]

303. Nú skal lýst hvé Lista   létuð (hjalms at holmi
     læskjarr konungr (harra   hríð spurðisk sú víða)
     gerðisk afreksorða   (ofkúgi dó jǫfra)
     efnd) þíns fǫður hefndir: allvaldr Sigurð falla.

"Læskjarr konungr Lista, nú skal lýst, hvé hefndir fǫður þíns; efnd afreksorða harra gerðisk. Allvaldr, létuð Sigurð falla; sú hjalms hríð at holmi spurðisk víða; ofkúgi jǫfra dó."

Reliable lord of Listi [Lista], now I shall relate how you avenged your father; the king's courageous words came true. Lord, you had Sigurðr slain; far and wide, that storm of the helmet [battle] on the island became famous; the oppressor of princes died.

And again: (FJ 439)

304.   Magnús varð at morði   meir rak þik til þeira
       málsnjallr í bǫð falla   þreksterkr konungr verka
       réð fyr ræsis dauða   (flagðs hest hafið flestan
       ríkr þjóðkonungr slíkum: fylldan) nauðr an skyldi.

"Málsnjallr Magnús varð falla í bǫð at morði; ríkr þjóðkonungr réð fyr slíkum ræsis dauða. Þreksterkr konungr, meir nauðr, an skyldi, rak þik til þeira verka; hafið fylldan flestan flagðs hest."

Eloquent Magnús was to fall in the fighting at the battle; the mighty monarch caused that death of the leader. Powerful king, a greater need than was right forced you to commit those deeds; you have satiated many a horse of the sorceress [wolf].

305.   Þar fell allt ok ǫrvir
       (ulfr rauð á her dauðum
       teðr) í tognings veðri
       tveir jǫfrar lið þeira.

"Þar fell allt lið þeira ok tveir ǫrvir jǫfrar í tognings veðri; ulfr rauð teðr á her dauðum."

Two audacious kings and all their army fell there in that storm of the sword [battle]; the wolf reddened its teeth on the dead troops.

94. The Slaying of Óttarr birtingr

After the fall of King Haraldr gilli Queen Ingiríðr was married to Óttarr birtingr, a district chieftain and a great leader. His family was from Þrœndalǫg, and he was a powerful supporter of King Ingi's rule during his minority. But King Sigurðr was not a friend to him and thought that he was biased in favor of his kinsman King Ingi.

Óttarr birtingr was killed north in Kaupangr in a single encounter. It happened in the evening as he was going to vespers. When he heard the whine of the ax, he raised his hand and cloak to protect himself, thinking that a snowball had been thrown at him, as boys will do.[1] The blow felled him. At that moment his son Álfr hroði came into the churchyard and saw his father fall as his killer ran east by the church. Álfr pursued him and killed him at the corner of the choir. People thought that was a manly vengeance, and he seemed to be a much more important figure than before. (FJ 440; U 223)

95. [no heading]

When the brothers Ingi and Sigurðr had possessed the title of king for six years, a man came from Scotland in the west named Eysteinn.[1] As Einarr Skúlason says:

> 306. Jǫfurr fýstisk austr
> ǫrlyndr ok hraustr.

The lord, liberal and bold, was eager to journey east.

He was attended and accompanied by Árni sturla, Þorleifr Brynjólfsson, and Kolbeinn hrúga. Eysteinn was acclaimed king at the Eyrarþing in the Rogation Days, and a third part of Norway was sworn over to him in joint rule with his brothers. The brothers were able to settle the matter when they met, and Eysteinn submitted to no ordeals or tests in Norway concerning his ancestry. The matter was accepted on faith because Haraldr himself had asserted it.

Eysteinn was ruling in Þrándheimr at the time Óttarr birtingr was killed. He immediately called out the militia and went out to Kaupangr (Niðaróss). Óttarr's kinsmen and friends charged King Sigurðr with the slaying, since he was also in town, and the farmers raged against him. But he offered to undergo an ordeal and undertook to carry hot iron to prove his innocence. They agreed on that. King Sigurðr then traveled to southern Norway, and the ordeal was never performed.

Queen Ingiríðr had a son by Ívarr Sveinsson. His name was Ormr, and he was later called "King's Brother." He was a very handsome man and became a great chieftain, as will later be recounted.[2] Queen Ingiríðr was married to Árni, who was called "King's Kinsman." Their children were named Ingi, Níkolás, Filippús, and Ingigerðr, who was married to Bjǫrn bukkr and later to Símon Kárason.

There was a district chieftain serving the brothers Sigurðr and Ingi. His name was Erlingr, the son of Kyrpinga-Ormr and Ragnhildr, the daughter of Sveinki. (FJ 441) Kyrpinga-Ormr's mother was named *Ragna*, and her mother was Ragna, the daughter of Jarl Ormr Skoptason and Ingibjǫrg, the daughter of Hákon jarl the Powerful.[3] Erlingr was a wise man and a great friend of King Ingi. With the king's sponsorship he was married to Kristín, the daughter of King Sigurðr jórsalafari.

Erlingr had an estate at Stuðla (Støle) in Sunnhǫrðaland.[4] He was called Erlingr skakki. He traveled abroad and was accompanied by Eindriði ungi (the Young) and several other district chieftains. They sailed west to Orkney. There Rǫgnvaldr jarl, called kali, and Bishop Vilhjálmr prepared to sail with them. They had a fleet of fifteen ships from Orkney and sailed to the Hebrides, and from there to France by the same route that Sigurðr jórsalafari had used.[5]

They sailed through the Straits of Gibraltar (U 224) and harried many places in Spain against the infidel. Soon after they passed the straits, Eindriði ungi split off with five ships. Rǫgnvaldr jarl and Erlingr skakki proceeded with ten ships and encountered a galley at sea. They joined battle and overcame the galley. Auðunn rauði (the Red), one of Erlingr skakki's first-rank warriors, was the first to board the galley, and that was reputed to be a great deed.[6] They captured a great deal of money and many treasures.

Rǫgnvaldr jarl and Erlingr went out to Jerusalem and the River Jordan. They returned in the fall and sailed to Constantinople, where they left their ships behind and went overland. Their luck held all the way to Norway, and their journey was much praised. Erlingr skakki was deemed to be a much more important man than before, both because of his expedition and his marriage. He was a man of great wisdom, and his friendship inclined most to King Ingi. (FJ 442)

96. Concerning King Sigurðr

We are told that once when King Sigurðr was riding from a feast east in Vík with his retinue and passed a farm owned by a wealthy man named Símon, he heard such beautiful singing in a certain house that he was much affected. He rode up to the house and saw that there was a woman standing by a handmill and singing wondrously well. The king dismounted and told his men to wait outside while he went in alone to the woman. When he went away again, the landowner Símon was aware of what business he had transacted with this woman. Her name was Þóra, and she was one of Símon's workers. Subsequently he made provision for her, and some time later she gave birth to a child who was named Hákon and was said to be the son of King Sigurðr.[1] Símon fostered the boy. At the same time Símon's sons Ǫnundr and Andréás were growing up there. The three of them were greatly attached to each other, and only death parted them.

97. Concerning King Eysteinn

King Eysteinn had a disagreement with the farmers residing in Ranríki[1] and Hising (Hisingen) when he was east in Vík. They gathered forces against him, and he met them in battle and won the victory. He killed many of them, took hostages, and exacted payments, though some were permitted to ransom themselves. Einarr reports as follows: (U 225)

307. Víkverjum galt   flest folk varð hrætt
         varð þannig hallt   áðr fengi sætt (FJ 443)
         gǫrræði gramr   en gjǫldin jók
         gjafmildr ok framr: sás gísla tók.

The king, generous and clever, repaid the people of Vík [Viken] for their high-handed ways—they suffered for that—; most men were scared before a settlement was reached, but he who took hostages increased the payments.

308. Vann siklingr sótt   Remir flýðu ríkt
     með snarpa drótt   ok reiddu slíkt
     leyfðs lýðum kær   ǫld festi auð
     Leikbergi nær: sem ǫðlingr bauð.

With his brave company, the king fought a battle close to Leikberg; the praise is dear to the people; the "Remir" fled in force and paid out what the king exacted; people promised riches.

Sometime later King Eysteinn sailed west across the sea to Caithness and learned that Jarl Haraldr Maddaðarson was anchored in Thurso. The king advanced with three ships and took them by surprise, though the jarl had twenty-five ships and enormous treasure. Since the jarl was unprepared, Eysteinn and his men were able to board the ship. They captured the jarl and brought him to their ship. He ransomed himself for seven marks of gold. With that, they parted. In the words of Einarr:

309. Váru sogns með sára   þrimr skútum tók þreytir
     syni Maddaðar staddir   þann jarl drasils hranna
     mágrenni (fremsk) manna   hraustr gaf hræskúfs nistir
     (máttugr) tigir átta: hǫfuð sitt spǫkum jǫfri.

"Átta tigir manna váru staddir með sára sogns mágrenni, syni Maddaðar; máttugr fremsk. Þrimr skútum tók þreytir drasils hranna þann jarl; hraustr hræskúfs nistir gaf hǫfuð sitt spǫkum jǫfri."

Eighty men stood by the feeder of the seagull of the sea of sores [blood, bird of prey, warrior], Maddaðr's son; the powerful one achieves fame. With three ships, the tester of the waves' steed [ship, sea warrior] captured that jarl; the bold feeder of the corpse bird [bird of prey, warrior] surrendered his head to the sagacious king.

From there King Eysteinn sailed south along the east coast of Scotland and anchored at the town called Aberdeen. There he killed many men and plundered the town. In the words of Einarr: (FJ 444)

310. Frétt hefk at fell
     folks brustu svell
     jǫfurr eyddi frið
     Apardjónar lið.

I have heard that the men of Aberdeen fell; the swells of battle [swords] burst; the king broke the peace.

He fought another battle to the south at Hartlepool and put the enemy to flight.[2] According to Einarr:

311. Beit buðlungs hjǫrr   Huginn gladdi heit
     blóð fell á dǫrr   hruðusk Engla beit
     hirð fylgðisk holl   óx vitnis vín
     við Hjartarpoll: valbasta Rín.

The king's sword bit; blood fell on spears; the retainers followed faithfully at Hartlepool; the steaming Rhine of the sword hilts [blood] gladdened Huginn [raven]; English ships were cleared; the wolf's wine [blood] increased.

After that he sailed to Whitby and fought. He won the victory there and burned the town, as this stanza relates: (U 226)

312. Jók hilmir hjaldr   ríkt lék við rǫnn
      þar vas hjǫrva galdr   rauzk ylgjar tǫnn
      hjósk hildar ský   fekksk fyrðum harmr
      við Hvítabý: fyriskógar garmr.

The king intensified the fighting at Whitby; there was a chant of swords [battle]; the cloud of battle [shield] was cloven; the hound of the fir forest [fire] played powerfully against houses; the she-wolf reddened her tooth; people suffered harm.

After that he harried far and wide in England. At that time Stephen was king in England.[3] Then King Eysteinn fought a battle at Skǫrpusker against certain knights and put them to flight, as Einarr tells us:

313. Drap dǫglingr gegn   rauf styrjar garð
      dreif strengjar regn   þars støkkva varð
      við Skǫrpusker   randǫlun sótt
      skjaldkœnan her: (FJ 445)   reiðmanna gnótt.

The valiant king killed the shield-keen company by Skǫrpusker; the rain of the bowstring [arrows] streamed; the yard of strife [shield] burst where a host of horsemen, attacked by the rim fish [swords], was obliged to scatter.

Then he fought at Pílavík (Willoughby?) and won the victory, as Einarr relates:[4]

314. Rauð siklingr sverð   vann vísi allt
      sleit gylðis ferð   fyr vestan salt
      prútt Parta lík   brandr gall við brún
      í Pílavík: brennt Langatún.

The king reddened the sword in Pílavík [Willoughby?]; the wolf's band tore the proud corpses of the Partar; the leader burned all Langton west of the sea; the sword rang against brows.

Langton was the last place he burned before they sailed away *in the fall and* returned to Norway.

There were differing opinions about this expedition. King Eysteinn believed that he had undertaken it in vengeance for King Haraldr Sigurðarson, who had fallen in England.

The three brothers got on well as long as their foster fathers were alive. King Ingi and Sigurðr had a combined retinue, and Eysteinn a separate one. [One after the other] Gyrðr, Ámundi, Þjóstólfr, Óttarr birtingr, Ǫgmundr sviptir, and Ǫgmundr Kyrpinga-Ormsson, Erlingr skakki's brother, died—Erlingr was not much honored as long as Ǫgmundr was still alive.[5] When they were all dead, King Ingi and King Sigurðr quickly separated their retinues. King Sigurðr was altogether a very overbearing and contentious man in his youth, and his brother King Eysteinn was not very different except that he was also a very covetous man. King Ingi was in poor health. His back was crooked and one foot (FJ 446) was withered so that he was very lame, but still he was very popular with the people.[6]

Einarr Skúlason was in the company of the brothers Sigurðr and Eysteinn, and King Eysteinn was a great friend of his. Eysteinn asked (U 227) him to compose a poem in honor of Saint Óláfr, and he did so. He presented it north in Þrándheimr in the very confines of Christ Church, and it was accompanied by great miracles. A sweet fragrance rose in the church, and people say that there were intimations from the king himself that he thought well of the poem.[7]

King Eysteinn honored Einarr greatly. We are told that once King Eysteinn had seated himself, but Einarr had not yet come to his seat. At that time King Eysteinn had made him his marshal. This happened north in Þrándheimr. Einarr had been at Nunnusetr at Bakki (Bakke).[8] The king said: "You shall be fined, skald, since you have not taken your seat, even though you are the king's poet. We will not be reconciled unless you compose a stanza before I empty my tankard." Then Einarr recited this stanza:

315. Oss lét abbadissa   enn til áts með nunnum
    angri firð of svanga   (ógnar rakks) á Bakka
    (dygg þótt víf en vígðu   (drós gladdit vin vísa)
    víti fyrðar) gyrða: vasat stallari kallaðr.

"Angri firð abbadissa lét oss gyrða of svanga, þótt fyrðar víti dygg víf en vígðu. Enn stallari vasat kallaðr til áts með nunnum á Bakka; drós gladdit vin ógnar rakks vísa."
The blameless abbess made me tighten the belt, yet men may reproach the faithful ordained women. For the marshal was not invited to eat with the nuns at Bakki [Bakke]; the woman did not gladden the friend of the battle-brave king.

It pleased the king greatly.

We are also told that when King Sigurðr was in Bjǫrgvin, it happened that there were minstrels in the town. One was named Jarlmaðr. Jarlmaðr ate goat meat on Friday. The king wanted to punish him and ordered him (FJ 447) to be whipped.[9] When Einarr arrived, he said: "You are treating our companion Jarlmaðr harshly." The king said: "It is in your hands. Compose a stanza, and as long as it takes you to compose he will be whipped." Einarr replied: "Jarlmaðr will wish me not to be overly tongue-tied." They gave him five strokes, then Einarr said: "Now the stanza is done."

316. Austr tók illa kristinn   vǫndr hrǫkk (vámr lá bundinn)
    Jarlmaðr frá búkarli   (vísmáll) (á skip þíslar)
    (gráðr vas kjǫts á kauða)   (sǫng leikara lengi
    kiðling (hinns slær fiðlu):   líma harðan príma).

"Illa kristinn Jarlmaðr, hinns slær fiðlu, tók austr kiðling frá búkarli; gráðr kjǫts vas á kauða. Vǫndr hrǫkk; vámr lá bundinn á skip þíslar; vísmáll líma sǫng leikara lengi harðan príma."
Jarlmaðr, the poor Christian who plies the fiddle, took a goat kid from a farmer in the east; the greed for meat overcame the churl. The whip coiled; the loathsome fellow lay bound on the ship of the wagon shaft [wagon]; for a long time the eloquent lash sang a harsh service over the minstrel.

It happened one summer that a prominent woman named Ragnhildr came to Bjǫrgvin. She was married to Páll Skoptason, commanded a longship, and traveled in the style of a district chieftain. She stayed in the town for a while, and when she made ready to leave, the king saw her preparations and said: "Is there a skald here?"

Snorri Bárðarson was present.[10] He was not quick on his feet, and he did not compose as rapidly as the king wished. (U 228) The king said: "It would not be this way if Einarr were here." At that time he was somewhat estranged from the king because of discord. The king asked whether he was in town and sent people to summon him. When he came to the quay, the king said: "Welcome, skald. Look at this woman's splendid departure. Compose a stanza now and finish it before the ship gets out to Hólmr."

Einarr replied: "That won't happen without negotiations." The king asked: "What sort of negotiations?" Einarr answered: "You and seven of your retainers will be obligated to memorize one line each in the stanza, and failing that (FJ 448), you must give me as many casks of honey as there are lines you do not remember." The king agreed, and Einarr recited the stanza:

317. Hola báru rístr hlýrum   varla heldr und vildra
    hreystisprund at sundi   víkmarr á jarðríki
    (blæss élreki of ási)   (breiðr viðr brimsgang súðum
    Útsteins (vefi þrútna):   barmr) lyptingar farmi.

"Hreystisprund rístr hola báru hlýrum at sundi Útsteins; élreki blæss þrútna vefi of ási. Varla heldr víkmarr á jarðríki und vildra lyptingar farmi; breiðr barmr viðr brimsgang súðum."

With the prow the capable woman carves the hollow wave toward the straits of Útsteinn [Utsteinen]; the storm chaser [wind] fills the swollen sails above the sail yard. There is hardly another bay horse [ship] on earth that sails beneath a more precious burden of the deck [cargo]; the broad breast gains good speed for the ship boards.

Then the king said: "I think I remember 'Hola báru rístr hlýrum.'"

"That's right."

"And then 'barmr lyptingar farmi.'"

But they could never remember what was in between.[11] Einarr was subsequently in the king's company and had the same privileges as the king's men.

98. The Slaying of Geirsteinn

The most faithful counselors of the two brothers had now died. It happened that there was a man named Geirsteinn living in northern Norway, a rich and inequitable man, assertive and contentious. One of his sons was named Hjarrandi and another Hísingr. They were overbearing men like their father and very full of themselves. Their sister was the mistress of King Sigurðr Haraldsson, and they were on terms of friendship with him, so that father and sons were all in the king's confidence.

Not far from Geirsteinn a distinguished woman of high lineage and many good qualities owned property. Her name was Gyða, and she was the sister of Ragnhildr, who was married to the great eastern chieftain Dagr Eilífsson and owned land in the east near Túnsberg. Geirsteinn became much enamored of her, but (FJ 449) that was not to her liking, and when he realized that, he was furious and became hostile toward her. He said that she was more likely to end up with a bad marriage.

Then he began to drive his cattle onto her fields and do a great deal of damage to her property, blaming her for rumors to the detriment of his reputation.[1] When she saw the damage, she said: "I am not getting the benefit of my distinguished kinsmen if I have to (U 229) suffer such injustice." She had a foster son named Gyrðr, a handsome and valiant man. He replied: "What you say is true, and you have suffered much injury at the hands of Geirsteinn. I think your comment is aimed at me, and I am indeed obligated to take revenge. But whoever does it should give some thought to what will ensue because of King Sigurðr's involvement."

It happened one day that Gyða saw a herd of cattle standing on her fields. They had done a lot of damage. She became very angry, picked up a spear, and ran to the herd. There she was met by her kinsman Gyrðr. He took the spear and drove off the cattle across a bridge over a river that ran between the farms. There he ran into Geirsteinn. Geirsteinn said: "We are now being opposed by insignificant men with no lineage, who think they are our equals." With that he aimed a thrust at him, but Gyrðr turned it aside and struck a blow on his left side that was the death of him.

After that he met Gyða. She thanked him and had readied two horses for him. He rode one and loaded his baggage on the other. She sent him to her sister Ragnhildr with tokens requesting that she protect him against his enemies. The message was also directed to Ragnhildr's son Grégóríús: "It is certain that there will be a vigorous pursuit of vengeance."

Gyrðr arrived in the east and met with Grégóríús. He had a large body of men, but at first he seemed rather hesitant,[2] and people were not of the same mind as to who (FJ 450) *....* [Gyrðr presented] the matter to Ragnhildr with authentic tokens. She communicated it to Grégóríús and said that it was crucial that *he should give the man aid. Grégóríús answered: "I have not* yet become much involved in disputes, but I am not reputed to be without leadership qualities. But the man who is to oppose King Sigurðr must have a great deal of support. We should take more account of our own disadvantage than of the matter facing us."

She said: "Give the man aid so that he may be granted life for the deed he has done, for he has washed away a great shame from our kinsmen. You should respect my words and your own honor."

Grégóríús answered: "It is hard to oppose the king, and it seems to me more disgraceful to promise help when none can be rendered."

Then she spoke in anger: "You are destined to be of no account for a long time when you pay no attention even if your kinsmen are killed. You are a far cry from your worthy kinsmen, and the deed that has been committed was amply justified."

Grégóríús said: "You are pressing me very hard, mother. Let me talk to the man."

Gyrðr stepped forward and presented the case skillfully, explaining the whole sequence of events and showing him the tokens. He said how important it was for his kin that he consider the matter. He also said that if he (U 230) was ever to be a chieftain, he would have to begin by testing himself.

Confronted with this account, the pressing need, and his mother's urging, Grégóríús said: "You are making a vehement case, mother. If what we are undertaking turns out honorably, it will benefit us. But I want the men who are with me to agree to support me if I take on this problem. Let them assume the responsibility with me, and let them swear to defend (FJ 451) his life. If so, I may be of some assistance to him."

There were sixty free men in his company. He and his companions now received the man into their keeping. Geirsteinn's sons learned of this and became furious. They told King Sigurðr that they wanted to burn Gyða's farm and seize all her possessions. The king asked them to refrain for the moment, saying that he would seek compensation and ascertain the true situation. The brothers went north and did many misdeeds, but because of the king's prohibition they did not dare do as much damage as they wished.

When they learned that their father's killer had been taken in by Grégóríús, they told the king and asked for a company of men to seek him out and kill him, together with all those who backed him. They said that the district chieftains had a lot of nerve opposing the king. The king replied that they should first proceed with moderation, and he sent a man named Loðinn to Grégóríús. He was known for his intelligence and many other good qualities.

He met with Grégóríús and inquired wisely and with great good will on the king's behalf, saying that it was fitting that he should defer to the king. He asked what Grégóríús would offer for the killing of Geirsteinn. He replied: "The king should determine the penalty for whatever he deems to be an offense against himself, but Geirsteinn was responsible for what happened, and his sons have conducted themselves very dishonorably in the sequel."

Loðinn departed and told the king what had happened. When the brothers heard this, they were very inflamed, but the king wished to send another man to Grégóríús, a man named Rauðr, together with thirty men. They met with Grégóríús and delivered their message with more vigor and vehemence than before. They said that the king wanted more authority than the district chieftains, and that Grégóríús was recalcitrant—"But you have a greater obligation to consider your situation."[3] (FJ 452)

Grégóríús replied: "There has already been a good man here, who delivered this message with wisdom and good will, though I could not agree with his view. You, on the other hand, present the matter aggressively, but you seem no more likely to accomplish anything here."

When they departed they took counsel, and Rauðr was disinclined to let things stand as they were. He told them to wait for him in the woods while he returned to the house—"It may be that we can catch the man when they are least prepared." They returned (U 231) fifteen strong and sat down on the benches in the hall where Grégóríús was accustomed to drink. They put on beggar's garb over their armor.[4]

In the evening when Grégóríús and his followers entered the hall, he asked what the beggars were doing there. Then he looked them over and realized who they were. He had them seized and fettered, and in the morning they were driven out into the woods to their companions. Then a thingmeeting was convened, and Grégóríús told what treachery these men wished to commit. Then they were condemned to death and were hanged.

King Sigurðr and Geirsteinn's sons learned of this. The latter were enraged and asked the king for an armed force, which he provided. They marched east to Vík, and there was no advance intelligence. They plundered as they went. At that time Grégóríús was in Túnsberg. Some say that it was Christmas Eve when Grégóríús was least on his guard. He nonetheless marched out against them and sent messengers in every direction so that troops gathered.

There were casualties in the encounter, and it ended with the flight of Geirsteinn's sons back to the king. We are told that they learned at one time that Grégóríús was going to be entertained at the residence of a kinsman. They kept a lookout and came to the feast, where they killed the men who were to host it. Then they sat down to feast themselves. Grégóríús got no word of this and arrived (FJ 453) at the bay below the farm. They intended to lay to in the anchorage.

Then Grégóríús said: "It looks to me as though there is a great company here, and it may be that hostilities are afoot. We will make a test and head for the next promontory. If they are hostile, they will go out to meet us, but it may be that we can make a quick maneuver back to the landing and get to the house first, so that we can meet the attack there."

It turned out as he thought. As soon as they pushed off, the others headed for the promontory, but Grégóríús switched back and got to the house first. They now clashed, and the fight resulted in many casualties. Grégóríús was a powerful warrior. Hísingr challenged him. They met and fought, and Hísingr fell in an encounter that has since become famous. Grégóríús took his sword and continued to fight. Then Hísingr's brother advanced and wanted to avenge his brother. The end of it was that Grégóríús killed both of Geirsteinn's sons and gained great honor and glory.

After these great deeds Grégóríús went to King Ingi and placed himself under his command. They became fast friends and Grégóríús was a faithful mainstay to the king all his days. Grégóríús was wealthy and spared neither himself nor his money in supporting King Ingi.[5] It was generally thought that he was the greatest and most outstanding of the district chieftains in Norway in living memory. (U 232)

A good many things happened that caused dissension between the brothers, but I will only make mention of the thing that seems to me to have been most momentous.

99. [no heading]

During the reign of the brothers Cardinal Nicholas came north from Rome *to Norway* on the orders of the pope.[1] The cardinal visited his wrath on King Sigurðr and King Eysteinn, and they were obliged to make their peace with *him. But he was* always on good terms with King Ingi and called him (FJ 454) his son. When they had made their peace with him, he allowed them to consecrate *Jón Bir*gisson as archbishop in Þrándheimr and gave him the garment called a "pallium."[2] He determined that the archbishop's seat should be located north in Kaupangr at Christ Church, where Saint Óláfr is laid to rest. Before that there were only suffragan bishops in Norway.

The cardinal ruled that no man should bear arms in the town with impunity except for the twelve men who accompanied the king. He improved the conduct of the Norwegians in many ways during his stay there. No one had come to Norway who was so honored as he was or who accomplished so much for the people. He returned south with great honor and gifts of friendship, saying that he would always be a great friend to Norway.

When he reached Rome, the pope died soon afterward, and all the people of Rome wanted Nicholas as pope. He was consecrated and given the name Hadrian, though he was previously named Nicholas. The people who traveled to Rome during his time related that he was never so busy talking to others that he did not give the Norwegians the priority if they wished to speak to him. But he was not pope for long and is now regarded as a true saint.

100. Concerning the Death of King Sigurðr

One winter King Sigurðr and King Eysteinn arranged a meeting in Upplǫnd in order to bring about a reconciliation because King Sigurðr had killed two of King Eysteinn's friends and retainers, Haraldr from Vík, who had a residence in Bjǫrgvin, and another man named (FJ 455) Jón Tábarðsson, a priest. The two kings conferred for a long time, and it was determined that all three brothers should meet the following summer in Bjǫrgvin. The upshot was that they wanted King Ingi to keep two or three residences and sufficient resources so that he could maintain a retinue of thirty men. But they thought that he did not have the physical health to be king. (U 233)

When King Ingi and Grégóríús learned of this, they went to Bjǫrgvin in force. King Sigurðr arrived there a little later and had a smaller force. At that time Ingi and Sigurðr had ruled Norway for nineteen years.[1] It took Eysteinn more time to arrive from Vík in the east than it took the others to arrive from the north. Then King Ingi had the signal sounded for a meeting out on Hólmr. Both the other kings and a multitude of people assembled, and the thing-meeting was well attended.

Grégóríús had two longships and more than ninety men, all maintained at his expense. He maintained his followers better than any of the other district chieftains. He never drank at taverns without having all his retainers with him. He went to the thingmeeting with a gilt helmet, and all his followers wore helmets as well.

King Ingi arose and delivered a speech, telling the men that he had learned how his brothers wished to deal with him. "And now I wish to seek counsel and ask for the aid and support of my friends. But I would rather lose my life than abandon my patrimony." The people at large applauded his words and said they wished to support him.

Then King Sigurðr stood up and spoke, saying that they were innocent of the charge that King Ingi brought against them. He said that Grégóríús was behind it, and he went on to predict that it would not be long, if he had his way, before they had a meeting in which his gilt helmet took a tumble. He ended his speech by saying (FJ 456) that they would not both prosper for long.

Grégóríús replied by saying that he would not have to wait long and that he was ready for him. With that the meeting broke up, but a few days later one of Grégóríús's retainers was killed by one of King Sigurðr's retainers on the street. Grégóríús wanted to attack King Sigurðr and his men, but King Ingi and many other men demurred.

A few days later Queen Ingiríðr, King Ingi's mother, was leaving vespers and passed by as King Ingi's retainer Sigurðr skrúðhyrna was killed.[2] He was old and had served many kings. King Sigurðr's retainers Hallvarðr Gunnarsson and Sigurðr Gunnarsson killed him, but people thought that King Sigurðr was behind it. The queen went directly to King Ingi and told him the news, saying that he wasn't much of a king if he would undertake nothing even though his retainers were slaughtered one after the other like pigs. The king was angered by her speech, and they exchanged words.

Then Grégóríús entered clad in helmet and byrnie. He begged the king not to be angry, but said that the queen spoke the truth. "I have come to back you if you will make an attack on Sigurðr. In the courtyard outside there are more than a hundred of my retainers fully armed, and they are prepared to attack from the most difficult approach." Most people tried to dissuade the king and said that Sigurðr (U 234) would want to pay compensation for the misfortune.

When Grégóríús saw that the dissuasion would work, he spoke to King Ingi: "They are lopping away our strength by first killing my retainer and now yours. Then they will kill me or some other district chieftain who seems to them to be the greatest loss for you. And when they see that you do not react, they will dethrone you as soon as all your friends are slain. Regardless of what your other district chieftains wish to do, I do not wish to wait for the slaughter. Sigurðr and I will transact our business this very night, however it turns out. It is apparent (FJ 457) that you are both at a physical disadvantage and have little stomach to protect your friends. I am now more than ready to march against Sigurðr, for my standards are raised just outside."

Now the king stood up and called for his robes and asked all who wished to follow him to ready themselves. He said that there was no point in deterring him and that he had counseled moderation long enough. He bade them join him in cutting to the core of the situation. King Sigurðr was drinking in Sigríðr sæta's hall and prepared for the onslaught, but he thought that the attack would come to nothing.

Then they approached the hall, King Ingi from the smithy above it, Árni "King's Kinsman" from out at Sandbrú, Áslákr Erlendsson from his own hall, and Grégóríús from the street, where the approach seemed hardest. Sigurðr and his men kept up a rain of arrows from the upper story and broke out the furnace bricks to pelt them. But Grégóríús and his men broke down the gate. In King Sigurðr's following Einarr, the son of Laxapáll, fell at the gate. Hallvarðr Gunnarsson was brought down by a shot through a window, and no one grieved his loss.

King Ingi and his men cut their way through the houses to them, and Sigurðr's troops deserted him and asked for a truce. Then King Sigurðr went to an upper room and wanted leave to speak. He had a gilt shield, and people recognized him immediately. They had no wish to listen and loosed a hail of arrows at him so that he could not remain there.

By this time his troops were much depleted *and the buildings in shambles. King Sigurðr then went out* together with his retainer Þórðr húsfreyja, *a man from Vík.³ He went to the place where King Ingi was located*. King Sigurðr called on his brother King Ingi to grant him a truce, but both were hewn down. Þórðr húsfreyja fell there with great renown.

King Sigurðr was buried at Christ Church at Hólmr. Many men fell there in Sigurðr's company, though I mention only a few cases. Some of King Ingi's men fell too, and four of Grégóríús's followers, as well as *many men* who were on neither side (FJ 458) but were struck by arrows down by the quays or out on the ships. The battle was fought two weeks before the feast of Saint John the Baptist (June 24), and *that was a Friday*. King Ingi gave Grégóríús a ship that King Sigurðr had owned.

Two or three days later King Eysteinn arrived from the east with thirty (U 235) ships and had Hákon, King Sigurðr's son, with him. He did not dock in the town but anchored out in Flóruvágar (Florvåg).[4] Mediators passed back and forth and wished to reconcile them. King Eysteinn was reluctant to be reconciled and consulted Einarr Skúlason. He asked who *he thought* had had the greatest part in the killing of King Sigurðr. He said:

318.   Alls engi þarf Inga   bǫð gatat stillir stǫðvat
      arngrennir þat kenna   styrjar mildr (þótt vildi)
      (hverr spyri satt frá snerru   fús vas fjǫrspell vísa
      seggr) at gram bitu eggjar: fylkis sveit at veita.

"Alls engi arngrennir þarf kenna Inga þat, at eggjar bitu gram; hverr seggr spyri satt frá snerru. Styrjar mildr stillir gatat stǫðvat bǫð, þótt vildi: fylkis sveit vas fús at veita vísa fjǫrspell."

No eagle feeder [warrior] can blame Ingi that sword blades bit the king; let every man hear the truth about the attack. The battle-generous leader was unable to stop the onslaught, although he may have wanted to: the king's retinue was eager to inflict death upon the ruler.

The king asked: "Who had the standards brought out if you *. . .* for King Ingi?" Einarr said:

319.   Út lét stǫng á stræti   hnigu menn í gný Gunnar
      sterkr dýrligra merkja   gagls fyr strengjar hagli
      (dúðusk dǫrr af reiði)   brœðr hafa barzk á víðri
      Dags sonr bera fagra: Bjǫrgyn fyr ósynju.

"Sterkr Dags sonr lét bera fagra stǫng dýrligra merkja út á stræti; dǫrr dúðusk af reiði. Menn hnigu í gný Gunnar gagls fyr strengjar hagli; brœðr hafa barzk á víðri Bjǫrgyn fyr ósynju."

Dagr's strong son let the fair pole of the precious standard be carried out on the street; spears shook with wrath. Men died from the hail of the bowstring [arrows] in the din of Gunnr's [valkyrie] goose [bird of prey, battle]; the brothers fought in wide Bjǫrgyn [Bergen] without cause.

". . . to the town. I would gladly have forestalled that misdeed." Then Einarr answered: (FJ 459)

320.   Myndit seima sendir   ef alkostigs austan
      svá brátt hafa látit   Eysteins flota þeysti
      (spjót flugu langt í ljótri)   beinn at Bjǫrgyn sunnan
      líf sitt (boga drífu):   byrr tveim dǫgum fyrri.

"Seima sendir myndit hafa látit líf sitt svá brátt—spjót flugu langt í ljótri boga drífu—ef beinn byrr sunnan þeysti alkostigs Eysteins flota austan at Bjǫrgyn tveim dǫgum fyrri."

The giver of gold [generous king] would not have lost his life so soon—spears flew far in the hideous storm of bows [battle]—if, two days before, a steady wind from the south could have sped the fleet of splendid Eysteinn west to Bjǫrgyn [Bergen].

Grégóríús wanted to go out and attack them, saying that there would be no better opportunity later on. He said he would take the lead. "But you should not go, sire, for there is no lack of manpower." But there were many who advised against it, and the attack was abandoned.

Eysteinn went east to Vík and King Ingi north to Þrándheimr. They were nominally reconciled with one another, though they did not meet in person. Grégóríús went east a little after King Eysteinn and stayed at his estate at Hǫfund on Bratsberg.[5] King Eysteinn was in Ósló and had his ships drawn more than two sea miles across the ice because the bay was frozen hard.[6] He went up to Hǫfund and wanted to capture Grégóríús, but Grégóríús realized what was afoot and retreated to Þelamǫrk with ninety men, then north across the mountains and down to Harðangr, whence he came to Stuðla (Støle).[7]

Here Erlingr skakki had a residence. He had gone north to Bjǫrgvin, but (U 236) his wife Kristín was at home and offered Grégóríús all possible hospitality. He was given a longship that belonged to Erlingr and everything else he needed. He thanked her warmly and said that she had acted splendidly, as was to be expected. Then they proceeded to Bjǫrgvin and met Erlingr, who approved of Kristín's action. Then Grégóríús traveled north to Þrándheimr and arrived before Christmas. King Ingi greeted him with great delight and offered him any of his possessions that he might want.

King Eysteinn burned (FJ 460) Grégóríús's residence and laid waste the farm. In the winter the ship sheds built by King Eysteinn the Elder north in Kaupangr (Niðaróss), which were magnificent structures, along with some excellent ships in King Ingi's possession, were burned. That was a most unpopular deed, and King Eysteinn and King Sigurðr's foster brother Phillipús Gyrðarson were held responsible.

The following summer King Ingi went south with a large force. King Eysteinn came from the east and levied troops. They met in the east at Seleyjar (Seløyane), and King Ingi had a great advantage in numbers.[8] They were on the point of fighting, but they settled the matter with the agreement that King Eysteinn would commit himself to pay forty-five gold marks because he had contrived the burning of the ships and sheds. In addition, Philippús and the other men who had been present at the burning were to be outlawed. Those men who could be proven to have wounded King Sigurðr were also to be outlawed, because King Eysteinn blamed King Ingi for harboring them. Grégóríús was to have fifteen marks for the property of his that King Eysteinn had burned. King Eysteinn was not pleased and thought that this was an imposed settlement.

King Ingi left the meeting and went east to Vík, and King Eysteinn went north. They did not meet, and the only words that circulated were not conciliatory. Both kings arranged the killing of men on the other side, and King Eysteinn did not pay the compensation that had been agreed on. Each accused the other of not holding to the agreement.

King Ingi lured many men from the service of King Eysteinn. King Eysteinn was deserted by Bárðr standali, the son of Brynjólfr, Símon skálpr, the son of Hallkell húkr, Halldórr Brynjólfsson, and many other district chieftains. But when two years had passed, both sides gathered armies. King Ingi came from the east with eighty ships and Eysteinn from the north with forty-five ships. King Ingi anchored south at Mostr (Moster) and King Eysteinn (FJ 461) a little farther north in Grœningarsund (Grønning).[9]

At that point King Eysteinn sent Áslákr the Young, the son of Jón, and Árni sturla, the son of Sæbjǫrn, to meet with King Ingi. They set out with a single ship, but as soon as Ingi's troops recognized them, they attacked and killed many of their men. They seized the ship and everything on board.

Áslákr and Árni together with a few men (U 237) escaped and returned to tell King Eysteinn what had transpired. Then King Eysteinn summoned a special meeting and told his men of the violence done by King Ingi. He asked them to steel themselves: "We have forces that are sufficiently elite and numerous that I have no intention of fleeing." But his words were met with no applause. Hallkell húkr was there with his two sons, Símon and Jón. Hallkell answered loud enough for many to hear: "Let your chests of gold lend you support and defend your land."

During the following night many ships rowed away in secret, some to join King Ingi, some headed for Bjǫrgvin, and some into the fjords. In the morning when the sun rose, the king was left with ten ships. He abandoned the great dragon vessel that the prior Eysteinn had constructed, because it was heavy to row. They abandoned several other ships and largely dismantled the dragon ship. They also dumped their casks of ale and wrecked whatever they could not take with them.

King Eysteinn boarded the ship of Eindriði, the son of Jón mǫrnefr, and they sailed north to Sogn. From there they traveled east over the mountains to Vík, but King Ingi took his ships and made for Vík by sea. King Eysteinn was to the east of Foldin and had nearly twelve hundred men.[10] They saw King Ingi's ships and thought that they had insufficient numbers to risk an encounter. They ran off into the woods, every man for himself, so that the king was left with a single man.

When King Ingi and his men realized that King Eysteinn was isolated, they organized a search for him. (FJ 462) Símon skálpr found him as he was fleeing in the scrub brush with his lone companion. Símon spoke and greeted him: "Greetings, lord," he said. The king replied: "I imagine that you now think you are lord." "It will be as it may," he said. The king asked for his help in escaping and said that such help behooved him—"For we have long been . . ."[11] [friends, though it is now otherwise." Símon said that it would not turn out this way.

The king asked to hear mass first, and this was done. Then he lay down prostrate, stretched out his arms, and asked that he be struck in the form of a cross between the shoulders. He said that they could then test whether or not he could endure steel, as Ingi's companions had discussed. Símon told the executioner to proceed; he said that the king had been creeping about the undergrowth long enough. He was then executed and was judged to have borne it bravely.

His body was moved to Fors (Foss) and was laid out for the night under the ridge south of the church. King Eysteinn was buried at the church of Fors, and his tomb is in the middle of the church floor with a fringed cover over it. He is reputed to be a saint. Where he was executed and his blood fell on the earth, a fountain sprang up, and another under the ridge where his body was laid out for the night. Many people are thought to have benefited from the water of both springs. The people of Vík say that many miracles occurred at King Eysteinn's tomb before his enemies dumped dog broth on the tomb.

It was known far and wide that Símon skálpr was greatly despised for this deed. Some say that when King Eysteinn was captured, Símon sent a messenger to King Ingi, and the king bade Eysteinn stay out of his sight. This is the way King Sverrir had it written down, but Einarr Skúlason composed the following:

> *Hkr 3.* Mun (sás morði vanðisk)
> margillr (ok sveik stilli)
> síð af slíkum ráðum
> Símon skalpr of hjalpask.

"Margillr Símon skalpr, sás vanðisk morði ok sveik stilli, mun síð of hjalpask af slíkum ráðum."

Wicked Símon skalpr (Sword-sheath), who made murder his trade and betrayed the king, will hardly obtain absolution for such actions.

Textual Notes

The following notes are not aimed at the general reader, for whom we have sought to provide a readable text that requires no recourse to the apparatus. It is, however, also our wish to provide the historian and the literary historian with a clear picture of what is in the main manuscript and what must be added to make it readable. C. R. Unger proceeded by filling in illegible and damaged portions of the text from other manuscripts (*Flateyjarbók, Hulda-Hrokkinskinna* as printed in *Fornmanna sögur, Fríssbók*), setting off these passages in small print and usually brackets. Finnur Jónsson sometimes included other readings in his apparatus but usually left the illegible passage blank in the main text. For the sake of readability, we have elected Unger's procedure, but we have clearly identified the illegible passages in the main manuscript by enclosing them in asterisks and referring the reader in the following notes to the most probable sources of Unger's readings in the printed texts of the alternative manuscripts.

This is a very partial solution. We do not know whether Unger worked from manuscripts or, to the extent they were available, printed editions. He failed not only to identify his sources for individual readings but he appears sometimes to have put forward conjectures without identifying them as such. In these cases we do not know whether he could make out letters or groups of letters in the main manuscript that guided his surmise but could not be deciphered by Finnur Jónsson half a century later, or whether he engaged in pure conjecture. All we can do is to signal where such questions arise. On the whole, such difficulties do not threaten the sense of the text. Alternative readings in other manuscripts are likely to be very close to what was in the MskMS, and even in cases where the correspondence in wording may not be exact, the narrative is not seriously affected.

Unger's treatment of the verse is discussed in the notes to the stanzas. Very minor lacunae in the MS, involving part of a word, a conjunction, or a pronoun, are not noted below. For vocalic <v> we have substituted <u>. We use the following abbreviations:

F (the 1871 edition of Codex Frisianus [*Fríssbók*])
FJ (Finnur Jónsson's 1928–1932 edition of MskMS)

Flat   (the 1860–1868 edition of *Flateyjarbók*, vol. III)
FmS   (*Hulda–Hrokkinskinna* as printed in *Fornmanna sögur*, vols. VI–VII)
U   (C. R. Unger's 1867 edition of MskMS)

The passages in our text are identified by asterisked phrases.

Chapter 1

Here Begins the Saga: The chapter heading in the MS is illegible. U follows *Flat* 251.

toppled the boy from: U 2.26 inserts "feldi hann ofan," which does not correspond exactly to *Flat* 253.2 or *FmS* VI, 6.5. FJ 4.11 follows U and notes that the MS is "very indistinct."

–ners sat there: U 2.30 inserts ". . . enninir sato þar eptir," again not corresponding exactly to *Flat* 253.6 or *FmS* VI, 6.10–11. FJ 4.16 follows U.

Some of his tablemates: U 2.32 fills in "Sumir logunautar hans villdo drepa sveininn," again not corresponding exactly to *Flat* 253.7–8 or *FmS* VI, 6.13–15. FJ 4.19 leaves a blank with the *Flat* text in a note.

the king loved him: U 2.33–34 fills in "konungr unni honom. Siþan [*Flat:* hleypr einn maðr ok] tekr maðr sveininn i fang ser oc leypr," abbreviating *Flat* 223.9–11. *FmS* VI, 6.16–17 differs. FJ 4.21 leaves a partial blank with *Flat* in a note.

another time: U 2.36 inserts "oþro sinni. Konungr segir. Opt velit þer honom osømilig orþ," which appears to conflate *Flat* 253.12–13 and *FmS* VI, 6.20–21. FJ 4.23 leaves a blank with *Flat* in a note. We follow *Flat*.

The king asked how: U 2.38 inserts "Konungr spyrr með hveriom atburþ þat hefði orðit" as in *Flat* 253.15–16 with "spyrr" for "spurde." *FmS* VI, 6.24 differs. FJ 5.2 leaves a blank.

Then the king arranged: U 3.1–2 inserts "Siþan settiz konungr viþ frendr hins vegna," very close to *FmS* VI, 6.27–28 but different from *Flat* 253.18–19. FJ 5.4 leaves a blank with *Flat* in a note. We follow *Flat*.

more and more: U 3.34 inserts "ollom hugþeccri sem alldr hans oc vizmunir drogoz fram," which is very close to both *Flat* 253.20–21 and *FmS* VI, 7.1–2. FJ 5.7 leaves a blank with *Flat* in a note.

At this time: At this point *Flat* 253 has the chapter heading "Um ofrid miken." *FmS* VI, 7 and FJ 5 have no heading. U takes his heading from the first sentence of the following paragraph.

[Karl said: U 4.10–19 inserts a long passage from *Flat* 254.29–255.1, but with a few changes. FJ 7.11 appends the passage in a note.

exaggerated. Grímr is: U 7.23 inserts "i vo[xt førþir. Konungr melti]" as in *Flat* 257.37 (with "segir" for "melti"), but omits the sentence in *Flat* following "førþir." FJ 12.19 includes it in his note, and we include it in the text.

I will pardon you: U 7.4 inserts "[þa mon ec gef]a" as in *Flat* 258.2–3 or *FmS* VI, 14.19. FJ 13.1 includes *Flat* in a note.

that you can get: U 7.16 prints only "þeir segia. Ecki," but FJ 13.17 includes a fuller text from *Flat* 258.18–19, which we follow.

Then he gave them: U 7.18 inserts "at halldi. [Fecc þeim siþan fe] oc baþ" as in *Flat* 258.25 (with an adjustment of tense). FJ 13.19 leaves a blank.

After a bit: U 7.20 inserts "Oc litl[o siþar kendi Karl meþ þeim] drycciar oc melti" as in *Flat* 258.27 (with an adjustment of tense). FJ 14.1 leaves a blank.

They do: Here begins a six-leaf lacuna in the main MS, which is left blank by U 7.21 but filled in from *Flat* 258.27–298.37 by FJ 14.3–70.24.

Chapter 12

familiar]: MskMS resumes.

the walls were too thick: U 10.3 notes a hole in the MS and inserts "veggir of þyccir við," which corresponds neither to *Flat* 301.22 nor to *FmS* VI, 156.18. FJ 75.12 leaves the space blank and notes Unger's reading.

he had advised: U 10.4 notes a hole and fills in "sem hann hafþi raþ" as in *Flat* 301.24. FJ 75.14 leaves a blank and notes *Flat.*

told the townspeople: U 10.5 inserts "[segia þeir borgar]monnom andlat hof[þingia]" as in *Flat* 301.26. FJ 75.16 leaves a blank and notes *Flat.*

would make a: U 10.8 inserts "ofra scyldo" as in *Flat* 301.28. FJ 75.19 leaves a blank and notes *Flat.*

in the town: U 10.10 inserts "varþvei[to i borgi]nne" as in *Flat* 301.30. FJ 75.22 leaves a blank and notes *Flat.*

Chapter 13

not: U 13.5 inserts "Snorrason. Eigi" as in *Flat* 304.22. FJ 81.5 leaves a blank and notes *Flat.*

awakening. What: U 13.7 inserts "vacni. eþa hvat" as in *Flat* 304.24. FJ 81.8 leaves a blank and notes *Flat.*

"That is good: U 13.9 inserts "[þat er gott] rað segir Halldorr . . . ." FJ 81.10 leaves a blank and notes *Flat* 304.25–26: "Festa sidan heit sitt. en hier er eigi greint hueriu þeir hietu."

. . . : U 13.9–11 has gaps that cannot be remedied from *Flat* 304 or *FmS* VI, 165. U 13.10 [hann søfr] is supplied from *FmS* VI, 165.3–4 "meðan hann sefr."

Sveinn proposed: U 17.1–2 inserts "oc be[iddi Sveinn at] þeir scyldi binda saman lag sitt" from *Flat* 306.23.

Chapter 14

wish: U 20.14 inserts "vilit er [þiggia]" from *Flat* 309.15.

the realm: U 20.16 inserts "gefom ver yþr halft Noregs [konungs] veldi" from a conflation of *Flat* 309.17 and *FmS* VI, 181.24.

of three days: U 20.26 inserts ".iii. dogom þa hefir" as in *Flat* 309.29. FJ 95.3 leaves a blank and notes *Flat.*

On the first day: U 20.28 inserts "Oc enn fyrsta dag hans" as in *Flat* 309.31. FJ 95.6 leaves a blank and notes *Flat.*

Chapter 15

The Slandering of Þorkell: U 23.4 adds the illegible heading from *Flat* 312.

Chapter 20

with him: U 30.10 inserts "oc Þorsteinn meþ [honom oc] voro saman .xii." from *Flat* 320.6–7: "og Þorsteinn med honum. fara nu heiman og voru saman .xij."

came back in: U 30.12 inserts "com inn" as in *Flat* 320.8 "og kemr inn aptr." FJ 113.18 leaves a blank and notes *Flat.*

Chapter 24

Concerning Hreiðarr heimski: U 35.33 provides the chapter heading on his own since the *þáttr* is missing in *Flat* and untitled in *FmS* VI, 120.

I can see: U 36.38 inserts "ec seia sem flesta menn" as in *FmS* VI, 202.13. FJ 125.33 leaves a blank.

have no intention: U 37.1 inserts "h[vergi fara. Ecci tiar sl]ict" as in *FmS* VI, 202.16. FJ 126.2 leaves a blank.

this trip: U 37.3 inserts "þessarrar farar" as in *FmS* VI, 202.21. FJ 126.5 leaves a blank.

They found many: U 39.39 inserts "oc breytto [þeir marga] vega orþom" as in *FmS* VI, 209.6: "ok leituðu sér marga vega við hann." FJ 130.20 reads "þeir marga" and indicates only that the words are "somewhat indistinct."

but he: U 40.2 inserts "við [hann. oc var hann] iafnan hleiandi." *FmS* VI, 209.8–9 reads somewhat differently. FJ 130.22 follows U and notes "somewhat indistinct."

tests of strength: U 40.4 reads "beþi um męlgina oc allr . . . þvi." FJ 130.25 reads "beþi um męlgina oc allra hellzt . . . en firi þvi." *FmS* VI, 209.11 supplies "bæði í margmælgi ok einkanliga í aflraunum."

. . . . : U 40.5–6 reads "þa þvarr þat allt af þeim hirðm[. . .] hirðinni." FJ 130.27–28 is identical. *FmS* VI, 209.11–12 provides the sense with "þa léttu þeir af áleitni við hann."

between the kings because: U 40.8–9 reads "þa hofþo sacar gør[zc til missattar með konungom þvi a]t hirðmaþr." FJ 130.30 leaves a blank. *FmS* VI, 209.16–17 supplies "þaðan af urðu sjálfir konungar missáttir," which appears to offer the basis for Unger's conjecture.

meet: U 40.10–11 reads "konungar scy[lldo finnaz]" as in *FmS* VI, 209.18 "konungarnir sjálfir skyldu finnast." FJ 130.32–33 reads "konungar scylldo . . . oc scipa malino."

and showed the king: U 43.21–22 fills in "oc synir konungi" as in *FmS* VI, 217.5–6 "ok sýndi konúngi svínit." FJ 135.32 leaves a blank.

see what King Haraldr: U 44.4–6 signals difficulties with small print but no brackets (we use brackets): "ec þicciomc [sia] hvernn Haralldr konungr [vill] þinn lut. ef [hann a at] raþa ef [þú ert] lengi i Noregi." This is roughly equivalent to *FmS* VI, 218.11–13: "þvíat auðsærr er þinn kostr, ef hann má ráða, sem hann mun ráða, ef þú dvelst hèr lángvistum." FJ 136.24–27 indicates in a note that some words are indistinct but readable.

Chapter 26

[King Magnús Dies]: U 46.9 takes the heading from *Flat* 328.

I wish: U 46.24–25 inserts "vil ec" as in *FmS* VI, 226.24. FJ 141.7 leaves a blank.

at me: U 46.26–27 reads "en mioc ero þeir ser ørnir [en mer no]cqvot ofscynia" as in *FmS* VI, 226.27–28. FJ 141.9 leaves a blank.

King Haraldr said: U 46.28 inserts "nu. Haralldr konungr melti" as in *Flat* 329.19. FJ 141.12 leaves a blank.

your majesty: U 46.30 inserts "herra konungr er," thus conflating *Flat* 329.23 and *FmS* VI, 227.4–5. FJ 141.14 leaves a blank.

your ancestral lands: At this point there is a missing leaf filled in from *Flat* 329.26–335.4. The inserted passage from *Flat* ends at the next asterisk. The rest of the missing text is supplied from *ÍF* 5, 265–68.

Chapter 30

fill]: Here the insert from *ÍF* 5, 265–68 ends and our text returns to the main manuscript at U46.33 and FJ 148.37.

six ships: U 49.27 inserts ".vi. skip" as in *FmS* VI, 247.16. FJ 153.3 leaves a blank.

he fled to the coast: U 49.29 inserts "le[tr hann] elltaz." *FmS* VI, 247.18 has "Sveinn" for "hann." FJ 153.5 leaves a blank for "elltaz at landi."

concluded, the king proceeded: U 49.31 reads "Oc er veizlom var lo[kit ferr konungr] norþr," which appears to be a conjecture. FJ 153.8 reads "oc er veizlom var lo[. . .] með landi."

abandon his claim: U 49.33 reads "hann vill gefa [upp allt mal um] scipit," which appears to be a conjecture based on *FmS* VI, 247.24 "at hann vildi allt sitt mál um skipit leggja á hans vald." FJ 153.10 reads "vill gefa . . . leggia a konungs valld."

Chapter 31

Kind Haraldr's Campaign: U 51.9 takes the chapter heading from *Flat* 335.

seized: U 56.12 inserts "toco [nu þar] hondom allt slict sem þeir villdo" as in *Flat* 339.38–340.1.

mention is made: At U 59.21 and FJ 169.22 there is a missing leaf in the main MS. It is filled in from *Flat* 343.14–349.24.

Chapter 35

affectionate terms.⁵]: The main text picks up again at FJ 178, U 59.22.

Chapter 36

lord: U 63.35 reads "herra," but FJ 185.2 reads "nerra," which appears to be a misprint.

Chapter 42

woman: U 81.28 reads "þat ma enn vera kerling segir hann" as in *Flat* 365.13. FJ 215.1–2 omits "kerling" and reads "þat ma enn vera s. hann." The facsimile is not legible at this point.

tents: U 82.23 reads "tǫðr" and conjectures "tiǫlld." FJ 216.14 reads "rǫðz" and surmises "tiold."

I did not foresee it: U 88.28 and FJ 226.23–24 read (normalized) "En þá gat ek þat eigi at mér." *Flat* 372.28–29 makes the sense a bit clearer with "En þá gat ek þat eigi at mér, er þú hafðir nýdrepit Ásmund frænda minn . . . ."

Chapter 47

It is not easy: Leaf 17 of the main MS is defective at the bottom and the missing portion is supplied from *Flat* 380.15–381.2, which is inserted in U 104.25–105.11 and included in the apparatus of FJ 252–53.

Chapter 48

and asked whether: The verso of the defective leaf is supplied from *Flat* 384.2–25. That text is inserted in U 107.23–108.4 and is found in the apparatus of FJ 258–59.

Chapter 53

-dles as: U 126.12 inserts "ker[tom sem ti]gnir menn varo til." This is presumably a conjecture since *Flat* breaks off at U 123 and the passage is not found in *FmS* (VI, 440–41). FJ 290.12 leaves a blank.

men into his service: U 126.14 inserts ".c. malam[anna. Þeir]," presumably also a conjecture. FJ 290.14 leaves a blank.

Chapter 55

You: U 133.8 inserts "yðr" as in *FmS* VII, 8.20. FJ 301.2 leaves a blank.

says Gísl Illugason: U 133.10 inserts "Sva [s]egir [G]isl [Jllu]ga son," as in *FmS* VII, 8.27. FJ 301.5 deciphered only "Sva . . . ga s."

Chapter 59

victorious: U 153.8 inserts "ok hafþi iafnan [sigr]," presumably by conjecture. FJ 332.14 leaves a blank.

well known: U 153.10 inserts "þat er monnom [kunnict]," also by conjecture. FJ 332.17 leaves a blank.

again to the honor: U 153.12 inserts "ma þat nu vera [enn til sømþar] varo riki Noregi." See note 59.3. FJ 332.19 leaves a blank.

Chapter 61

things will: U 158.29–30 inserts "oc segir mer gott hugr um liþit þat er mer fylg[ir oc mun þat] vel reynaz" apparently by conjecture. FJ 341.5 leaves a blank.

with a large force: U 158.31 inserts "Nu for Sigurþr konungr með [miclu liþi til ca]stalans" based on *FmS* VII, 78.17 but with "miclu liþi" from *F* 281.35. FJ 341.7 leaves a blank.

a large amount of food: U 158.33 inserts "Toc nu Sigurþr konungr þar af [castalanom vist m]icla" based on *FmS* VII, 78.19 but with "castalanom" conjectural. FJ 341.10 leaves a blank.

when he left: U 158.35 inserts "[er hann for af Jacob]slandi" with no warrant in *FmS*. FJ 341.12 leaves a blank.

he composed about: U 158.37 inserts "er hann q[uaþ um Jorsalaferþ] Sigurþar" with no warrant in *FmS*. FJ 341.14 leaves a blank.

maintained: U 159.28 inserts "oc kolloþo [oc sogðo] at konungr þessi enn utlendi" without warrant in *FmS*. FJ 342.22 leaves a blank.

and had an elite force: U 159.29–30 inserts "[oc hafa mannval] gott" without warrant in *FmS*. FJ 342.24 leaves a blank.

captured: U 159.31 inserts "oc toc[o þeir nu i] sitt valld" without warrant in *FmS*. FJ 342.26 reads "oc toco þeir . . . sitt valld."

have taken has brought: U 159.33 inserts "er þer h[ofot her hefir mor]gom goþum manni" without warrant in *FmS*. It looks as though Unger may have omitted some word such as "unnit."

those in the cavern: U 161.33 inserts "En [hellismenn] ottoðosc." There is no equivalent in *FmS*. FJ 346.10 leaves a blank.

Now King Sigurðr cast: U 162.2 inserts "N[u leitar Sigurþr konungr se]r raþa" as in *FmS* VII, 82.6 (with tense adjustment). FJ 346.13 leaves a blank.

made fast with: U 162.4 inserts "oc l[et drengia með] kauþlom digrom" as in *FmS* VII, 82.8–9. FJ 346.15 leaves a blank.

lowered them down: U 162.6 inserts "leto siþan sig[a batana ofan] fyr bergit," as in *FmS* VII, 82.12, which, however, reads "skipin" rather than "batana." FJ 346.17 leaves a blank.

storm of arrows: U 162.7–8 inserts "h[arþa hriþ með scotom]" with no warrant in *FmS*. FJ 346.19 leaves a blank.

succumbed: U 163.5 inserts "oc [f]alla [nu]," not found in *FmS*. FJ 348.8 could not read "alla" and leaves the space blank.

the island that: U 163.10 inserts "til [eyiar þeirar er]" as in *FmS* VII, 8.23. FJ 348.15 leaves a blank.

[After that: At this point there is a missing leaf and the text is supplied from *Fríssbók*. See note 61.13.

Chapter 61d

preparations had been made.]: The insert from *Fríssbók* ends.

Chapter 63

his ship: At this point there is an indication of a marginal note in the MS that has been cut away. See U 165n2 and FJ 351.15.

and was well received: U 166.3 inserts "oc [var honom vel] fagnat" as in *FmS* VII, 99.19 (with "þar" after "honom"). FJ 352.18 reads "oc . . . gnat."

accomplished. The skald: U 166.4–5 inserts "er Sigurþr konungr [for. sem sca]lldit segir" by conjecture but echoing *F* 289.45 ". . . meiri frægðarfor enn þessi er Sigurðr konungr for." FJ 352.20 reads "meire fregþar for en þessi var er Sigurþr . . . segir." Unger's reading indicates that "sem scalldit segir" is to be taken with the illustrious voyage, but that would leave the following sentence without a subject. We therefore omit U's "sem" and take "scalldit segir" to introduce the rejoicing at Sigurðr's return.

Chapter 64

He had: U 166.11 inserts "[hann let reisa Mic]hals kirkio" as in *FmS* VII, 100.7–8. FJ 352.28 leaves a blank.

most magnificent monastery: U 166.12 inserts "it veg[ligsta steinmustari. hann let ge]ra" as in *FmS* VII, 100.9–10 (with "þar" after "let"). FJ 352.30 leaves a blank.

and a harbor: U 166.14 inserts "oc hofn oc kirkio" approximating *FmS* VII, 100.13–14. FJ 353.1 leaves a blank.

after the model of: U 166.15–16 inserts "gørr [var i glicing þess sem] verit hafþi" as in *FmS* VII, 100.20. FJ 353.3 leaves a blank.

Chapter 65

many men: U 167.14 inserts "oc naut þar mioc fra [morgom monnom] broþor sins" from a presumed marginal note later cut away. FJ 354.15 assumes a marginal note but does not include the words although they are found in *FmS* VII, 103.8–9.

King: U 168.34 inserts "með Eysteini [konungi]" as in *FmS* VII, 103.25–26. FJ 356.24 leaves a blank.

Chapter 66

and outstanding king. U 169.2 inserts "rikr konungr [oc agetr. hann atti M]almfriþi" as in *F* 290.31. FJ 357.1 leaves a blank.

King Yaroslav and: U 169.3 inserts "Valldamarr þessi var sonr [Jarizleifs konungs. oc J]ngigerþar." See *FmS* VII, 111.7–8. FJ 357.2 leaves a blank.

-winson. The mother of: U 169.5 inserts "dottir Harallz Goþ[ina sonar. Moþir Ma]lmfriþar." See *FmS* VII, 111.10–11. FJ 357.4 leaves a blank.

Haraldr Valdimarsson's second daughter: U 169.7 inserts "Aunnor dottir Harallz [Valldamars sonar var Jngibiorg er atti] Knutr konungr." See *FmS* VII, 111.13–14 and *F* 290.36–37. FJ 357.6 leaves a blank.

-rét, Kristín: U 169.9 inserts "Marg[ret oc Cristin]" as in *FmS* VII, 111.19 and *F* 290.37. FJ 357.8 reads "Margret . . . oc Katerin."

Chapter 68

reward: U 171.31 inserts "at qveþ[islaunom]" as in *FmS* VII, 113.18–19. FJ 361.7 leaves a blank.

England: U 171.32 inserts "En[glandi]" as in *FmS* VII, 113.22. FJ 361.9 reads "af . . . lagþi hann."

his house. At: U 171.35 inserts "oc var þat fire garþi Þ[orþar. Þa] var Eysteinn" as in *FmS* VII, 113.24. FJ 361.11 leaves a blank.

-arr of Askr: U 171.36 inserts "Jngim[arr af Aski]" as in *FmS* VII, 113.27. FJ 361.13 leaves a blank.

people remarked: U 171.38–39 inserts "rǫddo menn um viþ," differing slightly from *FmS* VII, 114.1–2 ". . . ok tǫluðu menn um, at Þórði myndi eigi duga." FJ 361.15 leaves a blank.

Þórðr paid no attention: U 172.1 inserts "en Þorþr gaþi," differing from *FmS* VII, 114.3–4 "Þórðr lèt sem hann heyrði eigi." FJ 361.16 leaves a blank.

Chapter 69

who was named Sigurðr: U 174.12 inserts "er Sigurþr [het oc] siþan kallaþiz" as in *F* 292.25. FJ 365.1 leaves a blank.

Eilífsson: U 174.14 inserts "Dags [Eilifssonar]" in line with *F* 292.27. FJ 365.3 leaves a blank. *after the death of:*

divided: U 174.16 inserts "Eptir andl[at Olafs konungs scipto] þeir brøþr." It is unclear what the source of this reading is, unless it is the apparatus in *FmS* VII, 109n4. FJ 365.5 leaves a blank.

the northern part: U 174.18 inserts "[enn nørþra l]ut" perhaps also from *FmS* VII, 109n4. FJ 365.8 reads ". . . þra lut."

Chapter 70

An Account of Legal Dealings: U 174.21 inserts the heading "Þ[inga]saga milli Sigurþar konungs oc Eyst[eins konungs]." The heading is not found in the other MSS.

When Jer-: U 174.22 inserts "[þa er Jor]sala Sigurþr" presumably by conjecture. FJ 365.13 leaves a blank.

the country among themselves: U 174.23 inserts "oc scipto með [ser landino]" presumably by conjecture. FJ 365.14 leaves a blank.

We are told that: U 174.24–25 inserts "sagt eitt sinn at Sigurþr konungr," but may have been able to read a little more than his square brackets indicate judging from FJ 365.16 "Þat er oc sagt . . . konungr."

His kinsman by marriage: U 174.26 inserts "Hrana son magr hans oc" as in *FmS* VII, 123.25, but here too he may have been able to read a little more than he indicates judging from FJ 365.18 "þar var S. Hrana son magr . . . ."

men in charge: U 177.8 reads "setti hann sina menn [þa]r ifir," but FJ 369.9 was able to make out only "setti hann sina . . . Sigurþ." *FmS* VII, 129.8–9 reads "setti konungr þar menn sína Sigurð, etc."

elsewhere: U 177.9 reads "annarsta[þar]," but FJ 369.11 again deciphered a little less and read "ann . . . ." *FmS* VII, 129.11 supplies the full "annarstaðar."

toward him: U 177.11 inserts "at Jngi konungr for at [honom] með uvigian her" in agreement with *FmS* VII, 129.14–15. FJ could read only "Ingi . . . með uvigian her."

moved: U 177.13 reads "er su niosn com. [for] þa konungr" as in *FmS* VII, 129.17. FJ 369.15 could read only "er su ni . . . þa konungr."

King Magnús took: U 177.15 reads "Siþan [virði Magnus konungr] sva at" as in *FmS* VII, 129.19–20. FJ 369.18 could not read "Siþan" and the three following words.

should have: U 177.17 reads "at ec scyllda hafa finnfor," but FJ 369.20 could not decipher "scyllda hafa."

army: U 179.36 reads "drosc honom mikit [lið]" as in *FmS* VII, 134.8. FJ 373.8 reads "sunnan or landi. oc drosc honom mikit . . . landi oc stefnir hann," where the second "landi" looks like a dittography of the first (both followed by an "oc"). The second "landi" is not visible in the facsimile.

taking: U 179.38 inserts "oc vill nu sva greypliga [at] ganga at gera Sigurþ utlagan" in line with *FmS* VII, 134.10–11: "ætlar nú sva greypiliga (at) at gánga, at gera Sigurð Hranason útlægjan." FJ 373.10 leaves a blank.

King Eysteinn also assembled: U 180.1 reads "Eysteinn konungr biosc," but FJ 372.17 leaves these words blank.

order, hold: U 180.3 reads "þioct við stafna taca vapn sin" in line with *FmS* VII, 134.17 "þykt við stafna," but FJ 373.15 could only make out "þioct við . . . ca vapn sin."

They did so: U 180.4–5 reads "oc syna sic buna til motz við Sigurð konung. Þeir gera sva. ganga at þingino." FJ 373.17 could only read "við S. konung . . . ganga at þingino."

whether the laws: U 180.11–13. The MS reads "oc eigimc við brøþr við malit er þat iafnara at konungar siaisc á oc reynim með ocr hvat laug ero osannindi." The form "hvat" must stand for *hvárt* 'whether' and the form "osannindi" must be the present participle of *ósanna* 'disallow.'

King Óláfr: Thus U 182.26, but FJ 377.11 omits "Óláfr konungr." "O. k." is, however, clear on folio 29a of the facsimile.

Óláfr: The MS has "oc," presumably a false resolution of "O." for "Óláfr." U 182.27 prints "Hann" and FJ 377.11 prints "oc" with a note suggesting "hann" or "Olafr."

many men joined in: U 182.37 reads "Nu atto margir menn," but FJ 377.24 could only decipher "Nu at . . . men." *FmS* VII, 141.3 corresponds to U.

guilty: U 182.39 reads "sannr at socinni," FJ 377.26 could decipher only "sannr . . ." *FmS* VII, 141.6 reads "sannr at sök."

it would ill: U 183.2 reads "at illa myndi hlyþa," but FJ 377.28 deciphered only ". . . ndi hlyþa." *FmS* VII, 141.10 corresponds to U.

unjust: U 183.4 reads "honom þotti allosannlict," but FJ 377.31 deciphered only "honom þotti allos . . . ." *FmS* VII, 141.12–13 corresponds to U.

heretofore: U 183.6 reads "hefþi rofit þa[r til]." FJ 377.33 reads only "hefþi rofit . . . ." *FmS* VII, 141.15 has "hertil" for "þar til."

Norway: U 185.35–36 reads "i Noregi," but FJ 382.4 deciphered only "i . . . ." *FmS* VII, 150.8 corresponds to U.

severe: U 185.38 reads "með miclo afelli," but FJ 382.7 deciphered only "m . . . afelli." *FmS* VII, 150.11–12 corresponds to U.

Chapter 72

singing: U 188.4 (= FJ 385.14) reads "oc s[ungo] aptansonginn." *FmS* VII, 152.13 reads "lásu aptansaunginn."

in a short cloak: U 188.5 (= FJ 385.16) reads "i felldi no[ccorom] stuttum," which corresponds to *FmS* VII, 152.16.

to the place where: U 189.2–3 fills in "ganga siþan þ[angat sem Arni sat. oc qvaþ hann] viso." FJ 386.28 reads "ganga siþan þangat . . . v." *FmS* VII, 154.10–11 differs.

Árni jumped up: U 189.8 inserts "[Arni hliop upp oc bra sverþi oc vill]di raþa til Þorarins" as in *FmS* VII, 154.20. FJ 387.5 leaves a blank.

remember that he would: U 189.9–10 inserts "qvaþ hann a þat mega min[naz at hann myndi bera legra lut ef þeir ettiz við]" as in *FmS* VII, 154.22–23. FJ 387.7 leaves a blank.

Chapter 73

King: U 189.17 conjectures "konungs." FJ 387.16 leaves a blank.

daughter: U 189.20 inserts "Gutthorm[s dottir]" as in *FmS* VII, 155.9. FJ 387.1 leaves a blank.

Chapter 75

to his senses: U 192.7 inserts "racnaði [við]" as in *FmS* VII, 166.9. FJ 391.14 leaves a blank.

Chapter 76

saying: U 192.14 inserts "[sagþi] at konungr hafþi reiþi" as in *FmS* VII, 166.12. FJ 391.22 read only ". . . hafþi reiþi."

His name was Loðinn: U 192.16 inserts "H[aralldi er Loþinn het maþr] ettsmar" as in *FmS* VII, 166.15–16. FJ 391.24 leaves a blank.

who he was: U 192.17–18 inserts "qvaz ogørla vita [hvat manna hann] var" as in *FmS* VII, 166.18. FJ 391.26 leaves a blank.

Now it happened: U 192.18–20 inserts "Nu bar sva til a þesso sama qvelldi at Haralldr sagþi sveininom at hann scylldi reccia i huðfati hans um nottina. En er" as in *FmS* VII, 166.19–22. FJ 391.26 leaves a blank.

endure pages occupying: U 192.21–22 inserts "þ[ola myndo at knapar gengi upp a hann. oc spurþi hverr honom visaþi at reckia hia dugandi] monnom" as in *FmS* VII, 166.23–25 (with "hefði vísat" for "visaþi"). FJ 391.28 leaves a blank.

chased him out: U 192.23–24 inserts "r[ac hann i brot or huðfatino. for sveinninn oc sagði til Haralldi. Hann reiddiz oc hliop ut a scipit oc hirþi] ecki um" as in *FmS* VII, 166.27–167.2, which, however, reads "til Haralds" rather than "til Haralldi." FJ 391.30 leaves a blank.

in the habit: U 192.25–26 inserts "qvaþ hann op[t vilia ser svivirþing veita. Haralldr segir at hann hafþi minni svivirþing en hann var macligr oc hio til] hans" as in *FmS* VII, 167.4–6 for the first sentence and *F* 303.5–6 for the second.

people ran to separate: U 192.27–28 inserts "oc hl[iopo menn a milli þeira. oc var Haralldr a landi þa nott. Um morgoninn varp konungr af] ser cleþom" as in *F* 303.7–8. FJ 391.32 leaves a blank.

Skúlason replied: U 192.29–30 inserts "Scula son svaraþi. Eigi vitom ver þat gørla eþa hverso mon honom fritt at coma a yðarn fund," combining *FmS* VII, 167.12–14 with *F* 303.9–11. FJ 392.2 leaves a blank.

The king said: U 193.1 inserts "Konungr melti" as in *F* 303.16. FJ 392.12 leaves a blank.

contest with your king: U 193.2–3 inserts "Hverso vel þottiz þu við konung þinn [leika i ger. Herra segir hann mioc eptir þvi sem þer gerþot] fyrir" as in *F* 303.17–18. FJ 392.13–14 leaves a blank.

Chapter 78

varied: U 195.18 inserts "menn logþo til þessa mals [misiaf]nt mioc" as in *F* 305.32. FJ 396.3 leaves a blank.

own lights than in: U 195.20 inserts "oc reð konungr meirr með sino ein[reþi en vilia] liðs-ens," elaborating on *F* 305.33. FJ 396.6 leaves a blank.

commit himself to: U 195.22–23 inserts "at hann vill[di þat binda með ei]þi," improvising on *FmS* VII, 164.9 and *F* 305.35. FJ 396.9 leaves a blank.

for the ordeal: U 195.25–26 inserts "Biosc [Haralldr siþan til scirslo oc er þat mal manna at su scirsla hafi ger verit mest i Noregi]" as in *FmS* VII, 164.13–15. FJ 396.12 leaves a blank.

and Haraldr walked over: U 195.27–28 inserts "[oc gecc Haralldr þar eptir berom fotom oc leiddo hann byscopar tveir. Hann callaþi a hinn helga C]olumba meðan" as in *F* 306.3–4. FJ 396.13 leaves a blank.

Then King Sigurðr's son: U 195.29–30 inserts "[Þa melti Magnus son Sigurðar konungs. Eigi treþr hann hugmannliga iarnin. Konungr svaraþi. Jll]a melir þu" as in *F* 306.5–6 and *FmS* VII, 164.19–22. FJ 396.14 leaves a blank.

because he has borne: U 195.31–32 inserts "hefir þetta mal [scoroliga framit. Siþan let Haralldr fallaz i recciona. Oc eptir þria daga var scir]saln reynd" as in *F* 306.7–8 and *FmS* VII, 164.23–24. FJ 396.15 leaves a blank.

King Sigurðr accepted: U 195.32–34 inserts "Eptir þat [toc Sigurþr konungr vel viþ frendsemi hans. en Magnus son hans oþoccaþiz mioc við Haralld oc margir hof]þingiar snero eptir honom" as in *F* 306.10–13. FJ 396.16 leaves a blank.

Norse and he stumbled: U 195.35 inserts "Haralldi var stirt malit no[rrøna kylfþi hann mioc til orþanna oc hofþo margir menn þat] at spotti" as in *F* 306.12–13. Cf. *FmS* VII, 165.3–5. FJ 396.17 leaves a blank.

Chapter 79

It was Haraldr's custom: U 196.23 inserts "[Þat var vanði at Haralldr fylgþi Sigurþi konungi til svefns a qvelldom. Oc eitt] sinn gato þeir" as in *F* 306.16–17. FJ 396.21 leaves a blank.

for a long time: U 196.3–4 inserts "oc sato þeir [lengi oc drucco. Magnusi hafþi sen]dr verit hestr einn gauzcr" as in *F* 306.18. FJ 396.22 leaves a blank.

Those who were present: U 196.5 inserts "rødde [þeir um er við voro at engi mondi hestr vera iafnsciotr oc] vico til Harallz malino" as in *F* 306.19–20. FJ 396.23 leaves a blank.

Chapter 81

out from the south choir: U 198.22 inserts "utar fra cornum syþra me[gin]" as in *F* 308.28. FJ 400.13 leaves a blank.

Chapter 82

being admitted: U 198.26 inserts "oc unnit eið aþr [hann neþi] scirslom" as in *Ágrip*, ch. 57 (*ÍF* 29, 50). FJ 400.19 leaves a blank.

confirmed: U 198.28 inserts "með þeim eiðst[af staþ]festan eiþ" as in *Ágrip*, ch. 57 (*ÍF* 29, 50). FJ 400.21 leaves a blank.

thus ensured: U 198.29 and FJ 400.22 show a lacuna, but the missing wording must have the sense of "ensure." *Ágrip*, ch. 57 (*ÍF* 29, 50–51), reads: "ok vildi konungrinn með þeim eið-staf staðfesta eið lýðsins ok ríki sonar síns."

faithful to: U 198.30 inserts "ef þeir helldi með trul[eic festar] oc søri," which appears to be conjectural. FJ 400.23 leaves a blank.

Ósló: U 198.32. On the missing leaf at this point see notes 82.1–2.

Chapter 82a

above the town: Here MskMS resumes.

Chapter 84

Jarl Haraldr. In: U 202.8–9 inserts "var staddr i Orcneyiom með [Haralldi iarli. sva segir Jvarr]." FJ 406.7–8 reads "var staddr iOrcneyiom meþ Haralldi . . . ."

to Scotland to: U 202.15 inserts "for hann upp [a Scotland a fund] Scota konungs." FJ 406.18 reads "for hann upp . . . Scota konungs." *Orkneyinga saga* (*ÍF* 34, 117) supplies "upp á Skotland."

Chapter 89

recited: U 212.27 inserts "qveþit" as in *FmS* VII, 214.2 and *F* 329.20. FJ 423.2 leaves a blank.

Kolbeinn: U 212.30 has "Kolbeinn" as in *FmS* VII, 214.6 and *F* 329.24. FJ 423.6 leaves a blank.

the winter in: U 212.32 inserts "um vetrinn i Alaborg" as in *FmS* VII, 214.10 and *F* 329.25. FJ 423.8 leaves a blank.

Chapter 91

while King Sigurðr: U 216.23 notes a lacuna and inserts "en Sigurðr konungr oc vinir hans sato kyrrir" as in *FmS* VII, 220.8–9 and *F* 331.36.

King Ingi sent: U 216.24–25 inserts "Jngi konungr bref með innsiglom" corresponding nei-ther to *FmS* VII, 220.14 nor to *F* 332.3 nor to *Heimskringla* (*ÍF* 28, 314). FJ 429.13 leaves a blank.

Sáða-Gyrðr, Ǫgmundr: U 216.26 inserts "raþoneyti [Saðagyrþi Ogmundi svipti] Ottari" as in *FmS* VII, 220.17 and *F* 332.5. FJ 429.15 leaves a blank.

tillers: U 216.29 inserts "buondom oc [buþegnom oc]," which is not found either in *FmS* or *F.* FJ 429.17 leaves a blank.

land: U 216.30 inserts "i þesso [landi]," which does not correspond to *FmS* or *F.* FJ 429.20 leaves a blank.

Chapter 95

Ragna: The MS leaves an open space here, filled in "Ragna" by a late hand. See U 223.26 and
   FJ 441.1.

Chapter 97

In the fall and: U 226.17–18 inserts "um haustit oc" (cf. *FmS* VII, 237.18 and *F* 340.8). FJ 445.15
   leaves a blank.

Chapter 98

. . . . : The first line of fol. 36b is illegible (U 229.21–22 and FJ 450.1). It must have related
   how the matter was referred to Ragnhildr.
he should give: U 229.24–25 inserts "[fyr Gregorius] oc segir micla nauþsyn at [hann veiti
   manninom asia. Gregorius svarar. Litt hefi] ec enn viþ bunndiz vandamal manna."
   FJ 450.3–4 leaves a blank.

Chapter 99

to Norway: U 232.6 inserts "i Noreg" as in *FmS* VII, 240.8 and *F* 341.18. FJ 453.30 leaves a blank.
him. But he was: U 232.8 inserts "at ganga til settar við [hann. en hann var] avallt sattr" as in
   FmS VII, 240.11–12. FJ 453.32 leaves a blank.
Jón Bir-: U 232.10 reads "Joan Birgis son" as in *FmS* VII, 240.14 and *F* 341.23, but FJ 454.3
   could make out only ". . . gis son."

Chapter 100

and the buildings: U 234.29 inserts "Oc er nu liþit mioc gengit af hondom honom [en husin
   hoggvin mioc. gecc þa Sigurþr konungr ut] oc Þorþr husfreyia" as in *F* 344.1–2. FJ 457.25
   leaves a blank.
a man from Vík. He: U 234.30–31 inserts "hirþmaþr hans [vicverscr oc sneri þangat sem Jngi
   konungr var fyrir] oc kallaþi Sigurþr konungr a Jnga" as in *F* 344.2–4. FJ 457.26–27 leaves
   a blank.
many men: U 234.36–37 inserts "[urþo margir] fyrir scotom" as in *FmS* VII, 246.1, but with
   added "margir." FJ 457.34–458.1 leaves a blank.
that was a Friday: U 234.38 inserts "en [þat var fria]dagr" as in *FmS* VII, 246.3 and *F* 344.8.
   FJ 458.2 leaves a blank.
he thought: U 235.4 inserts "oc spurþi [hvat hann et]laþi" with no correspondence in *FmS* or *F*.
   FJ 458.9 leaves a blank between "hvat" and "laþi."
. . . . : Both U 235.10 and FJ 458.21 show a lacuna: "Hverr let merkin ut bera ef þu hefir . . .
   Jnga konungi."
". . . : Both U 235.16 and FJ 458.30 show a lacuna: ". . . til bøiar."

Explanatory Notes

Chapter 1

1. On the career of Yaroslav the Wise (1015–1054), see Vernadsky 1948:74–83. Yaroslav had used Varangian troops during his struggles against his brothers and would therefore have had long-standing contacts with the Scandinavian world. He was a devout Christian and was reputed to be bookish. We may perhaps surmise that Magnús's stay in Kiev served to promote a pious disposition in the future king of Norway. Yaroslav also initiated an ambitious building program modeled on Constantinople. His architecture would presumably have made St. Óláfr's residence seem paltry indeed, so that the queen's comparison is pointedly insulting. See also Cross 1929, 177–97 and Stender-Petersen 1953:115–38.
2. The word translated here as "costly tapestries" is *pell*, ultimately from the Latin *pallium*. It suggests a silken or satin-like material. See Falk 1919: 67–69.
3. "Even though it only stands on posts." *Súlur* were the inner posts of a Norse house that supported the roof beams. See Valtýr Guðmundsson 1889:117–46 and 1894:5–8. The point here seems to be that a more advanced royal hall would have had a vaulted ceiling without inner buttressing. On the prehistory of Ingigerðr's affection for King Óláfr of Norway, see *Heimskringla* II, chs. 70–90 (*ÍF* 27, 90–134).
4. Queen Ingigerðr's departure is tantamount to a declaration of divorce. According to early Icelandic law, the first prerequisite for divorce is such a declaration (*segja skilit*). The grounds in the present episode might be construed as violence (cf. *Eyrbyggja saga, ÍF* 4, 26) or general irreconcilability (cf. *Víga-Glúms saga, ÍF* 9, 50, where the term for irreconcilability is *sundrlyndi*). On the law governing divorce, see Jochens 1995:55–61; Merschberger 1937:124–26; Schwerin 1930:283–99.
5. According to *Heimskringla* (*ÍF* 26, 143–45; trans. Hollander, pp. 92–93), King Æthelstan of England sent King Haraldr hárfagri of Norway a sword delivered to him hilt first in order to suggest Haraldr's vassal status. Haraldr retaliated by sending Æthelstan his child to be fostered, implying that his was the superior rank. It seems not unlikely that the author of *Morkinskinna* may have borrowed the motif from an earlier version of *Haralds saga hárfagra*. On the existence of such an earlier version, see Jónas Kristjánsson 1977:449–72.
6. Magnús's agility is not exactly paralleled elsewhere, but the importance of athletic accomplishments, especially in kings, is nicely illustrated by the flyting between King Eysteinn and King Sigurðr (Ch. 71). Snorri's version of this verbal contest (*Heimskringla, ÍF* 28, 259–60; trans. Hollander, pp. 702–4) emphasizes athleticism even more and adds wrestling, ice-skating, archery, and skiing to the repertoire. See also st. 61 below. In general, see Brynjulf Alver, "Idrottsleikar" in *KLNM* 7, 322–30; Björn Bjarnason 1905:101; Götlind 1933:3–53 (esp. 28 and Figure 17).
7. Magnús's precocious killing is reminiscent of Gestr Þórhallsson's revenge against Víga-Styrr while still a boy, in chs. 9–10 of *Heiðarvíga saga* (*ÍF* 3, 232–35). The comment on Gestr's deed may be indicative of the reaction to Magnús's killing: "Now the news of Styrr's

killing spread far and wide, and many were impressed that a man so young as Gestr, who had never killed before, should have committed such a great deed against such an arrogant champion as Styrr had been during his life." See also Óláfr Tryggvason's vengeance at the age of nine for his foster father in Oddr Snorrason's *Óláfs saga Tryggvasonar* (Ch. 8).

8. See Else Ebel, "Der Fernhandel," in *UHV,* p. 289; Gelsinger 1981:155, 178; Jón Jóhannesson 1974:241. Embargo seems to be used as a weapon during times of political tension. Below (Ch. 36), Auðunn vestfirzki proposes to travel between Norway and Denmark during a time of war, and King Haraldr asks him what sort of a fool he is to entertain such a thought. In 1219, when feelings ran high between Norway and Iceland, two annals note that no ships came from Norway to Iceland. See Gustav Storm, *Islandske annaler,* pp. 125, 185. Later in Ch. 1 it is specified that the local people in the Baltic refuse to trade with the Norwegians.

9. Jonna Louis-Jensen 1977:80–82 has dealt with the story of Karl vesæli, which begins here, and concludes that it is a later interpolation. She bases this conclusion on the contradiction between the idea that on the one hand, the Þrœndir ask for the return of Magnús and, on the other, the idea that King Yaroslav initiates Magnús's reinstatement. She assumes that one version was in the oldest version of *Morkinskinna* and that the other was in a separate "Karls þáttr vesæla." When "Karls þáttr" was interpolated, the difference was reconciled only awkwardly, and the situation was further confused when account was taken of the version in *Ágrip.* Other solutions are imaginable. "Karls þáttr vesæla" has none of the familiar features of the independent *þáttr* and seems more likely to come from a version of King Magnús's life. Because it has a distinct Þrœndalǫg orientation, the source might well be *Hlaðajarla saga,* in which the activity of the Þrœndir and Einarr þambarskelfir would be at home (cf. note 1.21 and Andersson 1998). It is generally supposed that *Hlaðajarla saga broke off before the events described in *Morkinskinna,* but it seems possible that this lost text (or a continuation) carried the narrative down to the death of Einarr þambarskelfir (see Andersson 1998). The confusion may have arisen when the author of *Morkinskinna* combined the version in *Hlaðajarla saga with the tradition underlying *Ágrip.* There seems, in any case, to be no compelling reason for a separate "Karls þáttr vesæla" or a later interpolation.

10. This question echoes a passage in "Auðunar þáttr" (Ch. 36). Compare the following: "Hyggr þú nǫkkut þína gæfu meiri en annarra manna, ok hyggr þú at þú munir hér draga fram kaupeyri þinn en aðrir fá eigi haldit lífinu?" (FJ 7.6–9) "Hvárt er, at þú ert maðr svá óvitr at þú hefir eigi heyrt ófrið þann, er í milli er landa þessa, eða ætlar þú giptu þína svá mikla, at þú munir þar komask með gǫrsimar, er aðrir fá eigi komizk klakklaust, þó at nauðsyn eigi til?" (FJ 181.28–32; the phrasing is somewhat different in *Flat* III, 411–12).

11. The question of who qualifies as a king's thane comes up at regular intervals in *Morkinskinna* and several times in this chapter (see notes 1.20, 1.25, 2.3, 19.2, 30.6, 30.8, 64.3 below). It is related to the question of whether the Icelanders are to be considered as the Norwegian king's thanes. This notion crops up as early as "Gísls þáttr Illugasonar" (*ÍF* 3, 337), which Jonna Louis-Jensen (1977:111–22) dates in the early thirteenth century. Here Jón Ǫgmundarson addresses King Magnús Óláfsson († 1103) as follows: "Sire, we are just as much your men (*þínir þegnar*) as those who live in this country [Norway]." See *Ljósvetninga saga* (*ÍF* 10, 97) and *Hákonar saga Hákonarsonar* (Ch. 47), and cf. "Toward a Profile of the Author." See also Ármann Jakobsson 1997:136, 254, 259, 263–64, 274.

12. "District chieftains" translates the term *lendir menn* (sing. *lendr maðr*). On the office and evolution of these chieftains, see Arne Bøe, "Lendmann," in *KLNM* 10, 498–505, and Bagge 1991:12, 65–66, 72, 78–79, 88, 92, 94, 118–19, 124–25, 127, 129, 133, 141, 155–56, 196.

13. The word "Kaupangr" (or "kaupangr") is used regularly in *Morkinskinna* to refer to the town of Niðaróss (modern Trondheim). If the word is understood to be a common noun, it means something like "trading center" or "town." It is symptomatic of the uncertainty that in Bjarni Aðalbjarnarson's edition of *Óláfs saga helga,* he twice prints the word lowercase and twice uppercase. On the problem, see Bjarni Einarsson's edition of *Fagrskinna*

(*ÍF* 29, cxxx–cxxxi). Bjarni settles in favor of capitalization, and we follow his practice. Kaupangr was the earliest name of the modern city of Trondheim; the city changed its name to Niðaróss after 1180. That change has been traced to archbishop Eysteinn (1161–1188) and to the remodeling of the cathedral that was initiated in 1152. For a thorough discussion, see Didrik Arup Seip (1930). On the word itself, see Heinrich Beck, "Kaufungen, Kaupangr und Köping(e)," in *UHV,* pp. 358–73.

14. On the Eyra(r)þing, see Jörn Sandnes, "Øreting," in *KLNM* 21, 11–12. This was one of the two assembly places in Þrœndalǫg (along with the Frostaþing). It cannot be precisely located but was somewhere near the mouth of the river Nið in the vicinity of Niðaróss.

15. The device of intoxicating the guards may be compared to an episode in Saxo Grammaticus's *Gesta Danorum* 13.11 (pp. 363–64); trans. Eric Christiansen, I, 139–40. In this episode Erik, later Erik Emune (or eymuni) finds himself imprisoned by the Norwegian king Magnús blindi (the blind), the ally of Erik's rival Magnus (son of King Niels). He intoxicates the men set to guard him and is able to escape and sail to safety. This event occurs during the internal strife in Denmark following the murder of Knútr lávarðr in 1131.

16. "Ok þegar þrífr Karl í herðar honum ok fœrir hann útanborðs ok rœr í brott skipinu" (FJ 15.1–3). The phrasing is reminiscent of Sigurðr slembir's similarly adventurous escape later: "En hann greip í herðar þeim báðum ok steypti þeim útanborðs . . ." (FJ 411.25–27).

17. Despite the king's suspicions, it seems unmotivated that Kálfr should suddenly be sent on a Uriah mission to England. What is perhaps alluded to is a brief episode at the end of Snorri Sturluson's *Óláfs saga helga* (*ÍF* 27, 414; trans. Hollander, p. 536) to the following effect: "A messenger of King Knútr (Cnut the Great) came to Kálfr Árnason bringing him Knútr's bidding that Kálfr should send him three dozen axes and make sure that they were of the best quality. Kálfr answered: 'I will send King Knútr no axes. Tell him that I will send his son Sveinn some axes, enough so that he will think there is no shortage.'" If the echo is intended, King Sveinn is reminding Kálfr of their previous hostility. A connection between these passages would also suggest that the author knew a version of *Óláfs saga helga* with the ax incident. See also *Fagrskinna* (*ÍF* 29, 207). We may ask ourselves to what extent the name "Eggjar-Kálfr" (Kálfr from Egg) gave rise to the ax anecdote (*egg,* "blade," or *pars pro toto* for "ax").

18. On the management of two simultaneous narratives in the sagas, see Clover 1982: 61–147.

19. On the nickname *bryggjufótr,* see Finnur Jónsson 1907:318. It means literally "bridgefoot" or perhaps "lower (shore) end of a gangplank or gangway." Finnur Jónsson also suggests the possibility of "clubfoot." Oddly, a Sveinn bryggjufótr also appears in "Sveinka þáttr" (Unger, 137.1, and 139.8 and 32; FJ 307.3, 310.15, 311.11). See also *Ágrip* (*ÍF* 29, 32).

20. ". . . at Magnús skyldi fara til Nóregs ok taka þar við landi ok þegnum." See note 1.11 above. The word *þegnar* implies that the Norwegians are Magnús's subjects.

21. On the contradiction between Yaroslav's dispatching of Karl early in the chapter and his change of heart here, see Finnur Jónsson's "Indledning" to his edition (p. xi) and Louis-Jensen 1977:80–82. See also note 1.9. The mission of the Þrœndir to Russia (cf. *Ágrip,* Ch. 34) to clear the way for Magnús's succession to the throne has strong political overtones. It suggests a special relationship between Magnús and the Þrœndir, which is emphasized by Magnús's benevolence toward his subjects later. This is a relationship that stands as a model for all future relationships between the Norwegian king and his people. That it should single out the Þrœndir suggests that it might derive from **Hlaðajarla saga* (or a continuation), a lost history that was no doubt partisan toward Þrœndalǫg. The fullest discussion of **Hlaðajarla saga* is by Bjarni Aðalbjarnarson 1937:199–224. Bjarni does not make allowance for the use of this saga by the author of *Morkinskinna,* but he dates the composition of **Hlaðajarla saga* around 1200 (p. 236). It would be odd if the

author of *Morkinskinna,* writing some twenty years later, did not know a work so central to his theme.

22. The oath of twelve is a technical legal term (*tylftareiðr*). See Halvard Bjørkvik, "Tylvt," in *KLNM* 19, 118–19. The oath of twelve was required of a man charged with serious crimes. He was obliged to perform it with eleven compurgators in order to clear himself. The point made by Einarr here is perhaps that he and his companions are being treated like criminals.

23. *Morkinskinna* provides relatively little in the way of chronological indications. This one is taken over directly from Arnórr's stanza. See "Toward a Profile of the Author" and "Notes on Stanzas." Other chronological matters will be noted along the way. On Snorri's more elaborate chronology, see Bagge 1991:49–57.

24. "The border mountains" translates *Kjǫlr* (the keel), a term used for the ridge of mountains between Norway and Sweden. Snorri's "Hákonar saga góða" (*ÍF* 26, 165; trans. Hollander, p. 106) refers it specifically to the terrain between Norway and the province of Jamtaland (Jämtland). See also Kválen 1925a:22.

25. "The land and people" translates "land ok þegnar." *Þegnar* again refers to the legal subjects of a king (cf. notes 1.11 and 1.20).

Chapter 2

1. On the so-called "levy arrow" (a signal for troops to gather under certain circumstances prescribed by the laws), see *KLNM* 10, 308 and 501. See also Falk, *Waffenkunde,* p. 102.

2. "Naval obligations" translates *leiðangr,* a term that specifies the obligation of local populations in Norway to come to the defense of king and country. See Halvard Bjørkvik, "Leidang," in *KLNM* 10, 432–42.

3. "The consent and agreement of all the people, rich and poor" translates "með vild ok vilja allra þegna, bæði ríkra ok fátœkra." The word *þegnar* is apparently taken over from st. 4 ("óðal þegna") and again suggests that the primary meaning was "subjects." The word seems not to have carried any class implication, because the subjects could be both "rich and poor."

4. Where something like Norwegian patriotism surfaces in *Morkinskinna,* we may suspect that it is seen through and perhaps magnified by an Icelandic lens. The image of Norwegians resisting Danish rule may have been inspired by Icelandic resistance to Norwegian intrusions into Icelandic affairs in the period just prior to the writing of *Morkinskinna* (1215–1220). See "Toward a Profile of the Author."

5. Knútr (or Cnut) the Great died on November 13, 1035. The Haraldr who succeeded him was Haraldr Harefoot, who died on March 17, 1040. On the succession described here and ensuing events, see Loyn 1977:95–97.

6. On the sources that record this peace, see Bjarni Aðalbjarnarson's note in *ÍF* 28, 13n.2. The word for "Russia" in the manuscript is Garðaríki. As Finnur Jónsson's edition notes (p. 22), it must be a mistake for Danaríki, "Denmark." The sentence is omitted in the *Hulda-Hrokkinskinna* redaction (*FmS* VI, 26) and in *Heimskringla* (*ÍF* 28, 13), which therefore do not serve to correct the error.

7. For the English version of this agreement, see Loyn 1977:91.

8. This episode is omitted in *Heimskringla* and *Fagrskinna.* It sounds as though Kálfr is compensating for some earlier failure in battle, but no such incident is recorded. He acquits himself bravely at the Battle of Stiklastaðir. Perhaps the gist is that Kálfr is getting old and feeble and fears that he will not be able to stand his man in battle as he once could. The device of tying the hand to the sword is also attributed to Haraldr harðráði, when he is urged to absent himself from the Battle of Stiklastaðir, but here it is the weakness of youth rather than old age that inspires the remedy (see *ÍF* 27, 364).

Chapter 3

1. On the round of feasts (*veizlur;* sing. *veizla*) to which the king was entitled in connection with his supervision of the country, see Halvard Bjørkvik, "Veitsle," in *KLNM* 19, 632–34.

2. On the dire consequences of a king's being susceptible to slander, see the story of Haraldr hárfagri and Þórólfr Kveld-Úlfsson in *Egils saga* (*ÍF* 2, 27–54). At one point Þórólfr enunciates the positive ideal in this regard (p. 37): "The king will not believe lies that are whispered to him because there is no reason for me to betray him; he has showed me very great favor and done me no harm." The sequel shows that Þórólfr is sadly mistaken.

3. On the situation in the Orkney Islands at this time, see *Orkneyinga saga*, Ch. 25 (*ÍF* 34, 63–65). The rule of Orkney was subject to a dispute between Þorfinnr Sigurðarson and Rǫgnvaldr Brúsason, the latter a foster brother of King Magnús. Rǫgnvaldr appeals to Magnús, who offers to reinstate Kálfr Árnason if he will support Rǫgnvaldr. The text tells us that Þorfinnr was married to Ingibjǫrg Árnadóttir, Kálfr's sister, but *Orkneyinga saga* states the relationship differently: "Þorfinnr átti þá Ingibjǫrg jarlamóður, dóttur Finns jarls Árnasonar." Accordingly Ingibjǫrg was the daughter of·Finnr and Kálfr's niece. She was born around 1015, and after Þorfinnr's death, she married Malcolm, king of the Scots, and bore him the son Dungað. The children of Ingibjǫrg and Þorfinnr were the jarls Páll and Erlendr of Orkney. On the chronology, see Finnbogi Guðmundsson's introduction in *ÍF* 34, lxxxiii.

4. This outburst of Þrœndalǫg independence and assertiveness may again put us in mind of *Hlaðajarla saga. See note 1.21.

5. On the skald Sigvatr Þórðarson, see Finnur Jónsson, *Litteraturhistorie* I, 590–612.

6. The words "wise and amenable" translate "vitr ok góðgjarn." This is high praise indeed and would be difficult to match in the description of any other Norwegian king. See Ármann Jakobsson 1997:204.

7. "Svá skorpnar skór á fœti mér, at hvergi má ek úr stað komask." See Halldór Halldórsson, *Orðtakasafn*, 2, 138. *Morkinskinna* has a real predilection for riddling dialogue (see notes 28.1, 48.7, 56.3–4, 68.8 below), but in this case, the riddle appears to be borrowed from *Ágrip* (*ÍF* 29, 32). The meaning seems to be that King Magnús's demands are so restrictive that the farmers have lost any independence of movement or, more broadly, any political independence. But see also Ármann Jakobsson 1997:239.

Chapter 4

1. On "The Sagas of the Jarls" (Jarla sǫgur), which are also mentioned in *Fagrskinna* (*ÍF* 29, 215), see Bjarni Aðalbjarnarson 1937:151–52. Scholars assume that some version of *Orkneyinga saga* is meant.

2. The Battle of Rauðabjǫrg is described differently and in somewhat more detail in Ch. 26 of *Orkneyinga saga* (*ÍF* 34, 65–70). *Orkneyinga saga* also cites three stanzas by Arnórr jarlaskald and one by Bjarni Gullbrárskald not found in *Morkinskinna*. *Orkneyinga saga* does not have Kálfr's rejoinder, however: "It will be as you ask, but I wanted to establish how important it was to you which side I chose." On the location of Rauðabjǫrg (Roberry?), see Alex. B. Taylor 1931:41–45 (esp. 43–44).

3. Hǫrðaknútr's ruse to get recognition in Norway is reported only here and in *Hulda-Hrokkinskinna* (*FmS* VI, 48–49).

4. "Hákon" here and four times below is clearly an error for "Hǫrðaknútr," perhaps a wrong resolution of an abbreviation beginning with an "h" and including a "k." *Hulda-Hrokkinskinna* has the correct Knútr or Hǫrðaknútr (*FmS* VI, 49–50).

5. On the proffering of poison by an evil queen in the drinking hall, cf. Ch. 44 of *Egils saga* (*ÍF* 2, 109). In the latter case, the queen is the prototypical witch Gunnhildr. According to *Bǫglunga sǫgur* (pp. 17–18, 25–26), Hákon Sverrisson was poisoned by Queen Margrete in

1204, and his nephew Guthormr was poisoned by Kristín the following year. The poisoning of kings by queens would therefore have been very much in the minds of readers in the early thirteenth century.

6. On the death of Hǫrðaknútr (June 8, 1042) and the succession of Edward, see Loyn 1977:97.

7. On the nickname *sprakaleggr*, see Finnur Jónsson 1907:222. He translates *knagben* from *knage*, "to creak," hence "creaky leg." The genealogical information corresponds with *Heimskringla* (ÍF 28, 36; trans. Hollander, p. 408) and *Fagrskinna* (ÍF 29, 182). The information in *Fagrskinna* is considerably reduced, but *Heimskringla* adds that Ástríðr had the same father as Knútr (Cnut the Great) and the same mother as Óláfr Svíakonungr, and also that Sigríðr's father was Skǫglar-Tósti. Our text goes on to tell how Sveinn remains unavenged against King Knútr (Cnut) for the killing of his father, Úlfr. *Heimskringla* (ÍF 28, 36) adds that according to the "Saga of Knútr inn gamli," Knútr had had Úlfr killed in Roskilde. The actual killing is related in *Heimskringla* (ÍF 27, 285) and *Fagrskinna* (p. 203) and must come from a common source, but *Knýtlinga saga* does not include the incident. According to Saxo (10.17, pp. 292–93), Knútr had Úlfr killed during a feast in Roskilde when Úlfr recited slanderous verses about the cowardice of the Danes.

8. "Too great a jarl" translates *ofjarl*. On the title "jarl," see Arne Bøe, "Jarl," in *KLNM* 7, 559–64. Ch. 48 of "Haralds saga Sigurðarsonar" (ÍF 28, 130; trans. Hollander, p. 615) tells us that in the time of Óláfr Haraldsson and Magnús, there was only one jarl in Norway. Such a jarl might therefore potentially be the king's most powerful rival.

9. This ship is referred to in "Óláfs saga helga" (ÍF 27, 267–69; trans. Hollander, pp. 433–34), where it is told that the prow was adorned with a golden bison head. The ship is named in a stanza by Sigvatr and an unattributed stanza (see also sts. 21, 25, 76).

10. This campaign is reported very briefly in *Fagrskinna* (ÍF 29, 220) and in greater detail in *Heimskringla* (ÍF 28, 38–40; trans. Hollander, pp. 559–60). Snorri cites two different stanzas by Arnórr but omits the one in *Morkinskinna*.

11. Ré is the German Baltic island Rügen off the coast near Stralsund and Greifswald. Vestland refers to western Pommerania. Smálǫnd (not to be confused with the central Swedish province of Småland) refers to the lesser Danish islands. A passage in *Heimskringla* (ÍF 28, 145; trans. Hollander, p. 625) suggests that the islands south of Fyn, chiefly Langeland and Ærø, are meant. See also the note on st. 28.

Chapter 5

1. The Skotborgará (or Skotborg River) is the modern Kongeå running into the North Sea in western Jutland between Ribe and Esbjerg. It seems clear from the context that the author imagines it to be farther south and closer to the Dano-German border in eastern Jutland. On the problem of simultaneous narration, see note 1.18 above.

2. On the chronology for the following events, see Bjarni Aðalbjarnarson in ÍF 28, xiii–xiv. King Magnús's campaign in Jutland is dated 1043 in the annals. The German emperor at this time was Henry III, who led campaigns against the Hungarians in 1042–1044. See Reuter 1991:255. No Duke Otto is recorded, but Adam of Bremen, p. 136, tells us that in 1042 King Magnús's sister Wulfhild was affianced to Duke Bernhard's son Ordulf. The story told on the following pages appears to be a garbled version of that event. The Icelandic annals record the death of Aðúlfr or Aðalúlfr, Duke of Brunswick, "who was married to Úlfhildr, the daughter of St. Olaf" in 1060 or 1072 (*Islandske Annaler*, pp. 109, 471). See also Ármann Jakobsson 1997:130.

3. A god decked out in silver and gold and placed on an altar is found in Ch. 69 of Snorri's "Óláfs saga Tryggvasonar" (ÍF 26, 317). It is not found in Oddr Snorrason's version. See also *Eyrbyggja saga* (ÍF 4, 9) and, on idols in general, Jan de Vries 1956:1.385–89.

4. The form Ragnhildr appears to be an error for the previously mentioned Úlfhildr,

perhaps suggested by Magnús's daughter Ragnhildr, who plays an important part in the story of Hákon Ívarsson, below. *Hulda-Hrokkinskinna* (*FmS* VI, 58) has the correct form.

5. This story of a purloined wife recurs in William of Malmesbury's chronicle (I, 178–79), where it is set in the time of King Edgar (973). Here Edgar dispatches the nobleman Athelwold to woo Elfthrida, the daughter of Duke Ordgar of Devonshire, if her beauty turns out to equal its reputation. Athelwold takes her for himself, and the matter eventually comes to light. In this version the deceitful nobleman is killed, and the king marries his intended. Both stories seem to have been elaborated according to the same folktale pattern, unless we imagine that the author of *Morkinskinna* had some access to William of Malmesbury.

6. On this motif, see Harris 1979:57–81.

7. Snorri includes this episode in the *Separate Saga of St. Olaf* (*ÍF* 27, 448) and notes that the bell Glǫð was given by St. Óláfr and hung in St. Clement's Church. On St. Clement, see Dietrich Hofmann 1987 and 1997.

8. Oddr Gellisson cannot be identified. Chronologically, he could be the son of Gellir Þorkelsson, who enjoyed the favor of Óláfr Haraldsson (see *ÍF* 27, 220, 240–41, 255, 292). His son might therefore have been of an age and a disposition to be in Magnús's service. Gellir was Ari Þorgilsson's grandfather and is praised by Ari for his good memory. The family is therefore likely to have been a reservoir of history. See "The Oral Sources."

9. When Magnús sheds his armor, the implication must be that Magnús is under St. Óláfr's special protection. Falk lists a few characteristic ax names like Hel (the goddess of the underworld) in *Waffenkunde*, p. 116. The information on the byrnie is taken from st. 31 (see the note to that stanza).

10. Invulnerable garments are particularly ubiquitous in the legendary sagas, for example, *Egils saga einhenda* (Ch. 15), *Gǫngu-Hrólfs saga* (Chs. 4, 30, 32), *Hálfdanar saga Brǫnufóstra* (Ch. 8), *Hervarar saga* (Ch. 3), *Ragnars saga loðbrókar* (Ch. 15), *Sǫgubrot af fornkonungum* (Ch. 4), *Sǫrla saga sterka* (Chs. 3, 6, 18), *Vǫlsunga saga* (Ch. 42), *Ǫrvar-Odds saga* (Ch. 11), *Þáttr af Ragnars sonum* (Ch. 3), *Þorsteins þáttr bæjarmagns* (Chs. 3, 5). See also Anne Holtsmark 1954:104–8.

11. The motif of corpses piled high to bridge a river (or stem the flow) is paralleled in "The Battle of the Goths and the Huns" (see Christopher Tolkien 1960:57).

12. This passage is borrowed from *Ágrip*, Ch. 35. Animals appearing in battle are a regular phenomenon, especially in the legendary sagas (see Inger Boberg, *Motif-Index*, B260 [p. 46]), but oxen rigged with spears are not paralleled in these stories. Somewhat similar are anecdotes in *Trójumanna saga* (*Hauksbók*, 199) and *Vápnfirðinga saga* (*ÍF* 11, 24), in which a bull is being bested by another bull and is equipped with a spear tied to its head in order to improve the odds. Closest of all is a passage in "Þáttr Styrbjarnar Svíakappa" in *Flat* II, 72. Here horses and oxen are equipped with yokes to which spears are attached.

13. The information that the battle was fought on Michaelmas (September 29) is taken from st. 39 below. The author of *Morkinskinna* attributes it to Þjóðólfr, but Snorri (*ÍF* 28, 63) attributes it with a variant line to Oddr kikinaskald.

14. The reigning emperor (Henry III) did not die until 1056, ten years after the death of King Magnús. He was succeeded not by an Otto but by Henry IV.

Chapter 6

1. The Battle of Helganes is dated 1045 in the annals but a year earlier in *Heimskringla*. See Bjarni Aðalbjarnarson, *ÍF* 28, xiv. Helganes is a tip of land across from modern Århus on the east coast of Jutland.

Chapter 7

1. Both *Fagrskinna* and *Heimskringla* make it appear that the Battle of Áróss (Århus) took place a couple of months after the Battle of Helganes in the same year. This dating is based on st. 39 ("Vas fyr Mikjálsmessu"), which is also recorded in *Heimskringla* (*ÍF* 28, 63–64). In describing the battle, Snorri cites none of the stanzas in *Morkinskinna* but cites ten different ones: seven full stanzas and three half stanzas. He attributes them all to Þjóðólfr and none to Arnórr. The author of *Morkinskinna* places Helganes in Skåne, a confusion that may have resulted from the collocation of st. 37 ("viðr Helganes") and st. 36 ("Uppgǫngu vann yngvi—á Skáneyju"). The author of *Morkinskinna* apparently did not know where Helganes was. He also staged two battles between Magnús and Sveinn at Helganes. The battle alluded to in st. 39 ("fyr sunnan Áros") may in fact be the same as the previous battle, so that the author of *Morkinskinna* actually made three battles out of one. *Fagrskinna* and *Heimskringla* posit two battles but follow *Morkinskinna* in separating Áróss and Helganes. The dependency on stanzas in these sequences may suggest that there was no written "Magnúss saga" to work from. It is indicative that Snorri chooses different stanzas to create an expanded narrative in this part of *Heimskringla*. *Ágrip* gives the sequence of battles as first Helganes and then Hlýrskógsheiðr, whereas Theodoricus gives Hlýrskógsheiðr, followed by Helganes and Áróss.
2. *Morkinskinna* uses "Flýði jarl af auði" to document that the Norwegians referred to Sveinn as "jarl" rather than "king" (also *Fagrskinna*, *ÍF* 29, 224). Snorri does not cite the stanza in question and does not refer to Sveinn either as "jarl" or "king."
3. "Næst rauð frán á Fjóni," from which *Morkinskinna* deduces Magnús's age, is also found in *Fagrskinna* (*ÍF* 29, 225–26, st. 181) but not in *Heimskringla*. See the note on this stanza.
4. *Fagrskinna* (with a different placement directly after Knútr's death) gives most of Edward's long letter (*ÍF* 29, 217–18), but *Heimskringla* (*ÍF* 28, 66) only a very abbreviated version. The intensity of the rhetoric in *Morkinskinna*'s version suggests that the sentiments lie close to the author's heart. See "Toward a Profile of the Author."

Chapter 8

1. On this passage see "The Native Sources": "En seglit var tvéfalt pell af enum dýrstum vefjum." Here the sail is alleged to be two layers of precious silken material. Elsewhere, *pell* seems to be imagined as an adornment sewn onto more traditional sailcloth. See Falk, *Kleiderkunde*, p. 69.
2. Such weathervanes are frequently depicted in books on the vikings. See, for example, Wilson and Klindt-Jensen 1966: plates 58–59 or, in color, Almgren et al. 1966:168.
3. Kings in disguise are not uncommon in *Morkinskinna*. Cf. Magnús circulating among his troops on Hlýrskógsheiðr (Ch. 5, at note 6), Sveinn Úlfsson before the Norwegian army (Ch. 25), or Harold Godwinson before the army of Haraldr harðráði in England (Ch. 50). Haraldr harðráði is, of course, in perpetual disguise during his time in Constantinople.
4. This passage seems to be an elaboration of a paragraph in *Ágrip* (*ÍF* 29, 36). The "great treasures" anticipate Haraldr's Byzantine adventures without explanation. This awkwardness is avoided in *Ágrip*.

Chapter 9

1. This paragraph looks like a continuation of the interpolation from *Ágrip*, although Hringaríki is substituted for Upplǫnd. The genealogy matches, but *Morkinskinna* adds information on Haraldr grenski (from Grenland, Norway), Ásta's previous husband. Snorri

mentions the marriage of Ásta and Guðbrandr (kúla) in Ch. 43 of "Óláfs saga Tryggvasonar" (*ÍF* 26, 287).

2. Haraldr's concealed identity makes good sense as he evades his enemies, but disguise and
deception become a way of life for him, as the previous episode illustrates.

3. "Heavy eyebrows" renders "skollbrún," which cannot mean dark-complexioned here
because Haraldr has already been described as pale ("fǫllitaðr"). See Detollenaere 1942:
85–86. The parting gift of knife and belt is frequent in the sagas. Haraldr's guide is not
identified by name, so that the tradition cannot be traced. It could have been passed from
King Magnús to Oddr Gellisson, mentioned as a source for the Battle of Hlýrskógsheiðr,
or it could have circulated in the Þrœndalǫg region and been available there to any number of Icelanders, including Halldórr Snorrason.

4. On the skalds Bǫlverkr and Þjóðólfr, see Finnur Jónsson, *Litteraturhistorie* I, 627–33.

5. See Blöndal 1978:54–55. Blöndal considers the statement that Haraldr became the commander of King Yaroslav's defense forces to be a great exaggeration of some modest role
in tax-collecting expeditions or border fighting. The exaggeration could have been inspired in part by a similarly grand account of Óláfr Tryggvason's youthful exploits in Russia in Ch. 8 of Oddr Snorrason's *Óláfs saga Tryggvasonar.*

6. Blöndal (1978:55) points out that Haraldr can hardly have wooed King Yaroslav's daughter Elisaveta so early because she would scarcely have been ten years old.

7. Blöndal (1978:56) suggests that the Frakkar referred to in Illugi's *helming* could be the
Normans of Sicily and that "Lombardy" refers to the Byzantine province of Longobardia
in southern Italy. *FmS* VI, 134 cite the following couplet from Þjóðólfr's "Sexstefja" (5; *Skj*
IA, 370) to corroborate Haraldr's itinerary:

> Sás við lund á landi
> Langbarða réð ganga.
> He who advanced in the land of the Lombards ("við lund"?).

It is very likely that the stanza was part of Msk2 and that the scribe of *Flat,* who failed to
make sense of the syntactically incomplete couplet, simply decided to omit it. On Illugi,
see Finnur Jónsson, *Litteraturhistorie* I, 634.

8. The emperor was Michael IV Katallakos (1034–1041). His empress Zoe (978/980–1050)
had previously been married to Romanos III Argyros (1028–1034) and was later married
to Constantine IX Monomachos (1042–1055).

9. Blöndal (1978:58–59) notes this name change but offers no explanation. We may wonder whether the suffix *-brikt/-brigt* is connected with the verb *brigða* and noun *brigð* "for-
feiture, breaking, breach, variant (?)," so that Haraldr is the man who has abandoned the
north or the northern land. *Brigð* is also a legal term meaning the right to claim forfeited
land. Haraldr would then be the man who has a claim on the north, and that would certainly be in keeping with his career and his foresightedness. The idea that foreigners of
royal descent are shunned is puzzling, but it may be a reflection of the Byzantine fear of
any and all pretenders to the throne. Contemporary Greek sources indicate, however, that
Haraldr's real identity was known in Byzantine circles. See Bjarni Aðalbjarnarson in *Heimskringla* (*ÍF* 28, xvi).

10. For the proposed explanations of the word *Væringjar* (Varangians), see Blöndal
1978:4–7.

11. Már Húnrøðarson does not figure in *Landnámabók,* but he is mentioned at the beginning of *Þorgils saga ok Hafliða.* For the genealogy, see *Sturlunga saga* (1988), III, 75. It
seems clear that the author of *Morkinskinna* had a considerable fund of information
from western Iceland, where Már lived. See Ch. 83 below and "Time and Place of Composition."

Chapter 10

1. Gyrgir is the Byzantine general Georgios Maniaces, who campaigned in Sicily and southern Italy in the years 1038 to 1041. Contrary to the caricature in *Morkinskinna*, he was an unusually accomplished military leader, but he was of humble birth and unlikely to have been Zoe's kinsman. See Blöndal 1978:65–67.
2. Blöndal (1978:69) points out that the dispute could have been over the undesirability of camping on marshy ground, with the attendant danger of malaria.
3. Haraldr departs with Varangians and "Latínumenn." Bjarni Aðalbjarnarson in *Heims-kringla* (*ÍF* 28, 74n.) notes that these "Latins" must have been Normans.
4. The idea that Haraldr raided in Africa could be inspired by the mention of Serkland in Þjóðólfr's stanza, although Serkland more properly refers to the land of the Saracens (Arabia). See Blöndal 1978:60–61, and Bjarni Aðalbjarnarson in *ÍF* 28, 75 (note to st. 81). *Fagrskinna* (*ÍF* 29, 231, st. 186) and *FmS* (VI, 140) preserve another stanza by Þjóðólfr ("Sexstefja" 3, *Skj* IA, 369) that refers specifically to the king of "Affríka":

> Dolgljóss (hefir dási   vasat Affríka jǫfri
> darrlatr staðit fjarri   Ánars mey fyr hánum
> endr) es elju Rindar   haglfaldinni at halda
> ómynda tók skyndir: hlýðisamt né lýðum.

"Darrlatr dási hefir endr staðit fjarri, es dolgljóss skyndir tók elju Rindar ómynda. Vasat hlýðisamt jǫfri Affríka né lýðum at halda haglfaldinni Ánars mey fyr hánum."
The spear-lazy sluggard stayed away earlier when the hastener of the battle gleam [sword, warrior] captured Rindr's [Óðinn's second wife] rival [Jǫrð; "earth"] without dowry. It was impossible for the king of the Africans and his people to withhold from him the hail-covered daughter of Ánarr [Jǫrð; "earth"].

This stanza is, no doubt, the source of the mention below of "the king in Africa," and we can surmise that the stanza was indeed part of ÆMsk and omitted in *Flateyjarbók*. Snorri resolves the problem at one point (*ÍF* 28, 74) by referring to "Affríka, er Væringjar kalla Serkland" (Africa, which the Varangians call Serkland).

Chapter 11

1. See note 9.9.
2. On the church dedicated to St. Óláfr in Constantinople, see Blöndal 1978:152–53 and 185–86.
3. St. Óláfr appears on a white horse as at the Battle of Hlýrskógsheiðr (see Ch. 4 above). This episode is also recorded in the earliest versions of St. Óláfr's miracles (see "Acta Sancti Olavi Regis et Martyris," *MHN* 135–36 and n.), and Snorri includes it in his "Hákonar saga herðibreiðs" (*ÍF* 28, 371–72).
4. The motif of substituting walnuts for firewood is repeated during Sigurðr jórsalafari's visit in Constantinople in Ch. 63 below (see note 63.1).
5. On the Icelandic monetary units, see Gelsinger 1981:36–42, and note 16.1 below. One hundred marks is an exceedingly large amount of money. Blöndal (1978:31, 60) assumes that the campaigners were to pay a hundred marks for each pirate ship captured, but the passage could just as well mean that they paid a hundred marks for each vessel in their own fleet, as a form of rental. That would accord better with the statement at the beginning of Ch. 12: "Even though we cannot pay the emperor the sum agreed upon, we do have some resources."

6. "Hér mun eigi þat til at taka et minna, er eigi fæsk et meira." The saying is not included in Halldór Halldórsson's *Orðtakasafn.*
7. "En þá hefir sá happ, er hlýtr ok auðit verðr." On such fatalistic phrases, see Hermann Pálsson 1975:140–41.
8. On Haraldr's tunneling stratagem, see Blöndal 1978:73.

Chapter 12

1. "Er illt at setjask optarr niðr en hann ríss upp." This saying is not registered in Halldór Halldórsson's *Orðtakasafn.*
2. This is the point at which the great lacuna in *Morkinskinna* (filled in from *Flat*) ends and the main MS resumes.
3. On the firebird stratagem, see Blöndal 1978:71, and Adolf Stender-Petersen 1934:127–55. Absurd as the stratagem may seem, it appears that the Americans experimented with the idea of dropping bats with incendiary devices on Japanese cities in the Second World War. See the report in *American Heritage* 33 (1981): 93–94.
4. "Beri herr merki fyrir þér rogum!" The tense relationship between Halldórr and Haraldr anticipates the gist of "Halldórs þáttr Snorrasonar" (Ch. 30 below).
5. On the coffin stratagem, see Blöndal 1978:72–73, and Klaus Rossenbeck 1970:70–74.

Chapter 13

1. On Haraldr's visit to the Holy Land, see Paul Riant 1865:185–95.
2. On Stúfr blindi, see Finnur Jónsson, *Litteraturhistorie* I, 633–34.
3. A number of skaldic stanzas make it evident that it was the preeminent duty of kings and, hence, perhaps also of future kings, to suppress robbers and brigands. Cf. the appeal to King Magnús berfœttr toward the end of Ch. 56 below.
4. The envy of a successful man is, of course, ubiquitous, but here it could be inspired by the envy of Óláfr Tryggvason described in Oddr Snorrason's *Óláfs saga Tryggvasonar* (Ch. 9).
5. This incident is closely paralleled in the section of *Grettis saga* known as "Spesar þáttr" (*ÍF* 7, 279–80).
6. This paragraph rehearses the end of Ch. 12. See Blöndal 1978:178. It is interesting that the author substantiates Zoe's desire for Haraldr from a special oral tradition. Perhaps he had his doubts about the commonplace that a Norseman abroad inevitably attracts the attentions of a foreign queen.
7. Both *Fagrskinna* and *Heimskringla* omit the great serpent, but there must have been a widespread tradition about it because Saxo Grammaticus states that King Valdemar the Great of Denmark was still in possession of the knife with which Haraldr slew the serpent. See Saxo's *Gesta Danorum* 11, p. 305 (trans. Eric Christiansen, I, 54) and cf. the confused reminiscence in William of Malmesbury's *De Gestis Regum Anglorum* (II, 318).
8. Although *Fagrskinna* and *Heimskringla* banish the serpent, they retain the Óláfr miracle. On the location of the dungeon, see Blöndal 1978:87, and on Haraldr's release, p. 91.
9. *Morkinskinna* makes an emphatic point of Haraldr's blinding of the emperor (Michael V Kalafates), as do *Fagrskinna* (*ÍF* 29, 236) and *Heimskringla* (*ÍF* 28, 86; trans. Hollander, p. 588). Blöndal (1978:93–94) makes a more plausible case from Byzantine sources that Michael V fell victim to a political uprising and that the Varangians, who were regularly assigned such unpleasant tasks, were ordered to carry out the blinding. The event took place in 1042. On Þórarinn Skeggjason, see Finnur Jónsson, *Litteraturhistorie* I, 637.
10. The location of these chains between the Golden Horn and the Bosporus may be seen on the map provided by Blöndal (1978:178). Such chains may still be viewed in the Military Museum in Istanbul.

11. The device is somewhat similar to Óláfr Haraldsson's maneuver when he winches up a cable across Sauðungssund under Jarl Hákon's ship at the Battle of Nesjar, upsetting the ship and leaving the jarl and his crew at his mercy (*ÍF* 27, 37; trans. Hollander, p. 265). For the Byzantine version of Haraldr's departure, see Blöndal 1978:96. His departure took place in the fall of 1042.

12. There is no real evidence that Haraldr was involved with this princess, but William of Malmesbury says that he was condemned by the emperor to face a lion "because of the debauching of a noble woman" (*WM* II, 318).

13. On Haraldr's marriage to Ellisif, see Blöndal 1978:55.

14. *Fagrskinna* (*ÍF* 29, 238–39) and *Heimskringla* (*ÍF* 28, 91) give essentially the same genealogy. It shows that Sveinn Úlfsson and Ellisif's mother Ingigerðr are first cousins. On Valgarðr ór Velli, see Finnur Jónsson, *Litteraturhistorie* I, 637–38.

Chapter 14

1. *Fagrskinna* and *Heimskringla* (*ÍF* 29, 239; *ÍF* 28, 96; trans. Hollander, p. 593) add an interesting moment of dialogue between Sveinn and Haraldr, in which Haraldr expresses anger at the prospect of doing battle against his kinsman Magnús. Whether this is an attempt to minimize Haraldr's machinations and emphasize kin loyalty or merely an added maneuver in Haraldr's plan to abandon his alliance with Sveinn is not altogether clear.

2. The "outer course" is the sea route outside Norway's coastal islands.

3. Both *Fagrskinna* (*ÍF* 29, 243) and *Heimskringla* (*ÍF* 28, 101; trans. Hollander, p. 596) include mention of this bowl. Snorri adds the information that it had been seen by Guðríðr, the daughter of Guthormr Steigar-Þórisson. See "The Native Sources." Guðríðr is cited as a source below (Ch. 14), with her information transmitted through a certain Þorgils. *Fagrskinna* (*ÍF* 29, 245) and *Heimskringla* (*ÍF* 28, 101) instruct us that this was Þorgils Snorrason at Skarð, who died in 1201.

4. "Þat var brúnn purpuri." See Falk 1919:69.

5. "The Danish islands" translates "smálond í Danmǫrk." See *Heimskringla* (*ÍF* 28, 145; trans. Hollander, p. 625), where the phrase "Fjón ok Smálǫnd" occurs, probably with reference to the islands south of Fyn.

6. *Fagrskinna* (*ÍF* 29, 243) refers to this place as Akr. *Heimskringla* (*ÍF* 28, 97) gives no place name, but note 2 supplies "Akr á Vangi" in Hedmark, an old assembly site. Thus the meeting did not take place in Vík but further inland, as is corroborated by Theodoricus (*MHN* 54), who specifies "Upplǫnd."

7. The floor was customarily strewn with straw to absorb the dirt. In the first stanza of "Eiríksmál" (trans. Lee M. Hollander 1936:64), Óðinn speaks the following words preparatory to his reception of King Eiríkr blóðøx (Bloodax) in Valhǫll: "I got Valhǫll ready / to make room for warriors; / I waked the einheriar, / asked them to rise up, / to put straw on benches, / and to rinse the beer-jugs; / and the valkyries to deal wine out / as though a warrior drew nigh."

8. The familiar scales, operated with two bowls and weights, were also known in medieval Scandinavia, but the instrument referred to here (*reizla, reiðsla*) appears to be different. See Poul Rasmussen and Aslak Liestøl, "Vejningsredskaber," in *KLNM* 19, 634–37, and Finnur Jónsson, "Islands mønt, mål og vægt," in *Nordisk kultur* 30, 159.

9. This remark might be compared to a remark that Óláfr kyrri makes about Haraldr himself in Ch. 51: "In the days of my father this people was in great fear and trembling, and many hid their gold and treasures." The latter comment is taken over from *Ágrip* (*ÍF* 29, 41).

10. See note 1.22 above. The word *sættareiðr*, "oath of reconciliation," is not otherwise registered in the dictionaries.

11. See note 14.3 above.

Chapter 15

1. "Þorkels þáttr dyðrils" is included by Heinrich Gimmler (1976:63) among his "Grenz-fälle" or near-*þættir*. Fritzner (s.v. *dýrðill*) connects the word with *dýrð*, "preciousness," or Modern Icelandic *dirðill*, "short tail." Finnur Jónsson (1907:241) proposes "lover of finery." The same story is told about Þorkell and King Óláfr Tryggvason in *Flat* I, 405–7.

Chapter 16

1. On the value of the mark, see note 11.5 above and Hans-Peter Naumann, "Warenpreise und Wertverhältnisse im alten Norden," in *UHV*, pp. 374–89.
2. This episode is somewhat reminiscent of "Auðunar þáttr" (Ch. 36 below), in which Auðunn contrives to present a valuable ring to King Haraldr.
3. Óláfr Haraldsson's viking career is described in Snorri's "Óláfs saga helga," Chs. 4–20 (*ÍF*, 27, 4–26), and in *The Legendary Saga of St. Olaf*, ed. and trans. Anne Heinrichs et al., pp. 40–64. The author of *Morkinskinna* presumably knew some version of this account.

Chapter 17

1. *Fagrskinna* (*ÍF* 29, 137–38) adds the information (conceivably from *Hlaðajarla saga) that Ormr's father was Skopti (or Tíðenda-Skopti), who was the brother of Hákon jarl's wife Þóra. Snorri makes no mention of Skopti.
2. This is the first of several interesting comments in *Morkinskinna* on why a particular tale is told. The recognition of a man's intrinsic worth is a recurrent value in the text. See notes 25.3, 42.3, 42.11, 42.13, and 68.12 below.

Chapter 18

1. The notion of being good to your friends and harsh to your enemies is commonplace in the sagas, for example, *Hrafnkels saga* (*ÍF* 11, 99). Cf. note 49.2 and Barlow 1970:161.
2. The MS (FJ 103.11) reads *vtlenzcr*, but Finnur Jónsson suspects *vpplenzcr*, a reading that appears in *Hulda-Hrokkinskinna* (*FmS* VI, 186).
3. On differentials in gift-giving, see Andersson and Miller 1989:52–55 and Miller 1990:82.
4. According to Falk, *Kleiderkunde*, p. 44, "dark clothes" ("svǫrt klæði") might suggest poverty. Mendicant monks, if that is what the author has in mind, are a considerable anachronism in the middle of the eleventh century.
5. In the sagas a man's intelligence is regularly gauged by the accuracy of his surmises. "It turned out exactly as he surmised" is a recurrent phrase in such situations.

Chapter 19

1. This accusation echoes the charge in Constantinople that Haraldr took more than was rightfully his (Ch. 13 above). On the previous charge, see Blöndal 1978:78.
2. The last clause reads ". . . at sá mun mest vald á oss eiga, þegnum sínum." On the recurrent issue of the king's *þegnar*, see note 1.11 above.
3. The exchange of injurious ditties is reminiscent of the often-discussed entertainment at the wedding at Reykjahólar in *Þorgils saga ok Hafliða*. See *Sturlunga saga* (1988), I, 19–21.
4. "Next there is mention of the kings' dispute" ("Ok nú er rœtt um síðan mál konunga")

sounds like a reference to a written text, but it is difficult to guess what that text may have been. Since the chieftain of the Þrœndir, Einarr þambarskelfir, is involved, perhaps the best guess is again *Hlaðajarla saga.

Chapter 20

1. Þorsteinn Hallsson figures in *Njáls saga* (*ÍF* 12, 239 [with an elaborate genealogy], 439, 442, 448, 451–52, 460). On the landing tax (*landaurar*), see Gelsinger 1981:71–75.
2. On the pitfalls of gift-giving, see note 18.3 above.
3. On the relations of fathers and sons in the sagas, see Paul Schach 1977:361–81, and Cathy Jorgensen Itnyre 1996:173–96.

Chapter 21

1. There has been some debate on whether skaldic verse was transmitted without historical comment or was embedded in a narrative frame. It seems likely that Arnórr is the ultimate source of his own anecdote and that it was most probably passed down in his own family. The meaningless detail that he did not bother to wash off the tar seems less likely to have been invented after the fact and therefore suggests that the verse was from the outset part of an anecdotal tradition.
2. The order of recitation is reminiscent of an episode in *Gunnlaugs saga* (*ÍF* 3, 79–81), in which Gunnlaugr and Hrafn dispute the order in which they will present their panegyrics at the court of King Óláfr of Sweden. Here, too, the order is determined by personality; Gunnlaugr is judged to be more willful and is therefore allowed to go first.
3. There is an implication in this passage that an important factor in the retention of skaldic verse was aesthetic: verse judged to be good had a better chance of survival, though perhaps in this case it was the metrical novelty of *hrynhent* that ensured the memory of Arnórr's praise of Magnús. Haraldr was right about his own poem—not a single stanza of "Blágagladrápa" ("black goose" or "raven poem") has survived.
4. "A spear inlaid with gold" ("spjót gullrekit"). On such inlaid spears, see Falk, *Waffenkunde*, pp. 88–89.
5. The text reads "Kom sjá til nøkkurs løngum orðinn" and is difficult to parse. Cleasby/Vigfússon, s.v. *løngumorðinn*, suggest "long-talker" (in the vocative). *Løngum* can also be an adverb. *Flat* III, 322 (bottom) reads: "Kom sia til nockurs longum ordgnogt."

Chapter 23

1. The estate in Vík at Stokkar is modern Norwegian *Stokke*, in Vestfold, between Sandefjord and Tønsberg (see Kválen 1925a:12).
2. The word translated "outstanding qualities" is "vaskleikr," which is normally used to describe male valor. See Clover 1993:372 and 386–87.
3. Margrét has been introduced as "a highly intelligent woman," and that quality is now confirmed by her ability to foresee trouble. Cf. note 18.5 above.
4. Margrét's words about loving King Magnús only to lose him are not altogether transparent. They could be straightforward, but they could also be an attempt to reject Magnús without giving offense or to move him to relent. If so, they fail.
5. The problem here is incest. In general, see Magnús Már Lárusson, "Incest (*Island*)" in *KLNM* 7, 374–76. There is a special preoccupation with incest in *Morkinskinna*, as a number of passages suggest (see notes 65.4 and 70.3). It is possible that the topic had become

particularly burning in the wake of the relaxation of the marital impediments in the decisions of the Fourth Lateran Council in 1215. See Baldwin 1994:78. On the transmission of the council's rulings to Iceland, see Torfi H. Tulinius 1996.

Chapter 24

1. For a very helpful introduction, notes, and glossary to "Hreiðars þáttr," see Anthony Faulkes 1968. Faulkes (p. 87) speculates that the Glúmr in question might be the hero of *Víga-Glúms saga*, although that saga makes no mention of the killing of Hreiðarr.

2. This scene is reminiscent of an episode in *Egils saga* (*ÍF* 2, 102–3), in which a willful Egill forces his older brother Þórólfr to take him with him to Norway. Either episode could have stood as a model for the other, but if "Hreiðars þáttr" belongs to the original redaction of *Morkinskinna*, it is likely to have been primary. On the dating of "Hreiðars þáttr," see Faulkes 1968:20–22.

3. The verb "to trouble" is *kœja* and is *hapax*. See Faulkes 1968:87n.1/36. The brothers are said to put in at Bergen, but that may be an anachronism since Bergen did not really emerge until the time of Óláfr kyrri.

4. The word translated "unsightly" appears in the MS as "osycnligr." Faulkes (1968) discusses it on p. 88n.1/102. It is listed in *Norrøn ordbok*, p. 474 (s.v. *úsyknligr*), with the meaning "fælsleg, uhyggeleg" (uncanny). It could be a scribal error for *ósýnligr*, but that would duplicate the sense of the previous adjective, "ljótr" (ugly). Ásdís Egilsdóttir 1993 conjectures *úskynligr (unintelligent).

5. On ankle breeches, see Faulkes 1968:89n.1/123, and Falk, *Kleiderkunde*, p. 119.

6. The word rendered "sly" is "hugkvæmr," which Cleasby/Vigfússon, p. 291, gloss "ingenious"; Fritzner II, 82, "betænksom, agtsom"; Faulkes 1968:130, "ingenious, perceptive"; and *Norrøn ordbok*, p. 205, "aktsam, omtenksam, gløgg." These renderings do not bring out the negative valence clearly intended in this passage. The negative sense is most nearly conveyed in the phrase "hugkvæmr ok margbreytinn" (sly and fickle) in *Vápnfirðinga saga* (*ÍF* 11, 23) and *Þorsteins saga hvíta* (*ÍF* 11, 18). The Norwegians had, of course, a range of ethnic slurs about the Icelanders. See note 68.6.

7. Magnús's accommodation of Hreiðarr's rather outrageous request is in line with the kingly ideal of the common touch. See Snorri Sturluson's comment on the legendary Skjoldung king Hrólfr kraki in *Edda*, trans. Anthony Faulkes 1992:110: "He was the most notable of ancient kings primarily for generosity and valor and humility [*lítillæti*]." Óláfr Tryggvason's reception of the cantankerous skald Hallfreðr in *Hallfreðar saga* might also be compared (*ÍF* 8, 154).

8. This sentence renders the rather crabbed "'Háttung er ǫðrum á, þá,' segir hann, 'at lofgjarnliga sé við mælt, ef þú átt þetta eigi at sǫnnu sem mér lízk á þik ok ek sagða áðan.'" The general sense seems to be, "If my compliment is not genuine, then no compliment is genuine." See Faulkes 1968:90n.1/167.

9. There is a tradition of one characteristic defect in medieval historical portraiture. See Lars Lönnroth 1965:90–91.

10. A prophetic ability once again characterizes the exceptionally intelligent man. See notes 18.5 and 23.3.

11. "Quite strapping" renders "greit vaxligr" in the MS (FJ 130.17). Faulkes 1968: 90n.1/233, considers the reading corrupt and suggests *greppr vaskligr, but the adverbial *greitt* (from the adj. *greiðr*) in the sense of "straightforwardly, readily, clearly" seems acceptable here. See Cleasby, s.v. *greiðr* (p. 213), and Fritzner, s.v. *greiðr* (I, 636). The corruption may lie in the preceding "ok" for "en."

12. Faulkes 1968:55/249 conjectures *sjálfir finnask ("meet themselves") for the small lacuna here.

13. "Unashamedly" renders "grópasamliga," which is *hapax*. See Faulkes 1968:126, s.v. *grópasamliga*.
14. Cf. Haraldr gilli's outdistancing of Magnús blindi on horseback (Ch. 79 below).
15. Cf. the style of roughhousing in *Ljósvetninga saga* (*ÍF* 10, 72–73).
16. "Metal scabbard tips" translates "sverðskór" (*hapax*). See Falk, *Waffenkunde*, p. 34.
17. For a discussion of the authorial "I," which recurs a number of times below, see "Toward a Profile of the Author."
18. The witticism here plays off the fact that King Haraldr's father was nicknamed Sigurðr sýr (Sow). See Ch. 33 in Snorri's "Óláfs saga helga" (*ÍF* 27, 41; trans. Hollander, pp. 267–68). Any real or implied comparison of a man with a female animal constituted *níð* (slander) and was subject to a severe legal sanction (full outlawry). See the note to st. 74; also Whaley 1993:138–39.
19. This "strange" poem is not preserved, but if it was still known around 1200, it could have been a nucleus for the whole *þáttr*.
20. Cf. the opposite prediction about Sigurðr jórsalafari's life (Ch. 63). Sigurðr's life is compared to a lion, grand in the forequarters but tapering toward the hindquarters.
21. The peculiar idea that Hreiðarr will use the island to link Iceland and Norway suggests some larger theme. It seems to invert the story of how Óláfr Haraldsson wanted to acquire the island Grímsey in Eyjafjorðr from the Icelanders. That story is told in Snorri's "Óláfs saga helga" (*ÍF* 27, 215–16; trans. Hollander, pp. 394–95). The moral seems to be that friction will be minimized if both countries keep their own islands. Hreiðarr's Norwegian island could have a real parodistic edge in this context.
22. Svarfaðardalr is a valley off the west coast of Eyjafjorðr. Hreiðarr's residence there suggests that his story was most likely to have been passed down in the region of Eyjafjorðr.

Chapter 25

1. The chronological note on Rognvaldr Brúsason is perhaps taken over from a version of *Orkneyinga saga*. On the circumstances of his death, see the extant version of that saga (*ÍF* 34, 73–75). The date of Rognvaldr's death was 1046.
2. Þorgils Birnuson is not known from Saxo's *Gesta Danorum* or other sources. He is mentioned neither in *Fagrskinna* nor in *Heimskringla*.
3. Contrast Finnr Árnason's angry refusal to accept his life from King Haraldr (Ch. 42 at note 11). In that scene the author is critical of Finnr's unbridled anger, not admiring of his biting wit. In the present case he no doubt wishes the reader to value the stylishness of Þorkell geysir's response. That the anecdote did not find its way into *Fagrskinna* and *Heimskringla* is indicative of the tendency in those works to neglect the moralizing accents in *Morkinskinna* and focus more exclusively on the events of political history.
4. Finnur Jónsson 138.20–22 reads: "Ok get ek at verði þat eitthvert sinn, er mér þykki þessu misráðit." There is clearly a missing negative, which is found in Unger 45.7 and *Flat* III, 327.23–24. It is clearly visible in the facsimile of MskMS, folio 7B: "Ok get ek, at þat verði eitthvert sinni, at mér þykki þessu *eigi* misráðit."
5. The woman's assertiveness in matters of lineage may be compared to the pride of Ragnhildr Magnússdóttir in her dealings with Hákon Ívarsson (Ch. 42 at note 18).
6. Intelligence is once more equated with a precise calculation of what the future holds. Cf. notes 18.5, 23.3, and 24.10.
7. This is the Þorgils referred to above (note 25.2).
8. Cf. the appearance of Harold Godwinson unidentified before the Norwegian army at York and his colloquy with Jarl Tostig (Ch. 50 at note 4). The word translated "prance" is *burdeigja* and is an early occurrence of a Continental chivalric term. It occurs also in the German-derived *Þiðreks saga*. See Fritzner, s.v. (I, 216).

Chapter 26

1. Both *Fagrskinna* (*ÍF* 29, 248) and *Heimskringla* (*ÍF* 28, 105) delete this conversation, thus glossing over the contrast between Magnús's interest in his friends and his nation and Haraldr's self-interest. Once again, the moral preoccupation in *Morkinskinna* does not carry over into the later redactions. Similarly, the maxim in the following paragraph ("and surely the loyalty and valor of a good man is better than a heap of money") does not appear in *Fagrskinna* or *Heimskringla*.
2. Even in death, Magnús, the long-term planner, is able to exercise his foresight to outwit his uncle. This moment is also missing from *Fagrskinna* and *Heimskringla*. Cf. note 25.6.
3. This must be Þorsteinn Síðu-Hallsson (see note 20.1 above). According to *Njáls saga*, Þorsteinn fought in the Battle of Clontarf (1014), but he could still have been alive at the time of Magnús's death in 1047. See also *ÍF* 11, cvii–cviii. Þorsteinn did indeed have a son named Magnús. See the genealogy in "Geirmundar þáttr heljarskinns" (*Sturlunga saga* [1988], I, 6). This Magnús is the grandfather of Bishop Magnús Einarsson at Skálaholt, who died in 1148 and is mentioned in Ch. 83 below. Whatever source the author of *Morkinskinna* had on Bishop Magnús may also have been the source of his information on Þorsteinn Síðu-Hallsson, including the very precise details of Magnús's death scene.
4. Both Gehl 1939 and Mundal 1974 omitted *Morkinskinna* from consideration and therefore did not deal with this unique occurrence of the *fylgja* (companion spirit) motif.
5. Cf. note 9.3 above.
6. The feast of Simon (the Apostle) and Jude is celebrated on October 28.
7. The Helgeå (called here "Áin helga") is a river in Skåne (Scania) in what is now southern Sweden (see also Ch. 29). On the differing accounts of Magnús's death, see *ÍF* 28, 105n.2.
8. Note that Þorkell appears as Þorkell geysir in the previous chapter but as Þorkell geysa here. See Finnur Jónsson 1907:326, who interprets the word to mean something like "big mouth."
9. On the author's preoccupation with the prerogatives of noblewomen, see note 25.5 above.
10. The author is fond of registering precious gifts, for example, the bowl and mantle given to Steigar-Þórir by King Haraldr Sigurðarson (note 14.3) or the drinking vessel and cushions given to Bishop Magnús Einarsson by King Haraldr gilli (note 83.1). In this case, we are given no hint of how the information was transmitted in Iceland.

Chapter 27

1. Einarr echoes and underlines the importance of the advice given by Magnús on his deathbed (p. 182).
2. The Borgarþing was located near the modern Sarpsborg, east of Oslofjorden. See Didrik Arup Seip, "Borgarting," in *KLNM* 2, 148–49. It comprised the southeastern districts of Ranrike, Vingulmork, and Vestfold. See the map in *Heimskringla* (1991), III, 219.

Chapter 28

1. The idiom here is "rautt myndi fyrir brenna" (it might burn red). The image is perhaps that from the unpromising ashes a red flame might still spring. See *Norrøn ordbok*, s.v. *rauðr* (p. 337).
2. The healing of blindness or eye disease is among the commonest of Icelandic miracles. See Diana Whaley 1994:2.855–56.

3. On the term "choir," see Erik Moltke and Elna Møller, "Kor," in *KLNM* 9, 107–12. For a floorplan of Christ Church, see Anders Bugge, "Norge," in *Nordisk kultur* 23, 201.
4. On Oddr kikinaskald, see Finnur Jónsson, *Litteraturhistorie* I, 627.

Chapter 29

1. On the Eyra(r)þing, see note 1.14 above.

Chapter 30

1. This point marks the end of the insert from *Flat*. What followed in the lacuna was "Halldórs þáttr Snorrasonar," the first part of which is, therefore, missing and must be supplied from the other redaction edited in *ÍF* 5, 265–68 (from AM 66, fol., and Hr). There is another *þáttr* about Halldórr Snorrason in *Flat* I, 506–8.
2. On Kaupangr, see note 1.13 above.
3. Cf. the trick used by Sneglu-Halli to get ship passage at the end of his story (Ch. 43).
4. On whores in medieval Norway, see Allan Karker, "Prostitution," in *KLNM* 13, 505–8.
5. A retainer who had committed a breach of decorum was forced to empty a penalty libation (*vítishorn*). The most famous reference to that custom in Old Norse literature occurs in the episode detailing the god Þórr's visit to Útgarða-Loki in the *Prose Edda* (*SnE* I, 156; see also Reichborn-Kjennerud 1947:159).
6. Although Haraldr is angered at Halldórr's genealogical comparison, he embraces the point himself when he tells Sveinn from Lyrgja (Ch. 30 at note 8): "His [Halldórr's] ancestry in Iceland is no worse than yours in Norway, and not that much time has elapsed since those who now live in Iceland were Norwegians themselves." Haraldr's real sensitivity may be about his father Sigurðr sýr (Sow), already the subject of Hreiðarr's palpable joke (see st. 74 and note 24.18 above).
7. The meaning is either not quite clear or perhaps intentionally ambiguous. "And there is not much at stake" translates "litlu hættir nú til." That could mean that there is not much at stake in offending the king or that the money is so trivial that there is not much at stake in losing it.
8. That the Icelanders were Norwegians in the recent past connects with the question of whether the Icelanders are also to be considered the *þegnar* of the Norwegian king. See note 1.11 above. Bárðr's shuttle diplomacy in this episode is reminiscent of the mediation between Magnús berfœttr and Sveinki Steinarsson in Ch. 56 below.
9. On the institution of *veizlur* (hospitality owed to the king), see note 3.1 above.
10. This sentence renders: "Ok lét, at eigi skyldi verit hafa hans virðing meiri en þá, ef hann vildi farit hafa" (FJ 154.30–32). The phrasing is peculiar and not quite clear, but the sense must be that Halldórr will be honored even more than in his previous period of service. The MSS AM 66 and Hr add "ok engan mann skyldi hann hæra setja í Nóregi ótiginn, ef hann vildi þetta boð þekkjask" ("and he would raise no nonnoble man higher in Norway if he would accept this offer"). See *ÍF* 5, 276.
11. Since Halldórr's experience with King Haraldr would have formed the core of the Icelandic traditions about Haraldr, it seems likely that this king had the reputation of being tricky and unreliable in Iceland. See Jan de Vries 1931:61–63.
12. Einar Ól. Sveinsson prints "Eldisk árgalinn nú" in *ÍF* 5, 277 and glosses "hani" (rooster), an understanding retained by Ármann Jakobsson 1997:126, but Sverrir Tómasson points out to us that "árgali" could have the meaning "penis" and refers us to Jón Helgason 1975. This meaning gives the necessary bite to the phrase, and we translate accordingly.

13. The remark that Halldórr is not mentioned again (though he is in fact mentioned at the end of Ch. 40), although he has had a prominent role up to this point, suggests that the writer is thinking of a large narrative entity, perhaps *Morkinskinna* as a whole. Such remarks might encourage us to believe that *Morkinskinna* represents a unified literary concept.

Chapter 31

1. The word for "levy" here is "almenning(r)," which narrows the sense of "leiðangr," used in Bǫlverkr's stanza later. See Halvard Bjørkvik, "Leidang," in *KLNM* 10, 432–37. The law (see *NGL* II, 33) specified that the king could call up the levy for defense purposes or half the levy in times of peace. Accordingly, Snorri (*ÍF* 28, 109) specifies more exactly that King Haraldr raised half the *almenningr*.
2. The word for "flukes" is "krókar" and for trunks (or anchor stocks), "leggjar." Wartime rape is not discussed as such in Norse literature but is implied in the verbs *hernema* and *hertaka*, "capture in war." See Knut Robberstad, "Voldtægt," in *KLNM* 20, 239–40.
3. On the skald Grani, see Finnur Jónsson, *Litteraturhistorie* I, 634–35.
4. The term for "poem" here is *flokkr*, indicating a longer poem without a refrain. On Þorleikr fagri, see Finnur Jónsson *Litteraturhistorie* I, 641–42.
5. That tending pigs was considered a menial chore is illustrated by an episode in the first chapter of *Valla-Ljóts saga* (*ÍF* 9, 235) or a passage in "Helgakviða Hundingsbana II" (st. 39; Neckel/Kuhn, *Edda*, p. 158).
6. Vendilskagi is the town of Skagen at the northernmost tip of Jutland. Þjóð is Danish Thy, the area to the southwest of Vendill (Vendsyssel).
7. Heiðabýr (modern Danish Hedeby, on the River Schlei in Schleswig) was an important trade center in the Viking Age and the site of important archeological excavations. See Poul Enemark, "Hedebyhandel," in *KLNM* 6, 273–78, and Herbert Jankuhn 1986.
8. The women were presumably abducted for ransom or perhaps for the slave trade. On this practice in the Viking Age, see Horst Zettel 1977:133–35. There is a reminiscence of the trade in female slaves in Ch. 12 of *Laxdæla saga* (*ÍF* 5, 22–25).
9. Limafjǫrðr is the modern Danish Limfjord, the deep fjord and inlet that nearly severs the northern tip of Jutland at the level of Ålborg. Sámsey (Samsø) off central Jutland is placed too far north here. Accordingly, *Heimskringla* (*ÍF* 28, 116) changes the text to Hlésey (Læsø), which lies off northern Jutland.
10. At this point, there is a missing leaf in the MS. The following text is supplied from *Flat* III, 343.14–349.24.

Chapter 32

1. This formulation belongs in the context of the "humility topos" in medieval prefaces. See Sverrir Tómasson 1988:155–63.
2. Gabriel Turville-Petre 1968 gives a brief survey of Haraldr's poets in his Dorothea Coke Memorial Lecture of 1966. Gustav Indrebø 1928:173–80 sought to distinguish between a favorable image of the king projected by the poets and a less favorable image in the prose of *Morkinskinna*.
3. On the *skippund*, see Gelsinger 1981:34. Gelsinger calculates a *skippund* to be about 275 pounds or 125 kilograms.
4. Þingvellir (the "parliament plains") was established in 930 in southwestern Iceland as the site for the annual "national assembly." See Jón Jóhannesson 1974:35–74.
5. *Heimskringla* (*ÍF* 28, 79) specifies that Úlfr was the grandson of Ósvífr enn spaki. Further genealogical particulars are given in *Landnámabók* (*ÍF* 1, 123, 182–85).

6. *Ágrip* (*ÍF* 29, 40), *Fagrskinna* (*ÍF* 29, 262, 301), and *Heimskringla* (*ÍF* 28, 121, 198, 230) also make mention of Haraldr's construction of St. Mary's Church. *Ágrip* specifies, and *Heimskringla* (p. 121) lets it be understood, that the church was constructed to house the remains of St. Óláfr.

7. On the family of the Arnmœðlingar, see *Fagrskinna* (*ÍF* 29, 371–73) and *Heimskringla* (1991), III, 160.

Chapter 33

1. The dispute over a thief is reminiscent of the story of Ásu-Þórðr in Ch. 68.

2. King Haraldr's observation of Einarr's procession and the relevant one and a half stanzas are also found in the fragments of *Hákonar saga Ívarssonar* (1952), pp. 8–9, as well as in *Fagrskinna* (*ÍF* 29, 262–63) and *Heimskringla* (*ÍF* 28, 124). On the relationship of these texts to each other, see "The Native Sources."

Chapter 34

1. It does not seem possible that the Icelander could have had such a view from his ship. That could support Eivind Kválen's view that the author had never been in Trondheim (e.g., 1925a:35).

2. For examples of runic labeling, see *Norges innskrifter med de yngre runer*, II, 55–56 (note 3), 157, 167, and 341. The usual formula is "X owns this [object]." The story of Hákon jarl was told in the lost *Hlaðajarla saga and in the various versions of *Óláfs saga Tryggvasonar*.

3. For laws governing treasure-troves see *NGL* I, 58 ("Ældre Gulathingslov"), 257 ("Ældre Frostathingslov"), II, 101–2 ("Den nyere Landslov"). There seems to be a trend toward a greater share for the king, and this trend may underlie the tension between Haraldr and Einarr in the present passage.

4. The conflict here between the letter of the law and the king's authority is worked out in fuller and more dramatic detail in "Þinga saga" (Ch. 70).

Chapter 35

1. This sentence concludes "mun ek ekki svíkja hann né land undan honum." The word "land" has none of the patriotic connotations we are conditioned to hear. It is rather a question of Haraldr's legal title to the land. Nonetheless, it seems significant that Einarr puts national solidarity ahead of his personal differences with the king.

2. Hǫgni Langbjarnarson is otherwise unknown.

3. The author seems to be richly informed on Steigar-Þórir. On the transmission of this information, see note 14.3 above.

4. This sentence reads: "Þat er mér ekki til virðingar, heldr til háðungar ok at athlœgi." The contrast *háðung/virðing* is a variant of the contrast *háð/lof* in Ch. 58 (note 8) below. The contrast acquired critical importance with respect to the authenticity of skaldic verse in Snorri's preface to *Heimskringla* (*ÍF* 26, 5). See Sigurður Nordal 1973:136–37.

5. At this point, the lacuna filled from *Flat* ends and the main MS resumes.

6. The king appears to be as eager to tell his adventures as he is to listen to them as they are told by another in Ch. 40 below.

7. On this anecdote, see Gade 1995c:153–62.

8. The account of Einarr's death is given with some verbal correspondence but in greater detail in *Hákonar saga Ívarssonar* (1952), pp. 10–11. See "The Native Sources."

Chapter 36

1. Polar bears are mentioned elsewhere in the sagas as precious commodities. In Chs. 15–
   16 of *Vatnsdœla saga* (*ÍF* 8, 44), Ingimundr Þorsteinsson brings such a bear to King Haraldr
   hárfagri. According to *Hungrvaka*, Bishop Ísleifr Gizurarson presented Emperor Henry III
   of Germany with such a bear in 1056, and in 1123 Einarr Sokkason brought a bear from
   Greenland to Sigurðr jórsalafari ("Grœnlendinga þáttr," *ÍF* 4, 275). In the same "Grœnlendinga þáttr" (*ÍF* 4, 291–92), we are told that Kolbeinn Þorljótsson af Bataldri brought
   a bear from Greenland to Haraldr gilli but felt cheated of the reward and joined forces
   with Sigurðr slembir (see also Behrmann 1996:30 and 43). He then participated in the
   killing of Haraldr gilli and later died by drowning. The attack on Haraldr gilli and the
   drowning are told in *Morkinskinna* (U 206, 212; FJ 413, 423). The present text does not
   specify why Auðunn chooses to bring the bear to King Sveinn rather than King Haraldr,
   although the whole story seems to hinge on that point.
2. It was common practice for people to own half interest in land, a house, a ship, or an animal. For laws pertaining to such arrangements, see *Grágás* I, 63, and II, 245. See also
   Gulaþingslǫg (*NGL* I, 26) and *Landslǫg* (*NGL* II, 8; "Kjöpebolken," Ch. 18).
3. On Icelandic pilgrimages, see Paul Riant 1865:45–87; Einar Arnórsson 1954–58:1–45;
   Jakob Benediktsson, "Pilegrim," in *KLNM* 13, 305–6; Fabrizio D. Raschellà 1985–86:541–
   86; Carla Cucina 1998:83–155.
4. Þorsteinn Gyðuson is mentioned several times in *Sturlunga saga* ([1988], I, 71, 182, 187)
   and is located on Flatey in Breiðafjǫrðr. He died in 1190. Guðni Jónsson (*ÍF* 6, cvi) calculates that Auðunn is likely to have been Þorsteinn's grandfather. "Auðunar þáttr" is a particularly popular text and has often been printed separately (*ÍF* 6, cvii–cviii). Because of
   its popularity, there is also a small critical literature: Stefán Einarsson 1939:161–71; Gert
   Kreutzer 1986:100–108; Arnold R. Taylor 1946–53:78–96; Stig Wikander 1964:89–114.

Chapter 37

1. The Battle of Nesjar was fought between King Óláfr Haraldsson and Sveinn Hákonarson
   in 1015 (see *ÍF* 27, lxxxix).
2. Investment appears to be a subtheme in *Morkinskinna*. See, in particular, the story of Ásu-
   Þórðr (Ch. 68). For a brief survey of the trading situation, see Gelsinger 1981:149–80.
3. A passage in "Færeyinga þáttr" (*Flat* I, 130) seems to indicate that two distinguished boys
   are dressed in white tunics to denote slave status. White could be the natural color of the
   fabric, so that these passages may mean that the material is completely untreated (for example, with dye) and is therefore of the cheapest quality. See Falk 1919:40.

Chapter 38

1. See Hermann Pálsson 1990:117–30. Hermann traces the motif of the "king of Iceland"
   to a comment made by King Haraldr about Bishop Gizurr Ísleifsson in *Hungrvaka* (see
   Ch. 46). The motif reappears in *Bandamanna saga* (*ÍF* 7, 348–49). Brandr was the son of
   Vermundr in Vatnsfjǫrðr and is mentioned in *Laxdœla saga* and *Sturlunga saga*. Another
   cloak anecdote is told about him in *Flat* II, 140–42.
2. "Fine tunic" translates "skarlatskyrtill." See Falk 1919:54–55.
3. The primary transmitters of this story must have been Brandr himself and Þjóðólfr. It
   could therefore have been handed down in Vatnsfjǫrðr, Brandr's home, or in Eyjafjǫrðr,
   where Þjóðólfr was located. If Hermann Pálsson is right (note 38.1) that the author of

Bandamanna saga took the motif of the king of Iceland from "Brands þáttr," that may serve as evidence that the story of Brandr, or even the text of *Morkinskinna*, was known in the vicinity of Vatnsfjǫrðr, where *Bandamanna saga* is likely to have been written (*ÍF* 7, cxii).

4. King Haraldr's skill in interpreting Brandr's meaning is somewhat akin to his ability to interpret Stúfr blindi's laughter (Ch. 47). The king clearly had a reputation in Iceland for intellectual penetration. Cf. the summary of his personality in Ch. 32: "He had a profound intelligence, and it is the opinion of well-informed men that no one in all the northern lands was more penetrating than King Haraldr."

Chapter 39

1. King Haraldr's intelligence appears to extend to the medical field as well, as he has already demonstrated once before (Ch. 22). It seems not unlikely that Haraldr acquired his medical reputation because of his contact with the more advanced medicine of southern Europe during his service in Constantinople. On kings as healers in general, see Ármann Jakobsson 1997:112–14.

2. The "Beati Immaculati" is Psalm 118, the longest of the psalms and therefore something of a chore. The seven psalms are the penitential psalms, nos. 6, 31, 37, 50, 101, 129, and 142 in the Vulgate numbering.

3. It seems mysterious but probable that King Haraldr is reserving the woman for himself. How exactly her demonic illness is connected to her relationship with the king is unclear. The story seems to form a matching contrast to King Magnús's desired liaison with Margrét in Ch. 23. King Magnús accedes to the miraculously revealed wishes of St. Óláfr and refrains from the liaison. King Haraldr engages in quasi-magical practices and persists in his designs. King Magnús surrenders Margrét to a qualified husband, but Haraldr refuses to follow suit.

Chapter 40

1. This "þáttr" is missing in *Flat* but transmitted in a differing redaction in several manuscripts. Jón Jóhannesson reprints the separate redaction in *ÍF* 11, 335–36 (see also pp. cxii–cxiv) with the title "Þorsteins þáttr sǫgufróða" because the protagonist in this version bears the name Þorsteinn. Nothing is known about his family connections. On the implications of the "þáttr" for the oral transmission of saga materials, see Andreas Heusler 1957:205, and Heinrich Matthias Heinrichs 1975:225–31, 1976:114–33. Note that the storyteller's ability is accounted a branch of learning ("frœði"), and see Preben Meulengracht Sørensen 1993:36–38. The same is true of Stúfr blindi's poetic accomplishments in Ch. 47 (FJ 253 [from *Flat*]): "Ok muntu vera frœðimaðr mikill" (You must be a very learned man).

Chapter 41

1. Eysteinn orri ("heathcock," *tetrao tetrix*) belongs to the family of the Arnmœðlingar. See *ÍF* 29, 371 and *Heimskringla* (1991), III, 160.

2. The word translated "lodgings" is "skemma." Since mention is made of Þorvarðr's cargo, it seems possible that the "skemma" is a storage shed, but see Hilmar Stigum, "Skemma," in *KLNM* 15, 466–68. See also *Harðarsaga*, Ch. 13 (*ÍF* 13, 35, and note 6).

3. Since Þorvarðr has not been identified to the king as an Icelander, we may wonder

whether he can be so identified by his accent. Cf. the episode at the end of Ch. 50 (note 8), in which a resident of the English Danelaw recognizes Styrkárr as a Norwegian by his speech. In general, see William Moulton 1988:9–28.

4. Cf. the competition in bestowing awards between King Haraldr and King Sveinn in "Auðunar þáttr" (Ch. 36).

5. The phrase "flensa í milli segla" is of uncertain meaning. *Flensa* in Modern Icelandic means to kiss or lick. Since Haraldr laughs, we may suspect some sexual innuendo. Perhaps the sails are being compared to bedclothes since they too might harbor lovers in a storm. Some such nautical pun as the one attempted in our translation might catch the tone.

Chapter 42

1. The Sea of Jutland (Kattegat) lies between northern Jutland and the Swedish province of Halland. The Lófufjǫrðr (modern Swedish Lagan) runs into Laholmsbukten on the southernmost coast of Halland near the province of Skáney (Skåne, Scania).

2. The word "hundred" (*hundrað*) in Old Norse can mean either 100 or 120 (the so-called "long hundred"). It is not always clear which is meant, and we adopt the solution of translating *hundrað* with the English "hundred" on the understanding that this may mean the larger number. For example, the 300 ships referred to here could be 360. See Magnús Már Lárusson, "Hundrað," in *KLNM* 7, 83–87.

3. This is another of the interesting passages that comment on the reason for the preservation of a particular piece of lore. Cf. note 17.2. The snake episode is taken over from *Ágrip* (*ÍF* 29, Ch. 40, p. 38). *Fagrskinna* omits it, and *Heimskringla* (*ÍF* 28, 139; trans. Hollander, p. 622) attaches it to an earlier episode in the Limfjord.

4. The story about Ívarr hvíti and Sigvatr is not preserved in other sources. The "Compendium" of *Hákonar saga Ívarssonar* (Appendix) gives no hint of it. One possible source might be *Hlaðajarla saga.

5. On other versions of the story that follows, notably *Hákonar saga Ívarssonar*, the "Compendium" (Appendix), and *Heimskringla*, see "The Native Sources."

6. Ketill af Hringunesi was married to Gunnhildr, sister of Haraldr. Their daughter Sigríðr married Eindriði, son of Einarr þambarskelfir. Ketill's son was Guthormr, who stayed in Dublin, and *Morkinskinna* (U 111; FJ 264) mentions him as an emissary in Jarl Tostig's efforts to solicit support from Haraldr for the invasion of England. See also *Heimskringla* (*ÍF* 28, 122, 135).

7. It was customary to maintain a formation in naval battle by chaining the ships together. See Falk 1912:116–17.

8. The presence of Þórólfr mostrarskegg is a chronological aberration that is difficult to explain. According to the chronology of *Eyrbyggja saga* (*ÍF* 4, xxx–xxxiv) Þórólfr lived in the second half of the ninth century, not the middle of the eleventh century. Perhaps a great (or great great) grandson also named Þórólfr was involved in this battle and was given the ancestral nickname by mistake, but the genealogies reveal no such Þórólfr (see *ÍF* 1, 2, Genealogy VIII [Þórsnesingar]). Neither *Fagrskinna* nor *Heimskringla* makes mention of him.

9. "Victory beacon" translates "sigrbákn," in which *bákn* is the Frisian or English word "beacon." Nothing is known about this allegedly foreign custom, but *sigrbákn* looks like a very common kenning type for "sword" (cf. Hrólfr kraki's sword "Sigrljómi" [Falk, *Waffenkunde*, p. 58]), and we may suspect that the foreign custom has been derived from a misunderstood kenning. See Rudolf Meissner 1921:150–51.

10. St. Lawrence's Day is celebrated on August 10. On Steinn Herdísarson, see Finnur Jónsson, *Litteraturhistorie* I, 639–41.

11. The observation that a stallion fights more fiercely in the presence of a mare appears to have a basis in reality. See Bjarni Vilhjálmsson 1990:20–21. The authorial comment on

the transmission of the anecdote is in line with other such comments (cf. notes 17.2 and 42.3 above). That the anecdote was remembered for a negative reason (because it demonstrated lack of control), as the author alleges, seems unlikely. It was more likely to have been remembered as an excellent example of the biting rejoinder, hence of control rather than lack of control. The author's moral comment may therefore be somewhat out of line with popular culture.

12. "You don't look promising" (i.e., you must have bad news) translates Finnur Jónsson's reading "þit látið óvænliga" (214.14), although he allows the possibility of "miceliga" for "óvænliga," as in Unger 81.14. Unger's reading "mikiliga" (boastfully) might be understood to mean "you have a boastful or grandiose way about you" or perhaps "you must have something important on your minds." *Flat* III, 364, reads "mikiliga."

13. On the anecdote in general, see Knut Liestøl 1930:232, Joseph Harris 1979:57–81, and Joaquín Martínez Pizarro 1996:319–26. The anecdote is mentioned in the "Compendium" (Appendix) and must therefore have been in *Hákonar saga Ívarssonar*. The author's subjoined comment is again interestingly moralistic (cf. notes 17.2, and 42.3, 11).

14. The word translated "breakfast" is "dǫgurðr" or "dagverðr." See Bertil Ejder, "Måltidsordning," in *KLNM* 12, 118–23.

15. Whoever this Þórólfr was, his exploit must have lived on in some detail in Icelandic tradition. On the face of it, the tradition seems most likely to have been transmitted in Þórólfr mostrarskegg's native Vatnsfjǫrð in the northwest. On the other hand, a chronological confusion is unlikely to have occurred in his native tract. That could constitute an argument that *Morkinskinna* was not written in nearby Þingeyrar but in some other area.

16. The feast of St. Vincent is celebrated on January 22. The connection between Sveinn and this saint is not clear, but it could be that this was the saint on whose relics Sveinn swore allegiance to Magnús (see Ch. 4). Cormack (1994:158) suggests that the Norwegian capture of the reliquary could have reflected the presence of the relics of St. Vincent in Norway.

17. It is unclear who the third leader was in the company of Þórólfr and Prince Magnús. That name seems to have been omitted by oversight.

18. On the ill repute of the viking, see Fritz Askeberg 1944:129–34, Kaaren Grimstad 1972:2.250–52, and Staffan Hellberg 1980:72–74. See also King Óláfr's admonition to Bjǫrn in *Bjarnar saga Hítdœlakappa* (*ÍF* 3, 133).

19. The conversation between Haraldr and Ragnhildr is closely paralleled in *Bǫglunga sǫgur* (p. 115).

20. It is almost commonplace that a man who leaves Norway at odds with the king kills or expels one or more of the royal stewards in retaliation. See *Egils saga* (*ÍF* 2, 69), *Eyrbyggja saga* (*ÍF* 4, 5), or *Hallfreðar saga* (*ÍF* 8, 139–40). See also note 68.12 below.

21. On the matter-of-factness of rape in wartime, see note 31.2 above.

22. It is true that Hákon sided with King Haraldr at the Battle of the River Niz, but the version of that battle differs here from *Hákonar saga Ívarssonar*, in which Hákon secured Sveinn's escape from the battle and would have had every reason to count on the Danish king's gratitude.

23. On gold embroidery, see Falk 1919:25.

24. Þorfinnr appears in the form Toruidus Crassus (Þorviðr enn digri) in the Latin "Compendium" (Appendix). In this version he is struck by a "tyrstage" (a Danish word is used), a "bullstake," or perhaps more generally, a "hitching stake." Unger (90.2) read "hel" (*hæll* 'stake'), but Finnur Jónsson (229.3) read "stein," though he noted that the word was unclear. A note in *ÍF* 28, 163 indicates that the name Þyrnir (instead of Þorviðr) appears in a Swedish source.

25. This ill-advised exploit is similar to the one undertaken earlier by Þórólfr and Prince Magnús. The moral seems to be that King Haraldr devises plans that are unexceptionable and are only compromised by his rash followers.

26. On the following episode, see "The Native Sources." It is paralleled in *Ljósvetninga saga*

(*ÍF* 10, 103) and *Heimskringla* (*ÍF* 28, 165), but the version in *Morkinskinna* may well be the point of departure. The events referred to took place in Eyjafjǫrðr, and it seems most likely that the story was transmitted there.

27. The Latin "Compendium" gives a somewhat different genealogical account, saying that Hákon had two daughters (both unnamed), one of whom was married to "Hákon the Norwegian," by whom she had Erik Lam. According to *Knýtlinga saga* (*ÍF* 35, 231), "Hákon the Norwegian," who was married to Ragnhildr, the daughter of Erik Ejegod, was the son of Hákon Ívarssons daughter Sunnifa. Their son was Erik Lam. *Fagrskinna* and *Heimskringla* give no genealogical information, but the "Arnmœðlingatal" (*ÍF* 29, 373) agrees with the "Compendium" that Hákon's daughter was married to Jarl Páll Þorfinnsson of Orkney and was the mother of Hákon jarl. See Genealogy V in *ÍF* 28 and *Orkneyinga saga*, Ch. 35 (*ÍF* 34, 89).

Chapter 43

1. The text of this story is printed from both *Morkinskinna* and *Flateyjarbók* (from a different exemplar) in *ÍF* 9, 263–95. The nickname "Sneglu" suggests irascibility. S.v. *sneglinn* Blöndal gives the Danish "hidsig, bidsk, trættekær," and Arngrímur Sigurðsson (1970, s.v. *sneglulegur*), gives "touchy, hasty-tempered, waspish, testy." See also Finnur Jónsson 1907: 297, and *ÍF* 9, 263n.1.
2. Agðanes (Norwegian Agdenes) is a promontory at the mouth of Trondheimsfjorden.
3. Gásir (or Gásar) was an important harbor on the west coast of Eyjafjǫrðr in northern Iceland (see Gelsinger 1981:32). Hitrar (Norwegian Hitra) is a large island facing Trondheimsfjorden.
4. On this sort of sexual banter, see Carol J. Clover 1979:124–45.
5. For comparable skaldic tasks, see the challenges to Þórarinn stuttfeldr in Ch. 72 and to Einarr Skúlason at the end of Ch. 97 below.
6. See the notes to sts. 119–20.
7. See the note to st. 122.
8. That gruel was considered meager fare is illustrated by a dismissive comment in *Eyrbyggja saga* (*ÍF* 4, 24) and *Gísla saga* (*ÍF* 6, 116), and a gruel joke is found as early as Charlemagne's circle of court poets (contrived by Theodulf of Orléans at Alcuin's expense). See Peter Godman 1985:11–12.
9. This passage apparently refers to the disbursement of tithes. According to the Icelandic tithe law, one fourth of the tithes was to be distributed among needy people with dependents, and the disbursement could be made in cloth, marketable furs, sheepskins, food, or any kind of livestock (except horses). However, tithes were not legislated until 1097, that is, considerably later than our story would imply. See Jón Jóhannesson 1974:169, 174.
10. Einarr fluga was the son of Hárekr ór Þjóttu and the grandson of Eyvindr Finnsson skaldaspillir (see Genealogy II in *ÍF* 28).
11. "Inequitable man" translates *ójafnaðarmaðr*, a widespread character type in the sagas. A refusal to compensate killings always brings with it public disapprobation, as in the case of Víga-Styrr in *Heiðarvíga saga*, Hrafnkell in *Hrafnkels saga*, or Þorbjǫrn Þjóðreksson in *Hávarðar saga Ísfirðings*. See Preben Meulengracht Sørensen 1993:195–97.
12. When, in *Heiðarvíga saga*, Barði Guðmundarson appeals for compensation three successive times in three successive years, it is understood to be a demonstration of admirable patience (*ÍF* 3, 259).
13. On the episode in Hákon jarl's life referred to here, see "Þorleifs þáttr" in *ÍF* 9, 213–29, and Bo Almqvist 1965:186–205.
14. In most Old Norse penal codes, theft was considered a serious offense that in some cases was punished by death (see Gade 1985:159–83).

15. This peculiar form of reward is reminiscent of st. 13 in "Hlǫðskviða" (Neckel/Kuhn, *Edda*, p. 305).

16. The comment about the poor quality of Halli's praise poem must derive from a *lausavísa* by Halli (lv. 7; *Skj* IA, 389; *Flat* III, 426; *ÍF* 9, 292–93), in which he enumerates the metrical mistakes in the encomium of the English "king" (apparently, Jarl Harold Godwinson). See Gade 1991:361–74.

Chapter 44

1. The heading is supplied by Unger. None is found in Finnur Jónsson's edition. There is a rather different version of the same story in *Fríssbók*. See the careful comparison by Bjarne Fidjestøl (1971). Fidjestøl considers the two versions to be a prime example of oral variants.

2. The metrical flaw in Þjóðólfr's line was caused by the rhyme "grǫm : skǫmm," in which the two rhyming syllables were of unequal length (see Gade 1995a:6).

3. The implication in this passage is that fishing is a subsistence occupation. *Bandamanna saga* (*ÍF* 7, 295–97) provides an interesting account of how a man works his way up from nothing, beginning with fishing, which was apparently at the bottom of the economic scale.

Chapter 45

1. The title of this chapter is supplied by Unger. The story of Tryggvi Óláfsson (the alleged son of King Óláfr Tryggvason) is told in *Heimskringla* (*ÍF* 27, 411–14). The principle that seems to connect Chs. 44–47 is their relevance to King Haraldr's retinue. Ch. 48 ("Odds þáttr") is also a retinue story to the extent that it concludes with Þorsteinn's departure from the retinue. Retinue stories may have figured as an oral subgenre.

Chapter 46

1. The title of this cameo chapter is again supplied by Unger. On the Icelander as king see note 38.1. Gizurr Ísleifsson was bishop at Skálaholt († 1118).

Chapter 47

1. The story of Þórðr Glúmsson's marriage to Guðrún Ósvífrsdóttir is told in *Laxdœla saga* (*ÍF* 5, 93–100 and Genealogy IV).

2. The text of MskMS is defective in the following passage and must be supplemented from *Flat* (Unger 104–5; FJ 252–53). That there is something funny about being "the cat's son" ("kattar sonr") is suggested by the line "óneiss sem kattar sonr" (blameless as a cat's son) in "Helgakviða Hundingsbana I," st. 18 (Neckel/Kuhn, *Edda*, p. 133).

3. Compare the reference to Haraldr's paternity in "Hreiðars þáttr" above (note 24.18). The testing of the king's intelligence is similar to the theme of "Brands þáttr ǫrva" (Ch. 38 above).

4. The defective passage ends here.

5. Stúfr's request for the king's letter and seal in order to obtain property is paralleled in *Bjarnar saga Hítdœlakappa* (*ÍF* 3, 126).

6. It is not recorded that the king was obliged to consult his retainers on such matters, but paragraph 18 of *Hirðskrá* (*NGL* II, 406–7) may intimate that such was the custom. See also *Jómsvíkinga saga*, ed. Ólafur Halldórsson, p. 134.

Chapter 48

1. This "þáttr" was edited with introduction and notes by Guðni Jónsson in *ÍF* 7, 367–74. Oddr Ófeigsson is a leading character in *Bandamanna saga*, but saga and "þáttr" appear to be independent of each other.
2. The fullest account of the Lapp trade in Norway is in *Egils saga* (*ÍF* 2, 24–54). It is also an important element in "Þinga saga" (Ch. 70). A passage in the *réttarbœtr* of Sigurðr, Eysteinn, and Óláfr (*Frostathingslov* 16.2 in *NGL* I, 257–58) addresses the matter of the king's monopoly in Hálogaland and the penalties for any infringement of his rights. The present *þáttr* may very well grow out of issues connected with the legislation of these kings.
3. Þjótta (Norwegian Tjøtta) is an island off the southernmost part of Hálogaland at the mouth of the present Vefnsfjorden.
4. Mjǫla is identified in *ÍF* 7, 369, as the island Meløya off Hálogaland. The author places Mjǫla south of Þjótta, but if the identification with Meløya is correct, that island is in fact north of Þjótta (see Eivind Kválen 1925a:24).
5. Much of Þórir hundr's story is told in *Óláfs saga helga*. In his "Magnúss saga ens góða" (*ÍF* 28, 22), Snorri tells us that shortly after the Battle of Stiklastaðir, in which he fought against King Óláfr, Þórir went to Jerusalem and was reputed not to have returned. On the legend in general, see Bjarne Fidjestøl 1997:168–83.
6. The following passage is again defective (the verso of leaf 17 noted above in 47.2) and must be filled in from *Flat* (Unger 107.23–108.4; FJ 258–59).
7. "Þat er fornt mál, herra, at opt verðr villr, sá er geta skal." The saying is not included in Halldór Halldórsson's *Orðtakasafn*.
8. The defective passage ends here. This story is very reminiscent of a sequence in *Njáls saga* (*ÍF* 12, 217–20) in which Njáll's sons hide Þráinn Sigfússon from Hákon jarl using similar tricks. *Njáls saga* is presumably the borrower. There are somewhat similar search routines with increasingly ingenious hiding places in *Eyrbyggja saga* (*ÍF* 4, 50–54) and *Fóstbrœðra saga* (*ÍF* 6, 243–48). When King Haraldr refers to the matter as a "capital crime," it is presumably because the king's revenue has been in effect stolen (or so he believes).
9. Oddr gives an interesting elaboration of the action here. Perhaps we should imagine that he has it from private conversations with Þorsteinn. It emphasizes that the story celebrates the Norwegian who befriends the Icelander as much as the Icelander himself. Thus it illustrates how personal benevolence could temper political strains in the minds of Icelanders. The fullest illustration of this principle is the story of Egill Skallagrímsson and his Norwegian friend Arinbjǫrn. The story of Oddr and Þorsteinn was no doubt handed down especially in his native region around Miðfjǫrðr in the northwest of Iceland.
10. In a similar episode in Ch. 26 of *Ljósvetninga saga* (*ÍF* 10, 85) the Ljósvetningar try to purchase the collaboration of Skegg-Broddi Bjarnason with a gold ring, although he is married to a kinswoman of their antagonists, the Mǫðrvellingar. Broddi tries to reconcile his wife to his new allegiance by pretending the ring is for her, but she sees through the deception.

Chapter 49

1. On the situation in England, see Loyn 1977:98. The Jarl Úlfr referred to here is the father of Sveinn Úlfsson, Haraldr harðráði's great antagonist. William of Malmesbury gives a much fuller account of the events at the end of Book 2 of the *Gesta Regum Anglorum*

(*WM* I, 280–82). *Morkinskinna, Fagrskinna,* and *Heimskringla* differ slightly on the dates of Edward's death and Harold's coronation. None of them matches William of Malmesbury's account exactly.

2. Tostig elaborates the logic of "Hávamál," st. 43 (Neckel/Kuhn, *Edda,* p. 23): "Vin sínum / skal maðr vinr vera / þeim ok þess vin; / en óvinar síns / skyli engi maðr / vinar vinr vera" (A man should be a friend to his friend, and to that friend's friend; but no man should be a friend to his friend's enemy). The next step is to be a friend to your enemy's enemy.

3. William of Malmesbury (I, 281) tells us that Jarl Tostig met with King Haraldr in Scotland. The statement in *Morkinskinna* that Tostig went to Normandy corresponds in some degree with Snorri's statement that he went to Flanders (*ÍF* 28.172). Of the Norman and Anglo-Norman historians, only Ordericus Vitalis mentions a mission by Tostig to Haraldr of Norway (*OV* II, 142–5; see also his interpolations in William of Jumièges [II, 162/3]).

4. On the *þingamenn,* see the note to st. 132 and Bjarni Guðnason in *Danakonunga sǫgur* (*ÍF* 35, xciii–xciv). See also Ólafur Halldórsson 1994:2.617–40.

5. The reference to Steigar-Þórir here is found only in *Morkinskinna* and again suggests that the author had special access to traditions about Þórir.

6. In the main MS, this sentence ends "at hann gerði þungan," but it looks as though something may be missing. *Flat* III, 389 reads: "Þat verðr þá, er konungr sté út á bátinn, at gerði svá þungan, at hann fekk varla borit hann" (It happened when the king stepped out onto the boat that he became so heavy that it could hardly bear him).

7. According to *Morkinskinna,* Haraldr leaves his wife Þóra and his daughter María behind in Orkney. *Fagrskinna* (p. 278) speaks of Ellisif and María, while *Heimskringla* (p. 179) speaks of Ellisif, María, and Ingigerðr (Þóra having been left in Norway).

8. Morkere (Mǫrukári) was the son of Ælfgar jarl of Mercia. Waltheof (Valþjófr) was the son of Siwarth jarl of Northumbria. Thus they were neither brothers nor sons of Godwin. Furthermore, Waltheof did not participate in the Battle of the River Ouse.

9. The Feast of St. Matthew is celebrated on September 21.

Chapter 50

1. Eysteinn orri belongs to the clan of the Arnmœðlingar (see note 41.1 above). The author of *Morkinskinna* seems to have had a good conduit of information on this group, but it is not possible to reconstruct the transmission.

2. On the Battle of Stamford Bridge in terms of military history, see Gelsinger 1988:13–29 and Hughes 1988:30–76.

3. On the motif of the ominous fall, see Ove Moberg 1940–42:545–75.

4. On the concept of "luck" in Norse literature, see especially Gehl 1939. The word used here is *hamingja.*

5. The author lapses here into the first person (see note 24.17).

6. On Þorkell hamarskald, see Finnur Jónsson, *Litteraturhistorie* II, 54–55.

7. The elaborate description of this battle sequence may betoken the author's special interest in military matters, which is also evident in his description of Haraldr's Mediterranean exploits and the careers of Sigurðr jórsalafari and Magnús berfœttr.

8. See note 41.3 above.

Chapter 51

1. King Haraldr and his daughter María die at the same moment, "and people said that they shared the same life." The same idea is found in *Fagrskinna* (*ÍF* 29, 290) and in *Orkneyinga saga* (*ÍF* 34, 87; also *Magnúss saga lengri,* p. 339), but the shared life is omitted by Snorri (*ÍF* 28, 197).

2. The word for "ergotism" is *reformr* (FJ 282.30). Ingvald Reichborn-Kjennerud 1942:118–21 argues that because this illness is fatal for Magnús, it cannot be the benign skin condition called ringworm. He equates it rather with ergotism, which begins with a red rash around the affected limb. See also his *VGT*, Pt. 3, 1940:155–60.

3. The town in which Óláfr resides is presumably Niðaróss (Trondheim) since it is mentioned in the next sentence, although we are told below in Ch. 53 (note 2) that a particularly fine trading center was established in Bjǫrgvin (Bergen) during his reign. Snorri (*ÍF* 28, 204) makes this trading center Óláfr's personal creation.

4. The following genealogical information is filled out in greater detail by Snorri (*ÍF* 28, 198). The fact that the author refers to Skúli as "Skúli jarl" is used as a dating index (see "Time and Place of Composition"). This is the first mention of King Ingi Bárðarson.

5. Rein is a farmstead located by Stadbygd in Rissa herred in Fosen, Sørtrøndelag (see Eivind Kválen 1925a:21).

6. Elgisetr (Elgeseter) was a monastery in the vicinity of Niðaróss (see the map in *Heimskringla* [1991], III, 232). *Ágrip* (*ÍF* 29, 40) tells us that Haraldr's body was first buried at St. Mary's Church and later moved to Elgisetr.

Chapter 52

1. On Odmarus, see M. van Uyfanghe, "Audomarus," in *LM*, 1, 1197–98. He died ca. 670 and survives in the name of the Flemish town Saint-Omer. His miracles are recorded in a *vita* published in *MGH: Scriptores Rerum Merowingicarum*, 5, 753–64. See also Gade 1997.

2. For a selection of English and Norman sources bearing on these momentous events, see R. Allen Brown 1984. William of Malmesbury (I, 279–80) relates Harold's stay with William in a different form, making mention of Harold's betrothal to William's daughter but not his love affair with William's wife. Snorri (*ÍF* 28, 169) has a curious reminiscence of William's account of Harold's storm-tossed passage to Normandy, but there has been little study of the relationship between the English and Norse sources. English accounts of the events surrounding the Norman Conquest do not refer to Norse sources. See, for example, Frank Barlow 1983:107–9; H. R. Loyn 1982:58–59, 85–89; D. J. A. Matthew 1966:73–79.

3. In actuality, the Battle of Hastings (October 13) followed the Battle of Stamford Bridge (September 25) by a mere three weeks.

Chapter 53

1. Konungahella, southeast of Oslofjorden on the Swedish border, came closest to being equidistant from the chief residences of the kings of Denmark, Norway, and Sweden. It was therefore well situated as a meeting place. It lay at the mouth of the Gòtaälv, which is more frequently referred to as the traditional meetingplace of kings (e.g., FJ 22, 165, 292, 329), as it is at the end of this chapter.

2. On Óláfr kyrri and the founding of Bergen, see Knut Helle 1982:87–113.

3. On these leg rings, see Marina Mundt 1993:31–32.

4. On the seating arrangements described here, see Wilhelm Holmqvist and Hilmar Stigum, "Högsäte," in *KLNM* 7, 290–93.

5. St. Knútr (Cnut) reigned 1080–1086 and was succeeded by his son Óláfr (Hunger) (reigned 1086–1095).

6. Snorri explains the bare-legged style adopted by Magnús and his men from their experience in the western (Celtic) countries (*ÍF* 28, 229; trans. Hollander, p. 681). Saxo Grammaticus (*Gesta Danorum* 13.1, p. 342; trans. Christiansen I, 108) gives a different explanation for Magnús's nickname.

7. The author mentions King Haraldr's construction of St. Mary's Church in Niðaróss in Ch. 32 above. On the question of height, see *Heimskringla* (*ÍF* 28, 199n.1).
8. In the kings' sagas generally, good kings are associated with good harvests. See Snorri's "Ynglinga saga" (*ÍF* 26, 23–25, 31–32, 74–75) and "Hákonar saga góða" (*ÍF* 27, 170, 176). See also Hans Hubert Anton 1968:103, 106, J. M. Wallace-Hadrill 1971:56, 105, and Ármann Jakobsson 1997:250.
9. Snorri (*ÍF* 28, 204, and note 4) explains that King Óláfr established a Miklagildi (Great Guild) in Niðaróss and other towns in the place of looser movable drinking occasions called *hvirfingsdrykkjur*. The guilds were regulated by detailed bylaws. See Grethe Authén Blom, "Gilde (Norge)," in *KLNM* 5, 308–13.
10. King Óláfr's policy is very much in line with that of King Magnús góði before him. In Ch. 7, Magnús had refrained from pressing his claim in England, and in Ch. 26 he advised his uncle Haraldr to refrain from pressing his claim in Denmark. The contrast between peaceful and aggressive foreign policy is thematic in *Morkinskinna*.
11. On this reference to a *Knúts saga, see Bjarni Aðalbjarnarson 1937:151. Bjarni thinks that it is probably a reference to *Knýtlinga saga*, which tells of King Óláfr's dealings with King Knútr Sveinsson in similar language (*ÍF* 35, 163–64) but is considerably later than *Morkinskinna*. The passage in *Morkinskinna* would then have to be an interpolation.

Chapter 54

1. The "þáttr" of the kráku-karl is omitted in *Fagrskinna* and some redactions of *Heimskringla* (but see Louis-Jensen 1977:37–39, 87–94). It is strange that a single such story should have been preserved about King Óláfr, especially one so out of keeping with the personality otherwise attributed to this king. The humor is so perverse that we may wonder whether an anecdote originally connected with Haraldr harðráði was somehow transferred to Óláfr kyrri. That surmise derives plausibility from the fact that a contest of intelligence is in line with Haraldr's literary personality.
2. This place name appears not as "Haukstaðir" but as "Haukbœr" in *Ágrip* (*ÍF* 29, 41), *Fagrskinna* (*ÍF* 29, 302), and *Heimskringla* (*ÍF* 28, 209). Haukbœr is modern Håkeby, between Kville and Vettaland in Bohuslän (medieval Ranríki). See Kválen (1925a:28), who stated that there had never been a farmstead Haukstaðir in Ranríki and that this form in *Morkinskinna* must therefore be an error.

Chapter 55

1. Permia (Bjarmaland) is the area in northern Russia abutting the White Sea (see the map in *Heimskringla* [1991], III, 214).
2. On St. Clement's Church in Niðaróss, see Dietrich Hofmann 1987 and 1997.
3. The Christmas contributions are referred to as "jólagjafar" (FJ 297.19), but they represent some sort of exaction rather than a festive exchange of gifts. See Peter Andreas Munch, *Det norske folks historie*, 1.2, 815–17, 852–53; 2, 269–70, 568–70. See also *NGL* I, 58, 257, and V, 327. The passage in *Morkinskinna* is taken over from *Ágrip* (*ÍF* 29, 52). Ch. 29 of *Ágrip* (*ÍF* 29, 28–29) describes how Christmas exactions were imposed by King Knútr (Cnut the Great) of Denmark on Norwegian farmers and were not rescinded until the time of Sigurðr jórsalafari. The matter is discussed by Bjarni Einarsson in *ÍF* 29, xii–xiii.
4. This policy may be compared to the way in which Magnús's sons seek to gain the favor of the people on their accession in Ch. 60 (note 60.1).
5. Candlemas falls on February 2.
6. Hefring (Høvringen) is a promontory west of Niðaróss. See the map in *Heimskringla* (1991), III, 271.

7. On the legal value of proffered friendship, see Andersson and Miller 1989:21–22 and Miller 1990:331–32 (note 47). Steinbjǫrg is Steinberget in the vicinity of Niðaróss (see the map in *Heimskringla* [1991], III, 232).

8. On the author's special knowledge of traditions about Steigar-Þórir, see notes 35.3 and 14.3 above.

9. On the skald Gísl Illugason, see Finnur Jónsson, *Litteraturhistorie* II, 55–59. There is a "Gísls þáttr Illugasonar" in *Hulda-Hrokkinskinna* (*FmS* VII, 29–41) and in *Jóns saga helga* (*Bisk* I, 221–27). On the relationship of these redactions, see Louis-Jensen 1977:111–22.

10. The place name Qrvahamrar has not been identified.

11. On the importance of royal blood in the succession, see Sverre Bagge 1991:130, 135, 148.

12. Here the scribe's mind seems to have reverted to Sveinn's father, Haraldr flettir.

13. Snorri identifies Sigurðr as a *lendr maðr* and the son of Loðinn Viggjarskalli (*ÍF* 28, 214).

14. Vagnvík (Vanvikan) is the shore directly across the fjord from Niðaróss (see the map in *Heimskringla* [1991], III, 271). Þexdalr (Teksdal) and Seljuhverfi (Jøssund sogn) are marked on the same map.

15. Harmr is the modern Velfjorden close to the island of Vega and a little south of Þjótta (Tjøtta).

16. Eivind Kválen (1925a:90) notes that Seljutún is an error for Hesjutún (modern Hesttun), which is found in *Ágrip* (*ÍF* 29, 44), *Fagrskinna* (*ÍF* 29, 304), and *Heimskringla* (*ÍF* 28, 216). Vambarhólmr is the island of Vomma (see the map in *Heimskringla* [1991], III, 269).

17. Snorri describes the construction of Óláfr Tryggvason's ship Ormr enn langi in his "Óláfs saga Tryggvasonar" (*ÍF* 26, 335–36; trans. Hollander, pp. 220–21).

18. Óláfr Tryggvason's last great battle on Ormr enn langi was fought at Svǫlðr in the year 1000. The battle is described in epic detail by Oddr Snorrason in his *Óláfs saga Tryggvasonar* (Chs. 69–75) and is celebrated as "the most famous battle in northern lands." The battle would therefore have been familiar to everyone quite apart from Oddr's written account, but his book may nonetheless have been available to the author of *Morkinskinna*. According to Oddr, no one on Ormr enn langi fled. The king himself is invited to do so but refuses (Ch. 73). On our author's possible knowledge of Oddr Snorrason's book, see also notes 1.7, 9.5, 13.4.

19. For the family of Viðkunnr and the Bjarkey people, see Genealogy IX in *ÍF* 28.

20. *Morkinskinna*, *Ágrip*, and *Fagrskinna* make Egill the son of Áskell, but *Heimskringla* (*ÍF* 28, 214) makes him the son of Áslákr af Forlandi. According to *Ágrip*, *Fagrskinna*, and *Heimskringla* he is married to Ingibjǫrg, daughter of Qgmundr Þorbergsson and sister of Skopti í Gizka. He was allegedly captured because he did not wish to leave his wife. But in *Morkinskinna* there appears to be a relationship between Steigar-Þórir and Egill, and the person mentioned in connection with Egill's refusal to flee is Steigar-Þórir's daughter. *Orkneyinga saga* (*ÍF* 34, 158) confirms the majority view by telling us that Steigar-Þórir's daughter was married to Erlendr ór Hernum, not to Egill (another of Steigar-Þórir's daughers, Ingibjǫrg, was married to King Eysteinn Magnússon). The version in *Morkinskinna* may therefore be based on some oral confusion. Egill's death fits into a long tradition of heroic postures (see Preben Meulengracht Sørensen 1993:312–27).

Chapter 56

1. The unusual image of gleaming ice was used once before in Ch. 50 (see Eivind Kválen 1925a:34).

2. On the importance of royal blood, see note 55.11.

3. Óláfr hvítaskald quotes this proverb in "The Third Grammatical Treatise" (*SnE* II, 182) in the form: "'Er-a hlums vant,' sǫgðu refar [or "kvað refr"], drógu hǫrpu á ísi" (There is no lack of an oar-handle, said the foxes, as they dragged a shell on the ice). The explana-

tion of this saying is given as follows: "Þat er mælt til þeirra manna er láta stórliga, en megu lítið; þar er framfœring ok óeiginlig líking milli manns ok horpu" (This applies to people who act big and do little; there is an equation and a metaphorical comparison between a man and a shell). The idea is that a man is boasting of rowing a ton when he is just scraping a shell on water that is frozen anyway. The saying is not included in Halldór Halldórsson's *Orðtakasafn*.

4. The proverb seems to mean that the Lapps are luring customers with false promises of snow. We are to understand that the king's words are equally false (Hermann Pálsson 1997:25). This saying is also missing from Halldór Halldórsson's *Orðtakasafn*.

5. Gilli's nickname, which he shares with a certain Shetland Islander named Erlendr bakrauf (*Íslendinga saga* [1988], I, 252), speaks for itself, but why "ullband" should be a nasty or comic variation on "ullstrengr" is not clear. Finnur Jónsson (1907:239) offers no guidance.

6. Sveinn bryggjufótr was also the name of one of the leaders in the mission to return Magnús Óláfsson to Norway in Chapter 1 (see note 1.19).

7. The story of how Erlingr Skjálgsson resisted King Óláfr, was reconciled to him, then defected again, and was finally cut down by one of the king's followers is told in Snorri's "Óláfs saga helga." Some version of that saga was almost certainly available to the author of *Morkinskinna*.

8. On the white shield as an invitation to parley, see Falk, *Waffenkunde*, pp. 128–29.

9. The story of Sveinki Steinarsson is not found in *Fagrskinna* and *Heimskringla*, though it is included in *Fríssbók* (pp. 265–68). If it was originally in *Morkinskinna* and was suppressed in later versions, we might speculate that a story about the legitimacy of provincial independence was acceptable to the Icelandic audience of *Morkinskinna* but less acceptable to the royal audience in Norway. But Snorri would surely have fancied himself in the tradition of those master diplomats who mediate between King Magnús and Sveinki. Furthermore, Sveinki was the grandfather of Erlingr skakki, who becomes an important figure in *Fagrskinna* and *Heimskringla* (see Genealogy XII in *ÍF* 28).

Chapter 57

1. Viskardalr (Swedish Viskedal) is in Halland east of Gothenburg and Kungsbacke. In *Fagrskinna* and *Heimskringla*, these raids in Denmark occur at the beginning of Magnús's reign prior to the uprising of Steigar-Þórir.

2. On St. Columba, see Michael Herren, in *DMA* 3, 485 (s.v. Columba) or D. W. Rollason in *LM*, 3, 63–65 (s.v. Columba). Icelandic sources use both the Celtic form "Columcille" and the Latin form "Columba." See Helgi Guðmundsson 1967:110–13. The Lesser Church of Columcille is now St. Oran's Chapel.

3. Hugh the Bold (Hugi enn prúði) may be identified as Hugh of Montgomery, Earl of Shrewsbury, and Hugh the Stout (Hugi enn digri) as Hugh of Avranches, Earl of Chester (see *ÍF* 28, 223, n.1). The present passage suggests that traditions were debated and disputed, therefore taken seriously. It also suggests strongly that a skaldic stanza could be the nucleus of such traditions. The battle is dated to the beginning of 1098.

Chapter 58

1. On King Malcolm and his son David, see A. A. M. Duncan, "Malcolm III of Scotland," in *DMA* 8, 56–57, and Bruce Webster, "David I of Scotland," in *DMA* 4, 110–11. The date of King Magnús's first expedition to the west was 1098–1099 (*ÍF* 28, li). Many of the sources for this period of Scottish history, though not *Morkinskinna*, are translated in *Early Sources of Scottish History, A.D. 500 to 1286*, trans. Alan Orr Anderson (Edinburgh: Oliver and Boyd,

1922), II, 89–125. For a detailed discussion of Magnús's two expeditions to the west, see Rosemary Power 1986.
2. The story of Giffarðr was omitted from both *Fagrskinna* and *Heimskringla*, although it is clear from what is said below (note 58.8) that Snorri knew it. See Gade [forthcoming].
3. Snorri (*ÍF* 28, 225) refers to Dalr as Sunndalr (Swedish Sundal) and Norðdalr (Swedish Nordal). Véar is the district of Vedbo and Varðynjar is the district of Valbo (see the map in *Heimskringla* [1991], III, 265).
4. Voxerni (elsewhere spelled Foxerni) is two thirds of the way up the Götaälv toward Lake Vänern (see the map in *Heimskringla* [1991], III, 265).
5. This skald is anonymous in all versions. See the note to the stanza.
6. There is a Húsavík on Tjörnes (Skjálfandi) and one in Steingrímsfjörður in the south-eastern corner of the Vestfirðir. Given the northern concentration of names and persons in *Morkinskinna*, the Húsavík mentioned here is perhaps more likely to be the former. On Eldjárn, see Finnur Jónsson, *Litteraturhistorie* II, 134–35.
7. See the note on st. 74.
8. See note 35.4 above. Although Snorri does not take over the Giffarðr story from *Morkinskinna*, he appears to derive from it the principle that poetry recited before a king was likely to be truthful, lest it be mockery (*ÍF* 26, 5; trans. Hollander, p. 4).
9. This is Erik Ejegod, king of Denmark (1095–1103).
10. *Fagrskinna* and *Heimskringla* make no mention of this Maktildr (or Mechthild, Matilda). The German emperor at this time was Henry IV (1056–1106). Henry's *Vita* makes no mention of a daughter Mechthild. On the identity of Maktildr, see Russell Poole 1985: 115–31, and the note to st. 212.
11. The identity of this skald is not known.

Chapter 59

1. This is one of the sparse chronological notes in *Morkinskinna*. On the chronology of Magnús's reign, see *ÍF* 28, xlix–li.
2. There is considerable variation among the sources on the list of chieftains, apparently re-sulting from a misreading of *Ágrip* and a conflation of chieftains participating in the Swedish and English expeditions. The poetic exchange above is also recorded in *Orkn-eyinga saga* (*ÍF* 34, 99–100), where it is assigned to Magnús's first campaign and involves Magnús and Kali, Rǫgnvaldr's father. At this point in our text, *Ágrip* follows Theodoricus (*MHN* 63). *Morkinskinna* misreads *Ágrip* and shifts the participants on the Gautland ex-pedition, listed immediately before the participants in the later expedition (*ÍF* 29, 45–46), to the Irish venture. *Morkinskinna* also misreads the line in *Ágrip* that names "Úlfr Hranason, brother of Sigurðr, father of Nicholas" and produces "Sigurðr Hranason, Úlfr Nicholasson." *Fagrskinna* omits Úlfr Hranason, possibly because the compiler read "Úlfr Nicholasson" in *Morkinskinna* and did not know who he was. Snorri, in keeping with *Ágrip*, restores him. *Morkinskinna* adds Sigurðr Hranason to the list (a good informant on Magnús's last stand), as well as Serkr ór Sogni (the son of Brynjólfr; see *ÍF* 2, 103). *Morkin-skinna* also adds Eyvindr ǫlbogi (in the form "ǫlboli"), who appears later in *Ágrip* as Eyvindr Finnsson (*ÍF* 29, 46). It is clear that the *Morkinskinna* author did not connect the names and therefore treated them as two separate characters. According to *Ágrip*, *Morkin-skinna*, and *Fagrskinna* (also *Orkneyinga saga*), Erlingr of Orkney was also present and fell in the battle. *Heimskringla* follows *Ágrip*'s account of the first expedition and attaches both jarls (Erlingr and Magnús) to King Magnús. According to Snorri, Magnús escapes (cf. the earlier account in *Morkinskinna* and *Fagrskinna*), but Erlingr dies. *Orkneyinga saga* (*ÍF* 34, 95) lists the following participants on the first expedition (in addition to Magnús and Erl-ingr): "Viðkunnr Jónsson, Sigurðr Hranason, Serkr ór Sogni, Dagr Eilífsson, *Skopti ór Gizka, *Ǫgmundr, *Finnr ok *Þórðr [Skopti's sons], Eyvindr ǫlbogi, *Kali af Ǫgðum Sæ-

bjarnarson, Þorleifs sonar ins spaka, er Hallfreðr meiddi, ok *Kolr sonr hans." About Erlingr, *Orkneyinga saga* (p. 101) adds the interesting note: "Erlingr, sonr Erlends jarls, segja sumir menn at felli í Qngulseyjarsundi, en Snorri Sturluson segir hann fallit hafa á Úlaztíri með Magnúsi konungi" (Some men say that Erlingr, the son of Jarl Erlendr, fell in Menai Strait, but Snorri Sturluson says that he fell in Ulster with King Magnús). There were, in other words, conflicting accounts about these expeditions.

3. Unger (153.12) filled a small lacuna after "That may turn out . . ." with the words "enn til sømðar" (again to the honor, *scil.* of our Norwegian realm). Finnur Jónsson (332.19) left the lacuna blank. Since *Hulda-Hrokkinskinna* (*FmS* VII, 67) omits Magnús's speech, it appears that Unger's phrase is conjectural. We may wonder whether national honor is an anachronistic concept here, more appropriate to Unger's Norway than to Magnús's. The idea of "honor" (*sæmð*) is clearly picked up from Sigurðr Sigurðarson's reply, but in the latter case it is a question of Magnús's personal honor, not national honor.

4. Such stratagems are, of course, reminiscent of Haraldr harðráði's adventures in the Mediterranean.

5. On King Muirchertach Ua Briain (Mýrkjartan; † 1119) see Anderson, *Early Sources,* II, 133, and 138, and Power 1986. Muirchertach betrothed his daughter Blathmuine to Sigurðr jórsalafari in 1102, and Sigurðr was later made king of Man (not Orkney, as in Norse tradition) (see also Curtis 1921).

6. St. Bartholomew's Day falls on August 23.

7. The word "breechlings" (*bræklingar*) appears to be *hapax.* The derogatory term clearly refers to the sartorial style that gave Magnús his nickname, but it is curious that the king would mock a style that he imitated. The mockery no doubt reflects a later attitude among the Norsemen.

8. This expression of animosity toward the people of Upplǫnd is isolated but interesting. It suggests a West or Northwest Norwegian bias in the author's sources, and that would certainly be in line with the larger presence of western and northwestern Norway in the text. Sigurðr hundr (in the next sentence) is mentioned only here in *Morkinskinna.* His greatgrandfather Þórir hundr fought against Ólafr Haraldsson at Stiklastaðir (*ÍF* 28, 22; trans. Hollander, p. 549). Þórir's son Sigurðr was married to Unnr, the daughter of the Icelandic chieftain Snorri goði. Their daughter married Jón Árnason and bore Sigurðr hundr, who was thus also a great-grandson of Snorri goði (see Genealogy IX in *ÍF* 28).

9. On the Irish ax, referred to here as a *sparða,* see Falk 1914:112.

10. The author slips into the first person again (cf. notes 24.17 and 50.5).

11. We may fairly surmise that Viðkunnr is the ultimate source for the account of Magnús's last expedition, all the more so because the author has much to say about Viðkunnr in "Þinga saga" (Ch. 70).

Chapter 60

1. Cf. note 55.4. There is no prior reference to "harsh treatment and exactions" in *Morkinskinna,* only in *Ágrip* (*ÍF* 29, Chs. 27–29, pp. 28–29). That makes it clear that the present passage is taken over from *Ágrip* (*ÍF* 29, Ch. 51, p. 47).

Chapter 61

1. On Þórarinn stuttfeldr, see Finnur Jónsson, *Litteraturhistorie* II, 61–62.

2. See the note to st. 222. The skald in question is not Þorvaldr blǫnduskald but Þórarinn stuttfeldr (cf. *Heimskringla* [*ÍF* 28, 239n.1]).

3. The reference here is to Henry I (1100–1135). William of Malmesbury (*WM* II, 485–86) corroborates that Sigurðr got permission from Henry to winter in England. The year of

Sigurðr's arrival in England has been debated, and it is unclear whether he actually met King Henry on that occasion (see Koht 1924a:153–55).

4. On Sigurðr's remarkable voyage in general, see Paul Riant 1865:173–215.

5. This passage tells us something about the interaction between Norse history and Norse narrative and about what was deemed memorable and saga-worthy.

6. On the skald Halldórr skvaldri, see Finnur Jónsson, *Litteraturhistorie* II, 60–61.

7. The MS first states that there were seven pirate vessels (FJ 341.22) and now that there were eight (FJ 342.2). The half-stanza supports "eight." The scribes used Roman numerals, which are quite frequently subject to error.

8. Sintré is modern Portuguese Sintra just west of Lisbon.

9. The historical atlases make it clear that this information is surprisingly close to the truth. The line between the Christian and Muslim kingdoms around 1107–1108 did indeed run very close to Sintra and Lisbon. Henry, duke of Portugal, won Sintra back from the Muslims in 1109 and probably had secured Sigurðr's support. In 1110 he made an unsuccessful attempt to recapture Lisbon (see *ÍF* 28, 242–43, notes on sts. 189–90).

10. There is a certain similarity between Sigurðr's numbered military coups (some characterized by stratagems and culminating in plunder) and those of Haraldr harðráði. The similarities may be merely generic, but if there is oral or literary influence, we may imagine that Sigurðr's exploits were in fresher memory and may have colored Haraldr's adventures in retrospect.

11. Alkassa has been identified as Alcácer do Sal, southeast of Lisbon on the river Sado, but see Riant 1865:181n.1.

12. Forminterra (Formentera) and Íviza (Ibiza) (below) are islands in the Balearics. On the episode on Formentera, see Jan de Vries 1931:72, and Doxey 1996.

13. At this point there is a leaf missing in the MS, and we insert the corresponding account from *Fríssbók*, pp. 284.23–287.8.

14. On Roger II of Sicily, see James M. Powell, in *DMA* 10, 440–41. He was count of Sicily from 1101 to 1130 and king from 1130 to 1154. According to Icelandic reckoning, Sigurðr would have been in Sicily in the spring of 1109. For chronological as well as common-sense reasons it is, therefore, not possible that Sigurðr was involved in Roger's elevation to king.

15. In this passage there appears to be some conflation between William I and William II of Sicily. William II was childless but did marry his aunt Constance (daughter of William I) to Henry (later Henry VI). Manuel Komnenos was married not to a daughter of King Roger but to Agnes of France (*LM*, 1, 386). Their son was indeed Alexios II. On Berengar, see *ÍF* 28, 248n.5. See also the sources given in Koht 1924a:158–60.

16. On Sigurðr's trip to Jerusalem, see *ÍF* 28, 250n.1, Riant 1865:185–90, and Koht 1924a: 160–64.

17. On Sigurðr at the siege of Sidon, see Riant 1865:192–93, Koht 1924a:162–64, and Kenneth M. Setton 1969:386–87. Cf. the reference in Ch. 71 (note 4) below.

18. On this sailing maneuver, see *ÍF* 28, 252n.1, and cf. *Fagrskinna* (*ÍF* 29, 226) and *Orkneyinga saga* (*ÍF* 34, 235). In general, compare the reception of the Danish king Erik Ejegod at Constantinople in *Knýtlinga saga* (*ÍF* 35, 236–37).

19. Kirjalax is Alexios I Komnenos (1081–1118). On Gullvarta, see *ÍF* 28, 252n.3, and on Laktjarnir, *ÍF* 28, 253n.1.

20. The insertion from *Fríssbók* ends here. For Continental parallels to the story of the golden horseshoes, see the interpolated B-version of William of Jumièges (II, 82/3), van Houts 1985:544–45, and Koht 1924a:164–66.

Chapter 62

1. On the real or alleged linguistic abilities of the Norsemen, see Marianne Kalinke 1983:850–61.

2. We are told elsewhere that a similar grand offer was made to the Danish king Erik Ejegod. See Saxo Grammaticus, *Gesta Danorum* 12.7 (p. 339), trans. Eric Christiansen, I, 104; and note 31 (p. 275). The story is also told in *Knýtlinga saga*, Chs. 79–81 (*ÍF* 35, 232–39) (see also Riant 1865:160, 199). On the *skippund*, see note 32.3 above.

3. This is an interesting effort at visualizing the grandeur of the hippodrome, the outlines of which are still distinguishable in Istanbul, in local Icelandic terms. The homefield is the enclosed yard around an Icelandic farmhouse.

4. See the notes on sts. 21 and 151. The Æsir are a race of gods, the Volsungs and Gjukungs the chief families of Scandinavian heroic legend. See Claiborne W. Thompson, "Æsir," in *DMA* 1, 62–63, and R. G. Finch, "Vǫlsung-Niflung Cycle," in *MSE*, pp. 707–10. Perhaps the author is merely interpreting Greek gods and heroes with Norse counterparts, but it is possible that he is already familiar with the etymological idea that the Æsir came from Asia. See "Ynglingasaga" (*ÍF* 26, 11) and Snorri's *Edda*, trans. Faulkes, p. 4. If so, the author logically places the Æsir at the gateway to Asia. See also Heinrich Beck 1994:37–38, 48–59.

5. On these stringed instruments, see in particular Fabrizio Raschellà 1982:104–6.

Chapter 63

1. On the device of substituting walnuts for firewood, which also appears in the B-version of William of Jumièges's *Gesta Normannorum Ducum* (I, 82–84), see Riant 1865:200–1, Gaston Paris 1880:515–46, Jan de Vries 1931:51–79 (esp. 69–72), René Louis 1958:391–419 (esp. 396–99), and Elisabeth M. C. van Houts 1985:544–59. Cf. note 11.4 above.

2. The emperor at this time was Henry V (1106–1125), not Lothar (1125–1137). See the note in *ÍF* 28, 254n.1, and Koht 1924a:166.

3. This is King Niels (1104–1134), who is often referred to as Nicholas. For Eilífr, Niels's governor in Schleswig, see Saxo Grammaticus, *Gesta Danorum* 13.2, pp. 343–44 (trans. Christiansen I, 110–12).

4. Another minimal notation on chronology. Cf. notes 1.23 and 59.1.

5. This donation looks as though it should refer to the piece of the cross mentioned in *Heimskringla* (*ÍF* 28, 250), but the reference is so casual that it seems unlikely that the cross was mentioned earlier in *Morkinskinna*. *Ágrip* (*ÍF* 29, 48) tells us that Sigurðr did not keep his commitment to deposit the relic in the Church of St. Óláfr, and *Fagrskinna* (*ÍF* 29, 320) has a lacuna in the corresponding section. *FmS* VII, 96–100, makes no mention of the cross. It seems most likely that the story originated in *Ágrip* and was taken over from that source by Snorri. This sequence would be in accord with the view that the author of *Morkinskinna* did not himself use *Ágrip* but that the text of *Morkinskinna* was later interpolated from *Ágrip*.

6. The quarter-stanza does not appear to say what the prose indicates. *Ágrip* and *Fagrskinna* have lacunae, and *Heimskringla* omits the stanza. Presumably, it went on to document the people's delight at Sigurðr's return. The skald is unidentified, but the stanza is most likely from "Stuttfeldardrápa" (see the note to st. 234).

Chapter 64

1. On Eysteinn's building program, see Knut Helle 1982:115–16. On Ormr enn langi, see note 55.17.

2. The kings of Norway and Sweden had traditionally disputed the province of Jamtaland (Jämtland). See Snorri's "Óláfs saga helga" (*ÍF* 27, 28, 242, 255–61; trans. Hollander, pp. 288, 413–14, 424–27), and Bjarni Aðalbjarnarson 1937:24–26.

3. On the question of thanes, see note 1.11.

4. See Ch. 11 in *Hákonar saga Hákonarsonar*.

5. See note 55.20. The son of Maria and Guðbrandr was Óláfr ógæfa (the Unlucky), a pretender to the Norwegian crown who was defeated by Erlingr skakki in the Battle of Stangir (Stange) in 1168 (see *ÍF* 28, 407–10).

Chapter 65

1. For other reversions to the authorial first person, see notes 24.17, 50.5, and 59.10.
2. This is presumably the skald Ívarr Ingimundarson, whose verse is cited below as well as in *Fagrskinna* and *Heimskringla*. His "important family" does not, however, figure in *Landnámabók* (see Finnur Jónsson, *Litteraturhistorie* II, 59–60).
3. The love triangle underlies several "skald sagas," including *Hallfreðar saga*, *Kormáks saga*, and *Gunnlaugs saga*. The closest analogue, in which one of the rival suitors knowingly steals the bride by giving misinformation, is *Bjarnar saga Hítdœlakappa*. It is interesting that this plot model was attached particularly to poets.
4. The author adverts once more to the problem of incest, as in the story of King Magnús góði and Margrét (cf. note 23.5).
5. On the therapeutic approach to lovesickness through conversation, see Mary F. Wack 1990: 41–45, 89–90, 142.

Chapter 66

1. Snorri (*ÍF* 28, 258) gives essentially the same genealogy but does not include Óláfr the Swede, Ingigerðr, Yaroslav, or Jón Sørkvisson (who is important for the dating of our text). Snorri adds that Knútr lávarðr was the son of Erik Ejegod and grandson of Sveinn Úlfsson.
2. See note 55.19. It seems clear that in the latter parts of *Morkinskinna* the author has special access to traditions deriving from Viðkunnr and his family. It also seems quite plausible that Ásu-Þórðr from the East Fjords (in Ch. 68) and his descendants were the link between these events and Icelandic tradition.

Chapter 68

1. "To the town" translates "í kaupbœinn" (FJ 359.30). The town is presumably Niðaróss. The phrasing suggests that the author is so oriented toward Niðaróss that for him, it is "the town," pure and simple.
2. Notes 55.19 and 66.2.
3. An interest in investment strategies surfaces again, as in Chs. 34, 36 (Auðunn), and 48 (Oddr Ófeigsson). Assuming that the author himself had been in Norway, we may also assume that he had commercial interests, inasmuch as any travel between Norway and Iceland would have been to some extent commercial in nature (cf. note 37.2).
4. On the value of friendship, see note 55.7 above.
5. This story in effect inverts a previous story about how Einarr þambarskelfir asserts himself by saving a thief from King Haraldr's justice (Ch. 33 above). Here the underdog asserts himself by insisting on justice for the thief.
6. Þórðr is referred to here as a "landi," short for *mǫrlandi*, "suet-eater." Two sentences later he is referred to as an Icelandic beggar and, at the end of the chapter, again as a "mǫrlandi" (FJ 364.13). It clearly delighted the Icelanders to counteract such slurs with tales of their own success in Norway. See also "Halldórs þáttr Snorrasonar" (*ÍF* 5, 253n.1), the miracle of St. Þorlákr in *Biskupa sögur* I, 357, and *FmS* VII, 35.21.
7. The term *lǫgmaðr* is not used in the *Gulaþingslǫg* and occurs only once in the *Frostaþingslǫg*

(*NGL* I, 127). In later law texts codified in the twelfth century it is used only in the plural, about a collective body of "law men," that is, men skilled in the law who exacted fines on behalf of the legal district (see *NGL* I, 121). Not until the thirteenth century, in the laws issued by Hákon Hákonarson and his son Magnús, is the term used in the singular, referring to a specific judicial office. See *NGL* V, 421–23; Konrad Maurer 1875:esp. 24–30 and 41–42; and Torfinn Tobiassen, "Lagman," in *KLNM* 10, 153–62.

8. FJ 362.22: "'Stikk í mér,' kvað reka." A rough equivalent to this proverb might be, "If digging's the job, the spade's the tool" ("If it's litigation you want, I'm your man"). The saying is not included in Halldór Halldórsson's *Orðtakasafn.*

9. FJ 363.13–14: "Erat hera at borgnara, at hœna beri skjǫld." This saying is also not included in Halldór Halldórsson's *Orðtakasafn.*

10. See Ch. 59 above.

11. For the custom of fastening stolen goods to the back of a thief caught red-handed, see Gade 1985:161–68.

12. The response here is in the same spirit as Kálfr Árnason's response to Haraldr harðráði (Ch. 42, note 11), although not so witty. The author's moralizing about Eysteinn's forbearance is also similar to the authorial comment on Kálfr Árnason, leading us to surmise that perhaps the same author is at work in both passages.

Chapter 69

1. The chronological indications seem to cluster in the saga of Magnús's sons, and we may wonder whether there was a special source for these indications, skaldic or otherwise.

2. Austrátt (Norwegian Austrått) lies on the north shore of Stjørnfjorden at the mouth of Trondheimsfjorden. See the map in *Heimskringla* (1991), III, 263.

3. *Slembi-, slembir* appears to be related to the Icelandic *slambra, slembra,* "chop awkwardly, hack." The force of "slembidjákn" might be something like "hack deacon" or "half-baked deacon." Finnur Jónsson (1907:263) is more inclined to connect the word with the Icelandic *slembilukka,* "unexpected and undeserved luck," with the emphasis more on "unexpected." That would suggest the translation "fortuitous deacon."

4. For the genealogy of King Ingi Bárðarson, see note 51.4 above. Snorri gives a somewhat fuller but matching genealogy (*ÍF* 28, 297), adding at the end that Sigríðr was the sister of King Ingi "and Duke Skúli." We might speculate that the omission of Skúli in *Morkinskinna* suggests that the genealogy antedates the elevation of Skúli to a jarldom in 1217 (hence Snorri's title of "duke").

Chapter 70

1. The family connections are as follows:

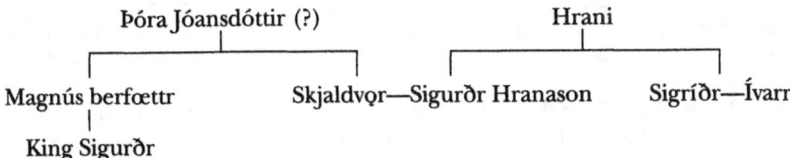

King Sigurðr is thus Skjaldvǫr's nephew and Sigríðr is his aunt by marriage, or "filletante." On Ívarr of Fljóðar, who is not mentioned elsewhere, see Gustav Storm 1877:54.

2. The Uriah mission is a frequent motif in the sagas, usually attributed by Icelandic writers to Norwegian kings with Icelandic victims (e.g., *Egils saga* and *Hallfreðar saga*). The "Þáttr

frá Sigurði konungi slefu syni Gunnhildar" (*Flat* I, 19–21) parallels the story of Sigurðr and Ívarr (the seduction of a wife by sending the husband to England on a tax-raising expedition).

3. The criminality of incest (King Sigurðr sleeps with his "aunt") preoccupies the author elsewhere (see notes 23.5 and 65.4). Here it is compounded by the problem of family honor.

4. On the Lapp tax, see note 48.2.

5. Valdísey (for Kvalðinsey [Kållandsö] in Lake Vänern [*ÍF* 28, 226 and 231]) is not mentioned in the account of King Magnús's campaign in Gautland in Ch. 58. Sigurðr ullstrengr and Finnr Skoptason are mentioned as commanders, but there is no mention of Sigurðr Hranason's service.

6. Bjarkey (Norwegian Bjarkøy) is located to the far north in the Lofoten Islands. See the map in *Heimskringla* (1991), III, 290.

7. Jonna Louis-Jensen (1977:98) notes that Keflisey is not known from other sources but that Storm (1877:49) identified it as Kjefsø (Kjepsø) in Vågan on Senja, north of the Lofoten group. Steig, mentioned two sentences below, is located just south of the Lofoten group.

8. On these "lawmen" (*lǫgmenn*), see note 68.7 above. See also Storm 1877:65–68.

9. Þrándarnesþing is located just to the south of Bjarkey (see the map in *Heimskringla* [1991], III, 287).

10. The MS has "Arnarheims þings." Louis-Jensen (1977:98n.16) notes that no Árnarnes can be located in Norway. Editors correct to "Árnarnesþing" on the basis of another occurrence below (FJ 378.12). See also Storm 1877:49–50.

11. On the problem of legal jurisdiction here, see Storm 1877:50–51.

12. On the areas of these law districts, see the map in *Heimskringla* (1991), III, 219.

13. On the skald Einarr Skúlason, see Finnur Jónsson, *Litteraturhistorie* II, 62–73.

14. A naval battle was fought at Sekkr (Norwegian Sekken) in Romsdalsfjorden in 1162. On this passage, see Louis-Jensen 1977:95–96. Snorri indicates that Eindriði Jónsson did not fall in this battle but in the Battle of Elfr (Götaälv) in 1160 (*ÍF* 28, 252–60).

15. Nothing is known for certain about Sigurðr, son of Sigurðr of Hvítasteinn (see *ÍF* 28, 269n.2, and Genealogy II.2; Koht 1924b:140), but this somewhat unmotivated mention of him suggests that he may be the ultimate source for the story or, at least, for the final phase of it. It seems quite possible that he is identical with the Sigurðr Sigurðarson who campaigns with Magnús berfœttr in Gautland (*Ágrip* [*ÍF* 29, 45]) and with the Sigurðr Sigurðarson who advises King Magnús Sigurðarson (blindi) in *Fagrskinna* (*ÍF* 29, 323). The latter is described as "mikill hǫfðingi ok allra manna vitrastr" (a great chieftain and the wisest of men) in line with *Morkinskinna*'s "lendr maðr, er einna var vitrastr í Nóregi" (FJ 376.4). Sigurðr Sigurðarson accompanies King Magnús on his last expedition to Ireland in *Morkinskinna* (FJ 332.6; see note 59.2 above), but this may be an error because he survives to appear as a close adviser to King Sigurðr Sigurðarson and King Magnús Sigurðarson in *Heimskringla*. Louis-Jensen 1977:108 believes that the original of "Þinga saga" was a Norwegian text. If so, it was based on a strictly Norwegian tradition, stemming perhaps from Sigurðr Sigurðarson. Storm 1877:55 locates Hvítasteinn (Hvitstein) in Follo on the east side of Oslofjorden, but Eivind Kválen (1925a:96) locates it in Jondal, east of Bergen on Hardangerfjorden.

16. The "lawmen" act here not as legal authorities, as in previous cases, but as jurors or judges. It is possible to think in terms of some Icelandic influence on this usage.

17. Louis-Jensen 1977:98n.15 notes that this rule is otherwise unknown, but a somewhat similar procedural trick is described in Ch. 2 of *Ljósvetninga saga* (*ÍF* 10, 7). Here a man's legal status is restored by taking him surreptitiously to three consecutive district thing-meetings, suggesting that some sort of statute of limitation was in effect.

18. On "belted in trousers" ("gyrðr í brøkr"), see Falk 1919:117, 121.

19. On this sort of halberd ("hǫggspjót"), see Falk 1914:78.

20. This locution occurs at the end of Ch. 24 in *Ljósvetninga saga* (*ÍF* 10, 82) in almost identical form.

21. There is an element of compulsory generosity in King Sigurðr's rueful words, reminiscent of the contest in generosity between King Haraldr and King Sveinn in "Auðunar þáttr" (Ch. 36).

22. The author writes here: "Ok þó var þat, er á leið ævi hans, at varla fekk hann gætt skaplyndis síns né hugar, at eigi yrði þat stundum með m . . . áfelli ok þungligum hlutum." The phrase "með m . . . [U 185.38 read "miclo"] áfelli" echoes King Eysteinn's interpretation of Sigurðr's dream at the end of Ch. 67 (FJ 359.19–20): "En vera kann, at þú mœtir nǫkkuru þungu áfelli." Whatever the immediate source of "Þinga saga," the main author seems to revert here to his own voice. The alternative would be that the phrase originates in "Þinga saga" and is carried over into the main text by the *Morkinskinna* author, but that would imply that "Þinga saga" formed part of the original and was not an interpolation, as is commonly thought.

Chapter 71

1. The word translated as "serving men" is "þjónustumenn" (FJ 382.19). It probably refers to the noncombatant servants in Sigurðr's train.

2. Cf. st. 279 and Ármann Jakobsson 1997:115.

3. "Tourneying" ("at ríða í turniment") imagined in the year 1130 is clearly anachronistic in the north, and very early even in the south. See Joachim Bumke 1991:247–51. Cf. note 25.8 above.

4. "I tied a knot for you" (FJ 383.31: "ok knýtta ek þér knút") seems to be an idiom meaning "to outdo someone." Fritzner, s.v. *knútr*, gives a slightly analogous usage. The same practice is alluded to in *Orkneyinga saga* (*ÍF* 34, 231–32 and 231n.3) in connection with Jarl Rǫgnvaldr kali's visit to the Holy Land, where the "tying of knots" quite clearly is to be taken in a literal sense (see Rudolf Meissner 1925:148–51).

5. On the location of Vágar (Vågan), see note 70.7 above.

6. On these projects, see note 64.1 above.

7. On this episode as a whole, see Lars Lönnroth 1978:53–80; Helgi Þorláksson 1979:174–80; Marianne Kalinke 1984:162–65; Sverre Bagge 1991:156–57; Diana Whaley 1991:101.

Chapter 72

1. Árni fjǫruskeifr is also mentioned in *Þorgils saga ok Hafliða* (Chs. 14–16) and is said to have spent a winter with Þorgils Oddason. Although he spent time in Iceland, he seems unlikely to have told the following anecdote at his own expense. On the nickname "fjǫruskeifr" (Shore-skewed), see Finnur Jónsson 1907:323.

Chapter 73

1. The curiosity here is that a stanza should be set down with such a negligible context. It sounds as though the context may have been forgotten and then remedied in this minimal way.

2. This is another of the chronological notices that seem peculiar to the saga of Magnús's sons (see note 69.1 above). *Fagrskinna* (*ÍF* 29, 320) and *Heimskringla* (*ÍF* 28, 262) do not place Eysteinn's death at Askstaðir but "á Stimi [or Stim] á Hústǫðum." Snorri dates the death on August 29 [1122] (*ÍF* 28, lviii and 262n.3). Kválen 1925a:89 considers Askstaðir to be an error for Hústaðir (in Romsdal).

Chapter 74

1. On the price of books, see Lars Lönnroth 1964:43–51. The precious book in question was most likely a "plenarius" inscribed with gold letters, which Sigurðr, according to Snorri, had received as a gift from the patriarch of Constantinople (see ÍF 28, 276).
2. "Birtingr" is a kind of trout named for its light color (*trutta albicolor*). The word is cognate with English "bright." When the author says that Óttarr was so named because he was dark, we must believe that the nickname was conferred as a joke.
3. The story is one of how a man made his fortune by dint of firm principle and despite a dangerous monarch. In structure it is therefore very much like the *þættir* of Icelanders, although the protagonist is a Norwegian. The same pattern obtains in the story of Áslákr hani in Ch. 77.

Chapter 75

1. The splendors of Konungahella were later burned to the ground by the heathens, as Snorri relates in *Heimskringla* (ÍF 28, 288–96). One source of information on Konungahella in Iceland would have been Snorri's foster father Jón Loptsson, who, Snorri notes (ÍF 28, 288), was in Konungahella in 1135 at the age of eleven.
2. Einarr Skúlason, here as elsewhere, would seem to be the most logical link between the Norwegian event and the Icelandic transmission.
3. "He was thumped" translates "ok var þøfðr" (FJ 391.13). "Þøfðr" seems most likely to be the past participle of *þœfa*, "to pound," presumably to get the water out of his lungs. *Hulda-Hrokkinskinna* (FmS VII, 159) omits the episode and *Fríssbók* (302.24–25) omits the phrase.

Chapter 76

1. "Gilli" is a Celtic word meaning "servant." Gillicrist is therefore "servant of Christ." Hallkell húkr below is (according to Snorri ÍF 28, 265 and 332) the son of Jón smjǫrbalti, a district chieftain in Mœrr, and the father of Símon skálpr.
2. Einarr would appear to be the transmitter of this anecdote as well as the previous one.

Chapter 78

1. The closest analogue to this dream is the tree-dream that appears to Queen Ragnhildr before the birth of Haraldr hárfagri in "Hálfdanar saga svarta" (ÍF 26, 90; trans. Hollander, p. 56).
2. The ordeal is also recounted by Saxo Grammaticus (13.11, p. 363; trans. Eric Christiansen I, 139). Ordeals seem to have been resorted to in paternity cases especially. See William Ian Miller 1988:189–218. On St. Columba, see note 57.2 above.
3. Cf. the sport made of the Flemish speaker Jón and his attempts to speak Norse in *Laurentius saga*, Chs. 11–12 (*Bisk* I, 801–2).

Chapter 79

1. Here and several times below, Magnús is referred to as "king" rather than "prince." It almost seems that the author took over the narrative from a source that described King Magnús's reign and therefore always titles him "king."

2. On stirrup trousers (*nafarskeptar brœkr*), see Falk, *Kleiderkunde*, p. 120. The trousers reached down around the soles of the feet like a type of legging.
3. The feat of outrunning a horse is not common in the sagas, but it echoes Hreiðarr's swiftness of foot (note 24.14 above). Saxo (14.5, p. 368; trans. Eric Christiansen II, 352) gives a rather different version of the episode.

Chapter 80

1. Sigurðr died in 1156 or 1157. See Storm, *Islandske annaler*, pp. 115, 475. He was the founder of Lyse kloster near Bergen. See "Fundatio Lysensis Monasterii," in *MHN* 171–72.
2. On the custom of playing with one's fingers as a sign of pleasure, see Gade 1994:137 and n.6.
3. All the interventions in connection with King Sigurðr's madness test the moral fiber, either secular or ecclesiastical, of those who oppose him. These interventions represent a moral streak in *Morkinskinna* not imitated in *Fagrskinna* or *Heimskringla*.

Chapter 81

1. On Sigurðr's burial place and later fate, see *ÍF* 28, 276n.6.

Chapter 82

1. At this point there is a missing leaf in the MS, and we insert the corresponding section from *Heimskringla* (*ÍF* 28, 276–86).
2. The insert from *Heimskringla* ends at this point.
3. For the location of these sites, see the map in *Heimskringla* (1991), III, 268. On caltrops (*hersporar*), see Falk, *Waffenkunde*, p. 198. They were spiked contraptions strewn on the ground as a primitive type of landmine.
4. On maiming as a means to eliminate royal contenders, see Gade 1995b:123–26, 129–30. See also the variant version in Saxo, p. 369; trans. Eric Christiansen, II, 353.
5. Snorri (*ÍF* 28.287) adds that Reinaldr was English and acquisitive, thus changing the heroic tone of *Morkinskinna* appreciably. Nothing is known of Reinaldr apart from this episode, but his death at the hands of Haraldr gilli is recorded by Henry of Huntingdon in his "Letter to Walther" of 1135 (*HH* 313), and also by Roger of Hoveden, who mentions that Reinaldr (Reginald) was bishop of Bergen (*RH* II, 213).
6. Most of these places can be located on the map in *Heimskringla* (1991), III, 268. For Frosta, see the map on III, 208.
7. Snorri provides a much fuller and somewhat differing genealogy (*ÍF* 28, 331–32).

Chapter 83

1. According to the Icelandic annals, Magnús Einarsson, bishop in Skálaholt, died in 1148 or 1149. On his life, see *Hungrvaka*, Chs. 13–15 (*Bisk* I, 75–79). As in Chs. 14 (note 3) and 26 (note 10), there seems to be a tendency for traditions to cluster around particular objects. Magnús Einarsson was a great-grandson of the Þorsteinn Hallsson who asked King Magnús Óláfsson for his name in Ch. 26 (see Genealogy 2 in *Sturlunga saga* [1988], III, 74), and some of the transmissions may have been routed through this family.

Chapter 84

1. For a fuller genealogy, see note 69.4. That Þóra should sleep with her sister's husband is, of course, a serious case of incest and reason enough for secrecy. On the concern with incest, see note 23.5 above. On the question of Sigurðr's legitimacy, see Bjarni Guðnason 1978:116–18.
2. On the skald Ívarr Ingimundarson, see Finnur Jónsson, *Litteraturhistorie* II, 59–60. Bjarni Guðnason (1978:47) argues the probability that Ívarr's stanzas were not in Eiríkr Oddsson's *Hryggjarstykki* but were added in by the author of *Morkinskinna*.
3. Jarl Haraldr is Haraldr Maddaðarson, who figures in *Orkneyinga saga*. See Michael Chesnutt 1981:33–55.
4. The killing of Þorkell fóstri is also mentioned in *Heimskringla* (*ÍF* 28, 298) and *Orkneyinga saga* (*ÍF* 34, 116). See also Bjarni Guðnason 1978:92.
5. See Bjarni Guðnason 1978:133. See also "The Poetic Corpus of ÆMsk and the Question of Interpolation."

Chapter 85

1. On Sigurðr's winter in Saurbœr, see Bjarni Guðnason 1978:119–22.
2. The sentence here seems somewhat elliptical: "Eigi leita fleiri til traustsins til vár, en at trausti skal þat verða." *Hulda-Hrokkinskinna* (*FmS* VII, 329 n.7) has a reading "en at trausti skal *þeim* verða," which improves the sense slightly.
3. The text here reads (FJ 410.24–25): "Ok því er þessa getit, at hann þótti nær sér taka bragðit." This looks like one of the authorial explanations of why a particular anecdote is told (see notes 17.2, 42.3, 42.11, and 42.13). It is not clear why Sigurðr should take the part of the foppish Norwegian. Perhaps the anecdote was remembered only because the Icelandic victim was so indignant that he never tired of telling the story, but it sheds no light on Sigurðr.

Chapter 86

1. On the relationship between rulers and chieftains, see Bagge 1991:133–37.
2. Holdhella is perhaps Norwegian Hella, north of Bergen on Sognefjorden. See also Eivind Kválen 1925a:72–73.
3. "Ek vil ganga á borð ausa bát minn" (a colorful euphemism for urinating).
4. This sentence echoes a passage in Ch. 1 above (see note 1.16).
5. "Section from the seat of his trousers" translates "setgeiri" (see Falk, *Kleiderkunde*, p. 122).
6. On the possible Danish role in Eiríkr Oddsson's *Hryggjarstykki*, see Bjarni Guðnason 1978:137–39, and cf. note 93.3. This would appear to be the same oath that is referred to in st. 259.
7. *Morkinskinna* states only that King Haraldr was "in the town," but Snorri specifies that it was Bergen (*ÍF* 28, 300).
8. Snorri mentions Sigurðr's parentage (*ÍF* 28.279) at a point where *Morkinskinna* is defective (p. 359).
9. Sigurðr's compurgators ("eiðsvarar") are presumably those who supported his paternity claim by oath.
10. The Eve of St. Lucy falls on December 13.
11. On these individuals, see Bjarni Guðnason 1978:128. The Icelander Erlendr cannot be identified. Kolbjǫrn Þorljótsson is probably identical with Kolbeinn Þorljótsson in

Fagrskinna (*ÍF* 29, 332) and *Heimskringla* (*ÍF* 28, 310). The latter is well known from "Grœnlendinga þáttr" (see also note 36.1).

12. On the importance of "ancestry among kings," see notes 55.11 and 56.2.

13. On the Borgarþing, see note 27.2.

14. Haraldr and, at the very end of *Morkinskinna*, his son Eysteinn, appear to qualify for sainthood only by virtue of being kings who succumb to assassination or execution.

15. The Battle of Fyrileif (Swedish Färlev in Ranríki [Bohuslän]) was fought between Magnús (blindi) and Haraldr gilli in August 1134. See the account in *Heimskringla* (*ÍF* 28, 280–82). On the chronological note, cf. 1.23, 59.1, 63.4, 69.1, 73.2.

Chapter 87

1. The author again states only that King Sigurðr was "in town" (FJ 415.14). For the sake of clarity, Snorri specifies that we are now in Kaupangr (Niðaróss) (*ÍF* 28, 304).

2. For the location of Mynni (north of Oslo), see the map in *Heimskringla* (1991), III, 275.

3. On the skald Kolli enn prúði, see Finnur Jónsson, *Litteraturhistorie* II, 75.

4. Krókaskógr is the modern Swedish Sörbygden in Bohuslän. See the map in *Heimskringla* (1991), III, 281. According to *Morkinskinna*, Magnús flees east to Karl Sǫrkvisson, who was king of Sweden for eight years and died in 1162. *Fagrskinna* (*ÍF* 29, 331) and *Heimskringla* (*ÍF* 28, 306) speak of Karl Sónason, a Swedish jarl, and that seems more likely to be correct.

5. Eiríkr eimuni (Erik Emune) ruled Denmark in 1134–1137.

6. On St. Hallvard, see Lilli Gjerløw, "Hallvard," in *KLNM* 6, 63–66. Hǫfuðey is the Norwegian Hovedøya in Oslofjorden. Fors is Foss in present-day Romerike.

7. For the location of the Straits of Hornbori (Homborsund), see the map in *Heimskringla* (1991), III, 275.

Chapter 88

1. On the sources for Eiríkr Oddsson's *Hryggjarstykki and Hákon magi in particular, see Bjarni Guðnason 1978:17, 77–80. Nothing is known of Hákon beyond his role in *Hryggjarstykki, which is also noted in *Heimskringla* (*ÍF* 28, 319).

Chapter 89

1. See st. 273.

2. Finnur Jónsson's index of names (p. 476) places this Mœre in Sweden. It appears to be the district "Meore" on the Swedish mainland, on the inner side of Kalmar, mentioned by Wulfstan to King Alfred of England in his travelogue (*Orosius 16:* "7 þonne æfter Burgenda lande wæron us þas land þa synd hatene ærest Blecingaeg 7 Meore 7 Eowland 7 Gotland on bæcbord, 7 þas land hyrað to Sweon"; "and then after Bornholm those lands were on our port which are called as follows: first Blekinge and Möre and Öland and Gotland, and those lands belong to the Swedes").

3. Snorri (*ÍF* 28, 309) adds the information that Óláfr was Sigurðr's nephew. The genealogy in *Heimskringla* (1991), III, 179, shows the relationship. On the nickname "hvínantorði," see Finnur Jónsson 1907:331, and *ÍF* 28, 309n.1. The element "hvínan" is cognate with English "whine" and "torði" with English "turd." The sense is not transparent.

4. On Úlfheðinn Sǫxólfsson, see Bjarni Guðnason 1978:128. Bjarni points out that Sǫxólfr

is a rare name, connected with the Fornungar in Øxnadalr and Hǫrgardalr, and that Úlf-heðinn may belong to this family. That would certainly fit well with his northern origin and the general concentration of northern Icelanders in *Morkinskinna*.

5. Portyrja is Norwegian Portør, and Límgarðssíða (*recte* Lungarðssíða) is Norwegian Lyngør on the coast of Aust-Agder, midway between Sandefjord and Kristiansand (see the map in *Heimskringla* [1991], III, 275).

6. On the outer course, see note 14.2 above. Kolbeinn Þorláksson is Kolbeinn Þorljótsson, as in note 86.11 above.

Chapter 90

1. Listi (Norwegian Lista) is on the southern coast of Norway in Agðir (Vest-Agder) (see the map in *Heimskringla* [1991], III, 249).

2. On *pungeltr* (*pungelta*), see Finnur Jónsson 1907:343 ("tanner"?). *Storkr* means "stork" and *kelduskítr* probably "well-fouler" (but see Finnur Jónsson 1907:299). *Skjappa* below means "measure" (as in a measure of grain).

3. Ægisfjǫrðr is the Norwegian Øksfjorden, on the northernmost west coast. Sigurðr presumably chops off the prow because of the special value of the carvings or even the gilding (see Falk, "Seewesen," pp. 40–41).

4. On Guðrún and her family (the Reyknesingar in western Iceland), see Bjarni Guðnason 1978:125–26.

5. On these *skútur* (sing. *skúta*), see Falk, "Seewesen," pp. 95–96.

6. On the location of Vágar (Vågan), see note 70.7.

7. Víkar is the Norwegian Vik in Brønnøy herred in Sør-Helgeland, on the peninsula of Sømna.

8. Þóraldi's name *keptr* (more often, *kjaptr*) is a word for the lower part of the face with some such connotation as "mug," or perhaps "loudmouth" (see Whaley 1993:128). *Skinnari* is simply "skinner" or "tanner." Finnur Jónsson (1907:298) translates *glæsirófa* as (Danish) "pragthale" (literally "show-tail"), or what we might call a peacock in referring to someone who is vain about his appearance. Byrða is the Norwegian Børøya, between Roan and Osen in Sør-Trøndelag.

9. "Hvalsnes" is a misspelling for "Valsnes," as the following stanza shows.

10. *Harðmagi* means "hard stomach." Finnur Jónsson (1907:215) suggests that it could refer to constipation, as it does in modern Scandinavian. *Klingruauga* (or *kringluauga*) means "round eye" (Finnur Jónsson 1907:199). The Finnr who is captured in the next sentence is Finnr Sauða-Úlfsson, who is recaptured and hanged at the very end of the chapter. The duplication may have occurred when the stanzas were incorporated into the prose of *Hryggjarstykki, as in the case of the double paternity oaths (note 86.6 above).

11. Snorri (*ÍF* 28, 313) refers to Jón kúza as Jón kaða ("hen"). Finnur Jónsson (1907) does not list "kúza." *Rangi* means "crooked" (Finnur Jónsson 1907:231), and *smyrill* (Finnur Jónsson 1907:309) is a kind of falcon (*falco aesalon*). *Hreinn* can occur as a common noun meaning "ship," but it appears to be a proper name here. See Falk, "Seewesen," p. 87.

12. Herðla (Norwegian Herdla) is on the island Askøy in Hordaland, near Bergen (see the map in *Heimskringla* [1991], III, 279).

13. The Rogation Days are April 25 and the three days before Ascension Day. They are devoted to processions of penance and supplication. Hamarr (Norwegian Hamar) lies north of Oslo in the interior, but the previous sentence makes it seem likely that Hamarr is an error for Hamarsfjǫrðr in Hǫrðaland. Both *Fagrskinna* (*ÍF* 29, 333) and *Heimskringla* (*ÍF* 28, 313) suggest as much.

Chapter 91

1. On Ingi's letter, see Bjarni Guðnason 1978:72–73.

Chapter 92

1. St. Martin's Day falls on November 11. The conflict described here is, as *Fagrskinna* (*ÍF* 29, 334) and *Heimskringla* (*ÍF* 28, 316) specify, the Battle of Holmengrå, located in southeastern Norway, now Sweden (see the map in *Heimskringla* [1991], III, 275).
2. The author reverts to his admiration for faithful service to a lord (cf. notes 26.1, 45.1, and 98.5). *Heimskringla* (*ÍF* 28, 452) places Línustaðir (Linnestad) near Tønsberg.
3. On Sigurðr and Klémet, see Bjarni Guðnason 1978:125–28. The nickname *skrauthanki* means something like "ornamental handle" or "ring" (Finnur Jónsson 1907:240). Ívarr Kálfsson was bishop from 1140 to 1150 and the father of Eiríkr erkibyskup (1188–1205; died 1213).
4. Þorsteinn at Auðsholt is otherwise unknown. Auðsholt was located at Biskupstunga between Brúará and Hvítá at Skálaholt in Iceland. The nickname *ambi* appears to be a diminutive of "Arnbjǫrn" (Finnur Jónsson 1907:301). The same source (p. 321) describes *dynta* as "a conceited, pompous, insincere, self-important, and mawkish person."
5. On Archbishop Jón Birgisson (1152–1157), see also Ch. 99.

Chapter 93

1. The story of Sigurðr's last day is also told by Saxo Grammaticus 14.29 (pp. 445–46); trans. Eric Christiansen, II, 466–68. On the relationship to Eiríkr Oddsson's *Hryggjarstykki, see Bjarni Guðnason 1978:55–66. Bjarni arrived at the conclusion that Saxo made direct or indirect use of *Hryggjarstykki. Note the use of the authorial first person and cf. notes 24.17, 50.5, 59.10, 65.1. See also Bjarni Guðnason 1978:20–21.
2. On Hallr Þorgeirsson, see Bjarni Guðnason 1978:79–80.
3. There is a quite standard and unrevealing "Vita et miracula sancti Ketilli," ed. Martinus Clarentius Gertz, in *Vitae sanctorum Danorum* (Copenhagen: Gad, 1908–1912), pp. 260–75. On Sigurðr's Danish connections, see Bjarni Guðnason 1978:80, 137–39.
4. On the skald Bǫðvarr halti (*recte* balti), see Finnur Jónsson, *Litteraturhistorie* II, 75.

Chapter 94

1. Because Óttarr had died, he could not have reported that he heard the whine of an ax, and because his assailant remained undetected, he apparently did not transmit such a surmise. This sort of narrative freedom is noted by Knut Liestøl (1930:85–86). Álfr hroði was later responsible for burning the farm Erdla (*ÍF* 28, 360) and was killed by Erlingr skakki (*ÍF* 28, 402).

Chapter 95

1. This chronological indication may be compared to notes 1.23, 59.1, 63.4, 69.1, 73.2, and 86.15.
2. It will be remembered that Ingiríðr is the widow of Haraldr gilli. Not much is told of Ormr

Ívarsson, but the story is carried on in *Fagrskinna* and *Heimskringla* and must therefore have been in the original *Morkinskinna*. Ormr participated in the Battle of Ré (Re in Vestfold; see the map in *Heimskringla* [1991] III, 282) in 1177, and that is one of the reasons for believing that *Morkinskinna* carried the history down at least to that date.

3. The blank in this sentence was filled in by a late hand with the name Ragna (FJ 441.1) (see the genealogy in *Heimskringla* [1991], III, 180, where the parents of Ormr and Ragnhildr are not included). On *kyrpinga*, see Finnur Jónsson 1907:337. It may suggest a wrinkled or decrepit person.

4. For Stuðla (Støle), see the map in *Heimskringla* (1991), III, 279, and Eivind Kválen 1925a:63.

5. The expedition of Rǫgnvaldr jarl and Erlingr skakki is told at greater length in *Orkneyinga saga* (ÍF 34, 208–37).

6. *Orkneyinga saga* (ÍF 34, 227) cites a stanza attributed to Rǫgnvaldr and confirming Auðunn rauði's deed. The passage is interesting because it illustrates how skaldic verse might be used to stabilize a particular tradition. In this case, the question of what actually happened is left up to Rǫgnvaldr, and he codifies his decision in a stanza.

Chapter 96

1. This Hákon is Hákon herðibreiðr, whose story does not survive in *Morkinskinna* but may be read in *Heimskringla*. (*Fagrskinna* has a lacuna.)

Chapter 97

1. At this point, *Heimskringla* (ÍF 28, 326) states: "Hann var ósáttr við bœndr, Reni ok Hísingsbúa." The form "Remi" in *Morkinskinna* (FJ 442.21) is clearly a misunderstanding of "Reni" (that is, "Renir," the residents of Ranríki [Bohuslän]) (see the note on st. 308). Hísing (Hisingen) is an island in Elfr (Götaälv) (see the map in *Heimskringla* [1991], III, 275).

2. *Heimskringla* (ÍF 28, 328) uses the form "Hjartapollr" (see the note on st. 311).

3. Stefnir is King Stephen, whose troubled reign extended through the years 1135–1154.

4. On the identification of Pílavík (Willoughby), see the note on st. 314.

5. On the nickname *sviptir*, see Finnur Jónsson 1907:274. It could apply to someone who twists or jerks something, but the reference is unclear.

6. On the pro-Ingi sentiments in *Morkinskinna*, see "Time and Place of Composition."

7. The reference is to Einarr Skúlason's "Geisli," which was commissioned by Eysteinn and recited in Christ Church (Kristkirken) in Trondheim in 1153. The poem, 71 stanzas in *dróttkvætt*, is printed in *Skj* IA, 459–73. The poem is preserved in *Flat* I, 1–7 (minus sts. 31–33) and in *Bergsbók*. The performance alluded to in *Morkinskinna* is omitted in *Fagrskinna* and *Heimskringla*.

8. For the location of Bakki (Bakke), see the map in *Heimskringla* (1991), III, 232.

9. On the status of minstrels in Old Norse society, see Seip, "Leikarar" in *KLNM* 10, 462–64, and Wallén, "Leikarar" in *KLNM* 10, 464–67. For a comprehensive discussion of minstrels in general, see Wareman 1951.

10. On the skald Snorri Bárðarson, see Finnur Jónsson, *Litteraturhistorie* II, 170.

11. The question of whether a skaldic stanza could have been understood by the audience during the first recitation has been debated by scholars (see Gade 1995a:23–27). This anecdote suggests that by the middle of the twelfth century, at least some listeners may have had problems in that respect (but we must also bear in mind that King Eysteinn had been raised outside of Scandinavia).

Chapter 98

1. The running of cattle onto a neighbor's field is reminiscent of the quarrel between Þorsteinn Egilsson and Steinarr Qnundarson in *Egils saga* (*ÍF* 2, 277–88). The episode is omitted from *Hulda-Hrokkinskinna* as well as from *Fagrskinna* and *Heimskringla*. It was included in *Ágrip*, but most of it is lost because the last leaves of the manuscript are missing.
2. The word *vafskiptasamr* is not recorded in the dictionaries but must mean something like "irresolute."
3. The negotiations between King Sigurðr and Grégóríús are similar to those between Magnús berfœttr and Sveinki Steinarsson, and the moral of the story is perhaps the same (see note 56.9 above).
4. This part of the story is very similar to Ch. 18 above.
5. Although Grégóríús defects from King Sigurðr for good reason, he becomes an exemplary retainer to King Ingi, thus illustrating again the theme of loyal service (cf. note 92.2).

Chapter 99

1. On the momentous visit of Cardinal Nicholas Breakspear in 1152, see *ÍF* 28, 333n.1, and Arne Odd Johnsen 1945.
2. On Jón Birgisson, see note 92.5.

Chapter 100

1. Cf. note 95.1.
2. On the nickname *skrúðhyrna*, see Finnur Jónsson 1907:240–41. *Hyrna* refers to something horn-shaped. Finnur Jónsson suggests a three-cornered scarf or a certain type of ax.
3. The nickname *húsfreyja* simply means "housewife" (Finnur Jónsson 1907:267).
4. For the location of Flóruvágar (Florvåg) in relation to Bergen, see the map in *Heimskringla* (1991), III, 268.
5. Hǫfund is a town in the Norwegian district of Gjerpen (Opp- and Uthaven) in Telemark (see the map in *Heimskringla* [1991], III, 275).
6. The word for "sea mile" is *vika*, "week" (FJ 459.18). See Poul Rasmussen, "Uge søs," in *KLNM* 19, 248–49, and "Mil," in *KLNM* 11, 626–27. Rasmussen notes N. E. Nørlund's calculation of a sea mile at somewhere between 8 and 8.5 kilometers.
7. This is the same Stuðla in Sunnhordaland mentioned above in note 95.4.
8. The Seleyjar (Seløyane) are an island group off the south coast of Norway (Agder) (see the map in *Heimskringla* [1991], III, 279).
9. Mostr (Moster) is an island south of Bergen off the mouth of Hardangerfjorden. Grœningarsund (Grønning) refers to the straits between the coast south of Bergen and the offshore islands (see the map in *Heimskringla* [1991], III, 279).
10. Foldin refers to Oslofjorden (see the map in *Heimskringla* [1991], III, 282).
11. The balance of the chapter is filled in from *Heimskringla* (*ÍF* 28, 345–46). The story is continued in *Heimskringla* down to 1179 and can be read in Hollander's translation (pp. 768–821).

Notes on Stanzas

St. 1: Arnórr Þórðarson jarlaskald: "Magnússdrápa" 1. FJ 19; *Flat* III, 262; *FmS* VI, 21–22; *F* 168; *ÍF* 28, 3, st. 1; *ÍF* 29, 208–9, st. 165; *Skj* IA, 338; *Skj* IB, 311; EAK 158.

The second half-stanza echoes the first half-stanza of "Óláfsdrápa Tryggvasonar" by Hallfreðr Óttarsson vandræðaskald (the cantankerous poet) (*Skj* IA, 156):

> tolf vas elds at aldri
> ýsetrs hati vetra
> hraustr þás herskip glæsti
> Hǫrða vinr ór Gǫrðum.

The enemy of the fire of the bow seat [arm, gold, generous king] was twelve years of age when the audacious friend of the Hǫrðar [people of Hordaland] handsomely outfitted his warships from Russia.

St. 2: Arnórr Þórðarson jarlaskald: "Magnússdrápa" 2. FJ 19–20; *Flat* III, 263; *FmS* VI, 22; *F* 168; *ÍF* 28, 4, st. 2; *SnE* I, 498 (ll. 5–8); *Skj* IA, 338; *Skj* IB, 311; EAK 158; *NN* §3082.

In l. 4, "bredía" (Flat; Hr "bræðir") has been emended to "bræðis" (Hkr), and "beinlogs ryre" in l. 7 has been emended to "brimlogs rýri" (mover of the wave flame) in keeping with the other MSS.

St. 3: Arnórr Þórðarson jarlaskald: "Magnússdrápa" 4. FJ 21; *Flat* III, 264; *FmS* VI, 26; *ÍF* 29, 210, st. 166; *Skj* IA, 339; *Skj* IB, 312; EAK 158; *NN* §817.

Flat gives the poet as "Skúli," whereas the other versions correctly attribute the stanza to Arnórr. The first half-stanza is corrupt: the translation of "gellir" (contender) is conjectural, and "hata" (oblique case) is emended from "hate" (nominative). The reading follows *NN* §817.

St. 4: Arnórr Þórðarson jarlaskald: "Magnússdrápa hrynhenda" 8. FJ 21; *Flat* III, 264; *FmS* VI, 26; *Skj* IA, 334; *Skj* IB, 307–8; EAK 156; *NN* §812.

"Magnússdrápa hrynhenda," which Arnórr presented to King Magnús on the occasion described in Chapter 21, is the first panegyric composed in *hrynhent* meter. The only earlier poetry preserved in *hrynhent* is one half-stanza and a couplet from "Hafgerðingadrápa" ("the poem of large breakers"; *Skj* IA, 177), but the authenticity of those lines is doubtful.

St. 5: Sigvatr Þórðarson: "Bersǫglisvísur" 1. FJ 26; *Flat* III, 267; *FmS* VI, 38–39; *Skj* IA, 251; *Skj* IB, 234; EAK 121–22; *NN* §§1113A, 2259, 2338B, 2463E.

For the interpretation of the first half-stanza, see *NN* § 2259 (= Hr). The second half-stanza follows *Skj* IB. For the order of Sigvatr's "Bersǫglisvísur" in Hkr and *MskMS, see Vestlund 1929.

St. 6: Sigvatr Þórðarson: "Bersǫglisvísur" 2. FJ 26; *Flat* III, 267; *FmS* VI, 39; *Skj* IA, 251; *Skj* IB, 235; EAK 122; *NN* §1853A.

In l. 5, "hæl" (heel) has been emended to "her" (army), in keeping with earlier editions.

St. 7: Sigvatr Þórðarson: "Bersǫglisvísur" 3. FJ 26–27; *Flat* III, 267; *FmS* VI, 39; *Skj* IA, 252; *Skj* IB, 235; EAK 122.

Óláfr Haraldsson enn helgi (St. Óláfr), Magnús's father, was king of Norway (1016–1028).

St. 8: Sigvatr Þórðarson: "Bersǫglisvísur" 4. FJ 27; *Flat* III, 268; *FmS* VI, 39–40; *ÍF* 28, 27, st. 26; *Skj* IA, 252; *Skj* IB, 235; EAK 122; *NN* §2776.

The stanza has been interpreted in accordance with the Hkr version (see *NN* §2776). Hákon Haraldsson enn góði (the good) was king of Norway ca. 933–960. He was fostered by Aðalsteinn (Æthelstan), king of England (924–939) (see note 1.5), and died in 961 from the wounds he received in the Battle of Fitjar in Stord, Norway.

St. 9: Sigvatr Þórðarson: "Bersǫglisvísur" 5. FJ 27; *Flat* III, 268; *FmS* VI, 40; *ÍF* 28, 27–28, st. 27; *Skj* IA, 252; *Skj* IB, 235; EAK 122; *NN* §1864.

The two Óláfrs mentioned in the stanza are Óláfr Tryggvason, king of Norway, ca. 995–1000, and Óláfr Haraldsson, Magnús's father.

St. 10: Sigvatr Þórðarson: "Bersǫglisvísur" 6. FJ 27; *Flat* III, 268; *FmS* VI, 40–41; *Skj* IA, 252–53; *Skj* IB, 236; EAK 122; *NN* §§1865, 2476, 3097H.

Magnús Óláfsson returned to Norway from Russia in the autumn of 1035.

St. 11: Sigvatr Þórðarson: "Bersǫglisvísur" 7. FJ 28; *Flat* III, 268; *FmS* VI, 41; *Skj* IA, 253; *Skj* IB, 236; EAK 122; *NN* §1114.

St. 12: Sigvatr Þórðarson: "Bersǫglisvísur" 8. FJ 28; *Flat* III, 268; *FmS* VI, 41–42; *ÍF* 28, 28, st. 28; *ÍF* 29, 213, st. 167 (ll. 5–8); *Skj* IA, 253; *Skj* IB, 236; EAK 122; *NN* §1866.

The text follows the versions in Flat, Hr, and AM 66. Ll. 1–2 in Hkr read "skulut ráðgjǫfum yðrum reiðask" (you should not get enraged at your counsellors). The reference to Magnús's earlier promises in Ulfasund (Ulvesund, Nordfjord, Norway) is obscure. According to the Norwegian law of the Gulathing (*NGL* I, 58), Magnús emended that law in Langeyjarsund (Langøysundet, Møre, Norway). None of the prose texts mentions that occasion, however, and neither Ulfasund nor Langeyjarsund is otherwise connected with Magnús.

St. 13: Sigvatr Þórðarson: "Bersǫglisvísur" 13. FJ 28; *Flat* III, 268; *FmS* VI, 42; *ÍF* 28, 29–30, st. 31; *ÍF* 29, 213, st. 168 (ll. 1–4); *Skj* IA, 255; *Skj* IB, 237; EAK 123.

The Hkr version of the second half-stanza differs from that of Hr, AM 66, Flat and reads as follows: "vinr es sás" (l. 1); "teitir" (l. 3), that is, "vinr es, sás býðr vǫrnuð, en hlýðið til, teitir varmra benja tármútaris" (he is a friend, who offers a warning, but you must heed, warrior). The phrase "the hand must be measured by moderation" implies that no one should reach further than moderation prescribes.

St. 14: Sigvatr Þórðarson: "Bersǫglisvísur" 11. FJ 29; *Flat* III, 269; *FmS* VI, 42–43; *ÍF* 28, 29, st. 30; *ÍF* 29, 213–14, st. 169; *Skj* IA, 254; *Skj* IB, 237; EAK 123; *NN* §1867.

Flat, AM 66, and Hr all have "hjaldrgegna" ("battle-brave"; l. 2) as an adjective modifying "þegna." Hkr and Fsk have "hjaldrgegnir" (nominative), which is interpreted as a form of address (battle-brave one). The translation of ll. 3–4 follows *NN* §1867.

St. 15: Sigvatr Þórðarson: "Bersǫglisvísur" 12. FJ 29; *Flat* III, 269; *FmS* VI, 43; *ÍF* 28, 30, st. 32; *ÍF* 29, 215–16, st. 171 (ll. 5–8+1–4); *Ágrip, ÍF* 29, 33; *SnE* II, 176 (ll. 1–4); *Skj* IA, 254–55; *Skj* IB, 237; EAK 123; *NN* §§1868; 1982.

In l. 4, the Flat reading "Haralldz menn" (Haraldr's men) has been emended to "hárir menn" (mature men) in accordance with the other MSS. The term "lawmen" (*þingmenn*) refers either to men who attend the legal assembly (*þing*) or to men who belong to a specific Norwegian legal district (*þing*).

St. 16: Sigvatr Þórðarson: "Bersǫglisvísur" 10. FJ 29; *Flat* III, 269; *FmS* VI, 43; *ÍF* 28, 28–29, st. 29; *ÍF* 29, 214, st. 170; *Skj* IA, 254; *Skj* IB, 237; EAK 123; *NN* §654.

The reading of the first half-stanza follows that of Flat, Hr, and AM 66. L. 3 in Hkr and Fsk is rendered slightly differently.

St. 17: Sigvatr Þórðarson: "Bersǫglisvísur" 14. FJ 29; *Flat* III, 269; *FmS* VI, 43–44; *ÍF* 28, 30, st. 33; *Skj* IA, 255; *Skj* IB, 238; EAK 123.

The text of the second half-stanza has been emended in accordance with Hkr. The versions in Hr, AM 66, and Flat show an increasing degree of corruption, with clumsy attempts to restore the text: l. 6 in Flat has "duelia" ("delay"; = Hr, AM 66) for "telja" (call); l. 7 has "frans" (Hr, AM 66) or "fáárs" (Flat) for "flaums"; and l. 8 in Flat reads "fulleidr konungr greifum," which in Hr and AM 66 is rendered as "fulleið konungs reiði" in an attempt to restore internal rhyme (-leið:reiði). Some of those readings must have been present in the common exemplar of *H and Flat (m), and it is impossible to know whether Msk2 contained the same mistakes.

*St. 18: Sigvatr Þórðarson: "Bersǫglisvísur" 18. FJ 29–30; Flat III, 269; F 177; Skj IA, 256; Skj IB, 238–39; EAK 124; NN §655.

The kenning "Haraldr's hawk isle" for Norway is unusual (see NN §655). In Steinn Herdísarson's "Óláfsdrápa" 12 (see st. 156), Norway is called "the lofty land" ("hár fold"), and "hawk isle" is apparently also intended to evoke the image of a mountainous region. The Haraldr mentioned in the kenning is the consolidator of Norway, Haraldr Halfdanarson hárfagri (fairhair).

*St. 19: Sigvatr Þórðarson: "Bersǫglisvísur" 16. FJ 30; Flat III, 269; Skj IA, 256; Skj IB, 238; EAK 123; NN §§2477, 3218.

The first half-stanza is interpreted according to NN §2477, while the second follows Louis-Jensen (1970:210). For the meaning of "jafnt" in l. 5, see NN §3218. Óláfr Haraldsson, Magnús's father, was also known by the nickname "enn digri" (the stout). Sts. 19–20 are recorded in Flat (*MskMS) only, and Louis-Jensen (1977:84) argues that they were not part of Sigvatr's "Bersǫglisvísur." According to her, their tenor suggests that they belonged to another poem and were inserted by a scribe at some point in the Msk transmission.

*St. 20: Sigvatr Þórðarson: "Bersǫglisvísur" 17. FJ 30; Flat III, 269; Skj IA, 256; Skj IB, 238; EAK 123; NN §3067.

L. 1 in Flat is corrupt ("Siguazs hugir er hítteg") and has been emended in accordance with NN §3067.

*St. 21: Arnórr Þórðarson jarlaskald: "Magnússdrápa hrynhenda" 9. FJ 32; Flat III, 271; FmS VI, 47; Skj IA, 335; Skj IB, 308; EAK 156.

"Visundr" (bison) was the name of Magnús's famous warship, which he inherited from his father, Óláfr Haraldsson (see note 4.9). King Gjúki is known from Old Norse heroic literature. He was the father of Gunnarr, Hǫgni, and Guðrún (see Vǫlsunga saga and the eddic lays of Sigurðr).

*St. 22: Arnórr Þórðarson jarlaskald: "Magnússdrápa hrynhenda" 10. FJ 32–33; Flat III, 271; FmS VI, 47–48; F 179; ÍF 28, 34, st. 36; Skj IA, 335; Skj IB, 308; EAK 156; NN §§813–14.

In l. 6, earlier editors have emended "fyri" (Hkr) or "fyris" (Flat) to "fyrir" and taken it as an adverb modifying the verb "bifǫusk" (trembled) with "álar" (sea streams) as the subject ("the sea streams trembled"). However, the verb-adverb collocation "bifask fyrir" is not attested elsewhere, and "a trembling sea" is out of keeping with skaldic imagery. The present reading preserves the text of the MS ("fyris álar," "eels of pine" = "ships") as well as the imagery of the first half-stanza ("the red gold [adornment on the ship] trembled").

*St. 23: Arnórr Þórðarson jarlaskald: "Magnússdrápa" 5. FJ 34; Flat III, 272; FmS VI, 49; F 178; ÍF 28, 32–33, st. 34; ÍF 29, 216, st. 172; Skj IA, 339; Skj IB, 312: EAK 158; NN §§818, 819A, 2989A.

In l. 1, Hkr and Flat have "jarla" (jarls') for "árla" ("early"; Hr, AM 66), which is taken as a qualifier to "dróttinn" (the lord of jarls).

*St. 24: Arnórr Þórðarson jarlaskald: "Magnússdrápa" 7. FJ 35; Flat III, 272–73; FmS VI, 51; Skj IA, 340; Skj IB, 312–13; EAK 159.

*St. 25: Arnórr Þórðarson jarlaskald: "Magnússdrápa" 6. FJ 35; Flat III, 273; FmS VI, 50–51; F 179; ÍF 28, 34–35, st. 37; Skj IA, 340; Skj IB, 312; EAK 158–59; NN §§1295, 1853B.

In Hkr, Hr, and AM 66 the stanza is attributed to Arnórr. L. 3 in Hkr reads "hallr ok hrími sollinn" (steep and bursting with frost) as appositions to the ship ("hléborðs visundr"). In l. 5, Hkr has "bjóðr" (giver) for "blíðr" ("benevolent"; Hr, AM 66, Flat) and "brynþings fetilstinga" for "brynþings meginhringa" (Hr, AM 66) or "byrdings meginþinga" (Flat).

*St. 26: Þjóðólfr Arnórsson: "Magnússflokkr" 5. FJ 36; Flat III, 274; FmS VI, 53; F 180; ÍF 28, 38, st. 38; ÍF 29, 219, st. 173; Skj IA, 362; Skj IB, 333; EAK 168.

In Hkr and Fsk, the stanza is attributed to Þjóðólfr Arnórsson.

St. 27: Arnórr Þórðarson jarlaskald: "Magnússdrápa" 8. FJ 37–38; *Flat* III, 275; *FmS* VI, 55; *Skj* IA, 340: *Skj* IB, 313; EAK 159; *NN* §820.

Earlier editors have construed l. 3 as "sveið ófám at Jómi" (scorched many at Wollin), which is metrically impossible. The Flat version ("suefns ofan af Jomni") is corrupt; AM 66 has "of ám" and Hr, "ofám." The present reading is supported by the fact that the adjective "ámr" (dark) occurs twice in Arnórr's poetry ("Þorfinnsdrápa" 7: "í ámu blóði," "in the dark blood" [*Skj* IA, 345]; "Erfidrápa Haralds harðráða" 10 [see *st. 140*]: "ámt grjót" "dark stones").

St. 28: Arnórr Þórðarson jarlaskald: "Magnússdrápa" 9. FJ 38; *Flat* III, 275; *FmS* VI, 55, 75; *F* 184; *ÍF* 28, 46, st. 43; *Skj* IA, 340; *Skj* IB, 313; EAK 159.

The name of the poet is given in Hkr. The MSS of Hkr have "valska" (Norman) for "virðum" ("warriors"; l. 3) and "Vestlandi" (l. 4) for "Vinðlandi." The latter reading also occurs in the prose texts. Hr and AM 66 record the half-stanza twice: the first time (*FmS* VI, 55) the reading of Flat is retained ("virðum," "Vinðlandi"). In keeping with Flat (*MskMS), the prose gives the place name as "Vestlandi," and the stanza is anonymous. The second variant of the half-stanza (*FmS* VI, 75) follows that of Hkr ("valska," "Vestlandi"), and the lines are attributed to Arnórr. The place name is corrupt in the prose text, which reads "fyrir vestan Aren"—a scribal error for Hkr's "fyrir Vestlandi á Ré" (by western Pomerania at Rügen) (see note 4.11). Thus *FmS* preserve the text of both Msk and Hkr. The Hkr version of the half-stanza apparently originated with Snorri, who emended the line in keeping with the prose ("Vestlandi"). See also *ÍF* 28, 46n.

St. 29: Þjóðólfr Arnórsson: "Magnússflokkr" 6. FJ 45; *Flat* III, 281; *FmS* VI, 64; *Skj* IA, 362; *Skj* IB, 333; EAK 168; *NN* §§849, 3083.

See *ÍF* 28, 42n for the importance of the place names in this stanza and in our *st. 32*. Ella was king of Northumbria (ninth century) and the slayer of Ragnarr loðbrók (hairybreeches). Later (867?), he himself was killed by the sons of Ragnarr (see *Ragnars saga loðbrókar* and *Þáttr af Ragnars sonum*). In the *kenning* "Ella's kinsman" (Magnús), the name denotes "king" in general.

St. 30: Þjóðólfr Arnórsson: "Magnússflokkr" 7. FJ 46; *Flat* III, 281; *FmS* VI, 67; *F* 183; *ÍF* 28, 44, st. 42; *ÍF* 29, 222, st. 174; *Skj* IA, 362–63; *Skj* IB, 333–34; EAK 168.

In Hkr, Hr, AM 66, and Fsk, the stanza is attributed to Þjóðólfr Arnórsson.

St. 31: Arnórr Þórðarson jarlaskald: "Magnússdrápa" 10. FJ 46–47; *Flat* III, 281; *FmS* VI, 65; *F* 183; *ÍF* 28, 43–44, st. 41; *ÍF* 29, 223, st. 175; *Skj* IA, 340–41; *Skj* IB, 313; EAK 159.

"Hel" was the name of Óláfr Haraldsson's battle-ax, which later was inherited by his son Magnús. According to Theodoricus, the ax was partly destroyed in the Battle of Lyrskovshede and later preserved in a church in Nidaros: "quæ et ibi confracta est et modo servatur in Nidrosiensi ecclesia" (*MHN* 49).

St. 32: Arnórr Þórðarson jarlaskald: "Magnússdrápa hrynhenda" 13. FJ 47; *Flat* III, 281; *FmS* VI, 68; *Skj* IA, 336; *Skj* IB, 309; EAK 157; *NN* §816.

The interpretation of the second half-stanza is uncertain. In l. 1, AM 66 has "vári"; Hr, "vaxi"; Flat, "vorru." Finnur Jónsson (*Skj* IB) emends to "verja" with the unattested meaning "son," which he takes as the base word for "grams ens digra" (son of the stout king). Ernst A. Kock (*NN* §816) keeps that emendation but translates "verr" as "champion" (also unattested). According to his reading, "verja valkǫstr" would mean "heap of fallen champions." However, "vári" (AM 66) either means "relative" (Björn M. Ólsen 1903:108) or "guardian," and "vári grams ens digra" must then be translated as "relative of the stout king" (Magnús) or "guardian of the stout king," where the latter interpretation could refer to Magnús in his capacity of keeper of St. Óláfr's shrine (see *ÍF* 28, 20; trans. Hollander p. 548). In l. 7, "kunn" ("famous"; accusative) has been emended to "kunnr" (nominative). If "kunn" is kept, it modifies "varga ætt" (family of wolves), which is not in keeping with Arnórr's practice: he frequently uses the adjective, but always as an apposition to a person (e.g., "þjóðum kunnr"; *st. 37*).

St. 33: Arnórr Þórðarson jarlaskald: "Magnússdrápa" 11. FJ 47; *Flat* III, 281–82; *FmS* VI, 68; *Skj* IA, 341; *Skj* IB, 313–14; EAK 159; *NN* §821.

In l. 4, "firar" ("people"; nominative) has been emended to "fira" (genitive). Finnur Jónsson connects "fira" with "siklingr"; Ernst A. Kock (*NN* §821) has "hrækǫst fira." The latter interpretation causes a redundant translation: "hrækǫst fira af ulfa barri" (stack of corpses of men from corpses). However, Hr and AM 66 have "firar," which makes no sense, and the reading in Flat, "fira ræfi" (fira_ræfi), indicates that the words in positions 4–6 formed a syntactic unit. The combination "vísi" plus qualifier is not uncommon (see *LP* 626), and the extra -r on "firar" could have arisen in hiatus during oral performance.

St. 34: Arnórr Þórðarson jarlaskald: "Magnússdrápa" 14. FJ 49; *Flat* III, 283; *FmS* VI, 84; *Skj* IA, 342; *Skj* IB, 314; EAK 159; *NN* §823.

The interpretation of the second half-stanza follows *NN* §823. Hǫgni is the name of various persons known from heroic literature, for example, Hǫgni Gjúkason (see note on *st. 21*), Sigrún's father in the eddic lays of Helgi, and a sea king, the father of Hildr (*SnE* I, 432–36).

St. 35: Þjóðólfr Arnórsson: "Magnússflokkr" 21. FJ 50; *Flat* III, 283; *FmS* VI, 84; *F* 189; *ÍF* 28, 57, st. 61; *Skj* IA, 366; *Skj* IB, 337; EAK 170.

Hkr assigns this stanza to Þjóðólfr Arnórsson.

St. 36: Arnórr Þórðarson jarlaskald: "Magnússdrápa" 16. FJ 50; *Flat* III, 283; *FmS* VI, 87; *ÍF* 29, 225, st. 179; *Skj* IA, 342; *Skj* IB, 315; EAK 160; *NN* §2520.

L. 2 is corrupt in Flat ("tyr log noga"). Hr and AM 66 have "ítrlógandi," and Fsk B reads "arflógandi" (spender of inheritance), which is kept in the Fsk edition. Finnur Jónsson (*Skj* IB) emends to "auðlógandi" (spender of wealth), whereas Ernst A. Kock (*NN* §2520) has "ýs lógandi" (spender of the bow). "Lógandi" should technically have a qualifier (hence the various emendations).

St. 37: Arnórr Þórðarson jarlaskald: "Magnússdrápa hrynhenda" 15. FJ 50; *Flat* III, 284; *FmS* VI, 85; *Knýtlinga saga*, *ÍF* 35, 132, st. 27; *Skj* IA, 336–37; *Skj* IB, 310; EAK 157; *NN* §§816n.1, 2019.

The names of the poet and the poem are given in *Knýtlinga saga*.

St. 38: Þjóðólfr Arnórsson: "Magnússflokkr" 22. FJ 51; *Flat* III, 284; *FmS* VI, 84–85; *F* 189; *ÍF* 28, 57–58, st. 62; *ÍF* 29, 223, st. 176; *Skj* IA, 366–67; *Skj* IB, 337; EAK 170; *NN* §§806, 854, 1817.

The reading of the first half-stanza follows the *Fornrit* editions. The appended clause (*hjástælt*) in l. 8 is modeled on a similar construction in Kormákr Ǫgmundarson's "Sigurð-ardrápa" 6:8 (*Skj* IA, 80): "[fens] vá gramr til menja" (the lord strove for treasure).

St. 39: Oddr kikinaskald: "poem about Magnús enn góði" 1. FJ 51; *Flat* III, 284; *FmS* VI, 90; *F* 191; *ÍF* 28, 63–64, st. 73; *Skj* IA, 354–55; *Skj* IB, 327; EAK 165.

The correct name of the poet is given in Hkr. In Hkr, l. 4 reads "vápnhljóði mjǫk þjóðir" (people [grew accustomed to] the sound of weapons), which is kept in the other editions. In the second half-stanza, all editions take "lítlu" (a little) with "fyr jól" (a little before Christmas) and translate "óhlítulig" either as "undecided" (*Skj* IB) or as "fought hero-ically" (Hkr). The first translation makes no sense in the prose context, and the second is unattested. In the present edition, "lítlu" (by little, by no means) is taken as an adverb modifying "óhlítulig." Michaelmas falls on September 29 (see note 5.13).

St. 40: Arnórr Þórðarson jarlaskald: "Magnússdrápa" 15. FJ 51; *Flat* III, 284; *FmS* VI, 85–86; *Skj* IA, 342; *Skj* IB, 314; EAK 159–60.

St. 41: Arnórr Þórðarson jarlaskald: "Magnússdrápa" 13. FJ 51; *Flat* III, 284; *FmS* VI, 85; *ÍF* 28, 58, st. 63; *ÍF* 29, 224, st. 178; *Skj* IA, 341–42; *Skj* IB, 314; EAK 159.

The translation of the half-stanza follows the *Fornrit* editions. The meaning of "þeirar tíðar" (at the right time) is uncertain. Bjǫrn Úlfsson, Sveinn's brother, was an English earl who, in 1049, was murdered by Swegn Godwinson, Harold Godwinson's older brother.

St. 42: Arnórr Þórðarson jarlaskald: "Magnússdrápa" 12:1–4. FJ 52; *Flat* III, 285; *FmS* VI, 83 (ll. 1–8); *F* 188–89 (ll. 1–8); *ÍF* 28, 56–57, st. 60 (ll. 1–8); *ÍF* 29, 224, st. 177 (ll. 1–8); *Skj* IA, 341; *Skj* IB, 314; EAK 159; *NN* §822.

The full stanza is given in Hkr, F, Fsk, Hr, and AM 66. In l. 1, Hkr and Fsk have "heiti" (present tense) for "héti" (preterite; Hr, AM 66, Flat).

*St. 43: Arnórr Þórðarson jarlaskald: "Magnússdrápa" 17:1–4. FJ 52; *Flat* III, 285; *FmS* VI, 89 (ll. 1–8); *F* 190 (ll. 1–8); *ÍF* 28, 62, st. 71 (ll. 1–8); *ÍF* 29, 225, st. 180 (ll. 1–4); *Skj* IA, 342–43; *Skj* IB, 315; EAK 160.

The name of the poet is given in Hkr, F, Hr, and AM 66, all of which also cite the full stanza.

*St. 44: Arnórr Þórðarson jarlaskald: "Magnússdrápa" 18. FJ 52; *Flat* III, 285; *FmS* VI, 89–90; *F* 190–91; *ÍF* 28, 63, st. 72; *ÍF* 29, 225–26, st. 181; *Skj* IA, 343; *Skj* IB, 315; EAK 160; *NN* §§824, 1134.

The reading of the first half-stanza follows Hr, AM 66, Flat, and Fsk. In l. 5, Flat, Fsk, AM 66, and some MSS of Hkr (Hkr x) have "annarr" for "annan" (Hr and Hkr y), which is at odds with the prose.

*St. 45: Haraldr harðráði: lv. 2:5–8. FJ 57; *Flat* III, 289; *FmS* VI, 130–31; *F* 193; *ÍF* 28, 69, st. 77 (ll. 5–8); *Orkn*, *ÍF* 34, 53, st. 16; *Skj* IA, 356; *Skj* IB, 328; EAK 166; *NN* §§1137, 3227.

L. 3 is unmetrical, and the insertion of the expletive particle "of" would restore the reading: "hverr of veit nema verðak." However, "of" occurs in none of the variants.

*St. 46: Bǫlverkr Arnórsson: "poem about Haraldr harðráði" 1. FJ 58; *Flat* III, 289; *FmS* VI, 131–32; *F* 193; *ÍF* 28, 69–70, st. 78; *ÍF* 29, 227, st. 182; *Skj* IA, 385; *Skj* IB, 355; EAK 178.

In l. 7, Hkr and Fsk have "ár et næsta" (the next year) instead of "ár en næstu" ("the next years"; Hr, AM 66). The latter reading is in keeping with the prose text.

*St. 47: Þjóðólfr Arnórsson: "Haraldsdrápa runhenda" 1:5–8. FJ 58; *Flat* III, 289; *FmS* VI, 132; *F* 193; *ÍF* 28, 70, st. 79 (ll. 5–8); *Skj* IA, 368; *Skj* IB, 338; EAK 171.

Hkr, Hr, and AM 66 give this and the next half-stanza (**st. 48*) as one full stanza, but in the reverse order (**st. 48* + **st. 47*). Fsk only cites **st. 48* (see below). The meter is *run-hent*, and the remaining three extant half-stanzas are preserved in *SnE* (I, 462). "Læsir" is the Old Norse term for the Ljachar, a people near the Vistula in Poland.

*St. 48: Þjóðólfr Arnórsson: "Haraldsdrápa runhenda" 1:1–4. FJ 58; *Flat* III, 290; *FmS* VI, 132; *F* 193; *ÍF* 28, 70, st. 79 (ll. 1–4); *ÍF* 29, 228, st. 183; *Skj* IA, 368; *Skj* IB, 338; EAK 171.

Jarl Eilífr Rǫgnvaldsson was the son of the Swedish jarl Rǫgnvaldr Úlfsson and Ingibjǫrg, sister of the Norwegian king Óláfr Tryggvason. "Fylkja hamalt" means to marshal the troops in a wedge-shaped formation, also known as "svínfylking" (*porcinum caput*), that was protected on the sides by shield walls (see *LP* 225; *Konungs skuggsiá* 59–60). See also *st. 195*.

*St. 49: Illugi bryndœlaskald: "poem about Haraldr harðráði" 3. FJ 59; *Flat* III, 290; *FmS* VI, 133; *Skj* IA, 384; *Skj* IB, 354; EAK 178.

The extant portion of Illugi's panegyric to Haraldr consists of four half-stanzas (the first two are recorded in *SnE* I, 478; the fourth in *ÍF* 28, 75–76, st. 82, and *ÍF* 29, 230, st. 185). All the half-stanzas are characterized by embedded clauses occupying ll. 2–3. These inserted clauses relate episodes in the eddic cycle of poems about Sigurðr Fáfnisbani (the slayer of the dragon Fáfnir) and the sons of Gjúki. Illugi must have used these allusions to eulogize Haraldr Sigurðarson by juxtaposing his merits to those of Sigurðr the Dragonslayer. The embedded clauses in stanzas 1–2 and 4 read as follows:

1. "Menskerðir stakk sverði myrkaurriða markar" (the necklace diminisher [generous king, Sigurðr] pierced the dark trout of the forest [dragon, Fáfnir] with his sword).
2. "Mildr gramr helt beisku eiskaldi orms eldi" (the generous king [Sigurðr] held the acrid heart of the snake [Fáfnir] over the fire).
4. "Buðla sonr bauð mágum sínum heim, sem frágum" (Buðli's son [Atli] invited his in-laws home, as we have heard).

Because the embedded clause in the second half-stanza contains the word "eiskald" (heart), which is otherwise recorded in poetry only in "Fáfnismál" (when Sigurðr fries

Fáfnir's heart: 27:4–5, "eiscǫld ec vil etinn láta"; Neckel/Kuhn, *Edda*, p. 185), Illugi must have known that stanza in its present form and put it to use in his eulogy (see also *SnE* II, 430, 493).

St. 50: Bǫlverkr Arnórsson: "poem about Haraldr harðráði" 2. FJ 59; *Flat* III, 290; *FmS* VI, 134; *F* 193; *ÍF* 28, 71, st. 80; *Skj* IA, 385; *Skj* IB, 355; EAK 178; *NN* §§806, 2035.

The first half-stanza follows *NN* §806. "Malmr" (iron) in the second half-stanza is translated in accordance with *ÍF* 28, 71.

St. 51: Bǫlverkr Arnórsson: "poem about Haraldr harðráði" 3. FJ 62; *Flat* III, 292; *FmS* VI, 135; *Skj* IA, 385; *Skj* IB, 355; EAK 178; *NN* §2036.

St. 52: Þjóðólfr Arnórsson: "Sexstefja" 2. FJ 64; *Flat* III, 294; *FmS* VI, 138–39; *F* 195; *ÍF* 28, 75, st. 81; *ÍF* 29, 230, st. 184; *Skj* IA, 369; *Skj* IB, 339; EAK 171.

St. 53: Þjóðólfr Arnórsson: "Sexstefja" 4. U 8; FJ 72; *Flat* III, 299; *FmS* VI, 154; *Skj* IA, 370; *Skj* IB, 340; EAK 171.

St. 54: Stúfr Þórðarson enn blindi: "Stúfsdrápa" 2. U 11; FJ 78; *Flat* III, 303; *FmS* VI, 161; *F* 199; *ÍF* 28, 83, st. 84; *ÍF* 29, 233, st. 187; *Skj* IA, 404; *Skj* IB, 373; EAK 186; *NN* §§880, 3396S.

L. 8, which in the Hkr versions reads "hafi ríks, þars vel líkar," is a part of a *klofastef* (split refrain). The complete refrain reads as follows ("Stúfsdrápa" 2:8, 3:8, 6:4):

> Hafi ríks þars vel líkar
> vist of aldr með Kristi
> Haralds ǫnd ofar lǫndum.

"Hafi ǫnd ríks Haralds vist of aldr með Kristi ofar lǫndum, þars vel líkar."

May the spirit of powerful Haraldr reside forever with Christ above the earth, where it is good to be.

See also *sts. 55* and *92*.

St. 55: Stúfr Þórðarson enn blindi: "Stúfsdrápa" 3. U 11–12; FJ 78–79; *FmS* VI, 162; *F* 200; *ÍF* 28, 84, st. 85; *ÍF* 29, 234, st. 188; *Skj* IA, 404; *Skj* IB, 373–74; EAK 186.

The first half-stanza follows Fsk. For l. 8, see the note on *st. 54,* above.

St. 56: Þórarinn Skeggjason 1. U 14; FJ 83; *FmS* VI, 167; *F* 201; *ÍF* 28, 86, st. 86; *ÍF* 29, 235, st. 189; *Skj* IA, 400; *Skj* IB, 368; EAK 184; *NN* §879.

The full name of the poet, Þórarinn Skeggjason, is given in Hkr, Hr, and AM 66 (Fsk has "Þórarinn"). The term "stólþengill" or "stólkonungr" (chair king) is the Norse version of Russian "stolnyi knyazi" ("great princes"; see Blöndal 1978:3, 177).

St. 57: Þjóðólfr Arnórsson: "Sexstefja" 6. U 14; FJ 83–84; *FmS* VI, 167–68; *F* 201; *ÍF* 28, 86–87, st. 87; *ÍF* 29, 235, st. 190 (ll. 1–4); *Skj* IA, 370; *Skj* IB, 340; EAK 171.

In l. 7, "a" (apparently caused by the preposition "á" in the previous line; MskMS, Hr) has been emended to "en" in keeping with AM 66 and the Hkr versions.

St. 58: Haraldr harðráði: lv. 4. U 15; FJ 85; *FmS* VI, 169; *F* 201; *ÍF* 28, 89, st. 88; *ÍF* 29, 237, st. 192; *SnE* I, 444 (ll. 1–4); *Skj* IA, 357; *Skj* IB, 329; EAK 166; *NN* §§ 2023, 2266.

The stanza is the first of the so-called "gamanvísur" (jesting verses), which are characterized by a recurring refrain occupying ll. 7–8. According to the prose text (*ÍF* 28, 89; *ÍF* 29, 237; *FmS* VI, 169; *Msk* 148), the poem originally consisted of sixteen stanzas. Five stanzas are recorded in MskMS, Hr, and AM 66, whereas Hkr and Fsk give only the first (*st. 58*), and Flat omits them altogether. The interpretation of the first half-stanza follows *NN* §2023. In l. 3, Hkr reads "brýnt" (quickly) for "brúnn" (Hr: "brun"; Fsk: "bryn").

St. 59: Haraldr harðráði: lv. 3. U 15; FJ 85; *FmS* VI, 169–70; *Skj* IA, 357; *Skj* IB, 328; EAK 166.

In l. 4, "vitz" (scribal error) has been emended to "víst" ("truly"; Hr, AM 66). The stanza alludes to the Battle of Stiklestad in 1030, where the fifteen-year old Haraldr and his half-brother, Óláfr Haraldsson, were overcome by the army of farmers from Trøndelag.

St. 60: "Haraldr harðráði: U 15; FJ 86; *FmS* VI, 170; *SnE* I, 498 (ll. 1–4); *Skj* IA, 139 (ll. 1–4); *Skj* IB, 130 (ll. 1–4); EAK 72 (ll.1–4).

The first half-stanza is recorded in *SnE* I, 498, where it is attributed to Brennu-Njáll Þorgeirsson, the protagonist of *Brennu-Njáls saga* (*ÍF* 12, *passim*). The second half-stanza is a repetition of ll. 5–8 of *st. 58*, above. L. 3 in the *Edda* version reads: "dreif á hafskips húfa" (battered the sides of the ocean-going ship).

St. 61: Haraldr harðráði: lv. 5. U 15; FJ 86; *FmS* VI, 170; *Orkn, ÍF* 34, 130, st. 34 (ll. 5–8); *Skj* IA, 357, 505; *Skj* IB, 329, 478; EAK 166, 235; *NN* §§2203B; 2989B.

In *Orkn*, the second half-stanza is part of a *lausavísa* (loose stanza) attributed to jarl Rǫgnvaldr kali Kolsson of Orkney (1139–1158). The first four lines of that stanza read as follows:

> Tafl emk ǫrr at efla
> íþróttir kannk níu
> týnik trauðla rúnum
> tíðs mér bók ok smíðir.

I am a daring chess player; I have nine accomplishments; I hardly forget the runes; I am accustomed to books and smith craft.

In MskMS, this stanza is the only jesting verse that leaves out the refrain. Hr and AM 66 add the refrain to conform with the prose text, which states that "they [the "gamanvísur"] all end in the same way" (*FmS* VI, 169 = *ÍF* 28, 89, *ÍF* 29, 237). Because the stanza then omits two of Haraldr's eight accomplishments, it hardly represents the original version. According to MskMS, most (not all) of the "gamanvísur" have the same ending, which would account for the lack of refrain in this stanza.

St. 62: Haraldr harðráði: lv. 7. U 16; FJ 86; *FmS* VI, 171; *Skj* IA, 358; *Skj* IB, 329; EAK 166; *NN* §2024A.

"Eygarð" ("island enclosure"; l. 6) is taken as an accusative of place. In Hr and AM 66, the order of this and the next stanza has been reversed. Upplǫnd (Opplandene) comprised present-day Hedmark, Hadeland, Romerike, Gudbrandsdalen, and Østerdalen in Norway. Haraldr's father, Sigurðr sýr (Sow), was a petty king of Upplǫnd.

St. 63: Haraldr harðráði: lv. 6. U 16; FJ 86; *FmS* VI, 170–71; *Skj* IA, 357–58; *Skj* IB, 329; EAK 166; *NN* §2524.

L. 1 in Hr and AM 66 has "enn" ("yet"; AM 66) and "ein" ("one"; Hr) for "oss" (us). Both readings restore the missing internal rhyme.

St. 64: Stúfr Þórðarson enn blindi: "Stúfsdrápa" 4. U 16; FJ 87; *Flat* III, 306; *FmS* VI, 172; *F* 202; *ÍF* 28, 90, st. 89; *ÍF* 29, 238, st. 193; *Skj* IA, 405; *Skj* IB, 374; EAK 186.

In l. 1, the Hkr versions read "allvaldr Egða" (the ruler of the people of Agder) for "ǫðlingr eiga" (MskMS, Fsk, Flat, Hr, AM 66) and, in l. 3, "gumna spjalli" (the friend of the people), for "gauta spjalli" (MskMS, Fsk, Flat, Hr, AM 66).

St. 65: Valgarðr á Velli: "poem about Haraldr harðráði" 5. U 16; FJ 87–88; *FmS* VI, 172; *F* 202; *ÍF* 28, 91, st. 90; *ÍF* 29, 238, st. 194; *Skj* IA, 391; *Skj* IB, 361; EAK 180–81; *NN* §§806, 875, 1144.

For the interpretation of the first stanza, see *NN* §§806, 1144. In the second half-stanza, the Hkr versions read "hvardyggr" (trustworthy) for "hugdyggr" (l. 6; MskMS, Fsk, Hr, AM 66). In l. 7, MskMS has the separate reading "snedrif" (snowstorm) where the other MSS have "sædrif" (sea spray); in l. 8, MskMS has "hnigþi" (singular) instead of "hnigðu" (plural; all other MSS). The different forms of the verb are reflected in the prose texts: according to MskMS, Haraldr sailed to Sweden with one ship, while Fsk (*ÍF* 29, 239) states that he went with three ships. Ll. 2 and 7 in MskMS are partly damaged by a hole in the vellum. Unger adds "frami veittiz þer" (l. 2) and "sattv þar er" (l. 7): the first reading is in keeping with Hkr, Hr, AM 66; the second must have been taken from Fsk A. (Hr, AM 66, Hkr all have "þá er"; F has "er".)

St. 66: Valgarðr á Velli: "poem about Haraldr harðráði" 6. U 17; FJ 88; *Flat* III, 306; *FmS* VI, 174; *F* 203; *ÍF* 28, 92–93, st. 92; *ÍF* 29, 239, st. 195; *Skj* IA, 391; *Skj* IB, 361; EAK 181.

The name of the poet is given in Hkr, Hr, and AM 66. Ll. 5 and 8 are damaged in MskMS. Unger's additions, "h[und]" and "[ey Donom nanar]," are taken from Flat. (Hkr, Fsk, Hr, AM 66 have "hynd," l. 1.) In l. 7, "skeiþr" (plural) has been emended to "skeið" (singular), in keeping with the verb forms ("bar," "rendi"; both singular).

St. 67: Valgarðr á Velli: "poem about Haraldr harðráði" 7. U 17–18; FJ 89–90; *FmS* VI, 175; *F* 203; *ÍF* 28, 93, st. 93; *ÍF* 29, 240, st. 196; *Skj* IA, 392; *Skj* IB, 361; EAK 181; *NN* §§806, 2989E.

St. 68: Valgarðr á Velli: "poem about Haraldr harðráði" 8. U 18; FJ 90; *FmS* VI, 175; *F* 203; *ÍF* 28, 93–94, st. 94; *ÍF* 29, 241, st. 197; *Skj* IA, 392; *Skj* IB, 362; EAK 181.

L. 8 in MskMS reads "hliott til scogs til flotta." The second "til" has been emended to "á," in keeping with the other MSS. The word "reykvell" (smoldering) is otherwise unattested.

St. 69: Valgarðr á Velli: "poem about Haraldr harðráði" 9. U 18; FJ 90; *FmS* VI, 176; *F* 203; *ÍF* 28, 94, st. 95; *ÍF* 29, 241, st. 198; *Skj* IA, 392; *Skj* IB, 362; EAK 181; *NN* §§876, 2989E.

In the first half-stanza, the Hkr MSS have "dvalði" (singular) with "ferð" (company) as the subject; Fsk has "dvǫlðum" (first person plural).

St. 70: Valgarðr á Velli: "poem about Haraldr harðráði" 10. U 19; FJ 92; *Flat* III, 308; *FmS* VI, 180; *ÍF* 29, 242, st. 199; *Skj* IA, 393; *Skj* IB, 362; EAK 181.

St. 71: Valgarðr á Velli: "poem about Haraldr harðráði" 11. U 19; FJ 92; *Flat* III, 308; *FmS* VI, 180; *ÍF* 29, 242, st. 200 (ll. 5–8); *SnE* I, 500 (ll. 1–4); *Skj* IA, 393; *Skj* IB, 362–63; EAK 181; *NN* §877.

The first half-stanza is cited in *SnE* I, 500, and Fsk gives the second half-stanza only. The last word in l. 1 is corrupt in MskMS and reads "bebi," whereas Flat, Hr, and AM 66 have "bæði." The interpretation of this word is uncertain; the present edition follows *NN* §877. In l. 6, "ricr" (FJ; U; Flat, "rict") is emended to "rístr," in keeping with Fsk, Hr, and AM 66.

St. 72: Bǫlverkr Arnórsson: "Haraldsdrápa" 7. U 21; FJ 97; *Flat* III, 311; *FmS* VI, 185; *F* 207; *ÍF* 28, 101–2, st. 98; *ÍF* 29, 246, st. 201; *Skj* IA, 386; *Skj* IB, 356; EAK 178–79; *NN* §2037A.

L. 5 in MskMS (and Flat) reads "yðvar frenda" (your kinsmen), which makes little sense and has been emended to "ykkar," in keeping with the other MSS. For the translation of "rómalda," see *NN* §2037A and *ÍF* 28, 102n.

St. 73: Haraldr harðráði: lv. 8. U 28; FJ 109; *Flat* III, 317; *FmS* VI, 193; *Skj* IA, 358; *Skj* IB, 330; EAK 166.

Magnús and Þórir had the same mother, Álfhildr, but different fathers. Nothing is known about Þórir's father and about how he obtained his nickname, "Hvinngestr" (Thief-guest). "Hvinn" was the Norse term for a person who committed petty theft (*NGL* I, 253), which was considered a shameful crime in medieval Scandinavian society. According to Norwegian law, a person who accused another person of petty theft and failed to substantiate the allegation by witnesses was subject to outlawry (*NGL* I, 273, 311, 331) or fines (*NGL* II, 70; IV, 223).

St. 74: Magnús enn góði: lv. 1. U 28; FJ 110; *Flat* III, 318; *FmS* VI, 194; *Skj* IA, 330; *Skj* IB, 304; EAK 154.

In Hr and AM 66, the stanza opens with two additional lines, "enn þótt héti || Hvinngestr faðir minn" (but even if my father was called "Thief-guest"), that are not in MskMS or Flat. The meter is *fornyrðislag*. The phrase "gera garð of hestreðr" apparently meant "to wrap the phallus of a horse so that it could not mate" (*LP* 173). Erik Noreen's attempt to explain the phrase as referring to a pagan phallus cult is not persuasive (Noreen 1922:51). The insult in Þórir's (Magnús's) stanza must have alluded to Sigurðr sýr's (Sow) unkingly fondness for farm activities (see *Flat* II, 12; *ÍF* 27, 41). As *Hreiðars þáttr heimska* shows (n. 24.18), Haraldr could be quite sensitive to references to his father and his nickname. Verbal insults in the form of poetic exchanges were quite common in Norse society. In some cases, derogatory stanzas incurred severe legal penalties (see *Grágás* I, 181–85; II, 390–94; *NGL* II, 70; IV, 222–23).

St. 75: Arnórr Þórðarson jarlaskald: "Magnússdrápa hrynhenda" 1. U 31; FJ 116–17; *Flat* III, 322; *FmS* VI, 196; *SnE* II, 116, 218 (ll. 3–4); *Skj* IA, 332–33; *Skj* IB, 306; EAK 155.

St. 76: Arnórr Þórðarson jarlaskald: "Magnússdrápa hrynhenda" 16. U 31; FJ 117; *Flat* III, 322; *FmS* VI, 196; *SnE* II, 498 (ll. 1–4); *Skj* IA, 337; *Skj* IB, 310; EAK 157.

In l. 7, Hr and AM 66 (*H) replace "frægra" (more glorious) with "fríðra" (more beautiful), in an attempt to restore internal rhyme.

St. 77: Arnórr Þórðarson jarlaskald: "Magnússdrápa hrynhenda" 17. U 32; FJ 117; *Flat* III, 322; *FmS* VI, 197; *Skj* IA, 337; *Skj* IB, 310; EAK 157–58.

St. 78: Arnórr Þórðarson jarlaskald: "Magnússdrápa hrynhenda" 18–19. U 32; FJ 117–18; *Flat* III, 322; *FmS* VI, 197; *Skj* IA, 337; *Skj* IB, 310–11; EAK 158.

Ll. 1–8 are rendered as one stanza in MskMS and Flat, whereas Hr and AM 66 divide it into two separate half-stanzas. In l. 3, MksMS reads "osamt" (unwilling). Finnur Jónsson (*Skj* IB) emends to the unattested "ofsamt," and Ernst A. Kock has "ásamt" (together).

St. 79: Magnús enn góði: lv. 2. U 33; FJ 119–20; *Flat* III, 323; *FmS* VI, 200; *Skj* IA, 330; *Skj* IB, 304; EAK 155; *NN* §808.

For the interpretation of the first half-stanza, see *NN* §808. It has been suggested that this stanza was mistakenly attributed to Magnús enn góði and that in reality, it was part of a sequence of love stanzas (including *st. 212*) composed by Magnús berfœttr (see Poole 1985:116–18).

*St. 80: Anon. st. 5. FJ 147; *Flat* III, 334; *FmS* VI, 236; *Skj* IA, 425; *Skj* IB, 395; EAK 195–96; *NN* §§908, 1147, 2787.

The first half-stanza follows *NN* §908; for the interpretation of the second, see *Skj* IB.

*St. 81: Oddr kikinaskald: "poem about Magnús enn góði" 2. FJ 147; *Flat* III, 334; *FmS* VI, 236; *F* 209–10; *ÍF* 28, 106, st. 99; *ÍF* 29, 249, st. 202; *Skj* IA, 355; *Skj* IB, 327; EAK 165.

*St. 82: Oddr kikinaskald: lv. 1. FJ 148; *Flat* III, 334; *FmS* VI, 237; *Skj* IA, 355; *Skj* IB, 327–28; EAK 165.

In l. 4, all MSS have "stillir" ("king"; nominative) which can only be construed as a form of address. Because Oddr is hardly addressing Haraldr at this point, the nominative has been emended to a genitive ("stillis"). The second half-stanza follows AM 66.

St. 83: Haraldr harðráði: lv. 9; Þjóðólfr Arnórsson: lv. 11. U 51; FJ 156; *Flat* III, 335; *FmS* VI, 251–52; *F* 211; *ÍF* 28, 109, sts. 100–1; *ÍF* 29, 250–51, st. 203; *Skj* IA, 358, 379; *Skj* IB, 330, 349; EAK 166, 175; *NN* §§846, 1854B; 3086.

In MskMS, the whole stanza is attributed to Haraldr, whereas in Hkr, Hr, AM 66, and Fsk A, the stanza is the result of alternate composition; that is, Haraldr and Þjóðólfr recite one half-stanza each (cf. the similar practice in *sts. 91* and *122*). According to Fsk B, Þjóðólfr was the sole composer of the stanza. For the interpretation of the first half-stanza, see *NN* §846. In Fsk and Hkr (= Hr, AM 66, F), the second half-stanza reads as follows:

> sumar annat skal sunnar
> (segik eina spá) fleini
> (vér aukum kaf króki)
> kaldnefr furu halda.

Next summer the cold beak [anchor] with its claw will secure the ship still farther south; that I predict; we'll plunge the hook deeper.

That reading is clearly superior to the MskMS variant, which may have been caused by the scribe's misreading of "kaldnefr" (rendered as "calldnez") in l. 8.

St. 84: Bǫlverkr Arnórsson: "Haraldsdrápa" 8. U 51; FJ 156; *Flat* III, 335; *FmS* VI, 252; *F* 211; *ÍF* 28, 109–10, st. 102; *ÍF* 29, 251, st. 204; *SnE* I, 498 (ll. 1–4); *Skj* IA, 386–87; *Skj* IB, 356–57; EAK 179; *NN* §§1793C, 3396Q.

The translation of "skokkr" (l. 5) is conjectural (see *NN* §§1793C, 3396Q). The word can mean "coffin," "box," "sheath on a knife," and something on a ship—"bottom boards" (see *Norrøn ordbok* 384). "Skokkr" also occurs in Arnórr Þórðarson's "Þorfinnsdrápa" 21 (*Skj* IA, 347–48) and in Kolli's "Ingadrápa" 4 (*st. 296*).

St. 85: Anon. st. 6. U 52; FJ 157; *Flat* III, 336; *FmS* VI, 253–54; *F* 211; *ÍF* 28, 110–11, st. 103; *ÍF* 29, 252, st. 205; *Skj* IA, 425–26; *Skj* IB, 395; EAK 196; *NN* §§909, 1953A.

The first half-stanza is interpreted according to *NN* §909.

St. 86: Grani: "poem about Haraldr harðráði" 1. U 53; FJ 158; *Flat* III, 336–37; *FmS* VI, 254; *F* 212; *ÍF* 28, 111, st. 104; *ÍF* 29, 252, st. 206; *Skj* IA, 387; *Skj* IB, 357; EAK 179; *NN* §806.

The first half-stanza follows *Skj* IB. In l. 8, Hkr and Fsk read "faðir Dóttu" (Dótta's father), where Dótta is taken as a personal name. MskMS, Hr, and Flat all have "dóttur" (daughter), which is kept in the present edition. To "pay out the riches of his daughter" could imply paying out her dowry as ransom. Hrólfr kraki (Pole) was a legendary Danish king, and the *kenning* refers to the episode in which Hrólfr, pursued by the Swedes, threw gold on the ground to distract his enemies (see *SnE* I, 392–98; *Hrólfs saga kraka ok kappa hans* 88–90; and the similar ruse described in Msk [*st. 96*]).

St. 87: Grani: "poem about Haraldr harðráði" 2. U 53; FJ 158–59; *FmS* VI, 254–55; *SnE* I, 524 (ll. 1–4); *Skj* IA, 387; *Skj* IB, 357; EAK 179.

L. 3 in Hr reads "hord verk hilmir giordí"; AM 66 has "horð veitk hilmí." Two MSS of the *Prose Edda* (748, 757) have "hirð" (retainers) for "hríð" (storm, battle), a reading that is adopted by Finnur Jónsson (*Skj* IB) and Ernst A. Kock but requires the unsupported emendation of "hilmi" (accusative) to "hilmis" (genitive: "hirð hilmis," "the retainers of the king"). Þjólarnes was a place on the river Gudenå in Jutland.

St. 88: Stúfr Þórðarson enn blindi: "Stúfsdrápa" 5. U 54; FJ 160; *Flat* III, 338; *FmS* VI, 255; *F* 212; *ÍF* 28, 112, st. 105; *ÍF* 29, 253, st. 207; *Skj* IA, 405; *Skj* IB, 374; EAK 186; *NN* §881.

In l. 3, Fsk, Hr, and AM 66 have "gladdr" ("gladdened"; Fsk A, AM 66) and "glaðr" ("happy"; Fsk B, Hr) for "gœddr" (MskMS and the Hkr versions), and in l. 4, Fsk has "búendr" (farmers) for "Danir" (Danes).

St. 89: Þorleikr fagri: "Sveinsflokkr" 2. U 54; FJ 161; *Flat* III, 338; *FmS* VI, 256–57; *F* 212; *ÍF* 28, 113, st. 106; *ÍF* 29, 254, st. 208; *Skj* IA, 397; *Skj* IB, 365; EAK 183.

St. 90: Þorleikr fagri: "Sveinsflokkr" 3. U 55; FJ 161–62; *Flat* III, 338; *FmS* VI, 257; *F* 213; *ÍF* 28, 113, st. 107; *ÍF* 29, 254, st. 209; *Skj* IA, 397; *Skj* IB, 366; EAK 183.

St. 91: Haraldr harðráði: lv. 10 (l. 1). Þjóðólfr Arnórsson: lv. 12 (ll. 2–8). U 55; FJ 162; *Flat* III, 338–39; *FmS* VI, 257–58; *ÍF* 29, 256, st. 212; *Skj* IA, 358, 379–80; *Skj* IB, 330, 349; EAK 166, 176; *NN* §§870, 1079D.

St. 92: Stúfr Þórðarson enn blindi: "Stúfsdrápa" 6. U 55; FJ 163; *Flat* III, 339; *FmS* VI, 258; *F* 213; *ÍF* 28, 114, st. 108; *ÍF* 29, 256, st. 213; *Skj* IA, 405; *Skj* IB, 374; EAK 186.

For the split refrain (l. 4), see the comments on *sts. 54–55*, above. In l. 3, "rett" (second person singular) has been emended to "réð" (third person singular) in keeping with Fsk and the Hkr versions. ("Stúfsdrápa" was composed after Haraldr's death.)

St. 93: Anon. st. 7. U 56; FJ 164; *Flat* III, 340; *FmS* VI, 259; *F* 213; *ÍF* 28, 114–15, st. 109; *ÍF* 29, 257, st. 214; *Skj* IA, 426; *Skj* IB, 396; EAK 196.

St. 94: Þorleikr fagri: "Sveinsflokkr" 6. U 56; FJ 164; *Flat* III, 340; *FmS* VI, 259; *F* 213; *ÍF* 28, 115, st. 110; *ÍF* 29, 257–58, st. 215; *Skj* IA, 398; *Skj* IB, 366; EAK 183; *NN* §2039.

St. 95: Þorleikr fagri: "Sveinsflokkr" 7. U 57; FJ 165–66; *Flat* III, 341; *FmS* VI, 261; *F* 213–14; *ÍF* 28, 116, st. 111; *ÍF* 29, 258, st. 216; *Skj* IA, 398; *Skj* IB, 367; EAK 183.

In Hkr, Fsk, Hr, and AM 66, the stanza is attributed to Þorleikr fagri, whereas MskMS and Flat assign it to Þjóðólfr. Because it is unlikely that Þjóðólfr, Haraldr's own court poet, would praise Haraldr's archenemy Sveinn, the attribution in MskMS (Flat) must be erroneous. In l. 1, "tirar," is emended to "tíðar," in keeping with the other MSS.

St. 96: Þorleikr fagri: "Sveinsflokkr" 8. U 59; FJ 168; *Flat* III, 342; *FmS* VI, 264; *F* 214; *ÍF* 28, 117, st. 112; *ÍF* 29, 260, st. 217; *Skj* IA, 398; *Skj* IB, 367; EAK 183.

In l. 6, MskMS, Fsk, and Hr read "letto" ("lettu"), whereas Hkr, Flat, and AM 66 have "létu" ("they lost more ships"). For this ruse, see the note on *st. 86*, above.

St. 97: Þorleikr fagri: "Sveinsflokkr" 9. U 59; FJ 169; *Flat* III, 343; *FmS* VI, 264; *F* 215; *ÍF* 28, 118, st. 113; *ÍF* 29, 260–61, st. 218; *Skj* IA, 399; *Skj* IB, 367; EAK 183.

St. 98: Haraldr harðráði: lv. 12. FJ 171; *Flat* III, 344; *FmS* VI, 270; *F* 218; *ÍF* 28, 124, st. 116; *ÍF* 29, 262, st. 219; *Skj* IA, 359; *Skj* IB, 330; EAK 167.

St. 99: Haraldr harðráði: lv. 11. FJ 171–72; *Flat* III, 344–45; *FmS* VI, 270; *F* 218; *ÍF* 28, 124, st. 115; *ÍF* 29, 263, st. 220; *SnE* I, 458 (ll. 5–8); *Skj* IA, 358–59; *Skj* IB, 330; EAK 167.

St. 100: Þjóðólfr Arnórsson: "Sexstefja" 11:3–4. U 61; FJ 180; *Flat* III, 351 (ll. 3–4); *ÍF* 29, 264, st. 221; *Skj* IA, 371; *Skj* IB, 341; EAK 172; *NN* §§857, 3084.

MskMS and Flat have ll. 3–4 only; Hr and AM 66 omit the half-stanza. In our text, ll. 1–2 are added from Fsk A. The interpretation follows *NN* §857.

St. 101: Þjóðólfr Arnórsson: "Sexstefja" 19. U 65; FJ 188; *Flat* III, 351; *FmS* VI, 339; *ÍF* 29, 271–72, st. 230; *Skj* IA, 373; *Skj* IB, 343: EAK 173; *NN* §§806, 1902.

In l. 6, "þ[eim]" is damaged in the MS. To "break twigs in the shoes" means to cause trouble for someone.

St. 102: Þjóðólfr Arnórsson: "Sexstefja" 20. U 66; FJ 188; *Flat* III, 351; *FmS* VI, 340; *F* 237–38; *ÍF* 28, 166, st. 145; *ÍF* 29, 272, st. 231; *Skj* IA, 373; *Skj* IB, 343–44; EAK 173.

In MskMS, only l. 1 ("toc holmbva hneccir") is recorded in the text; the whole poem is added below the text by the first hand. In l. 3, MskMS reads "frᵉgsta" ("the most famous"; = Fsk B, A, Hr, AM 66); Hkr x (K, 39, F) has "frœkna" (audacious). Garmr is a mythological dog mentioned in the eddic poem "Vǫlospá" (see Neckel/Kuhn, *Edda*, pp. 10–11, 14).

St. 103: Þjóðólfr Arnórsson: "Sexstefja" 21:5–8, 10:5–8. U 66; FJ 188; *Flat* III, 351; *FmS* VI, 339 (ll. 5–8), 340 (ll. 1–4); *F* 217 (ll. 5–8), 238 (ll. 1–4); *ÍF* 28, 166, st. 146 (ll. 5–8), 123, st. 114 (ll. 5–8); *ÍF* 29, 272–73, sts. 232–33; *Skj* IA, 371, 374; *Skj* IB, 341, 344; EAK 172–73.

In MskMS, ll. 1–2 are recorded in the text; ll. 3–8 are written in the top margin by the first hand. L. 8 is damaged: "[konvngr bioþa]" is added by Unger (Finnur reads "þioð oll konvngr . . ."). In Fsk, the stanza is divided into two separate, consecutive half-stanzas, and in Hkr the two half-stanzas are given as sts. 146 (ll. 5–8) and 114 (ll. 5–8), respectively. In Hr and AM 66, the second half-stanza is cited separately after "Sexstefja" 19 (*st. 101*), while the first half-stanza is given as ll. 5–8 of "Sexstefja" 21, in keeping with Hkr. In l. 3, MskMS reads "neþi" (= Fsk B, Hr, AM 66, Flat, F); Hkr (K, 39) has "næmiz." Hálfr was a legendary Norwegian king who died after his rival Ásmundr had attempted to burn him inside his hall (see *Hálfs saga ok Hálfsrekka* 114–16).

St. 104: Haraldr harðráði: lv. 17. U 68; FJ 193; *Flat* III, 354; *FmS* VI, 346–47; *Skj* IA, 360; *Skj* IB, 331; EAK 167; *NN* §§2445B, 2989B.

The versions of this stanza in Flat, Hr, and AM 66 have couplets three and four (ll. 5–8) in the reverse order. The meter is an irregular variant of *dróttkvætt*.

St. 105: Sigvatr Þórðarson: lv. 9. U 76; FJ 206; *Flat* III, 360; *FmS* VI, 288; *Skj* IA, 268; *Skj* IB, 248; EAK 128; *NN* §§674, 2480D.

For the interpretation of the first half-stanza, see *NN* §674. In l. 5, other editors emend "hlýða" (listen) to "heyra" (hear) to achieve internal rhyme (þérs:heyra). However, that reading is not warranted by the MSS and the rhyme "-r-": "-ð-" (þérs:hlýða) is legitimate.

St. 106: Steinn Herdísarson: "Nizarvísur" 1. U 77; FJ 208; *Flat* III, 361; *FmS* VI, 313; *F* 227; *ÍF* 28, 145–46, st. 127; *ÍF* 29, 264–65, st. 222; *Skj* IA, 407; *Skj* IB, 376; EAK 187; *NN* §§886, 2247D, 3262A.

The interpretation of the first half-stanza follows *NN* §886.

St. 107: Steinn Herdísarson: "Nizarvísur" 2. U 78; FJ 208–9; *Flat* III, 362; *FmS* VI, 313; *F* 228; *ÍF* 28, 148, st. 131; *ÍF* 29, 265 st. 223; *Skj* IA, 407; *Skj* IB, 377; EAK 187.

In l. 1, MskMS and Flat have "hitti" (found), which makes no sense in this context. Hkr reads "hætti" (put at risk) (cf. Fsk A: "hæitu"; AM 66: "hrætiz"; Hr: "hvattiz"). The line has been emended in accordance with the Hkr version.

St. 108: Steinn Herdísarson: "Ulfsflokkr" 1. U 78; FJ 209; *Flat* III, 362; *FmS* VI, 314–15; *F* 228; *ÍF* 28, 147, st. 130; *ÍF* 29, 266, st. 224; *Skj* IA, 409; *Skj* IB, 378; EAK 188; *NN* §1146.

The name of the poet is given in Hkr, Fsk, and in Hr and AM 66, which here follow Hkr. For the interpretation of the first half-stanza, see *NN* §1146.

St. 109: Þjóðólfr Arnórsson: "Sexstefja" 14:1–4. U 78; FJ 209; *Flat* III, 362 (ll. 1–4); *FmS* VI, 316; *F* 229; *ÍF* 28, 149–50, st. 134; *ÍF* 29, 266, st. 225 (ll. 1–4); *Skj* IA, 372; *Skj* IB, 342; EAK 172; *NN* §§2030–31, 3230.

The whole stanza is given in Hkr, Hr, and AM 66. In l. 4, Hkr and Fsk have "landreki" (chieftain) for "oddviti" (war leader; MskMS, Hr, AM 66, and Flat). "Hlífr" (shields) is otherwise unattested as a plural form.

St. 110: Steinn Herdísarson: "Nizarvísur" 5. U 79; FJ 211; *Flat* III, 363; *FmS* VI, 317; *ÍF* 29, 267, st. 226; *Skj* IA, 408; *Skj* IB, 377–78; EAK 188; *NN* §§ 887, 1145.

In l. 5, "selldo" (gave) is emended to "heldu" (protected; Hr, AM 66, Flat) to restore alliteration, and in l. 6, "hrafns" (genitive) has been emended to "hrafn" (nominative) in keeping with the other MSS. Fsk presents a slightly different version of the second half-stanza.

St. 111: Þjóðólfr Arnórsson: "Sexstefja" 15. U 79; FJ 211; *ÍF* 29, 267, st. 227; *Skj* IA, 372; *Skj* IB, 342; EAK 172; *NN* §§860, 1853D.

MskMS has l. 1 only, which reads "flest var hirþ með .h." The line is omitted in *FmS* (VI, 319) and in Flat, but Fsk records the whole stanza. In the present edition, ll. 2–4 have been added from Fsk.

St. 112: Þjóðólfr Arnórsson: "Sexstefja" 16. U 79; FJ 211; *Flat* III, 363; *FmS* VI, 319; *F* 229; *ÍF* 28, 151, st. 136; *ÍF* 29, 268, st. 228; *Skj* IA, 372; *Skj* IB, 342–43; EAK 172.

L. 1 in MskMS reads "Sangs quoþv gram gengin" (= Flat, Hr, AM 66), which is corrupt. Hkr and Fsk have "Sogns" and "gegnan." In l. 2, MskMS, Flat, and F have "et næsta" (next), while Fsk, Hr, AM 66, and the other Hkr-MSS have "et fæsta" (at least).

St. 113: Arnórr Þórðarson jarlaskald: "Erfidrápa Haralds harðráða" 2. U 79; FJ 211–12; *Flat* III, 363; *FmS* VI, 318; *Skj* IA, 349; *Skj* IB, 322; EAK 163; *NN* §837.

In MskMS, the verbs "láta" and rjóða" in the first half-stanza are in the second person singular ("letz," "ra/tt"), and "tyggi" (king) would then be a form of address. Because the poem was composed after the death of Haraldr and such posthumous forms of address are unattested in *erfidrápur* (commemorative poems), the verbs have been emended in accordance with Flat.

St. 114: Arnórr Þórðarson jarlaskald: "Erfidrápa Haralds harðráða" 3. U 80; FJ 212; *Flat* III, 363; *FmS* VI, 318; *Skj* IA, 349; *Skj* IB, 322; EAK 163; *NN* §838.

In l. 5, "ra/þz" (was reddened) has been emended to "raufsk" (broke), in keeping with Hr and AM 66 and to preserve internal rhyme. In l. 8, Finnur Jónsson and Ernst A. Kock silently emend "buðlungr" (nominative) to "buðlungs" (genitive) against all MSS and take it to modify "skjaldborg" (shield wall; *Skj* IB) or "skúfar" ("swords"; *NN* §838). The present edition keeps the nominative and takes it as an apposition to "hoddglotuðr" (treasure breaker).

St. 115: Arnórr Þórðarson jarlaskald: "Erfidrápa Haralds harðráða" 4. U 80; FJ 212; *Flat* III, 363–64; *FmS* VI, 319; *F* 229; *ÍF* 28, 150–51, st. 135; *Skj* IA, 349–50; *Skj* IB, 322; EAK 163.

St. 116: Þjóðólfr Arnórsson: "Sexstefja" 17. U 80; FJ 213; *Flat* III, 364; *FmS* VI, 320; *F* 230; *ÍF* 28, 151–52, st. 137; *ÍF* 29, 268–69, st. 229; *Skj* IA, 373; *Skj* IB, 343; EAK 173; *NN* §§806, 861.

The name of the poet is given in Hkr, Fsk, Hr, and AM 66. The text of the latter two MSS follows Hkr at this point. For the interpretation of the first half-stanza, see *Skj* IB.

St. 117: Þjóðólfr Arnórsson: "Sexstefja" 22. U 88; FJ 225; *Flat* III, 372; *FmS* VI, 341; *F* 238; *ÍF* 28, 167, st. 147; *ÍF* 29, 273, st. 234; *Skj* IA, 374; *Skj* IB, 344; EAK 173; *NN* §§806, 862.

For the plural form, "rendr," of "rond" (shield), see *ÍF* 28, 167n.

St. 118: Þjóðólfr Arnórsson: lv. 25. U 91; FJ 231; *Flat* III, 375; *FmS* VI, 336; *F* 237; *ÍF* 28, 164, st. 144; *Skj* IA, 383; *Skj* IB, 352–53; EAK 177.

In l. 1, "sv" is emended to "sús" for syntactical reasons and in keeping with the other MSS. L. 3 in MskMS and Hr reads "styr" (battle), which is unmetrical (three alliterating staves in the line) and has been emended to "því" ("that"; Hkr, Flat, AM 66). "Reynduz" (plural; l. 5) has been emended to "reyndisk" (singular; Hkr, Hr, AM 66, Flat) for syntactical reasons.

St. 119: Þjóðólfr Arnórsson: lv. 14. U 94; FJ 235; *Flat* III, 417; *FmS* VI, 361–62; *ÍF* 9, 267–68, st. 1; *Skj* IA, 380; *Skj* IB, 350; EAK 176; *NN* §1140.

In l. 3, "hvatt" (MskMS, Hr, AM 66) has been emended to "hvápt-." Flat, whose version of *Sneglu-Halla þáttr* is different and more extensive than the version recorded in MskMS and *FmS*, has "huafft." In l. 6, "or" has been emended to "af," in keeping with Flat. In Flat, *sts. 119* and *120* occur in reverse order. For the story of Þórr's encounter with the giant Geirrøðr, see Eilífr Goðrúnarson's "Þórsdrápa" (*Skj* IA, 148–52), and *SnE* I, 284–302.

St. 120: Þjóðólfr Arnórsson: lv. 15. U 94; FJ 236; *Flat* III, 417; *FmS* VI, 362; *ÍF* 9, 268, st. 2; *Skj* IA, 380; *Skj* IB, 350; EAK 176; *NN* §2989C.

In l. 5, "mann sasc" (singular) is emended to "menn sáusk" (plural) with AM 66. Flat and Hr have "monnom leiz ormr." The interpretation of l. 6 is uncertain: "kilja" can mean "strife," "nourishment," or "garment" (*LP* 338). The present translation follows those of *Skj* IB and *ÍF* 9. Sigurðr's famous fight with the dragon Fáfnir is recorded in "Fáfnismál" (Neckel/Kuhn, *Edda,* pp. 180–88), *Vǫlsunga saga,* 150–56, and *SnE* I, 356–58.

St. 121: Sneglu-Halli: lv. 1. U 94; FJ 236–37; *Flat* III, 418; *FmS* VI, 363; *ÍF* 9, 270, st. 3; *Skj* IA, 388; *Skj* IB, 358; EAK 179; *NN* §3222.

"The cleaver of rye loaves" is a play on such *kenningar* for warrior as "cleaver of shields" and is a derogatory term for "man."

St. 122: Haraldr harðráði: lv. 14; Sneglu-Halli: lv. 4. U 94–95; FJ 237; *Flat* III, 419; *FmS* VI, 363; *ÍF* 9, 271, st. 4; *Skj* IA, 359, 389; *Skj* IB, 359; EAK 167, 179.

The text of the stanza reads as follows:

> Hvert stillir þú Halli.
> Hleypk framm at skyrkaupi.
> Graut munt gǫrva láta.
> Gǫrr matr es þat smjǫrvan.

St. 123: Þjóðólfr Arnórsson: lv. 16. U 95; FJ 238; *Flat* III, 419; *FmS* VI, 364; *ÍF* 9, 273, st. 5; *Skj* IA, 380–81; *Skj* IB, 350; EAK 176.

In MskMS, Hr, and AM 66, this half-stanza is attributed to Sneglu-Halli. Flat gives Þjóðólfr as the poet, which is more likely in view of the derogatory content.

St. 124: Sneglu-Halli: lv. 5. U 96; FJ 238–39; *Flat* III, 420; *FmS* VI, 365; *ÍF* 9, 275, st. 6; *Skj* IA, 389; *Skj* IB, 359; EAK 180.

In l. 5, "rvdna" is emended to "runa," in keeping with the other MSS and for metrical reasons. (Two short syllables are required by the meter.) In MskMS, l. 6 reads "reþ ec sciott gorfo," which has been emended to "ræðk skjótgǫru" (AM 66). In l. 7, MskMS has "asvini"; the other MSS read "af svíni."

St. 125: Sneglu-Halli: lv. 6. U 101; FJ 246; *Flat* III, 426; *FmS* VI, 376; *ÍF* 9, 292, st. 7; *Skj* IA, 389; *Skj* IB, 359; EAK 180; *NN* §2038.

In l. 1, "þaz" (MskMS, Hr, AM 66) has been emended to "þars" (Flat). In l. 2, MskMS reads "sellt," but "hellt" ("hafan þangul hellt vm") has been added in the lower margin by the first hand: the other MSS have "heldk." L. 9 is abbreviated "b. m. þ. of h." in MskMS but is written in full in AM 66. The repetition of the final line is characteristic of dream stanzas and prophetic stanzas and of a specific eddic meter (*galdralag*) associated with sorcery and incantations (see *SnE* I, 714–16) (see also the note on *st. 133,* below).

St. 126: Þorgils fiskimaðr: lv. 1. U 101; FJ 247; *Flat* III, 377; *FmS* VI, 385; *F* 255; *Skj* IA, 400; *Skj* IB, 369; EAK 184.

L. 4 in Flat, F, Hr, and AM 66 reads: "hlǫmm en þat var skǫmmu." In l. 8, "drengr" ("warrior"; nominative) has been emended to "drengs" (genitive; Hr, AM 66, Flat). The poetic exchanges are also recorded in F, but the accompanying prose, as well as the sequence of stanzas (*sts. 127, 128, 126*), is different.

St. 127: Haraldr harðráði: lv. 15. U 101; FJ 248; *Flat* III, 377; *FmS* VI, 385; *F* 255; *Skj* IA, 359; *Skj* IB, 331; EAK 167; *NN* §§806, 847A, 1902, 2026.

St. 128: Þjóðólfr Arnórsson: lv. 13. U 102; FJ 248; *Flat* III, 378; *FmS* VI, 385–86; *F* 255; *Skj* IA, 380; *Skj* IB, 350; EAK 176; *NN* §2268.

In l. 2, MskMS reads "mótr" (or "mótt"); the other MSS correctly have "mót" (encounter). MskMS, Hr, and AM 66 have "mót(r) illt" (a terrible encounter), whereas F and Flat read "mót hart" (a hard encounter). "Spiotom" ('spears'; dative plural, l. 2) has been emended to "spjóta" (genitive plural; F) to provide a qualifier for "móðu" (river).

St. 129: Þorgils fiskimaðr: lv. 2. U 102; FJ 249; *Flat* III, 378; *FmS* VI, 386; *Skj* IA, 400; *Skj* IB, 369; EAK 184.

In l. 3, AM 66 has "goll et vafða" (the wound gold), a reading that retains the internal rhyme and seems to have been inspired by l. 6 in *st. 126* ("hǫfðum golli vafðan"). In Flat, that line reads "gæddir gull raudan," which is unmetrical and clearly corrupt.

St. 130: Haraldr harðráði: lv. 16. U 102; FJ 249; *Flat* III, 378; *FmS* VI, 387; *F* 256 (ll. 5–8); *Skj* IA, 360; *Skj* IB, 331; EAK 167; *NN* §§847B, 2026.

The translation of "hrauðung" ("landing"; l. 1) is uncertain (see *NN* §847B). Ll. 7–8 ("ristin skalf í rǫstum || rǫng" "the carved frame quivered in the currents") echo l. 3 of *st. 217:* "vestr bifask rengr í rǫstum" (in the west, ship frames quiver in the currents). In F, ll. 5–8 are given as the second half-stanza of a verse spoken by a salt burner, one of Þorgils's sons. Ll. 1–4 of that stanza are recorded in F only (*Skj* IA, 426).

St. 131: Þorgils fiskimaðr: lv. 3. U 102; FJ 249; *Flat* III, 378; *FmS* VI, 387; *F* 256; *Skj* IA, 401; *Skj* IB, 369; EAK 184; *NN* §§806, 847D.

L. 4 in the other MSS reads "rǫmm en þat var skǫmmu" (see the note on *st. 126*). In F, this stanza is attributed to Þjóðólfr. In addition to *sts. 126–28, 130* (ll. 5–8), and *131,* the episode as recorded in F contains a stanza recited by a young man, another son of Þorgils (*Skj* IA, 426). The differences in prose and poetry between the Msk and F redactions suggest that we are dealing with two oral variants of the same story (see Louis-Jensen 1977: 85–87, and Fidjestøl 1971). See also note 44.1.

St. 132: Ulfr stallari: lv. U 111; FJ 265; *Flat* III, 388; *FmS* VI, 401; *F* 242; *ÍF* 28, 175, st. 149; *Skj* IA, 403; *Skj* IB, 372; EAK 185; *NN* §806.

In l. 2, "iafna" has been emended to "jafnan," in keeping with the other MSS, and "hreíns" ("fair"; genitive, l. 6) has been emended to "hrein" (feminine nominative singular). The English company of "þingamenn" was instituted by Knútr enn ríki (Cnut the Great) around 1018 and disbanded after the Norman Conquest in 1066. It consisted of six thousand chosen men (see Saxo Grammaticus, *Gesta danorum,* X.18, 292–98; trans. Christiansen I, pp. 36–44). See also note 49.4.

St. 133: Anon. "dream stanzas and prophetic stanzas" 10. U 112; FJ 266; *Flat* III, 389; *FmS* VI, 403–4; *F* 243; *ÍF* 28, 177, st. 151; *ÍF* 29, 277–78, st. 236; *Skj* IA, 430; *Skj* IB, 400; EAK 198.

In l. 1, MskMS (and Hkr, Hr, AM 66) has "scoð," Fsk A "scæð," and Flat "sked." L. 5 clearly presented problems for the various redactors. In the Hkr versions, the line reads "sviptir sveiflankjapta" ([the woman] tears [men's flesh] with quick movements of the jaw). Fsk has "suipt hefer svæiflangæfta" and Flat "suiptir sier skipta," none of which makes sense. Hr and AM 66 follow the MskMS reading. In l. 8, "olat" has been emended to "óðlát," in keeping with Hkr and to preserve internal rhyme. The last line is repeated in Hr, AM 66, and Hkr (not so in MskMS, Fsk: see the note on *st. 125,* above). In Hkr and *FmS,* the sequence of this and the following stanza has been reversed. Flat follows MskMS.

St. 134: Anon. "dream stanzas and prophetic stanzas" 8. U 112; FJ 266; *Flat* III, 389; *FmS* VI, 403; *F* 242; *ÍF* 28, 176, st. 150; *Skj* IA, 430; *Skj* IB, 400; EAK 198.

St. 135: Anon. "dream stanzas and prophetic stanzas" 11. U 112; FJ 267; *Flat* III, 389; *FmS* VI, 404; *F* 243; *ÍF* 28, 178, st. 152; *ÍF* 29, 277, st. 235; *Skj* IA, 430–31; *Skj* IB, 400–1; EAK 198; *NN* §§3096, 3234.

The MskMS variant of this stanza is problematic. In the other MSS, "feigþar" ("doomed to die"; l. 1) is replaced by "fremðar" (fame). The version in MskMS could have been caused by the word "feigþ" in l. 6. In Hkr and Fsk, l. 2 reads "hlautk þvít heima sátum," with King Óláfr as the speaker, which is clearly the better reading: "I died a holy death on the battlefield, because I stayed home." L. 5 in Hkr and Fsk reads "uggik enn at tyggi" (yet I believe, king, [that death is in store for you]), while Hr, AM 66, and Flat follow MskMS. The other MSS replace the verb "ráða" (cause, have power over) in l. 8 with "valda" (cause, have power over). In Fsk, *st. 135* is placed before *st. 133.*

St. 136: Steinn Herdísarson: "Óláfsdrápa" 4. U 113; FJ 268; *Flat* III, 390; *FmS* VI, 408; *F* 244; *ÍF* 28, 180–81, st. 153; *ÍF* 29, 279, st. 237; *Skj* IA, 410; *Skj* IB, 379; EAK 189.

In l. 5, Hkr, Hr, and Fsk have "fira" (men) for "Fila" ("people of Fjaler"; MskMS, AM 66, Flat). The last line is part of a *klofastef* (split refrain) that is completed (or repeated) in the final line of *sts. 154–56, 158–59, 163, 167–68.* The entire refrain reads as follows:

ríklundaðr veit undir
sik beztan gram miklu
Óláfr borinn sólu.

"Ríklundaðr Óláfr veit sik miklu beztan gram borinn undir sólu."

Proud-minded Óláfr knows he is the foremost king born beneath the sun.

The various scribes and redactors clearly failed to understand the nature of the refrain and tried in various ways to integrate the last line syntactically into the half-stanza. The different MSS give the following variants: "veit vndir" (MskMS); "vítt undan" (AM 66); "veik undan" (Flat); "hellt undan" (Fsk A); "vatt undir" (Hkr). MskMS is the only MS to preserve the correct reading.

St. 137: Steinn Herdísarson: "Óláfsdrápa" 2. U 113; FJ 269; *Flat* III, 390; *FmS* VI, 407; *Skj* IA, 409–10; *Skj* IB, 379; EAK 188.

In l. 5, "þess" (genitive; MskMS, Hr, AM 66) has been emended to "þeim" (dative; Flat) to preserve internal rhyme. Flat has "lengi" (long) for "Englum" (Englishmen) in l. 6.

St. 138: Steinn Herdísarson: "Óláfsdrápa" 3. U 114; FJ 269; *Flat* III, 391; *FmS* VI, 407; *Skj* IA, 410; *Skj* IB, 379; EAK 188.

St. 139: Arnórr Þórðarson jarlaskald: "Erfidrápa Haralds harðráða" 9. U 114; FJ 269; *Flat* III, 391; *FmS* VI, 407; *Skj* IA, 351; *Skj* IB, 323; EAK 163; *NN* §806.

St. 140: Arnórr Þórðarson jarlaskald: "Erfidrápa Haralds harðráða" 10. U 114; FJ 270; *Flat* III, 391; *FmS* VI, 409; *Skj* IA, 351; *Skj* IB, 323; EAK, 163–64; *NN* §§839, 2523.

The interpretation of the stanza follows *NN* §2523.

St. 141: Arnórr Þórðarson jarlaskald: "Erfidrápa Haralds harðráða" 11. U 114; FJ 270; *Flat* III, 391; *FmS* VI, 409; *Skj* IA, 351; *Skj* IB, 324; EAK 164; *NN* §1135.

In l. 4, MskMS and Flat have "hreinscialldar," which has been emended to "hreinskjaldaðr," in keeping with Hr. L. 5 in MskMS ("dyndo . . . vndar") is emended to "dunðu . . . undan" with Flat.

St. 142: Arnórr Þórðarson jarlaskald: "Erfidrápa Haralds harðráða" 12. U 116; FJ 273; *Flat* III, 393; *FmS* VI, 413–14; *Skj* IA, 351; *Skj* IB, 324; EAK 164.

The first two lines of this stanza are repeated in Þorkell hamarskald's encomium to Magnús berfœttr ("Magnússdrápa" 5:1–2; see *st.* 220).

St. 143: Arnórr Þórðarson jarlaskald: "Erfidrápa Haralds harðráða" 13. U 116; FJ 273; *Flat* III, 393; *FmS* VI, 417; *Skj* IA, 352; *Skj* IB, 324; EAK 164; *NN* §2022.

Because "valda" (cause, have power over) takes the dative, "þat" (accusative; l. 2) has been emended to "því."

St. 144: Þjóðólfr Arnórsson: lv. 26. U 116; FJ 274; *Flat* III, 393; *FmS* VI, 417; *F* 248; *ÍF* 28, 188–89, st. 157; *ÍF* 29, 285, st. 240; *Skj* IA, 383; *Skj* IB, 353; EAK 177.

In l. 6, "sniallrað" has been emended to "snjallráðs," in keeping with Hr, AM 66, and Flat. (Hkr and Fsk have "snarráðs" "quick-witted".)

St. 145: Haraldr harðráði: lv. 18. U 117; FJ 276; *Flat* III, 394–95; *FmS*, VI, 416; *F* 248; *ÍF* 28, 187–88, st. 155; *ÍF* 29, 284, st. 238; *Skj* IA, 360; *Skj* IB, 332; EAK 167.

The meter of this stanza is *fornyrðislag*, which Haraldr obviously considered inferior to *dróttkvætt*.

St. 146: Haraldr harðráði: lv. 19. U 118; FJ 276; *Flat* III, 395; *FmS* VI, 416; *F* 248; *ÍF* 28, 188, st. 156; *ÍF* 29, 284–85, st. 239; *Skj* IA, 360–61; *Skj* IB, 332; EAK 167–68; *NN* §2027.

This is the last stanza attributed to Haraldr. In l. 8, Hkr has "hjalmstofn" (helmet stump) for "hjalmstall" ("helmet stem"; MskMS, Hr, AM 66, Flat, Fsk A).

St. 147: Stúfr Þórðarson enn blindi: "Stúfsdrápa" 8. U 118; FJ 277; *Flat* III, 395; *FmS* VI, 419; *ÍF* 29, 286, st. 241; *Skj* IA, 405; *Skj* IB, 374; EAK 186; *NN* §§806, 2040.

In l. 4, "orrostor" has been emended to "orrostu" (Hr). The different MSS have the following variants of l. 6: "søm ef þess ero dømi" (MskMS); "sœm en þess eru dœmi" (Flat); "sœm ef þess væri dœmi" (Fsk; metrically incorrect); "sœm eru þess of dœmi" (Hr). The line has been emended in accordance with Hr, which offers the better reading.

St. 148: Arnórr Þórðarson jarlaskald: "Erfidrápa Haralds harðráða" 14. U 118; FJ 277–78;

Flat III, 395; *FmS* VI, 418; *F* 249; *ÍF* 28, 189–90, st. 158; *ÍF* 29, 286–87, st. 242; *Skj* IA, 352; *Skj* IB, 324; EAK 164.

Ll. 5–6 in Hkr and Fsk read "þars til þengils hersa ‖ þat sá herr" (where the army observed that about the king of nobles).

St. 149: Arnórr Þórðarson jarlaskald: "Efidrápa Haralds harðráða" 15. U 119; FJ 278; *Flat* III, 396; *FmS* VI, 420; *F* 249; *ÍF* 28, 191, st. 160; *ÍF* 29, 288, st. 243; *Skj* IA, 352; *Skj* IB, 325; EAK 164; *NN* §§1136, 2989A.

In l. 4, Hkr has "roðnir oddar" (reddened spear points) for "reknir broddar" ("gold-adorned spears"; MskMS, Hr, AM 66, Flat); Fsk A has "roðnir broddar." L. 5 in Fsk and some MSS of Hkr (J2, 47 = Hkr y) have "ens mæra" (the glorious) for "ens milda" ("the generous"; MskMS, Hr, AM 66, Flat, Hkr x).

St. 150: Þjóðólfr Arnórsson: lv. 27. U 119; FJ 279; *Flat* III, 396; *FmS* VI, 420; *F* 249; *ÍF* 28, 190, st. 159; *ÍF* 29, 288, st. 244; *SnE* I, 526 (ll. 5–8); *Skj* IA, 383; *Skj* IB, 353; EAK 177; *NN* §2039.

L. 1 echoes ll. 5–6 of "Vǫlospá" 23 ("hvárt scyldo æsir ‖ afráð gialda" "whether the gods should pay restitution" [Neckel/Kuhn, *Edda*, p. 6]), which describe the aftermath of the battle between the races of gods. This verbal reference is probably not fortuitous, and there is ample evidence that Haraldr's skalds were familiar with eddic poetry (e.g., sts. 49, 152, and Arnórr's Þórðarson's "Þorfinnsdrápa" 24 [*Skj* IA, 348]). L. 7 in Hkr, Fsk, and Flat reads "lofðungr fekk [beið, Fsk] enn leyfði" where "enn leyfði" ("the commendable"; nominative) modifies "lofðungr" (lord).

St. 151: Arnórr Þórðarson jarlaskald: "Erfidrápa Haralds harðráða" 16. U 120; FJ 281; *Flat* III, 397; *FmS* VI, 422; *Skj* IA, 352; *Skj* IB, 325; EAK 164.

Vǫlsungr was a legendary king, the ancestor of Sigmundr and his son, Sigurðr the Dragon-slayer. "Vǫlsungr" is used to designate the king as well as his descendants, and in this stanza Arnórr uses the name to establish a connection between Haraldr Sigurðarson and the heroic Sigurðr (see the note on *st. 49*, above).

St. 152: Arnórr Þórðarson jarlaskald: "Erfidrápa Haralds harðráða" 17. U 120; FJ 281; *Flat* III, 397; *FmS* VI, 422–23; *Skj* IA, 353; *Skj* IB, 325; EAK 164; *NN* §§840–41, 1934A.

In l. 7, "costot" has been ememded to "kostat" (*NN* §841). The neuter plural form in the MSS must have been caused by a misinterpretation of the word "minni" (taken as neuter plural rather than as a comparative adjective, feminine accusative plural). In l. 3, "harðrs í heimi" echoes "Vǫlospá" (45:5 "hart er í heimi" "it is hard in the world" [Neckel/Kuhn, *Edda*, p. 10]), a line that describes the conditions in the world leading up to the doom of the gods (see the note on *st. 150*, above).

St. 153: Arnórr Þórðarson jarlaskald: "Erfidrápa Haralds harðráða" 18. U 120–21; FJ 281; *Flat* III, 397; *FmS* VI, 423; *Skj* IA, 353; *Skj* IB, 325; EAK 164; *NN* §842.

In l. 3 in MskMS, Finnur Jónsson reads "dagglingr" in keeping with all other MSS, whereas Unger has "dýrlingr." For the interpretation of the second half-stanza, see *NN* §842.

St. 154: Steinn Herdísarson: "Óláfsdrápa" 5. U 121; FJ 282; *Flat* III, 398; *FmS* VI, 427; *Skj* IA, 410; *Skj* IB, 380; EAK 189; *NN* §888.

In l. 5, "borþveg" (plank road) has been emended to "borðvigg" (plank steeds) with all other editions, and "brimsgangr" (nominative; l. 6) has been emended to "brimsgang" (accusative; Hr). For the split refrain in l. 8 in this and the following stanzas, see the note on *st. 136*.

St. 155: Steinn Herdísarson: "Óláfsdrápa" 6. U 121; FJ 282; *Flat* III, 398; *FmS* VI, 428; *Skj* IA, 410; *Skj* IB, 380; EAK 189; *NN* §§806, 889–90, 1936, 1991.

"Sæ" (sea) in l. 4 can technically either go with "straum" (sea flow) or be taken as the first element of a compound "sækonungr" (sea king).

St. 156: Steinn Herdísarson: "Óláfsdrápa" 12. U 121; FJ 283; *Flat* III, 398; *FmS* VI, 438; *ÍF* 29, 298, st. 250 (ll. 5–8); *Skj* IA, 412; *Skj* IB, 381; EAK 190; *NN* §2530.

The first half-stanza is interpreted in keeping with *NN* §2530. In the other MSS, "veit vndir" (l. 8; MskMS) reads "velt" (Fsk B) or "veik undan" (Hr). MskMS preserves the correct reading (see the note on *st. 136*). For the interpretation of "the lofty land" as Norway, see the note on **st. 18*. The second half-stanza is repeated in MskMS (see *st. 158* below).

St. 157: Steinn Herdísarson: "Óláfsdrápa" 10. U 124; FJ 286–87; *FmS* VI, 436–37; *F* 254; *ÍF* 28, 202, st. 167; *ÍF* 29, 297, st. 249; *Skj* IA, 411; *Skj* IB, 381; EAK 189; *NN* §§892, 2041n1.

St. 158: Steinn Herdísarson: "Óláfsdrápa" 12:5–8 = *st. 156* (ll. 5–8). U 124; FJ 287.

See the note on *st. 156* above. The half-stanza is repeated with one variation: "veʀ" ("defends"; l. 1 [5]) has been replaced with "feʀ" (goes). The first variant is supported by the other MSS. The half-stanza is not repeated in *FmS*.

St. 159: Steinn Herdísarson: "Óláfsdrápa" 7. U 124; FJ 287; *FmS* VI, 435–36; *ÍF* 29, 298, st. 251; *Skj* IA, 411; *Skj* IB, 380; EAK 189.

The MskMS version of this stanza is somewhat garbled. The stanza is not in Flat, and Hr and AM 66 follow MskMS. In l. 1, Fsk has "Egða stillir" (subjugator of the Egðir) for "Engla stillir" (subjugator of the English). The last couplet has been drastically changed in the MskMS version. L. 8 originally belonged to the split refrain, but in the course of the Msk transmission, the line was reinterpreted syntactically as being part of the couplet, and l. 7 was changed to provide a subject and a verb—"sóknherðir veit sverða" (the strengthener of the swords' attack knows). Fsk preserves the original reading, where l. 7 ("sǫngherðǫndum sverða") functions as a dative object to "auðsótt" (l. 6): "the earth . . . will not be easy to conquer for the strengtheners of the swords' song [battle, warriors]."

St. 160: Steinn Herdísarson: "Óláfsdrápa" 8. U 124; FJ 287; *Skj* IA, 411; *Skj* IB, 380; EAK 189; *NN* §891.

The stanza is preserved in MskMS only. In l. 8, "litvþ" is emended to "litat" (*NN* §891). The neuter plural in the MS may have been caused by the neuter plural "sverð" (swords) in the previous line.

St. 161: Steinn Herdísarson: "Óláfsdrápa" 9. U 124; FJ 288; *FmS* VI, 436; *Skj* IA, 411; *Skj* IB, 381; EAK 189.

St. 162: Steinn Herdísarson: "Óláfsdrápa" 11. U 125; FJ 288; *FmS* VI, 437; *Skj* IA, 411–12; *Skj* IB, 381; EAK 189; *NN* §893.

St. 163: Steinn Herdísarson: "Óláfsdrápa" 13. U 125; FJ 288–89; *FmS* VI, 439; *F* 256; *ÍF* 28, 203, st. 168; *ÍF* 29, 299, st. 252; *Skj* IA, 412; *Skj* IB, 382; EAK 190.

In l. 1, the other MSS have "þengill Þrœnda" for "Þrœnda þengill."

St. 164: Arnórr Þórðarson jarlaskald: "Þorfinnsdrápa" 1. U 126; FJ 290; *FmS* VI, 439; *ÍF* 29, 300, st. 253; *Skj* IA, 343; *Skj* IB, 316; EAK 160; *NN* §826.

The chieftain mentioned in Arnórr's stanza is Jarl Þorfinnr Sigurðarson of Orkney († ca. 1064).

St. 165: Anon. st. 11. U 127; FJ 292; *FmS* VI, 437; *F* 254, 259; *ÍF* 28, 202, st. 166; *Ágrip, ÍF* 29, 41; *Skj* IA, 426–27; *Skj* IB, 396; EAK 196.

St. 166: Anon. st. 13. U 129; FJ 295; *FmS* VI, 446–47; *F* 260; *Skj* IA, 427; *Skj* IB, 397; EAK 196; *NN* §2983.

Ll. 1–2 are damaged in MskMS, and Unger adds "[mol ve]." L. 3 in F (= J2, 47) reads "segir tvevétr," which is metrically incorrect. (The line is too short.) The meter is an irregular *fornyrðislag*.

St. 167: Steinn Herdísarson: "Óláfsdrápa" 14. U 129; FJ 295; *FmS* VI, 447; *F* 260; *Skj* IA, 412; *Skj* IB, 382; EAK 190; *NN* §2983.

St. 168: Steinn Herdísarson: "Óláfsdrápa" 15. U 130; FJ 296; *FmS* VI, 441; *F* 260–61; *Skj* IA, 412; *Skj* IB, 382; EAK 190; *NN* §2531.

St. 169: Steinn Herdísarson: "Óláfsdrápa" 16. U 130; FJ 296; *FmS* VI, 447–48; *F* 261; *Skj* IA, 413; *Skj* IB, 382; EAK 190.

L. 4 in F has "jǫfurr" (lord) for "firum" ("men"; MskMS, Hr, AM 66), and in l. 8, F reads "Háalfs" (Hálfr's) for "Háars" ("Hárr's"; that is, "Óðinn's").

St. 170: Steinn Herdísarson: "Óláfsdrápa" 17. U 130; FJ 296; *FmS* VI, 448; *Skj* IA, 413; *Skj* IB, 383; EAK 190; *NN* §§894–95, 1853D, 2041n.2, 2983.

The interpretation of this stanza follows *NN* §§894–95. In l. 5, "gramr" ("lord"; nominative) is emended to "grams" (genitive), and in l. 8, "boriɴ" (masculine nominative singular) is emended to "borin" (feminine nominative singular).

St. 171: Þorkell hamarskald: "Magnússdrápa" 1. U 132; FJ 299; *FmS* VII, 5; *F* 262; *ÍF* 28, 214, st. 172; *ÍF* 29, 303, st. 254; *Skj* IA, 438; *Skj* IB, 407; EAK 201; *NN* §1150.

All five extant stanzas of Þorkell's poem are recorded in MskMS. L. 5 is damaged in MskMS, and Unger adds "[við]" with the other MSS. In l. 7, MskMS, Fsk, Hr, AM 66, and F read "morðvals" (strife falcon); the other Hkr MSS have "morðhauks" (strife hawk).

St. 172: Gísl Illugason: "Erfikvæði Magnúss berfœtts" 1. U 132; FJ 299; *FmS* VII, 6; *F* 262; *Skj* IA, 440; *Skj* IB, 409; EAK 202.

MskMS, Hr, AM 66, and F record twenty stanzas of Gísl's commemorative poem. The meter is a regularized *fornyrðislag*. In l. 8, MskMS has "iofri" (chieftain), but "hiorvi" (sword) has been added in the margin.

St. 173: Gísl Illugason: "Erfikvæði Magnúss berfœtts" 2. U 132; FJ 300; *FmS* VII, 7; *F* 262; *Skj* IA, 440; *Skj* IB, 409; EAK 202.

St. 174: Gísl Illugason: "Erfikvæði Magnúss berfœtts" 3. U 132; FJ 300; *FmS* VII, 7; *F* 263; *Skj* IA, 440; *Skj* IB, 410; EAK 202.

In l. 5, F has "eyiar" (islands) for "Yrjar" (Ørlandet), obviously a result of the scribe's failure to recognize the Norwegian place name.

St. 175: Gísl Illugason: "Erfikvæði Magnúss berfœtts" 4. U 133; FJ 301; *FmS* VII, 8–9; *F* 263; *Skj* IA, 440; *Skj* IB, 410; EAK 202.

St. 176: Gísl Illugason: "Erfikvæði Magnúss berfœtts" 5. U 133; FJ 301; *FmS* VII, 15; *F* 263; *Skj* IA, 441; *Skj* IB, 410; EAK 202.

St. 177: Gísl Illugason: "Erfikvæði Magnúss berfœtts" 6. U 133; FJ 301; *FmS* VII, 9; *F* 263; *Skj* IA, 441; *Skj* IB, 410; EAK 202.

St. 178: Anon. st. 16. U 134; FJ 303; *FmS* VII, 12; *F* 264; *Skj* IA, 428; *Skj* IB, 398; EAK 197.

St. 179: Steigar-Þórir: "kviðlingr." U 135; FJ 304; *FmS* VII, 12; *F* 264; *ÍF* 28, 216, st. 174; *ÍF* 29, 305, st. 255; *Ágrip*, *ÍF* 29, 44; *Skj* IA, 434; *Skj* IB, 403; EAK 198.

In l. 2, MskMS, Hr, AM 66, Fsk B, F, 47, and Ágrip all have "fœrðum" (MskMS "førþom") for the correct "forðum" (Hkr [K, 39, J2]).

St. 180: Anon. st. 15. U 135; FJ 304; *FmS* VII, 10; *F* 264; *ÍF* 28, 215, st. 173; *ÍF* 29, 305, st. 256; *Skj* IA, 427–28; *Skj* IB, 397–98; EAK 197.

St. 181: Þorkell hamarskald: lv. 2. U 135; FJ 305; *FmS* VII, 13; *F* 265; *ÍF* 28, 217, st. 175; *ÍF* 29, 306, st. 257; *Skj* IA, 439; *Skj* IB, 409; EAK 201–2.

In Old Norse society hanging was considered a shameful punishment, and the higher the culprit hung, the greater the shame (see Gade 1985:159–83).

St. 182: Gísl Illugason: "Erfikvæði Magnúss berfœtts" 7. U 136; FJ 305–6; *FmS* VII, 15; *F* 265; *Skj* IA, 441; *Skj* IB, 410; EAK 202.

In l. 1, "settvsc" (plural; MskMS, Hr) is emended to "sættisk" (singular; AM 66, F) for syntactical reasons.

St. 183: Gísl Illugason: "Erfikvæði Magnúss berfœtts" 8. U 136; FJ 306; *FmS* VII, 16; *Skj* IA, 441; *Skj* IB, 411; EAK 202; *NN* §2269.

For the interpretation of the first half-stanza, see *NN* §2269. It is unclear whether "Elfr" here is a place name (Götaälv, Nidelven) or just denotes "river" in general.

St. 184: Bjǫrn krepphendi: "Magnússdrápa" 1. U 142; FJ 315; *FmS* VII, 4; *F* 268; *ÍF* 28, 213, st. 171; *Skj* IA, 434–35; *Skj* IB, 404; EAK 200; *NN* §§1148, 2785, 3217.

L. 5 in MskMS and F read "bles castar hręfasti," which is corrupt. The above emendation is in keeping with most MSS of Hkr, as well as with Hr and AM 66.

St. 185: Bjǫrn krepphendi: "Magnússdrápa" 2:1–4. U 142; FJ 315–16; *FmS* VII, 14 (ll. 1–8); *F* 269 (ll. 1–4); *ÍF* 28, 217, st. 176 (ll. 1–8); *Skj* IA, 435; *Skj* IB, 404; EAK 200; *NN* §3103.

L. 4 in MskMS and F has "armi" (arm) for "Harmi" (Hkr, Hr, AM 66). That mistake did not arise in MskMS but must have been a part of the exemplar (Msk2), because the half-stanza is misplaced in both MskMS and F. In Hkr, it describes Magnús's encounter with

Þórir in Harmr (Velfjorden) and the subsequent hanging of Þórir (see *st. 181*). The second half-stanza reads as follows:

> Frátt hvé fylkir mátti
> (fór svát hengðr vas Þórir)
> (fǫr vas gunnar gǫrvis
> greið) dróttinssvik leiða.

"Frátt, hvé fylkir mátti leiða dróttinssvik: fór, svát Þórir vas hengðr; fǫr gunnar gǫrvis vas greið."

You have heard how the king countered treason: it happened that þórir was
hanged; the campaign of the wager of battle [warrior] went well."

Hence, Snorri must have known the whole stanza and placed it in the correct context.

St. 186: Bjǫrn krepphendi: "Magnússdrápa" 3. U 143; FJ 316; *F* 269; *Skj* IA, 435; *Skj* IB, 405; EAK 200; *NN* §2046.

St. 187: Þorkell hamarskald: "Magnússdrápa" 2. U 143; FJ 316; *FmS* VII, 40; *F* 269; *Skj* IA, 438; *Skj* IB, 408; EAK 201.

St. 188: Bjǫrn krepphendi: "Magnússdrápa" 6:1–2, 7:7–8. U 143; FJ 316; *FmS* VII, 41, 43; *F* 269; *ÍF* 28, 220–21, st. 179 (ll. 1–2) + st. 180 (ll. 7–8); *Skj* IA, 436; *Skj* IB, 405–6; EAK 200.

In Hkr, Hr, and AM 66, the two couplets belong to two different stanzas, and the name of the poet is given. F follows MskMS. Whereas Snorri must have known the whole poem, the author of ÆMsk knew it imperfectly; hence lines, stanzas, and couplets are displaced in the text of MskMS (and F).

St. 189: Bjǫrn krepphendi: "Magnússdrápa" 5:5–8. U 143; FJ 317; *FmS* VII, 41 (ll. 1–8); *F* 270 (ll. 1–4); *ÍF* 28, 219, st. 178 (ll. 1–8); *Skj* IA, 435–36; *Skj* IB, 405; EAK 200; *NN* §1149.

The whole stanza and the name of the poet are given in Hkr, Hr, and AM 66. F follows MskMS.

St. 190: Bjǫrn krepphendi: "Magnússdrápa" 7:1–4, 6:5–8. U 144; FJ 317; *FmS* VII, 42; *F* 270; *ÍF* 28, 221, st. 180 (ll. 1–4); 220, st. 179 (ll. 5–8); *Skj* IA, 436; *Skj* IB, 405–6; EAK 200.

In the Hkr version (= Hr, AM 66), the name of the poet is given, and the two half-stanzas are assigned to different stanzas. F again follows MskMS. In l. 1, the other MSS have "bar" (preterite) instead of "berr" (present tense; MskMS, F). L. 7 in MskMS has "mvlsc" for "mylsk" (all other versions), and that form was copied into the prose text: "vt a Mvlsc."

St. 191a–b: Gísl Illugason: "Erfikvæði Magnúss berfœtts" 9. U 144; FJ 317–18; *FmS* VII, 43–44; *F* 270; *Skj* IA, 441; *Skj* IB, 411; EAK 203.

In Hr and AM 66, the two half-stanzas are given as one stanza. In keeping with F, Hr, and AM 66, ll. 3–4, "øgi" ("terror"; accusative) has been emended to "œgir" (nominative) and "gramr" ("lord"; nominative) to "gram" (accusative). The change is necessary from a contextual point of view, because Lǫgmaðr, not Magnús, was king of North Uist.

St. 192: Bjǫrn krepphendi: "Magnússdrápa" 8. U 144; FJ 318; *FmS* VII, 43; *F* 270; *ÍF* 28, 221–22, st. 181; *Skj* IA, 436; *Skj* IB, 406; EAK 200.

Guðrøðr crovan (small-hand), Lǫgmaðr's father, was the son of Haraldr svarti (the black) of Islay. Guðrøðr accompanied Haraldr Sigurðarson on his English campaign in 1066 and escaped after the Battle of Stamford Bridge. He later became ruler of the Hebrides, the Isle of Man, and parts of Ireland. He died in 1095 and was succeeded in power by his son Lǫgmaðr (see *ÍF* 28, 221n.1). The author of ÆMsk was obviously ignorant of the fact that Guðrøðr was no longer alive during Magnús's first campaign. In l. 6, "fenginN" (MskMS, Hr, AM 66) has been emended to "finginn" (F) to restore internal rhyme.

St. 193: Þorkell hamarskald: "Magnússdrápa" 3. U 145; FJ 319; *FmS* VII, 46; *F* 271; *ÍF* 28, 223, st. 183; *ÍF* 29, 308, st. 258; *Orkn*, *ÍF* 34, 96, st. 30; *Skj* IA, 438; *Skj* IB, 408; EAK 201; *NN* §2908.

L. 5 in MskMS has "stengs"; Unger adds "r" ("strengs"), with the other MSS.

St. 194: Bjǫrn krepphendi: "Magnússdrápa" 9. U 145; FJ 319–20; *FmS* VII, 45–46; *F* 271; *ÍF* 28, 222–23, st. 182 (ll. 1–4); *Skj* IA, 436–37; *Skj* IB, 406; EAK 200.

St. 195: Gísl Illugason: "Erfikvæði Magnúss berfœtts" 10. U 145; FJ 320; *FmS* VII, 44; *F* 271; *Skj* IA, 442; *Skj* IB, 411; EAK 203.

L. 2 in AM 66 reads "eyja dróttar" (genitive) for "eyja dróttinn" (nominative; MskMS, Hr, F), that is, "the guardian of the people conquered four ancestral countries of the islanders," which seems preferable because Magnús was not lord of the isles. L. 6 echoes a line from the eddic "Reginsmál" (23:8 "eða hamalt fylkia" [Neckel/Kuhn, *Edda,* p. 179]). For the practice of using that battle formation, see the note on **st. 48,* above.

St. 196: Gísl Illugason: "Erfikvæði Magnúss berfœtts" 11. U 145; FJ 320; *FmS* VII, 44–45; *F* 271; *Skj* IA, 442; *Skj* IB, 411; EAK 203; *NN* §87.

L. 6 in F has "ríklundaðir" (proud-minded) for "ríkisvendir" ("royal scepters"; MskMS, Hr, AM 66). The "Haraldr" referred to in l. 2 must be Magnús's grandfather, Haraldr Sigurðarson. According to *Gísls þáttr Illugasonar (FmS* VII, 40), Gísl accompanied Magnús on his expedition to the west.

St. 197: Gísl Illugason: "Erfikvæði Magnúss berfœtts" 12. U 145; FJ 320; *FmS* VII, 45; *F* 271; *Skj* IA, 442; *Skj* IB, 411; EAK 203.

St. 198: Gísl Illugason: "Erfikvæði Magnúss berfœtts" 13. U 146; FJ 320–21; *FmS* VII, 46–47; *F* 271; *Skj* IA, 442; *Skj* IB, 412; EAK 203.

The adverb "prúðliga" (boldly) in l. 4 plays on the nickname of Hugi enn prúði (the bold).

St. 199: Gísl Illugason: "Erfikvæði Magnúss berfœtts" 14. U 146; FJ 322; *FmS* VII, 49; *F* 272; *Skj* IA, 442; *Skj* IB, 412; EAK 203.

In l. 8, "hvno" (MskMS, F) has been emended to "húna" (Hr, AM 66).

St. 200: Gísl Illugason: "Erfikvæði Magnúss berfœtts" 15. U 146; FJ 322; *FmS* VII, 51; *F* 272; *Skj* IA, 443; *Skj* IB, 412; EAK 203.

St. 201: Gísl Illugason: "Erfikvæði Magnúss berfœtts" 16. U 147; FJ 322; *FmS* VII, 51; *F* 272; *Skj* IA, 443; *Skj* IB, 412; EAK 203; *NN* §2534.

L. 8 in MskMS reads "divps valfasti," and F has "dívpr salfasti." The word "valfasti" usually means "corpse flame" (sword). Ernst A. Kock (*NN* §2534) emends to "djúps svalfasti" ("the cool fire of the deep," that is, "gold"), while Finnur Jónsson (*LP* 589) merely notes that the word "valfasti" in this particular instance means "fire."

St. 202: Magnús berfœttr: lv. 2. U 148; FJ 324; *FmS* VII, 57; *F* 273; *Skj* IA, 432; *Skj* IB, 402; EAK 199; *NN* §2983.

In l.1, "vill hann eigi" has been emended to "villat," to preserve the meter.

St. 203: Anon. B st. 2. U 148; FJ 324; *FmS* VII, 57; *F* 273; *Skj* IA, 591; *Skj* IB, 591–92; EAK 288. The Msk y-branch (J2, 47, F) gives the name of the Norman knight as "Gipparðr" in both prose and poetry. L. 5 ("fram reiþ þar var fna/þi") is corrupt in MskMS. In AM 66, "framreið var" violates the meter, whereas F has "framreiðar var fra/ðe." Because both MskMS and AM 66 show the same mistake, the line must have been miscopied in the common exemplar of MskMS and AM 66 (Msk x), where the letter <þ> was doubled, thus creating a new morphemic boundary: "framreiþ (þ)ar var."

St. 204: Eldjárn: lv. 1. U 148; FJ 325; *FmS* VII, 59; *F* 273; *Skj* IA, 437; *Skj* IB, 407; EAK 201; *NN* §916.

In keeping with the readings of Hr, AM 66, and F, "verþr" (l. 3) has been emended to "vest" to retain internal rhyme, and for syntactical reasons, "breiðhvfoþo" (l. 6) has been emended to "breiðhúfuðum" (Hr, AM 66), and "of" (l. 7) to "í" (Hr, AM 66).

St. 205: Eldjárn: lv. 2. U 149; FJ 326; *FmS* VII, 60; *F* 274; *Skj* IA, 437; *Skj* IB, 407; EAK 201.

In l. 2, "fasc" (scribal error) has been emended to "falsk" (AM 66), and "varo" (l. 6; third person plural) has been emended to "váruð" (second person plural; F) for syntactical reasons.

St. 206: Þorkell hamarskald: "Magnússdrápa" 4. U 149; FJ 327; *FmS* VII, 53; *F* 274; *Skj* IA, 438–39; *Skj* IB, 408; EAK 201; *NN* §2533.

In l. 5, "herþir" (strengthener; all MSS) has been emended to "herðar" (shoulders), and "varþa" (MskMS, AM 66, F) to "varð á" (see *NN* §2533).

St. 207: Gísl Illugason: "Erfikvæði Magnúss berfœtts" 17. U 150; FJ 327; *FmS* VII, 53; *F* 274; *Skj* IA, 443; *Skj* IB, 412; EAK 203.

St. 208: Gísl Illugason: "Erfikvæði Magnúss berfœtts" 18. U 150; FJ 327; *FmS* VII, 57–58; *F* 274; *Skj* IA, 443; *Skj* IB, 413; EAK 204.

St. 209: Gísl Illugason: "Erfikvæði Magnúss berfœtts" 19. U 150; FJ 327; *FmS* VII, 58; *F* 274; *Skj* IA, 443; *Skj* IB, 413; EAK 204; *NN* §2534n.

In l. 3, "franum" (Hr: "franu") has been emended to "fránn of" (F): the scribe of the Msk x-branch mistook the adjective and the preposition "fránn um" for one word. This stanza also contains echoes from the eddic lays about Sigurðr the Dragonslayer, e.g., l. 2 "en Huginn gladdisk," compared to "Reginsmál," 18:2, "þá er Hugin gladdi"; 26:8, "oc Hugin gladdi"; "Fáfnismál," 35:6, "oc Hugin gleddi" (Neckel/Kuhn, *Edda,* pp. 178–79, 186). Gísl undoubtedly knew the *fornyrðislag* insertions in "Reginsmál" and "Fáfnismál" and must have used the eddic lines from the Sigurðr cycle deliberately in his praise poetry to Magnús, the grandson of Haraldr Sigurðarson and the father of Sigurðr jórsalafari. See also the notes on *sts. 49, 151, 195, 210, 271.*

St. 210: Gísl Illugason: "Erfikvæði Magnúss berfœtts" 20. U 150; FJ 328; *FmS* VII, 58–59; *F* 274; *Skj* IA, 444; *Skj* IB, 413; EAK 204.

L. 8, "þars vega þurfti," echoes l. 4 of "Reginsmál," 18, "ok vegit hafði" (Neckel/Kuhn, *Edda,* p. 178; see the notes on *sts. 209, 271*). The Haraldr in l. 6 must refer to Haraldr Sigurðarson (see *st. 196*).

St. 211: Anon. B st. 1. U 150; FJ 328; *FmS* VII, 54; *F* 275; *ÍF* 28, 226, st. 184; *ÍF* 29, 310, st. 259; *Skj* IA, 591; *Skj* IB, 591; EAK 288.

St. 212: Magnús berfœttr: lv. 3. U 151; FJ 330; *FmS* VII, 61; *F* 276; *Skj* IA, 432; *Skj* IB, 402; EAK 199.

In l. 1, all other MSS have "ein er su." It has been suggested that Maktildr was Matilda, the daughter of Malcolm of Scotland and Margaret, the great-granddaughter of Edmund Ironside (see Poole 1985:116–17). Matilda married Henry I of England shortly after his coronation in 1100. She was brought up in England under the care of her aunt Christina, abbess of Wilton (see Chibnall 1994:7–11). The reference in this stanza to her warlike activities is difficult to reconcile with reality.

St. 213: Magnús berfœttr: lv. 4. U 152; FJ 330; *FmS* VII, 61; *F* 276; *Skj* IA, 433; *Skj* IB, 402–3; EAK 199.

In l. 4, Hr and AM 66 have "vífit" (singular) for "víf en" (plural; MskMS and F).

St. 214: Magnús berfœttr: lv. 5. U 152; FJ 330–31; *FmS* VII, 62; *F* 276; *Skj* IA, 433; *Skj* IB, 403; EAK 199; *NN* §2532.

In l. 2, "ormliNz" has been emended to "Armhlín" (arm-Hlín). Hr has "armlins," AM 66 "armlín, " and F "armlinns." The *kenning* must have been misunderstood at an early point in the transmission of the stanza. The *kenning* "gollhrings Gerðr" (Gerðr of the gold ring) recalls the refrain of Haraldr harðráði's jesting verses (*sts. 58–63*).

St. 215: Anon. B st. 3. U 152; FJ 331; *FmS* VII, 66–67; *F* 276; *Skj* IA, 591; *Skj* IB, 592; EAK 288; *NN* §1226.

St. 216: Anon. B st. 4. U 152; FJ 331; *FmS* VII, 67; *F* 276; *Skj* IA, 592; *Skj* IB, 592; EAK 289; *NN* §2549.

The first line is problematic because "eggjendr" ("inciters"; masculine accusative plural) would normally require a qualifier. Finnur Jónsson (*Skj* IB) therefore emends to "eggviðu" (blade woods), while Ernst A. Kock has "eggsendi" (blade senders). However, both emendations are metrically impossible (resulting in a heptasyllabic line). If the MS reading is kept, "eggjendr" must be taken as a half-*kenning* for "warriors."

St. 217: Kali Sæbjarnarson lv. 1. U 152; FJ 331; *Flat* II, 429; *FmS* VII, 49; *Orkn, ÍF* 34, 99, st. 31; *Skj* IA, 434; *Skj* IB, 404; EAK 199.

In *Orkn* and in *FmS,* which at this point follow *Orkn* rather than MskMS or Hkr, the half-stanza is attributed to Kali Sæbjarnarson, the grandfather of Jarl Rǫgnvaldr kali Kolsson of Orkney. According to that saga, the verbal exchange between Kali and Magnús took place on Magnús's first expedition and not on the second, as described in MskMS. The fact that the identity of the poet was not known to the compiler of the Msk version must mean that the half-stanzas were not part of the version of *Jarlasǫgur with which he was familiar. The *Orkn* version has the following variant readings: l. 2: "þingríkir hǫfðingjar" (law-mighty chieftains); l. 4: "konungr" (king) for "iofvʀ" ("lord"; = Hr, AM 66).

St. 218: Magnús berfœttr: lv. 1. U 151; FJ 332; *Flat* II, 429; *FmS* VII, 49; *Orkn, ÍF* 34, 100, st. 32; *Skj* IA, 432; *Skj* IB, 402; EAK 199.

St. 219: Magnús berfœttr: lv. 6. U 154; FJ 334; *FmS* VII, 70; *ÍF* 29, 313, st. 260; *Skj* IA, 433; *Skj* IB, 403; EAK 199.

In l. 7, "velld ec" (first person singular) has been emended "veldr" (third person singular) in keeping with the other MSS. "Ingjan" (l. 6) is the Old Norse version of Old Irish "ingen" (girl, daughter). The identity of this Irish woman is unknown, but it is tempting to connect her with the mother of Haraldr gilli (see Ch. 76 and note 76.1).

St. 220: Þorkell hamarskald: "Magnússdrápa" 5. U 155; FJ 335–36; *FmS* VII, 71; *Skj* IA, 439; *Skj* IB, 408; EAK 201; *NN* §806.

The first two lines of this stanza repeat ll. 1–2 of Arnórr Þórðarson's "Erfidrápa Haralds harðráða" 12 (*st. 142*).

St. 221: Þórarinn stuttfeldr: "Stuttfeldardrápa" 1. U 157; FJ 338; *FmS* VII, 75–76; *Skj* IA, 489; *Skj* IB, 461–62; EAK 227; *NN* §3107.

The meter is *hagmælt*, a variant of *tøglag*, with regularized rhyme and alliteration, as in *dróttkvætt*. In some stanzas of "Stuttfeldardrápa," rhyme and double alliteration are missing in the first line. For Hrólfr kraki, see the note on *st. 86* above.

St. 222: Þórarinn stuttfeldr: "Stuttfeldardrápa" 2. U 157; FJ 339; *FmS* VII, 76; *F* 281; *ÍF* 28, 239, st. 185; *Skj* IA, 490; *Skj* IB, 462; EAK 227; *NN* §§2794, 3107.

Hkr attributes the stanza to Þórarinn stuttfeldr, and the meter (*hagmælt*) indicates that this is correct. L. 3 in MskMS has "margscaps" for "margspaks" (scribal error).

St. 223: Þórarinn stuttfeldr: "Stuttfeldardrápa" 3. U 157; FJ 339; *FmS* VII, 77; *Skj* IA, 490; *Skj* IB, 462; EAK 227.

L. 5 in MskMS has "þott," which has been emended to "þótti," in keeping with Hr and AM 66. L. 6, "þar lands sem hvar," is repeated as l. 8 in Sigurðr slembir's *lausavísa* (*st. 279*).

St. 224: Halldórr skvaldri: "Útfarardrápa" 1:5–8. U 159; FJ 342; *FmS* VII, 79 (ll. 1–8); *F* 282 (ll. 1–8); *ÍF* 28, 241, st. 188 (ll. 1–8); *Skj* IA, 486; *Skj* IB, 458; EAK 225; *NN* §§964, 2990C.

St. 225: Halldórr skvaldri: "Útfarardrápa" 2. U 160; FJ 343; *FmS* VII, 79–80; *F* 282; *ÍF* 28, 242, st. 189; *Skj* IA, 486; *Skj* IB, 458; EAK 225.

St. 226: Halldórr skvaldri: "Útfarardrápa" 3. U 160; FJ 344; *FmS* VII, 80; *F* 282; *ÍF* 28, 243, st. 190; *Skj* IA, 486; *Skj* IB, 458; EAK 225; *NN* §806.

In l. 3, MskMS has "k" (i.e., "konungr," "king"), which is corrupt and has been emended to "kundr" (descendant), in keeping with the reading of F. (Hr and AM 66 have "kind" [descendant]; feminine.)

St. 227: Haldórr skvaldri: "Útfarardrápa" 4. U 161; FJ 344; *FmS* VII, 80; *F* 282; *ÍF* 28, 243, st. 191; *Skj* IA, 486; *Skj* IB, 458; EAK 225.

The name of the poet is given in Hkr. In *FmS*, this and the next half-stanza are given as one. L. 2 in MskMS (and in Hr, AM 66) reads "Alcass i styr," which has been emended to "Alcassi styr" in keeping with the Hkr MSS.

St. 228: Halldórr skvaldri: "Útfarardrápa" 5. U 161; FJ 344–45; *FmS* VII, 80–81; *F* 283; *ÍF* 28, 243, st. 192; *Skj* IA, 487; *Skj* IB, 458–59; EAK 225.

"Fra" (l. 1; third person singular) has been emended to "frák" (first person singular) with the other MSS. In l. 2, the other versions read "til sorga" (plural).

St. 229: Halldórr skvaldri: "Útfarardrápa" 6. U 161; FJ 345; *FmS* VII, 81; *F* 283; *ÍF* 28, 244, st. 193; *Skj* IA, 487; *Skj* IB, 459; EAK 226.

St. 230: Halldórr skvaldri: "Útfarardrápa" 8. U 162; FJ 347; *FmS* VII, 84; *Skj* IA, 487; *Skj* IB, 459; EAK 226.

In l. 5, "ba/þ" (third person singular) has been emended to "bautt" (second person singular). The translation of "lífs aftíg" (death) is conjectural. According to *LP* (4), "aftíg" is etymologically related to OE *oftēon* (deny, deprive), and "lífs aftíg" would then be translated as "deprivation of life," that is, "death."

St. 231: Halldórr skvaldri: "Útfarardrápa" 7. U 162; FJ 347; *FmS* VII, 82–83; *F* 284; *ÍF* 28, 245–46, st. 195; *ÍF* 29, 317, st. 261; *Skj* IA, 487; *Skj* IB, 459; EAK 226.

In l. 1, "ba/þsterkir" ("battle-strong"; adjective, plural) has been emended to "bǫðstyrkir" ("battle strengthener"; noun, singular) with the other MSS. In l. 3 MskMS, has "gyiar" for "gýgjar" (giantess).

St. 232: Þórarinn stuttfeldr: "Stuttfeldardrápa" 4. U 162; FJ 347; *FmS* VII, 83; *F* 284; *ÍF* 28, 246, st. 196; *Skj* IA, 490; *Skj* IB, 462; EAK 227; *NN* §3107.

St. 233: Halldórr skvaldri: "Útfarardrápa" 9. U 163; FJ 348; *FmS* VII, 84; *F* 284; *ÍF* 28, 246–47, st. 197; *Skj* IA, 487; *Skj* IB, 459; EAK 226.

Ll. 1–2 are damaged in MskMS. Unger adds "me[kir me]rþ" (Finnur reads "mer . . . hiols"), but the reading "merð" is not supported by the MSS, which all have "morð." The translation of the half-stanza follows *Skj* IB. The *kenning* "fremðar ræsir" (advancer of honor) for "king" also occurs in Ívarr Ingimundarson's "Sigurðarbǫlkr" 4 (*st. 260*).

St. 234: Þórarinn stuttfeldr: "Stuttfeldardrápa" 7. U 166; FJ 352; *FmS* VII, 99; *Skj* IA, 491; *Skj* IB, 463; EAK 227; *NN* §§966, 2990D.

None of the MSS identifies the poet of this fragment, but the meter (*hagmælt*) suggests that it belongs to "Stuttfeldardrápa." The translation follows *NN* §§966 and 2990D. "Harðmóðigr" usually means "hostile," which is at odds with the prose text. Ernst A. Kock suggests a translation "cheerful," but such a meaning of "harðmóðigr" is unattested. The present translation (faithful) is chosen in keeping with "harðráðr," "harðúðigr" (steadfast).

St. 235: Gullásu-Þórðr: lv. 1. U 172; FJ 362; *FmS* VII, 114–15; *Skj* IA, 453; *Skj* IB, 421–22; EAK 208; *NN* §920.

"Lindbols" (l. 6; MskMS, AM 66) has been emended to "linnbóls" ("snake lair"; Hr), which preserves the internal rhyme; in l. 8, "vm" has been emended to "und" (Hr, AM 66).

St. 236: Einarr Skúlason: lv. 1. U 181; FJ 375; *FmS* VII, 137; *Skj* IA, 482–83; *Skj* IB, 454; EAK 223–24.

Earlier editors emend l. 7 to "bauga fægihrjóðr" ("person who destroys or portions out rings," that is, "generous king"). That reading is not supported by any MS, however, and "bauga fægirjóðr" (colorer of shields) is a *kenning* for warrior.

St. 237: Sigurðr jórsalafari: lv. 2. U 188; FJ 385; *FmS* VII, 152; *F* 299; *Skj* IA, 454; *Skj* IB, 422; EAK 209.

In l. 1, "hann" has been left out to preserve the meter, and in l. 2, the enclitic definite article has been omitted ("felldinom").

St. 238: Þórarinn stuttfeldr: lv. 1. U 188; FJ 385; *FmS* VII, 152–53; *F* 299; *Skj* IA, 491; *Skj* IB, 463; EAK 228.

In l. 5, "veri" (third person singular) has been emended to "værir" (second person singular; Hr, AM 66, F) for syntactical reasons. In l. 5, MskMS reads "Møra" (of the people of Møre) for the verb "mæra," which the scribe apparently regarded as a qualifier for "hildingr" (l. 8).

St. 239: Þórarinn stuttfeldr: lv. 2. U 188; FJ 386; *FmS* VII, 153; *F* 299; *Skj* IA, 491; *Skj* IB, 463; EAK 228.

L. 7 in MskMS reads "nv samir at miNazc," which violates rhyme and alliteration, as well as syllabic structure. The line has been emended in keeping with the readings of Hr and AM 66. F has "eN samir," which retains internal rhyme.

St. 240: Þórarinn stuttfeldr: lv. 3. U 189; FJ 386–87; *FmS* VII, 154; *F* 299; *Skj* IA, 491–92; *Skj* IB, 464; EAK 228; *NN* §967.

Ll. 4–5 are damaged in MskMS. Unger adds "gaml[a oc vantv eina]" from Hr and AM 66. (Finnur Jónsson reads "gamla . . . co.") For the myth behind the *kenning* "dung of the ancient eagle" (bad poetry), see *SnE* I, 216–24.

St. 241: Sigurðr jórsalafari: lv. 3. U 189; FJ 387; *FmS* VII, 155; *F* 300; *Skj* IA, 454–55; *Skj* IB, 422–23; EAK 209.

St. 242: Einarr Skúlason: lv. 2. U 192; FJ 392; *FmS* VII, 167; *F* 303; *Skj* IA, 483; *Skj* IB, 455; EAK 224; *NN* §§962, 3108A.

This stanza is badly damaged in MskMS. Unger adds ll. 2–4 "[allvallz gleþi halldit gramr scalattv gvmna gapamvnn vm]" and ll. 7–8 "[r þess fyr gotnom galldrs navþsyniar valldit]," in accordance with Hr. In *Skj* IA, Finnur Jónsson uses AM 66 as the main MS but lists the variant readings from Hr. In the present edition, "scalattv" (Hr; l. 3: "skallattv;" AM 66, F) has been emended to "skaltattu" for metrical reasons; and in l. 5, "heiþir iofrar" (nominative plural) has been emended to "heiðar jǫfra" (genitive+genitive; AM 66, F) as part of the *kenning* "hlíðrœkjandi galdrs heiðar jǫfra." The *kenning* "chant of the giant" (gold) refers to the story about a giant's wealth being measured in mouthfuls (see *SnE* I, 214).

St. 243: Einarr Skúlason: "Haraldsdrápa II" 4. U 199; FJ 401; *FmS* VII, 184–85; *F* 314; *ÍF* 28, 286–87, st. 206; *ÍF* 29, 325, st. 263; *Skj* IA, 457–58; *Skj* IB, 425; EAK 210; *NN* §2535.

The meter is *hagmælt*. In l. 3, MskMS has "biorgnyiar," a scribal error for "Bjǫrgynjar" (Bergen).

St. 244: Halldórr skvaldri: "Haraldsdrápa" 5. U 199; FJ 402; *Skj* IA, 489; *Skj* IB, 461; EAK 227.

St. 245: Einarr Skúlason: "Haraldsdrápa II" 5. U 200; FJ 402; *Skj* IA, 458; *Skj* IB, 426; EAK 210. For Ella, see the note on **st. 29.*

St. 246: Einarr Skúlason: "Haraldsdrápa I" 1. U 200; FJ 402–3; *FmS* VII, 196 (ll. 1–4); *F* 320 (ll. 1–4); *ÍF* 28, 296, st. 207 (ll. 1–4); *ÍF* 29, 329, st. 266 (ll. 1–4); *Skj* IA, 456; *Skj* IB, 424; EAK 210; *NN* §922.

L. 1 in MskMS has "let" (third person singular; = F); Hkr, AM 66, and Fsk have "léztu" (second person singular). In l. 2, MskMS and Hkr read "eljunfrár" (courageous), the other MSS have "eljunþrár" (defiant), and in l. 6, MskMS has "nisto," a scribal error for "misto."

St. 247: Einarr Skúlason: "Haraldsdrápa I" 2. U 200; FJ 403; *FmS* VII, 196 (ll. 1–4); *F* 320 (ll. 1–4); *ÍF* 28, 296, st. 208 (ll. 1–4); *ÍF* 29, 329, st. 267 (ll. 1–4); *Skj* IA, 457; *Skj* IB, 424–25; EAK 210.

In l. 1, "slettv" (neuter dative singular) has been emended to "sléttan" (masculine accusative singular; = Hr, AM 66, Fsk, Hkr) for syntactic reasons. In the same line, the other MSS read "áttuð" (second person plural), for MskMS "atti" (third person singular). In l. 2, Hr, AM 66, Hkr, and Fsk B have "Háars" (Óðinn's) for MskMS and Fsk A "Háalfs" (Hálfr's). For the legendary king Hálfr, see the note on *st. 103* above.

St. 248: Einarr Skúlason: "Haraldsdrápa II" 2. U 200; FJ 403; *Skj* IA, 457; *Skj* IB, 425; EAK 210. This stanza is recorded in MskMS only. As to the identity of the poet, the codex has "h," which Unger reads as "Halldórr" (skvaldri) and Finnur Jónsson as "hann" ("he"; *Skj* IA). The meter (*hagmælt*) indicates that the stanza was part of Einarr's "Haraldsdrápa." In l. 3, MskMS reads "hveŋþ," a scribal error for "Hveðn" (Hven), and "hamoþro," (?) which has been emended to "hánǫðru" (tall snake), in keeping with earlier editions.

St. 249: Einarr Skúlason: "Haraldsdrápa II" 3. U 200; FJ 403; *Skj* IA, 457; *Skj* IB, 425; EAK 210; *NN* §2049.

St. 250: Ívarr Ingimundarson: "Sigurðarbǫlkr" 1. U 201; FJ 405; *Skj* IA, 495; *Skj* IB, 467; EAK 229.

The meter is a regularized *fornyrðislag*. Hkr (*ÍF* 28, 297; trans. Hollander, p. 731), Hr, AM 66 (*FmS* VII, 199) and MskMS mention the name of Aðalbrikt, Sigurðr's foster father. The name is not given in Fsk (*ÍF* 29, 326).

St. 251: Ívarr Ingimundarson: "Sigurðarbǫlkr" 6. U 202; FJ 406; *Skj* IA, 496; *Skj* IB, 468; EAK 229.

The stanza is only recorded in MskMS, and the damaged parts (ll. 7–8) cannot be restored. The meaning of the last half-stanza must be gleaned from the prose.

St. 252: Ívarr Ingimundarson: "Sigurðarbǫlkr" 7. U 202; FJ 406; *Skj* IA, 496; *Skj* IB, 468; EAK 230.

For Vilhjálmr and his death, see *st. 282*. For King David of Scotland, see note 58.1.

St. 253: Ívarr Ingimundarson: "Sigurðarbǫlkr" 8. U 202; FJ 407; *Skj* IA, 496; *Skj* IB, 468; EAK 230.

The name "Dáfinnr" is an Old Norse folk-etymological variant of "Davíð," following the pattern of the variants "Finnr" and "Fiðr" (see *st. 116*).

St. 254: Ívarr Ingimundarson: "Sigurðarbǫlkr" 9. U 202; FJ 407; *Skj* IA, 496; *Skj* IB, 469; EAK 230.

St. 255: Ívarr Ingimundarson: "Sigurðarbǫlkr" 10. U 203; FJ 407; *Skj* IA, 496; *Skj* IB, 469; EAK 230.

In l. 3, " or" has been emended to "ór."

St. 256: Ívarr Ingimundarson: "Sigurðarbǫlkr" 11. U 203; FJ 407; *Skj* IA, 497; *Skj* IB, 469; EAK 230.

St. 257: Ívarr Ingimundarson: "Sigurðarbǫlkr" 2. U 203; FJ 408; *Skj* IA, 495; *Skj* IB, 467; EAK 229.

St. 258: Ívarr Ingimundarson: "Sigurðarbǫlkr" 3. U 203; FJ 408; *Skj* IA, 495; *Skj* IB, 467–68; EAK 229.

St. 259: Ívarr Ingimundarson: "Sigurðarbǫlkr" 12. U 203; FJ 408; *FmS* VII, 200; *F* 322; *ÍF* 28, 298, st. 209; *ÍF* 29, 326–27, st. 265; *Skj* IA, 497; *Skj* IB, 469; EAK 230; *NN* §1154.

The stanza is also recorded in the Hkr MSS and in Fsk, Hr, and AM 66. In l. 8, the other MSS read "ens milda" (genitive) for MskMS "en milldi:" "Magnús was judged to be the father of that mighty, generous king."

St. 260: Ívarr Ingimundarson: "Sigurðarbǫlkr" 4. U 204; FJ 409; *Skj* IA, 495–96; *Skj* IB, 468; EAK 229.

St. 261: Ívarr Ingimundarson: "Sigurðarbǫlkr" 5. U 204; FJ 409; *Skj* IA, 496; *Skj* IB, 468; EAK 229.

In ll. 1 and 4, Unger emends "hell" to "hellt" and "vesta" to "vestr" (scribal errors).

St. 262: Ívarr Ingimundarson: "Sigurðarbǫlkr" 13. U 207; FJ 414; *FmS* VII, 205; *F* 325; *ÍF* 28, 302, st. 210; *ÍF* 29, 330, st. 268; *Skj* IA, 497; *Skj* IB, 469; EAK 230.

The stanza is also cited in the Hkr MSS and in Fsk, Hr, and AM 66. In l. 3, MskMS has "horða," which Unger and Finnur Jónsson emend to "Horðar," in keeping with the other MSS. In Hkr, Fsk, Hr, and AM 66, ll. 1–2 read: "tóku við mildum ‖ Magnúss syni" ([they] received the generous son of Magnús); F reads: "Toko margir ‖ við Magnus seyni" (many received Magnús's son).

St. 263: Kolli enn prúði: "Ingadrápa" 1. U 208; FJ 416; *FmS* VII, 208–9 (ll. 1–4); *F* 326 (ll. 1–8); *ÍF* 28, 305, st. 211 (ll. 1–4); *Skj* IA, 503; *Skj* IB, 476; EAK 234; *NN* §969.

In l. 4, "ferþar" ("company"; MskMS, F) has been emended to "verðar" ("food"; Hr, AM 66, Hkr). In l. 6, "orsynia þic" is a corruption of "ǫrr synjaðir." The clause "en ǫrr synjaðir brynju eirar," "and, bravely, you refused to spare the byrnie," could also be construed as "and, bravely, you refused the sparing of the byrnie [peace]."

St. 264: Kolli enn prúði: "Ingadrápa" 2. U 208; FJ 416; *FmS* VII, 209 (ll. 1–4); *F* 326 (ll. 1–8); *ÍF* 28, 305, st. 212 (ll. 1–4); *Skj* IA, 503; *Skj* IB, 476; EAK 234.

In l. 1, "haʀa" ("ruler"; oblique, MskMS, Hr) has been emended to "harri" (nominative) in keeping with the other MSS, and "song fvss" (song-keen) in l. 6 has been emended to "sóknfúss" ("battle-keen"; F). L. 8 in MskMS has "hersciptir" (army divider), which creates a heptasyllabic line and has been emended to "herskriptr" (colored shields), in accordance with the F variant. L. 4 is part of a split refrain of which only this line remains.

St. 265: Kolli enn prúði: "Ingadrápa" 3. U 209; FJ 417; *FmS* VII, 210; *F* 327; *ÍF* 28, 306–7, st. 213; *Skj* IA, 503; *Skj* IB, 476; EAK 234.

St. 266: Ívarr Ingimundarson: "Sigurðarbǫlkr" 14. U 210; FJ 419; *F* 328; *Skj* IA, 497; *Skj* IB, 469; EAK 230.

St. 267: Ívarr Ingimundarson: "Sigurðarbǫlkr" 15. U 211; FJ 420; *F* 328; *Skj* IA, 497; *Skj* IB, 470; EAK 230.

In l. 1, "roþo" has been emended to "rotu-." (The MskMS reading is metrically and se-
mantically impossible.)

St. 268: Ívarr Ingimundarson: "Sigurðarbǫlkr" 16. U 211; FJ 420; *Skj* IA, 497–98; *Skj* IB, 470;
EAK 230.

The last line echoes lines from the "First Lay of Guðrún" (Gðr I, 1:4; 13:2; 27:8;
Neckel/Kuhn, *Edda,* pp. 202, 204, 206). See also the note on *st. 288* below.

St. 269: Ívarr Ingimundarson: "Sigurðarbǫlkr" 17. U 211; FJ 420; *F* 328; *Skj* IA, 498; *Skj* IB,
470; EAK 231.

L. 4 in MskMS and F reads "oc ramir stra/mar," which is metrically correct but phonetically
wrong ("rammir" is phonetically long). If the correct consonant quantity is preserved, "oc"
must be deleted for metrical reasons.

St. 270: Ívarr Ingimundarson: "Sigurðarbǫlkr" 18. U 211; FJ 421; *F* 328; *Skj* IA, 498; *Skj* IB,
470; EAK 231.

St. 271: Ívarr Ingimundarson: "Sigurðarbǫlkr" 19. U 211; FJ 421; *Skj* IA, 498; *Skj* IB, 470;
EAK 231.

L. 2 ("sás vega þorði") echoes formulaic lines from the Sigurðr cycle that always occur in
alliteration with "Vǫlsungr ungi" ("the young descendant of Vǫlsungr," i.e., Sigurðr): e.g.,
"Reginsmál," 18:3–4, "Vǫlsungr ungi ‖ oc vegit hafði"; "Sigurðarqviða en scamma,"
1:3–4, "Vǫlsungr ungi ‖ er vegit hafði"; 3:5–6, "Vǫlsungr ungi ‖ oc vega kunni"
(Neckel/Kuhn, *Edda,* pp. 178, 206) (see the note on *st. 209*). The allusions to Sigurðr the
Dragonslayer in Ívarr's poem to Sigurðr slembir also must have been intentional.

St. 272: Ívarr Ingimundarson: "Sigurðarbǫlkr" 20. U 211; FJ 421; *Skj* IA, 498; *Skj* IB, 470;
EAK 231.

Two lines are missing from the second half-stanza.

St. 273: Ívarr Ingimundarson: "Sigurðarbǫlkr" 21. U 211–12; FJ 421; *Skj* IA, 498; *Skj* IB,
470–71; EAK 231.

St. 274: Ívarr Ingimundarson: "Sigurðarbǫlkr" 22. U 212; FJ 422; *F* 329; *Skj* IA, 498–99; *Skj* IB,
471; EAK 231.

St. 275: Ívarr Ingimundarson: "Sigurðarbǫlkr" 23. U 212; FJ 422; *Skj* IA, 499; *Skj* IB, 471;
EAK 231.

St. 276: Anon. B st. 17. U 212; FJ 423; *FmS* VII, 214; *F* 329; *ÍF* 28, 310, st. 214; *Skj* IA, 594; *Skj* IB,
595; EAK 290.

The couplet is damaged in MskMS. Unger adds "[varð eigi vel við styr]" in keeping with
Hr and AM 66. In the present edition, "varð eigi" has been emended to "varðat" with the
other editions. The meter is a hexasyllabic variant of *runhent.*

St. 277: Ívarr Ingimundarson: "Sigurðarbǫlkr" 24. U 213; FJ 424; *F* 330; *Skj* IA, 499; *Skj* IB,
471; EAK 231.

St. 278: Ívarr Ingimundarson: "Sigurðarbǫlkr" 25. U 213; FJ 424; *F* 330; *Skj* IA, 499; *Skj* IB,
471; EAK 231.

In l. 1, "dref" has been emended to "dreif" (F) and "meþan" (l. 6; "while") to "með"
("with"; F). The phrase "dǫrr roðin" (reddened spears) is an onomastic pun on the name
"Benteinn" (wound rod).

St. 279: Sigurðr slembir: lv. 1. U 214; FJ 425; *FmS* VII, 216; *F* 330; *ÍF* 28, 312, st. 215; *Skj* IA,
495; *Skj* IB, 467; EAK 229.

This is the only stanza attributed to Sigurðr slembir. In l. 8, "var" has been emended to
"hvar," in keeping with the Hkr version (K). The meter is an irregular variant of *tøglag,*
with an intricate system of rhymes and verbal repetitions that have a distinct non-Norse
appearance:

Gótt vas í g**amm**a	vasa þar g**am**ans vant
þars vér gla**ð**ir dr**ukk**um	at g**am**ansdry**kk**ju
ok gla**ð**r gr**am**s sonr	**þegn** gladdi **þegn**
gekk me**ð**al be**kk**ja:	**þar** lands sem hv**ar**.

The last line repeats l. 6 of Þórarinn stuttfeldr's "Stuttfeldardrápa" 3 (*st. 223*).

St. 280: Ívarr Ingimundarson: "Sigurðarbǫlkr" 26. U 214; FJ 425; *FmS* VII, 216; *F* 330–31; *ÍF* 28, 312, st. 216; *Skj* IA, 499; *Skj* IB, 471; EAK 231; *NN* §3109n.

The stanza is anonymous in all MSS, and Finnur Jónsson hesitantly assigns it to Ívarr's "Sigurðarbǫlkr" because of the meter (*fornyrðislag*). In l. 3, "meþ" (with) has been emended to "und" (beneath) with the other MSS.

St. 281: Ívarr Ingimundarson: "Sigurðarbǫlkr" 27. U 214; FJ 426; *Skj* IA, 499; *Skj* IB, 472; EAK 231; *NN* §3109.

L. 1 in MskMS reads "þaN vetr eN nesta" (that next winter), which is ungrammatical (the verb is omitted). Furthermore "vetr" (winter) duplicates the *kenning* "naðra deyði" ("snake slayer," that is, "winter") in the next line. Hence, the scribe must have failed to understand the *kenning* and accordingly added "vetr" from the prose. L. 3 has "fall" ("fall"; accusative), which is syntactically incorrect ("valda" takes the dative) and makes the line too short.

St. 282: Ívarr Ingimundarson: "Sigurðarbǫlkr" 28. U 214; FJ 426; *Skj* IA, 499–500; *Skj* IB, 472; EAK 232.

There is a discrepancy between the information given in the prose text and in the poetry. According to the prose, Vilhjálmr was killed in Víkar (Vik, Helgeland), which is in keeping with the Hkr version of the event (*ÍF* 28, 312; trans. Hollander, p. 742). It is possible that the poem originally had "norðr í Víkum" (l. 8) and that the place name "í Vágum" was repeated from the preceding stanza.

St. 283: Ívarr Ingimundarson: "Sigurðarbǫlkr" 29. U 215; FJ 426; *Skj* IA, 500; *Skj* IB, 472; EAK 232.

St. 284: Ívarr Ingimundarson: "Sigurðarbǫlkr" 30. U 215; FJ 427; *Skj* IA, 500; *Skj* IB, 472; EAK 232.

"Hnefa" (fist) in l. 6 has been emended to "nefa" (nephew). The word "hnefa" must have been caused by "handar" (hand) in the following line.

St. 285: Ívarr Ingimundarson: "Sigurðarbǫlkr" 31. U 215; FJ 427; *Skj* IA, 500; *Skj* IB, 472; EAK 232.

The stanza has been misplaced in the prose text: Sigurðr captured and hanged Finnr at Kville (county in northern Bohuslän, Sweden).

St. 286: Ívarr Ingimundarson: "Sigurðarbǫlkr" 32. U 215; FJ 427; *Skj* IA, 500; *Skj* IB, 472–73; EAK 232.

In l. 2, MskMS reads "tecr" for "tecinn" (scribal error).

St. 287: Ívarr Ingimundarson: "Sigurðarbǫlkr" 33. U 215; FJ 428; *Skj* IA, 500; *Skj* IB, 473; EAK 232.

St. 288: Ívarr Ingimundarson: "Sigurðarbǫlkr" 34. U 215; FJ 428; *Skj* IA, 500; *Skj* IB, 473; EAK 232.

L. 8 ("of vegǫndum") echoes "Guðrúnarqviða ǫnnur" 4:8 "und [of] vegondom" (Neckel/Kuhn, *Edda*, p. 224). For the eddic equivalents of l. 2 ("fyr Sigurði"), see the note on *st. 268*.

St. 289: Ívarr Ingimundarson: "Sigurðarbǫlkr" 35. U 217; FJ 430–31; *Skj* IA, 500–1; *Skj* IB, 473; EAK 232.

St. 290: Ívarr Ingimundarson: "Sigurðarbǫlkr" 36. U 217; FJ 431; *Skj* IA, 501; *Skj* IB, 473; EAK 232.

In l. 5, the MS has "sciod," which Unger and Finnur Jónsson emend to "sciolld" (shield).

St. 291: Ívarr Ingimundarson: "Sigurðarbǫlkr" 37. U 218; FJ 431; *Skj* IA, 501; *Skj* IB, 473; EAK 232.

St. 292: Ívarr Ingimundarson: "Sigurðarbǫlkr" 38. U 218; FJ 431–32; *Skj* IA, 501; *Skj* IB, 474; EAK 233.

St. 293: Ívarr Ingimundarson: "Sigurðarbǫlkr" 39. U 218; FJ 432; *Skj* IA, 501; *Skj* IB, 474; EAK 233.

In l. 7, "rvþvsc" (were reddened) has been emended to "hruðusk" (were cleared).

St. 294: Ívarr Ingimundarson: "Sigurðarbǫlkr" 40. U 218; FJ 432; *Skj* IA, 501; *Skj* IB, 474; EAK 233.

St. 295: Ívarr Ingimundarson: "Sigurðarbǫlkr" 41. U 218; FJ 432; *Skj* IA, 501; *Skj* IB, 474; EAK 233.

St. 296: Kolli enn prúði: "Ingadrápa" 4. U 219; FJ 433; *Skj* IA, 504; *Skj* IB, 477; EAK 234.

The stanza is recorded in MskMS only. Earlier editors assign it to Kolli's "Ingadrápa." "Oll" (all; l. 2) has been emended to "ǫld" (men), which restores the internal rhyme. In l. 7, "doct" has been emended to "dǫkk" (water). In l. 8, the short form of the name "Sigurð-ar" has been replaced by the long form "Sigvarðar," for metrical reasons.

St. 297: Kolli enn prúði: "Ingadrápa" 5. U 219; FJ 433; *Skj* IA, 504; *Skj* IB, 477; EAK 234; *NN* §970.

The stanza is recorded in MskMS only. "Hrosar" (third person singular; l. 3) has been emended to "hrósak" (first person singular). In l. 4, "valkost" ("corpse heap"; accusative) has been emended to "valkǫstr" (nominative) to furnish the missing subject. The last half-stanza follows *NN* §970. The decisive battle between Sigurðr and Ingi took place near Hol-mengrá by Hvaler on November 12, 1139 (see *ÍF* 28, 316 and note 92.1; trans. Hollander, p. 745). Langeyjarsund (Langósund) is most likely the strait between Langóarna and Hol-mengrá in Hvaler.

St. 298: Ívarr Ingimundarson: "Sigurðarbǫlkr" 42. U 220; FJ 435; *Skj* IA, 502; *Skj* IB, 474; EAK 233.

For syntactical reasons, "sneckio" ("ship"; oblique, l. 4) has been emended to "snekkja" (nominative), and "son" (accusative; l. 5) has been emended to "sonr" (nominative).

St. 299: Ívarr Ingimundarson: "Sigurðarbǫlkr" 43. U 220; FJ 435; *Skj* IA, 502; *Skj* IB, 475; EAK 233.

St. 300: Ívarr Ingimundarson: "Sigurðarbǫlkr" 44. U 221; FJ 436–37; *Skj* IA, 502; *Skj* IB, 475; EAK 233.

St. 301: Ívarr Ingimundarson: "Sigurðarbǫlkr" 45. U 221; FJ 437; *Skj* IA, 502; *Skj* IB, 475; EAK 233.

St. 302: Ívarr Ingimundarson: "Sigurðarbǫlkr" 46. U 221; FJ 437; *Skj* IA, 502; *Skj* IB, 475; EAK 233.

St. 303: Bǫðvarr balti: "Sigurðardrápa" 1. U 222; FJ 438; *Skj* IA, 504; *Skj* IB, 477; EAK 234; *NN* §971.

St. 304: Bǫðvarr balti: "Sigurðardrápa" 2. U 222; FJ 439; *Skj* IA, 504; *Skj* IB, 478; EAK 234; *NN* §972B.

In ll. 7–8, "flestom fylldom" (dative) has been emended to "flestan fylldan" (accusative) for syntactical reasons.

St. 305: Bǫðvarr balti: "Sigurðardrápa 3. U 222; FJ 439; *Skj* IA, 505; *Skj* IB, 478; EAK 234.

L. 3 in the MS has "tavgnvngs," which was corrected in the text by the insertion of an <i> above the last <v>.

St. 306: Einarr Skúlason:" Runhenda" 1. U 223; FJ 440; *Skj* IA, 473; *Skj* IB, 445; EAK 219.

The meter is *runhent.*

St. 307: Einarr Skúlason: "Runhenda" 2. U 225; FJ 442–43; *FmS* VII, 234; *F* 338; *ÍF* 28, 326, st. 219; *Skj* IA, 473; *Skj* IB, 445–46; EAK 219; *NN* §3107.

In l. 4, "giafmilld" (generous; accusative) has been emended to "gjafmildr" (nominative), in accordance with the other MSS. In the Hkr versions (and in Hr, AM 66), ll. 7 and 8 oc-cur in the reverse order.

St. 308: Einarr Skúlason: "Runhenda" 3. U 225; FJ 443; *FmS* VII, 234; *F* 338; *ÍF* 28, 326–27, st. 220; *Skj* IA, 473; *Skj* IB, 446; EAK 219; *NN* §1986.

L. 3 in Hkr, Hr, and AM 66 have "bær" (suitable to be spread) for MskMS "kǫr" (dear). In l. 5, Hkr, Hr, and AM 66 have "Renir" [people of Ranríki; that is, Bohuslän in Sweden]: MskMS's "Remir" are unknown (see note 97.1). The place name Leikberg has not been identified.

St. 309: Einarr Skúlason: "Eysteinsdrápa" 1. U 225; FJ 443; *FmS* VII, 235; *F* 339; *ÍF* 28, 327, st. 221; *Skj* IA, 475; *Skj* IB, 447; EAK 220; *NN* §955.

The first half-stanza is garbled in MskMS. In keeping with the other MSS, "songs" ("song"; l. 1) has been emended to "sogns" (sea); "maNe" (dative singular; l. 3) has been emended to "manna" (genitive plural); "hattom" ("manners"; l. 5) has been emended to "skútum" (ships). In l. 3, "mogreNir" (nominative) has been emended to "mágrenni" (dative).

St. 310: Einarr Skúlason: "Runhenda" 5. U 225; FJ 444; *FmS* VII, 235; *F* 339; *ÍF* 28, 328, st. 222; *Skj* IA, 473–74; *Skj* IB, 446; EAK 220.

St. 311: Einarr Skúlason: "Runhenda" 6. U 225; FJ 444; *FmS* VII, 235–36; *F* 339; *ÍF* 28, 328, st. 223; *SnE* I, 524 (ll. 1–2); *Skj* IA, 474; *Skj* IB, 446; EAK 220.

St. 312: Einarr Skúlason: "Runhenda" 7. U 226; FJ 444; *FmS* VII, 236; *F* 339; *ÍF* 28, 328–29, st. 224; *SnE* I, 524 (ll. 3–4); *Skj* IA, 474; *Skj* IB, 446; EAK 220.

In l. 5, Finnur Jónsson reads "lec," whereas Unger has "let."

St. 313: Einarr Skúlason: "Runhenda" 8. U 226; FJ 444–45; *FmS* VII, 236–37; *F* 339 (ll. 1–4); *ÍF* 28, 329, st. 225 (ll. 1–4); *Skj* IA, 474; *Skj* IB, 447; EAK 220; *NN* §3107.

In l. 7, "raNdølom" has been emended to "randolun" (rim fish) with earlier editions. The place name Skorpusker is unknown.

St. 314: Einarr Skúlason: "Runhenda" 9. U 226; FJ 445; *FmS* VII, 237; *F* 340; *ÍF* 28, 329, st. 226; *Skj* IA, 474–75; *Skj* IB, 447; EAK 220; *NN* §954.

Poole (1980:276) suggests that the "Partar" in Einarr's stanza referred to the inhabitants of Partney in Lincolnshire. On the identification of the other English place names in *sts. 310–14,* see Poole 1980.

St. 315: Einarr Skúlason: lv. 5. U 227; FJ 446; *Skj* IA, 483; *Skj* IB, 455; EAK 224; *NN* §§963, 2489.

The following three *lausavísur* by Einarr Skúlason (*sts. 315–17*) are recorded in MskMS only. In l. 4, "fyr þat" ("for that"; scribal error) has been emended to "fyrðar" (men), and in l. 6, "rarat" (scribal error) has been emended to "varat" (following Unger and Finnur Jónsson).

St. 316: Einarr Skúlason: lv. 6. U 227; FJ 447; *Skj* IA, 483–84; *Skj* IB, 455–56; EAK 224.

In l. 6, "velmall" has been emended to "vísmáll" ("eloquent"; Unger's emendation), which restores the internal rhyme.

St. 317: Einarr Skúlason: lv. 7. U 228; FJ 448; *Skj* IA, 484; *Skj* IB, 456; EAK 224; *NN* §3108.

In l. 7, "við" (preposition) has been emended to "viðr" (verb) for syntactic reasons.

St. 318: Einarr Skúlason: " Ingadrápa" 2. U 235; FJ 458; *ÍF* 29, 337, st. 269; *Skj* IA, 476; *Skj* IB, 448; EAK 220.

In l. 7, "fiarspell" (destruction of property) has been emended to "fjorspell" ("death"; Fsk). Fsk has "ulfgrennir" ("wolf feeder"; l. 2) for MskMS "arNgreNir" (eagle feeder), and "ræsi" ("ruler"; l. 6) for "visa" (ruler).

St. 319: Einarr Skúlason: "Ingadrápa" 3. U 235; FJ 458; *ÍF* 29, 337, st. 270; *Skj* IA, 476; *Skj* IB, 448; EAK 221; *NN* §§2538, 2990B.

L. 4 is damaged in MskMS, and Unger adds "[bera fagra]" in accordance with Fsk. L. 7 reads as follows in Fsk: "brœðir hafa barz miðri" (brothers have fought [in] the middle [of Bergen]).

St. 320: Einarr Skúlason: "Ingadrápa" 4. U 235; FJ 459; *ÍF* 29, 338, st. 271; *Skj* IA, 476; *Skj* IB, 448; EAK 221.

In l. 6, "EysteiN" (nominative) is emended to "Eysteins" (genitive), in accordance with the Fsk variant. L. 7 is damaged in MskMS, and Unger adds "[beinn at]" with Fsk.

Concordance of Episodes in
Fagrskinna and *Heimskringla*

Morkinskinna established a new literary type, the historical compendium. Previous kings' sagas took the form of biographies of individual monarchs, notably Óláfr helgi (Saint Óláfr), Óláfr Tryggvason, and King Sverrir. The author of *Morkinskinna* took the next step and constructed a chronicle extending from the reign of King Magnús Óláfsson to (in all probability) the reign of Magnús Erlingsson. This move was not without precedent because *Ágrip* had already initiated the chronicle form, albeit in a very limited compass. The difference in dimensions is, indeed, so great between *Ágrip* and *Morkinskinna* that the former can hardly be regarded as a model for the latter.

Whatever the precedents, *Morkinskinna* revolutionized history writing almost immediately. The chronicle form was imitated in *Fagrskinna* about five years later and in *Heimskringla* about a decade later. In these two works, *Morkinskinna* was the chief source for the relevant time period. Both works were more historically disciplined and less enthusiastically anecdotal, but they capitalized extensively on the narrative provided in *Morkinskinna*. Because this book presents only *Morkinskinna* and not the later literary developments, we will not propose an overall analysis of how *Morkinskinna* was used. Gustav Indrebø (1917) has analyzed *Fagrskinna*'s treatment of *Morkinskinna,* and Bjarni Aðalbjarnarson has done the same for *Heimskringla* in his introduction to *ÍF* 28. Instead, we will provide a sort of concordance in tabular form for the convenience of readers who wish to compare the texts. We refer to Bjarni Einarsson's edition of *Fagrskinna* (abbreviated *Fsk*) and Bjarni Aðalbjarnarson's edition of *Heimskringla* (abbreviated *Hkr*). Page numbers in *Morkinskinna* (*Msk*) refer to our translation. We begin with *Fagrskinna*, tabulating chapter by chapter (chapters 44–101).

Morkinskinna and *Fagrskinna*

Fsk 44 omits the quarrel of King Yaroslav and his queen and her demand that he foster Magnús, as well as Magnús's childhood in Russia. *Fsk* also omits "Karls þáttr vesæla" (*Msk* 91–96). In *Fsk,* the Þrœndir send a delegation to fetch

Magnús from Russia. This is in line with *Msk* 97, a version that conflicts with the account in "Karls þáttr" to the effect that the initiative in securing the throne for Magnús came from King Yaroslav (*Msk* 92).

Fsk 45 = *Msk* 99 (Magnús's return to Norway).

Fsk 46 (¶ 1) = *Msk* 100 (the acceptance of Magnús). *Fsk* 46 (¶ 2–3) = *Msk* 100 (Sveinn Álfífusonr fails to win over the Norwegian chieftains).

Fsk 47 (¶ 1) = *Msk* 100. *Fsk* 47 (¶ 2) = *Msk* 101–2 (the Danish succession, war between Norway and Denmark, and a negotiated peace). *Fsk* omits an incident concerning Einarr þambarskelfir and another concerning Kálfr Árnason (found in *Msk* 102).

Fsk 48 = *Msk* 103 (but omits Kálfr Árnason at Stiklastaðir). *Fsk* 48 (pp. 212–15, on Sigvatr's "Bersǫglisvísur") = *Msk* 104–9. *Fsk* 48 (p. 215) = *Msk* 109 (Rǫgnvaldr made Jarl of Orkney; reference to "jarla sǫgur"). *Fsk* omits Kálfr's choice of sides between Rǫgnvaldr and Þorfinnr (*Msk* 110). *Fsk* also omits an episode involving Magnús and Álfífa (*Msk* 111). *Fsk* 48 (pp. 216–17) = *Msk* 111. *Fsk* 48 (pp. 217–18, on Magnús's decision not to dispossess King Edward) = *Msk* 127–28.

Fsk 49 (pp. 218–19) = *Msk* 113–14 (on Magnús's appointment of Sveinn Úlfsson as jarl, but omits Einarr þambarskelfir's comment "too great a jarl"). *Fsk* 49 (p. 220) = *Msk* 114–15 (on how Sveinn Úlfsson has himself declared king of Denmark and Magnús's punitive campaign).

Fsk 50 (pp. 221–22) = *Msk* 115–23 (on the Battle of Hlýrskógsheiðr, but omits the digression on Duke Otto's wooing of Magnús's sister). *Fsk* 50 (pp. 224–25) = *Msk* 123–26 (Magnús defeats Sveinn again).

Fsk 50–51 (pp. 226–27) = *Msk* 130–31 (Haraldr Sigurðarson goes to Russia, but *Fsk* omits the details of Haraldr's secret escape and his preliminary betrothal of Ellisif).

Fsk 51 (pp. 228–34) = *Msk* 132–44 (Haraldr's campaigns in the Mediterranean, but *Fsk* omits the "Norðbrikt" subterfuge, Haraldr's request for a "lock of Empress Zoë's hair," the story of how Haraldr healed a woman with a demon lover, Haraldr's great feast to celebrate the dedication of a church, and one of the campaign stratagems [access by tunneling]).

Fsk 51 (p. 234) = *Msk* 144 (Haraldr goes to Jerusalem and secures the route to the River Jordan). *Fsk* 51 (p. 234) = *Msk* 145 (Haraldr accused of consorting with Zoë's niece Maria, but *Fsk* omits Haraldr's fabliau-like escape from the emperor's spies). *Fsk* 51 (p. 235) = *Msk* 145–46 (Haraldr consigned to a dungeon and rescued). *Fsk* 51 (pp. 235–37) = *Msk* 147 (Haraldr blinds the emperor and abducts Maria). *Fsk* 51 (pp. 237–38) = *Msk* 147–49 (Haraldr returns to Russia and marries Ellisif). *Fsk* 51 (pp. 238–39) = *Msk* 150 (Haraldr confers with Sveinn Úlfsson).

Fsk 52 (pp. 239–40) = *Msk* 151 (Haraldr confers with Magnús, is rejected, and allies himself with Sveinn Úlfsson). *Fsk* 52 (pp. 241–43) = *Msk* 152–54 (Haraldr goes to Norway and is accepted by Þórir at Steig, but *Fsk* omits Haraldr's deceitful abandonment of Sveinn Úlfsson). *Fsk* 52 (pp. 243–45) = *Msk* 154–55 (Haraldr and Magnús divide the realm).

Fsk 53 (p. 246) adds a paragraph on Haraldr hárfagri's dynasty. *Fsk* 53 (pp. 246–48) = *Msk* 156–57 (the kings dispute the royal anchorage). Here *Fsk* omits a long sequence of episodes:

1. "Þorkels þáttr dyrðils" (*Msk* 157–58)
2. the return of Magnús's adviser at the Battle of Hlýrskógsheiðr (*Msk* 158)
3. Magnús's bestowal of a jarldom on Ormr Skoptason (*Msk* 158–59)
4. Þrándr upplendingr's special invitation to Magnús and "Þrándar þáttr upplendings" (*Msk* 159–61)
5. Einarr þambarskelfir's collision with Haraldr over excessive exactions (*Msk* 161–62)
6. Haraldr's baiting of Magnús's brother Þórir (*Msk* 162)
7. "Þorsteins þáttr Hallssonar" (*Msk* 163–65)
8. "Arnórs þáttr jarlaskálds" (*Msk* 165–67)
9. "The Good Counsels of King Haraldr" (*Msk* 167–68)
10. the story of King Magnús and Margrét (*Msk* 168–70)
11. "Hreiðars þáttr" (*Msk* 171–79)
12. the story of how Magnús secures a safe haven in Denmark for his mother (*Msk* 179–81)
13. the episode in which Sveinn Úlfsson caracoles before the Norwegian army (*Msk* 181)

Fsk 54 (p. 248) = *Msk* 181 (Sveinn Úlfsson flees). *Fsk* 54 (p. 248) = *Msk* 181 (Magnús dies; *Fsk* omits all the details and recounts the actual death in parts of two sentences). *Fsk* 54 (pp. 248–49) = *Msk* 184–86 (Haraldr is declared king at Vébjǫrg [Viborg]; Einarr þambarskelfir is more interested in returning Magnús's corpse to Norway; *Fsk* omits the poor man on Samsø seeking alms from Magnús).

Fsk 55 treats material that must have been in the lacuna of MskMS as follows: Sveinn Úlfsson is declared king in Denmark (*Fsk* 250); *Fsk* drastically abbreviates the story of Þorkell geysa and his daughters (*Msk* 187–94, 195–96); *Fsk* omits "Halldórs þáttr Snorrasonar" (*Msk* 187–94). *Fsk* 55 (p. 253) = *Msk* 194–97 (Haraldr harries in Denmark). *Fsk* 55 (p. 253) = *Msk* 198 (the kings agree to do battle at the Götaälv). *Fsk* 55 (pp. 253–55) (Þorleikr fagri leaves Iceland for Norway at this time—four stanzas not in *Msk*). *Fsk* 55 (pp. 256–57) = *Msk* 199–200 (Sveinn fails to show up for the appointed battle, and Haraldr harries as far south as Hedeby). *Fsk* 55 (pp. 258–61) = *Msk* 199–203 (Haraldr returns to Norway and eludes Sveinn's pursuit by throwing goods and captives overboard).

Fsk 56 (pp. 261–62) = *Msk* 204–5 (King Haraldr and the Icelanders). *Fsk* 56 (pp. 262–63) = *Msk* 205 (but *Fsk* summarizes all of Haraldr's dealings with

Einarr þambarskelfir, including Einarr's death). *Fsk* omits the story of an Icelander who shares in the discovery of Hákon jarl's treasure (*Msk* 206–8), the
story of how Haraldr tests the loyalty of his district chieftains (*Msk* 208–10),
and the events leading up to the death of Einarr þambarskelfir and his son
(*Msk* 210–11).

Fsk 57 (pp. 263–64) = *Msk* 211 (Finnr Árnason deserts to Sveinn Úlfsson).
Here *Fsk* omits a series of episodes:

1. "Auðunar þáttr" (*Msk* 211–15)
2. "Úlfs þáttr auðga" (*Msk* 215–19)
3. "Brands þáttr ǫrva" (*Msk* 219–20)
4. King Haraldr's healing of Ingibjǫrg Halldórsdóttir (*Msk* 220–22)
5. "The Storytelling of an Icelander" (*Msk* 222–23)
6. "Þorvarðs þáttr krákunefs" (*Msk* 223–25)
7. the introduction of Hákon Ívarsson and some introductory matter before the
   Battle of Niz (*Msk* 226–28)

Fsk 57 (pp. 264–68) = *Msk* 228–31 (the Battle of Niz). *Fsk* 57 (pp. 268–69)
= *Msk* 231–32 (Finnr Árnason's verbal exchange with King Haraldr). *Fsk* 57
(p. 270) = *Msk* 232–33 (Sveinn Úlfsson takes refuge with the old couple).
Fsk omits Þórólfr mostrarskegg's exploit (*Msk* 233–34) and King Haraldr's
dealings with Hákon Ívarsson (*Msk* 234–36). *Fsk* 57 (p. 271) = *Msk* 237
(Hákon takes service with Sveinn Úlfsson). *Fsk* omits Hákon's killing of
Ásmundr (*Msk* 237–38). *Fsk* 57 (pp. 271–72) = *Msk* 215 (*Fsk* backtracks to King
Haraldr's falling out with the Upplendingar). *Fsk* 57 (p. 273) = *Msk* 238–39
(King Haraldr and King Sveinn make peace). Here *Fsk* omits several more
episodes:

1. the fighting between King Haraldr and Hákon Ívarsson in Gautland (*Msk* 239–
   43)
2. "Sneglu-Halla þáttr" (*Msk* 243–52)
3. King Haraldr's encounter with a fisherman in a boat (*Msk* 252–54)
4. Haraldr's avenging of Tryggvi Óláfsson (*Msk* 255)
5. a note on Gizurr Ísleifsson (*Msk* 255)
6. "Stúfs þáttr blinda" (*Msk* 255–57)
7. "Odds þáttr Ófeigssonar" (*Msk* 257–61)

Fsk 58 (p. 274) = *Msk* 261–62 (Edward the Confessor dies and Harold Godwinson succeeds him, but Tostig feels equally entitled).

Fsk 59 (pp. 274–75) = *Msk* 262 (Tostig seeks to enlist Sveinn Úlfsson, without success).

Fsk 60 (pp. 275–76) = *Msk* 262–63 (Tostig persuades King Haraldr to campaign with him; Úlfr stallari dies).

Fsk 61–62 (pp. 276–78) = *Msk* 264 (King Haraldr makes his preparations—monitory dreams).

Fsk 63 (pp. 278–79) = *Msk* 265–66 (Haraldr defeats the jarls Morkere and Waltheof).

Fsk 64 (p. 280) = *Msk* 267 (King Haraldr takes York).

Fsk 65 (pp. 280–81) = *Msk* 267 (King Harold Godwinson retakes York).

Fsk 66 (pp. 281–82) = *Msk* 268 (King Haraldr sights the English army).

Fsk 67 (p. 282) = *Msk* 268–69 (King Haraldr makes his battle dispositions).

Fsk 68 (pp. 282–85) = *Msk* 269–70 (Harold Godwinson is unable to detach Tostig from the opposing army and promises King Haraldr seven feet of earth).

Fsk 69 (pp. 285–87) = *Msk* 271–72 (King Haraldr falls).

Fsk 70 (pp. 287–89) = *Msk* 272–73 (Jarl Tostig falls).

Fsk 71 (pp. 289–90) = *Msk* 273–74 (the "Orrahríð" and the anecdote about Styrkárr stallari).

Fsk 72 (p. 290) = *Msk* 275 (Óláfr and Magnús succeed Haraldr on the throne).

Fsk 73 (pp. 290–91) = *Msk* 275 (the death of Magnús). *Fsk* omits some information on Tostig's sons Ketill krókr and Skúli and his descendants (*Msk* 276).

Fsk 74–76 (pp. 291–95) = *Msk* 276–77 (William's conquest of England and the death of Harold Godwinson).

Fsk 77–78 (pp. 295–97) = *Msk* 276 (genealogical material).

Fsk 79 (pp. 297–99) = *Msk* 279–80 (peace negotiations between Norway and Denmark). *Fsk* 79 (pp. 299–302) = *Msk* 280–82 (the reign of Óláfr kyrri). *Fsk* omits the story of King Óláfr and the kráku-karl (*Msk* 282–85).

Fsk 80 (pp. 302–03) = *Msk* 285–86 (the succession of Magnús and Hákon, Hákon's sudden death, and Steigar-Þórir's support of Sveinn, the son of Haraldr flettir, against Magnús). *Fsk* 80 (pp. 304–6) = *Msk* 286–91 (Þórir and Egill Áskelssonr resist Magnús, are captured and hanged). *Fsk* omits "Sveinka þáttr Steinarssonar" (*Msk* 291–97).

Fsk 81 (pp. 307–10) = *Msk* 297–303 (Magnús harries in the western islands and Scotland).

Fsk 82 (pp. 310–11) = *Msk* 303–5. *Fsk* omits the story of the knight Giffarðr.

Fsk 83 (pp. 311–12) = *Msk* 306–7 (the three Scandinavian kings make peace).

Fsk 84–85 (pp. 312–15) = *Msk* 309–13 (Magnús harries in the west again and falls in Ireland. His three sons Sigurðr, Eysteinn, and Óláfr succeed him, but Óláfr dies young).

Fsk 86–90 (pp. 315–19) = *Msk* 313–24 (King Sigurðr's adventures in the Mediterranean). Here *Msk* has a lacuna between Minorca and Constantinople. It can be filled in approximately from Codex Frisianus.

Fsk 91 (pp. 319–20) = *Msk* 324–25 (Emperor Alexios [Kirjalax] gives King Sigurðr a choice between either gold or games). Here *Fsk* has a lacuna of four leaves (equivalent to *Msk* 324–26). *Fsk* omits "Ívars þáttr Ingimundarsonar" (*Msk* 326–28).

Fsk 92 (p. 320)—six lines following the lacuna and reviewing Eysteinn's public works. This matter is skimmed from the flyting between Eysteinn and Sigurðr (*Msk* 345–47), which is otherwise omitted in *Fsk*.

Fsk 93 (p. 320) = *Msk* 334 and 349 (the deaths of Óláfr and Eysteinn). Here *Fsk* excises several episodes:

1. King Sigurðr's dream (*Msk* 329–30)
2. "Ásu-Þórðar þáttr" (*Msk* 330–34)
3. "Þinga saga" (*Msk* 334–45)
4. the flyting between Sigurðr and Eysteinn (*Msk* 345–47)
5. "Þórarins þáttr stuttfeldar" (*Msk* 347–49)
6. the episode of King Sigurðr and Óttarr birtingr (*Msk* 350–51)
7. the episode of Erlendr gapamunnr (*Msk* 351–52)

Fsk 93 (pp. 320–21) = *Msk* 352 (the arrival of Haraldr gilli). *Fsk* omits the story of Haraldr and Loðinn (*Msk* 352–53), the story of King Sigurðr and Áslákr hani (*Msk* 353–54), and the story of King Sigurðr and the whore (*Msk* 354–55). *Fsk* 93 (p. 321) = *Msk* 355–56 (Haraldr gilli's paternity ordeal). *Fsk* omits the race between Haraldr and Magnús Sigurðarson (*Msk* 356–57) and King Sigurðr's dealings with Bishop Magni (*Msk* 357–58). *Fsk* 93 (p. 321) = *Msk* 358.

Fsk 94–95 (pp. 321–26) tells of the hostility between Haraldr and Magnús, Magnús's victory at the Battle of Fyrileif, Haraldr's victory at Bergen, and the capture and maiming of Magnús. Almost all of this is missing in *Msk* 359–63 because of a missing leaf, but see *Hkr* (*ÍF* 28, 276–86).

Fsk 95 (p. 326) = *Msk* 366 (Haraldr's progeny, notably Ingi and Sigurðr, but the texts diverge). *Fsk* omits King Haraldr's gifts to Bishop Magnús (*Msk* 366–67).

Fsk 96 (p. 326) = *Msk* 368 (*Fsk* says that Sigurðr slembir submitted to a paternity ordeal witnessed by five bishops in Denmark, but *Msk* seems to suggest that it took place in Jerusalem). *Fsk* 96 (p. 327) = *Msk* 370–71 (Sigurðr is captured by Haraldr's men but escapes with an epic swimming feat). *Fsk* omits Sigurðr's stay with Þorgils Oddason at Saurbœr (*Msk* 369–70). *Fsk* 96 (pp. 328–29) = *Msk* 371–72 (Sigurðr kills King Haraldr). *Fsk* 96 (p. 330) = *Msk* 372–73 (Sigurðr goes north and takes Magnús blindi from his monastic arrest).

Fsk 97 (p. 331) = *Msk* 373–74 (Ingi is declared king, and his men win two victories on his behalf).

Fsk 98 (pp. 331–32) = *Msk* 374–75 (King Eiríkr eimuni of Denmark joins Magnús in an attack on Norway and is driven off). *Fsk* omits *Msk* 375 with its mention of Eiríkr Oddsson.

Fsk 99 (pp. 332–33) = *Msk* 376–81 (Sigurðr campaigns in Denmark and executes his enemies in northern Norway). *Fsk* omits Ingi's letter (*Msk* 381–82). *Fsk* 99 (pp. 333–34) = *Msk* 382–85 (Ingi and his brother Sigurðr defeat and kill Magnús). *Fsk* omits Sigurðr slembir's martyrdom and the killing of Óttarr birtingr (*Msk* 385–88). *Fsk* 99 (pp. 334–35) = *Msk* 389 (Eysteinn arrives from Scotland and gets a third of the realm). Here *Fsk* drops a number of episodes:

1. the introduction of Erlingr skakki and his voyage to Jerusalem with Rǫgnvaldr (*Msk* 389–90)
2. King Sigurðr's begetting of a son Hákon (*Msk* 390)
3. King Eysteinn's raiding in the west (*Msk* 391–92)
4. anecdotes involving Einarr Skúlason (*Msk* 393–94)
5. the slaying of Geirsteinn (*Msk* 394–98)

Fsk 99 (p. 335) = *Msk* 398 (the visit of Cardinal Nicholas from Rome). *Fsk* 99 (pp. 335–39) = *Msk* 398–401 (King Ingi kills King Sigurðr at the behest of Grégóríús). *Fsk* 99–100 (pp. 338–39) = *Msk* 401–2 (Eysteinn is greatly displeased, but he and Ingi settle their differences at Seleyjar).

Fsk 100–1 (pp. 339–41) = *Msk* 403–4 (Ingi routs Eysteinn's forces, and Eysteinn is slain by Símon skálpr).

Morkinskinna and *Heimskringla*

Snorri Sturluson was able to make use of both *Morkinskinna* and *Fagrskinna* when he composed the third part of *Heimskringla*. For his use of *Fagrskinna* the reader may refer to Gustav Indrebø (1917). Because Snorri dealt more freely with the narrative and made more additions than *Fagrskinna*, it will be practical to reverse the procedure employed above and use the narrative outline of *Morkinskinna* as a point of departure, followed by a tabulation of the differences in *Heimskringla*. Like *Fagrskinna*, *Heimskringla* omits "Karls þáttr vesæla" at the outset. Magnús's return to Norway is punctuated by a stop in Sweden and the support of Queen Ástríðr, underpinned by three stanzas of Sigvatr Þórðarson. From that point, the correlation with *Morkinskinna* is closer.

Msk 100 = *Hkr* 7–9 (Magnús accepted as king of Norway).

Msk 100–1 = *Hkr* 10–11 (Sveinn Álfífuson fails in his appeal to the Norwegians). *Hkr* adds some details on Knútr inn ríki in England (*Hkr* 11–12).

Msk 101–2 = *Hkr* 12–13 (Magnús and Hǫrðaknútr make peace). *Hkr* omits Einarr þambarskelfir's insistence on his seat (*Msk* 102) and an anecdote on Kálfr Árnason's courage (*Msk* 102). At the same time, *Hkr* adds a good deal of new material:

1. Queen Ástríðr and Magnús's mother Álfhildr compete for status (*Hkr* 13–14).
2. Sigvatr returns from Rome and stays with Ástríðr in Sweden, then with Magnús in Norway (*Hkr* 14–20).
3. Magnús commemorates King Óláfr (*Hkr* 20–21).
4. Þórir hundr goes to Jerusalem (*Hkr* 22).
5. Ásmundr Grankelsson kills Hárekr ór Þjóttu, with a reference to a rich oral tradition (*Hkr* 22–23).
6. A certain Þorgeirr ór Veradal af Súlu chides Magnús for befriending his father's enemies, with one stanza (*Hkr* 23–24).

Msk 103–4 = *Hkr* 24–25 (Magnús and Kálfr Árnason at Stiklastaðir).

Msk 103–4 = *Hkr* 25–26 (Magnús takes a hard line against his father's enemies [*Msk:* the Þrœndir]).

Msk 104–9 = *Hkr* 26–31 (Sigvatr's "Bersǫglisvísur"). *Hkr* omits the hostilities between Rǫgnvaldr Brúsason and Þorfinnr jarl in Orkney (*Msk* 109–10) and Álfífa's attempt to poison Magnús (*Msk* 111).

Msk 111 = *Hkr* 31–32 (differing versions of dynastic developments in England).

Msk 111–12 = *Hkr* 32–36 (Magnús campaigns in Denmark and has himself declared king).

Msk 113–14 = *Hkr* 36–38 (Magnús names Sveinn Úlfsson jarl in Denmark). *Hkr* 38–40 expands a brief notice in *Msk* 114–15 on Magnús's reduction of Jómsborg.

Msk 114 = *Hkr* 40–41 (Sveinn Úlfsson has himself declared king in Denmark). *Hkr* omits Magnús's punitive expedition in Denmark (*Msk* 114).

Msk 115–21 = *Hkr* 41–45 (the Battle of Hlýrskógsheiðr). *Hkr* omits the story of Duke Otto's courtship in Norway.

Msk 123 = *Hkr* 46 (the Battle of Ré [Rügen]).

Msk 125–26 = *Hkr* 47–52 (Magnús defeats Sveinn at Áróss [Århus]).

Msk 126 = *Hkr* 52–56 (Magnús pursues his victories on Fyn). *Hkr* retrieves the victory of Magnús over Sveinn at Helganes (*Hkr* 56–65).

Msk 127–28 = *Hkr* 65–67 (Magnús decides not to contest King Edward's rule in England).

Msk 130–31 = *Hkr* 68–69 (how Haraldr escapes from Stiklastaðir).

Msk 131–32 = *Hkr* 69–71 (Haraldr in Russia).

Msk 132–34 = *Hkr* 71–72 (Haraldr in Greece). Here *Hkr* omits a number of matters:

1. stops in Wendland, Saxony, France, Lombardy, Rome, and Apulia (*Msk* 132)
2. Haraldr's disguise as Norðbrikt (*Msk* 132)
3. Haraldr's request for a "lock of hair" from Empress Zoë (*Msk* 133)
4. Haraldr's healing of a woman with a demon lover (*Msk* 133–34)

Msk 134–35 = *Hkr* 72–74 (Haraldr disputes a tenting ground with Gyrgir).

Msk 135–36 = *Hkr* 74–76 (Haraldr displaces Gyrgir, campaigns in Africa, and sends his profits to Russia.) *Hkr* omits Haraldr's building of a church in Constantinople (*Msk* 136–37).

Msk 139–41 = *Hkr* 76–77 (Haraldr destroys a town in Sicily by fire).

Msk 137–38 = *Hkr* 77–78 (Haraldr reduces a town by tunneling). *Hkr* adds the reduction of a town by men pretending to engage in athletic games before the walls; Snorri notes that two Icelanders (Halldórr and Úlfr) were among the players (*Hkr* 79–80).

Msk 141–43 = *Hkr* 80–81 (Haraldr reduces a town with a mock burial procession).

Msk 144 = *Hkr* 81–84 (Haraldr goes to Jerusalem).

Msk 145–46 = *Hkr* 85–86 (Haraldr is suspected of commerce with the empress's niece Maria, is thrown in prison, and effects his escape).

Msk 147 = *Hkr* 86–87 (Haraldr blinds the emperor).

Msk 147–48 = *Hkr* 88–89 (Haraldr abducts Maria and escapes).

Msk 148–49 = *Hkr* 89–91 (Haraldr returns to Russia and marries Ellisif).

Msk 150 = *Hkr* 91–95 (Haraldr allies himself with Sveinn and, in *Hkr*, with the Swedes; in *Msk*, Haraldr defers the alliance until he has consulted Magnús).

Msk 151 = *Hkr* 95–96 (peace overtures between Magnús and Haraldr).

Msk 152–53 = *Hkr* 96–98 (Haraldr invents a deception to justify abandoning his alliance with Sveinn). *Hkr* omits Steigar-Þórir's special alliance with Haraldr and Sveinn's continued harrying (*Msk* 153–54).

Msk 154–56 = *Hkr* 98–101 (Magnús and Haraldr divide the realm). *Hkr* 102–3 adds a note on St. Óláfr's relics and a note to the effect that Sveinn seizes all the revenues in Denmark.

Msk 156–57 = *Hkr* 103–4 (Magnús and Haraldr clash over the royal anchorage). At this point, *Hkr* suppresses a great deal of material:

1. "Þorkels þáttr dyrðils" (*Msk* 157–58)
2. the visit of a man who advised Magnús at the Battle of Hlýrskógsheiðr (*Msk* 158)
3. the conferral of a jarldom on Ormr Skoptason (*Msk* 158–59)
4. "Þrándar þáttr upplendings" (*Msk* 159–61)
5. Haraldr's mockery of Magnús's brother Þórir (*Msk* 162)
6. "Þorsteins þáttr Hallssonar" (*Msk* 163–65)
7. "Arnórs þáttr jarlaskálds" (*Msk* 165–67)

8. King Haraldr's healing of a boy's memory (*Msk* 167–68)
9. the story of King Magnús and Margrét (*Msk* 168–70)
10. "Hreiðars þáttr" (*Msk* 171–79)
11. King Magnús's provision for his mother's safety (*Msk* 179–81)
12. details of King Magnús's death scene but adds (*Hkr* 105) a dream in which Magnús is summoned by St. Óláfr (*Msk* 181–83)
13. the narrative about Magnús's brother and mother after his death (*Msk* 183–84)

Msk 184–85 = *Hkr* 106–107 (Haraldr presents himself at the Vébjargar-þing, but Einarr þambarskelfir deems it more important to return Magnús's body to Norway). *Hkr* omits the funeral voyage and the poor blind man's last request on Samsø (*Msk* 185–87).

Msk 187 = *Hkr* 107 (Haraldr is declared king in Norway—according to *Msk*, also in Denmark—but in *Hkr*, he must temporarily abandon his claim). *Hkr* omits "Halldórs þáttr Snorrasonar" (*Msk* 187–94).

Msk (lacuna) = *Hkr* 108 (Sveinn Úlfsson reclaims the throne in Denmark).

Msk 194–96 = *Hkr* 108–11 (Haraldr campaigns in Denmark and punishes Þorkell geysa). *Hkr* 112 adds a note on Haraldr's marriage to Þóra Þorbergs-dóttir and his progeny.

Msk 197–98 = *Hkr* 112–13 (Haraldr renews his harrying expeditions, and Sveinn challenges him to meet at the Götaälv). *Hkr* 113 (= *Fsk* 253–55) notes the arrival of Þorleikr fagri from Iceland.

Msk 199–200 = *Hkr* 114–15 (Sveinn does not keep the appointment; Har-aldr plunders at will and burns Hedeby).

Msk 200–4 = *Hkr* 115–18 (Haraldr returns to Norway and eludes Sveinn's pursuit by distracting the pursuers with precious jetsam).

Msk 204–5 = *Hkr* 118–19 (general assessment of Haraldr and his relation-ship to the Icelanders). At this point, Snorri makes both subtractions and ad-ditions. He omits the following:

1. the tension between Haraldr and Einarr þambarskelfir (*Msk* 205)
2. the story of an Icelander who shares in the discovery of Hákon jarl's treasure (*Msk* 206–8)
3. the story of how Haraldr tests the loyalty of his district chieftains (*Msk* 208–10)
4. Haraldr's mockery of Einarr þambarskelfir (*Msk* 210)

The additions are as follows:

1. *Hkr* 119–20 adds notes on Halldórr Snorrason and Úlfr Óspaksson.
2. *Hkr* 121 adds a note on Magnús's and Haraldr's building projects.
3. *Hkr* 121 introduces Hákon Ívarsson.
4. *Hkr* 122 retrieves Einarr þambarskelfir.

5. *Hkr* 122 retrieves Jarl Ormr (here Eilífsson rather than Skoptason).
6. *Hkr* 123–25 retrieves briefly some of the moments in the hostility between Haraldr and Einarr þambarskelfir.

Msk 210 = *Hkr* 125–26 (Haraldr kills Einarr and his son). Here, too, there are omissions and additions. Omitted are:

1. "Auðunar þáttr" (*Msk* 211–15)
2. Haraldr's retaliation against the Upplendingar and "Úlfs þáttr auðga" (*Msk* 215–19)
3. "Brands þáttr ǫrva" (*Msk* 219–20)
4. Haraldr's healing of Ingibjǫrg Halldórsdóttir (*Msk* 220–22)
5. "Íslendings þáttr sǫgufróða" (*Msk* 222–23)
6. "Þorvarðs þáttr krákunefs" (*Msk* 223–25)

Added are the following:

1. Haraldr cajoles Finnr Árnason to make peace between him and the Þrœndir, and Hákon Ívarsson stipulates marriage to Magnús's daughter Ragnhildr (*Hkr* 126–29).
2. Haraldr is prepared to marry Ragnhildr to Hákon but refuses to grant him the necessary jarldom (*Hkr* 129–30).
3. Hákon kills Sveinn Úlfsson's marauding nephew Ásmundr (*Hkr* 130–32).
4. After the death of Jarl Ormr, Haraldr gives Hákon the coveted jarldom and marries Ragnhildr to him (*Hkr* 132).
5. Haraldr is reconciled with Kálfr Árnason (*Hkr* 132–33).
6. Haraldr arranges to have Kálfr Árnason killed in battle in Denmark (*Hkr* 133–35).
7. Snorri inserts three miracles worked by St. Óláfr (*Hkr* 135–38).

Msk 225–26 = *Hkr* 139–40 (Haraldr is trapped in Lófufjǫrðr but escapes). Here Snorri omits Sigvatr's skaldic recitation before Ívarr hvíti (*Msk* 226) and adds a section on Haraldr's building of a giant ship and assembling of a fleet (*Hkr* 141–45).

Msk 227–31 = *Hkr* 145–52 (the Battle of Niz).

Msk 231–32 = *Hkr* 154–55 (King Haraldr's verbal exchange with Finnr Árnason).

Msk 232–33 = *Hkr* 152–54 (Hákon Ívarsson helps Sveinn Úlfsson escape from the battle and reach the cottage of a poor couple). Here Snorri omits Þórólfr mostrarskegg's exploit (*Msk* 233) and Haraldr's dealings with Hákon Ívarsson, because these latter have already been accounted for (*Msk* 234–36). At the same time, he adds the conclusion of the story about Sveinn Úlfsson and the poor couple (*Hkr* 155–56) and a revelation of Hákon's complicity in

Sveinn Úlfsson's escape. This prompts Haraldr to devise a plan to kill Hákon (*Hkr* 157–58). Haraldr and Sveinn conclude a peace (*Hkr* 158–62).

Msk 238–43 = *Hkr* 162–65 (Haraldr and Hákon wage war against each other in Gautland). Here again, there are a number of deletions and additions. Omitted are:

1. "Sneglu-Halla þáttr" (*Msk* 243–52)
2. Haraldr's encounter with a fisherman in a boat (*Msk* 252–54)
3. Haraldr's avenging of Tryggvi Óláfsson (*Msk* 255)
4. a note on Gizurr Ísleifsson (*Msk* 255)
5. "Stúfs þáttr blinda" (*Msk* 255–57)
6. "Odds þáttr Ófeigssonar" (*Msk* 257–61)

The new material is as follows:

1. Haraldr's punitive expeditions in various provinces (*Hkr* 165–66)
2. a chronological note on the time elapsed since Magnús's death (*Hkr* 167)
3. genealogical notes on Edward the Confessor and William the Conqueror (*Hkr* 168)
4. Harold Godwinson woos William's daughter (*Hkr* 169–70).

Msk 261 = *Hkr* 170–71 (Harold Godwinson succeeds Edward the Confessor).

Msk 262–63 = *Hkr* 172–75 (Jarl Tostig represents his claim unsuccessfully in Denmark and successfully in Norway).

Msk 264–65 = *Hkr* 175–78 (King Haraldr marshals his forces under the shadow of ill omens).

Msk 264 = *Hkr* 178–79 (Haraldr stops off in Orkney and leaves his wife [*Msk:* Þóra; *Hkr:* Ellisif] and daughter [*Hkr:* daughters]).

Msk 265 = *Hkr* 179 (Haraldr lands at Cleveland and begins his campaign).

Msk 265–66 = *Hkr* 179–83 (Haraldr defeats Jarls Morkere and Waltheof).

Msk 267 = *Hkr* 182–83 (Haraldr takes the surrender of the English, but the town is secretly occupied by Harold Godwinson at night).

Msk 268–72 = *Hkr* 183–91 (The initial battle ends with the fall of King Haraldr).

Msk 272–74 = *Hkr* 191–93 (The second battle ends with the fall of Eysteinn orri and the escape of Styrrkárr stallari).

Msk 274–75 = *Hkr* 197–98 (Óláfr returns to Norway).

Msk 276–77 = *Hkr* 193–97 (the story of William's conquest of England). *Hkr* 198–201 adds a general assessment of Haraldr.

Msk 278–80 = *Hkr* 201–2 (King Óláfr makes peace with Sveinn Úlfsson).

Msk 280–82 = *Hkr* 203–9 (King Óláfr's appearance, manner, and customs). *Hkr* omits "Kráku-karls þáttr" (*Msk* 282–85).

Msk 285–86 = *Hkr* 210–12 (After the death of Óláfr, the realm is shared between Magnús berfœttr and Hákon Þórisfóstri, but Hákon dies while hunting). *Hkr* 212–13 adds a passage on Magnús's raiding in Halland, which anticipates *Msk* 297.

Msk 286 = *Hkr* 213–14 (The Þrœndir declare for Sveinn, the son of Haraldr flettir, in concert with Steigar-Þórir and Egill Áskelsson). *Hkr* 261 omits Magnús's speech against Sveinn.

Msk 288 = *Hkr* 214–15 (The Þrœndir defeat Sigurðr ullstrengr).

Msk 288–91 = *Hkr* 215–17 (Magnús defeats the Þrœndir and hangs Þórir and Egill).

Msk 291 = *Hkr* 218 (Magnús takes reprisals against the Þrœndir, and Sveinn Haraldsson flees to Denmark). *Hkr* omits "Sveinka þáttr Steinarssonar" (*Msk* 291–97).

Msk 298–302 = *Hkr* 219–25 (Magnús harries in the west).

Msk 303–7 = *Hkr* 225–28 (Magnús campaigns against King Ingi Steinkelsson in Gautland). *Hkr* omits the story of Giffarðr (assuming that it was in Snorri's version of *Msk*).

Msk 307 = *Hkr* 228–29 (The three northern kings make peace). Here *Hkr* adds several items:

1. information on Magnús's progeny, dress, and stature (*Hkr* 229–30)
2. Magnús's quarrel with Skopti Ǫgmundarson (*Hkr* 230–32)
3. two miracles worked by St. Óláfr (*Hkr* 232–33)

Msk 309–13 = *Hkr* 233–37 (Magnús's last campaign and death in Ireland).

Msk 313 = *Hkr* 238 (Magnús is succeeded by his sons Eysteinn, Sigurðr, and Óláfr). *Hkr* omits that the brothers give their people new privileges (*Msk* 313) but adds that they appoint Hákon Pálsson jarl in Orkney (*Hkr* 239).

Msk 314–22 = *Hkr* 239–47 (Sigurðr campaigns in the Mediterranean; a lacuna in *Msk* is covered by *Hkr* 247–53).

Msk 322–24 = *Hkr* 253 (Sigurðr and his men entertained in Constantinople). *Hkr* omits the feast that Sigurðr arranges for the emperor (*Msk* 324–25).

Msk 325 = *Hkr* 253–54 (Sigurðr returns to Norway).

Msk 326 = *Hkr* 254–56 (Eysteinn's accomplishments in Norway during Sigurðr's absence). *Hkr* omits "Ívars þáttr Ingimundarsonar" (*Msk* 326–28) but adds summary descriptions of Sigurðr and Óláfr and anticipates Óláfr's death from *Msk* 334.

Msk 328–29 = *Hkr* 257–58 (Sigurðr's wife Málmfríðr and concubine Borghildr Óláfsdóttir). *Hkr* omits Sigurðr's dream (*Msk* 329–30), "Ásu-Þórðar þáttr" (*Msk* 330–34), and "Þinga saga" (*Msk* 334–45).

Msk 345–47 = *Hkr* 259–62 (Sigurðr and Eysteinn measure their accomplishments in a flyting). *Hkr* omits "Þórarins þáttr stuttfeldar" (*Msk* 347–49) and adds a note on the marriage of King Magnús berfœttr's daughter Ragnhildr to Haraldr kesja, the son of Eiríkr góði (Erik Ejegod).

Msk 349 = *Hkr* 262–63 (King Eysteinn dies). *Hkr* omits two fits of madness suffered by Sigurðr (*Msk* 350–52) and adds his crusade in Sweden (*Hkr* 263–64).

Msk 352 = *Hkr* 264–65 (the arrival of Haraldr gilli). *Hkr* omits an incident involving Haraldr and a man named Loðinn (*Msk* 352–53) and two more fits of madness (*Msk* 353–55).

Msk 355 = *Hkr* 265 (Sigurðr's political dream).

Msk 355–56 = *Hkr* 266 (Haraldr gilli's paternity ordeal).

Msk 356–57 = *Hkr* 269–70 (Haraldr gilli and Prince Magnús wager on a race). *Hkr* omits King Sigurðr's dealings with Bishop Magni (*Msk* 357–58) but adds several other items:

1. an incident in which Sigurðr saves Haraldr from hanging (*Hkr* 270–71)
2. a miracle worked by St. Óláfr to restore a boy's tongue (*Hkr* 271–72)
3. a second miracle that frees a Christian from the heathens (*Hkr* 272–75)
4. Sigurðr's building projects at Konungahella (*Hkr* 276–77)

Msk 358 = *Hkr* 276–77 (the death of King Sigurðr). *Hkr* omits Sigurðr's last-minute divorce (*Msk* 357–58).

Msk has a lacuna of one leaf = *Hkr* 278–86 (with the following content):

1. The contrast between Magnús and Haraldr; Haraldr takes half the realm.
2. The two kings gather forces and meet at Fyrileif.
3. Haraldr's smaller force is routed. He takes refuge in Denmark, and Magnús subdues all of Norway.
4. Haraldr raises forces in Halland and Vík.
5. Magnús seeks advice from Sigurðr Sigurðarson but rejects all options and remains in Bergen.
6. Haraldr arrives at Bergen at Christmas; both sides prepare.

Msk 363–64 = *Hkr* 286–88 (Haraldr wins the victory and has Magnús maimed). *Hkr* omits King Haraldr's gifts to Bishop Magnús Einarsson (*Msk* 366–67).

Msk 367–69 = *Hkr* 297–98 (introduction and travels of Sigurðr slembir). *Hkr* omits Sigurðr's stay at Saurbœr (*Msk* 369–70).

Msk 371 = *Hkr* 300–1 (Sigurðr kills Haraldr).

Msk 371–72 = *Hkr* 301–4 (Sigurðr tries to gain acceptance in Norway).

Msk 372–74 = *Hkr* 304–5 (Sigurðr frees Magnús from his monastic arrest, but they are defeated by Ingi's forces at Minne).

Msk 374 = *Hkr* 306 (Sigurðr and Magnús incite Karl Sǫrkvisson [*Hkr:* Karl Sónason] against Norway, but he is defeated by Ingi's forces).

Msk 374–75 = *Hkr* 307–8 (Sigurðr and Magnús incite King Eiríkr eimuni against Norway, but the campaign fails).

Msk 376–78 = *Hkr* 309–10 (Sigurðr campaigns in Danish waters).

Msk 378–79 = *Hkr* 310 (Sigurðr kills Benteinn Kolbeinsson).

Msk 379–81 = *Hkr* 311–13 (Sigurðr spends a winter in Finnmark, then takes reprisals against the chieftains of northern Norway).

Msk 381–82 = *Hkr* 314–15 (Ingi addresses a letter to his brother Sigurðr).

Msk 382–85 = *Hkr* 315–19 (The followers of Ingi and Sigurðr defeat Magnús and Sigurðr at the Battle of Holmengrå).

Msk 385–87 = *Hkr* 319–20 (the martyrdom of Sigurðr slembir).

Msk 388 = *Hkr* 322 (the slaying of Óttarr birtingr).

Msk 389 = *Hkr* 322–23 (King Eysteinn is given a share of the realm alongside his brothers Ingi and Sigurðr; he blames Sigurðr for the death of Óttarr birtingr).

Msk 389–90 = *Hkr* 323–25 (Erlingr Kyrpinga-Ormsson's expedition in the Mediterranean).

Msk 390 = *Hkr* 325–26 (King Sigurðr fathers a son Hákon).

Msk 391–92 = *Hkr* 326–30 (Eysteinn harries in the west).

Msk 392 = *Hkr* 330–32 (the retinues and character of the three brothers). *Hkr* omits two incidents involving King Eysteinn and Einarr Skúlason (*Msk* 393–94) and the slaying of Geirsteinn (*Msk* 394–98).

Msk 398 = *Hkr* 332–33 (the visit of Cardinal Nicholas). *Hkr* 334–37 adds two miracles worked by St. Óláfr.

Msk 398–404 = *Hkr* 341–46 (Hostilities between Ingi and Eysteinn end with Eysteinn's death).

APPENDIX B

The Latin Compendium
of Hákon Ívarsson

The Latin "compendium" (or summary) is preserved in a manuscript belonging to the prominent sixteenth-century Danish historian Anders Sørensen Vedel (1542–1616). It is assumed (*Hákonar saga* 1953:XV) that Vedel did not make the summary himself but took it over from an Icelander who had access to a complete version of *Hákonar saga Ívarssonar* in a manuscript differing somewhat from the manuscript that preserves the four fragments discussed in the Introduction (AM 570a 4 to). Since some of the material in Vedel's manuscript can be attributed to the Icelandic humanist Arngrímur Jónsson (1568–1644), Jón Helgason and Jakob Benediktsson suggest that Arngrímur may also be responsible for the compendium, which he could have executed in Copenhagen in the winter of 1592–1593 (*Hákonar saga* 1953:XVI). A comparison of the compendium with the differing summaries in *Morkinskinna* and *Heimskringla* shows clearly that it is in line with *Heimskringla*. Snorri also made use of *Morkinskinna*, but in his treatment of Hákon Ívarsson he seems to have relied largely on the independent *Hákonar saga Ívarssonar*. *Morkinskinna* is sufficiently divergent that it cannot very well come from the same source. Jón Helgason and Jakob Benediktsson (*Hákonar saga* 1953:XXXIX) allow for the possibility that the author of *Hákonar saga* knew *Morkinskinna*, but they are more inclined to accept Bjarni Aðalbjarnarson's view (1937:153–54) that the saga and *Morkinskinna* are independent versions of the same tradition. We have seen ("The Native Sources,") that Bjarne Fidjestøl demurred and returned to the idea that the saga author knew *Morkinskinna* and chose to depart from it in order to provide a fuller narrative.

The compendium is translated from the text in the 1953 edition (pp. 38–40). Since the summary is in somewhat telegraphic style, we have provided clarifications in square brackets. We also include in square brackets references to relevant comments in the 1953 edition (abbreviated simply "ed.").

The Latin Compendium of Hákon Ívarsson

Hákon Ívarsson received two ships and went to Denmark, [then to] England, [where he was] especially attached to Edward the Confessor.

Einarr, having at a certain meeting [in the margin: in Kaupangr, ed. XIX] rescued a thief from the gallows, incurred the wrath of King Haraldr, and after his son was overcome in the anteroom by the king's guards, he was himself killed at the king's behest but only after the king was wounded through his chain mail by Einarr's spear [ed. XIX].

The voice of his son was heard: "I feel the sharp fangs of the king's dogs [ed. XIX]."

[The king] was secretly angry at him [Einarr] because he had supported Magnus in refusing Haraldr part of the realm. For that reason, Haraldr was in the habit of saying that as long as Einarr was alive, he would not be recognized as sole king of Norway.

King Haraldr achieved a reconciliation with the farmers, who were in a fury over Einarr's killing, through the offices of Finnr Árnason. With a similar intent, and with the agreement of Hákon, who was guided by the representations and counsel of Ormr Eilífsson, Finnr's nephew, [Haraldr] set about betrothing Magnús's daughter Ragnhildr to Hákon Ívarsson under his own roof. The district chieftain Ormr married Sigríðr, the daughter of Finnr, and Haraldr married Finnr's granddaughter Þóra, the daughter of Þorbergr.

The dead were laid to rest in St. Oláfr's Church and the king departed from Kaupangr, leaving the reconciliation to be arranged by Finnr, with a double compensation committed for Einarr and a single one for Eindriði.

Having been entertained at a feast, Hákon proposed to Ragnhildr at the conclusion of the feast, but she refused on the ground that she was a princess and at the very least entitled to a marriage with a district chieftain. [Hákon] reported this back to Haraldr, who stated that he could not abolish the custom of having only one district chieftain, a custom that went back to the time of Magnús. With that, they parted.

Therefore [Hákon] went to Sveinn Úlfsson in Denmark and was well received.

There was an Ásmundr at Sveinn's court, a nephew on his sister's side, who debauched many women [ed. XX] and led a reprehensible life. Dismissed from the court as a result, he went to the provinces, where he joined forces with some companions and carried out villainous raids on the king's lands. Captured once, he escaped; captured again, he escaped a second time and engaged in piracy, inflicting many evils on the Danes. Therefore Hákon was sent to contain and apprehend him. Attacking him with one ship against three, he captured him and carried off his head, which he threw down at the feet of King Sveinn.

Sveinn, regretting the deed, later sent word to Hákon to leave the realm. Having returned to Norway, he was appointed district chieftain in the place of the deceased Ormr, and he was married to Ragnhildr. With intercession made on his behalf, Kálfr Árnason, having returned to his native soil, was accepted again into the king's good graces after he had been abroad as an exile in England and Orkney.

When a number of battles had been waged between Sveinn and Haraldr, Haraldr sailed with a fleet to Denmark and attacked Fyn (Fünen), where the farmers had gathered forces. He sent Kálfr Árnason ahead, saying that he would follow, but Kálfr fell before the superior forces of the farmers and was later found by Haraldr. After defeating the farmers, Haraldr returned to Norway in no very good odor with the farmers or the friends of Kálfr. Finnr was openly hostile and went over to Sveinn, who appointed him as the governor of Halland.

Haraldr subsequently challenged Sveinn to a naval battle in Vík [ad Vichensem amnem, ed. XXI], bringing with him Hákon Ívarsson with three ships. The fleet numbered 150 ships. Having raided in Halland, Óláfr [recte: Haraldr, ed. XXI] was found by Sveinn in Lófufjǫrðr. There they met at sea, and Hákon rallied the Norwegian fleet, which had thrice been put to flight.

Sveinn escaped with the aid of Hákon, after approaching his ship and calling himself Vandráðr. [Sveinn] was sent to a farmer in Halland, etc. Finnr was captured, etc.

This was the Battle of Niz. Later, Sveinn summoned the farmer to him and gave him the command of Zealand, granting him a fertile estate. His wife was forced to remain at home where she was, in Halland.

Eventually, Sveinn's escape from the battle with Hákon's help was revealed because of the quarreling of some drunken soldiers, with Hákon shown to be superior to all others in the science and practice of war and the cunning with which he rescued Sveinn. Avoiding the wrath of Haraldr, he fled to Sweden. Subsequently, he supported three of Haraldr's chieftains in Upplǫnd. The people of Upplǫnd refused tribute to Haraldr.

Peace between the kings Sveinn and Haraldr. Haraldr entered Sweden, with his ships brought into Lake Vänern. Hákon marched against him with a very precious banner given him by his wife, which she in turn had received from her father. With it came the warning either to return in possession of it or, in the event it was lost, not to return at all. Þorviðr the Stout fled when his horse pulled up a hitching stake [tyrstage, ed. XVII] that struck him in the forehead. The chieftain's [Hákon's] standard-bearer fell and the banner was taken from him, but he [Hákon] took it back, killing the man who had seized it. Later, Haraldr avenged himself in Upplǫnd.

When Haraldr was later killed in England, Hákon was taken into favor again by Óláfr kyrri and returned to his native country. He was survived by two daughters.

The first married Hákon the Norwegian, by whom she had Erik, called the Wise or Lamb, the King of Denmark.

The second married Páll, the chieftain of Orkney, by whom she had Hákon [ed. XXV].

1. Norway and Sweden

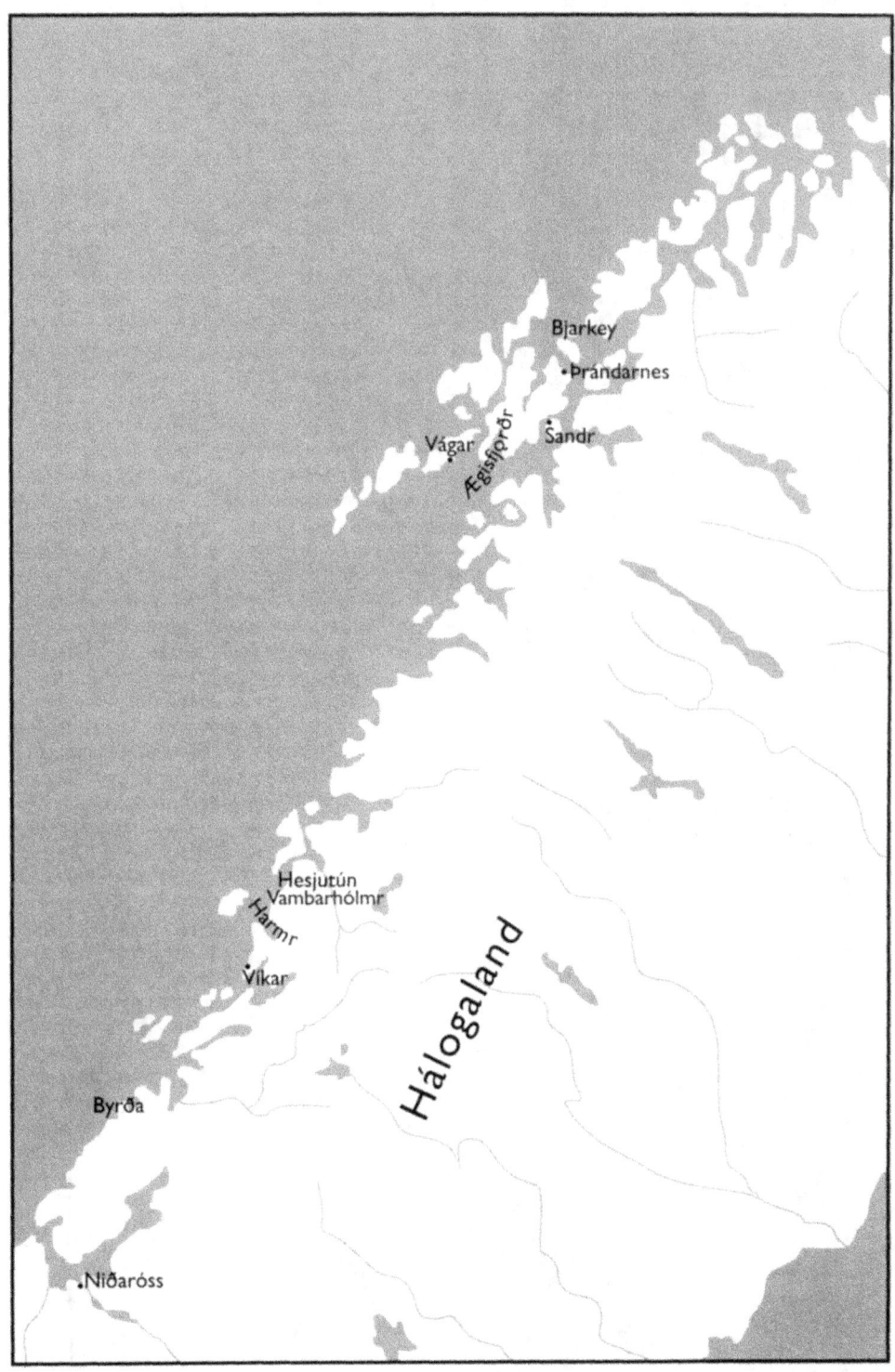

2. Northern Norway

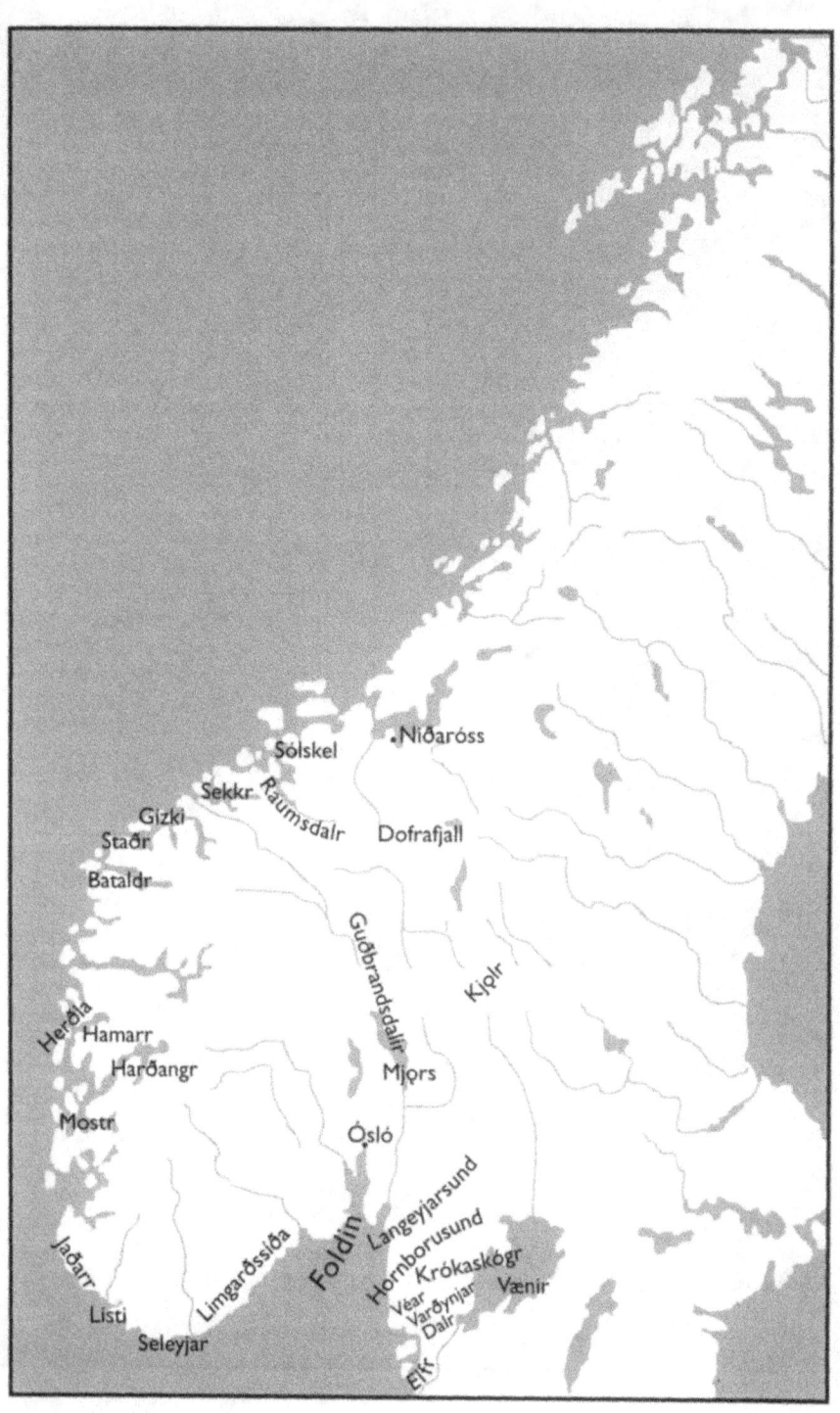

3. Southern Norway

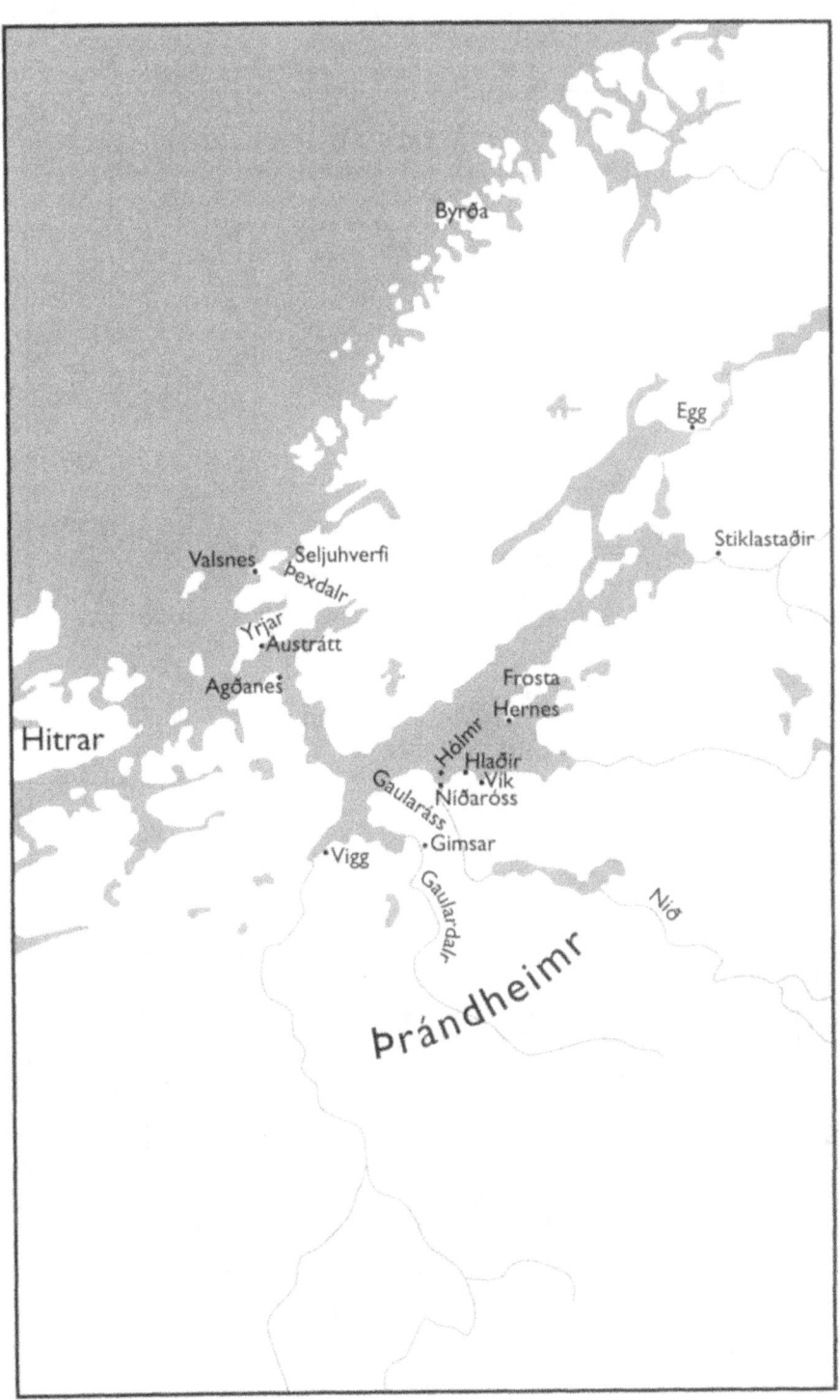

4. The Trondheim Environs

5. Sweden and Denmark

6. Iceland

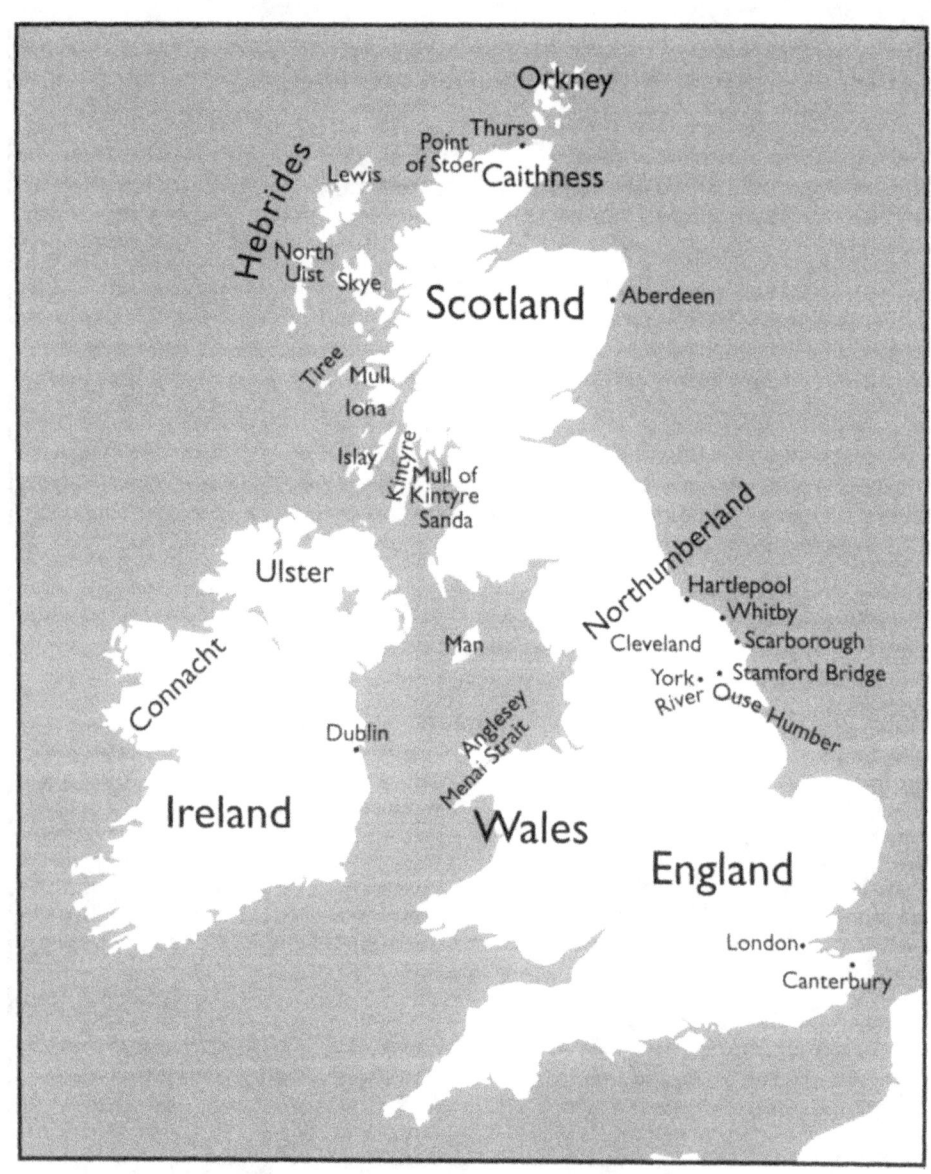

7. The British Isles and Ireland

Bibliography

Primary Sources

"Acta Sancti Olavi Regis et Martyris." In *Monumenta Historica Norvegiae: Latinske kildeskrifter til Norges historie i middelalderen.* Ed. Gustav Storm, 125–44. 1880. Rpt. Oslo: Aas & Wahl boktrykkeri a.s., 1973.

Adam of Bremen. *Gesta Hammaburgensis Ecclesiae Pontificum.* Ed. Bernhard Schmeidler. Hannover: Hahn, 1917; rpt. 1977.

Ágrip af Nóregskonunga sǫgum. Ed. Bjarni Einarsson, 1–54. Íslenzk fornrit, 29. Reykjavík: Hið íslenzka fornritafélag, 1984.

Anderson, Alan Orr, trans. 1922. *Early Sources of Scottish History, A.D. 500 to 1286.* 2 vols. Edinburgh: Oliver and Boyd.

Andersson, Theodore M., and William Ian Miller. 1989. *Law and Literature in Medieval Iceland: Ljósvetninga saga and Valla-Ljóts saga.* Stanford: Stanford University Press.

The Anglo-Saxon Chronicle: *Two of the Saxon Chronicles Parallel with Supplementary Extracts from the Others.* 2 vols. Ed. Charles Plummer. Vol I: *Text, Appendices and Glossary.* 1892. Rpt. Oxford: Oxford University Press, 1952.

Biskupa sǫgur. 2 vols. Copenhagen: S. L. Möller, 1858–78.

Bjarnar saga Hítdœlakappa. In *Borgfirðinga sǫgur.* Ed. Sigurður Nordal and Guðni Jónsson, 109–212. Íslenzk fornrit, 3. Reykjavík: Hið íslenzka fornritafélag, 1938.

Brennu-Njáls saga. Ed. Einar Ólafur Sveinsson. Íslenzk fornrit, 12. Reykjavík: Hið íslenzka fornritafélag, 1954.

Bǫglunga sǫgur. Ed. Hallvard Magerøy. 2 vols. Oslo: Solum forlag og Kjeldeskriftfondet, 1988.

Christiansen, Eric, trans. 1980. *Saxo Grammaticus: Danorum Regum Heroumque Historia.* 3 vols. BAR International Series, 84. Oxford: British Archaeological Reports, 1980.

Danakonunga sǫgur. Ed. Bjarni Guðnason. Íslenzk fornrit, 35. Reykjavík: Hið íslenzka fornritafélag, 1982.

Driscoll, M. J. [Matthew James], ed. and trans. 1995. *Ágrip af Nóregskonungasǫgum.* [London]: Viking Society for Northern Research, University College, London.

Edda: Die Lieder des Codex Regius nebst verwandten Denkmälern. Vol. I: *Text.* Ed. Gustav Neckel. 4th rev. ed. by Hans Kuhn. Heidelberg: Carl Winter Universitätsverlag, 1962.

Edda Snorra Sturlusonar: Edda Snorronis Sturlæi. 3 vols. Ed. Jón Sigurðsson et al. 1848. Rpt. Osnabrück: Zeller, 1966.

Egils saga Skalla-Grímssonar. Ed. Sigurður Nordal. Íslenzk fornrit, 2. Reykjavík: Hið íslenzka fornritafélag, 1933.

Eirspennill: AM 47 fol. Nóregs konunga sǫgur: Magnús góði—Hákon gamli. Ed. Finnur Jónsson. Kristiania [Oslo]: Den norske historiske kildeskriftskommission, 1916.

English Historical Documents. Vol. II: *1042–1189*. Ed. David C. Douglas and George W. Green-
away. London: Eyre & Spottiswoode, 1953.
Fagrskinna-Nóregs konunga tal. Ed. Bjarni Einarsson, 55–373. Íslenzk fornrit, 29. Reykjavík:
Hið íslenzka fornritafélag, 1984.
Faulkes, Anthony. [1968]. *Two Icelandic Stories: Hreiðars þáttr, Orms þáttr*. London: Viking
Society for Northern Research.
——, trans. 1992. *Edda*. London: J. M. Dent and Sons.
Finnur Jónsson, ed. 1912–15. *Den norsk-islandske skjaldedigtning*. Vols. IA–IIA: *Tekst efter
håndskrifterne*. Vols. I–IIB: *Rettet tekst*. 1908–15. Rpt. Copenhagen: Rosenkilde & Bagger,
1967–73.
*Flateyjarbók: En samling af norske konge-sagaer med indskudte mindre fortællinger om begivenheder i
og udenfor Norge samt annaler*. 3 vols. Ed. Guðbrandur Vigfússon and C. R. Unger. Oslo:
Malling, 1860–68.
Fornmanna sögur eptir gömlum handritum útgefnar að tilhlutun hins norræna fornfræða félags.
12 vols. Copenhagen: Popp, 1825–37.
Fríssbók: Codex Frisianus. En samling af norske konge-sagaer. Ed. C. R. Unger. Christiania [Oslo]:
P. T. Mallings forlagsboghandel, 1871.
Grágás: Islændernes lovbog i fristatens tid. 3 vols. Vol. I: *Konungsbók*. Vol. 2: *Staðarhólsbók*. Ed.
Vilhjálmur Finsen. 1852, 1879. Rpt. Odense: Odense universitetsforlag, 1974.
Grettis saga Ásmundarsonar. Ed. Guðni Jónsson. Íslenzk fornrit, 7. Reykjavík: Hið íslenzka
fornritafélag, 1936.
Gunnlaugs saga ormstungu. In *Borgfirðinga sǫgur*. Ed. Sigurður Nordal and Guðni Jónsson,
49–108. Íslenzk fornit, 3. Reykjavík: Hið íslenzka fornritafélag, 1938.
Hákonar saga Ívarssonar. SUGNL 62. Ed. Jón Helgason and Jakob Benediktsson. Copen-
hagen: J. Jørgensen, 1952.
Hálfs saga ok Hálfsrekka. In *Fornaldarsögur norðurlanda*. Ed. Guðni Jónsson. Vol. II, 93–
134. N.p.: Íslendingasagnaútgáfan, 1956.
Heimskringla. Ed. Bjarni Aðalbjarnason. 3 vols. Íslenzk fornrit, 26–28. Reykjavík: Hið ís-
lenzka fornritafélag, 1941–51.
Heimskringla. Ed. Bergljót S. Kristjánsdóttir, Bragi Halldórsson, Jón Torfason, and Örnólfur
Thorsson. 3 vols. Reykjavík: Mál og menning, 1991.
Henry of Huntingdon: *Henrici Archidiaconi Huntendunensis Historia Anglorum*. Ed. Thomas
Arnold. Chronicles and Memorials of Great Britain and Ireland during the Middle Ages,
published by the authority of Her Majesty's Treasury, under the direction of the Master of
the Rolls. 1879. Rpt. Wiesbaden: Kraus, 1965.
Historia Norwegiæ. In *Monumenta Historica Norvegiae: Latinske kildeskrifter til Norges historie i middelalderen*. Ed. Gustav Storm, 69–124. 1880. Rpt. Oslo: Aas & Wahl boktrykkeri a.s., 1973.
Hollander, Lee M., trans. 1936. *Old Norse Poems: The Most Important Non-Skaldic Verse Not Included in the Poetic Edda*. New York: Columbia University Press.
——, trans. 1991. *Heimskringla: History of the Kings of Norway*. 1964. First Paperback printing,
1991. Austin: University of Texas Press.
Hrólfs saga kraka ok kappa hans. In *Fornaldarsögur norðurlanda*. Ed. Guðni Jónsson. Vol. II,
1–105. N.p.: Íslendingasagnaútgáfan, 1956.
Jómsvíkinga saga. Ed. Ólafur Halldórsson. Reykjavík: Jón Helgason, 1969.
Jón Þorkelsson, ed. 1895. *Sex sögu-þættir*. 2nd ed. Copenhagen: Skandinavisk Antiquariat.
Kock, Ernst Albin, ed. 1946–49. *Den norsk-isländska skaldediktningen*. Vol. I. 2 vols. Lund:
Gleerup.
Konunga sögur. 3 vols. Ed. Guðni Jónsson. N.p.: Íslendingasagnaútgáfan, 1957.
Konungs skuggsiá. Ed. Ludvig Holm-Olsen. Norrøne tekster, 1. Olso: Kjeldeskriftfondet,
1983.
Laxdæla saga. Ed. Einar Ólafur Sveinsson. Íslenzk fornrit, 5. Reykjavík: Hið íslenzka forn-
ritafélag, 1934.

Morkinskinna: Pergamentsbog fra første halvdel af det trettende aarhundrede. Indeholdende en af de ældste optegnelser af norske kongesagaer. Ed. C. R. Unger. Oslo: Bentzen, 1867.

Morkinskinna. Ed. Finnur Jónsson. SUGNL 53. Copenhagen: J. Jørgensen & Co., 1932.

Morkinskinna. Ed. Jón Helgason. Copenhagen: Levin & Munksgaard, 1934.

Norges gamle love indtil 1387. 5 vols. Vol. I: *Norges love ældre end Kong Magnus Haakonssöns regjerings-tiltrædelse i 1263;* Vol. II: *Lovgivningen under Kong Magnus Haakonssöns regjeringstid fra 1263 til 1280, tilligemed et supplement til förste bind.* Ed. R. Keyser and P. A. Munch. Christiana [Oslo]: Chr. Gröndahl, 1846–48.

Olafs saga hins helga. Die "Legendarische Saga" über Olaf den Heiligen (Hs. Delagard. saml. nr. 8¹¹). Ed. and trans. Anne Heinrichs et al. Heidelberg: Carl Winter, 1982.

The Old English Orosius. The Early English Text Society S.S., 6. Ed. Janet Bately. New York: Oxford University Press, 1980.

Ordericus Vitalis: *The Ecclesiastical History of Orderic Vitalis.* Ed. and trans. Marjorie Chibnall. 6 vols. Oxford Medieval Texts. Oxford: Clarendon Press, 1969–80.

Orkneyinga saga. Ed. Finnbogi Guðmundsson. Íslenzk fornrit, 34. Reykjavík: Hið íslenzka fornritafélag, 1965.

Ragnars saga loðbrókar. In *Fornaldarsögur norðurlanda.* Ed. Guðni Jónsson. Vol. I, 219–85. N.p.: Íslendingasagnaútgáfan, 1956.

Raschellà, Fabrizio. 1982. *The Second Grammatical Treatise.* Filologia Germanica, testi e studi, 2. Florence: Felice le Monnier.

Roger de Hoveden. *Chronica Magistri Rogeri de Houedene.* Ed. William Stubbs. Vols. I–II. 4 vols. Chronicles and Memorials of Great Britain and Ireland during the Middle Ages, published by the Authority of Her Majesty's Treasury, under the direction of the Master of the Rolls. 1868. Rpt. Wiesbaden: Kraus, 1964.

Saga Óláfs Tryggvasonar af Oddr Snorrason Munk. Ed. Finnur Jónsson. Copenhagen: Gad, 1932.

Saxo Grammaticus. *Saxonis Gesta Danorum.* Ed. J. Olrik and H. Ræder. Vol. I. 2 vols. Copenhagen: Levin & Munksgaard, 1931.

"Sneglu-Halla þáttr." In *Eyfirðinga sǫgur.* Ed. Jónas Kristjánsson, 261–95. Íslenzk fornrit, 9. Reykjavík: Hið íslenzka fornritafélag, 1956.

Storm, Gustav, ed. *Islandske annaler indtil 1578.* Christiania [Oslo]: Grøndahl & søns bogtrykkeri, 1888.

Sturlunga saga. Ed. Örnólfur Thorsson et al. 3 vols. Reykjavík: Svart á hvítu, 1988.

Sverris saga etter Cod. AM 327 4°. Ed. Gustav Indrebø. 1920. Rpt. Oslo: Norsk historisk kjeldeskrift-institutt, 1981.

Theodrici Monachi Historia de Antiquitate Regum Norwagiensium. In *Monumenta Historica Norvegiae: Latinske kildeskrifter til Norges historie i middelalderen.* Ed. Gustav Storm, 1–68. 1880. Rpt. Oslo: Aas & Wahl boktrykkeri a.s., 1973.

"The Third Grammatical Treatise." See *SnE* II, 62–189.

Trójumanna saga. In *Hauksbók.* Ed. E. Jónsson and F. Jónsson, 193–226. Copenhagen: Thieles bogtrykkeri, 1892–96.

Vitae sanctorum Danorum. Ed. Martinus Clarentius Gertz. Copenhagen: Gad, 1908–12.

Vǫlsunga saga. In *Fornaldarsögur norðurlanda.* Ed. Guðni Jónsson. Vol. I, 107–218. N.p.: Íslendingasagnaútgáfan, 1956.

Þáttr af Ragnars sonum. In *Fornaldarsögur norðurlanda.* Ed. Guðni Jónsson. Vol. I, 287–303. N.p.: Íslendingasagnaútgáfan, 1956.

William of Jumièges. *The Gesta Normannorum ducum of William of Jumièges, Orderic Vitalis, and Robert of Torigni.* 2 vols. Ed. and trans. Elisabeth M. C. Van Houts. Oxford Medieval Texts. Oxford: Clarendon, 1992–95.

William of Malmesbury. *Willelmi Malmesbiriensis monachi de gestis regum Anglorum.* Ed. William Stubbs. 2 vols. Chronicles and Memorials of Great Britain and Ireland during the Middle Ages, published by the authority of Her Majesty's Treasury, under the direction of the Master of the Rolls. London: 1887.

Secondary Sources

Almgren, Bertil et al. 1966. *The Viking.* Gothenburg: Tre Tryckare.

Almqvist, Bo. 1965. *Norrön niddiktning. Traditionshistoriska studier i versmagi.* Vol: 1: *Nid mot furstar.* Stockholm: Almqvist & Wiksell.

Andersson, Theodore M. 1994. "The Politics of Snorri Sturluson." *JEGP,* 93:55–78.

———. 1998. "The Continuation of *Hlaðajarla saga.*" *JEGP,* 97:155–67.

Anton, Hans Hubert. 1968. *Fürstenspiegel und Herrscherethos in der Karolingerzeit.* Bonn: Röhrscheid.

Ármann Jakobsson. 1997. *Í leit að konungi: Konungsmynd íslenska konungasagna.* Reykjavík: Háskólaútgáfan.

———. 1998. "King and Subject in *Morkinskinna.*" *Skandinavistik,* 28: 101–17.

Arngrímur Sigurðsson. 1970. *Íslenzk-ensk orðabók.* Reykjavík: Prentsmiðjan Leiftur.

Ásdís Egilsdóttir. 1993. "Af óskynlegum Íslendingi." In *Orðaforði heyjaður Guðrúnu Kvaran 21 júlí 1993.* Reykjavík: n.p.

Askeberg, Fritz. 1944. *Norden och kontinenten i gammal tid.* Uppsala: Almqvist & Wiksell.

Bagge, Sverre. 1990. "Harald Hardråde i Bysants. To fortellinger, to kulturer." In *Hellas og Norge. Kontakt, komparasjon, kontrast.* Ed. Øivind Andersen and Tomas Hägg. 169–92. Skrifter utgitt av Det Norske Institutt i Athen, 2. Bergen: Klassisk Institutt, Universitetet i Bergen.

———. 1991. *Society and Politics in Snorri Sturluson's Heimskringla.* Berkeley: University of California Press.

Baldwin, John W. 1994. *The Language of Sex: Five Voices from Northern France around 1200.* Chicago: University of Chicago Press.

Barlow, Frank. 1970. *Edward the Confessor.* Berkeley: University of California Press.

———. 1983. *The Norman Conquest and Beyond.* London: Hambledon Press.

Beck, Heinrich. 1987. "Kaufungen, Kaupangr und Köping(e)." In *UHV,* 358–73.

———. 1994. "Snorri Sturlusons Sicht der paganen Vorzeit." In *Nachrichten der Akademie der Wissenschaften in Göttingen.* Philol.-hist. Kl. 1994, 5–60.

Behrmann, Thomas. 1996. "Norwegen und das Reich unter Hákon IV. (1217–1263) und Friedrich II. (1212–1263)." In *Hansische Literaturbeziehungen. Das Beispiel der Þiðreks saga und verwandter Literatur.* Ed. Susanne Kramarz-Bein. Berlin: de Gruyter. Pp. 27–50.

Bjarni Aðalbjarnarson. 1937. *Om de norske kongesagaer.* NVAOS, 1936, no. 4. Oslo: Jacob Dybwad.

Bjarni Guðnason. 1978. *Fyrsta sagan.* Studia Islandica, 37. Reykjavík: Bókaútgáfa menningarsjóðs.

Bjarni Vilhjálmsson. 1990. "Postulínsgerð og hestavíg." *Gripla,* 7:7–50.

Björn Bjarnason. 1905. *Nordboernes legemlige uddannelse i oldtiden.* Copenhagen: Prior.

Björn Magnússon Ólsen. 1903. "Til versene i Egils saga." *ANF,* 19:99–133.

Boberg, Inger Margrethe. 1966. *Motif-Index of Early Icelandic Literature.* Copenhagen: Munksgaard.

Brown, R. Allen. 1984. *The Norman Conquest.* London: Edward Arnold.

Bugge, Anders. 1934. "Norge." In "Kirkebygninger og deres udstyr." *Nordisk kultur* 23, 189–270. Copenhagen: J. H. Schultz.

Bumke, Joachim. 1991. *Courtly Culture in the High Middle Ages.* Trans. Thomas Dunlap. Berkeley: University of California Press.

Chesnutt, Michael. 1981. "Haralds saga Maddaðarsonar." In *Speculum Norroenum: Norse Studies in Memory of Gabriel Turville-Petre.* Ed. Ursula Dronke et al., 33–55. Odense: Odense University Press.

Chibnall, Marjorie. 1994. *The Empress Mathilda: Queen Consort, Queen Mother and Lady of the English.* 1993. Rpt. Cambridge: Blackwell Publishers.

Cleasby, Richard, and Gudbrand Vigfússon. 1874; rpt. 1957. *An Icelandic-English Dictionary.* London: Oxford University Press.

Clover, Carol J. 1979. "Hárbarðsljóð as Generic Farce." *SS*, 51:124–45.
——. 1982. *The Medieval Saga*. Ithaca: Cornell University Press.
——. 1986. "The Long Prose Form." *ANF*, 101:10–39.
——. 1993. "Regardless of Sex." *Speculum*, 68:363–87.
Cormack, Margaret. 1994. *The Saints in Iceland: Their Veneration from the Conversion to 1400*. Subsidia Hagiographica, 78. Brussels: Société des Bollandistes.
Cross, Samuel H. 1929. "Yaroslav the Wise in Norse Tradition." *Speculum*, 4:177–97.
Cucina, Carla. 1998. "Il pellegrinaggio nelle saghe dell'Islanda medievale." In *Atti della Accademia Nazionale dei Lincei*, classe di scienze morali, storiche e filologiche. *Rendiconti*. Ser. 9, vol. 9, fasc. 1, 83–155.
Curtis, E. 1921. "Murchertach O'Brien, High King of Ireland, and his Norman Son-In-Law, Arnulf de Montgomery, *circa* 1100." *Journal of the Royal Society of Antiquaries of Ireland*, 51:116–24.
Detollenaere, F. 1942. *De schildering van den mensch in de oudijslandsche familiesaga*. Leuven: De Vlaamsche Drukkerij.
Doxey, Gary B. 1996. "Norwegian Crusaders and the Balearic Islands." *SS*, 68:139–60.
Ebel, Else. 1987. "Der Fernhandel von der Wikingerzeit bis in das 12. Jahrhundert in Nordeuropa nach altnordischen Quellen." In *UHV*, 266–312.
Einar Arnórsson. 1954–58. "Suðurgöngur íslendinga í fornöld" *Saga*, 2:1–45.
Ellehøj, Svend. 1965. *Studier over den ældste norrøne historieskrivning*. Bibliotheca Arnamagnæana, 26. Copenhagen: Munksgaard.
Falk, Hjalmar. 1912. "Altnordisches Seewesen." *Wörter und Sachen*, 4:1–122.
——. 1914. *Altnordische Waffenkunde*. In NVAOS, 1914. No. 6. Kristiania [Oslo]: Jacob Dybwad.
——. 1919. *Altwestnordische Kleiderkunde, mit besonderer Berücksichtigung der Terminologie*. In NVAOS, 1918. No. 3. Kristiania [Oslo]: Jacob Dybwad.
Fidjestøl, Bjarne. 1971. "Tåtten om Harald Hardråde og fiskaren Þorgils." *MM*. Pp. 34–49.
——. 1982. *Det norrøne fyrstediktet*. Universitetet i Bergen Nordisk institutts skriftserie, 11. Øvre Ervik: Alvheim & Eide akademisk forlag.
——. 1997. "The Legend of Þórir hundr." In his *Selected Papers*. Ed. Odd Einar Haugen and Else Mundal. Trans. Peter Foote. Odense: Odense University Press, 1997. Pp. 168–83.
Finnur Jónsson. 1894–1901. *Den oldnorske og oldislandske litteraturs historie*. 2 vols. Copenhagen: Gad.
——. 1907. "Tilnavne i den islandske oldlitteratur." *ÅNOH*, 22:161–381.
——. 1936. "Islands mønt, mål og vægt." In *Nordisk kultur*, 30. Copenhagen: J. H. Schultz. Pp. 155–61.
Foote, Peter. 1955. "Notes on the Prepositions *of* and *um*(*b*) in Old Icelandic and Old Norwegian Prose." *Studia Islandica*, 14. Reykjavík: H. F. Leiftur; Copenhagen: Munksgaard. Pp. 41–83.
Fritzner, Johan. 1886–96. *Ordbog over det gamle norske sprog*. 3 vols. Kristiania [Oslo]: Den norske forlagsforening.
Gade, Kari Ellen. 1985. "Hanging in Northern Law and Literature." *MM*. Pp. 159–83.
——. 1991. "*Fang* and *fall*: Two Skaldic *termini technici*." *JEGP*, 90:361–74.
——. 1994. "On the Recitation of Old Norse Poetry." In *Studien zum Altgermanischen: Festschrift für Heinrich Beck*. Ed. Heiko Uecker. Ergänzungsbände zum Reallexikon der Germanischen Altertumskunde, 11. New York: Walter de Gruyter. Pp. 126–51.
——. 1995a. *The Structure of Old Norse dróttkvætt Poetry*. Islandica, 49. Ithaca: Cornell University Press.
——. 1995b. "1236: Órækja meiddr ok heill gerr." *Gripla*, 9:115–32.
——. 1995c. "Einarr þambarskelfir's Last Shot." *SS*, 67:153–62.
——. 1997. "Northern Lights on the Battle of Hastings." *Viator*, 28:65–81.
——. "*Morkinskinna's* 'Giffarðsþáttr': Literary Fiction or Historical Fact?" *Gripla* [forthcoming].
Gehl, Walther. 1939. *Der germanische Schicksalsglaube*. Berlin: Junker und Dünnhaupt Verlag.

Gelsinger, Bruce E. 1981. *Icelandic Enterprise: Commerce and Economy in the Middle Ages*. Columbia: University of South Carolina Press.

———. 1988. "The Battle of Stamford Bridge and the Battle of Jaffa: A Case of Confused Identity." *SS*, 60:13–29.

Gimmler, Heinrich. 1976. *Die Thœttir der Morkinskinna. Ein Beitrag zur Überlieferungsproblematik und zur Typologie der altnordischen Kurzerzählung*. Diss. Frankfurt am Main.

Gísli Sigurðsson. 1994. "Another Audience—Another Saga: How Can We Best Explain Different Accounts in *Vatnsdœla saga* and *Finnboga saga ramma* of the Same Events?" In *Text und Zeittiefe*. Ed. Hildegard L. C. Tristram. ScriptOralia, 58. Tübingen: Gunter Narr Verlag. Pp. 359–75.

Godman, Peter. 1985. *Poetry of the Carolingian Renaissance*. Norman: University of Oklahoma Press.

Götlind, Johan. 1933. "Idrotter och friluftslekar." *Nordisk kultur*, 24. Copenhagen: J. H. Schultz. Pp. 3–53.

Grimstad, Kaaren. 1972. "A Comic Role of the Viking in the Family Sagas." In *Studies for Einar Haugen Presented by Friends and Colleagues*. Ed. Evelyn Scherabon Firchow et al. The Hague: Mouton. Vol: 2:243–52.

Halldór Halldórsson. 1968–69. *Íslenzkt orðtakasafn*. 2 vols. Reykjavík: Almenna bókafélagið.

Harmer, Florence E. 1989. *Anglo-Saxon Writs*. 2d ed. Stamford: Paul Watkins.

Harris, Joseph. 1979. "The King in Disguise: An International Popular Tale in Two Old Icelandic Adaptations." *ANF*, 94:57–81.

Heinrichs, Heinrich Matthias. 1975. "Die Geschichte vom sagakundigen Isländer (Íslendings þáttr sǫgufróða). Ein Beitrag zur Sagaforschung." In *Literaturwissenschaft und Geschichtsphilosophie. Festschrift für Wilhelm Emrich*. Ed. Helmut Arntzen, Bernd Balzer, Karl Pestalozzi, and Rainer Wagner, 225–31. Berlin: de Gruyter.

———. 1976. "Mündlichkeit und Schriftlichkeit. Ein Problem der Sagaforschung." *Jahrbuch für internationale Germanistik*. Series A, 2:114–33.

Helgi Guðmundsson. 1967. *Um Kjalnesinga sögu. Nokkrar athuganir*. Studia Islandica, 26. Reykjavík: Bókaútgáfa menningarsjóðs.

Helgi Þorláksson. 1979. "Hvernig var Snorri í sjón?" In *Snorri. Átta alda minning*. Reykjavík: Sögufélag, 174–80.

Hellberg, Staffan. 1980. "Vikingatidens víkingar." *ANF*, 95:25–88.

Helle, Knut. 1982. *Bergen bys historie*. Vol: 1: *Kongssete og kjøpstad—fra opphavet til 1536*. Bergen: Universitetsforlaget.

Hermann Pálsson. 1975. "Um gæfumenn og ógæfu í íslenzkum fornsögum." In *Afmælisrit Björns Sigfússonar*. Ed. Björn Teitsson et al., 135–53. Reykjavík: Sögufélag.

———. 1990. "Brands þáttr örva." *Gripla*, 7:117–30.

———. 1997. "Úr landnorðri. Samar og ystu rætur íslenskrar menningar." *Studia Islandica*, 54. Reykjavík: Bókmenntafræðistofnun Háskóla Íslands.

Heusler, Andreas. 1957. *Die altgermanische Dichtung*. Darmstadt: Wissenschaftliche Buchgesellschaft.

Hofmann, Dietrich. 1987. "St. Clemens im frühchristlichen Skandinavien." In *Arbeiten zur Skandinavistik, 7. 1987 Arbeitstagung der Skandinavisten des deutschen Sprachgebietes 4.8–10.1985 in Skjeberg/Norwegen*. Ed. Ulrich Groenke. Frankfurt a. M.: Peter Lang. Pp. 67–91.

———. 1997. *Die Legende von Sankt Clemens in den skandinavischen Ländern im Mittelalter*. New York: Peter Lang.

Holtsmark, Anne. 1954. "Olav den hellige og 'seierskjorten.'" *MM*. Pp. 104–8.

Houts, Elisabeth M. C. van. 1985. "Normandy and Byzantium in the Eleventh Century." *Byzantion*, 55:544–59.

Hughes, Shaun F. D. 1988. "The Battle of Stamford Bridge and the Battle of Bouvines." *SS*, 60:30–76.

Indrebø, Gustav. 1917. *Fagrskinna*. Avhandlinger fra universitetets historiske seminar, 4. Kristiania [Oslo]: Grøndahl & søns boktrykkeri.

——. 1922. "Aagrip." *Edda*, 17:18–65.

——. 1928. "Harald Hardraade i Morkinskinna." In *Festskrift til Finnur Jónsson 29. Maj 1928*. Copenhagen: Levin & Munksgaard, 173–80.

——. 1939. "Nokre merknader til den norrône kongesoga." *ANF,* 54:58–79.

Itnyre, Cathy Jorgensen. 1996. "The Emotional Universe of Medieval Icelandic Fathers and Sons." In *Medieval Family Roles: A Book of Essays*, Ed. C. J. Itnyre, 173–96. New York: Garland.

Jankuhn, Herbert. 1986. *Haithabu. Ein Handelsplatz der Wikingerzeit*. 8th ed. Neumünster: Wachholtz.

Jochens, Jenny. 1995. *Women in Old Norse Society*. Ithaca: Cornell University Press.

Johnsen, Arne Odd. 1945. *Studier vedrørende kardinal Nicolaus Brekespears legasjon til Norden*. Oslo: Fabritius.

Jón Helgason. 1975. "Vísa í Svarfdælu." In *Opuscula*, 5. Ed Jón Helgason, 291–94. Bibliotheca Arnamagnaeana, 31. Copenhagen: Munksgaard.

Jón Jóhannesson. 1974. *A History of the Old Icelandic Commonwealth*. Trans. Haraldur Bessason. N.p.: University of Manitoba Press.

Jónas Kristjánsson. 1977. "Egilssaga og konungasögur." In *Sjötíu ritgerðir helgaðar Jakobi Benediktssyni 20. Júlí 1977*. Ed. Einar G. Pétursson and Jónas Kristjánsson. Reykjavík: Stofnun Árna Magnússonar. 2:449–72.

Kalinke, Marianne. 1983. "The Foreign Language Requirement in Medieval Icelandic Romance." *MLR*, 78:850–61.

——. 1984. "*Sigurðar saga Jórsalafara*: The Fictionalization of Fact in *Morkinskinna*." *SS*, 56:152–67.

Kock, Ernst Albin. 1923–44. *Notationes norroenae: Anteckningar till Edda och skaldediktning*. Lunds universitets årsskrift, n.s., sec. 1, 19–39. Lund: Gleerup.

Koht, Halvdan. 1924a. "Kong Sigurd på Jorsal-ferd." *HT* (N), 26:153–68.

——. 1924b. "Hvem var Tore Ingeridson?" *HT* (N), 26:138–41.

Kreutzer, Gert. 1986. "Von Isländern, Eisbären und Königen. Anmerkungen zur Audun-Novelle." *Trajekt*, 5:100–8.

Kválen, Eivind. 1925a. *Den eldste norske kongesoga*. Oslo: n.p.

——. 1925b. "Tilhøvet millom Morkinskinna, Fagrskinna, Ágrip og Orkneyinga saga." *Edda*, 24:285–335.

Lexicon Poeticum antiquæ linguæ septentrionalis: Ordbog over det norsk-islandske skjaldesprog oprindelig forfattet af Sveinbjörn Egilsson. Ed. Finnur Jónsson. 2d ed. 1931. Rpt. Copenhagen: Atlas, 1966.

Liestøl, Knut. 1930. *The Origin of the Icelandic Family Sagas*. Oslo: Aschehoug.

Lönnroth, Lars. 1964. "Tesen om de två kulturerna—kritiska studier i den isländska sagaskrivningens sociala förutsättningar" *SI*, 15:1–103.

——. 1965. "Det litterära porträttet i latinsk historiografi och isländsk sagaskrivning." *APS*, 27:68–117.

——. 1978. *Den dubbla scenen. Muntlig diktning från Eddan till Abba*. Stockholm: Prisma.

——. 1998. "The Man-Eating Mama of Miklagard. Empress Zoe in Old Norse Saga Tradition." In *Kairos: Studies in Art History and Literature in Honour of Professor Gunilla Åkerström-Hougen*. Ed. Elisabeth Piltz and Paul Åström. 37–49. Jonsered: Paul Åströms förlag.

Louis, René. 1958. "A propos du pèlerinage de Robert le Libéral à Constantinople et Jérusalem: les ducs de Normandie dans les chansons de geste." *Byzantion*, 27:391–419.

Louis-Jensen, Jonna. 1969. "Den yngre del af Flateyjarbók." *Afmælisrit Jóns Helgasonar 30. júní 1969*. Ed. Jakob Benediktsson et al. Reykjavík: Heimskringla. Pp. 235–50.

——. 1970. "En strofe af Bersǫglisvísur." *Opuscula*, 4. Bibliotheca Arnamagnæana, 30: 208–10.

——. 1977. *Kongesagastudier: Kompilationen Hulda-Hrokkinskinna*. Bibliotheca Arnamagnæana, 32. Copenhagen: C. A. Reitzels boghandel A/S.

Loyn, H. R. [Henry Royston]. 1977. *The Vikings in Britain*. London: Batsford.

——. 1982. *The Norman Conquest*. London: Hutchinson.

Martínez Pizarro, Joaquín. 1996. "Kings in Adversity: A Note on Alfred and the Cakes." *Neophilologus*, 80:319–26.

Matthew, D. J. A. [Donald James Alexander]. 1966. *The Norman Conquest*. New York: Schocken.

Maurer, Konrad. 1875. "Das Alter des Gesetzsprecher-Amtes in Norwegen." In *Festgabe zum Doctor-Jubiläum des Herrn Hofraths und Professors Dr. Ludwig Arndts*. Munich: Christian Kaiser.

Meissner, Rudolf. 1902. *Die Strengleikar. Ein Beitrag zur Geschichte der altnordischen Prosalitteratur*. Halle: Niemeyer.

——. 1921. *Die Kenningar der Skalden*. Bonn and Leipzig: Kurt Schröder; rpt. Hildesheim: Georg Olms, 1984.

——. 1925. "Ermengarde, Vicegräfin von Narbonne, und Jarl Rögnvald." *ANF*, 41:149–91.

Merschberger, Gerda. 1937. *Die Rechtsstellung der germanischen Frau*. Leipzig: Curt Rabitzsch.

Meulengracht Sørensen, Preben. 1993. *Fortælling og ære. Studier i islændingesagaerne*. Aarhus: Aarhus University Press.

Miller, William Ian. 1988. "Ordeal in Iceland." *SS*, 60:189–218.

——. 1990. *Bloodtaking and Peacemaking*. Chicago: University of Chicago Press.

Moberg, Ove. 1940–1942. "Olav Haraldssons hemkomst. En historiografisk undersökning." *HT* (N), 32:545–75.

Moulton, William. 1988. "Mutual Intelligibility among Speakers of Early Germanic Dialects." In *Germania: Comparative Studies in the Old Germanic Languages and Literatures*. Ed. Daniel G. Calder and T. Craig Christy, 9–28. Wolfeboro, N.Y.: D. S. Brewer.

Munch, Peter Andreas. 1852–59. *Det norske folks historie*. 6 vols. Christiania [Oslo]: C. Tønsberg.

Mundal, Else. 1974. *Fylgjemotiva i norrøn litteratur*. Oslo: Universitetsforlaget.

Mundt, Marina. 1993. *Zur Adaptation orientalischer Bilder in den Fornaldarsögur Norðrlanda*. Frankfurt am Main: Lang.

Naumann, Hans-Peter. 1987. "Warenpreise und Wertverhältnisse im alten Norden." In *UHV*, 374–89.

Noreen, Erik. 1922. *Studier i fornvästnordisk diktning: Andra samlingen*. Uppsala universitets årsskrift 1922. Filosofi, språkvetenskap och historiska vetenskaper, 4. Uppsala: A-B. akademiska bokhandeln, 1–77.

Norrøn ordbok. 3rd ed of *Gamalnorsk ordbok*. Ed. Leiv Heggstad, Finn Hødnebø, Erik Simensen. Oslo: Det norske samlaget, 1975.

Ólafur Halldórsson. 1987. *Færeyinga saga*. Reykjavík: Stofnun Árna Magnússonar á Íslandi.

——. 1994. "Þingamanna þáttur." In *Sagnaþing helgað Jónasi Kristjánssyni sjötugum 10. apríl 1994*. Reykjavík: Hið íslenska bókmenntafélag. Vol. 2:617–40.

Olsen, Magnus B., ed. 1941–54. *Norges innskrifter med de yngre runer*. 3 vols. Oslo: I kommisjon hos Dybwad.

Paris, Gaston. 1880. "Sur un épisode d'Aimeri de Narbonne." *Romania*, 9:515–46.

Perkins, Richard. 1989. "Objects and Oral Tradition in Medieval Iceland." In *Úr Dölum til Dala: Guðbrandur Vigfússon Centenary Essays*. Ed. Rory McTurk and Andrew Wawn. Leeds Texts and Monographs, New Series, 11. Leeds: Leeds Studies in English. Pp. 239–66.

Poole, Russell. 1980. "In Search of the Partar." *SS*, 52:264–77.

——. 1985. "Some Royal Love-Verses." *MM*. Pp. 115–31.

——. 1991. *Viking Poems on War and Peace*. Toronto: University of Toronto Press.

Power, Rosemary. 1986. "Magnus Bareleg's Expeditions to the West." *Scottish Historical Review*, 65:107–32.

Pulsiano, Phillip, ed. 1993. *Medieval Scandinavia: An Encyclopedia*. New York: Garland.

Raschellà, Fabrizio D. 1982. *The So-called Second Grammatical Treatise: Edition, Translation, and Commentary*. Florence: Felice Monnier.

——. 1985–86. "Itinerari italiani in una miscellanea geografica islandese del XII secolo." *Filologia Germanica*, 28–29:541–84.

Reichborn-Kjennerud, Ingvald. 1942. "Gamle sykdomsnavn." *MM*. Pp. 118–21.

——. *Vår gamle trolldomsmedisin.* In NVAOS in five parts: (1) 1927, no. 6:1–284; (2) 1933, no. 2:1–212; (3) 1940, 1:5–221; (4) 1944, no. 2:3–263; (5) 1947, no. 1:3–253.

Reuter, Timothy. 1991. *Germany in the Early Middle Ages, 800–1056.* London and New York: Longman.

Riant, Paul. 1865. *Expéditions et pèlerinages des scandinaves en Terre Sainte au temps des croisades.* Paris: Imprimerie de Ad. Lainé et J. Havard, 1865.

Rossenbeck, Klaus. 1970. *Die Stellung der Riddarasǫgur in der altnordischen Prosaliteratur—eine Untersuchung an Hand des Erzählstils.* Diss. Frankfurt am Main.

Schach, Paul. 1977. "Some Observations on the Generation-Gap Theme in the Icelandic Sagas." In *The Epic in Medieval Society: Aesthetic and Moral Values.* Ed. Harald Scholler. Tübingen: Niemeyer. Pp. 361–81.

Schwerin, Claudius von. 1930. "Die Ehescheidung im älteren isländischen Recht." *Deutsche Islandforschung,* 1 (no more published). Ed. Walther Heinrich Vogt. Breslau: Ferdinand Hirt. Pp. 283–99.

Seip, Didrik Arup. 1930. *Trondhjems bynavn.* Trondheim: Trondhjemsforeningen.

Setton, Kenneth M., ed. 1969. *A History of the Crusades.* Vol. 1. Ed. Marshall W. Baldwin. Madison: University of Wisconsin Press.

Sigfús Blöndal. 1920–24. *Islandsk-dansk ordbog.* Reykjavík: I Kommission hos Verslun Þórarins B. Þorlákssonar.

——. 1978. *The Varangians of Byzantium.* Trans. and rev. Benedikt A. Benedikz. Cambridge: Cambridge University Press.

Sigurður Nordal. 1953. "Sagalitteraturen." *Nordisk kultur,* 8B, 180–273. Copenhagen: J. H. Schultz.

——. 1973. *Snorri Sturluson.* 2nd printing. Helgafell: n.p.

Stefán Einarsson. 1939. "Ævintýraatvik í Auðunarþætti vestfirzka." *Skírnir,* 113:161–71.

Stender-Petersen, Adolf. 1934. *Die Varägersage als Quelle der altrussischen Chronik.* Acta Jutlandica, 6.1. Copenhagen: Reitzel.

——. 1953. "Jaroslav und die Väringer." In *Varangica.* Aarhus: Bianco Luno. Pp. 115–38.

Storm, Gustav. 1877. *Sigurd Ranessøns proces.* Kristiania [Oslo]: Det Mallingske bogtrykkeri.

Sverrir Tómasson. 1988. *Formálar íslenskra sagnaritara á miðöldum. Rannsókn bókmenntahefðar.* Reykjavík: Stofnun Árna Magnússonar.

Taylor, Alex. B. 1931. "Some Saga Place-Names." *Proceedings of the Orkney Antiquarian Society,* 9:41–45.

Taylor, Arnold R. 1946–53. "Auðunn and the Bear." *Saga-Book of the Viking Society,* 13:78–96.

Tolkien, Christopher. 1960. *The Saga of King Heidrek the Wise.* London: Nelson.

Torfi H. Tulinius. 1996. "Guðs lög í ævi og verkum Snorra Sturlusonar." *Ný saga. Tímarit sögufélags,* 8:31–40.

Turville-Petre, Gabriel. 1968. *Haraldr the Hard-Ruler and His Poets.* Dorothea Coke Memorial Lecture 1966. London: University College London.

Untersuchungen zu Handel und Verkehr der vor- und frühgeschichtlichen Zeit in Mittel- und Nordeuropa. Teil I: Methodische Grundlagen und Darstellungen zum Handel in vorgeschichtlicher Zeit und in der Antike: Bericht über die Kolloquien der Kommission für die Altertumskunde Mittel- und Nordeuropas in den Jahren 1980 bis 1983. Ed. Klaus Düwel, Herbert Jankuhn, Harald Siems, and Dieter Timpe. (= Abhandlungen der Akad. der Wiss. in Göttingen. Philol.-Hist. Kl. Series 3. No. 156). Vandenhoeck & Ruprecht, 1985.

Valtýr Guðmundsson. 1889. *Privatboligen på Island i sagatiden.* Copenhagen: Høst.

——. 1894. *Den islandske bolig i fristatstiden.* Copenhagen: Gad.

Vernadsky, George. 1948. *Kievan Russia.* New Haven: Yale University Press.

Vestlund, Alfred. 1929. "Om strofernas ursprungliga ordning i Sigvat Tordarsons 'Bersǫglisvísur.'" *Studier tillägnade Axel Kock.* In *ANF,* 40:281–93.

Vries, Jan de. 1931. "Normannisches Lehngut in den isländischen Königssagas." *ANF,* 47:51–79.

———. 1956. *Altgermanische Literaturgeschichte.* Rev. ed. Berlin: de Gruyter. 2 vols.

Wack, Mary F. 1990. *Lovesickness in the Middle Ages: The Viaticum and Its Commentaries.* Philadelphia: University of Pennsylvania Press.

Wallace-Hadrill, J. M. [John Michael]. 1971. *Early Germanic Kingship in England and on the Continent.* Oxford: Clarendon.

Wareman, Piet. 1951. *Spielmannsdichtung: Versuch einer Begriffsbestimmung.* Amsterdam: N. V. Drukkerij Jacob van Campen.

Whaley, Diana. 1991. *Heimskringla: An Introduction.* [London]: Viking Society for Northern Research, University College London.

———. 1993. "Nicknames and Narratives in the Sagas." *ANF,* 108:122–46.

———. 1994. "Miracles in the Biskupa sǫgur: Icelandic Variations on an International Theme." In *Samtíðarsögur (The Contemporary Sagas).* Akureyri: n.p. 2:847–62.

Wikander, Stig. 1964. "Från indisk djurfabel till isländsk saga." *Vetenskaps-Societetens i Lund Årsbok,* 89–114.

Wilson, David M., and Ole Klindt-Jensen. 1966. *Viking Art.* Ithaca: Cornell University Press.

Zettel, Horst. 1977. *Das Bild der Normannen und der Normanneneinfälle in westfränkischen, ostfränkischen und angelsächsischen Quellen des 8. bis 11. Jahrhunderts.* Munich: Fink.

Index to Introduction and Explanatory Notes

Index to *Morkinskinna*